Voyage Across the Stars

DAVID DRAKE

KT-546-560

TOWER HAMLETS
LIBRARIES

TOWER HAMLETS LIBRARIES	
91000001141183	
Bertrams	16/02/2012
SCI	£8.99
THBET	TH11002405

VOYAGE ACROSS THE STARS

This is a work of fiction. All the characters and events portrayed in this book are fictional, and any resemblance to real people or incidents is purely coincidental.

Preface copyright © 2012 by Cecelia Holland. Introduction copyright © 2012 by David Drake. *Cross the Stars* copyright © 1984 by David Drake. *The Voyage* copyright © 1994 by David Drake

All rights reserved, including the right to reproduce this book or portions thereof in any form.

A Baen Book

Baen Publishing Enterprises
P.O. Box 1403
Riverdale, NY 10471
www.baen.com

ISBN: 978-1-4516-3771-7

Cover art by Sam Kennedy

First Baen paperback printing, January 2012

Distributed by Simon & Schuster
1230 Avenue of the Americas
New York, NY 10020

Library of Congress Cataloging-in-Publication Data

Drake, David.
  Voyage across the stars / by David Drake.
    p. cm.
  ISBN 978-1-4516-3771-7 (omni trade pb)
  I. Title.
  PS3554.R196V73 2012
  813'.54--dc23

                                    2011040759

Printed in the United States of America

10 9 8 7 6 5 4 3 2 1

TABLE OF CONTENTS

GODS AND MONSTERS: DRAKE'S NEW MYTHOLOGY

They still call to us, the old stories. Cocooned in our air-conditioned, insulated buildings dozens of feet from the earth, the sky obscured, we still hear the ancient tales and in them we can still remember who we were. The human hero, caught between the monsters and the gods, uses courage, strength and boldness to restore the fundamental order. This satisfies our deepest sense of justice, of virtue.

That in our time, courage, strength and boldness seem to have priced themselves out of the virtue market makes this kind of exercise even more valuable. From Joyce to the Coen Brothers the story of Odysseus comes at us from all angles, and the story of the Argonauts appeals ever more to the special-effects-besotted movies.

In the hands of a master like David Drake the old tales echo with unexpected meanings and analogies, a sly reference to a rosy fingered dawn, the monster with fewer than two eyes. His own monsters are sensational, as always. Nobody does monsters better than David Drake; they are forever bursting terrifically up from the sea or out of the earth itself, all spines and tentacles and horrible teeth.

Much of the delight of these two works is the way Drake manipulates the original to fit his space-opera setting, like the evolution of the Golden Fleece into some kind of instantaneous transporter, in *The Voyage*, or any of the weird worlds in *Cross the*

Stars that mark Don Slade's desperate struggle to get home. These are gifts of a resourceful mind conversant in both worlds, and illuminate both: the magical elements of the Greek myth become a technological marvel in the space-opera and you see how both fit into their cultures' value systems.

The deeper message is in the differences between the Greeks and us, because Don Slade may seem to be operating in some parallel universe, but these books, like all fiction, are ultimately about us, about our moral universe.

The Greek gods control what happens in both the originating myths. These gods are real, are outside human existence, are other. The moral dilemmas they represent are beyond the ability of mortals to address; the order which determines right or wrong belongs to the gods, not to men.

So the Greeks needed to purge the common mind of terror and pity, but not guilt.

The modern world has turned that all inside, and made the irreconcilable demands of life into a constant test, and one we often fail. Exchanging magic for technology makes the human hero suddenly liable for a lot more. Now we're alone, and the monsters are still there, in the dark, rising furious from the depths. Drake roars back through his indomitable heroes, he blasts out his rockets of words, but the monsters never die. As he says of Don Slade, "they are part of what had forged him," and all of us, those monsters from within. But we are our own gods now, and we can't escape.

Cecelia Holland

STARTING A LONG WAY FROM HERE

This volume collects *Cross the Stars* and *The Voyage*, two cases where I recast an Ancient Greek epic as an SF adventure novel (a space opera). My undergraduate (double) majors were History and Latin, so that may seem an obvious thing for me to try; in fact it wasn't. (I've missed seeing a lot of things that seem obvious after the fact.)

In 1980, I quit lawyering and was driving a bus for the Town of Chapel Hill. While sitting in the bus garage between runs, I wrote a letter to a friend in which I commented that the *Odyssey* could be rewritten as a Western, though of course I didn't write Westerns. As the words came off my pen, it struck me that I *did* write SF; what was true for a horse opera would probably work for a space opera as well.

Nothing happened for a few months. Then Jim Baen called and offered me a two-book contract: a big book for $10K and a little book for $7,500. I said "Yes!" immediately. (I've done a lot of dumb things, but I was never dumb enough to turn *that* down. I made $6,100 during my year of bus driving).

Then, because at the time both Jim and I thought that we ought to know what the books would be about, I said the big book would be what became *Birds of Prey* (my working title was *The Warm Summer Rain*; note what I said above about doing a lot of dumb things) and the little book would be a rewrite of the *Odyssey*. That was off the top of my head, but it seemed like a good idea on reflection also. (Almost immediately thereafter I became a full-time writer, though the decision didn't have as direct a connection as it may seem to.)

I wrote *Birds of Prey* first (I had been trying to write it for more than a decade). Then I reread the *Odyssey* (for the umpteenth time, of course), making a précis of everything that happened in it.

Until I made the précis, I didn't have a real understanding of the way the *Odyssey* is paced and connected. Almost all the incidents which people (myself included until then) think of as being the *Odyssey* occur in one book: after dinner on the island of Scheria, Odysseus recounts to his hosts the things he claims have happened to him since he left Troy. Homer doesn't tell the reader about the Cyclops: that's a story which Odysseus tells to King Alcinous and his other guests.

I mentioned this development to Jim in one of our regular phone calls. "But you don't have to do it that way," he said.

Which took me aback. Of course I had to do it that way! It's that way in the original.

Then I actually thought about the situation instead of just reacting. I wasn't going to be graded on my understanding of the *Odyssey*; my present job was to tell a good story in English. That meant the *form* of the story had to be translated, as surely as the language in which I told it.

This was a typical case in which I benefited from being Jim Baen's friend (because we were chatting as friends, not as editor and writer). There were many similar instances on both sides. Over the years, Jim and I saved one another from ourselves as a regular thing.

I already understood that I would have to adapt the incidents of the *Odyssey* functionally, not simply copy them. A one-eyed giant is a credible threat to an Iron Age chieftain, but such a creature doesn't read the same in relation to the commander of a high-tech combat unit.

Finally, I had to allow for cultural as well as technological differences. Odysseus caps his victory by slowly strangling—the process is described in some detail—the female servants who have been sleeping with Penelope's suitors.

This is only one example (although a pretty striking one) of normal behavior in an Iron Age culture which is unacceptable in a society that I (or anybody I want as a reader) would choose to live in. I might've been stupid enough to follow the structure of an ancient epic in a modern space opera, but I wasn't going to describe a hero with the worldview of a death camp guard.

Adapting the *Odyssey* was the second most important lesson I got writing. (The *most* important was learning that I needed to outline.)

Since *Cross the Stars* I use the same process on all material, historical as well as fiction. First I consider the requirements of my medium; space opera, military SF, and fantasy all start from different assumptions. Then I look at the functional effect of every element of the original.

Only when I've completed those basics do I begin to plot my novel. *Paying the Piper* is military SF based in Hellenistic history; *The Voyage* (included in this volume), is space opera based on the *Argonautica* of Apollonius of Rhodes. I developed both of them and many other stories by using the technique I learned by writing *Cross the Stars*.

There's one other thing to mention: I don't forget the original while I'm writing. In *Cross the Stars* you'll find hints of Homer's words as well as his story. I'll never be the writer Homer was (nobody else will either, but that's another matter), but I'm better for having read him than I would have been without his example.

Dave Drake
david-drake.com

CROSS THE STARS

DEDICATION

To Jim Baen,
for ten years of making me a better writer,
and for acting as a friend.

ACKNOWLEDGMENTS

This novel began in discussions with Glenn Knight, while we were some thousands of miles apart. Jim Baen and Bernadette Bosky were of inestimable help in matters of direction. Karl Wagner—kindly old Doc Wagner—provided technical data as always. When my nerves were frazzled, Sharon Pigott spent an evening keying in the last of the rough draft and saving me a further day and a half of crushing work. And my wife, Jo, made friendly, dispassionate, enormously helpful comments on that rough.

Blessings to you all.

CHAPTER ONE

A hologram of a tank, bow-on as it plowed through a brushfire, filled most of the wall behind President Hammer's desk. Either by chance or through Hammer's deliberation, the tank was *Two Star*— Danny Pritchard's unit twenty years before, when he had been a sergeant in the Slammers and not Hammer's chosen successor.

"Hey, snake," the President called cheerfully when he saw it was Pritchard who had entered the office unannounced.

Hammer tilted away the desk display which he had been studying. He had not let age and the presidency blunt all the edges of his appearance. If Hammer's hair was its natural gray now, then it was still naturally his own. His shoulders and wrists would have done credit to a larger, younger man. There was a paunch below desk height that had not been there five years before, however. No practical amount of exercise could wholly replace the field work of the lifetime previous. "Had a chance to glance over the proposal from Dominica?"

"Glance, yes," Danny said, perching himself on the arm of an easy chair instead of the seat. The fabric responded to his weight, squirming in an attempt to mold itself to his contours. Pritchard preferred a solid bench, so he gave as little purchase as possible to the luxury with which Hammer disarmed visitors. "I like the idea of having somebody else pay for part of our army, sure . . . and, well, train it while things are quiet here on Friesland. But I think Dominica's too far if we—needed the guns back in a hurry."

Danny popped the rolled notes he held against his knee. It was a sign of the nervousness which he otherwise controlled. "Thing is, Alois," he continued to the older man, "that isn't what was on my mind right at the moment." He smiled. "Even though it should have been."

Hammer snorted. He spun his desk display toward his Adjutant and heir presumptive. "Teitjens sent this over as background before he briefs me on the slump in heavy equipment export projections. I'd sooner listen to you, on the assumption that I'll at least understand your problem when you've finished."

"Yeah, well," the younger man agreed. "The problem's easy."

He slid down into the cup of the chair after all. The office walls were a slowly-moving fog-blue, almost a gray. Pritchard slitted his eyelids. The hologram behind the President could have been a real tank on a skyswept plain. "We got a homeworld query on one of our veterans. Do you remember Captain Don Slade?"

Hammer nodded calmly over his clasped hands. "Mad Dog Slade? Sure, I remember him. He was the one man I really wanted who insisted on retiring when he heard his father'd died. Home to Tethys, wasn't it? The Omicron Eridani Tethys, I mean. I offered him a duchy here on Friesland, too, Danny."

"Via, he was a duke back home, Colonel," Pritchard said to the blurred man and to the tank. "He was the next thing to a king there if he'd wanted to be." The Adjutant opened his eyes again and sat as erect as the cushions would permit him. "We were—well, he did me a favor. We were friends, Don and me. Tell the truth, he didn't much like to be called Mad Dog."

"Well," Hammer said with a laugh, "if he'll come back, I'll call him Duke Donald or any curst thing he chooses. Not because he's a friend of yours, Danny—though that too—but because you can't have too many people like Slade on your side." The President did not precisely frown, but his face lost most of its laughter. "Among other reasons, because if they're on your side, they aren't on the other guy's."

"I think Don had had about enough of sides when he left here," Pritchard said. He looked up at the ceiling and remembered his big,

black-haired friend in the spaceport at their last meeting. "He said he was ready to spend the rest of his life fishing like his grandfather."

"*Fishing?*" Hammer repeated in angry amazement. "He was going to go from one of *my* tank companies to fishing?"

It was his Adjutant's turn to laugh. Danny gestured with his notecards and said, "Well, fishing on Tethys isn't that different from the sort of jobs we gave M Company, Alois. There's a lot of water there, and the things that grow in it are pretty much to scale, from what Don told me. . . ."

"But the thing is," Pritchard added, sobering, "Don didn't get there. We got a query from—" he checked the uppermost card from habit rather than from present need— "Marilee Slade, asking if Don were still on our establishment."

"Not in two years," Hammer said with a frown. "Mother? Or Via! Not his wife, is she? Don didn't take home leave in, well, at least the ten years since I promoted him to ensign."

"Seems to be his sister-in-law," the younger man said. Hammer had already swung the display back around. The President's fingers were calling up Slade's personnel file and planetary data on Omicron Eridani II—one of a trio of worlds named Tethys by their original settlers. "Brother's widow, I'd guess, from the way the query was worded," Pritchard continued. "Never talked much to Don about why he'd joined the Slammers, but I sort of gathered this lady had something to do with it. Also he was the younger son, that sort of hereditary nonsense." The Adjutant's eyes met those of the childless President. There was iron in the grin of each man.

Hammer grunted approval at whatever he saw on his display. "Council of Forty runs the place," he muttered. "Hereditary oligarchy. You know, I like the look of some of these average metal prices. Might be worth our while to ask for quotes, especially on the manganese. Either they sweat their workers like I wouldn't dare, or they've got a curst slick operation."

He gestured over the desk with an upraised palm. "But I don't suppose you thought you needed me to clear a trace on Don Slade, did you? Shoot."

"He left here on a tramp full of hard-cases. He was in a hurry and he wouldn't listen to reason," Pritchard said to the ceiling. "Golf-Alpha-Charlie Five Niner. I located a survivor on Desmo and got the story. Fellow'd gotten to Desmo on an Alayan ship. Don had been aboard the Alayan, too, but he'd gotten off at a place called Terzia. Produces medicinals. Place got one or two tramp freighters a month, so it shouldn't have been a bad place to trans-ship."

Pritchard shrugged himself out of the chair again and began to pace the large, austere office. "No question of coercion," he continued. "The survivor says Don tried to talk them all into working their butts off in the jungle or some such thing. Don was free to go, just like the others he was with—and *they* all lifted off."

Compared to Hammer, the brown-haired Adjutant was tall. He slapped the notes on his left palm. "What the problem turned out to be is that Terzia's refused landing rights to every ship that's approached it since the Alayans lifted off. It could be chance; but chance or not, the result's the same. For over a year, Don's been caged there as sure as if he was behind bars . . . and he may be that, too, for anything we know otherwise."

Hammer was playing with the controls of his display again. "Terzia's got real-time commo," the President said in the mild voice that he used when his brain was busy with something besides the words he was speaking.

"Yeah, and that's funny," said Pritchard. "I got the impression that the place was virtually pre-industrial. Exports some high-purity natural medicinals, but nothing in quantity. No quantity that there'd be a Stadtler Communications System, unless the economic pyramid comes to a pretty sharp point."

The President nodded. "One projection system, one Transit launch, one of a lot of things. One Don Slade right now, though that wasn't going to show up on a Commercial Movements Summary, was it?" Hammer's fingers tapped the surface of the display gently. "Though that may be a flaw in the compiler's outlook, not Terzia's."

Hammer got up from his chair also. He ambled past the hologram. Beyond that wall of his office were the grounds of the Presidential Palace, lushly beautiful and maintained for no purpose but the President's enjoyment. Hammer did not object to the gardens, but it was at his orders that the crystalline window giving onto them had been replaced by the hologram. He saw the palace grounds only through the windows of his armored limousine as an incident of travel. "Right now, it's the projection system that matters," he said aloud. "You'll have Margritte handle it?"

Danny nodded at the reference to his wife. "We've got a few other people supposed to be trained on the Stadtler rig," he said. He rubbed his lower back and ribs absently with both hands. "Sometimes it works for them, sometimes it doesn't. With Margritte, it works, and I hope to blazes there's somebody on Terzia that good too. . . ."

Danny Pritchard had made a point of wearing civilian garments ever since the day of Hammer's inauguration. His present suit was as soft and smooth as the creamy shimmer of its color . . . and it was acutely uncomfortable on a body that suddenly felt the need for battle-dress again. "Alois," the Adjutant continued, "that leaves a couple questions."

"Margritte has a blank check," Hammer said. "If they won't listen to reason about Slade until she threatens that we'll land a Field Force regiment, she can do that."

"Terzia's a full seventy Transit minutes away from us," Pritchard said flatly. "They may think they're far enough away to be safe, so they don't have to listen to us."

Hammer turned. He was no longer the paunchy ruler of a complex industrial world. He was a commander whose troops had stormed Hell a score of times before and might do it again.

"If they won't listen to *us*, they'll listen to our guns, won't they?" Hammer said. His voice was as hard and sincere as the bow of the tank behind him. "Slade broke up a Guards Regiment with one tank company and a battalion of half-trained militia. If the Guards had taken the port behind us, Danny, you and I wouldn't be standing here, would we? Though our skulls might still be on poles out front."

Pritchard shrugged like a dragonfly beginning to pull free of its cocoon of soft, cream fabric. "I'd roughed out some contingency plans," he said as he turned to the door. "I'll work on specific movement orders while Margritte tries to get a connection with Terzia."

"'Tell them," Hammer called to his Adjutant's back, "that I don't know if we can release Don Slade alive by force. But I'll promise to burn their planet for his funeral pyre if we can't."

For some moments after the door closed, Hammer continued to stand where he was: silhouetted against the bow of the tank.

CHAPTER TWO

The Citadel was a spike in relief against the mottled turquoise sky. There was no bulky starship on the landing platform beside the tower.

Don Slade swore very mildly, his voice as leaden as his heart. He stepped aside to let the work gang pass him as the trail dipped back into the jungle.

This was the one vantage point on the trail's length. Slade had cradled the short barrel of his powergun in the crook of his left arm as he marched ahead of the column. Now he held the weapon vertical for safety. The butt was against his hip, and the muzzle touched at eyebrow height the tree against which the tanker leaned wearily.

Bedyle, the foreman, stopped beside his superior. "Problems, sir?" the lightly-built humanoid asked in Spaceways English. The language differed radically from the version of English Slade had learned to speak as a boy on Tethys, but it—Spanglish—provided a medium of trade throughout the human universe . . . and beyond that universe, as on Terzia. Though it was sometimes difficult for Slade to remember that he and the Terzia herself were the only two humans on the planet.

"No problem, Bedyle," Slade said. "Nothing new, at any rate. There's just no ship. Still."

Slade's black hair was cropped short on his head and jaw for comfort. Hair coiled like strands of honeysuckle over his bare chest and splashed down his limbs to the backs of his hands and feet. From a distance, he had a bestial appearance which the calm of his expression belied. Slade was taller by forty centimeters than the tallest of the work gang; taller and stronger besides than most of the humans whom he had met in a life of knocking about the universe.

"You know, Bedyle . . ." the big man said. His eyes were on the distant spire, but his mind was much farther away. "You'd think after nine days in the copper-pod jungle, that place would look good. But . . . if there was a Palamede slave-ship docked there, I'd ship out in its hold before I'd take another step through the gate of the Citadel."

"Your life is so very bad, then?" the foreman asked softly.

The workers were filing past, chanting something melodious and without meaning. Slade had been unable in a year to learn a word of the native language. The Terzia swore that when her ancestors had landed on the planet, the autochthones already spoke Spanglish. There was no reason to believe that she was lying . . . or that she was telling the truth, for that matter. Slade had no way to judge the Terzia's statements.

The locals, males and females alike, carried fifty-kilo burdens of copper-pods without signs that their frail-looking bodies were being strained. They were nude. Only in the greenish cast underlying their brown skins, and in the lack of external genitals in the males, were they demonstrably inhuman.

Slade had personal experience of the human characteristics of some of the females.

"Bad?" Don Slade said, echoing the foreman. The sounds of lesser animals seeped from the jungle and merged with the voices of the work gang. "Via, no, Bedyle. Life isn't bad. I've got every luxury I could dream of, and the most beautiful woman I've ever met. I've got a job I'm needed at—" he nodded toward the workers he supervised and protected—"and it keeps me on my toes besides. I don't even get bored, what with all the different habitats we crop. I'd have to say my life is perfect."

The man paused. He turned to scan as much of his surroundings as he could see through the broad-leafed, ten-meter plants that made up the basic vegetation of this spot. A train of colorful, multi-legged creatures chased itself around one fleshy stem. The joints of the beasts' exoskeletons clattered softly.

"The only problem is," Slade went on, "it's not the life I want to live. And there's not a curst thing anybody can do about that until another ship sets down."

The sucking sound of a tree being pushed up from beneath was overlaid by the scream of the worker caught in the first pair of pincers.

Slade pumped the fore-end to charge his weapon as he pivoted the butt to his shoulder. The monster's emerging head was toward the back of the file. It curved from the ground, dripping loam from its compound eyes and from the agate-melded segments of its broad carapace. A workman, streaming blood where the knife-edged pincers entered his body, was being transferred to the maw that gaped sideways to receive him. Slade had no time to pick his shot there, however. The real danger lay at the other end of the carnivore's rising body.

Along ten meters of the trail, pairs of pincer-tipped legs slashed out of the soil like sprouts in time-lapse. Three other work-men had been caught and were being swung toward the head end for ingestion. The survivors of the file screamed and leaped into the jungle. Their burdens tumbled in the air behind them.

At the further end, toward the Citadel, waved the tail and the slim, meter-long cone of the creature's sting. Slade fired at the base of it.

The carnivore lay ambushed on its back beneath the trail. As the pincers struck upward, the tail arched toward its prey. Large prey would be dispatched by a sting, while numbers of smaller victims—like the file of laborers—would be immobilized by sprayed venom even if they had escaped the first thrust of pincers. Now the impact of the bolt caused the tail to spasm. It drove a stream of chartreuse venom from the sting a moment before it would have been properly aimed at the work gang.

Slade was turning toward the monster's head again even as the jet of poison splattered onto the foliage above. The ground beside the man was cracked and heaving. A jointed leg as thick as his wrist lashed toward him, pincers clicking. The carnivore was squirming to turn its body upright.

Slade fired, stepped sideways, and fired twice more in rapid succession. A drop of poison struck his right shoulder and splashed upward across his neck, ear, and biceps.

The first three bolts from the powergun had shattered the creature's armor. The sting hung askew, one of the foremost pair of legs had been blown from its socket, and the cyan flash of the third round had cratered the curve of the head shield. The bolts liberated their energy instantaneously, however. Despite the amount of surface damage the powergun did, no single shot could penetrate to the vitals of this huge, loosely-organized carnivore. Slade's fourth round was aimed at the ulcer left by the third. The bolt struck in a gout of vaporizing internal tissue as the poisoned gunman screamed and dropped his weapon.

Skin was already sloughing where the venom drop had struck. Over the areas of secondary contact the skin was turning gray and black. Slade slapped his chest injector plate with his left hand because his right arm and side had gone numb. Leaf mold steamed beneath the hot iridium barrel of the gun he had dropped. The injector dumped stimulant and anti-allergenic directly into Slade's anterior vena cava. Under its impact and that of the venom, he staggered. He fumbled a medicated compress out of the kit at his belt and scrubbed at the damaged area. The fire in Slade's blood damped down as the compress debrided, then covered, the swatches where the skin was dead.

Although Slade had not lost consciousness, his conscious mind was surprised to find that he was kneeling beside his gun. His torso felt as if it swelled and relaxed with every beat of his heart. There had been enough breeze to carry one droplet of the unaimed venom to him. It had almost been enough to be fatal.

The creature was dying with the noisy lethality of a runaway truck. It hammered its surroundings. The middle part of its body was still within the trench in which it had lain hidden, while both ends lashed the vegetation above. Across the trail and the heaving exoskeleton from Slade, a stunned laborer tried to drag himself further into the jungle. A pincered leg gouged the earth beside him. Slade cursed and tried to leap to the injured worker's aid.

Slade had forgotten the amount of damage done to his own system by the drugs and counter-drugs that roiled within him.

Instead of clearing the monster as he had intended, the man landed on the blotchy carapace. His feet slid out from under him. The carnivore was trying to arch its center segments from the trench. Its weight pinned Slade's shins to the soft loam. The laborer scuttled safely behind the bole of a tree. The leg whose wild thrashings had endangered the native now recoiled toward the man. The creature's optic nerves and central ganglion had been destroyed, but its autonomic nervous system was making a successful attempt to heave the great body erect reflexively.

The powergun would have been useless even if Slade still held it. The carnivore was dead, but only time or a nuclear weapon would keep its corpse from being dangerous. Slade grabbed the limb as it swung for him. His biceps swelled as they directed the pincers down onto the dirt a hand's breadth short of his chest. They dug into the soil like the recoil spades of projectile artillery. That gave the leg purchase against the massive thrust it exerted a moment later.

The creature squirmed wholly clear of the trench. Its meter-thick body carried Slade up with it as its weight released him. There were tiny chitinous projections where the carapace armor joined that of the belly. They flayed the big man's calves through the tough, loose trousers that had covered them.

Slade threw himself out of the way. He was limited to the strength of his upper body because his legs were still numb. The creature was squirming off mindlessly into the jungle like a giant centipede. One of the legs of a rear segment still impaled a laborer. The corpse's drag kept that limb out of synchrony with the fluttering fore-and-aft motion of the others. The body segment itself twitched out of the line the remainder of the creature was trying to take.

In the dirt behind the carnivore dangled its sting. The plates that should have held and directed the weapon were shattered. Chartreuse venom still dripped and left a dark trail on the ground.

In the wake of the creature's clattering exit, the jungle came alive with the moans of injured laborers.

Slade staggered to the fallen bundle that held the main medical supplies. When he had an opportunity, he would do something about the bloody agony of his own calves. They would wait—would have to wait—for Slade to treat the laborers who were already going into shock from trauma or poisoning.

The Citadel was temporarily only a memory behind a curtain of sweat and adrenalin.

CHAPTER THREE

At the top of her tower, the Terzia shuddered because a human would have shuddered in reaction to the scene she had watched. The breaking earth, the pincers stabbing upward with enough force to penetrate wood . . . the venom drifting forward in a haze, burning like lava the bare flesh it contacted. . . .

Everything that happened was out of her control once it began. But the danger had to be real or the exercise was pointless . . . as it seemed to be pointless anyway, to judge from the bleakness of Slade's remarks to Bedyle.

The Terzia's awareness extended across all the life forms native to the planet. She watched from her tower and through the eyes of the laborers in Slade's gang, both the hale and the dying. When the brain-blasted carnivore stumbled against the tree trunk, the Terzia felt the impact both through the chitin and through the bark. Sunshine and starglow, breezes and rain all over the world simultaneously, were as much a part of her consciousness as was her terror of a moment before.

Like the wind, the chime of the Stadtler Communications Device was a stimulus external to the Terzia in all her facets. The human simulacrum in the tower turned the unit across from her in the open room.

The Stadtler Device consisted of a massive chair which faced a niche surrounded by a bank of cabinets. The smooth surfaces of chair and cabinets covered electronics as sophisticated as any other array in the present human universe. There was, in fact, no certainty that the original provenance of Stadtler Devices was human at all. A glaucous light on one chair-arm pulsed in harmony with the three-note chime.

The Terzia stepped toward the unit without hesitation and without any dimming of her awareness of every other factor sensed by the planet's native life. Stadtler Devices were almost solely the prerogative of governments, and generally governments of the richest worlds and nations. The units, built on or at least shipped from Stadtler, provided instantaneous communications over astronomical distances—at astronomical cost. A planet like Terzia could scarcely have afforded such a bauble, were Terzia not capable of directing its entire volume of extra-planetary exchange in as narrow a focus as it desired.

The Terzia seated herself in the chair. She touched the light to end its pulsing and to activate the projection circuits of the device. Her garment swirled as she moved. The fabric appeared to be layers of diaphanous gauze, gathered and pinned at the shoulders by crystalline brooches. In fact, the layers were sheets of light polarized by the crystals, and there was no fabric at all in the ensemble.

An image was beginning to form in the alcove across from the chair, just as a more-than-physical simulacrum of the Terzia would be awakening in the caller's unit, parsecs or kiloparsecs away. The Stadtler Device could not be used to receive alone. Its principle, whatever it was, required balance: a biological intellect at either node of a communication.

It did not require a human intellect. That was why the link worked as well for the Terzia as it could have worked for the human she counterfeited.

A woman on a couch like the Terzia's own gazed from the alcove. The soft focus of the caller's form sharpened as the electronic cabinets, the room, and the world beyond the room blurred and disappeared. The universe of the moment had shrunk to a pair of facing couches and the females upon them.

The caller was shorter than the Terzia and dressed in a soft, one-piece garment. She leaned forward and said, "I am Life Baron

Margritte Pritchard." That rank flowed from Margritte's duties as Minister of State for Communication. "I speak with the authorization of President Hammer and the State of Friesland. This is a matter of highest importance, both to our world and to your own. The information you are about to receive must be forwarded for immediate response by your chief executive."

The Terzia's hair was a rich brown, falling in waves to her upper back. It rippled as she nodded. "I am the chief executive of Terzia."

The statement was true in a way that only the Stadtler Device made possible. In the field of the communications unit, there was a being called the Terzia who was separate from all other beings on the planet. Separate from the being that *was* all other life on the planet. The Terzia's face had been modeled on a fine-boned hybrid of French and Southern Oriental. It began to glow with the arrogance of individuality.

Visual and auditory contact had been complete almost immediately. The two personalities, those of Margritte and the Terzia, were still integrating. That process would continue, had to continue, throughout the communication to prevent the link from breaking up into static and sheets of color. For the moment, however, all Margritte was aware of was the fact that Terzia's ruler acted as her own communications officer. That was not an uncommon circumstance for the few who could afford a Stadtler Device. "There is a man being held on your planet," Margritte said. "You must release him immediately or risk the anger of—" she paused "—of Colonel Alois Hammer. The man's name is Donald Slade of Tethys."

The Terzia had known what must be coming. The name was still a numbing blow. Like a spark in her mind popped an image of Don Slade, back from the field. *His gun lay on the table by the door. It was safe, with its magazine ejected beside it, but it had not been cleaned and put up until other business had been attended to. Slade's black hair was long enough to wave as his head tossed with his laughter. His shirt lay in the hallway and he was stepping out of his trousers. The blaze of his smile and personality flooded the Terzia watching him from the bed.*

The Stadtler Field was momentarily a bloom of mauve static. Then it was peopled by entities whose mutual sharpness was beyond their own self-knowledge. Both minds had recoiled for an instant, then merged. The memory that had flashed into Margritte's mind was nearly identical to that of the Terzia. *A younger Don Slade, a shell crater and not a luxurious bed-chamber; a uniform spattered with the blood of the corpse at the crater's lip. But the same laughter and the same fiery intensity . . . and the same sinewy hands loosing the trouser fly.* "Oh dear Lord," Margritte whispered. "Oh Danny." She looked at the Terzia, seeing and being seen as never before.

"So that is why you want him back," said the alien with human features and a bitter human smile. "Reasons of state."

"No!" Margritte shouted, angry and cold with a lower-brain fear. Intellectually she knew that the Stadtler Device was proof against eavesdropping. Nothing which did not merge with the field could withdraw information from it after the link was established. What she did not herself report would not exist to Hammer; or to her husband. But certain reflexes are much older than the human intellect. "It was only once, under fire. It didn't mean anything, except that we were alive."

"Yes, alive," the Terzia agreed. She would have stood and paced if the logic of the Stadtler Device had permitted it. Instead, images of Don Slade wandered around the edges of the field, visible to both communicators.

The big man walked along the jungle edge beside the tender on which he had arrived. He had a pair of imaging goggles, but they were pushed high on his forehead. With his lips pursed, Slade was trying to duplicate the notes of something that had called to him from the undergrowth. The song hung in the Stadtler Field. It was not sound but the shadow of a memory.

In a second ghost-like moment, Don Slade was making love to one of the members of his work gang, a girl with bright eyes and skin the color of oak bark. They were all Terzia, all objects tailored to the needs of the planet in a universe over which humans swarmed with their mechanical responses to questions and their violence toward threats and toward excessive strangeness. The autochthones were a part of Terzia's defense system. So were the plants that produced complex drugs in wild profusion. And so was the "human" mistress of the world; the Terzia, who dealt with human traders and who controlled the hardware which kept less peaceful wanderers at a distance. *The image of the man astride the alien girl shouted with joy as unexpected muscles clamped. It showed a delight which the merely-human exoticism of the Terzia had not aroused in him for many months; and which itself had soon palled into despondency.*

The third image which flickered and trailed the others into the neutral background was that of the present morning, Slade leaping the thrashing carnivore to save a laborer who was not a man. To Terzia, the workman was no more than a skin cell, a fleck of spittle voided during a charade. To the man putting himself at risk, the victim was his responsibility . . . and even if someone had told him the truth, he might have reacted with the same furious determination, because his duty was not a matter over which Don Slade gave power to any other to determine.

The Frisian and the Terzia—the women—were alone again.

Margritte tongued her upper lip, dry with tension. She said, "You have to release Don Slade. We order it."

"Do you think he's kept in a cage?" the Terzia blazed. "He has *everything,* luxury, excitement—love, damn you, love if you will, for a soul like a jewel in the sunshine!" She paused and added in a whisper, "I am very old, and that is . . . useful to me."

"Bring Don Slade here," Margritte said. "Put him on line with me. Have him tell me himself that he doesn't see the bars."

The Terzia tossed her head as if the wash of her lustrous hair could wipe away the words she was hearing. Margritte continued inexorably, "Or else let him go, lady. You have no other choice."

"Do you think you could take him from me?" the Terzia demanded. Her voice and bearing were those of the arrogant queen whose whim made the planet a danger spot for roistering spacers, a world whose profits barely balanced the harsh justice of its ruler. On the edge of the Stadtler Field flashed gunpits. They were armed with high-intensity weapons that could rip a ship from orbit or scar the face of a moon.

Margritte Pritchard's eyes were as cold as her smile. "Do you think," she said, "that Hammer's Slammers haven't dropped on a hot landing zone before?" *The Stadtler Field went black and red and saffron. Through it all spiked the blazing cyan of powerguns. Landing craft sprayed the perimeter from their gun tubes as the blunt iridium bows of tanks slid through cargo doors to hunt in a burning city.*

"That was M Company clearing an LZ on Cronenbourg," said Margritte's voice through the flashing darkness. "Don Slade was in the lead tank." Then she added, "Our panzers will bring him out of here alive, lady. Or they will sear this world to glass. I swear it, and Colonel Hammer swears it."

Tears were a human thing, but the Terzia was almost fully human as the Hell-lit carnage cleared.

"He doesn't want to go back to you," said the Terzia as her throat cleared. She looked at her fingernails and not the face of her tormentor. "He left you. He says he wants to go home."

"Then send him home," said the woman on Friesland, with a garden unseen outside and an ache in her own heart.

The Terzia looked up again, amber eyes behind long lashes. "There's trouble there, you know," she said steadily. "Those who want to kill him."

It could have been a lie. Hammer himself had no data beyond the bare bones of the request, and there was no evident way that the Terzia would be better informed. But it fit, the Lord knew; and Margritte was by no means sure that either of them could lie to the other on a link as intense as this one.

"That may be," Margritte said at last. "Maybe he'd be better to stay where he is or to come back to Friesland. We want him, the Colonel wants him. But Don's an adult. He can make his choices, even if they're mistakes."

"All right," said the Terzia. Her muscles bunched to raise her from the chair, a motion that would have broken the contact. She was human enough to scream against fate, but not in front of this messenger, this rival.

Margritte raised a hand to hold the Terzia one final moment. When she spoke, it was not as Life Baron, not as the representative of Friesland—if it had ever been, since the link had been forged so strongly. "Lady," Margritte said, "others have planned to kill Don Slade, you know. And the mistake has always been theirs."

She nodded, and the gray envelope of the Stadtler Field brightened for both into separate living worlds.

*

CHAPTER FOUR

An armed man in the crimson livery of the Dyson family waved. His helmet speakers boomed, "All right, clear to land."

The air car sagged gratefully into the courtyard of Slade House. The vehicle's bright caparisoning had been stained by spray and perhaps a storm in its journey from one of the more distant of the Council Islands—baronies, in effect—of Tethys. There were more shouted orders from the man in crimson. The driver lifted minusculely and slid the car sideways. It joined the line of other cars parked along the courtyard's southern wall.

More than a score of Councilors had already arrived. Teddy Slade did not recognize the trappings of this vehicle, nor could he place the youngish man who got out of it with his entourage of flunkies.

"Wasn't used to be like this, Teddy," rasped Coon Blegan. The old man shifted on the skirt of the gun drone to take some of his belly's pressure off his belt. "If your great grand-dad'd learned a Dyson was giving orders in the compound, he'd have reached for his boat gun. And their tarted-up bully boys running things at Slade House, well. . . ."

Blegan morosely scratched his left armpit. Thomas Slade had ordered Blegan to stop wearing his illegal shoulder holster when he appointed the old retainer as servant to his son Edward. Increasingly since Master Thomas had died, the old man had felt the lack of a burden he had thought he had forgotten. "Didn't call the old man Devil for nothing, you know," Coon went on. "Devil Don. Always wondered how it came they named your uncle after him, Teddy. Wouldn't have thought there was any way to know how a little baby like that was going to grow up."

The youth's control was born of a lifetime's experience with Blegan. He said, "Perhaps Uncle Donald had a chance to grow into a perfectly decent, useful human being like Father, Coon. Only he heard too much talk by old farts about the grand days of the Settlement, when a Slade could shoot a man for looking cross-eyed. I'd be obliged if nobody tried to repeat the experiment with me."

Three more cars were approaching over the perimeter wall; the Rices and the Mortons, trailed by a larger van carrying additional retainers for Madame Morton. Even when everyone arrived, however, the most noticeable livery would be crimson. The Dysons shared Main Island with the Slades—and the Port, which was supposed to be neutral ground for all the Councilors. Even if Beverly Dyson had needed to bring his men in from half across the planet, however, they would have been here in strength for the present occasion.

"It was never like that, Teddy," Blegan said.

"Via!" the youth shouted. "All the rest of the world can remember to call me 'Edward', Coon—at least part of the time. How come you can't?"

Blegan looked at young Slade reproachfully. "Perhaps I didn't think the rest of the world knew you the way I do, Master Edward," he said. "But I'm an old man and ready to be cut up for bait, I'm sure."

"Oh, Lord and Martyrs, Coon," Teddy muttered. He squeezed Blegan's hand. "What's a word matter? But I wish . . ." He looked up. A supply truck was balancing awkwardly in the air, waiting for landing permission from the man in crimson. The truck's color was weather-beaten blue-green, Slade Blue. "But I wish. . . ." the youth repeated, and he let his voice trail off again.

"Things were hard during the Settlement, they tell me," Coon Blegan said. He did not look at Slade, just squeezed the lad's hand and released it. "I'm not that old, not even Coon, but they told me. These—" he patted the skirt of the gun drone. For all the old man's apparent flabbiness, the metal rang with authority. "These weren't for men, they were for the orcs and the knife-jaws. I know you don't believe it because they steer clear of Council Islands by now, but I myself saw an orc come right over this wall."

Coon waved toward the three-meter perimeter barrier, then back up at the gun of the drone the pair of them leaned against. "Ten centimeter bolts cooked her just fine, same's they did during Settlement when the orcs came in packs."

"Those days are over, Coon," Slade said quietly as he watched liveried hangers-on rumaging through the provisions truck. They were squabbling, each of a dozen parties trying to snare any special delicacy for the Councilor whom they served.

"Ooh, aye," Blegan agreed, "and glad I am, too, an old man like me doesn't need excitement." He paused. "But I didn't need to carry your father back dead from the Port, either, with a knife through his belly and half his ribs. He'd not have gone there alone had he an ounce of sense, not the way things are now."

Teddy swung in front of the old servant and took him by the hands. "Don't you see, Coon?" he demanded. "It won't make this a better world to live in if people like *us* help tear down civilization the way the thugs at the Port do. We need order here, but we won't get it by the two of us buckling up like vigilantes and getting ourselves killed too. If the only way to keep decent men from dying in the street was to make Beverly Dyson the President, then—I'm glad of that too."

"*That* one," said Coon Blegan, but he smiled and did not spit as young Slade had expected. The youth did not recognize the smile any more than he had recognized Coon's gesture toward his armpit for what it was.

Blegan was watching the crowd around the truck. A knife had flashed, then gone sailing through the air as a coda to the crack of wood on bone. Men cheered as the group broke apart. Durotige, a big man in Slade coveralls marked as well with a crimson stripe, roared triumph. He was swelling in the congratulations of livery-men who stayed clear of his artfully-spinning nunchaku. Durotige fed the chain-linked batons in a figure-8, between his legs and over his shoulders alternately.

His opponent of a moment before wore shabby green and scarlet livery. He was hunched over, holding a right forearm that was probably broken. The injured man backed and cursed as the outward arch of the nunchaku snapped just short of his nose. Durotige had been a Slade Under-Steward a month before. That his constituency had now changed was shown by the stripe on his trousers—and by the enthusiasm with which the crimson Dyson claque supported him.

"Beverly Dyson," the old servant repeated grimly. "That one wants to piss with the big dogs, but I don't think he can raise his leg high enough. One of these days Master Donald'll come home . . . and there'll be some to learn why your Uncle was nicknamed what he was."

CHAPTER FIVE

"Oh, come, Marilee," said Beverly Dyson in a reasonable tone of voice. "Why shouldn't I call him Mad Dog? It's what his own father called him, isn't it?"

Councilor Dyson touched the base of a stim cone to his left wrist. The disposable injector wore the black and gold striping of a powerful euphoric. In fact, the stock which Dyson carried was loaded with a mild stimulant. It did nothing to disturb the Councilor's plans or the ruthless speed with which he could execute them.

"Don's father hated him, as you well know," snapped Marilee Slade as she stared through the window. The family apartments were on the third floor of Slade House. The Trophy Room in which she sat with Dyson looked across the broad courtyard to the Council Hall beyond. The truck which had for all practical purposes been looted in the courtyard was just getting under way again. It would stop at the service dock behind the House for proper unloading. Ever since a driver had been beaten within an inch of his life, the provisions vehicles touched down in the courtyard first. "That's why," Marilee continued on a rising inflexion, "his father falsified the birth records thirty years ago to make it appear that Thomas was the elder twin."

"Marilee, my dear, we've been over this," said Dyson in a patronizing sing-song. It rasped the woman's nerves like wind on an aspen. Dyson knew that, and his smile was all the broader for that fact. "Legally, your late husband was the Slade Councilor—as your son Edward will be when he comes of age. There's no point trying to overturn a Council decision, especially a decision made so long ago. And after all, if you claim your father-in-law lied to the Council, why do you presume his dying words to his son were the truth? That's not logical, my dear."

"Well, it's the curst truth!" the woman blazed. She turned. Her heels clacked on the mosaics of imported marble which overlaid a floor of sand-finished concrete dating back to the Settlement. The widow was tall, man-tall, though most of her height was from the waist down. The garment she wore had legs when she strode, but it was a single glittering cocoon when she chose to stand straight. The fabric shaded from black at the lower gathering to a flame-shot scarlet on the woman's slim neck. "Listen, Dyson," she snapped along a pointing finger, "even if—"

"Beverly, my dear, please," the handsome man interrupted. "After all, we've known each other all our lives." He too stood, dropping the flaccid stim cone back into the waist pouch from which he had taken it. There was a trash chute in the pedestal table beside him. Using the chute would have permitted others to examine the container, to penetrate a facet of the disguise in which Dyson wrapped himself.

"*Councilor* Dyson," retorted Marilee Slade. "Look, if you want me to treat you as a human being, then you've got to stop this nonsense about appointing yourself guardian for Edward. He's not a child, he's almost twenty—and if he *needs* a guardian, it can be me!"

The tall woman pivoted back to the window. Beverly Dyson permitted his face to lose the mobility he maintained when others were watching him. "I don't appoint anyone guardian, Marilee," he said. "That's what the Council meeting is being held to discuss. Though of course I won't deny that many of the Council do believe there should be—a—I'm sorry, but facts are facts—a strong male hand at the helm of the Slade Estate during these troubled times."

When the woman did not respond, Dyson stepped carefully closer to her. He had been beautiful as a child and as a youth. When he reached adulthood, Dyson had been wise enough to eschew the cosmetic treatments that would have frozen that youthful beauty. Twenty-odd years of natural ageing had left Councilor Beverly Dyson ruggedly handsome. He was as attractive to men as to women, and he had none of the smooth cuteness that destroyed respect when power was being discussed.

There was a mark on Dyson's left forehead where age had begun to undo some expensive plastic surgery. The skin there was a trifle shinier than the rest, and there was a path that could be traced back in whorls along Dyson's short-cut hair. "You know, my dear," he went on in a carefully modulated voice, "there's a simple solution. We were friends when we were younger. I still want to be your friend, and more than friend." His hand reached out toward the woman in a gesture that deliberately stopped short of her arm.

The curving crystal surface of the window had been treated during extrusion to permit no reflection on the inner side. There was obvious awareness of the outstretched hand in Marilee's voice, however, as she said, "If you want a strong male hand running the Slade Estate, then wait for Don to return. It can't be long, now that Friesland says they've traced him."

"Marilee," said Dyson sadly. "Even if I believed that weren't one of your little games to delay the Council, my dear, I scarcely think that Mad Dog Slade is what is required on a world already having difficulties with violence among the *lower* orders." He had difficulty keeping his tone light, and his arm lowered slowly.

"Mad Dog," the woman repeated with seeming amusement. She continued to face the activity in the courtyard below. "You know, I knew Don Slade pretty well, Bev . . . and I never knew him to lose his temper."

"I'm the wrong one to tell *that* silly lie, lady!" shouted Councilor Dyson. His fresh, bubbling anger drew Marilee's gaze as his attempted tenderness had not. Dyson touched the scar on his forehead. "I'm not going to forget, you see, what he did to *me* for a childhood prank!"

Marilee smiled. His rage was her victory. "I haven't forgotten that either Bev," she said. "It must have been quite a surprise when

Don popped to the surface after you thought you'd bolted the escape hatch over him. But I really don't think he lost his temper when he came for you with the wrench. I think he had just decided the world would be a better place with you dead. Don was never the one to leave dirty jobs for other people when he could handle them himself."

Laughter pursued Councilor Dyson as he strode from the room.

CHAPTER SIX

"We had a bad one," Don said without preamble as he opened the door of the Terzia's chamber. "I left all the harvest so we could get back quicker with the wounded. Brought the dead; I know it didn't matter, but I did and I don't care cop what you think about it."

The big man paused for the first time since he entered the room. He swallowed and said, "There were two missing. We searched, but there's two missing."

"That doesn't matter, Don," said the Terzia from the bed itself. "Come—come sit by me while I talk."

The poison burns on Slade's upper body were white with the SpraySeal which now covered them. Besides the sweat-streaked dust on his skin and trousers, Slade's hands had a black patina. He had changed the barrel of his powergun as soon as he entered the Citadel. The one he had used on the giant carnivore was by no means shot out; but there was no reason to skimp on equipment, and a millimeter's tighter focus on a bolt might mean a life.

"Lady," Slade said, "the harvest's all over the trail and beside it. I'm going out with another gang. I'll be back as soon as we've gathered up the copper-pods—"

"They don't matter, Don. Sit down."

"—and found the bodies; Terzia, it matters to me," Slade concluded. His weariness was no veil over the angry determination in his voice.

The Terzia lay on a glade-green spread in a pool of light muted to duplicate forest shadows. Slade had never been sure of the process by which Terzia controlled the light. At other times, it had seemed to him to be extremely sensual.

"Don," the Terzia began. Then she lowered the hand with which she had beckoned him. In a changed, business-like voice, she said, "Both the bodies are with the carnivore, as you call it, some three kilometers from where it was shot. A party of workers has been sent out to retrieve the remains from the seventeenth-segment limb on the animal's right side and from its gullet. That business does not require you. This does. Sit down, please."

Slade's lips worked—silently, because he could not decide quite what words he wanted them to form. His left hand, smudged already with carbon and metal, touched the fresh and gleaming barrel of his powergun for reassurance. "I don't . . ." Slade said without the haste or hostility of a moment before.

"Don, come here if you think you might ever want to leave Terzia," the other said. She held out her hand again.

Slade moved as he would have moved to mount his tank in an alert: quickly, but with the caution that kept haste from being a danger. He laid his weapon on the table that had held it in the past and stepped toward the bed. He wiped his palms nervously on the dirty fabric of his trousers. Slade was not fit to see a woman, to make love on a sleek, resilient bed to a beauty herself so sleek and as capable of innovation as of response.

He did not hesitate, because he knew by more than words that the Terzia cared for the customary graces only as it pleased her lover to provide them. Slade had made love in alleys and in trenches, once even on his own stretcher in the casualty holding station as an affirmation to himself of his intention to survive. The Terzia was a jewel, not some fellow-swimmer in the maelstrom as those other partners had been. Or again—

Slade's groin was quickening with new excitement as he slid onto the bed.

"Is . . ." he said as his hands cupped her left shoulder and right buttock, calluses over smooth skin and the muscles supple beneath each. "Is there word of a ship coming in?"

"And any ship would be enough," said the Terzia sadly. Her arms circled him, drawing her naked chest against the big man's. His body quivered with a vibrancy she had not drunk from it in months. "You want to leave me so badly."

"Lady," Slade said. He squeezed her tighter in unconscious reaction to the words he was framing. "I don't want to leave you, but I want to go home. I'd. . . . You're a princess here, a queen." He arched back slightly so that he could look at the Terzia's face. "It'd be crazy for you to leave all this to come to Tethys. Gravel and sea, that's all it'd be to you. But it's my home."

"No, I couldn't leave my world, even with you," the Terzia said. Her eyes were on Slade's chest, on the black, springy delicacy of the hairs that doubled by their shadows on his skin. "I'll arrange for you to leave, then, Don. I think you should know—" she looked up to meet his puzzled expression— "that matters on your homeworld are very unsettled. You might find yourself safer—and happier—if you chose some other destination in which to settle down. If not here, then—" the assumed humanity of the Terzia caused her voice to catch— "perhaps back on Friesland. Your friends there have not, have not forgotten you."

Disbelieving, as tense and as careful as when he disarmed booby-traps, Don Slade said, "Lady, I thank you, but . . . it's been a long road to get here, and I don't think I'll turn back now. If there's trouble on Tethys, then I guess there's trouble anywhere, one way or the other. I'm as used to it as the next man. And I'd—" he bent forward again and nuzzled the Terzia's hair— "really like to go home."

"You will," said the almost woman. She shifted her body to free Slade's trouser catches. "You will very soon, my darling."

CHAPTER SEVEN

There was a bay concealed in the Citadel's flank. Its doors slowed, then latched open. Slade stared at the vessel hangared within. Then he looked back at the Terzia. He was not sure whether she had made a mistake through ignorance or whether he was the butt of a joke grim even by the standards of mercenary soldiers. "Terzia," Slade said in a voice that he worked to control, "this is only a lifeboat. It can't carry me back home."

"Not directly," agreed the Terzia off-handedly. For the first time since Slade had met her, she had not dressed before leaving her chamber. Intellectually, Slade knew that there was no more reason to dress for the autochthones than there was to dress before being seen by so many dogs . . . and there was no more reason to dress for one's lover than for one's mirror. Terzia's nonchalance surprised Slade, however, and the fact that nudity was a change bothered him. "It has a range of forty-five Transit seconds, though," she continued. "That will take you to Elysium."

Slade had stepped into the bay to touch the boat's nose. The hull's spongy coating was perfectly fresh. The only marks on the vessel's white surface were consistent with jostling during loading and shipment. The boat had very clearly never been moved under its own power. "I don't recall an Elysium in this sector," the man said as he paced cautiously along the vessel's seven-meter length. Like "Tethys," Elysium was a name of some frequency among the scattered human settlements.

"It's not in your indices,"said the Terzia. Something she did caused a motor to whine. The lifeboat began to ease out of the bay on its docking cradle. The low sun stained the ablative coating a pinkish color as the nose inched into the light. "The inhabitants are human, though they have no open traffic with the rest of the galaxy. They'll help you home for my sake; and perhaps for your sake as well."

Slade let the vessel slide past him. He stepped around its stern. He continued to examine the boat, even though his expertise would scarcely have let him discover gross damage to the structure. Slade was no rocket jockey. The thought of leaving in this contraption frightened him even against his hopes of escape from plush captivity. Only the fact that lifeboats were designed for use by the ignorant gave him any confidence at all in the coming operation.

The Terzia stood in the open. To Slade, she was framed between the bulk of the vessel and the doorpost. Her waist tucked in above hips that felt firmer than their fullness suggested. The shadow of one breast lay across the cone of the other. Her nipples were dark and still erect, though the Terzia's face was in repose as she met Slade's eyes.

The motor's whisper died back into silence. The lifeboat halted, now clear of the bay.

A tendril of vine squeezed a switch in a control box. The boat's hatch began to clamshell open. The Terzia had no non-mechanical control over machinery or other inanimate objects. Mechanical control was not limited to that exerted by her humanoid body, however. The result had to it a touch of magic or implanted electronics. It was new to Don Slade; and it was being shown him now only because the whole mime was ending.

"It's programmed to Elysium," the Terzia said. She was facing Slade, smiling at him as he walked slowly out of the building. "Food and water for twelve, there'll be no difficulty that way. You will have to bring her down yourself, though; there aren't any over-ride docking facilities on Elysium."

"I . . ." said Slade. His eyelids lowered as he stepped back into the sunlight. "Lady, I've never landed one of these. I guess you're sure that there'll be no freighters down soon?"

"That's beyond my control," said the Terzia coolly. "I can prevent ships from landing, but I can't make them come. And I can't be sure how much time I have. How much time your friends will permit me. I must consider the risk to Terzia now, you see."

"Of course," said the man, though the words made only grammatical sense to him. Something had changed, but Slade could not imagine what.

A year on Terzia had not rotted Slade's mind, but the year had its own parameters, as did any long time spent in a habitat. Slade was somewhat disoriented by being faced here with a sort of urgency that was familiar when he was a mercenary soldier. "Well, I've hit dirt on the likes of these before, so. . . ."

"At first I thought the ship itself was alive," said the Terzia with her face turned up to the sky. It was still blue in the west, but it shaded imperceptibly to magenta on the further rim of the horizon. A few bright stars waited there, above the gently-waving jungle canopy. "Then I learned it was the men, not the ships; but it was very long, very long indeed before I realized that the men were different among themselves in such a way."

"I'm not—Via, I don't understand what you mean," Slade said.

A ladder began to extend from the open cockpit. It was swinging wide enough to clear the hull's soft coating. Half-deployed, the ladder began to jerk as the motor protested. Burrs on an untested cam or lubricant congealed in the step-down gears were hanging up the system. Slade jumped, caught the bottom rung, and let his weight jerk the ladder over the rough spot before he let go.

The Terzia had still not answered him. It was becoming clear that she did not intend to do so; and the man's words had not precisely been a question, anyway. "You will be able to land it?" she asked.

"Sure," said Slade. He rubbed his palms together, the one slick with grime of some sort from the ladder. "I, I'll just get some of my gear together, I guess."

"No," said the Terzia. "There is clothing aboard, and the Elysians will provide you with whatever you need there. Tell them I sent you, to help you go home. You had nothing of particular note with you when you decided to—visit here, did you? Your wealth is still on Friesland, waiting for a bank transfer?"

Turning to the open hatch and not to the Terzia's rich, dark hair, Slade said, "Ah, I wonder if I could, ah, buy one of the guns in the armory. I know there can be some problems with arms shipments, and you don't know when you'd raise another freighter, like you say. But I'd be obliged—"

"Oh, Don," the Terzia said. Her arms encircled him from behind. Her hair and perfume flowed over Slade like the love that was back in her voice. "You could have the planetary defense battery if you could carry it, but not to Elysium. They would be offended, and you won't need a gun anyway, not there. . . . Not here, either, except for the sake of your own wants. I'll keep the guns you used so well, and perhaps there'll be another visitor who will want them and want me . . . and whom I will want in turn. I don't think you can imagine how rare—"

Slade turned. Her breasts were warm against him; a runnel of perspiration on his own chest dammed and spilled sideways as the two embraced. "I wish," Slade whispered before their mouths met. There was nothing more he could have said in any event.

It was the Terzia who gave the extra squeeze, then stepped away. "You are welcome here," she said. "You will always be welcome here, while you remain—the Captain Donald Slade that you are. While you live." She turned and began to walk briskly away from the open lifeboat.

Slade licked his lips, then nodded to no particular purpose. The ladder was ten rungs to the hatch, but he mounted them with only six long, deliberate movements of his arms and legs.

At the rim of the hatch, the man looked back and found the Terzia was watching him again from an open gateway of the Citadel. "You must remember," she said distinctly, "that I am not really human, Don Slade." Then she disappeared within the black, towering building.

It seemed somehow to Slade that the Terzia had been talking to herself; and in the softening light, he could not really have seen tears on the lovely cheeks anyway.

CHAPTER EIGHT

"Number two thruster has failed to trip," said the console, in Spanglish and with a decidedly cheerful tone.

"Via!" Don Slade said. The boat's control console was supposed to have brought them out of Transit space with momentum calculated for a feather-light thruster landing on Elysium. "Why—" Wrong question, save it for later. "Cancel. Does the other thruster have enough power to bring us down safely?"

"The other two thrusters," the console said, supercilious now as well as cheerful, though Slade could imagine a programmer thinking the correction might be useful to the pilot, "have more than enough power to execute the landing within the original parameters."

Praise the Lord, even if the initial announcement had taken a year off Slade's life. He didn't have much head for heights, and the rate at which Elysium was swelling in the analog displays did nothing for his heart rate, either. The planet appeared blue in the onrushing holograms. Tethys would have been gray at the same distance; though on Tethys' surface, the moaning seas were blue and green and sometimes a maroon like an emperor's robe, when the sun and the life within the waters were just right. "What happened to Number Two?"

"An error in assembly," the console said. "A three-oh-three-seven board was installed in the control circuit instead of the four-oh-three-seven board proper for this model."

"Via," Slade repeated. The vessel was beginning to shudder now with the atmospheric buffeting he recognized from a score of light-craft insertions. However, Slade did not usually have a display to remind him of the terrifying height and speed.

"The feed valve in number two thruster did not shut off when the unit failed to trip," said the console's happy voice. "We are losing reaction mass at the maximum rate of flow for that unit. We will be at approximately twenty-one thousand meters above the planetary surface when thrusters one and three shut off for lack of reaction mass."

"Blood and death," said Don Slade in open-eyed horror.

"Unless there is a failure in those unit controls also," the console added in a caveat which it might have programmed into itself during the past seconds.

"All right," said Slade. He rose from the pilot's seat in front of controls he did not understand and could not in any case have used as effectively as the console itself had done. "Run through recommended procedures for this emergency—and if you say there isn't one, I'll come through a bulkhead to find you!"

"Unlock and press the red lever on the underside of your right chair arm," the console said. "The chair will drop into the escape capsule. I will deploy the capsule when thrust ceases. I am broadcasting a Mayday, giving course and altitude particulars on five bands carrying local communications traffic. I am adding the information that the Terzia has asked that you be afforded aid."

Slade interlaced his fingers behind his neck and jerked back, cracking stiffness out of his shoulder muscles. Then he sat down again in front of the console. The short hop from Terzia had required three weeks of perceived time, because the boat's instruments were not powerful enough to lop off large chunks of Transit space. During that time, the console had gotten on Slade's nerves badly. Its cheerful voice had seemed to sneer at all his questions as at those of an ignoramus . . . as Slade indeed was, in the craft of space-faring.

But the machine's exposition now reminded the man uncomfortably of his training officer long years before. The officer was Major With, an Academy graduate from Friesland and a professional with no sympathy for recruits who had not grown up with organized warfare the way he himself had done. Major With had discussed failures in target practice or personal hygiene in a dispassionate voice that cut a recruit like a trip to the flogging block.

With's voice had remained just as cool, his appraisals just as accurate, the night enemy commandos hit the Operations Center because local traitors had sabotaged the perimeter warning system. None of the commandos survived after they wiped out the head-quarters cadre. With precision, Major With had disposed his half-trained recruits by radio even as the commandos blasted through a wall of the room in which he was barricaded.

Control consoles were not human, of course. But Slade hadn't been sure that Major Frikki With was human either, before that night he saved so many of the trainees he had scorned.

"Dust to dust," Slade muttered as he sat down again. He threw the concealed lever. His stomach lurched with the drop, and the light went out. Something slammed shut overhead.

The lifeboat had bunks for twelve, but it did not surprise Slade to learn that there was only one escape capsule. Spacers and those who built to spacers' specifications had a tendency to regard out-siders as cargo, not humans. This boat had been intended for an immigrant ship in which a single crewman would have commanded a load of lay freight.

The lurching darkness in which Slade was now confined was oddly comforting. He no longer had displays and meaningless controls to worry him. What waited on the ground did, sure, but it wasn't a hot LZ. The familiar state of mind excluded the other concerns over which he had no control. Slade's right palm sweated for a gunswitch to rest on, but that was no great lack.

Ejection was downward and sudden, sharp enough to lift Slade against the restraints that had wrapped him to the seat without his will or notice. The capsule was not blind, as he had thought and secretly hoped. Screens, black because their pickups had been shrouded in the belly of the lifeboat, flared when the capsule spat free. Three digital displays and a horizon with arrow came to life at the same instant of uncoupling. The shock of the drogue chute deploying snapped Slade back into the seat. His feet and the base of the capsule jerked up against the drag. Then the main canopy banged open, forcing Slade's weight through the cushions and against the metal backing of the seat.

That was the point at which everything went to hell again.

It was probably nobody's fault that the boat's fuel-starved thrusters cut out a half second apart instead of simultaneously. That skewed impulse was enough to send the vessel rumbling at 90° to its programmed slant away from the capsule. If the timing had been slightly worse, the separated objects would have merged again and reached the planetary surface as an amalgam of metal and extruded flesh. Instead, the lifeboat rotated through the capsule's parachute with the motion of a hawker winding cotton candy onto a cone. Then the vessel passed on, releasing the chute with a last playful tug. The fabric streamed behind the capsule. It was a shroud for Slade's corpse and no longer a canopy that could slow his impact to a safe degree.

The castaway had a brief hint of what must have happened. The display whose pick-up had shown the canopy's black fabric across the violet of space suddenly changed. It filled with the streaked white coating of the lifeboat's belly. Then the black was gone and the white was a spark. Images spun to match the sudden fury of the capsule from which they were observed.

The digital displays went wild. The attitude arrow blurred from its own spinning and from Slade's failing consciousness. He never wholly blacked out, but there was no task he could have accomplished had one been set him. Slade was at the point of a high-speed corkscrew. Centrifugal force darkened his face and hands with blood. Across him played the light of the downward screen. The screen was verdant with the image of a meadow through which the capsule would crush its path.

The first hint of relief was a tug too gentle to have been noticed, even if Slade had his full faculties. The canopy had been stopped from spinning, but it was some seconds before that stasis was transmitted through the line to brake the capsule's own rotation. Even before that happened, there was a shift of perceived weight downward as Slade's body translated deceleration into gravity. The unread altimeters that had been clicking off a descent of over fifty meters per second began to slow at an increasing rate. The capsule was being controlled as an angler controls the rush of a fish against a light line. The attitude arrow steadied into a sway that matched the way the globe rolled in the lower screen.

In the upper screen was a daisy-chain of four air cars, each with a line of the canopy looped over a stanchion. The cars were so light that even under full power they should not have been able to halt Slade's plummeting descent. With intelligence and equal care, they had re-extended enough of the canopy to take the initial shock of deceleration. The cars must have dived nose-first to make the pick-up, but now their bellies were to the capsule and their fan modules were directed straight down. It would have taken skill and great strength to control such a vehicle with one hand and with the other to reach out into a two-hundred kph air-stream to snag the canopy.

Now that the descent was slow and controlled, the drivers leaned over to peer at the capsule between their vehicles and the black curve of the canopy. Either the pick-up lied, or Slade's rescuers were a group of young girls.

CHAPTER NINE

Because the capsule was supported by four separately-controlled vehicles, it lurched the last hand's-breadth to the ground. That was still a softer landing than many that Slade had made behind professionals . . . and only seconds before, he would have traded his hope of salvation for the chance to awaken in a hospital, much less to walk away from the capsule. There was a quick-release lever in the center of the panel in front of the seat. Slade was still searching for it when his rescuers turned the dogs from outside and the walls fell away. Slade was surrounded by nymphs on a sunlit meadow.

Slade's first thought was that they were girls and very pretty. A moment's further consideration showed that in fact, his four rescuers were women and beautiful—but there was a level of truth to the initial impression as well. Three of them were dark-haired and stood nearly as tall as the man's shoulder. The fourth had the same elfin features, but she was fifty millimeters short of the others' height and her hair was red. None of them were as old as eighteen standard years, so far as the castaway could judge. The red-haired girl reached to hand Slade out of the capsule. If the others were nymphs, then surely the fourth was a pixie princess.

A girl giggled. "Lord have mercy!" Slade muttered. He had been too logy until that moment to remember that he was still as naked as he had been during the long, lonely Transit from Terzia.

All of his rescuers were laughing, now, though it was not a cruel sound. "Here, you've come this far," said the red-haired one as Slade tried to hide back in the capsule. She gave his hand an encouraging tug. "We shouldn't laugh," she said. "Liet, toss me my wrap from under the seat."

Slade swallowed. He should have learned more about Elysium before he left Terzia, but Lord! he'd been launched and gone before he really had time to think about what was happening to him. You don't really cross cultures when you have a gun in your fist and orders to execute. Your culture is that of your unit, and what surrounds your unit is so much glassware—to be spared where practical. This was different; and a gun, while intrinsically useless, would have made a useful pacifier for Slade's soul.

"Thank you, lady," he said to the girl who handed him the wrap. It was just that, a cape with a brooch fastener. The metal was a copper alloy, hand-worked and very delicate. With the cape upended, what would have been the lower hem for the owner could be pinned around Slade's solid waist. The rest hung down as a tawny apron, a natural wool of some sort, and quite adequate for modesty. Slade had soldiered too long to have any personal taboos about nudity. He had, however, a lively appreciation of how the parents of these girls might react to the naked man who suddenly appeared with them. He stepped carefully out of the capsule.

Flustered, Slade had last spoken in his birth tongue. In Spanglish, "lady" would have been replaced by "donya" in the vocative. It was in the same true English that one of the girls now said, "But how are we going to carry him, Risa? He must weigh two hundred and—" She flicked her eyes back to Slade in a glance that appraised more than his weight, correcting the phrase already begun. "A hundred and ten kilos at least."

"Oh, that'll be all right, Sare," said the red-haired girl, the leader as the castaway's instincts told him. "He'll ride with me. We'll stay low and slow. If the drain's still too much for my power, you can jumper me."

"Ah, ladies?" Slade said. "You're going to take me to your government? I was sent here by the ruler of a neighboring world—" Via! The Mayday had mentioned Terzia, and they must have heard it or they couldn't have snagged him out of his streaming plunge.

Think! "Ah, I was sent here by the Terzia, who thought your rulers could help me."

The air cars, though light, showed a heartening sophistication that belied the wool wrap and the hand-crafted brooch. Dainty bronze-ware wasn't going to get Don Slade home in his lifetime.

Liet giggled again, but Risa said, "We'll take you to the city, of course. There aren't many visitors here on Elysium, not many people know about us; but I'm sure we'll be able to help any friend of the Terzia."

They were all looking at Slade in some wonder. He had suspicion that Risa's "not many visitors" was an understatement. "It's not in your charts," the Terzia had said of this Elysium, and Slade had no reason to believe that she was wrong.

Certainly the cursory navigational data supplied with the lifeboat did not mention the place. The girls' eyes made Slade feel something like a side of meat, but he had at least the consolation that it was pretty good meat.

Slade was past his first youth, but he had no inclination to have become inactive. He had seen too many line officers leave a tank turret for a desk and go to seed with appalling suddenness. Slade's build would permit that if he let it, the great ropes of muscle growing marbled with fat, the hard belly beginning to sag to match the wobbling buttocks. The tan of Terzia's sun had faded somewhat during the voyage, but improvised exercise had kept up the muscle tone of his big body. Sare's estimate of his weight was short by five kilos, perhaps because so much of Slade's bulk was dense muscle.

Also . . . early in his service with the Slammers, before a former nickname had resurfaced, Slade had been known as "Tripod." He knew quite well that in love-making, as in any other craft, the workman's skill is more important than his tool. From the way their eyes flickered to Slade's groin, it seemed that these girls were not aware of that as yet.

"Well, I think we'd better get back," Risa said. "If you wouldn't mind, sir, we'll trim better if you sit sideways in the luggage space instead of in the other seat. I'm afraid you'll have to put your knees up."

Risa was leading the way to the open car. She stretched back an index finger as if to draw Slade physically along. The other three girls scattered at once to their own vehicles. All of them were landed neatly beside the collapsed parachute. The chute's monomolecular fabric should have been of interest to locals who seemed to wear no synthetics. The girls scampered over the canopy without a glance down, and Slade knew enough to doubt their disinterest stemmed from ignorance.

The hull of Risa's car was molded in pastel swirls. The pattern was not quite garish up close, and at any distance it would mute into a blur more natural than any equal expanse of a solid color could be. The meadow's vegetation was more varied than the screens could suggest, but only an occasional stalk was more than a meter high. There were no thorns to jab Slade's legs or bare feet.

The car was little more than two seats and, behind them, a cargo space narrow enough to be a strait fit for Slade's chest sideways. "Lord and Martyrs," he exclaimed as he seated himself gingerly. "You dived this at two hundred kays?"

"We had to," said Risa, hopping into the driver's seat. "Nobody else was anywhere around, and we couldn't just let you fall."

The car staggered a little on a sliding lift-off, but its fans had a surprising amount of power for an open vehicle. Risa trimmed them manually at three meters, then slipped upward to ten where there was a better view of the rolling landscape.

The planet was not entirely open meadow as Slade's subconscious had been trying to convince him. Mountains were now visible astern in the near distance, and the broad band of darker green to the left was surely a forest fringing a watercourse. In addition, mixed herds of animals, none of them familiar to Slade, cropped the vegetation. Occasionally, the whine of fan blades or the shadow of one of the cars flitting above would spook a whole section of the plain. Hundreds of beasts, the largest species up to half the size of the lifeboat, would rush off across the sward like dark surf. They showed no signs of being domesticated.

It was a matter of increasing concern to Slade that, apart from the cars, there were no signs of civilization at all.

"You settled here recently?" he asked. That would explain both the low population and the Terzia's remark about the planet being uncharted.

The car was traveling at fifty kph or less, so wind noise was no impediment to normal speech. Risa glanced back at her passenger and gave him a broad smile. "We've been here longer than you might think," she said. "But if you mean Elysium doesn't show— signs of much development, well, that's true. Our ancestors picked this world to settle because it seemed to them a paradise, a—" she dimpled— "an Elysium. They were determined to keep it that way, and every generation since then has agreed. There aren't many of us on Elysium—that's part of why the planet has stayed, well . . ." She took her left hand from the controls to gesture in an evocative semi-circle. "But we're happy with our world and happy with our lives, almost all of us."

Slade nodded and tried to keep the questions behind his eyes. Early migrant ships did not pick and choose planets. They had drives which frequently failed, leaving them between stars with no way to re-enter Transit space, or—and this could only be surmised because it left only negative evidence in the human universe— stranded them forever in Transit, in an envelope crushed slowly inward by a palpable grayness.

Risa either read or deduced the doubt in the castaway's mind. "Our ancestors were slow-ship colonists," she said. "That wasn't working for many reasons, so they found a way to escape from their vessel. But I guess it'd be better if you heard the details of all that from my parents."

"This seems a very lovely world," Slade said carefully, "and a very peaceful one." He did not know whether the girl was lying to him or if she were merely retailing the lie which had been told her in the guise of history. That was not important, but it *was* crucial for Slade to learn enough of the present situation for him to tailor his own lies to meet it. He was a lone traveler, and his hopes of getting home depended on the impression he made on the people he was about to meet.

"Oh, very much so," Risa agreed with another bright smile.

"That's the main reason we don't mix very much with other, well, cultures. There'd be problems—sometimes not even everybody here on Elysium agrees about what to do or how. If we opened ourselves to the rest of the galaxy, some of the problems might become violent. Avoiding violence was very important to our ancestors, and to us."

"Well," said Don Slade, "a merchant like me who's bounced around on a lot of planets sees violence, I'm afraid. And I can only respect the way you folk have managed to avoid it." There was, Slade realized, as much truth to that statement as not.

Risa had not called her base, home, whatever, so far as Slade could tell. He had noticed that the girls in the accompanying cars were speaking. Though there were no microphones evident, it was obvious that they were reporting to someone. Six or eight kilometers ahead, on the shore of a lake that reflected the clouds above it, was a settlement of a few hundred houses and a probable public building or two. None of the structures looked particularly impressive, though that opinion might be affected by distance and the way the walls managed to blend with their surroundings. "This is the nearest town, then?" Slade asked.

"This is the town," Risa said, "though we call it the city." For a moment the girl's smile was replaced by something gentle but wistful. "We've seen real cities, you know," she said. "But none of us have visited one."

Risa touched a plate in the dashboard. It glowed green, reassuring her about the state of the power-pack. The car's instrumentation was unobtrusive but very slick, certainly nothing some farmer had cobbled together during a long winter. "This isn't everyone," the girl said. "Lot of families like to live alone or with just a few neighbors. But there aren't very many of us, as I said."

"Well, the . . ." Slade said, frowning now in open puzzlement. "These air cars. They are made on Elysium, aren't they? Or do you—?"

"Oh, the machinery!" Risa said delightedly. "Oh, my goodness, you thought you'd see that! All of that is underground, right here, most of it, under the houses and some distance beyond, I believe.

I'm sure they'll show it to you if you'd like, but it isn't the sort of thing we—on Elysium—wanted in the open. My goodness," she repeated, her laughter bubbling into the sky as an image occurred to her. "You must have thought you were on a planet where you'd have to grow a long white beard and learn to card wool. Really, I'm sure my parents can help you get home."

"Risa," said some undifferentiated part of the dashboard in a bass voice, "why don't you bring our guest by the house first. We have some clothes for him. After he's had a chance to bathe and change, your mother and I will walk him over to the Hall for dinner."

"All right, Dad," the girl replied. Slade could not see how she was keying the mike, but there could have been a button on the control stick. Risa made a moue over her shoulder at the man. "I hope you like red," she said. "Kelwin dearly loves it, and I doubt anyone else in town has clothes to lend that might fit you. Not that you're as *heavy* as Kel. . . ."

People were standing on porches or against vine-covered fences, watching the car approach. The individual yards were separated by walkways, but there did not seem to be any provision for ground vehicles. That was not completely inexplicable, but the only air cars Slade had seen were the quartet that had rescued him. Additional transport should have been parked in the yards, even if none of it happened to be airborn at the moment.

Then Risa guided her vehicle—a trifle too fast at first, because she was unused to compensating for Slade's considerable mass—around a house of weathered stone. An older man and woman waved from where they stood, well clear of the opened back wall. Risa tilted the fans forward to balance momentum with their thrust. Then she drove neatly into the building and parked beside two very similar cars.

The garage was well lighted. Slade had expected the floor and walls to be stone or concrete. It was with a sense of surprise that he realized these were some synthetic which glowed without any external light source.

The older couple had walked in as Risa shut the fans down. They could have passed as Slade's age or less, but the castaway's instinct was that they were much older. The man had Risa's hair and features, while the woman was nearly blond and somewhat less fine-drawn. Both smiled warmly at the girl and her passenger. "I'm Nan," said the woman as she stretched out a hand to Slade, "Risa's mother; and this is my husband Onander. I'm sure our daughter has welcomed you to Elysium, but let me assure you that the welcome was from the whole community."

The hull and seat-back flexed beneath Slade's weight when he levered himself out of the space in which he had ridden. He touched Nan's hand as he stepped from the vehicle, though he was careful not to put any strain on her. "Lady," he said, conscious of his image but able nonetheless to be sincere, "your daughter and her friends saved my life. I can't think of any welcome better than that one. And if there's any way you might help me get home, the way the Terzia thought you might, I—well, how could I owe you for more than my life? But I would appreciate it."

"Of course we'll help you," said Onander. He clasped the bigger man, hand to biceps, in a gesture that brought their left wrists together as if they were mingling blood. "But I hope you'll accept a night of our hospitality here. We dare allow few visitors, but someone the Terzia recommended is welcome not only as a guest but also as a font to slake our curiosity. But you will—" he glanced down at Slade's garment with a smile and not censure—"be more comfortable in proper clothes, won't you? They're right upstairs in the bathroom."

Nan and Onander were already leading the way around the parked cars to the staircase in a corner. The outside door had pivoted shut unnoticed. That was the sort of effortless control to be expected in a room with smoothly-gleaming surfaces; but the stairs took Slade aback again. They were of dark wood, old enough to show wear in the gentle bowing of the treads. Each tread was pegged, not nailed or glued, to the stringers. The fit appeared flawless.

"Via, this is a fine piece of work," Slade said aloud as he let his fingers brush the balustrade. He felt that he had to be as careful with it as he had been with his hostess, though the dense wood barely flexed beneath his foot. It struck him that the Elysians themselves might be less fragile than his nervousness seemed to be warning him.

Nan glanced back at the big man. "My mother's mother built it," she said. "To replace the extruded one. I'm told that it was almost six years before she called it finished—not that she was working on it full time."

Nan paused at the stair head and rapped the balustrade. The sound had a life that masonry or synthetics would not have duplicated. "They were both, this and the plastic, utilitarian in that they permitted people to walk between the garage and the first floor," the woman continued. "But this had a utility for my grandmother while she was working on it, too . . . and for us, to remember her every time a step sounds on the tread."

As he mounted the last step himself, Slade glanced over his shoulder and smiled. Risa still waited at the foot of the stairs, watching the play of the castaway's muscles. When his eyes caught hers, the girl blushed before she grinned back.

CHAPTER TEN

"The seat of honor, Mister Slade," Onander said as he pointed to the chair at the center of the cross table. The chair to either side of the central one was empty also. Nan took the guest's hand lightly to bring him forward, much as her daughter had led Slade to the car.

There were about thirty adults already sitting at the two side tables and at the seats to either end of the table that crossed them into a square-based U. They clapped lightly as the castaway entered the room. There were decanters and covered dishes on the tables, but the meal had waited for Slade's arrival.

Slade's tunic and shorts were red, as he had been warned. The garments were comfortably light in the warm evening, and they were loose enough to give him occasional twinges as he remembered his garb on landing. Other Elysians were wearing similar clothing, though mostly of printed cloth. There was no certain cut or style. One man was nude at least from the tabletop to his cap of iridescent feathers.

Nan sat in one of the flanking chairs. Onander pulled out the central one and gestured Slade into it. Before the Elysian himself sat down, however, he called, "Friends? Our guest would probably be better for a meal in him. Afterwards, we hope he'll join us in the other room and tell us something about himself and the things he's seen; but for now, let's all eat in peace."

There was another patter of hands beneath a rainbow of Elysian smiles.

The Slammers were normally fed with ration packs, standardized food. It might once have had a Dutch emphasis, but when reconstituted it tended to be as featureless as a hooker's thirtieth trick of the night. The mercenary troops themselves came from worlds as varied as those on which a contract might station them. It was better to accept the cost and inconvenience of standardized rations than to lose thirty percent of your effectives to diarrhea or constipation every time you shifted planets.

Slade, however, had made a practice of eating on the local economy wherever possible. He hadn't joined Hammer to be bored, and he'd always figured he pulled his weight even when he had the runs. The big man therefore appreciated the meal before him as few of his fellows would have been able to do.

Not that the food was exotic in any normal sense. There was roast meat, vegetables both raw and cooked—nothing Slade recognized, and nothing particularly striking except a dish that looked like cole slaw and tasted like napalm—and bread, which was almost certainly baked from Terran wheat. The wine was probably better than Slade had a palate to enjoy. He had grown up on Tethys with stim cones, not alcohol. His introduction to the latter as a low-ranking trooper had been regimental stash, valued for reasons apart from its piquant subtleties of flavor.

"You know," he said around a bite of roast—from the end, where it was cooked gray, not pink—"I sort of thought you might be vegetarians. It, well, I thought you might."

"Some of us are," Onander said as he forked more meat from the tray between the two men. "Down at the far end," he noted, with a gesture toward one of the side tables, brief enough to be unobtrusive. "We haven't a large population on Elysium, but neither is it a monolithic one. You wouldn't prefer, ah, vegetable protein, would you? Really, I should have checked."

Slade had not been conscious of being the center of attention. The other people in the hall had been eating and chatting in normal fashion. Now, however, the big wood-paneled room had noticeably stilled. "Oh, not at all," the castaway said in embarrassment. "It's mostly seafood of one sort or another . . . a lot of it compressed and textured plankton, but animals to start out even if they were little ones."

He grinned and looked around the room. "Tell the truth, a lot of what I was raised to eat was about as bland as regimental food." He raised a bite of roast on his fork. "Nothing as good as this," he closed, putting an obvious period to the explanation by eating the morsel.

Slade had not done any physical labor since his last bout of exercise on the lifeboat. The tension of the landing, however, had itself kept his metabolism cooking at a high rate. He plowed on through repeated servings, vaguely conscious without focusing on it that those around him continued to eat though at a much lower rate. When Slade finished, covering a belch with his hand, there was almost simultaneous movement among his hosts to push their plates away and lean back.

Nan stood. "I think," she said, "that if we've all eaten, we can adjourn to the Assembly Room to listen to our visitor. If he wouldn't mind?" she added, looking down at Slade. The question was real and hopeful, not a rhetorical exercise.

"Ah, I'd be delighted," said the big man. When he got up, he found that his muscles were wobbly with exhaustion and the pleasant burden of food being digested. Natural courtesy aside, Slade owed these friendly people a duty for their hospitality. It did not occur to him to shirk his duties simply because he was tired.

"Of course everyone couldn't gather to meet you directly tonight," said Onander as he opened the door behind his own chair. A two-meter long hallway, open at the further end, lay beyond. "But from the Assembly Room, we can broadcast and share your talk with the whole community."

Slade had noticed that the dining room into which he had first been ushered was only half the exterior size of the building. The Assembly Room filled the remainder, save for the length of the hall between them. Too narrow for a kitchen, he would have thought . . . and none of his business; Slade wasn't searching this city for contraband.

The Assembly Room took his breath away with its abruptness.

They had dined beneath bare rafters, seated on wood and eating from hand-thrown pottery. The Assembly Room was by contrast as technically advanced as anything Slade had seen. It was of a style that was wholly new to him as well.

Elysians who passed as Slade stepped aside were reclining on what seemed to be a bare floor. The surface rose and mounded, not only beneath their weight but by meeting their bodies at comfortable angles. The feet of those walking to places to sit did not affect the floor in any visible manner.

But it was the walls that made Slade pause just inside the doorway. They held his attention in growing horror. The covering material had its own light as had that of the air car garage. This time the wall was not a wash of blank color but rather a mural painting with life and depth and movement.

"It's a scene from our history," Nan said with quiet dignity. "Our ancestors were slow-ship colonists. There was a higher level of radiation aboard than the designers had allowed for, or perhaps they just failed to allow for the passage of time on a closed system. There was, at the end, fighting between our ancestors and other passengers who had—deviated further from the original stock."

More than Slade's eyes were absorbed. He could not have seen the objects on the black background more clearly: rusty iron, the golden gleam of a join brazed instead of welded, the silvery polish of the lands against the shadowed grooves of a gun barrel. To another man, they would have been crude steel boxes, crawling their way one at a time through narrow darkness. But Slade was a tanker. His palms sweated and his heart began to race. "No," he whispered. It was not only other men in those tanks, it was him again.

The lead vehicle disintegrated. There was a spark on the glacis, then a globe of orange fire. Fuel and ammunition had exploded. For that brief instant, the surroundings were more than hints in shadow: girders interlacing, reaching far beyond visibility. Nowhere in sight was there a longitudinal connection except the catwalk down which the armored boxes struggled.

"The main drive was in East Section," Nan was saying. All the others who had dined with Slade were now seated on the floor. "For generations, our ancestors had used auxilliary units in West for power, but at the end it was necessary to tap the main drive."

The next vehicle clumsily shoved aside the remains of the first. Glowing fragments slipped over the edge of the catwalk and pirouetted, as softly as thistle seeds, toward the black that swallowed them and their warmth. Flashes lighted slots in the bulkhead at the walk's far end. Projectiles rang and splashed from girders, from the walkway, from the armored targets waddling forward.

"You can't just bull your way in!" Slade said. "Not if they're waiting, not if they're hardened and you give them time to pick and—"

The leading vehicle had been firing toward its goal with three automatic weapons. Now a pale amber beam threaded through the girders at an angle and touched the vehicle's flank.

"—choose, it's—"

Another orange explosion.

"—suicide!"

"There was no choice," the Elysian said. Her firm hands held one of Slade's to keep the castaway from gouging himself with his cropped nails. "There was only one vehicular connection between East Section and West. The crews knew what they were doing."

The third vehicle might have been lighter than its fellows, or perhaps even machinery could feel and react to desperation. The tank rocked through the wreckage at speed. The laser touched it but did not bite out the vehicle's heart. The beam left only a scar that glowed white, then red, as it cooled. As the tank neared its goal, the guns in the bulkhead fired at an increasing deflection. Shots still hit. The weapons replying from the vehicle's bow fell silent. But there were not so many hits, and they did not have the seam-splitting accuracy of moments before.

"At the time this was going on—" Nan continued. A white flash beneath the lumbering vehicle scattered the three iron road-wheels on the left side. They spun off the catwalk as the tank lurched the other way. Their edges glowed and disappeared.

"—a team was entering the power room from outside, unnoticed by the inhabitants who were concentrating on the bulkhead."

A door from somewhere ahead of the disabled vehicle spewed others onto the catwalk. The remaining gun on the tank fired until the barrel shone. Weapons from West Section itself must have joined, because the flecks of projectiles ricochetting patterned the vehicle's quarter for the first time. It made no difference. The others were over the tank like maggots on the third day's corpse. They were humanoid, but they had huger bodies and fewer eyes than men. They began to devour the vehicle's crew even as they dragged them through the prized-open hatches.

"If they had known, you see," Nan said as the mural faded to swirls of dark pastel, "they would have cut the connection. The power had to be on for three full days before all the passengers in West Section could escape to Elysium. All the survivors."

Slade shuddered to bring himself out of the waste of fear and memory where he had lived for the past moments. Music of some sort was a soothing undercurrent in the hall. Patient, friendly faces were turned up to his. "Dear Lord have mercy," the tanker said. He released his hand from the woman's. He managed a smile. "I'm Don Slade," he said. "I was a merchant. . . ."

CHAPTER ELEVEN

"I think we've got a balance," said the blonde technician. Her voice whispered out to every human on Elysium except for Don Slade. "We're going to begin coupling in." Her fingers played over the banks of rocker switches before her.

"A little up in the thirties, I think," said her bald companion. The blonde's fingers replaced a nod. They touched controls and sharpened the color of the images forming in her mind, her companion's mind, and in those of the other thirteen thousand Elysians with right-brain implants.

The bald technician rubbed his temples. "Blessed Lord," he grumbled. "That spike almost took the top off my skull. And just the mural, not something he'd been through himself."

"How's this?" asked the blonde as the images firmed.

"Perfect," said her companion. He touched one of his own controls, minusculely changing the attitude of the hidden probe aimed at the back of Slade's head.

"I had the controls set down, just cracked enough to get a reading, I thought. Really."

"I'm not blaming you," the bald technician said. He had closed his eyes. "I never knew an affect to peak like that either. I just hope the shunts catch the next spike the way they're supposed to. Or—" he smiled, covering a wince of remembered pain— "our guest is going to be very surprised when his audience starts to scream just as he gets to the good part."

Then the two of them relaxed behind their instruments. With the ease of long experience, they let Don Slade's words and the thoughts like sharks beneath those words hiss simultaneously through their own minds.

"The ship on which I hired passage," the speaker was saying, "had a lot of military types aboard. There'd been a lot of fighting on Friesland in the recent past. Hard-cases had signed on with one side or another. Now that things had settled down, they were leaving; and sometimes one step ahead of the White Mice, the authorities. Passes weren't being checked very carefully. The Colonel—ah, President Hammer, the new executive, seemed to figure that it was as cheap to ship the trash out as it was to cull them and shoot them.

"Or just shoot them, I guess—" A vivid image of bound figures collapsing against a shot-burned wall; a smile on the speaker's face that matched the image much better than it did his merchant persona. "I hear that might've been discussed before a fellow named Pritchard, close to the President, put his foot down."

Elysium watched the men with the uniforms and bearing of military men who filled a small, tense room. Young men in battle-dress stood beside the door. The seated men had the age and rank. They were scowling, several of them ready to jump to their feet. Danny Pritchard in civilian clothes was clicking off, coldly as an abacus, the long-term effects of a present resort to terror.

Don Slade was not a figure in his own vision. The scene was tinged red with suppressed violence. Beneath the physical details ran an awareness of the weight of Slade's pistol holster and the smooth hardness of the mini-grenade concealed in his left hand. The big man was poised to clear the room if Hammer ordered his friend's arrest.

"I wasn't too worried about the other passengers," Slade was saying. His voice was a pleasant tenor, sharply at variance with the jagged images in his mind. It was always the striking memories that remained, of course. But what the subject found striking depended on the life that had brought him to them.

"I'd turned all my, ah, wares to cash, and I figured to arrange a

bank transfer when I got home to Tethys. The others aboard the ship, a tramp with just the registry number GAC 59, weren't the sort of folks I'd have wanted to go to sleep with if I'd had anything worth stealing. But I didn't, and they knew it, and I figured I could handle minor annoyances about as well as the next guy." The smile again, and the great, scarred fingers of one hand caressing the knuckles of the other.

"Thing is," Don Slade continued, "there *was* one thing I had that the others turned out to want: my—trading experience, for the venture they were planning. . . ."

CHAPTER TWELVE

"Nice of you to come see us, Slade," said the leader of the men with their hair dyed blue.

"Hello, Blackledge," said Don Slade in a voice as cold as his expression. The tanker did not know why he had been called to the bridge. Likely it had something to do with the fact that the most recent Transit had been four hours ago, far too long for a normal computation.

It did not concern Slade to find that there were four other passengers on the bridge, along with the normal trio of crewmen. What Slade disliked was the fact that the four were Reuben Blackledge and three of his henchmen from Aylmer's Guards. That unit had been known for its members' blue hair and the abnormal brutality with which it conducted its affairs. Hammer had proscribed the Guards as soon as he thought he could spare their manpower. Individual soldiers had shaved or redyed their hair. The smart ones found passage off Friesland while the going was good. It was a bad sign that the outlaws were sporting their old color. It was worse that they lounged on the bridge as if they now owned it.

"Hey, hang loose, trooper," Blackledge said, tense to his own surprise when the tanker looked at him. All four of the outlaws had guns. The detector at the bridge hatchway had shown that Slade was unarmed . . . but no one with hands and a mind like Mad Dog Slade was really unarmed. "Look," Blackledge continued, "this isn't any hijacking or anything like that, is it?"

He looked around for support. His fellows nodded. They too had been shocked by the physical presence of the tank officer whom they had expected to overawe. The crewmen nodded also. Levine, the Captain, said, "These are hard times, Mister Slade. I have responsibilities, too, to do what's best for my crew and my backers."

"There's the matter of responsibility to your passengers, too, Levine," Slade said. He walked over to the bulb of the navigational display which was now dark and empty. It looked like a harmless motion, because Slade's back was to four of the Guards; but everyone on the bridge was now within reach of the tanker's arms. "There's three hundred of us who've paid to be hauled home on schedule and in order, right?"

"Happens the rest of us," said Blackledge, "want to change the schedule a little, Slade. Look—" his voice rose in nervous anger, though Blackledge was not a small man either— "it's fine for you, the fares pay the cost of Transit and the ship makes its profit off odds and sods of cargo it picks up on the way. But there's a lot of us aboard, your highness, people who spent their last sparkler to cheat the hangman one more time. You get off and transfer a fortune back into your pocket. But what d'ye think happens to most of *us?*"

Slade turned slowly to face the outlaw leader. Well, he'd never really believed he was meant to die in bed, for all his determination a month ago that he would go home and live as quietly as a shore-side mussel.

Blackledge's face was suffused. In that state it was marred by a scattering of white, hair-thin scars. "I don't suppose," said Slade in a reasonable voice, "that you called me here to see if I'd split my pay—" he had more than that, but less than the fortune in loot that Aylmer's Guards would have expected from someone with Slade's opportunities—"with everybody at our first landfall."

If Blackledge said they *did* intend such extortion, it was going to get tense. Slade doubted that these blue-haired clowns had the subtlety that would be needed to actually break Slade to their will; but he did not care to be around for them to practice on, either.

"Naw, we don't want your money," the outlaw said. Slade relaxed, and the outlaws relaxed. The ship's crewmen looked quizzical, but they did not realize how close they had been to a maelstrom of bodies and gunfire. Blackledge was trying to find an alternative to the bantering superiority with which he had opened the interview and to the frightened hostility into which his tones had degenerated. "We're all mercs, right? We don't rob each other."

Which was a lie, but one whose telling was an olive branch that Don Slade was willing to accept with a smile. "There's a lot of us, you see," the outlaw continued, "who didn't figure on Hammer getting holier than thou once he'd shot his way into the presidency. We figure we're owed something, and there's plenty of places out there just waiting to pay us."

Places like Tethys, Slade thought as he nodded false approval. Places that hadn't had an internal war since they were settled. Places whose emergency alert system was cobwebbed from disuse. The chances of this lot getting away with significant loot were slim, but Via! the damage they'd do before the locals mopped them up!

Via. . . . If Slade grabbed the submachine gun of the nearest outlaw, he could empty it into the control panel before they stopped him. "I don't know, though," the big man said as if he were considering. "Three hundred effectives won't give you much of a perimeter. I suppose everybody's pretty well agreed on this, though?"

Another man with scarcely a stubble to dye nodded furiously. It was Blackledge, however, who answered by saying, "This is just one ship of twenty-two, Slade. Isn't that right?"

"That's right," agreed Captain Levine with a bob of his head. "Ready and waiting. It's hard to make it on unscheduled loads, stony hard. I owe it to my backers to take a chance when it offers. . . ."

A chance to be slagged down with your rusty hull, the tanker thought. But he was accustomed to the ravening bite of powerguns, and to the short shrift they gave any but the most refractory armor. Levine did not have that experience; and the outlaws, who probably did understand, would not dwell aloud on the vulnerability of the chariots hauling them to fantasy loot.

But it meant that whether or not GAC 59 survived, the raids were going to occur. Good soldiers have to be willing to die, but suicidal men have little purpose in a well-run army. They just leave you with another damned slot to train for. "Sounds like you've thought things through pretty well," said Don Slade. "Now I'm just waiting for the other shoe to drop, hey?"

"We want you to command us," said Blackledge. He vomited out the words with a forward thrust of his head. The outlaw's hair waved above his scarred, red face.

Slade was genuinely surprised for the first time since he stepped onto the bridge. He jerked away from the words.

"Look, I don't mean we'd make you God," Blackledge continued hastily. He gestured toward Slade with his left hand. "There's a Ship's Meeting, same as there's a Fleet Meeting. You won't have cop to do with that, it's us that plan things. But after we hit ground, well—" The outlaw frowned across the company of his fellows. "Look, we've heard of you, you're used to commanding things. Most of the other ships, they've got their own officers, they left as formed units. Us here don't. We're bits and pieces from twenty outfits, and nobody the rest'd listen to. We *know* we're headed for some heavy traffic, Slade. You're going the same place. If you're smart, you'll be willing to help steer for a triple share of the loot."

Slade began playing again with the navigation bulb. It gave him a look of aimless placidity. "Whatever happened to Aylmer?" he asked. "General Aylmer, I think he called himself, didn't he?"

One of Blackledge's companions began to snicker. Blackledge hushed him with a punch on the shoulder and a molten glare. "Aylmer thought he'd make a deal for himself that'd leave some people hanging," said the outlaw leader. "Some people got to know about that. I think they may've greased Aylmer before they bugged out themselves."

A stubble-haired outlaw broke the silence he had maintained until then. "It's the same thing you've been at," he said. His lips flicked saliva. "Only we don't have tanks, is all. And don't worry about what your buddies who stayed on Friesland with the cushy jobs might say. *They* knew about this. We kept it quiet as we could, but there's no way a deal this big could have been put together without their high and mightinesses learning, was there?"

"All right," said Don Slade. His skin felt as though he were being crushed by an avalanche of needles. But choose Life, even when Life has a gun-stock. "It won't work, because I don't think any of your lot have the discipline to make it work. But I'll give you as much leadership as you're ready to take."

CHAPTER THIRTEEN

Slade was the first man through the cargo hatch, because there was no one else aboard he had trusted to lead the rush on the gun position. In fact, half a dozen of his thirty-man assault company were pounding across the rammed-earth field as more pirate freighters roared in to land and the personnel of Desireé Port reached for weapons they had forgotten.

The field was defended by a pair of heavy powerguns on opposite sides of the perimeter. The ball-mounted weapons were hardened, but not to the point that Slade would not have preferred to take them out with bursts from a tribarrel. None of the ships in this rag-tag assemblage would admit to having more than small arms aboard, however.

Levine had landed a full seventy-five meters from the gun Slade was to assault. The chill air and icy footing effectively doubled the distance that was already too long. Shots were being fired, some at random, some in the attack on the control tower that another vessel had been told off for. A bolt ripped a long gouge through the snow near Slade. One of the pirates following the tanker threw away a pistol and began to run back toward the ship.

The door to the gun turret was flush-fitting and locked. One of the pirates fired at it from a meter away. Steel crashed and sprayed. The gunman howled as he danced back. He began swatting at the sparks that had ignited his tousled hair.

"Back, Via!" Slade shouted. The oval gouges in the door surface were bright orange, but the lime core within still glowed white and smooth. Gimbals squealed above the attackers as the gun tube shifted from its vertical alignment. Slade wore a set of back-and-breast armor, too small for him and so joined along the right side with leather straps. The armor prodded him over the collarbone as he slapped the home-made limpet mine over the lock plate of the door. The tanker had a helmet but no commo. He was point-man, not commander, might they all burn in Hell!

The gun fired above them. It was a sharp crack and a cone of heat that fanned across the snow. A pirate freighter, fifty meters up and settling on thrusters, collapsed inward around a cyan flash. The ship hit the field hard enough to bury half of itself before it blew up.

"Fire in the hole!" Slade shouted into the ringing pandemonium. He was unreeling the four meters of wire between the battery pack and the blasting cap in the mine. That length should take him safely around the curve of the gun emplacement. "Fire in the hole! Fire in the hole!"

Somebody in the Control Tower blew divots from the concrete to either side of Slade's head. The tanker threw the switch, knowing that if he ducked he would be back in the blast cone. Two of the outlaws who had followed Slade did duck. They were hurled sideways as the mine blew in the door. Slade was through the gap while the smoke still roiled. His submachine gun hosed a long burst as if the bolts were a knotted cord dragging the big man into the gun emplacement.

There were three men in civilian clothes within. One was on his back, unconscious. Two were screaming and frightened, with their hands rising even as the bolts savaged their torsos. . . .

"But after we traded on Desireé, they decided to touch down on a place called Mandalay," Don Slade said to the Elysian citizens before him.

The castaway's nails were tight against his palms because of his memories of the raid. The initial butchery, and then the savage counter-attack which the locals were able to mount because no one would listen to Slade shouting they should cut and run before

Desireé had time to organize. Looting and raping . . . and then, for many of the outlaws, dying. The universe was better for that result, of course.

"I was against it," Slade's mouth said, "but all I could get was a delay for GAC 59. We held a light-minute out while the rest of the fleet landed."

"This is crazy!" Blackledge cried. He threw up his hands for emphasis. The outlaw was careful to speak toward the commo screen and not toward Don Slade who sat against a bulkhead on the edge of a plotting can. "There's five *thousand* of us, that's more'n in the whole settlement down there. They're not going to ladle cop on us, even if we weren't allies, like to say."

"The fact they're a bunch of bandits and you—we're a bunch of bandits," said the black-haired tanker, "doesn't make anybody allies. Besides—" He absently fingered the fresh scab on his biceps, a memento of concrete flying during the Desireé raid. "I could tell you stories about allies."

The main bridge screen was slaved to one of the exterior pick-ups on the flagship. An Awami League hasildar named Al Husad styled himself Fleet Admiral now. He was accepted as such in much the same way that Slade was a captain. Al Husad owed much of his position to hints that his vessel mounted ship-killing guns in one cargo bay. The Admiral had denied that loudly during planning for the Desireé attack; and Slade's duties had not kept him too busy to see that the flagship landed on Desireé after both gun emplacements were in pirate hands.

The digital signal feeding the screen was riddled with static. The view of the spaceport and the ships landing with various levels of skill was made pale by the white static flares of individual receptors.

"Curse it, they'll have all the women," moaned one of Blackledge's henchmen, with him on the bridge. The outlaw would have muttered about liquor, but Slade had reprogrammed the waste processor. The unit could now turn out ethanol, diluted by its own hygroscopic tendencies to about 95% but otherwise chemically pure.

"You think they're going to grow shut, Dobler?" Slade gibed. Dobler's blue hair looked particularly silly because it fringed his bald spot. Many of the mercenaries aboard GAC 59 had taken up the Aylmer fashion when they turned pirate. A few had changed back after the raid, though. Seal rings like the one Don Slade wore were having a certain vogue. "I tell you, if any of you had the sense to *really* listen to me, we'd wait here three days instead of three hours. We'd be the only suckers on Mandalay with money to spend—and you'd be amazed how much cheaper you can go around the world, then."

"What is this cop?" demanded a crackly voice. Mandalay Control was talking again to Al Husad. The weak signal was rebroadcast by the flagship, but the static was amplified as well. "You say twenty-one and there's only twenty."

Service vehicles of some sort were flitting through the field of the vision blocks feeding the screen. Steam and dust drifted from the score of vessels. Anyone who had been present at a landing could imagine besides the hiss and pinging as metal cooled.

"They'll flood the market, though," said Captain Levine dolefully. None of the ex-mercenaries save Slade had an appreciation for the economics of being first to port. "Because you're afraid, we'll get cop for our cargo."

"Nope," said Slade. He had convinced the wrangling leaders of his vessel to go along with the delay. Now, faced with the fact of it, there was a chance that the only consensus left would be to lift the tanker's head. Slade held to his wrist the last of the cache of stim cones he had looted during the raid. "Our cargo's thrusters from the Desireé repair docks, not jewelry and trash like most of the others loaded. Our price won't go down."

"Had one drop its navigational computer," said Al Husad's voice. "If it don't get on line in a couple days, maybe we'll send help. But say, what about clearance? You come on with all this cop about staying sealed till you clear us, and then you sit on your thumbs. I got boys been in Transit three weeks, ready to tear the roof off this little burg."

"Do you?" replied Mandalay Control. The audio link roared into garbage. The image on the vision screen rocked, but it still showed bombs blowing in the hulls of every ship in sight.

Men with grenade projectors and full atmosphere suits leaped from the beds of the service vehicles which had earlier set the explosives. The grenadiers began firing projectiles into the jagged openings. From the way the Mandalay troops were dressed, Slade was sure they were lobbing gas rounds into the pirate fleet.

"B-b-but God in heaven!" babbled Captain Levine. "They aren't, I mean—Mandalay's a pirate haven, *everybody* knows that, they *trade*, they don't—" His circling hand indicated the carnage on the screen.

The local forces were not very numerous, probably no more in total than the few hundred men carried by any ship in the fleet that had just landed. That was quite large enough a force for the present purpose. The outlaws of the fleet were trapped like so many sheep in a slaughter pen.

The cargo hatch of one of the ships began to rise slowly on its hydraulic jacks. It had opened a little more than a hand's breadth when a trio of directional mines went off in the gap. The hatch continued to rise. Shrapnel had painted the interior of the cargo bay with the blood and brains of the men huddled to rush through it. With an almost leisurely calm, one of the Mandalayan troops turned toward the bay and shot in two grenades. On impact they began to gush black fumes, one of the skin-absorptive nerve poisons like KD2.

"Remember how Al Husad was talking?" Slade asked, from his corner. The tanker was calmer for being proven right. None the less, he had to hide the fact that the butchery on the screen horrified him as much as it did the gaping outlaws around him. It had not always been possible to be a Slammer and be choosy about the cause for which you were fighting. Slade was a civilian now, and in another context he could have laughed as he pulled the plug on the pirates the way someone on Mandalay had just done it.

But right now, there was nothing intellectual involved. Slade was watching his peers die in an ambush that had been meant for him as well.

Everyone on the bridge continued to stare at the screen. The tanker was not even sure any of the outlaws were aware that he had spoken. He went on anyway. "Like I heard here, as a matter of fact. 'Might just take the place over, nothing they could do with so many of us. Hell with using Mandalay just for trade.' They're hard boys here, friends, and it seems they're not stupid ones either. *They* know there were too many of us to be safe if they let us swarm all over the place. One ship, maybe three . . . but not twenty-odd together. So they did something about it, is all."

Slade pointed toward the screen. The suited attackers were beginning to clamber aboard the ships they had disabled. There would be some resistance, some casualties, but panic and disorganization would have exposed almost all the pirates to the touch of the gas bombs. KD2 needed little more than that. One touch and nerve cells would begin to die in shrivelled black traceries until the rot reached the brain stem.

"I'd as soon," the big man said, "be gone when they come to finish the job." But his great, scarred hands were twisting as if they wished they held a weapon.

"Cunning has value," noted one current of the community.

"It's scarcely a virtue, though, is it?" demanded the other viewpoint. It was an amalgam like the first, of every mind; not a segment polarized against the rest of the body politic. "A human virtue, that is."

"Have we been wholly open with him, then?" rejoined the first viewpoint. It was hard to say which advocacy was the Devil's. "Or are we being . . . cunning?"

CHAPTER FOURTEEN

"With the S—" Don Slade caught himself. "With the large trading organizations," he continued, "there's a lot of information available. It's expensive, but mistakes can be a lot more expensive. You don't think about it, the—man on the ground doesn't. The poop's just there when he needs it. Not always right, and never a hundred percent up to date; but a lot better than fumbling in the dark.

"Which is what we were left to do on Levine's tub, of course," the castaway continued. The smile he flashed was a pleasant one, not his predator's grin. He looked a trifle rueful, but more engaging for that; the sort of fellow who tells you any catastrophe is an adventure when you've lived through it. "There was diddly-squat for background in GAC 59's data base. Tell the truth, I doubt there'd been anything much better anywhere in the fleet, which may be why their leaders decided to try Mandalay, of all places. They'd all heard something about it besides the coordinates.

"Be that as it may, some of the folks aboard had heard about a place called Toler. Supposed to be a funny culture, but peaceful and some attractions as a liberty port. We still had a cargo to unload and Via! I didn't have any better suggestions. The straight run to Tethys was more than our recycling system could have handled. And besides, these types weren't the sort I wanted to bring home with me; it's a quiet place, Tethys. So we landed on Toler. . . ."

"Three by twenty-kilotonne thruster units," said the tall port official. He was jotting notes with a stylus and paper instead of

punching the data into a computer link. Toler—there seemed to be
only one settlement on the planet—had a gritty, run-down look to
it. It consisted of one-story buildings with courts surrounding
snaky-limbed trees. Vegetation was sparse. Most of it had the same
yellowish cast as the dry soil and the dust that the wind blew in curls
across the flat landscape. "One by fifteen KT unit, five by ten KT,
three fivers. That's all? Spares?"

The port official was blond and very thin. He was only two-thirds
of Slade's bulk, though their eyes met on a level. "No spares," the
tanker admitted, "but they're first-quality units, Goldstein &
Trumpener, still crated." Slade did not understand why the official
was making written notes. GAC 59's landing approach had been
fully automated and flawless, so the port *did* have a master computer.
Maybe the linking system was down.

"Passengers and crew?" the blond man said, making another
notation. His voice sounded edgy, but he had displayed no more
than professional interest in the vessel. A tic raised the local's right
cheek fractionally.

"Two hundred thirty-seven," said Slade. Virtually all the men
had poured out of GAC 59 as soon as the thrusters shut down. The
attraction of dives and mere solid ground had something to do with
the exodus; but so did graphic retellings of what had happened to
the rest of the fleet, buttoned up on Mandalay. "Ah, it's sort of a
cooperative trading arrangement, a lot of veterans pooling our
severance bonuses. Won't be any trouble beyond, you know, a little
wildness. I guess most of the boys are already anticipating their
profits a little in your bars and knock shops." Slade essayed a smile.
It was warm enough, even in the shadow of the lifted cargo hatch,
but there was something in the local man's demeanor that made the
tanker shiver.

"Yes, we have those," the official said. His right hand teased the
stylus across the back of his neck. Something flickered in his eyes, a
moment's cloudiness like the nictitating membrane of a reptile—but
over the surface of the mind, not the pupil. "More of our visitors
prefer the sorm once they've tried it, though, the tree. Not expensive,
and very . . . satisfying." The man's stylus twitched again.

"Yeah, well . . ." said Slade. This was the only ship on the ground at the moment. That wasn't surprising—they'd known Toler was pretty much of a backwater—but it didn't augur well for a good price on the thrusters. "When I've got this business taken care of, maybe I'll give it a try. Ah, who should I talk to about selling our cargo?"

"I'll take care of that," the official said with the absent look in his eyes. "You'll be made a fair offer, as soon as I have, have fed in the data." To Slade's surprise, the man reached out and touched the tanker on the wrist. "You should try the sorm," the local said in unexpected animation. "Not everyone can appreciate it, the rabble you've arrived with. But—"

The blond man cocked and lowered his head so that Slade could see the back of his neck. At the base of the hairline, the skin puckered into a wrinkled mound as large as the first joint of Slade's thumb. A tiny droplet of blood and clear fluid leaked from the scab.

"I know what you think," the official said as he straightened. "I did too, at first. But there's no harm, no tissue damage, a trivial puncture. And it opens a universe, Mister Slade, that minds like yours and mine can appreciate." He tongued his dry lips, again a reptilian gesture and not a sensual one.

Abruptly, the local man shuddered. His hair danced like a spill of chalky water. "I have to get back," he said. He was already walking toward what seemed to be the port office. It was a low, inner-facing structure like all the other buildings. "Don't forget what I've said."

"Right," Don Slade muttered to himself. "No bloody fear of that."

Something was chirruping in the depths of the hold, a bird or lizard; probably neither, possibly not local to this planet, and Lord! how empty it made the ship sound.

The big man unsealed the hip pockets of his coveralls and thrust his hands in to occupy them. Nothing was moving on the earthen field since the official had gone inside. From the streets curving among the courtyard houses came raucous cries and an occasional glimpse of carousing outlaws on the way from one entertainment to another. Via, Slade had been on enough strange worlds not to get nervous about docking in on some backwater. He was a man, a human being, whether or not he had the hundred and seventy tonnes of a panzer wrapped around him.

He began whistling under his breath; not a full song, just catches from a tune that had been old when space travel was a dream. He began to walk toward the sprawling settlement.

"If I was to leave my husband dear
And my two babes also. . . ."

Slade did not carry a weapon, not a hidden knife, not the pistol that had been part of his clothing during twenty years of service.

"Oh, what have you to take me to,
If I with you should go?"

The individual houses were as regular as could be maintained with the differing levels of skill with which they had been constructed. The streets which connected—and indeed, separated—the blank house walls seemed to be more what remained of the area when the building went up on it than part of a plan. Each of the buildings had a single outer door. There was nothing Slade could recognize as advertising or even identification, but all the buildings with an open door were devoted at least in part to the desires of the men who had just landed.

The tanker stepped into a house at random. The room beyond the arched doorway was dim. It felt less dry than the outside. There was a bar to the left where two mercenaries drank. Why they wanted to pay for something the ship offered free was beyond Slade. The door leading to the right was ajar, but the big man could hear nothing meaningful from beyond.

"Yes sir?" said the woman in the armchair facing the outside door. There was a glow-strip on the wall beside her, but it was faint enough that Slade could not be sure whether her hair was blond or brown or a pale, friendly russet. "Whatever's your pleasure, we have it. And the first touch of sorm is on the house." She gestured easily toward the door to Slade's right.

The outlaws at the bar shifted abruptly. They strode down the hall to the left and out of sight around one of the internal corners.

"There's women?" Slade asked. He was rubbing his fists in recollection and present discomfort.

"Of course," said the greeter. She stood up. Her age was as indeterminate as the color of her hair. She was no longer young, but the body she displayed as she raised her patterned smock was firm and attractive. Because her breasts had been small to begin with, they had not sagged noticeably with age. Her belly twitched with a shudder of ecstasy; faked, no doubt, but—

"Lord!" Slade blurted. There was a wire from the wall to the back of the woman's neck. Not a wire, a tendril, the sorm the official had talked about.

"The root bothers you?" the greeter asked without concern. "It's not necessary." She tossed her head forward. Her hair was indeed russet. The shudder that wracked her body for an instant now was neither ecstatic nor counterfeit. But it was brief, and the smile was back on the woman's face even as the tendril subsided to the wall through which it grew. Slade noticed, however, the change in the woman's nipples. They had been as erect as bullet noses. Now they were relaxing almost as suddenly as the root had dropped away from the woman's spine.

"You're a strong man," she said. She stepped toward the tanker with the front of her dress still lifted to shoulder height. "Your children would have fine, sharp minds, too, wouldn't they?"

"Maybe another time," said Slade. He dodged back into the sunlight. He was furious with his body because it insisted on shivering for several more minutes.

A heavy air-cushion truck was grumbling down the street. It was almost the first vehicle Slade had seen on Toler. It pulled up beside one of the closed buildings.

The building's door opened. People from within joined the two men on the truck in unloading sacks of vegetables and flour or legumes. They worked without expertise, but they seemed to be in good health. The locals glanced at Slade as he walked past, but their attention was primarily focused on their task. No one spoke. The tanker half expected to see roots trailing back into the dwelling, but there was nothing of the sort. All the locals bore the puckered scars of the sorm tree, but they were free now and functioning normally.

Slade walked faster. "He took her to the topmast high," trembled the words in his mind. "To see what she could see."

Slade was whistling through his teeth, but the result would have been a monotone to anyone not inside his mind as well. "He sunk the ship in a flash of fire," snarled the ballad to its conclusion. "To the bottom of the sea!"

Three soldiers stumbled out of a doorway ahead of Slade. They were blinking in the sunlight. Two of them dabbed at the backs of their necks. "You don't *know*, Donnie-boy," said one of that pair.

Slade jumped, but the third outlaw was the subject of the address, not the tanker who stood unnoticed as the others approached. "The most beautiful girl in the world could lie there with her legs spread, and it wouldn't be as good."

"Listen!" snapped the third soldier, "I *watched* that thing poking into you. It ain't natural."

"Never put anything in a vein yourself, Donnie?" asked the other of the pair who had tried the sorm trees. Then the outlaw bumped into Slade, although the tanker had flattened himself against a building to give the others more room.

Instead of the curse and violence Slade had bunched his fists to respond to, the outlaw patted the bigger man on the chest. "Scuse, brother," the fellow said as he stepped around the human obstruction. Not only had the outlaw himself responded mildly, he seemed to have forgotten that such a collision on a liberty night could bring a savage reaction from the other party.

"But I don't care, man," the outlaw was saying as the three of them continued on their way. His fingers had spread blood in roseates across his neck, but there was no real damage, nothing an injection might not have left. "You're chicken, but it doesn't hurt anybody but you. And you'll never know how much you're pissing away. . . ."

Slade cursed, very softly. Then he stepped into the building the three soldiers had just left.

The interior was much like that of the first dive Slade had

entered, though the greeter here was male. "Good day, sir," the local said from his chair. "How can we help you?"

The automated bar in this entry lounge was unoccupied. Slade had been concerned that the hundreds of outlaws would overwhelm Toler with consequent disaster, but the cribs and dives were in adequate supply. What they did in the long intervals between landings was another question. For that matter, most freighters would have a score or fewer crewmen. Only fifteen of GAC 59's complement were actually Levine's men. "Stim cones?" Slade asked through dry lips.

The greeter shrugged. "Sorry, not on Toler," he said. He gestured to the bar. "There's alcohol, of course. And the sorm."

"Yeah," said the tanker. He opened the right-hand door and entered the sorm parlor he had expected to find there. "I'm not a coward," he said, but the sounds Slade's lips and tongue formed were too soft for even the speaker to hear them.

"Yes, sir?" said a local, one of the two men within the good-sized room. The other man wore ship's coveralls. Blaney, Slade thought his name was, one of the drive operators. The man lay on one of six narrow couches. He was flaccid except for rhythmic shudders moving from his torso to his extremities.

"He's all right?" the tanker asked. His finger traced the path of undulations. Slade was trying desperately to keep his voice normal.

"Certainly," said the attendant without a sneer or condescension. He was changing the covering of the end couch. The cushion was overlaid with a thin, hard sheet that might have been either vegetable or synthetic. A pair of used sheets lay crinkled on the floor. "The sorm makes his muscles shudder at intervals to keep up their tone. Not that there's any need for that in a short touch, but the plant does its best for its clients." The attendant gave Slade a glass-smooth smile. "After a time," he added, "one can work perfectly well without uncoupling, you see."

The attendant's own tendril waggled back to the wall as he tucked in the sheet.

There was a grommetted hole in the cushion. It was at about the point where a man's neck would rest if he lay supine on the couch.

The sheet covered that hole, but the material was too thin to stop a tendril probing up, through it and skin and into the base of the brain. "I see," said the tanker. He was sure his voice was squeaking. "How much does a touch cost?"

"The first is free," said the attendant. He gathered up the used sheets and stuffed them into a chute in the wall beneath his tendril. "After that—" the local man turned around. "You're from Friesland, sir?"

"I've been there," Slade answered guardedly.

"Then the equivalent of thirty Frisian talers per touch," the attendant explained with a smile. "The length varies. This man and two others were touched at the same time." He gestured at Blaney. The crewman was quiescent again after his bout of "exercise." "The others have left—not dissatisfied, I'm sure. But this man's mind permitted a greater level of interaction with the sorm, and consequently even greater—pleasure—for the client."

The local man must have correctly interpreted Slade's grimace, for he shook his head at the tanker and added gently, "No, Captain Slade. The client can sever the connection at will." The attendant arched his neck back slightly as if he were baring his throat to a razor.

"No!" said the tanker. "No, I've seen that, you don't have to show me again." Then he said, "You know my name, friend?"

The local man's body relaxed. There may have been a hint of relief in his expression. "We aren't peasants here on Toler, Captain Slade," he said with dignity. "Our culture doesn't lend itself to crystal and metal, but we have a very satisfactory data bank. The Port Commandant entered information on our visitors, and the information was made available to potential users. You are, of course, a noteworthy man."

In a sharper tone of voice, the attendant went on, "You don't have to stand here and feed your fears, Captain. You can walk away. There's no sin in being afraid."

"I'm not afraid," said Slade harshly. "I just lie down here?" He sat, swinging his legs onto the nearest couch, even as the attendant nodded agreement.

The sheet rustled beneath Slade's neck. The big man relaxed all his muscles. He had been operated on without anesthetic. This pain would be nothing.

But the pain had nothing to do with his fear, either. Hairs prickled as something brushed past them, but even so Slade did not feel any touch on his skin proper. Then a sense of euphoria swept away every other feeling. He was still aware of his former fears, but his mind held them up to his detached appraisal and his laughter.

Slade slipped deeper into an outside awareness with the ease of a diver entering a blood-warm lagoon.

The attendant had been quite truthful about Toler's data bank, but the statement was a joke as well. The sorm's joke, in a way, because the sorm colony connected all those humans who were in fact that data bank.

The tree had developed its properties as a means of ensuring pollination and good planting locations on a dry and windswept world. Some of the runners by which the sorm colonies spread learned—and the term could not be understood to imply intellection—to contact the nervous systems of small burrowing animals. This gave the adapted sorms a degree of mobility unmatched by any other plants on the world. Moreover, as a colony added symbiotes, it gained a level of consciousness which no single animal mind could equal.

The adapted colonies spread and flourished. Tendril-dragging animals scampered from anther to distant pistil. When the symbiosis became more complete, animals could carry out tasks without being in immediate contact with the sorm. They would return after they had scrambled over barriers to plant nuts or whatever other task had been set them. It was less the attitude of a junkie seeking another fix than it was the thankful longing of a laborer returning home after a hard day. The result was a true and flawless partnership for the individual animals and for the sorm species as a whole.

The human settlement of Toler provided an increase of potential knowledge and reasoning power of a magnitude which humans had taken several million years to develop. That the amalgam outstripped in its way any single human was inevitable.

And that the amalgam none the less resembled a human society was perhaps also inevitable. After contact, the Toler colony needed further human contacts to survive; and in any case, the amalgam built from the instincts and memories of its animate partners.

The sorm's problem was that its symbiotes could not reproduce themselves. Male symbiotes lost the capacity to ejaculate and, after a few days or weeks of linkage, no longer even produced sperm. By the time the symbiosis was complete enough for the sorm to guide its partner in the complex operation, the animal was sterile.

Ovulation was not affected, perhaps because its cyclic nature recovered more quickly from suppression of hormones which the sorm's touch entailed. Prostitutes—female members of the colony in estrus—provided an indigenous birthrate when the sparse interstellar traffic cooperated. Recruits directly from that traffic made up the rest of the colony's requirement.

Slade's body trembled. His muscles massaged themselves and squeezed the blood in his veins back to feed his heart's slow pumping. Slade was unaware of that movement save as a datum reported through the eyes of the smiling attendant.

The Toler colony never stripped a visiting ship. It was common on any port for one or two of the crew to go missing: jailed or floating in a ditch or simply jumping ship to await a better berth on a future vessel. On Toler, the minds that stayed behind in blissful comfort were those with a particular sharpness of focus which fused best with the structure of the sorm. They were not always the minds that would have rated highest in human tests of intelligence, though that was often a concomitant.

And all but the core of Slade's being rejoiced to know that his was one of the minds that would be permitted to merge with the colony.

The feeling was not simply that of drug euphoria or the instant before orgasm, though it encompassed those things. There was also an enormous sense of physical well-being and the triumphant riding-down of an opponent. There was no dream quality to Slade's perceptions. They had the clarity of cells in a diamond lens. The tanker was barred from the control of his own body only by his multiplicity of viewpoints as a part of the sorm colony. The physical Don Slade was a needle among thousands of needles, safe and discrete but unnecessary for the moment.

"I am," insisted Slade's being. "*I* am."

And of course he was, healthy still and happier than every man who had not been to Toler, had not merged with the sorm. But Slade's mind was drawing away, plunging toward the roiling sea of Tethys.

Slade hit the surface and tendrils of the sorm recoiled from the droplets of the harsh gray salt. A shudder wracked the tanker's body. His arms drove him upward, clutching madly for the spray-drenched air.

Slade had fallen off the couch. The big man hyperventilated. His arms swam several flailing strokes before consciousness reasserted itself. "Blood and Martyrs," he wheezed as he stared at the impassive attendant. "Blood and Martyrs!"

Blaney was trembling again on the next couch. There were tiny speckles of blood on the sheet on which Slade had lain. Through the hole in the sheet gently quested the sorm tendril. Its tip was not a single tube as Slade had expected. It was a brush of tiny filaments, now drawn to a ghostly point and slick with fluids from Slade's neck.

Slade rocked to his feet. His limbs worked. He had his sense of balance. Don Slade had a body and soul once more. He gave the attendant an open-handed slap that rocked the smaller man against the wall without stunning him as it should have. Slade's hand throbbed beneath its calluses.

The tanker strode through the door and the lobby, then back into the street. The greeter's expression had the same drugged calm as the attendant's when Slade recovered from the couch.

There was some activity around the ship when Slade returned. The tanker had seen no sign of food-shops, now that he thought about it. Hunger must have driven back at least some of the outlaws. At the entry hatch stood one of the crewmen with a ration packet in his hand.

"Get me Levine," Slade said. They were his first words since his whispered prayer in the sorm parlor. "It he's not on board, raise him through his implant."

"Implant?" the crewman repeated as if he had never heard of a bio-electrical commo link implanted in the user's mastoid. Maybe he hadn't. This ship was crewed by trash as ignorant as most of its passenger list.

"Via!" the tanker snarled. He strode aboard with his boots clanging on the deck and short shrift for the man who had half-blocked his way. "He's got *some* sort of radio with him, doesn't he?"

Captain Levine was scurrying down the corridor toward Slade already.

"Slade, praise heaven I've found you," the spacer called. "We have troubles!"

"Curst true we've got troubles," the tanker agreed. He looped Levine in an arm to turn the smaller man back to the bridge with him. "Sound recall, however you do that, and we've got to lift ship fast."

"That's what I'm trying to *tell* you!" Levine insisted. "We *can't* lift ship. I haven't got enough crew."

Slade took his arm away from the spacer. "Come on," he said quietly. "We may as well talk on the bridge anyway. Tell me about the problem."

"It's the sorm trees," Levine explained as he scurried along. "You know about them?"

Slade's brief nod was all the affirmation he trusted himself to make.

"Well, a lot of my boys went under and didn't come back," the captain explained. "They seem all right—" The pair of leaders entered the bridge where three nervous-looking spacers already waited. "But they won't rouse for shaking or cold water. The attendants just shrug and look away."

"Right," Slade said. He glanced around the four spacers. "You tried it? Tried the sorm?"

"I did," said one man slowly. "It didn't make anything to me. I mean, I just felt good. But my buddy's still there on the table." He waved generally toward the settlement beyond the bulkhead.

"This isn't a ship that—" Levine began. "Well, we need three people each in Navigation and Drive when we Transit. The controls aren't slaved to one master, each unit's separate and it has to be synched within parameters. Right now we've got a shift in Drive, but only me and Keltie in Navigation. And look, you don't run with a single shift very long. Shift and shift's bad enough."

"All right, sound recall anyway," the tanker said. "You've got a siren or something, don't you? I know where Blaney is, at least. I'll round up half a dozen mercs and see what I can do."

The big man paused in the hatchway on his way to the hold where the arms were stored. "And Levine?" he said. "Wait for me to come—no, you come along too. I wouldn't want to get back here and find the ship had left me in this hellhole. And believe me, the people who left me would live to regret it too."

And even without reading Slade's mind, no one who heard him could doubt the truth of that threat.

Slade had no difficulty finding the building in which the sorm had touched him. He might not have been able to give directions, however, to find it in the skewed checkerboard of identical walls. The building's door was now closed.

"Should I blast it?" demanded Blackledge. Slade had picked the first outlaws he met to accompany him and the captain. The other mercs carried pistols or submachine guns. The big tanker himself had chosen a 2 cm shoulder weapon this time.

"No," said Slade. He kicked at where he judged the latch would be, though nothing was visible from the outside. The panel exploded inward ahead of the tanker's boot-heel.

The greeter had disappeared, leaving the lobby empty. There was a small hole in the wall above the greeter's arm-chair, but the tendril was gone also. Slade had taken a certain pleasure in kicking the door down. Before he could smash into the sorm parlor the same way, however, the attendant opened the door from within. The local stepped back. "Your pleasure, sirs?" the man asked.

"Blaney," said Slade. He strode through the door with his gun in a patrol sling, muzzle forward. He did not expect that kind of trouble here, but he would have welcomed the excuse to open up. The crewman lay much as Slade had left him. "How do we bring him back?" Slade demanded. *"Fast,* and no cop. We're right on the edge here, you know it yourself."

The remainder of the group was filing into the parlor. They were nervous, even the three like Blackledge and Slade whose necks were scabbed from a tendril puncture. Their hands tightened on their guns as the attendant said, "The client can separate at will, Captain Slade. You know that. There is no other way to separate him that will not cause the individual's death."

"Cop!" said Blackledge. He slid a long knife from his boot. His left hand gripped Blaney's hair and drew the crewman's head off the couch. The tendril slid further through the cover sheet without relaxing its hold on the comatose human.

"Wait, *please,"* said the attendant. The local man's voice held emphasis but no real concern. "If the trunk is injured or the root severed, the orphaned filaments will—"

Blackledge drew his blade across the tendril. The knife had a razor edge, and the steel was density-enhanced to retain that keenness. The cut ends of the root flipped up with a drop of sap on either of them.

Blaney spasmed on the couch like a pithed frog. His jaw was opening and clopping shut again to pass gulping sounds. That was not an attempt to scream, nor were his arms trying to wave help closer as they flailed. The brain itself has no pain receptors.

The thrashing stopped. Blaney lay still. His eyes were open and his body was as flaccid as if his skin were filled with hot wax. The crewman's face was growing freckled. Then the tips of the filaments waved through in a hundred places above the skin, gleaming with blood.

One of the outlaws screamed and emptied his submachine gun into the attendant's body. The cyan flashes lighted the close room and heated it in a gush of vaporized flesh. The local man slumped. His eyes were calm until they glazed. As the outlaws bolted from the sorm parlor, the tendril withdrew from the attendant's neck. It whisked itself back within the bolt-scarred stone.

Slade's finger was on the trigger as he stood, alone of living men, within the parlor. He did not fire.

The black-haired man was not even particularly angry as he walked back into the street. The sorm had its ways, just as Don Slade had his. The sorm had caused some difficulties just now by being the way it was, but the weather did that . . . and only fools got mad at the weather.

The trick in this case was going to cause some difficulties right back for the sorm. That was a lot more useful than losing your temper and going berserk.

The refrain trailed again through Slade's mind: "Down to the bottom of the sea!"

The wail of the ship's siren had gathered in most of the complement by the time Slade returned to the vessel. The bridge hatch was closed. Slade had to hammer on it and shout his name into a sound-plate before a crewman would admit him.

"Slade," said the harrassed-looking Captain Levine. "I think we'll be all right if we're left alone for a while. M'kuru here knows a little about navigation—" one of the four Drive crewmen nodded to Slade— "and I'm giving him a crash course that'll let us lift. After what happened in there, I'd say the quicker we all got off here, the better we were. Even with a short crew."

"No," said the tanker simply. "We're going to get your people back." A tic lifted a corner of his mouth. "Not Blaney, but the others. I've been into the system."

Slade touched the switch that winched down a ladder from the ceiling. The access port to the gangway along the top of the hull doubled as the bridge escape hatch when GAC 59 was in normal space. Levine watched with a puzzled look on his face as the big tanker slid the inner hatch back within the pressure hull. Slade activated the outer clamshell seal. "What do you plan to do?" the spacer called after Slade's disappearing legs.

When Slade did not reply, Levine scrambled up the ladder after him. The tanker was stretching his gun sling from carrying length to a shooting brace. "If we kill the trees," Levine said, "it's the same thing as Blackledge cutting the root. For God's sake, I don't want them killed that way!"

"I knocked open doors till I found a local who was still—attached," the tanker explained. On the catwalk, the two men were ten meters above the ground. They had a good field of view across the houses of Toler. "To explain it to the sorm. When it took one or two men from a crew, it didn't matter much. This time it took the same percentage, I guess, from our people, but too many of them were crew instead of mercs. Mind-set, I guess. And I couldn't get through to the sorm either; the fellow I talked to just stared and no more of our people were turned loose. Well, they weren't dumped out—I know they want to stay, but the colony *can* dump them, whatever that attendant said."

Slade sat carefully on the sun-heated catwalk. He locked his ankles and braced his elbows inside his knees. The gun was a cheap one without the electronic analog sight of the Slammers' shoulder weapons. A simple post and aperture would serve for this, however, so long as the alignment was accurate.

"But if you blow up trees," the spacer pleaded, "won't you—"

Slade fired and the air popped closed along the bolt's dazzling track. The nearest structure was the port control building. It had never been opened to the outsiders. The sorm in its courtyard started to branch about two meters above the ground. The scale-barked trunk at that point was about thirty centimeters in diameter before the bolt hit. The trunk was a cloud of blazing splinters a moment later.

The blond port official must not have been coupled to the tree when the powergun sawed it off. He was able to run out of the building shrieking as the stump smouldered and the tips of severed branches thrashed at random above the wall.

The Toler colony could afford to be larger than its conspecifics which depended on lower life forms to advance their needs. Each of the five hundred trees in the spaceport colony had deep-well irrigation and courtyard walls to break the force of the winds. Subsurface runners welded the colony together. The sorm trees were none the less discrete individuals whose life did not depend on that of the other members of the colony.

Whose life or death was individual.

Slade shifted his aim to a distant tree. The outlaws had probably not scattered too far from the ship in their quest for pleasure. The first bolt blew chunks from a wall coping. The second, after Slade corrected his aim, shattered another sorm. The courtyards were not built high enough to protect the trees from the gunman's brutal pruning.

Another hit. Another. Three shots in a row before the next tree sagged away from a half-severed trunk. Another hit. A miss, and Slade's hand slipped a fresh magazine from his coveralls to reload his weapon. The iridium barrel glowed, setting dust motes adance above the sight plane.

"You have to stop!" screamed the blond official from the ground. His face and teeth were white.

"Turn them loose," Slade called back. He locked the magazine home with the heel of his hand. "I'll give you time enough to stick a bloody root back in your skull. But if my people don't start coming back in the next five minutes, it's *gone*—every curst tree in this colony." He raised the powergun and clapped its fore-end for emphasis.

The Toler official blinked, struggling to form coherent thoughts. Then he began to shamble toward the building in which the nearest undamaged sorm still grew. To his back, Slade shouted, "I don't care cop about what you do with other ships. But you leave my people alone!"

The tanker turned, panting with the release of tension. Captain Levine was staring at him.

The tanker's face bore a look of surprise. It stemmed less from his success than from the possessive he had just heard himself use to refer to the cut-throats below.

CHAPTER FIFTEEN

"Clear-sighted," suggested one current of Elysian thought. "A response almost before he knew the problem."

"A ruthless response," amended the other viewpoint. "All those deaths accepted—caused—so long as they were not of his tiny caste."

"Can anything human be responsible for all humans?" protested the first. "Can we . . . ?"

"Well, welcome to Stagira," said Don Slade to the scouting party he had assembled in Bay 4.

The only sounds beyond were the ping of cooling metal and the breeze hissing above the docking pit. "Via, we should never have come here," grumbled Reuben Blackledge. The outlaw's mouse-blond hair was beginning to grow out beneath its blue tips. "The whole colony's died off."

"They landed us, didn't they?" said another of the outlaws staring out of the hold. But the long corridors facing the heavily-armed party were empty, and even the glow-strips lighting them seemed pale from encrusting grime.

"That was on automatic codes," said Slade. The ship's crewmen were too valuable to risk in scouting, but Slade had been on the bridge during the landing. "The machines work, at least some of them. If there aren't any humans to trade with, then we'll just have to pick up what we can, won't we?" To the microphone on his belt, Slade added, "Leaving the bay. You can secure in thirty seconds." To the score of mercenaries with him, "Come on, boys." The big tanker stepped off with his left foot.

The idea had been Slade's. In the confusion of the last hour on Toler, the others were stumbling back to the ship or aiding the sorm's victims to do so. The tanker had dragooned Levine and another navigator to help search the Port Office. It had been a grisly job for Slade and a far worse one for the spacers. They gagged at the thirty-odd corpses, some of them still twitching like frogs on a dissecting pan.

In the end, the search had paid off with a case of navigational microfiches which had probably accompanied the original settlers to Toler. There was electronic equipment which might have been nearly as old in storage. The colony had obviously shifted to symbiosis and biological data-storage very shortly after landing. It would have been almost impossible to decipher obsolete machine codes with the resources of GAC 59, however. There was no reason to assume that background radiation would not by now have degraded the stored data to random uselessness anyway.

By comparing the ancient microfiches with the vessel's own navigational data, Levine and his crew had found a nearby colony with a high technical rating which was no longer listed in current files. With luck, this one—Stagira—would be unfrequented but would have useful items that even GAC 59 alone could loot.

"I hadn't," Slade admitted aloud as he and his men echoed down the broad corridor, "expected the hardware to be in such good shape and *nobody* around."

"Any sign of farms when we landed?" asked one of the men.

"No sign of nothing," said Blackledge, who had also been on the bridge. "Place is bare as a whore's bum."

"Didn't seem to be any native life at all," Slade agreed. "Hydroponics would've been simpler than surface farming, no lack of raw materials. That doesn't explain why they didn't build at all on the surface . . . but there wasn't any lack of odd-ball notions when the first colonies cut loose from Earth, either."

"Here's a door!" called one of the men who had ranged furthest ahead.

"Then let's see what's behind it," Slade said in a calm voice. As he walked toward the portal and his clustering men, the tanker hitched up his equipment belt. The others carried shoulder weapons of one sort or the other. Slade wore only a holstered pistol—and, on his back, a satchel of plastic explosive. Fiddling with his belt gave him a surreptitious chance to wipe his sweaty palms on his coveralls.

"Shall I blow it in?" demanded one of the outlaws. Each man carried either a block of explosive like Slade or several blasting caps. The caps were touchy and bloody dangerous, but it was the men who carried the—quite inert—blocks of explosive who seemed most interested in shedding their burdens.

"Via, let's just try the touch plate," Slade said. When nobody else moved, he tapped the square in the center of the panel himself. There was no blast, no paralyzing shock as they had all managed to psych themselves into expecting. Instead, the door whispered sideways. It gave onto a scene in sybaritic contrast to the bleak corridor outside.

"Bingo," Slade called on his commo unit. Its signals would be drunk by the walls when he stepped inside, so the tanker wanted to tell those on the ship of the good fortune. "We've got our roughage and probably our protein besides. I'll scout around, see what we can raise, and report in a moment."

The air that puffed from the verdant interior was humid enough to condense noticeably in the corridor. The vegetation was varied. At least most of it was Earth-standard stock. There were no walls visible save the fifty centimeters between the corridor and the interior. The carefully-tended pathway felt like real sod beneath Slade's feet as he stepped inside.

"Just for the hell of it," the tanker said as the last of his men were following him into the artificial environment, "let's put something solid in the door's slideway. Pergot, your gun'll do. Just something to block it if it decides to close itself. Gives us room to set a charge."

The outlaw obeyed. He was unhappy about disarming himself, but he was unwilling to make an issue of the fact. The shoulder weapon's heavy iridium barrel should at worst only deform under the stresses that the closing mechanism could exert on it through the massive door.

As the men started to turn, secure in their retreat, the gun sank into the trackway's gray, nondescript lining. The door began to slide shut as quietly as it had opened.

Pergot lunged back, either to snatch up his disappearing weapon or to get into the corridor again. He accomplished neither. Or, at any rate, most of the outlaw did not reach the corridor. Pergot's left boot and right leg from mid-thigh lay inside the cavern when the door hissed to rest. Very possibly Pergot's head and hands were clear on the other side, so that only the half-meter of his torso had disappeared within the tonnes of door.

Something burst out of the undergrowth behind the party. The men were already tense with the horror before them. They spun, several of them screaming. The pig that had appeared now disintegrated in a squeal and cyan glare.

"Put 'em up!" Slade shouted as he bulled forward. The pig was scattered gobbets. Wallace, who had jumped aside at the animal's appearance, was on the ground also. The garish tunic the outlaw wore was afire, and there were two cratered holes in the small of his back. A companion's submachine gun had raked him.

Slade smothered the fire with his own broad chest, then ripped the smoldering remnants free. "Poles for a stretcher—Kuntz, Reecee," he ordered, naming two of the men who wore heavy knives.

The SpraySeal from the tanker's medical pouch was closing off the wounds, but it could do nothing for the internal damage. Powergun bolts had limited penetration, but abdominal wounds like these would be bordered by cooked flesh as much as a centimeter deep. There was nothing Slade could do about that. He was not even sure the ship's medicomp was up to the task. The Slammers could have handled it; anybody who got back to a Battalion Aid Station with his brain alive was going to make it.

But right now, Friesland seemed about as close as the ship, with that massive door separating both from the scouting party.

Slade set a cone of Hansine against the base of Wallace's spine. The wounded man trembled slightly as the drug entered his system.

It would disconnect his sensory apparatus until the dose was counteracted. That would not keep ruptured blood vessels from leaking, and it would not keep Wallace's belly from swelling as his intestines writhed around patches of dead muscle in their walls.

"What happened to Pergot's gun?" asked Blackledge, now that there was leisure again for recollection. "That molding looked just like zinc sheet, but the gun slipped through it like water." After a pause, the outlaw added, "You know, the whole wall looks like it's covered with the same stuff. Howes, poke at it, why don't you? Maybe we can slip right through."

"Screw yourself, why don't you?" Howes snapped. He leveled his 2 cm weapon at the door, however.

"Hold up, dammit," Slade said as he stepped out of his coveralls. The tanker had worn standard battle-dress for the sake of its pockets and attachments. Most of the party was in looted finery of one sort or another. The tough fabric of the coveralls would make a much better bed for the stretcher.

Howes fired. The air sizzled in a blue-green flash. The door's sheathing acted as a reflex reflector, splashing the bolt back in the direction from which it had come.

The reversal was imperfect enough that the whole party caught some of the charge. Howes, the gunman, was at the center of the spreading cone, however. Foliage beyond the men hissed. Slade shouted at what felt like a bath of nettles over his bare calves and buttocks.

Howes dropped his gun. The skin of his hand was fiery, and the surface of his eyes had baked in the glare that seared away his brows. When the gunman began to scream, his cracked lips gemmed with blood.

"All right," Slade said. He immobilized Howes with one hand while his other fumbled the SpraySeal from the kit again. The spray contained a surface analgesic that would take care of Howes' immediate pain, though the blindness was another matter. "We're going to move out," the tanker continued with both volume and authority. "We're going to find out who's behind all this. And then we're going to change it."

The tanker put the sealant back into the kit. His own buttocks and the similar burns of other pirates could wait for better supplies, though his harness chafed angrily as he moved.

"Marshal and Dobbs, first shift on the stretcher," Slade said. "Broadfoot, you guide Howes here. Let's move it, boys, we've got some convincing to do."

As the party moved off down the path, Slade scooped up the gun Howes had dropped.

They found the first building a hundred meters away, in a glade. Because it was windowless and completely unadorned, the leading outlaws drew up abruptly and raised their guns at an apparent fortification.

Stoudemeyer had been born on Telemark. "Hey!" he said in wonder, giving two syllables to the exclamation. He slung his submachine gun and pushed past the others to reach the door.

"Via, yeah," Stoudemeyer said as his hand caressed the door without touching the latch plate. "Captain, do you know what this is? It's a true to God bubble house! There's only five of them on Telemark, and I'd have said there wasn't another in the galaxy!"

"Well, what's it do, then?" Blackledge demanded. He gestured toward the man and building alike with a prodding motion of his gun muzzle.

"It does everything," Stoudemeyer said. He palmed the latch. "It does every curst thing you could imagine."

The others, even Slade, twitched a hair to the side as the door slid open. It was too reminiscent of the cavern's outer portal. The man from Telemark strode through without hesitation. "I tell you," he called over his shoulder, "being caught in here is like a bee drowning in honey. It don't hurt a bit. . . ." The door closed behind Stoudemeyer, then opened again before the babble of fear could even start. "The latch works fine from this side too," said Stoudemeyer, "but suit yourselves."

Blackledge was the first to follow Stoudemeyer. Slade was the last, and he decided not to order someone to stay back with Wallace. Never give orders you know will be ignored . . . and the tanker did not want to miss his own first look into this candy store, either.

The interior walls were a neutral gray when Slade first glimpsed them through the open door. By the time he was inside, however, Stoudemeyer had activated a control orally. The house was running through a series of panoramas, three or four seconds apiece, in which the walls seemed to melt into the far distance. Then the whole scene would dissolve into a radically different one. Slade did not appreciate the level or realism until the third example, a knoll of sere grass beneath a sky of cloud and purple lightning. Hard-spitting raindrops began to lash the men from hidden outlets. Among the curses and shouts of anger, Stoudemeyer's voice cried, "Cancel climate! Cancel sound!"

The sparkling desert that followed—in a few seconds, for a few seconds—did so without the blast of heat that would otherwise have probably accompanied the blue-tinged sunlight.

"Tell it to find something and hold it, Stoudemeyer," Slade directed irritably. The tanker could not hear Stoudemeyer's response over the general rumble of so many men in a small building.

The background segued to a glade much like the outside. Via, it *was* the glade outside; there lay Wallace twitching under stimulus of the breeze that ruffled the grass beside him. It was as if the party had been covered by a glass bubble thick enough to block out all sound.

"What do you sit on?" an outlaw demanded.

Stoudemeyer shrugged. "Ask for a chair," he said.

"All right, give me a chair," said the other man. He stumbled forward and the fellow behind him jumped away. The floor between them rose into a sculptured chair mounted on a pedestal that seemed too thin to support itself and a seated man. Neither Slade nor anyone else doubted that the construct *would* hold; but prodding at it with a finger was as much of a trial as anyone would make for the moment.

The Telemark mercenary was basking in his sudden importance. "Swivel chair," he said, pointing at the floor in front of him. From the point indicated extended a seat with the liquid grace of an amoeba. The seat looked like the one earlier called to life; but when Stoudemeyer sat in this one, he was able to spin it in further display. "Everything," he repeated, "anything. All you have to do is ask."

Outlaws were moving apart as far as the four-meter diameter of the floor permitted them. They were experimenting with shapes. Some of the more imaginative were creating subtle forms from their home worlds. They could even mime wood grains and basketry.

"Food?" asked Slade. He could simply have checked for himself. He did not, however, care to push buttons—even verbal ones—at random when there were directions available.

Stoudemeyer waved expansively. "Ask," he said as if he himself were the provider.

"Bring me Tethian rock-cruncher in a pepper sauce," the tanker said firmly.

"I'm sorry," responded a voice. It seemed only millimeters from Slade's ear. "That is not in my inventory. You may describe the dish by reference to others; or, if you prefer, you may make another selection."

Stoudemeyer must have heard the house's response, or at least enough of it to extrapolate the remainder. He hopped out of his chair with the smug expression replaced by one of concern. "Hey, I'm sorry, sir, I forgot. This place is probably as old as the ones back home. I mean—maybe eight hundred standard years. Can you believe it? That old and work like this still? He was a genius, a bloody genius."

"You mean try Earth food, not Tethys', because this place was built before the Settlement," Slade said to clarify what he had just been told. One point at a time.

"Right, or Telemark food," Stoudemeyer agreed. In test and demonstration, the man from Telemark said, "Bring me hassenpfeffer and a mug of, oh, any lager."

Slade could hear the voice saying from beside the other mercenary, "Yes sir, your food will be brought in forty—three—seconds."

"And this isn't half of it," Stoudemeyer confided to Slade. All around the room, outlaws were exploring this new capacity of the dwelling. Some of the men were demanding protein rations after a series of failures to come up with any other meal from the hidden menu. "The real thing about bubble houses is the dream-code feature." He kept his voice very low. "It's supposed to be as good as, as, you know—the sorm."

Stoudemeyer turned his head. He looked somewhat embarrassed. "I wouldn't really know, you know. On Telemark, you've got to own a province, practically, to even think of owning a bubble house. I mean, there's *five* that Kettlemann built before he disappeared. But everybody knows about them."

"Your dinner, sir," said the voice that was as cunningly projected as the rain had been some minutes earlier. The floor bulged like asphalt bubbling in the sun. The bulge rose on a stem like those that lifted chair seats. It halted with a hydraulic, not mechanical, smoothness at the height of Stoudemeyer's mid-chest. The bulge then irised open from the top to form a platter around a poultry-in-gravy dish which Slade presumed was hassenpfeffer. At any rate, the man from Telemark seemed satisfied as he took a thigh bone and began nibbling at the dark meat. "It's good," he said. "Try it."

Rather than attempt the meat right at that moment, Slade lifted the half-liter beer mug from the center of the tray. He expected the gravy to cling to the gray alloy of the container. The gravy did not, but the tray itself exuded a flexible tendril by which it retained the mug. Just, come to think, as the floor retained the tray. The tanker's pause was only mental. There was no obvious break in the slow progress of the mug to his lips. The lager, when he drank it, was cool and sharp and in no discernible way frightening.

"He was a genius," Stoudemeyer repeated around a mouthful of his pickled rabbit. "Certified Scientist Theodor Kettlemann. Started building bubble houses for the richest men on Telemark. I mean, nobody can figure *now* how this stuff works. And it still works." His gesture around the room spattered Slade with some of the tart gravy.

"Thing is," Stoudemeyer went on, "we had a planetary government then but not really, you know? And Kettlemann had some notions about genetics that didn't sit well with some people. He wouldn't work for anybody of Italian stock, for instance, even if they could trace their line right back to Landfall. And they were willing to pay his price. There was trouble about that. So when Kettlemann disappeared, a lot of people thought he'd been snatched—or wasted—by somebody he wouldn't build a house for."

"And instead, he recolonized," Slade said. He looked at the tangle of furniture and men wrangling over food of various types. "Picked a barren world that wasn't of interest to anybody else but gave him raw materials. And peace. Via, though, this must have cost a *fortune* to set up, the transport and the processing equipment alone."

Stoudemeyer nodded. "Kettlemann might have had that," he said. "Around the time he disappeared, so did a lot of other people. Rich people with their families. There was a lot of talk about it, all the way from mass murder to secret bases that were going to wipe out all the wops when the time was right. The whole business didn't cause the Partition Wars, exactly. But it didn't help things one bit, either."

"Well," said Slade. "Maybe it's time to go find what passes for a government here. And get our butts off-planet. Doesn't look like there's a whole lot of this—" he released the mug which snapped back onto the tray of which it was part, "—that we could dismantle and carry with us. Though the protein and vegetation still is handy for our synthesizers."

As Slade turned to the door, he adjusted his slung weapon out of habit. What he saw in the wall caused him to pump the gun live and to kick the latch-plate with the toe of his boot. That was the quickest way of opening the door without interfering with the business of shouldering his weapon.

Wallace and the makeshift stretcher were disappearing into the ground.

The scene was not an artifact of the wall display. The drugged man had sunk a centimeter further by the time Slade could see him through the open door. "Contact, you bastards!" the tanker roared to the startled remainder of the scouting party. None of them had noticed what was going on outside. "Everyone out!" As he spoke, Slade launched himself into the glade behind his gun muzzle.

The turf was beginning to close over Wallace in a neat seam.

Slade fired twice into the ground, aiming a hand's breadth above the peak of Wallace's head even as the seam covered that head. Point blank, the big powergun would shatter ceramic armor and burn a hole through eight millimeters of iridium.

The soil gouted upward, blasted by the vaporizing water trapped within each clod. Fifty centimeters down, the second bolt gouged bare a different layer. Not clay, as on a normal world, nor the bedrock overlain by manufactured soil as Slade had rather expected here. There was instead a dull gleam that covered itself as soil fell into the hole. Wallace lurched completely out of sight.

Slade did not fire again. He had seen what happened when that omnipresent alloy took a bolt from a powergun. Howes was enough of them to be blind and partly flayed from that nonsense.

Pirates were pouring out of the bubble house in panic. They lacked, in general, any notion of what was going on. Wallace's disappearance was not obvious except to one who had seen it in process; and that was Slade alone of the party. One man began to hose the undergrowth. A dozen others took up the activity. They flushed out a variety of birds and small animals as the succulent foliage burned.

"Hold your fire!" the tanker ordered. He had to shout three more times before he was at last obeyed. The volleying powerguns did not make enough physical racket to overwhelm a voice as strong as Slade's. The whole incident had a level of psychic noise that had to run its course, however.

Even as the last shot sizzled from a submachine gun, Slade was saying, "Reecee, give me your knife." The party had no proper entrenching equipment, but the long fighting knife would serve.

Slade probed with the borrowed weapon, gingerly at first though he was sure there was no harm the blade could do to Wallace now. Other pirates crowded around. The hot barrels of their weapons added an angry tinge to the stink of ozone. The turf through which the blade cut appeared perfectly normal. The halves of a severed worm flexed to either side of the knife. Soil crumbled from a yellow insect larva the size of a man's thumb-joint.

With a curse and an order snarled to the men closest, Slade dug the blade through the sward in a vicious circle. Outlaws who were late in obeying the order now leaped aside to save their toes. The tanker used his broad left hand as a spade to fling up the turf the knife had cut. Then he slashed again, deeper. The soil was still rich-looking and crumbly. Roots no longer bound it in their web-work this far below the surface. Slade scattered two double handfuls, then cursed and began to scoop deeper with his helmet. The blunt edge and padded interior of the helmet made a bad shovel, but the loose soil did not fight his efforts.

The helmet thudded on metal like that which the shots had uncovered before. There was no sign of Wallace, his clothing, or the stretcher on which he had lain. Slade used his bare hands again to squeeze a patch of metal clear. The gray surface was now covered with iridescent ripples like those of oil on still water. The colors blurred and fused and sank to neutral gray again even as the men watched. The surface had its usual metallic sheen . . . but Slade was no longer sure that it was metal at all.

Most of the men around Slade had no idea what was going on. Stoudemeyer had seen some and guessed more, perhaps much more. "There's a thing about Kettlemann that didn't make a lot of sense," said the man from Telemark. "He already had a reputation when he got into building bubble houses. But he wasn't an engineer. He was a geneticist."

Slade stood up, swearing very softly. He wiped dirt from the blade on his own thigh before he handed the knife back to Reecee. The party watched the tanker apprehensively, though they had not all realized that Wallace was missing.

"All right," Slade said. "We break up into groups of three. Every group has a radio. Reecee, Stoudemeyer, you're with me. We'll lead Howes. We're going to cover as much of this place as we have to to find who's in charge. Or at least where it's being run from. Report anything funny, and we'll all check in every quarter hour."

As Slade separated and numbered the remaining groups, he could feel Stoudemeyer staring at him somberly. The man from Telemark did not believe that the search would uncover what they needed to find to escape.

Slade could not very well object to his subordinate's pessimism. Not when the two of them were completely of the same opinion.

Four hours of searching disappointed Slade's hopes if not his expectations. The cavern was large but not endless. The parties sent in opposite directions around the wall had met on the other side of the circle. They had not found a door besides the one by which they had all entered, nor was there anything else that looked promising.

The groups had located thirty-seven bubble houses. There might have been some duplication before Slade directed groups to turn up a clod at the doorway of each house they found. Even so, it was probable that the cursory search had failed to find all the unobtrusive structures.

It was even possible that there was a headquarters building somewhere, a planetary capital—but by now, Slade and Stoudemeyer were not alone in doubting that.

The team Slade led personally sat around a table in the seventh bubble house they had found. The houses had been identical; though of course identical in their infinite variety. Howes had recovered enough to eat with the rest of them. He was still blind. His face had swollen like a pumpkin, but contact analgesics remained adequate for pain.

Slade gestured with a chicken drumstick. "The system works fine," he noted aloud. "Not just mechanically, but the life forms, vegetation, animals up to the size of pigs. At least to the size of pigs," he corrected himself.

"Only no people but us," Stoudemeyer said.

"Blood, we know why *that* is," said Reecee angrily. "Same curst thing killed them as killed Wallace after we'd lugged him all that way. Your Kettlemann just *thought* this planet was empty, Stoudemeyer. Something got him and something's going to get us if we don't get the hell out."

"You know, I thought about Wallace," said the man from Telemark. He put down his fork in order to give full attention to what he was hoping to explain. "I think he was dead. It's this food, you see?"

"Go on," prompted the tanker. His expression was non-committal.

"Well, it's not magic, you know," Stoudemeyer explained. He raised his fork again as an example. "There's a synthesizer, but it starts with advanced constituents—proteins and carbohydrates, not rock dust and water. On Telemark they're fed by plankton, the bubble houses are, mostly. But here, where the whole place is controlled—not just the house—the system acts as, well. . . ."

Every eye was focused on the lump of meat on the fork. "As a clean-up system too."

Reecee gagged. He lurched away from the table.

"I think you've got something very close," Slade said. His mouth had dried up, but he continued to chew away at the morsel already taken. You could not let—ultimate sources—get to you, or you'd never be able to eat fish from a sea in which men drown. "Only Wallace wasn't dead. I heard him mumbling as the soil zipped itself over his face. And Team Two said Pergot was still there at the door, what was left of him. The system doesn't recycle carrion. This was set up for very rich people, remember. It crops fresh meat as required."

"No, that's crazy—" began Stoudemeyer. His chair seat extended itself upward like tube-stock being drawn from a billet. As the man's knees lifted toward his chest, his whole body dropped. The chair pedestal was being reabsorbed by the floor, even as the seat enfolded the man who had been sitting on it.

Sliding from his own chair and reaching around the table should have been two motions for the tanker. He accomplished his goal of grasping Stoudemeyer's hand with a fluid grace that would have done credit to a gymnast in free-fall. Slade's whole body, legs and back and muscle-knotted shoulders, reacted together as he pulled Stoudemeyer from the gray maw that was engulfing him. The victim was off-balance and unable to extricate himself in the seconds available to him. For the moment, however, his body was held by little more than gravity. Slade's brutal snatch-lift dislocated the smaller man's shoulder, but it popped him from the tube like the cork from sparkling wine.

"Outside fast!" the tanker roared. His left hand slapped the latch plate. Momentum and the continuing pull of Slade's arm cracked the whip with Stoudemeyer. The man from Telemark snapped through the opening, wheezing with fear and gratitude.

As Slade turned back, Reecee caromed off his chest. Their legs tangled as Reecee fell. It was probably too late for Howes already, even if Slade had not been tripped.

The blinded man's screams reverberated as what had been his chair closed over him. The action must have been triggered when Stoudemeyer shot free. The mechanism was more similar to a tar pit than to a mouse-trap; but it was quick enough to take Howes, fuddled by pain and drugs.

Reecee scrambled to his feet to run again. Slade caught the outlaw by the shoulder with one hand—there was no time to talk— and retrieved Reecee's fighting knife with the other. Should've brought a blade of his own, Via. . . .

Stoudemeyer's chair had reformed. Howes' chair and the man himself were a bubble on the floor, a giant copy of the shape from which the house extruded furniture and food. This bubble was shrinking. Howes' whimpering had been shut off instantly when the metal closed over him. Slade struck at the seam joining the bubble to the floor proper.

The atomic shells of the knife's point and edges had been shrunk in a magnetic forging process more rigorous than that which contains the plasma in a fusion plant. The result would stay needle-sharp as it was rammed through steel plate or ceramic body armor. It was not sharp enough to penetrate the fluid surface that had just swallowed the blind man, however. The blade skidded and rang. Slade shouted a curse and struck again. When the knife slipped away this time, it took a thumb-nail-sized circuit from the toe of Slade's right boot. The bubble was almost flat by now.

Howes was a pompous ass, a fool before he blinded himself and a useless burden since. Slade caught up the shoulder weapon slung on his own chair. He ran outside. His nostrils stung with suppressed tears.

"What are we going to do?" Reecee blubbered. "It can take us out here just as easy, can't it? What are we going to do?"

"We're all right if we keep moving," Slade said.

"But why's it taking *people?*" Stoudemeyer asked. He spoke in a normal voice, but the words were more an apostrophe to his own doubts than a question to his companions. "There's plenty of animals out here, the pigs and the rabbits. They must be here as food stocks. Why does it take us instead?"

"You're not going to sleep, Captain?" Reecee demanded. He was a big man also, but only blind panic could have driven him to bait Slade. The tanker stood with the knife naked in his hand. "You're such a hero that you're going to walk around laughing while the bloody *dirt* buries the rest of us like it did Wallace?"

"Don't guess it does take people," Slade said. He let out a shuddering breath. His hands were shaking, but there was no sign of his fear and adrenalin as he spoke. "I think your Professor Kettlemann just programmed the system with a narrower definition of human than you or I might've used. Different, that's sure a cop. Got any wog blood in you, Stoudemeyer? Bet your home-grown genius wouldn't approve. *May he burn in Hell!*"

"But what do we *do?*" Reecee repeated.

"We fucking *think* of something!" Slade roared back. As the outlaw stepped back, shocked as if by a slap in the face, Slade flung the knife.

It buried itself to the cross-guard in the sod between Reecee's boots.

It was usually easy to forget they were trapped in a chamber rather than a walled enclosure. The shock waves were a brutal reminder. The blast shuddered on and on until the noise that could not escape had damped itself to silence. Leaves had been stripped from the nearest trees. The ears of the scouting party continued to ring long after the cavern itself had ceased to do so.

The door by which the party had entered was still closed and still unmarked.

Slade set down the detonator. He began methodically brushing leaf-mold from his bare knees. When they were clean, he strode toward the door where other members of the group were already gathered and arguing. Slade's pack, with the shoulder weapon across it, lay by the tree which had sheltered him.

"Didn't do a *bloody* thing!" snarled one of the outlaws. He slammed the butt of his weapon against the dull metal. None of the men were too angry to remember what shooting into the door had brought Howes.

"We've got plenty more explosives," said Blackledge. "We'll put them all against this door and that'll do it."

"No," said Slade. "Not uncontained. Even if we did punch a hole, it'd seal before we could use it. We need to get the system itself. If we set our charge in one of these houses—" he waved beyond the trees, in the general direction of the nearest bubble house— "close it up with a time fuse, we might be able to kill the whole thing." The tanker took off his helmet and fanned himself with it.

"*Cop,*" said Blackledge. His tone cleared a broad aisle between him and the tanker two meters away. "We don't need a house blown up, we need a *door* gone. This didn't work, fine. We got ten times that much left. We'll set it all off together, right here." The blue-haired outlaw's submachine gun already pointed squarely at Slade's midriff.

"Ten times nothing is still nothing," the tanker said tensely. He rapped the door with the knuckles of his left hand, holding the helmet.

"I tell you something else that's bloody nothing!" Blackledge shouted. He waggled his gun in needless emphasis. "The way you've been bloody running things! *That's* nothing!"

Slade fired. His bolt clipped the rim of the helmet with which he had hidden the pistol. Enough of the energy got through to handle the job, however.

The outlaw's submachine gun blew up. Slade had fired at it rather than at the man for better reasons than misplaced mercy. Even a brain shot might not have kept Blackledge's trigger finger from one last spasm. The flash of the magazine exploding was a blue-green so intense that it was almost white. Flaming droplets of plastic and metal sprayed the men.

Blackledge lurched sideways and fell as if a truck had hit him.

His right hand and right side from shoulder to knee were charred black except where bone poked out. Blackledge did not scream because shock had not yet let the pain through. The only sound he made was the clicking in his throat as he tried to draw a breath.

Slade did not reach for his medikit, but he extended his pistol for careful aim. There was enough cruelty in the universe without letting someone suffer needlessly. Even Blackledge, even someone as useless as Blackledge. . . .

The tanker lowered his weapon again without firing the second shot. The rest of the scouting party relaxed unconsciously. None of them had thought to gainsay Slade. Even the pair of outlaws who had also been with Aylmer could see that a quick end was the best that Blackledge could hope for even if they managed to get him back to the ship.

"Petrie," said Slade, after the pause had allowed him to get his breathing if not his pulse back under control, "strip off your coveralls. Mine went off with Wallace, and we need another stretcher now."

Slade bent over the wounded man. The pistol's barrel was still too hot for the holster. Slade transferred the weapon to his left hand while his right took another cone of pain blocker from the limited medical supplies. Without the blocker, Blackledge would die of shock; and he might die too soon.

"Taylor, Hwang," the tanker went on as he straightened again, "you'll carry him. Be as easy as you can, but we may not have much time. Rest of you, gather your gear and let's get moving. We need one of those bubble houses to get out of this place."

In the confusion of movement and released tension, Stoudemeyer stepped closer to Slade. In a low voice the man from Telemark asked, "Do you really think there's a way, ah—Captain?"

"Lord help me," Slade muttered back, "I think there is."

"But what do I ask for?" called Taylor through the open door.

"Ask for any curst thing you want!" Slade shouted back. "Ask for raw beef. And keep asking, like I bloody told you!"

Beside the kneeling tanker, Reuben Blackledge began to

mumble the words to a song. It sounded as if it were in Latin, a hymn from deep in the outlaw's consciousness. The coveralls lumped misshapenly over the wounded man's body.

In the bubble house, Taylor was saying, "Raw beef. More raw beef. More raw beef." The house's response was inaudible to the rest of the party outside. Except for Slade, the outlaws' hands were clenched on the guns he had ordered them not to use.

"The system has to be centralized," Stoudemeyer said nervously. "It may not replenish itself here, just because Taylor's—"

Taylor screamed. He leaped with his boots pedaling like those of a man who hears a rattlesnake beneath him. The real stimulus was a negative one, the feeling of the floor beginning to drop away beneath his feet. Taylor was out the door even as the third platter of synthesized beef was beginning to unfold in front of where he had stood.

Another mercenary shouted and jumped sideways as the ground began to shift under him. Slade jerked the igniter wire. He prayed that the time pencil's stated thirty-second delay was fairly close to its reality. "All right, dammit," he said as he jumped to his feet, "let's get back a ways. *Don't separate!*"

When he watched the process from the beginning, Slade could see the wink of metal as tendrils parted the soil. Blackledge twitched his left arm. It was the only movement of which the drugged man was capable. His chanting trailed off into a one-sided argument of some sort as the grass closed over his face, then his swollen body.

"Twenty-four," Slade whispered, "twenty-five, twenty—"

Forty kilos of high explosive went off, literally in the bowels of Professor Kettlemann's closed system.

It was hard to determine the epicenter of the blast. The ground seemed to hump up about ten meters from the point it had fed itself Blackledge and his wrapping of explosive. The bulge hammered the cavern's interior as if the ground were the hard-struck membrane of an enormous drum. Light had been omnipresent in the high ceiling. Now the light died in a logarithmically expanding wave from the point above the blast. It was a reversed vision of an incandescent bulb going out, when the filament retains an orange glow for instants after it no longer illuminates its surroundings.

Slade picked himself up carefully. Somebody cried out at the darkness. Several of the team were switching on the light-wands they brought and had promptly forgotten in the lighted cavern. Streaks flickered through the fuzzy yellow glows. It was not rain but grit, oxidized metal raining from the ceiling.

The tanker wiped and lowered his upturned face hastily. "Let's move!" he shouted to the men of his party. "Bloody thing may regenerate, or it may come down on our heads like a drop forge. Curst if I want to be around either way."

The door that had crushed Pergot was crumbled open like a heap of smelter slag. It buried whatever was left of the dead outlaw. Flies buzzed away from the pig carcass as the men stumbled past behind their light-wands. The corridor beyond was still illuminated. Slade wondered vaguely where it led, whether to more self-contained habitats or to something quite different. He had no real interest in finding out.

Several of the group cheered as they bolted into the corridor. Birds fluttered past them, called to the light.

Be damned to replenishing stores, thought Don Slade. What GAC 59 needed now was *out*.

CHAPTER SIXTEEN

"Ruthless even to his own men!" shuddered the mind of Elysium.

"The only salvation of his men," it replied. "Not cruel, and ruthless only at need. Men use men. But mankind uses men for the species to survive. For our species to survive. . . ."

As if in answer, the first current of opinion recalled an image from the castaway's mind. It was his last look at Blackledge's face. The dark, dilated pupils met Slade's as the ground sagged down and the fuse hissed on the wounded man's chest. "Ruthless. . . ."

"Captain Levine didn't want to lift ship so suddenly," Don Slade said to the Elysian faces before him. "Some of the guys who hadn't been in the scout party sort of wanted to look around for themselves, too. Nobody had planned to go looking for us if we hadn't come back, though, any more than we'd thought they would."

The big man paused and cleared his throat. It wouldn't do to put his foot in his mouth now. These were nice folks, gentle folks, and the last thing he wanted to do was to give them an accurate glimpse of life in the universe from which he came. "Some of the people who'd been with me, though, they were pretty strong about getting off Stagira before something came through the hull to eat them. Used words like 'kill everybody on the bridge if the ship didn't lift ASAP.' Just panic, of course, but I wouldn't say they were joking right at that moment, either.

"While we were trying to get out of that cave, Levine and his navigators were thinking about their problem—crewing. Now, if we'd been able to touch down at some of the busier ports, there'd have been plenty of folks on the beach that we could have struck a deal with. But we were worried about competition, and besides . . . there was a problem about the manifesting of the cargo from Desireé. The bigger places with their red tape might have kept us a year in Customs Quarantine."

Well, it would have been about a year before the courts got through their rigamarole and everybody aboard GAC 59 was executed with due ceremony.

"But there was a place called Windward, where the colony modified autochthones to handle very complex tasks. Even starship crew jobs. So when the men of the scout party pushed matters, Levine already had a course plotted to Windward. . . ."

"So, assuming your cargo meets the manifest," said Senior Patriarch Bledsoe, "we have a deal." He offered his hand.

Captain Levine shook, but as he did so he said sourly to the Windward official, "The thrusters are in the original packing, Patriarch. There shouldn't be any problem with them. I'm a good deal more concerned about whether your crewman is going to function as well as the ten-tonne unit we're trading for him."

"For *it*, good sir," said the Windward official. Bledsoe's smile was wholly on his lips, not in his tone. "Human pronouns are as out of place for the Treks as they would be for so many, oh, thrust units. You'll see."

The local man had a fringe of white hair and a cherubic expression. He had driven a bargain, however, that obviously reflected the trouble the outlaws would have in selling their cargo on any world which did not wink at piracy. Bledsoe walked to the window. Don Slade already stood there, watching port activity. The two men were nearly of a size, but the tanker had a physical hardness which the other lacked. Muscles meant very little in modern, civilized warfare, however. Slade did not remember having seen a more heavily-defended spaceport on any world which was not in the midst of open warfare.

"We certainly expect you to test our merchandise as closely as we test yours, gentlemen," Bledsoe said. "There's a necessary programming period, of course, to interface the Trek with your system. About three days, I would judge, though there may be idiosyncrasies. After that, you can expect to have one of your control stations occupied at all times by a flawless, sleepless living machine. We'll modify your synthesizers to turn out a protein supplement that won't cause allergic reactions in a Trek; that won't be a problem. You'll find your purchase well worth the expense, I assure you."

"I don't wholly understand," said Slade. "How does what would be a six month cram-course for a human with top of the line hypnocubes turn out to be three days for a, a Trek?" He turned away from the bustle of planetary and intra-system traffic outside to pin the local man with his eyes.

Bledsoe shrugged. "There are advantages to being inhuman, Mister Slade," he said. "To being unintelligent in human terms. Your Trek will act within the parameters which it deduces from the equipment it operates and the task to which it is set. As I said, three days is generally enough time for the programming to be completed."

"Well, what I'd like," snapped Captain Levine, "is to have a look at one of these things. What are they, rocks with arms?"

"We'll have your unit delivered at once," the local man said with a narrowing of his eyes. "But surely you must have seen Treks working outside?"

Bledsoe motioned Levine over. Slade made room at the window with a grim smile on his face. The tanker had a notion as to what was about to happen. "There," said the local man. "Driving that truck."

"Good heavens, Patriarch!" Levine blurted. "Surely that's a human being?"

Like much of the labor force visible, the figure in the truck's open cab was a humanoid of medium height. A closer look disclosed that its gray color was not clothing but rather the skin or natural covering—fur or fine scales—itself. The gray figures differed significantly from the occasional true humans in only one respect:

the humans worked with the usual amount of waste motion and chattering. The others, the Treks, carried out their tasks without any such flaws.

"They are *not* human, Captain Levine!" the Senior Patriarch said sharply. "And you will *not* be given another warning about your language. We aren't hard to get along with, here on Windward; but if you persist in blasphemy, you'll find we have rules and ways to enforce them." Bledsoe nodded toward one of the visible barbettes. Its twin powerguns had tracked the ship all the way to landing. Now the squat tubes were trained on the engine room, ready to gut their target at the first sign of trouble. Presumably the defenses were crewed by "flawless, sleepless, living machines" also.

Levine had lapsed into shocked silence. The tanker spoke to fill the embarrassing gap. "I suppose," he said mildly, "that you have, ah, normal recreation facilities for the crew while our purchase is being programmed?" Slade almost said "programming itself," but he caught himself short of another possible blunder.

"Normal and abnormal," said the local man. His expression relapsed into a knowing smile. "We can put some activities off-limits to your personnel if you like. All the establishments are, so to speak, managed by Treks. If you don't care, though, the sky's the limit—liquor, drugs; boys, women, or combinations; honest games—anything. We on Windward believe men have a right and a duty to take pleasure, though of course we support your right as commander—" He glanced from Slade to Levine and back again. Their relationship had not been made clear to Bledsoe. "—to control your crew for the good of the vessel."

Slade nodded. "Wide open should be just fine," he said. "So long as you don't have sorm trees."

"Pardon?"

"Don't worry about it," tanker said. "Let's get a team to emptying our hold, and let's get our Trek started on learning the hardware." He grinned. "The other hardware."

"Here's the high-speed vector shift," said Riddle, the Midwatch navigator who was handling the training.

The Trek followed the human's pointing finger to the cylinder switch with click detents for band jumps. The gray-furred humanoid had been trying to follow the training simulation by using the rocker switch by which the three units were brought into synchrony. Amazingly, the Trek had been successful within safety parameters if not those of comfort. That was, after all, as much as one dared to hope from the regular navigation crew.

The exercise continued smoothly. The Trek used both three-fingered hands to make adjustments now that he no longer had to keep one glued to the rocker switch. Its motions had less of the manic intensity of a one-armed pianist, as a result.

"She's absolutely incredible," muttered Riddle.

Slade glanced sharply at the navigator, then back to the autochthone. "Any time you're in front of a local," the tanker said mildly, "you call Treks 'it.' I think the best thing that'd happen otherwise is we lift off short another navigator."

Though it was natural, the Lord knew, to think of the Treks as human, as people. Their thigh and upper arm bones were noticeably longer than those of the lower limbs. Their facial features were understated in the manner of primitive carvings in low relief. The fur was less obtrusive than it would have seemed, because it was so fine and clinging that even at arm's length it seemed more like clothing than it did some facet of alienness.

The Treks had no secondary sexual characteristics, however. Riddle might find the creature's lithe quickness to be feminine. Slade, however, was reminded of a gunman he had known, and whose sex was not an issue once you had seen him kill.

The conning room was designed around a three-sided pillar. The primary controls were arranged on the sides of the pillar. Behind each navigation console, the bulkhead was covered with banks of status read-outs whose information was echoed to the main screen when the central computer saw a need to do so. The Trek shot frequent glances over its shoulder.

Slade began to open a ration packet. It was sealed in a tough polymer with a metalized inner surface. The autochthone turned in soundless delight. It extended a hand palm-upward toward the tanker. The palm was not fur-covered. The Trek's skin was a smooth, rich sable.

"Food?" Slade asked. He broke off half the ration bar and offered it. The Trek reached past the offered portion and took the half still in its wrapper. It opened the polymer carefully and waggled it so that the inner surface reflected the ranks of gauges to the rear.

"You want a mirror?" Slade said in surprise. The autochthone nodded enthusiastically. "Via, we can do better than this. I'll see to it." Slade looked at Riddle and added. "Do you really have to watch all that stuff too?" He waved at the mass of dials and data windows.

The navigator shrugged. "Well, they're there, they've got some purpose. And the way things work on this trash-bucket, the more you know, the better. But Lord! She's so—" Riddle ran his hand over the Trek's shoulder and biceps. "Good isn't the word. And without being able to *speak.*"

Slade pointed at the Trek's throat with one blunt forefinger. The tanker was careful not to touch the smooth fur. "When the light catches it the right way," he said, "you can see there's a scar there. I suspect it could speak about as well as it does everything else, except for that."

Riddle leaped from his chair in an outburst of rage. "The bastards did *that?*" he shouted. The Trek nodded without apparent emotion. It resumed the activities of the training program. Riddle had not needed the confirmation anyway. "Those, those—animals!" he went on. His hand touched the Trek's shoulder again. "*She's* not an animal, *they* are."

Slade lifted the navigator's hand and dropped it back at the man's side. The tanker was tall enough to look down on Riddle's bald spot when they were both standing. "*I'm* telling you to watch your tongue, friend," Slade said. "If you can't learn to, you'll spend the rest of this landfall tied down and sedated."

When he felt the smaller man relax somewhat, Slade continued. "Now, how much longer are you on duty here?"

"Ninety-three minutes," the navigator said sullenly. He did sit down again.

"Fine," said Slade. "As soon as you're off, I want you to get over

to one of the knock shops on the Strip and have your ashes hauled.
Girls are a bit pricey, but don't worry about that, the first one's on
me." His eyes narrowed slightly as he watched the balding man. "Or
a guy, Via, take your choice. But you've got an order, mister, and
don't think I'm kidding."

The tanker slapped his thigh as he walked out of the conning
room. His hard palm cracked where the pistol holster would have
been had he bothered to wear one.

Behind Slade, the navigator glowered at the autochthone's
dancing arms.

"—what can the matter be?" Don Slade caroled as he walked
across the port apron. A cab would have brought him directly to the
main hatch, but the tanker felt good tonight, felt like walking. Area
floods made the port and the vessels in it shimmer in amber light.
"Seven old maids, locked in the lavat'ry."

"Slade, where've you been?" demanded a voice. Figures detached
themselves from the hatch. Captain Levine had been speaking.
"They've cheated us, there's something wrong with the Trek."

"They were there from Sunday to Saturd'y," Slade continued.
That was playfulness, however, not real disregard of the problem.
Windward had stim cones, real Cajumel blendings, and some of the
whores had carried professionalism almost to a level of enthusiasm.

The big man put his arms around his pair of greeters, Levine and
Riddle. The latter's bald spot gleamed like polished copper. "Let's go
see what the problem is," the tanker said.

"The problem is the curst thing's dying before we even shift
atmosphere," said Captain Levine as the trio stumbled up the ramp.
Slade kept hold of his two companions' waistbands as if they were
coolies and he a rickshaw. "I suppose we ought to be glad it didn't
happen in the middle of a Transit sequence, but dear heaven! the
cost, a whole *thruster,* and all wasted!"

"Lot of people got wasted when we got the thrusters, too," Slade
noted equably. "But we wanted them pretty bad. Want not, waste
not, d'ye suppose, Captain?"

The Trek lay on the shelf of the vessel's medicomp. The creature might as well have been laid on the broiler in the galley for all the use the primitive piece of hardware would do. The medicomp could not be reprogrammed to handle non-human life forms. Since GAC 59 lacked even the most basic parameters such as the Trek's normal heart rate and body temperature, a more flexible medicomp would not have helped anyway.

The Trek lay supine. Its body was so flaccid that the soles of its feet touched the shelf. The ankle joints obviously did not lock. The creature's eyes were covered with yellowish scum which matted the fur around the orbits as well. Fluid of some other description, possibly the Trek equivalent of blood, was leaking out of its nostrils and simple ears. The creature's breathing was rapid and louder than the stand-by hum of the equipment. It did not take experience as extensive as the tanker's to recognize imminent death.

Slade stepped to the communications unit on the wall beside the medicomp. He tapped a three-digit code into the key pad to access the ship-to ship radio; ten digits more to enter Windward's commo net through the port transponder; and finally the six digits of the Port Warden. At no time did Slade pause to check the number or to fumble with the key pad. His eyes narrowed over chill anger as he waited for the connections to go through. There was no sign of the evening's entertainment when he snapped at the men across from him. "Why in *Hell* didn't you get help from the locals before now? Do you *like* to watch things die?"

Riddle grimaced and looked away. He had not, come to think, spoken since Slade's return.

Captain Levine said bluntly, "I wasn't about to bring them in till I found you. I can deal with these people if I've got somebody like you standing behind me. But not by myself, not when they're sure to deny liability."

"Warden's Office, Third Son Tuburg speaking," said the commo unit.

"This is freighter Golf-Alpha-Charlie Five Niner," Slade replied. "Berthed on Pad Four. The Trek we purchased yesterday is in dying condition. Seems disease or poison. We need medical help right away or we're going to lose hi—ah, it."

"Roger," said the speaker. Slade was not sure whether it was a good sign or a bad one that the Windward watch officer broke the connection at once.

"All right, what happened?" the tanker asked. He might as well improve his time by getting the background while they waited. The Trek breathed with the harshness of a file on stone.

"Riddle buzzed me about three hours ago," said Captain Levine. He gestured with his thumb. "He said the thing's performance had deteriorated and now it wasn't moving at all."

Slade looked at the navigator. "Why were you still on duty then, Riddle?" he asked without expression.

The balding man looked away. "Hutchins didn't show up for his watch," he said.

"Didn't you say Hutchins paid you to stand a double?" the Captain interjected.

"No matter," said Slade. No matter that he was going to deal with at just this moment. "What happened then?"

Levine risked a puzzled glance at his navigator. "Well," he went on, "when I got to the conning room it was about like you see it here. Not quite so much, well, leaking, but sick. Limp as a coil of rope. So we brought him down here—" he nodded vaguely at the medicomp— "and called you. You weren't wearing your belt unit."

Slade wavered between anger and laughing, then laughed. "My belt unit's lying on my bunk, along with a lot of other garbage I didn't want to fool with tonight. And as for what I was wearing, Captain—for most of the night, I wasn't wearing a curst thing. And neither were the ladies I was with."

"Well, ah," Levine said. "We needed to get hold of you, you see."

"What did it eat, Riddle?" Slade said sharply.

"I gave her some water!" the navigator replied angrily. "Nothing to eat since *you* fed her."

"Then maybe we're all right," the tanker said as if he did not understand the attack. "If it wasn't fed anything but carbohydrates, then maybe it was just some bug it picked up. We're not responsible for that, not till we lift off, at any rate." He smiled wryly. What was the warranty on humanoids purchased by pirates? Especially under the seller's guns.

Help arrived in a growl of fans on the pad. Levine trotted down the corridor. "This way!" he shouted ahead. Moments later, the Captain was back. Two clashing pairs of boots and the bare-soled whispering of a Trek followed him.

One of the Windward humans was young and dishevelled. Slade did not recognize the symbol on the man's white cap. The tanker suspected that the fellow was not, by local law, a doctor. He and the Trek who carried the chromed medical case pushed past Slade and Riddle to the dying autochthone.

The other human was Senior Patriarch Bledsoe himself. In earlier dealings, the Windward official had covered the steel edges of his personality with a layer of bonhommie. That had not hidden the truth or even camouflaged it; but it showed the same willingness to deal rationally as did Slade's own careful control.

The bonhommie was gone now. "You were warned about certain rules, Captain Levine," said the Senior Patriarch harshly. Bledsoe must have pulled his uniform on in a rush, but his appearance was as sharp as it had been during the cargo negotiations. "I don't assume you have violated those rules—" not really a lie, so transparent were the words— "but if you have, you and your vessel will be expelled at once from Windward."

"But I don't understand, ah, Port Warden," Levine blurted.

Slade understood. So did Navigator Riddle. The balding man was pressing his palms fiercely against one another while his eyes focused on their trembling.

The medic muttered something cryptic to the autochthone which had accompanied him. That Trek made a quick gesture with its hands—sign language. It bore the laryngeal scar also, even though the speech that would otherwise be possible would clearly help in its duties. Job requirements are not always rational requirements, and a creature which speaks may too easily be thought of as human.

The healthy Trek rolled its wheezing fellow belly-down on the shelf. The Trek's strain at the activity suggested that the autochthones had less short-term strength than even human females of the same size. Despite that, the medic did not help his assistant turn the injured creature. The local man was instead pulling on a pair of disposable gloves. He bent forward as his Trek assistant spread the other autochthone's buttocks.

Slade knew too little about Trek physiology to guess whether the opening displayed was a cloaca or something more specialized than that. The black skin of its lips was distended. The surrounding fur was matted, though there was no sign of fluids leaking as they did from the creature's ears and nose.

"Well?" demanded Senior Patriarch Bledsoe.

The medic reached into his kit. Instead of speaking, he gave his superior a curt nod. The medic's face was a queasy contrast to the metallicly-calm expression of his Trek assistant.

Bledsoe's tongue touched dry lips. "Captain Levine," he said, "your crew will be delivered to you as soon as humanly possible. Humanly! You will lift off within five minutes of the last arrival." The official's eyes were as merciless as the twin-barreled gun turret aimed at the ship from outside.

"Senior Patriarch," Slade interrupted, "we'll clean our own house. You can watch if you like."

The tanker did not look at Riddle. The navigator stood in near catatonia by the bulkhead. Slade's words rang about him with deadly earnestness. Slade was going to beat the balding navigator within an inch of his life, because nothing short of that could be expected to satisfy the Windward authorities. "And we expect to pay a stiff penalty over and above the cost of a replacement Trek. But—"

"Are you mad?" Bledsoe demanded as if he and not the tanker were the man who had killed for a business. "Mister Slade, I will have them slag this ship down around me before I will consider placing another Trek into this *cesspool!*"

The gloved medic put an injector behind the dying Trek's ear. The creature convulsed mightily. The medic jumped back to avoid the flailing limbs. He dropped the empty injector on the shelf.

"Sir," said the tanker. His anger was obvious and as great as that of Bledsoe. "We won't leave because we *can't* leave that fast in our present state of crewing. If that means blasting us where we stand, then you might want to see how our powerplant's been rigged." That was a lie, but it would be the truth if Slade had half an hour's grace. "If you're willing to deal, though, we'll deal with you on any terms that give us a chance to survive."

The medic and his assistant were already leaving the cubicle. Riddle stared at the Trek. It ignored him. The other autochthone was dead, though its extremities continued to slap the shelf and walls. The injection had only speeded the process made inevitable when the Trek absorbed human proteins.

The Senior Patriarch swallowed, "All right," he said, staring fiercely back at the tanker. "I'll send aboard a navigational unit with a link to the central computer. They'll set and lock your controls onto the nearest inhabited world, that's Erlette. And if that isn't satisfactory, Mister Slade—then yes, we *will* see what you may have done to your powerplant. Good day!"

The Windward official turned and bounced Captain Levine out of his way. Bledsoe did not even seem to notice the contact as he strode back toward the hatch.

"Slade, Slade, Captain," Levine pleaded, "does he mean that Riddle—"

As if his name were a trigger, Riddle ran down the corridor. "You bastards!" he shouted. "You bastards! You know they're human! *You know they're human!*"

Levine and the tanker tried simultaneously to jump after the navigator. The instant's delay they caused each other permitted the balding man to reach the hatch before they could catch him.

Bledsoe had continued to walk toward the vehicle that had brought him to the ramp. The medic and his assistant were already seated and waiting. So were two other Treks. One was the driver.

The other crewed the pillar-mounted tribarrel. The air cushion vehicle was not an ambulance but a gun-truck.

Riddle caught Bledsoe by the sleeve while the local official was still half-way from his vehicle. Bledsoe had ignored the navigator's previous taunts. Now he turned. Harsh light at an angle threw his face into a sequence of cold ridges and cold valleys.

Slade saw and understood the look in the Senior Patriarch's eyes. Captain Levine tried to squeeze past to run to his crewman. The tanker's arm encircled Levine's waist and immobilized the smaller man by lifting his feet from the deck. This was no time to interfere. It would be like trying to stop lava with a barrier of brushwood.

"You're human!" Riddle screamed to the Trek at the automatic weapon. "You've got to free yourselves; *kill* the people who torture you! *Kill* them!"

The medic broke his stony reserve. He leaped from the truck seat with a cry of rage. Bledsoe turned also. He was trying only to restrain the other Windward human, but Riddle reacted as if the motion were a challenge. Riddle's fist clubbed the older, heavier man on the side of the neck. Bledsoe stumbled to his knees with a grunt.

The Trek gunner fired a long burst into Riddle's body. The hot-griddle hiss of the shots was obscured by the shattering disintegration of the navigator's chest. Then both ceased, discharge and impact. What remained of Riddle slumped to the ground. Its left hand was extended as if in entreaty.

The iridium muzzles of the tribarrel glowed, and there was a glowing track in the ramp's face where a bolt had struck because the thorax at which it was aimed had vaporized. Ozone and decomposition products from the expended cartridges warred with the animal odors of burned flesh and voided wastes.

Slade released Captain Levine.

The gun's cyan flickering had frozen the medic in a half crouch from which he slowly relaxed. Senior Patriarch Bledsoe got to his feet with the clumsiness of a reanimated corpse. The right side of his face and uniform were freckled by the navigator's explosive death. "Five minutes after we deliver your last *man*, Captain Levine," said Bledsoe.

He swung himself aboard the truck. As the vehicle whistled off toward the Operations Building, the dimly-glowing muzzles of the tribarrel continued to track Slade and Levine in the hatchway.

CHAPTER SEVENTEEN

"He would really have blown up his ship," thought Elysium. *"He would have killed everyone for kilometers around. And they had a right to expel the vessel, the folk of Windward. Their culture was threatened."*

"He saved the ship and saved his fellows," Elysium replied. There was, there could be, neither heat nor rancor in the exchange. It was more as if two currents met in the sea, swirling and mingling. *"He saved lives that would have been lost had he bluffed and been called on it."*

Then, with all the unity that so many minds could muster on any subject; *"He does not bluff when he threatens. When he offers slaughter, he means nothing short of it. . . ."*

"The Transit to Erlette was about as smooth as any I'd made," Slade was saying. "It was sure as smooth as anything I'd made in GAC 59. That didn't keep Captain Levine from being concerned, though. . . ."

"This is just asking for disaster, Captain Slade," said Levine. "We'll come out of Transit in an atmosphere! Or we'll wind up in, we'll never be able to figure out *where,* as tired as my people are going to be."

"They tell me," said Slade calmly, "that everything's spot-on with no problems. And they seem pretty relaxed, too, even if they have been pulling a rotating double."

"Oh, that's fine, surely," said the spacer. His tones of angry sarcasm would not usually have been directed against Slade. "Windward had a ground unit the size of Friesland's, *certainly* it can preset us across seventeen Transit seconds. What is there on Erlette? Will we find the Transit crewmen we need there? On a place nobody's ever heard of?"

"You know," said the tanker, "I *did* hear of Erlette. While I was with the Slammers. But I'm hanged if I remember why. Must've been a briefing, people we were operating with or against or some curst thing. *Hanged* if I remember just what, though."

A dozen of the bridge displays winked and changed in a sudden, organized fashion that meant nothing to Slade. The crewman with the throat mike and earpiece turned to Levine. "Want I should request landing clearance, Captain?"

"Yes, curse it, of course," Levine said. He twisted and punched up a line of figures on his own console. "Before something *worse* goes wrong." The Captain's lips pursed. "Though you know, that's not bad. Maybe the old girl's settling in and the misalignments are cancelling out."

Slade left the bridge as the spacers shifted into the critical minutiae of landing. He wore a puzzled expression. "Wonder if I saved anything with my souvenirs in the hold?" the tanker mumbled to himself. "Not even sure I'll be able to find the right box, of course. . . ."

The air still rocked with the echo of the thrusters. The landing site was in the flood plain of a creek. The water's encroachment could presumably be controlled by the dam at the valley's head, but there was no need of that now. The shallow water sprayed to either side of the service vehicle crossing to reach the starship.

The outlaws were restive. Their partying on Windward had been recent enough that there was not the need to let off steam that a longer Transit would have bred. Further, the party on Windward had ended sharply—brutally, for those who had the bad judgment to try to resist the local authorities. The men who could not be chivvied back were carried aboard the ship. Seven of them were dead. Now the survivors looked over the latest landfall in sullen frustration. The disaster that swallowed their fellows on Mandalay had left GAC 59 too weak to protest the treatment its complement earned.

Slade and Levine waited at the forward hatch. Bourgiby and Rooks, the two surviving members of the Ship's Meeting, were with them. The port's visible defenses were of the bare-bones variety to be met with on rural worlds: two powerguns on opposite sides of the valley. They were probably 15 cm, probably old; certainly able to open the ship like a ration packet if they were functional at all. Erlette would have been a good target for the original fleet to raid—if there were anything here to loot. The planet appeared to have nothing to recommend it to GAC 59 alone, except that the inhabitants did not seem to intend to slag the vessel.

Just yet, at least.

The service vehicle was a small bus. It pulled up at the ramp. Partly-uniformed personnel began jumping out of the cab and rear door. A few of them wore coveralls, but most made do with a flash-breasted jacket over nondescript civilian clothes. "Well, I'll be hanged," said Rooks.

There was no need for him to amplify his statement. A female driver/co-driver team was normal enough. That some of the port officials greeting the new arrivals were female was no cause for surprise either. However, there were about a dozen people in the service vehicle, and every one of them was a woman.

The trio which strode briskly toward the ship's command group was led by a lithe brunette. She was as leggy as Slade, though a decimeter shorter in the torso. "Captain Levine?" she said to the tanker as she approached.

Slade stepped back, thumbing toward Levine. The woman's extended hand shifted smoothly toward the spacer, though her eyes retained a glint of awareness of the bigger man. "Captain Levine," she repeated as they shook hands. "I'm Delores Rodrigues. I'm Mayor here on Erlette. This is Deputy Brandt and Deputy Morales. I can't tell you how thankful we are. And I assure you, there's been no recurrence of the disease in fifteen years. It's perfectly safe."

"*What?*" said Rooks angrily.

Levine's smile took a sickly cant. Instinct wiped on his trousers the hand that had just touched the woman.

"Why yes," said Rodrigues, looking across the eyes of the startled men. Slade was trying to place the comment with what he had heard of Erlette, but that heading was still all blank. "The officials on Windward gave us to believe that you were coming as a sort of, well, relief mission. Didn't they tell you?"

"Blood and martyrs!" Rooks snarled. "*Warn* us, you mean, those bastards! What do you mean, disease?" The outlaw had backed a step up the ramp. Bourgiby, his fellow, was silent but as clearly concerned.

"Ah, Mayor Rodrigues," said Slade, "I'm not sure how much garbling there might have been in your message from Windward." Message capsules were radio transmitters slung into on-stage Transit by a ground unit. They had considerable margin for error. "But this is simply a freighter with a cargo of landing thrusters and a need for some specialized crew . . . that we hope you could help us with."

"Well, yes, but . . ." the Mayor said. She turned her head. The main hatches had been opened also, against orders but inevitably. Outlaws and probably some of the ship's crew were beginning to exit warily. Though their total number was not yet obvious, it was already clear that they were greatly more numerous than the complement of an ordinary freighter. "They said you had over two hundred men aboard. Males. And surely you have, don't you?" She waved toward the groups spreading from the cargo hatches.

"Well, yes, but we're not specialists," the tanker said. Slade had concealed his surprise when the others froze at mention of disease. Via, he'd been in hellholes in service. Though the Slammers' excellent Med Section was no longer behind him, the big veteran's subconscious could not really believe in danger from microbes. Unreasoning confidence armored him against the unproductive fear that wracked the others. "We're not, ah, medical specialists I mean," he added.

Deputy Morales was a short, plump woman. Now she laughed briefly. "Via, mister," she said, "we don't *need* doctors. Like Delores said, there hasn't been a sign of the disease since it killed just about all the men on Erlette fifteen years ago. What we need is a little more variety for our sperm bank."

Morales pointed—her hands were surprisingly delicate—toward a white stone building. It was also one-story, but it was more imposing than the others of the community. Beside the building was a cooling plant, breathing a plume of vapor into the humid air. "And maybe some variety for us, too. What do you say, mister?" She popped Levine in the ribs and gave him a simultaneous leer. Her expression seemed to rock the Captain as much as the physical contact.

Brandt, the third of the greeting team, was brunette like the leader, but smaller and with fox-sharp features. "We've summoned citizens who might want to participate in, ah, direct methods," she said. Her voice was prim. Brandt kept her eyes focused so that they did not make contact with the eyes of any of the four men. "That isn't by any means all the, ah, women on Erlette. In the time we've been alone, we've made certain adjustments, of course."

Morales gave a coarse snicker and prodded Levine again.

Blushing but undeterred, the prim woman continued. "You and your crew will find an adequacy of entertainment, however. In exchange, we will expect cooperation with our efforts to increase the permanent gene pool." She too pointed toward the sperm bank. "There is no risk, of course. But we are aware that some males import an emotional significance to what is only a mechanical act, the transfer of sperm."

"Ah, Mayor," Slade said. "Sirs—" That was wrong, wasn't it, hell and blast this situation. "There's still the problem of our navigators. Our lack of them. Is there any chance that you have qualified people that might be hired on a temp—"

Rodrigues touched Slade's forearm to halt him. "Mister . . . ?"

"Slade," the tanker said. "I'm—well, it's complicated."

"Mister Slade," the woman resumed, "there's a great deal about the future to be discussed. Right now, there are organizational details to be handled. This is—" she turned up her palms with a smile—"an embarrassment of riches for us, incredible riches. But I'll call on you later this evening, if you don't mind. We'll be alone at my home, and we can work out a number of things."

The prim brunette beside the Mayor made a moue.

The memory of Mayor Rodrigues' smile lingered long after the trio of women had driven away.

"You know, Captain Slade," said Snipes, the ship's tall, bearded Administrative Officer, "I really respect you."

Slade put down the laser pencil. He had just completed soldering the final lead to a post on the non-functioning commo unit. Slade's palms were sweaty. It scared the bleeding cop out of him to work with electrical blasting caps. Even before they were inserted in the block of high explosive, they could shatter your hands or your eyes if something went wrong. And the one poor bastard Slade remembered, the fellow who had three caps in a front pocket of his trousers at the spaceport on Friesland . . . A maintenance crew had switched on a Transit generator for testing. The powerful field induced enough of a current in the leads to detonate the blasting caps.

The screen on the upper wall of the shop was fed by one of the external vision blocks. There was nothing in particular to see. Erlette's port and capital were quiet except for light vehicular traffic in the dusk.

"The way you run these, these soldiers," Snipes continued. He was a good-sized man, one of those who used the exercise machines more as a matter of religion than of muscle tone. "But without getting, well, hardened like most men in your position would be."

"Now, do you have some luggage that'll hold all this?" Slade asked. "A box might do if it had to, but I'd like something that looked like it was a change of clothing without anybody asked. And not military."

The crewman glanced at the assembly, phony electronics and ten very real kilos of plastic explosive. "Well," he said uncertainly, "there's my own leave bag. I guess you could borrow it."

"Might I?" said the tanker. "Fast?"

Snipes was back in less than a minute with the bag. It was a nice one, self-adjusting to hold its contents firmly but without crushing them. Slade began to pack it with care. First the gray, taped blocks of explosive, then the guts of the commo unit. All of them were connected by looped wires and the blasting caps buried in the mass of explosive.

"I can tell," said Snipes, "that you understand women, too." His mouth worked. "I swear, there was no decent woman ever born but my mother. Lord rest her soul."

"Oh, I don't know," said Slade. He was arranging the leads with great care. "I was set to be married once. Turned out she married my brother Tom . . . but the way I was then, I wouldn't say Marilee was indecent. Or even wrong."

"But it made you look at yourself, didn't it?" Snipes pressed. He reached out and touched the hand with which Slade was shifting the charge. "Made you realize there were things, that for you—for a real man like you—a woman couldn't do as well as a man."

"Tell the truth, Johnsie," the tanker said, "it was more the Slammers that did that." Slade folded over the top of the bag and watched it seal itself into the smallest six-sided prism that would hold its present contents. "In twenty years under Hammer, I met curst few women I'd trust to close my back in a firefight. For killing, I'll take a man any day."

He stood up. Snipes extended his arm to hold the fingers in contact, but the thought behind the Admin Officer's eyes was changing. "And that's fair, I guess," Slade went on, "because for screwing, I don't have a darned bit of use for men." He smiled. "Most other duties, I'm pretty well neutral."

"Well, why *are* you still on board, then?" Snipes demanded. "You could be out there, having a, having an *orgy* like the rest of them. Couldn't you? Even Webb. 'Come on Johnsie, it won't hurt. They'll be so *willing*.' It just makes me. . . ." He trailed off with a grimace.

Slade was studying the view screen, partly to avoid looking at his companion's face. "Well," the tanker said, "I checked some of the old briefing cubes in the hold luggage you found for me. Didn't like what I learned." He shrugged. "Most everybody else had gone off already, like you say. There wasn't any point in raising a fuss then. So I—" He smiled again, tense with pre-battle nerves. The apparatus was complete and he had nothing to occupy his mind but the future. "I called my date and told her I'd need a couple extra hours to clear up some business. Which was true."

Slade wiped his hands very carefully with a solvent towel from the dispenser on the bulkhead. The skin of his hands prickled for a moment as it was cleaned. The skin of his neck and biceps continued to prickle for reasons unconnected with the towel. "She ought to be—yeah. I think that might be Delores right now."

Slade shook himself to loosen his muscles. "Take care, trooper," he said. He wore a cape against the chill and beneath the cape a civilian suit of brilliant silk from T'ien. The only military touch was a heavy belt on which a commo unit balanced the weight of a slung wallet.

On the screen, Delores got out of the same small bus she had arrived in earlier. This time she was alone in the vehicle. The tall woman began walking toward the vision block over the bridge hatch, growing on the screen. The garment she wore covered but did not hide her breasts, even in the screen's blurred image.

"Hold the fort till I get back," the tanker called over his shoulder. As his boots echoed down the corridor, Snipes heard him add, "Won't say I'm not used to the work, but it's a curst strange context."

Mayor Rodrigues' house was a low dome sunk a meter deep in the soil. The skylights, now shuttered, would not open without noise. There was no door except for the one which the woman now opened onto a flight of steps.

"Ah, you don't have a, a roomate?" Slade asked huskily.

The tall brunette smiled. "Not tonight," she said. "Not unless you want one." Rodrigues stepped to the tanker. She swept his cape clear with her arms before she squeezed as much of her length against him as their position made possible. Slade shifted awkwardly at the woman's weight and strength. He returned the hungry kiss and felt his groin return it also, despite his tension.

"Come, dearest," Delores said. She broke away to lead Slade

down the short flight of stairs. Her fingers felt warm and moist on his. "You don't know how long I've wanted this."

Slade paused to lock the door. A twist of the handle set bolts in both transom and threshold.

"Some things I don't like disturbed," he muttered, nervous and seemingly embarrassed. His luggage was in the bus outside. Slade had not wanted to call attention to the case by bringing it inside at once.

The room they stood in was the whole front half of the circular dwelling. There was a table and a variety of cushioned benches for seating. The floor was of rush mats, fresh and green-smelling. In the wall bisecting the interior were three doors. Two of them were ajar. Slade could see the corner of a low bed in the center room. The room to the left had a tiled interior, surely a bathroom though the fixtures were of unfamiliar style. The third door would lead to the kitchen, closed off for no reason other than its inappropriateness to the intended activity.

Probably.

Delores was in Slade's arms again. His left hand flicked the brooch holding his cape. The fabric slithered away from his shoulders. The tanker's belt gear pressed against the woman's thrusting belly. She backed off, panting, and reached for the belt hook.

Slade caught her fingers with one hand. "Just a second, darling," he muttered. His free hand tucked down the indigenous lace of her blouse so that he could kiss one broad, dark nipple. "Just a second," he repeated as he straightened. He walked quickly to the right-hand door. One hand reached into his slung wallet.

"The bathroom's the other way," Delores said. She did not sound concerned, only out of breath. She was reaching behind her for the blouse fasteners.

Slade opened the door, onto the empty kitchen as he had expected. "Oh, to hell with that anyway," he said as he strode back to the woman. It was not particularly necessary that his movements make sense; only that they be seen as non-threatening to a woman in the Mayor's present circumstances. "Here," the tanker said as Dolores nuzzled his throat, "let me help with the blouse."

She turned willingly. As willingly, she extended her hands behind her. She gave a throaty chuckle as Slade guided the hands to his groin, and she did not first realize when the tanker taped her wrists that the program had changed abruptly.

"Dearest?" the woman said in puzzlement as she turned back to Slade. "If you like this, we can, of course . . . anything. But I hoped first . . . ?"

"Here, love," Slade said. He lifted the tall woman onto a bench. She still did not object, though she was frowning. "Just for a moment," he added as he taped her ankle to one leg of the bench. It was solid wood, fifteen or twenty kilos; heavy enough to keep Rodrigues from jumping quickly to a hidden weapon or communications device.

The tanker was breathing hard. His body had told no more lies than his victim's body had. "Via." he said. "Via." He drew the pistol from his wallet and held the small weapon loose in his hand. "Don't pull against that," Slade went on with a nod toward the obvious strain of the woman against her wrists behind her. "It's freight tape. You can cut it, and alcohol'll release the adhesive clean. But you couldn't pull it apart with tractors. The loops are tight enough that it won't help you to tear your skin loose."

"But *why?*" Delores said. She did not struggle for the moment, but her body was tensed for a last hysterical burst before expected death convulsed her. "Donald, almost anything. . . . If not me, then *somebody* on Erlette will—want whatever you want. Willingly."

Slade sat down on another bench, facing his captive. "I was on Sphakteria," he said. "Were you?"

Rodrigues shook her head without comprehension of either the words or what was happening to her. Her blouse hung free of one of the breasts it had not hidden very well to begin with.

"I was, the Slammers were," the tanker went on. "Both sides pretty well financed. We got a book from Central on a dozen or so merc units operating against us."

Delores' eyes began to widen. She tensed still further.

"You won't be hurt," Slade said sharply. In his calmer voice of moments before, he continued, "But you're right, there was a company of scouting specialists from Erlette. All women and ready to prove they had more balls than any man they were going to run into." Slade shrugged. "The background, though. . . . All the men on Erlette had died, not a few years before from a sex-linked plague, but thirty-odd years back even then. And they'd been killed by the women."

"Don, none of that's true!" the Mayor gasped. "At least, I mean about the men here on—"

"*Can it,* honey," Slade said. "I'm not going to hurt you, you hear?" He glared at the woman until she subsided. "It was true ten, twelve years ago when I heard it, and it's true now. Word was, no men were allowed to live on Erlette since that—incident. There was a sperm bank and normal reproduction to keep up the population at a viable level. . . . but male offspring got deep-sixed at birth."

The tanker shrugged again. "That's your business," he said. "I don't interfere. But I didn't much like the notion that the same thing happened to visiting spacers—after they'd contributed to the gene pool directly and through the sperm bank."

"Donald," the Mayor whispered, "that's all the most vicious lies. You and your men aren't in any danger, I *swear* it."

Slade nodded. "Then there won't be any trouble," he said. "All I want is for all the—all *my* men—to be sent back to the ship unharmed. And we'll leave. Anybody in the Sperm Bank tonight?"

Delores' face hardened. "Why?"

"Because it's solider than this place," Slade said, "and because I figure it's too important—" The glint in the woman's eyes agreed with his assumption even before he finished stating it. "—for any of your, ah, friends to try and be heroes around it. They might risk you, but if somebody puts a batch of holes through that place, your whole society goes down the tubes. Right?"

"There's no one there," the woman said. Her pause had stretched dangerously long. "You're completely wrong, Mister Slade . . . but I suppose we can humor you if you want no more than you say. I'm sorry that things had to work out this way."

"Oh, lady," said the tanker wearily. "I couldn't agree with you more." He snicked the short, keen blade of his work knife out of its nest between the scales. "Only thing is, I'd like even less for things to work out the way you and your friends planned."

With a single motion Slade cut the tape holding Mayor Rodrigues' ankles to the bench. Cradling her in his left arm, and using her body to shield the pistol from possible watchers, Slade walked out of the house.

Traffic was sparse. Slade was still concerned that the lights of another vehicle would show that he was driving the bus. The alternative risk was to tape Delores to the driver's seat and free her hands to drive. Slade was not silly enough to do that. The pistol he carried was a deadly weapon, but the bus in hostile hands was yet more dangerous.

There were no incidents on the way. The Sperm Bank was quiet on their arrival, save for the whine of its cooling plant. "I hope," said Slade to the woman beside him, "that you've got the key to this place. I can drive into the door a couple times—" He patted the control column. The fans were spinning at idle while the bus waited in front of the squat, stone building. "But that's likely to cause coolant leaks in your refrigeration system."

"The door has a key-pad lock," Delores said sullenly. "We can get in." Whether she would have said the same without the threat was uncertain.

Slade worked the punched combination as directed while the bus continued to purr. There was no alarm as the door opened. By now, an alarm would have done as much good as harm anyway.

The tanker slipped his pistol back in the pouch in order to lift Mayor Rodrigues with his left hand and the borrowed luggage with his right. As expected, the initial room was a lobby with a desk and more padded benches against the walls. The corridor beyond led to a laboratory and a series of cubicles where, presumably, the sperm could be implanted. Most of the hardware was ceramic rather than of metal or synthetics.

The rear half of the building was a rank of refrigerated, multi-drawer files. The air held a sharp trace of ammonia. On a stanchion in the center of the room was a voice communications unit. "Can you talk to your friends on that?" Slade asked. He turned so that the woman he held could see the phone.

"Yes." The syllable was more guarded, now, than angry. The Mayor had had time to consider the risk to her community that a madman *here* posed.

Slade taped the woman's left ankle to the stanchion. Then he cut free her wrists. "I want you to start calling people," the tanker said as he stepped back. "And first, I want you to tell them exactly what you see here."

With the care the apparatus deserved, Slade opened the case and tilted it so that Delores could see clearly what was inside. The Mayor was no demolitions expert, but the threat was utterly clear from context. Her gasp was proof enough of that.

"And I want you to tell them," the tanker went on as he slid his own commo unit from his belt sheath and keyed it, "that if I let up on this switch—" he pointed to the key his left thumb depressed— "the signal triggers the bomb." His index finger tilted down toward the case. "Ten kilos of Cylobar. If that doesn't ring a bell, tell them its propagation rate is ten kays per second."

The tanker sat down against the wall. He moved carefully, so that his thumb did not slip and he did not lose eye contact with the horrified woman. "When you've got their attention that way," Slade concluded, "then we'll move on to my instructions."

He smiled, and his face was more threatening than the way he gestured with the commo unit he held.

"Slade!" blurted Captain Levine as female guards ran him into the refrigeration room at gunpoint.

"Dear heaven, I'd prayed they wouldn't have gotten you, you *know* about these—but why's she tied? The Mayor?"

Half a dozen more of GAC 59's crew stumbled down the corridor. They were logy with the treatment they had received, but their condition seemed to be acceptable. The pair of guards fanned to either side of the doorway. Deputy Brandt followed the spacers with a bell-snouted weapon of her own. She trained the gun on the center of Slade's chest.

Slade remained seated. The gun muzzle looked no more angry and threatening than did the Deputy's eyes.

The tanker nodded to her. "Levine," he said calmly, "you're going back to the ship right now. The mercs are being delivered there already." The tanker raised an eyebrow toward Brandt, who nodded curtly. "You'll program the ship to Transit from ground—"

"*I* can't set a course alone," Levine broke in. "And a ground Transit, the gravity well could kick us seconds, *minutes* off course."

"I'd rather be lost by five Transit minutes," said the tanker dryly, "than be lifting off on thrusters when the Deputy here decides we're out of range for my handset."

Brandt's gun trembled.

Levine looked warily from Slade to the weapon. Then he trotted back down the corridor, toward the vehicle that had brought him. One of the power room crew started to follow.

"Hold it," said Slade in a voice that made gun muzzles twitch.

The crewman turned to Slade. "But why do we got to stay here?" he whined.

"Because," said the tanker, "I know Captain Levine won't take off with no crew. And I'm not quite so certain that you all would be careful to wait for me to board."

More guards and another group of crewmen clattered into the building. Slade looked at Deputy Brandt, who had been surreptitiously eyeing the open case. "Take a good look," the tanker said calmly.

The sharp-featured woman glared at him. Her front teeth nibbled her lips. "I need to talk to Delores," she said abruptly. Brandt took a stride toward the bound Mayor.

"Hold it!" Slade repeated, even more sharply than before. The Deputy turned. She pointed her weapon. Everyone in the room tensed. "You can talk with her," Slade continued, "but you do it aloud so I can hear."

"All right, *mister!*" the Deputy rasped. "I was going to tell Delores there'd been a few adverse drug reactions. What do you think of *that?*"

"Cele—" said the woman strapped to the stanchion.

"I think you'd better have the bodies brought to the ship," replied the tanker in an even voice. "Nobody stays."

"Why?" Brandt demanded shrilly. "Bother you that we'd roll them in with sheep-cop and use them for fertilizer? That's all they're bloody good for! All they ever were."

Slade got up slowly. His face was placid, though his jaw muscles bunched momentarily. The tanker held his commo unit at his side as he walked toward Brandt. The Deputy took one step back. She locked her left hand on the fore-end of her pointed weapon. No one in the room seemed to breathe.

"That for real?" Slade asked gently. "Or is it a toy?" He stepped forward. The bell muzzle bumped his chest. Another step. The woman tried to brace herself, but the tanker's size and strength thrust her back.

"Cele!" screamed Mayor Rodrigues.

With a cry of fury, the Deputy slashed her gun down to point at the floor. Slade slapped her, knocking the woman down with his open hand and all his strength behind it.

One of the guards almost fired at the gun-shot crack and Brandt crumpling sideways. Discipline held. The finger lifted trembling from the trigger.

"Now," said Slade to the dazed Brandt, "I think you and your guns had best get out of here. I'll wait to hear from Captain Levine—" he nodded toward the phone— "that the ship's ready and the men are aboard. Understood?"

He looked around the room at the women and at the crewmen edging back from the violence.

No one in the building would meet Slade's eyes, but they all understood.

"Touch her," said Slade to the crewman who reached for Delores' lacy blouse, "and we'll lift short one man more." The tanker did not bother to draw the pistol from his wallet.

"Well, I don't see—" the crewman began as he snatched his hand away.

The phone on the stanchion purred its summons.

The Mayor jumped as her concentration on other things broke. Before she could recover, Slade had stepped to the instrument and switched it live. "Sperm Bank," he said. "Slade speaking." The tall woman strapped to the post was a warmth and odor.

"Slade, they want me to tell you that everybody's back at the ship," said Levine. "Except me, they wouldn't string a line, so I'm across the creek at this curst *phone.*"

"Well, is it true?" the tanker demanded. "*Are* all the landmen back aboard?" Slade had great experience in projecting a facade of tank-like solidity. As with tanks, his interior was complex and had a way of displaying frustration at awkward times.

"Yes, yes," said Levine, "but—" and the words tumbled out through the background hiss— "Slade, there's eleven of them *dead,* corpses!"

"Do you know a way to bring the dead back to life, Captain Levine?" the tanker asked. He directed a bitter grimace at Delores Rodrigues. The captive woman had shrunk back when the phone spoke of the deaths her plan had caused.

"Of course not!" snapped Levine. "What do you mean?

"I don't know a way either," Slade replied, "so let's not worry about that. Get back aboard, and be ready to Transit the instant the hatch closes behind me." The tanker waited a moment longer, but the phone popped with the sound of Levine switching off without further comment.

"Time to leave, boys," Slade said to the men and the woman who had stared at him throughout the conversation. "Let's see what kind of transport they've got for us." He waved the crewmen down the corridor ahead of him.

As the men obeyed, Slade reached down and poised his knife over the strap holding Delores to the stanchion.

"Don't run," he said to the woman softly. "It'll be your life if you do, and I'd sooner avoid that."

He cut across the band of tape and stood, looping his left arm through Delores' as if they accompanied one another formally. She stared down at the tanker's left hand and his thumb on the switch.

Slade was smiling as she met his eyes. Delores raised her chin proudly. "Let's go, then, Mister Slade," she said.

The building's interior had been so isolated that the drizzle outdoors was a surprise to Slade. The guards whose hooded ponchos covered their guns were no surprise at all. The crewmen were already being loaded on a small bus like the one Slade had driven the night before.

Deputy Brandt stared at the tanker. Only her eyes moved in a face that shone white on one side, swollen red on the other.

"Wait," Slade said as his consort started to walk toward the bus. He shut the door of the Sperm Bank with a metallic crash. "Does it lock?" he asked and tried the door again before anyone could make a pointless reply to his question. The door was locked.

"Careful," Slade added, still holding Rodrigues as he dipped his pistol out of the wallet with his free hand.

"What—" called Deputy Brandt behind him. Slade had already fired.

The pistol was one he had chosen as being smaller and more concealable than an ordinary service weapon. It spat a light charge through a 5 mm bore. The sound it made was more unpleasant than threatening, like the squawk of a stepped-on kitten. Metal splashed from the key-pad of the lock. Three more shots, sparks in the rain-drops, followed to crater the pad's surface into uselessness.

Slade turned. He held the pistol muzzle-up because he could not return it to the wallet until the barrel had cooled. "There," he said to Deputy Brandt. "You can cut through that easily enough . . . but I don't think you're going to be inside the building before we're the Hell off your planet—unless you're willing to blast. Your choice, madam."

Brandt spat at the tanker's feet.

"All right, Mayor Rodrigues," Slade said to the woman at his side. "You'll be released at the ship. Right now, I'd as soon you rode with us. Just in case."

As the bus drove off, Slade could hear the harsh timbre of Deputy Brandt's voice. The guards around her were scurrying for hand tools with which they could break into the Bank—without risking its contents.

* * *

The driver brought her bus to a lurching halt well short of the ramp. Realizing that, she lifted the vehicle again in a blast of dust and gravel, hopping twenty meters closer.

"Now *move!*" Slade snarled to the crewmen as the bus door tonged open. There were a dozen women near the ship, but only one or two of them carried weapons openly. The men obeyed with alacrity handicapped by the narrow aisle.

"Feel like coming along yourself?" Slade added to Mayor Rodrigues in an undertone.

"Do you think you're that good, Mister Slade?" the Mayor answered. "You're not, you know." She swallowed angrily, as if she expected the big man to hit her.

"Guess we'll never know," Slade said mildly as he stepped to the door behind the other men. "You're probably making a good decision anyway."

The tanker did not look back as he pounded up the ramp to the bridge hatch. He held the commo unit high in his left hand. The women watched the crew scuttle aboard with only the interest an event brings, not a catastrophe. How many times had they used up and discarded the crew of a freighter? You could hate cultures, but that didn't help you any. . . . Evil wasn't the affair of a professional soldier.

By the Lord, though, it was the business of Don Slade.

The ramp was already lifting to close the hatch as the tanker threw himself aboard. "Go! Go! Go!" he bellowed down the corridor. The hatch sealed with a sigh and a shock that reflection said was Transit but clutching fear had identified as gunfire. GAC 59 was clear of Erlette; the Lord knew where, but clear.

There was chaos on the bridge. "Stations!" the tanker shouted as he bulled his way through smaller men. "First shift to Transit stations, everybody else the hell out of the operations area!" He had briefed them in the Sperm Bank. There was no time now for yammering indiscipline.

Crewmen scurried to their duty stations or out into the corridor again. That left Slade on the bridge with Levine, Snipes, and one of the Meeting members—Rooks. Slade wondered if Rooks' partner, Bourgiby, had been an overdose fatality on Erlette. The tanker seated himself on the analog tub which had become his usual spot. He looked at the commo unit which he still held. Sighing, he replaced it in its belt sheath.

"You should've taken your finger off just before we lifted," Levine said savagely.

"Wouldn't have changed a thing," said Slade. He rubbed his eyes. He had gotten no sleep for over thirty hours. "I'd cut the power lead to this thing," he said, tapping the unit without looking down, "so they wouldn't get a blip if my thumb slipped. That'd tell them it was a fake."

"A fake?" Rooks repeated. "You didn't really have a bomb like you said?"

Slade stood up angrily. "Look," he said, "I'm a tank officer, not a technician. Sure, I suppose you could rig a bomb and a command detonator out of even the gear available on this tub. But *I* couldn't, not in a couple of hours. Via! I put something together that looked real to me. And I prayed to the Lord that our friends down there—" he gestured toward a bulkhead. Only context could indicate that he meant the Erlette authorities—"couldn't prove it wasn't real except by daring me to fire it." Slade smiled past his restless irritation. "Things could've gotten interesting if they'd pushed."

"I was just about to stick it in," said Rooks. His voice built by stages from reflection to anger. "She patted me on the back of the neck and I thought 'The bitch ought to trim her nails.' And then I couldn't feel anything where she nicked me. Then my whole body. Couple hours ago I come around, my neck hurts and my butt hurts where they'd jabbed me again. And they load forty of us in a truck like cordwood, still half zonked and bare-ass naked. I wish you'd blown up every bloody one of the bitches!"

Levine and Snipes were nodding, perhaps for different reasons. Slade said, "It's not the people, it's their culture. And that's something their grandmothers locked them into. Ever been on Eutyche?"

Blank looks greeted the question. The tanker shrugged and

continued. "They lock women up there. From birth. When she's sold into marriage, the father and brothers carry the girl to the husband under guard. Let your daughter run on the street and she'll be stoned to death by your neighbors before they burn your house down over you. It's not people there, and it's not people here on Erlette. It's just the way people live."

"Well, that may be, Captain Slade," said Levine. He was showing a little more backbone than his previous norm. "But it's a problem that has to be solved, this culture. And the only way I see to solve it was as Mister Rooks says. Blow them all up."

"There's some might say the same about other things; like this ship, hey?" Slade gibed. He rang his knuckles off a console for emphasis. "Isn't true, though. Not about Erlette, anyhow."

Slade struck a stance in the middle of the deck with his left fist raised. He extended the index finger. "They don't need men, because they've got the Sperm Bank." He extended the middle finger with the fist. "There's enough traffic here to keep the gene pool fluid and it seems to scratch any itches for something beyond lips and prosthetics that may arise among the citizens."

Slade's ring finger flipped up also. "So male infants go for the chop. Nobody could hide their baby boy through puberty . . . and even then, it'd just be something to hunt for officials who get into that sort of thing. You've got a society maintained by people like Deputy Brandt."

"So blow it bloody up!" snapped Rooks.

Slade smiled. "No," he said, "blow up the bloody Sperm Bank." He folded his fingers back into a fist. "Then they've got to coddle every male they've got, infants or immigrants. Or else their whole world goes down the tubes when the population drops below a viable level. Like a lot of places did where there was too small a settlement to begin with. Like Stagira, I suspect. That's all it would take."

"Then it *is* too bad your bomb wasn't real," Snipes said. It was hard to tell if his sourness resulted from the fact that a gynocratic society had not been smashed, or if the tone belonged to his interaction with Slade earlier.

The tanker laughed as he seated himself again on the analog device. "Via," he said, "the bomb was real enough. It was the controls ·I had to fake."

The other three men stiffened. "The Cylobar was just as real as what we blew clear of Stagira with," Slade explained. "So were the blasting caps. Just how real, I guess they learned on Erlette when we jumped and the Transit fields generated a current in the leads."

Slade's lips smiled like a dog worrying flesh. "And I only hope Deputy Brandt and her crew had gotten into the building by that time."

CHAPTER EIGHTEEN

"He smashed the culture for spite," thought Elysium. "Not because he believed the replacement would be better."

"It will be better," the other current noted. Extrapolations flickering through the group consciousness supported that view.

"But all that mattered to him was bringing down the structure around the ears of those who had threatened him," pressed the flow that was too rigorous to be hostile, too chilling not to be negative.

"What he did," closed the other current, "benefitted individuals and Mankind. If he acted from instinct rather than belief, so much the better for him . . . and for his universe, which is our universe as well. . . ."

"When it's somebody else's specialty," Don Slade was saying, "and they've pulled it out every time despite the disaster they're predicting, then it's easy to discount what they say the next time. It happens—I'm told it happens—in military settings, too."

Those who knew as well as heard Slade were flashed a glass-edged vision: the doorway of a command post, three men in gray uniforms pistol-shot on the ground and the neck of the fourth being broken by Slade's bloody hands.

"They always think you can hold it if you've held before," Slade muttered. "They tell me."

The big man cleared his throat. "So it shouldn't have been a shock when we popped out of Transit only a kay above the ground the next time . . ."

* * *

The buzzer went off. All the instrument consoles were bathed in red lights. Such warnings were unnecessary, because only the dead could doubt there was an emergency when the starship flipped on its back in a gravity well.

Slade was on the bridge as usual during maneuvering. He was not strapped in. GAC 59 had no facilities to immobilize as many men as the ship now carried. Besides, the hot LZs on which the tanker was trained had no time for such frills.

Slade's legs shot up because his arms hugged the curve of the analog tub instinctively. Then Levine righted the ship in a corkscrew motion through a massive forward thrust. As a result, GAC 59 was moving at over a hundred kph when it plowed through the trees and into a field. Things began happening in a hurry. Slade probably lost his grip before the display unit shredded its clamps and flew into a console. By then the question was academic, even to Slade himself.

The sirens of the emergency vehicles merged in Slade's mind with the screams. Some of the screams were his own. . . .

"Because," Slade said, and the speakers amplified his voice so that it could be heard by all the hundred and three other survivors, "the authorities here think they're being exceptionally nice in not standing us against a wall and shooting us every one."

The tanker nodded toward the double doors of the hall. Many of the mercenaries turned to look also, though they all knew what they would see there. The detachment of Rusatan police wore neat, white uniforms. Some of them seemed unfamiliar with the submachine guns they had been issued for this detail. Those were the only guns in the room, however, and they were gripped the tighter when the local men felt the mercenaries looking at them.

"So," Slade continued from the dais, "staying here on Rusata isn't an option. Unless you figure to stay the way the folks will who were too late for the medics."

Men looked at one another, at themselves. The Rusatans had given the crash victims excellent medical treatment, but reconstruction had stopped with grafts of synthetic skin. Prosthetics, the locals had noted bluntly, were the business of the mercenaries themselves. The salvage value of GAC 59 would not cover the cost of necessary treatment—and the necessary shipment of the survivors off a world their presence would disrupt.

"It's not *fair!*" muttered Captain Levine. He sat beside Slade on the dais. "She was *my* ship. I ought at least to have had all she brought for scrap."

"That wasn't an option either, my friend," said the tanker in a low, dangerous voice. Slade cut on the amplifier again and continued, "So we have the choice of leaving on either of the ships in port right now. That's a human tramp out of Barmaki; and an Alayan ship."

"Those're the ones that look like bloody lightwands?" somebody demanded from the audience.

"The Alayans have exoskeletons, yes," Slade replied. He raised his voice so that it would ride over the disgust. "They have eight limbs, and they speak to humans through vocalizers. They also—" his voice went up a further notch; he rose to focus attention—"have extremely well-found ships, although they don't operate on the same principles that ours do. Captain Levine is going to talk to you now about the other choice."

Slade sat down. Levine glanced at the gathered men, then looked at his boots again. "It won't—" he began. Slade reached across the spacer and flicked the mike on his epaulette to 'ON.' "I've been over the ship," Levine resumed. "They want us bad, so they're making a price to Rusata. Doesn't do cop for us . . ."

He looked up. In a stronger voice, Levine continued. "It won't get us there. Not one more landing, not two or I'm the Messiah. They want us because they're worse-crewed than we were, and their captain thinks he can make Barmaki with me and what's left of my people." Levine nodded. Three or four of the audience nodded back, the remnant of GAC 59's crew.

"But they can't," Levine said. He stood up as Slade had done, but without the tanker's deliberation. Levine's hands washed each other unnoticed. "I don't know how they got here. One of their generators has kicked out three times, and it's heaven's own providence they weren't actually *in* Transit when it happened. Their captain hoped I could help fix it. You *can't* fix a generator except to pull out the boards and replace them. They're trying to use jumpers to the other generators, heaven blast me if I lie!"

Captain Levine paused, then sat down abruptly. In a lowered voice he closed, "I—I don't want the bugs either. But we'll all die if we ship with the Barmacids. I'm sure of it."

"The Alayans offer passage for as far along their route as the individual wants," Slade said over the worried murmur. "They won't alter their course, but they'll disembark passengers at any point. So long as the ground authorities are willing. They say that eighty to ninety percent of the worlds they touch are human, and—"

"And that's cop!" roared someone from the audience.

"All right, maybe it is!" Slade shouted back with the support of the amplifier. "But we know they *do* land on human worlds or they wouldn't be here, would they?"

Breathing hard, but in a more reasonable voice, the tanker went on. "People, this is no time to wedge our heads. We can take passage to someplace livable with the Alayans—or we can jump straight to Hell with the Barmacids. If anybody's that determined to die, there's people right here can probably oblige him." Slade waved again at the police.

The tanker had risen to a half crouch during his burst of anger. Now he settled himself again in his chair as the audience buzzed. "Oh," Slade added, "there's one other thing. Some of you may have the notion that going off in a human ship might leave the way open to—opportunities. Other than settling someplace." He nodded toward the police detachment, this time to explain why he had chosen a euphemism instead of saying piracy. "No guns leave here with us. Everything aboard GAC 59 except your asses and mine became government property when we crashed. If you don't like the word salvaged, you can say confiscated. It won't bother the locals a scrap, and it's how things are."

The buzzing lowered despondently.

"Now," Slade concluded, "you were each issued a ballot and a stylus when they marched you in. There's a box for your votes right here." He pointed to the foot of the dais. "We all go the way the majority decides. You mark A for Alayans, B for Barmacids. You drop it in the box. And if you want to live, you mark an A"

Levine shut off his microphone. As the hall rustled with men marking ballots, the spacer whispered, "I wonder what they'd vote if they knew the Alayan ship drives people crazy?"

Slade shut off his mike as well. "A chance of going crazy's better than near certainty of being lost in Transit," he whispered back. "So they'd for sure vote the same way they're going to now."

The first of the castaways were shuffling toward the box, clutching their ballots.

"Just as sure as I'm doing the counting," Don Slade concluded in a voice that did not move his lips.

The screams were attenuated by the hundred meters of corridor between Slade and their source. They were still easily loud enough to identify. The tanker was off his mattress and running for the sound even before his conscious mind was aware of the occurrence it had dreaded.

The Alayan starship was an assemblage of globes joined by tubes. The ship appeared to have as much and as little geometric certainty as a spider's web. That is, the basic form was certain, but the location of any single element within the whole might well have been random.

There was no way the ship itself could land or take off in a gravity well. Two of the globes carried lighters for ferrying cargo and passengers to the vessel in orbit. It had concerned Slade to realize that the lighters were of human manufacture though none of the vessel's other apparatus was. The situation suggested absurdly that the Alayans had not touched down on planets before their scattered vessels encountered humans some centuries before.

The survivors of GAC 59 were in three connected globes. The decks and fittings within were of plastic with evident mold marks. The globes themselves, like the tubular corridors which joined them, seemed chitinously natural.

Now men were running toward Slade down the corridor as if the screams were whips behind them. The fugitives were an incident of passage to the big tanker, an impediment through which he trampled as he would have a sleet storm.

There were no artificial weapons in the human sections of the ship. The Alayans had segregated even the slight personal effects the Rusatans had let the survivors take on board. Men played ball with wadded sheets and played checkers with scraps of fabric on a board scribed on the deck with fingernails. It was boring as Hell, but it should have been safe.

Stoudemeyer leaped from his victim, Captain Levine. Levine was the third, judging from the wrack in the blood-splattered room. The pearly glow from the ceiling glistened on Stoudemeyer's face. The man from Telemark now looked a bestial caricature of a man. Someone had clawed out Stoudemeyer's left eye so that it hung down his cheek by the nerve. Most of the blood on his face and bare chest had come from the throats of his victims, however—like Levine, now in spraying convulsions beneath his killer.

Slade snatched the blanket from an abandoned bunk. "Easy now, sol—" he began.

Stoudemeyer grinned wider and launched himself at the tanker.

The blanket had been extended for a makeshift net. Slade was wholly confident in his strength. He planned to wrap the madman in the fabric and hold him without further injury until more help dribbled back to view the excitement. Stoudemeyer's furious attack was no surprise, but the madman's strength was. Despite a conscious awareness of hysterical strength, Don Slade had met very few men who could overpower him under any circumstances.

As the short, pudgy Stoudemeyer proceeded to do.

The madman's clawed hands swept the blanket down. Slade caught Stoudemeyer's wrists and held him, but the blanket tangled both their legs. They staggered sideways and fell as a pair, Stoudemeyer on top. His face was marked with streaks and bubbles of blood. He glared at Slade with his good eye while the other bobbled on his cheek.

Slade shouted. He thrust upward against Stoudemeyer's wrists with all his strength. The madman giggled and continued to force his claws down toward his victim. Stoudemeyer's bloody gape was lowering toward Slade's throat inexorably.

Black with snarling madness himself, the tanker bit at Stoudemeyer's scalp. It was the only part of the shorter man Slade could reach with his teeth. They gouged hair and blood vessels aside before they skidded on bone. It was a useless attempt; but to Slade it was better than shouting for help that would not come.

Something bathed him in cold light.

Slade had been wounded before. He had even been left for dead on a field with hundreds of bomb fragments in his body. His flesh had chilled then and his mind had withdrawn to a single hot spark throbbing like an overloaded transformer.

He had never before been ice all over, though with full command of his senses. Slade could feel the tickling strands of Stoudemeyer's hair against the roof of his mouth. He could also feel the edge of the madman's incisors, against the pulse of the tanker's throat and just short of slashing through it.

The members that lifted Stoudemeyer gently away were blue and they were not hands. Slade could no longer control his field of vision. In and out of it drifted several Alayans. There were flickers of light at the violet end of the human range. It could have been cross-talk among the aliens . . . or synapses stuttering in Slade's own brain.

Sucker-tipped tendrils lifted the tanker upright. Something swabbed at the peak of his breastbone. The touch was cold momentarily as all things were cold. Then natural warmth and control flooded back through Slade's body.

"We regret," purred the vocalizer of one of the three Alayans, "that we struck you also, Mr. Slade." The Alayan waggled the device he held in one of his upper limbs. The object looked like petrified sea-foam, but it was not difficult to connect it with the stunning chill that had ended the fight. "We could not be sure in the haste of the moment which of you was the attacker."

"Umm," Slade said. He spat to clear his mouth, then rubbed his lips. "Yeah."

The other two Alayans had lifted Stoudemeyer. The madman

was still in a state of supple uncontrol as the Alayan device had left him. The Alayans were carrying Stoudemeyer toward the opening through which they had entered the passenger section. That passage was normally closed to humans.

"Wait a—" Slade began. Humans were entering the compartment again. Late-comers tried to push aside the earlier returnees who tended to conglomerate at the ends of the corridor instead of coming fully within the spattered compartment.

In a lower voice, the tanker continued. "Look, we've got to talk. I need to know—" his tongue paused between two questions, settled on the short-term one—"where you're taking him."

"Come," said the Alayan's vocalizer as he touched it. There was a flash of violet light from one of the six stalked projections—surely not heads—atop the alien's carapace. It might have been meant for a nod. "We will explain that to you. And now that you have more knowledge, we will explain again what you can expect to happen on the voyage."

The Alayan moved toward the exit after his companions and Stoudemeyer. His four lower limbs made delicate, twinkling motions so that his tall body seemed to roll rather than walk.

Slade wondered morosely as he followed whether the Alayan had made a lucky guess at the unspoken question, or whether they could read human minds.

The corridor blurred in both directions as soon as the door to the passenger chamber spasmed closed. There was no apparent beginning or end to the tube, and there was no sign of Stoudemeyer or the aliens who had carried him off.

"You've dumped him into—" Slade waved a hand at the glowing blue wall of the corridor. "Dumped him outside. Didn't you?"

"Assuredly not, Mister Slade," said the soft, mechanical voice. "He will be cared for, be repaired physically, as ably as possible. We will keep him sedated, or co—"

"You're going to use him to drive the ship," the tanker broke in again. Levine had told him the scuttlebutt about the Alayan drive, suggestions that the Alayans themselves had not denied in discussions before Slade made the survivors' decision for them. A warping of real space very different from the human technique of entering a separate Transit universe. A warping of space achieved through the warping of a human mind, the rumors went. . . .

"No, Mister Slade," replied the dancing fingers on the vocalizer, "we *have* used him to drive the ship. We cannot use his mind again, because it no longer has a basis in objective reality. That is always the case, I am afraid. You were aware of the situation when you accepted our offer of transport."

Slade ignored the last part of the statement. It was true; he simply did not care to dwell on it. "They always go—go berserk like Stoudemeyer just did?"

Light of no discernible hue played over one of the Alayan's— faces; a shrug of sorts. "Rarely that. We apologize. Generally catatonia, sometimes other forms of aberration. We did not expect this—" Warmth spread across the human's skin that implied the speaker had gestured in the infrared. "—but one cannot be certain what the ash will look like when one burns a log."

"And you can't—do this—travel—yourselves," Slade asked through a grimace that reflected his difficulty in finding words. Slade no longer believed he was simply in a tube connected to the passenger compartment, though he had no better explanation of where the Alayan might have taken him.

"Any sentient mind will serve the purpose," said the Alayan. "Any mind with a grasp of reality and the ability to change reality through—fantasy, if you will. We direct the fantasies so that they become real . . . and the vessel moves in objective reality through the—pressure of the subject's mind. Unfortunately, that mind moves as well, in a psychic dimension from which it cannot be retrieved. We could use ourselves as subjects, but we do not do so while we have minds aboard which are not ours. That is the main value for which we trade."

The listening human realized that there would have been no hostility or even emotion in the words whether or not they were the construct of a vocalizer. The Alayans did not hate their passengers; nor did they treat humans cruelly, the way humans were often wont to do to their own species. It was a simple operation, like *triage*: separating victims into those who would survive and those who would not. Nothing in the process implied a desire that some not survive . . . a wish for Kile Stoudemeyer to bite through his fellows' throats and to spend the rest of his life in total sedation.

But better that than similar destruction of an Alayan mind. The choice, after all, was the Alayans'.

"I knew," Slade said, aloud but more to himself than to the exoskeletal creature before him, "that people—some of us—might go nuts because of your drive. I mean, Transit hits some people like that, the sensation's different for everybody . . . and it makes some people snap. I didn't figure that it wasn't *may* go nuts, it was like firing a gun and watching the empty case spit out. I think we'd better, ah, disembark at the next landfall. Unless—I mean, how many stops can you make on the—" Slade did not pause, but his lips stuck momentarily in a rictus as he finished, "—present fuel?"

"Everyone who wishes to leave and is permitted to do so by the planetary authorities," said the Alayan, "may of course disembark on Terzia. There will have to be a second—impetus—to reach that world, Mister Slade. More than that to reach any other planet which could be suitable for your purpose, for your leaving the ship."

Slade hammered his fist into the corridor wall. The wall absorbed the blow with a massive resilience like that of deep sod. The hazy light seemed to fluctuate.

"You may do as you see fit, Mister Slade," the alien went on. His faces flickered, occasionally in the visible spectrum, "but I would suggest that you not discuss the situation in detail with your fellows until you have landed. It would cause distress, and it would probably lead to violence and injuries more serious than any the need of propulsion will cause."

"Who goes next?" the tanker demanded as he stared at his hand.

"The choice is generally random," the vocalizer said. "Not you, of course. Though if there is someone you would like to choose for the next segment? Or however far you choose to prolong the association after you have had time to reflect."

"Anyone?" Slade said. He turned and looked at the alien: the courteous, slim-bodied creature who was discussing his human cargo like lambs in a pen. "Shouldn't be hard to find somebody dead worthless in this lot, you'd think. . . ."

Not hard at all. Some of the outlaws were men Don Slade had been on the verge of killing a time or two himself. There were others, a few, whom the tanker still did not know by name. They were without personalities—to Slade. Without any of the factors that would have made them people instead of objects.

And there were those whom the crash of GAC 59 had disabled: paraplegics for whom no therapy could do more than maintain life, limbless torsos who would be shambling wrecks even with better prosthetics than they were ever likely to afford.

No problem for Don Slade. No problem for Captain Slade, who had hosed innocents with cyan fire during more operations than he cared to remember.

"All right," the tanker whispered to his clenched fist. "Take me." He turned his back on the Alayan. In the hollow distance, there was no sign of the door by which they had entered the corridor.

"You mean, Mister Slade—" began the mechanical voice. Its tone could not be hesitant, but the words' pacing was.

"I mean use me in your drive, curse it!" Slade shouted as he spun around. "I—"

He paused. The anger melted away from the fear it had been intended to cloak. Then the fear surrendered itself to the honesty of desperation. "There's none of them worth the powder to blow them away," the tanker whispered. "And I've sent men to die, the *Lord* knows. . . . But these're mine, like it or don't. And it's all too much like deciding who to butcher so that the rest of the lifeboat gets another meal. I'm not going to do that."

"Your principles do you credit, Mister Slade," said the Alayan, "but as the leader—"

"I don't have any bloody principles!" Slade said. "I'm just not going to axe one of *my* men for no better reason than to save my ass. Besides—" more calmly, now; almost diffident— "I don't see. . . . I mean, some of those fellows aren't bolted together real tight. Me, though . . . well, you'll see."

The Alayan's exoskeleton dulled for a moment to an almost perfect matte finish. Then the sheen that Slade had equated with health, but which probably indicated something else, returned. "All right, Mister Slade," the alien said. One of his tendrils played over an object on the belt around his midsection. The corridor began to fall in on itself. A door formed in the end of it as there had been when the pair entered. "You will not feel anything. There will be no pain. I cannot tell you exactly when it will happen, though it will not be soon."

Slade nodded. He stepped to the door. It was already opening onto the globe in which Slade had been sleeping when Stoudemeyer went berserk in the adjacent compartment.

"And Mister Slade," continued the voice which the tanker did not turn to face, "this passage will open for you if you wish to reconsider your decision."

"I won't," said Slade as he rejoined the wondering humans who called him their leader.

CHAPTER NINETEEN

Slade whuffled in his sleep. The blanket covered him for its feel rather than for need of warmth in the controlled climate of the passenger globe. Slade's hands tugged the fabric closer and his body shifted slightly. There was nothing to awaken the men snoring in darkness to either side of the tanker.

There was nothing to indicate to them that Don Slade was in Hell.

Slade was not sure how he had gotten there this time, though there was nothing unfamiliar about his surroundings. It was night, and thirty degrees of the horizon bubbled and writhed with the inverted orange funnel of a fire-storm. Somebody had been caught without nuclear dampers. A fusion bomb had gone off and had found fuel enough in the target area to multiply blast effect a thousandfold with winds of living flame.

But where was his tank? Where in *hell* was his tank, Hell was his tank . . .?

There was nothing nearby but mud and shattered trees. Powerguns slashed the distance with blue-green bolts. Occasionally they were answered or amplified by flares of high explosives that preceded their shock waves by many seconds. The mid-level overcast reflected the spire of the fire-storm into a soft, ghastly ambiance. It lighted the figure picking its way toward Slade across the mud and shell-holes.

Reflex moved the tanker's hand toward the pistol which should have been in his belt. The pistol was not there, however; and his hand was either missing or not responding to control. Slade could not be sure. Vision was no longer quite the accustomed process either.

"Sing out!" called Don Slade in warning. It was what he would have done if he were armed, if he could have slipped to cover behind a stump. What was *wrong* with his—

"What's the matter, Don?" called the oncoming figure. The voice was a pleasant tenor that cut through the hissing wind. "There's nothing more to fear, is there?"

"Via," said the tanker. "*Via!* Major Steuben!"

"Oh, call me Joachim, Don," said the other figure. "You did when we were alive, after all. And anyway, we're all equal here."

"Joachim," the big man begged. "Where are we?"

There could be no doubt that it really was Joachim Steuben. The uniform that rustled like a whore's undergarments; the boyishly-smooth face and the curly black hair, signs of wealth spent lavishly when they could no longer truly be signs of youth. The pistol in a cutaway holster high on Joachim's right hip, an ornamented bangle for a mincing queen—until he chose to kill. Joachim Steuben, slim and dainty as a white mouse . . . and the unit he commanded on the jobs for which no one else quite had the stomach, the White Mice. The Greeks, after all, had called their Furies the Kindly-Minded Ones.

Major Steuben commanded the White Mice until he died.

"Why Don," the trim figure said. "We're where people like you and I go when we die. We're in Hell." Steuben giggled, a sound that Slade remembered too well to mistake it for humor. "We're where everybody goes."

Something passed overhead with a freight-train rush, an artillery salvo aimed twenty kilometers down-range. The ground trembled to its passage.

"Joachim," Slade said. "I think we ought to get out of here." His legs would not move, he could not *see* his legs. "I think I'm going to need your help. I don't—"

"I thought loyalty was the answer," said Joachim. He spoke

conversationally. The dead major was ignoring Slade's words as one may ignore another's words at a party, where there will be plenty of time for the other to make his point later . . . and none of it makes any difference anyway. "Be perfectly loyal to a man, answer his needs even when his words don't admit those needs." Joachim gestured with a dainty hand. "Do you know what loyalty brings you, Donnie?"

"Joachim, I didn't—" Slade began. He respected Major Steuben, but he feared Steuben as well. Joachim was like a tank under the control of someone else; not necessarily hostile, but unstoppably lethal if it was chosen to be.

"Loyalty," Steuben continued in his smooth lilt and harsh smile, "brings you a shot in the back."

"I didn't shoot you, Joachim!" the tanker said.

"I know who killed me, Don," said the smiling figure. "And I know that nothing matters." Joachim reached out with his right hand, his gun hand, and made as if to stroke Slade's cheek. The smooth palm did not or did not quite touch the tanker. "Do you fancy me now, Donnie?" the slim man said.

Slade tried to lick his lips. "I don't think so, Joachim," he said.

Joachim giggled. "It's as good as any offer you'll get here, my friend," he said. "And as bad, of course. I'm not real, you know."

The slim figure turned. The back of the silk uniform rustled. The cloth was tattered and charred around the crater which a cyan bolt had left in killing the Major. "Nothing is real for you any more, Donnie," Joachim called as he walked back through the wasteland. The sky warmed the bright-work of his pistol's frame. "Nothing ever will be real," said the lilting voice as the wind swallowed it at last.

"I'm going home, Joachim," Slade called. "Home is real. Joachim Steuben! *I'm* real!"

Across the horizon from the fire-storm, a calliope began to rave at the sky.

"What's the matter, brother?" asked a voice behind Slade. "Don't feel like such a big man now, is that it?"

Don turned his attention with the care of a man who needs a

further moment to think. Via, do *I* look that old? Aloud he said, "Hello, Tom. I didn't expect to find you here."

"But it's just the place for Mad Dog Slade, isn't it, brother?" said Tom. He gestured at the shattered forest, at the shot-split night. "So it's the place for me, too, now that we're the same. Now that we're dead."

They were fraternal twins, not identical; but they shared some features, and they had the same deep, powerful chests. Tom Slade was stocky where his brother was simply big; and the years since they separated had not been kind to the man who had stayed on Tethys. The orange haze hid the change in hair color, from fair to white; but the individual strands were coarser, now, and they were strewn at wider intervals across Tom's scalp than they had been twenty years before. Tom's face was wrinkled. At the moment, the wrinkling was exaggerated by the bitter grimace into which Tom had screwed his mouth.

"No," Don said slowly. "I don't think it's the place for me, Tom. Or either of us. Let's see if we can't find a way out, shall we?"

"Why?" snarled Tom. He moved closer with his hands spread at his sides, as if to grapple with his bigger brother. A blade had entered beneath Tom's ribs on the left side. The edge had been sharp enough to be drawn up diagonally through bone and the organs of the thorax. Tom's shirt flopped away from the gash. The bloody stain on the fabric seemed glisteningly fresh. "So you could kill me yourself, Don? I know you've always wanted to, dear brother. Well, you're too late. I'm *dead.*" Tom's left hand deliberately spread the lips of his wound. "And you're dead too."

The tanker tried to reach out for his brother's dripping hand, but he still had no control over his own limbs. "Tom," he said softly. "I maybe wasn't what you wanted in a brother, but I never hated you. And . . . Via, Tom, if I'd wanted you dead, you wouldn't have had to wait around for it. Come on, help me and we'll get the hell out of here."

"We can't get out!" the shorter man shouted. "We can't! Don't you understand that?"

"No, I don't understand," Don said simply. "Look, I *have* been these places—" he would have gestured to the waste around them— "that's no more than the truth. And I'm not interested in standing around in another one, buck naked or whatever the *hell* I am. Now *help* me, curse it!"

The other figure slumped back from the tanker. "I can't even help myself," Tom said. "Any more than I could help my jealousy of you when we were alive. And I'd tell you I was sorry, Don, but it doesn't really matter now. Nothing—" and the figure turned, walking away from Don Slade as distant sirens howled—"ever mattered. I see that now. . . ."

"Tom!" the tanker called. *"Tom!"*

"Shouldn't bother you that he doesn't listen to you," said another voice. "After all, you never listened to anybody else, did you?"

The speakers always approached from behind; but Don Slade noticed that however he turned, the glare of the fire-storm was on his left side. "Hello, Father," he said. "I guess I could have figured that you'd be here."

Councilor Slade looked much the same as he had when Don last saw him on Tethys. That was not surprising. Though the Councilor had lived eighteen years after Don left home as a recruit for Hammer's Slammers, he had always seemed aged.

As with the son who had succeeded him, time and duties had taken a harsh toll from Councilor Slade. His hair was gone, save for a fringe, and his eyebrows were starkly white as they pinched together in the angry expression Don remembered so well.

"Then I'm sure I've given you some pleasure," the Councilor snapped in reply. "Cherish it, brat. You'll find no other pleasure ever again."

"I guess I am glad to see you," the tanker said. "I've regretted the way we parted often enough. I don't mean I'd have ever come back to Tethys if you were—" the swallow would not come—"still alive. But I wanted a chance to apologize for my part in the way things worked out. It wasn't all my fault, but I'm sorry for the part that was."

"You're a liar!" the Councilor screamed. He clenched his fist and shook it. His frailty would have made the gesture ridiculous were it not for the fury that glinted from the close-set eyes.

Three shells burst squarely overhead. They were so high that the pops of the charges were several seconds behind the red sparkle. Don cringed, equating the mild warning for the rain of fire and fragment the pops presaged. Aloud he said, "Do people tell lies here, Father? I don't feel like it myself." Then, "Why did Tom say he was jealous of me? He's the one who had it all."

"Did he?" Councilor Slade said with a gibing laugh. "You're the one who had Marilee, though, aren't you?"

"I knew the lady," Don admitted. He was surprised to learn that an anger hotter than mere frustration was still possible for him in his present guise. "And she brought me down about as hard as I care to remember. I don't say I didn't deserve it, but . . . she *married* Tom, he *knew* he'd won that one!"

"He knew much better than that, boy," said Councilor Slade. "But you've lost her forever, now."

There was a deadly hush across the wasteland. "Go on, brat!" Councilor Slade cackled. "Call me a liar! Call me a liar!"

And the bomblets from the firecracker rounds overhead began to burst across the landscape like the white heart of a furnace.

The scintillant blur was too bright and total for there to be any other sound or shape in Slade's universe. He should have felt the shrapnel gouging him apart, but the circumstances that prevented him from taking cover also seemed to shield him from the agony of dissolution. Slade rode on the white tide, buoyed up by the blasts whose crackling merged into a roar which in turn became cotton-flock silent.

And toward him through the fluffy silence walked Marilee in high boots and a flame-colored body suit.

"Oh, Via, girl," Slade whispered. "Oh my Lord. Are you dead too, Marilee?"

The wasteland was gone. The light that bathed the cloud-top ambiance was a soft white instead of the hellish orange of the previous scene. Marilee smiled. She looked older; but dear Lord, they all were older, it had been twenty years. "No, Don," the tall woman said. "I'm not dead, any more than you are."

She stretched out a long-fingered hand. Slade reached

instinctively to meet her, and he *did* have an arm that moved, a body he could see—

But their hands did not quite touch. As the big man took a step forward to fold Marilee into his arms, she raised a finger in warning and shook her head.

Slade froze. "You're not real," he said in a flat voice.

"I'm very real," Marilee said, "but what you see now isn't my physical body, Don." Her grin flashed in a way that tore him with the recollection. "For that matter, you're not really *seeing* anything . . . but I suppose you'd figured that out."

"More or less," Slade said. "What I'd mainly figured was I wanted to get out of this bloody place." He shrugged the shoulders he could now see and feel again. "That place, I mean. But I'd rather be on Tethys than here, too, so long as . . . well, you're still on Tethys, Marilee?"

"The part of me that isn't in your mind, yes," the woman said. "We could use you there. But there's a problem."

"Shoot," said the tanker. He could not solve all problems, but he knew that he could solve most of them if he had the time to mumble the details over in his brain.

Marilee lounged back onto haze that seemed to have no more solid reality than any other part of the surroundings. "You see, Don," she said, "your mind is driving an Alayan ship to a planet called Terzia. And at the same time, your mind is creating a false reality for itself. You'll be incurably insane when the ship reaches Terzia. You won't be able to recognize reality."

Slade's tongue touched one corner of his mouth, then the other. "I won't be able to recognize you?" he asked.

"Your reality will be within your mind," the woman said. She was smiling again. "As this is." Her spread fingers gestured. "As I am."

"Then I'll make a reality in which I'm sane," said Slade. He stepped forward. His voice rose as he added, "By the Lord, I *will!*"

Marilee's image receded from Slade without losing its infinite clarity. Her smile was broader. "That's right, Don," she called as she disappeared. "Remember that we need you on Tethys. . . ."

* * *

Slade grunted and swung to his feet. The men sleeping near him did not notice. The three Alayans who had entered the globe sprang to alertness like semaphore arms working. All the Alayans carried the frothy apparatus with which Stoudemeyer and Slade had earlier been subdued. The flickers of radiant cross-talk were strikingly obvious since the globe had been darkened for the passengers to sleep.

"Hey, stay calm," the tanker said. He raised his hands close to his shoulders, palms forward. It was a gesture of submission, but it was a pretty fair posture to strike from also. Slade knew he was not crazy, but he did not intend to be frozen into permanent silence before he could explain that to the Alayans.

"We apologize for disturbing you, Mister Slade," said the middle of the three aliens, "but we are now in orbit around Terzia. Would you please come with us so that we can make arrangements with the planetary authorities?"

Other humans were awakening in the compartment. The lights began to come up smoothly, though it was some hours before they would have done so in the normal cycle. There was a buzz of conversation. Somebody cheered.

"Listen, that's fine," said Slade with a false smile. "But there's no problem, you see? I'm all right. Why don't you just drop those things for the moment?" He twirled his index finger toward the glove-like stunners without lowering his hands from their position of defense. "I'm fine, believe me."

The Alayans did not need to turn to look at one another because of their multiple faces. The chamber danced with coded light for a moment. Then the alien in the center dropped his device on the floor. His vocalizer said as his companions followed his lead, "Of course, Mister Slade. If you'll just step this way."

The tanker was not surprised to find himself in a corridor without termini, facing a single Alayan instead of the trio with which he had left the globe. "Now, I know what you're thinking," Slade said hastily, "but it didn't work that way with me. I'm still sane."

"I will not argue definitions with you, Mister Slade," said the Alayan. "If you mean that you perceive the same reality that you did—earlier . . . the reality that I perceive—then I think you are wrong."

Slade gestured, tossing distinctions into the air. "Look," he said, "it doesn't matter. The main thing is that you know I'm not dangerous. Right?"

A scintillant pattern played across all of the Alayan's faces. Slade did not understand what had happened until the vocalizer spoke. With its mechanical lack of humor, it said, "We know that you are not dangerous, Mad Dog Slade?"

The tanker began to laugh. The tension of the past forty hours, while he waited to be driven mad, released itself in guffaws that doubled Slade over. "Via, Via," he wheezed when he could get his breath. "Somebody's been talking to you, haven't they? Well."

Calmer, but with a smile still cramping his cheeks, Slade went on. "Still, you know what I mean. I swear to goodness if it weren't for some of the things about your ship, I'd travel around with you just to get to know you people better."

The big man sobered fully. He added, "After I'd taken care of some things back home. I hear they need me there."

His face was as placid as a gun barrel.

CHAPTER TWENTY

"He led those who trusted him into Hell," noted the dispassionate mind of Elysium. "He decided for them, so that some died and some went mad without any knowledge of what they were being sent into."

"He led them," responded the other current. "He decided for men who had chosen him to decide. When it came to a clear choice, he was willing to sacrifice himself for those he led."

"I thought it was simple enough," Slade said to the Elysians facing him. "We'd disembark at the first world we hit, Terzia it was going to be. Now that we knew, *I* knew, I've got to admit—what sailing with the Alayans meant. And the tenders brought everybody down to the surface of the planet without argument.

"But the trouble started when I formed everybody up between the tenders and the Citadel to hear the new plans . . ."

"This might be worth it for booze and women, muttered Bourgiby as he mopped sweat from his neck, "but so far I've seen damn none of them around."

The landed castaways were watched over by native males whose powerguns were certainly not of native manufacture. The guards were not overtly threatening, but neither were they friendly. No one could say for sure whether the locals spoke any human dialect.

Slade stepped forward so that the men he had formed in double ranks could see him. The guards were watching closely. They did not interfere. Neither did the trio of Alayans who had come down in the tenders with their human cargo. "Ten-*shun!*" the tanker roared. He hoped that past habit would silence and focus the group on him, though few of them would have been from outfits noted for obedience to their officers.

"Excuse me," said a voice. "You will be allowed to speak, but first I have an announcement to make for the Terzia."

Slade turned. His mouth had been open already to unload grim truths on the castaways. The speaker was surprising enough that it was a moment before the big man remembered to reply.

The Spanglish phrasing had been human-standard, so far as there was such a standard, but the speaker was a male Terzian, an autochthone. He was a little stockier than most of his fellows; and his skin, while swarthy, lacked the olive tinge underlying the others'.

Besides his human trousers, the autochthone wore a commo helmet with a directional amplifier. Even if Slade had wanted to contest the local's right to speak, human lungs would have been hopelessly outclassed. The amp boomed out, "The Terzia, who rules this world absolutely, offers greetings and condolences to you who have been landed here. She offers honest employment to all who care to remain. Our exports here on Terzia are minerals and forest products. There are collector's positions open in both fields. A man who applies himself will be able to save the price of passage off-planet within a year."

The groan from the mercenaries needed no amplification to be heard.

Rooks broke from the ragged line. "Hey, what is this?" he called as much to his fellows as to Slade. "I thought the deal was—" he turned toward the trio of Alayans who were waiting near the human ranks—"we had passage as far as we wanted to go. And this sure as bleeding *hell* isn't where I want to go!"

The Alayan's vocalizer had a volume setting that permitted it to thunder over the chorus of support for Rooks. "That is correct, sir," boomed the machine voice. "You are welcome to travel with us as far as you choose." There was a brief pause. "Our eighth landfall following this one will be Desmo."

The tone of the pandemonium changed. There were cheers and a number of whistles. The ranks had already dissolved. Now there was a movement toward the Alayans. Men were demanding details of time and circumstances from the coolly-erect aliens.

Desmo was headquarters for a score of relatively small mercenary units. The planet acted also as a recruiting center for several of the larger ones. The world was by no means loosely gripped by the Military Tribunate which ran it. Still, Desmo's entertainment was varied and was geared toward the needs of young men in a dangerous line of work.

It struck Slade that he had never seen more than three Alayans at a time. Part of the tanker's mind held that thought and wrestled with it, while the reflexive part of him roared, "Hold up, curse you! If you get on that ship, it'll drive you nuts!"

Not all the assembly could hear the words, but Slade's bellow gave up less than the aliens might have hoped to their machinery.

"Yeah, that's what I said," the tanker went on grimly. He had their attention again. Slade stood arms akimbo, angry at the men for being fooled and angry at the way the Alayans and the Terzian authorities had combined to that end. "Their ship moves by snapping people right out of their skulls. Just like Stoudemeyer. That something you want to see happen to you?"

The mercenaries seethed like the water of a stone-lashed pool. The sun hammered them in this jungle-lapped clearing. Their skins were pale from the voyage and near-confinement on Rusata. Neither the Alayans nor the ground authorities had as yet provided protective gear. The series of assaults by the sun and various figures of power left the men enervated and afraid.

In the bright sun and the confusion, it was hard to tell how much the Alayans had been talking among themselves. Now the vocalizer of the central alien called, "Mister Slade?"

The loud question split the mercenaries between those looking at the Alayan and those looking at Slade himself. "Are you speculating?" the Alayan continued in the brief hush. "Or do you mean the voyage has affected your own mind?"

"You know what I've been through!" the tanker shouted. "I won't have you doing that to these others, do you hear me?"

Somebody in the crowd laughed. Slade took two strides toward the sound. He caught himself as mercenaries scattered or even braced themselves, secured by the armed guards.

"*Listen,* you people!" Slade said. The grip he kept on his temper showed in the tremble of his voice. "I've led you the best I know how—"

He was interrupted by the amplified voice of the Terzian official. "For those of you who will be transients on our world," the autochthone was saying, "follow me to the free entertainment center in which you may stay while cargo is being transferred to and from your vessel."

There *were* females on Terzia after all. An even dozen of them issued from a door in the tall spire which seemed the only building in the region.

Over the bellows of enthusiasm, the autochthone continued. "Those of you who intend to stay, fall in at those trucks." He pointed toward a pair of scabrous-looking stake-bed vehicles. "They will carry you immediately to the labor barracks."

The Terzian turned. The rush of the human audience to follow him was so immediate that the men forced their way past Slade in their haste.

The tanker bunched his shoulders momentarily. Then he simply got out of the way. The females had slipped into the building again. The male autochthone led the surviving mercenaries toward the same entrance as if they were the children of Hamelin—or the rats. At the very door, one man paused and looked back. Snipes, the Admin Officer. Then he sneered at Slade and disappeared with the others. The portal clicked shut behind him.

Slade closed his eyes. His lips pursed and flattened in a sort of exercise to work the feeling back into them. It was not anger that weighed on him, but the crushing sense of failure. The sun felt good, like the clean sun of Tethys burning away fatigue on a gravel strand. After a minute's stillness, Slade opened his eyes and stepped toward the empty trucks.

"Where will you go now, Mister Slade?" asked the voice behind him.

The big man turned. The Alayan was alone. His limbs held no weapon, only the vocalizer on which his tendrils expertly worked. The Alayan's six tiny heads goggled without human expression.

"I'm going to the labor barracks, I suppose," said Slade. "I thought about some other things I might do—" he looked up and down the spindly alien, wondering again whether the chitin would have cut as the exoskeleton splintered in Slade's grip—"but I need to get home. They tell me."

The alien mimed a human nod with his central pair of heads. "You can travel with us, you know," the vocalizer said.

Slade smiled. "I might," he said. "Would you use me for the fuel instead of the men? Now that we know it doesn't bother me?"

"You know we cannot," said the flat voice. "You are functional, Mister Slade—obviously functional. But our need is for reality, not function. We will get you to your homeworld at least as quickly as any other system of freighter connections is likely to do."

"Figured," said Slade. "Well, I'm not going to watch that, my friend."

He turned and stared up the glistening flank of the spire behind them. "You kept your bargain, and you didn't lie. Can't blame you for not wanting to lose your fuel supply, and I can't blame the folks here for discouraging immigrants." He shrugged. "Our sort of immigrants. But I'll work my passage out in a mine or any *curst* place before I watch you burn up my men!"

The Alayan nodded again. "I understand, Mister Slade," he said through his vocalizer.

Despite the emotions wracking him, Slade was quite convinced that the alien *did* understand.

"But please remember," the Alayan continued, "that—men—are lost during any long voyage. Because of our precautions, no one has been shot while gambling or been driven mad by adulterated stimulants. Most of your men will disembark on Desmo, Mister Slade, in better health than they will have a year later."

"What'll you do then?" Slade said harshly. "Send yourselves to Hell? Or rot for want of fuel?"

The Alayan's faces danced with a radiance only hinted in the sunlight. "We transport intelligent life forms among the stars faster and more cheaply than any rival," the vocalizer said. "We never lie about the terms, though we do not emphasize them either. We will find a cargo on Desmo, Mister Slade. And we will find fuel."

The Alayan walked back toward one of the tenders. He moved with the fragile dignity of an aged man. Lord preserve those men who would sail again with the creatures . . . but Don Slade had done all that he could himself.

Do you have to feel you have failed because outlaws won't take your word that a situation is dangerous? Cop!

A door snicked open at the base of the tower. Slade could not be certain whether it was the one through which his men had entered or a different one. The Citadel was huge. Its smooth surface and relatively small diameter to height tended to conceal its real bulk, however.

A woman stepped toward Slade. She was flanked by two guards. The guards were male autochthones, but the woman had to be human: the first human Slade had seen on this planet, besides the men with whom he had landed.

The woman was beautiful, beyond any questions of need or abstinence. The dress she wore was rich and clinging, and her dark, honey hair fell across her shoulders beneath a fillet of green crystal. A part of the tanker's mind was surprised that the woman's beauty and importance were not riding in a vehicle, even for the hundred meters or so which separated her from Slade. In fact, she did not even wear shoes. Her toes flexed liquidly against the sward as she walked.

"Dear Lord have mercy!" the tanker muttered. He had been seventeen the last time he felt as he did now.

"Captain Donald Slade?" the woman called. Her voice had the alto clarity of birdsong at evening.

"I once was that, yes," Slade said. He was suddenly aware of how sweat-stiffened and prickly were the clothes he wore. "You represent the Terzia? I'm here to sign on as a miner, I guess."

"I think we can do better than that, Captain," said the woman. She was close enough to extend a hand to grip Slade's warmly. She smiled. "I *am* the Terzia."

CHAPTER TWENTY-ONE

Don Slade slept in a comfortable room. If he wished, he could have opened it into a porch by cranking the roof and west wall into recesses. There was no need for that. This night on Elysium, Slade was tired enough to sleep on a heap of cinders.

No resident of the planet above the age of six was asleep.

The mental netting that linked the folk of Elysium was as real and as resilient as a spider's web, but it did not change the fact that humans evolved as social *individuals*. It was as individuals that they talked now in family groupings before they joined again in the decision that the society would make—as an individual.

Onander filled a mug that he had thrown and fired himself in youth. He handed it to his daughter. Nan already sipped from a similar mug at the astringent blend of coffee, cacao, and milk.

"Well, we certainly can't keep him here," said Onander. By watching himself fill the third mug, he did not have to catch the eyes of either woman.

"No, dear," said Nan in a tone which was further from agreement with her husband than the words themselves were. "That wouldn't be at all fair to him, would it?" In a slightly different voice she added, "The Terzia acts in such *human* ways on occasion. It's a little hard to believe, sometimes."

The surface of Risa's drink began to tremble until the girl set the mug down with a thump. The blush on her cheekbones clashed with the coppery tinge of her hair. "He's not something we have to be afraid of, you know," Risa said. "He's alone. And he's been acting quite nicely. Well? Hasn't he?"

"Well, he's certainly been acting," said her father. His tone was sharpened by the rasp of Risa's demand.

"Now, dear, that isn't fair," said his wife before Risa could respond. That would raise the emotional temperature still further. "Everyone tries to be pleasant to strangers. That's all Don's doing. But of course, Risa—" She looked calmly over to her daughter—"he is very dangerous. And we couldn't allow him to stay, even if he wanted to."

"Well, what *is* the mural in the Hall?" the girl demanded, more in frustration now than anger. "What sort of men—and women!— fought the mutants? Weren't they like him? *Our* ancestors. Why should we be afraid of Don?"

"Oh, Risa," Onander said softly. He reached out a hand. His daughter took it willingly, greedily. "The battle was no myth; but the mural is a warning, not a trophy. Those were our ancestors, yes. Some of our genes. . . . And we *all* of us, despite the unity we've begun to achieve; all of us could be back in that Hell of violence and slaughter, very easily."

"But the mutants aren't here, Father," Risa said. "They're still on the colony ship or they've died out. Or maybe they landed somewhere after all, have their own world—but they aren't on Elysium."

Onander turned his daughter's hand palm-upward. He cupped his own much larger hand above it on the table. "The mutants were half the war, my dearest. When our ancestors built the matter transmitter, they left the mutants behind. But they couldn't leave themselves behind."

He paused, looking from the paired hands to the eyes of his daughter. "Don Slade is a credit to the race in many ways," Onander continued softly. "And no, if it hadn't been for souls like his among our ancestors, we would never have survived to settle Elysium, to make it what we have for the past millennium. But there are things in us which if awakened would drop us back into chaos as suddenly as our ancestors escaped it. And you know that also, my Risa."

"He wouldn't be happy, dearest," Nan said sadly. It was hard to tell whether the sadness was on her daughter's behalf or for more personal reasons. "Not even for a little while, now that he's so focused on getting back to Tethys. He really does believe it will be home to him after twenty years, you know."

"Yes," Risa said with a sharp movement of her head, a nod or a peck. She slipped her hand from beneath her father's. When Risa drank from her mug, it was with loud gulping noises.

"I think," said Onander heavily, "that it's about time to make a decision." Nan met his eyes and nodded; Risa nodded to her mug of bitter drink.

The trio fell silent around the handsome kitchen table. The alcohol lamp burbled softly beneath the pot of drinks. Occasionally a local equivalent of insects would be batted away by the repulsion field guarding the open window.

Physically, the family was of three separate entities . . . but their minds were merging, and all over Elysium minds were merging to decide the fate of a sleeping castaway.

"Captain Slade?" the voice whispered. "Don?"

Hours of tension and a heavy meal had drugged Slade as thoroughly as a deliberate anesthetic. The reflexes were still there, however, even if they had to fight to the surface through meters of cotton batting. "Roger," the tanker said, groping for the equipment belt that should have been close to his head.

Risa touched Slade's hand with one of hers. He felt the edge of the bed give under her slight weight. "I came to tell you," the girl said, "that they—that we are going to send you to Tethys."

"That's—" Slade said. "Well, I don't know how I'll ever be able to thank you. But if Elysium ever—has need for what I have or what I am, it's yours."

Slade had been momentarily blind when he rolled out of sleep. Now the tanker's eyesight was returning with a rush. The door of his room was closed. Starlight through the window above the bed showed that Risa wore a pastel garment, high-necked and frothy. The garment covered a great deal more of the girl's skin than had the suit she wore in the air car, but it covered that skin with little more than the shadow it threw.

"Girl" was the wrong word. Dear Lord, but there could be no doubt but that Risa was a woman.

"You won't be able to remember us, though," Risa said as she sat primly. "We—we're peaceful here on Elysium, and they think that if word got around. . . ."

"Sure," the tanker said. He shifted so that he was upright with his back against the window ledge. His legs were tucked beneath him and covered with the sheet. "I, well. . . . There's some places like yours where I figure they wouldn't let a stranger go at all. For the reason stated. I'll admit I half thought. . . ."

Slade's voice trailed off. The woman beside him had been in his mind, however. She knew that the thought had been multiple, not partial. *A door closing and the hiss of lethal gas from vents. Burly men holding Slade on either side and the prick of an injection. A greeting, and as Slade turned, a blast of gunfire.* The tanker had known too many situations in which an individual did not fit the circumstances. It was never something he had liked; Slade preferred to think of his enemies as gunmen facing him. But he had heard the stories, sure he had.

Lord have mercy on the soul of Joachim Steuben; and on the soul of Donald Slade, who was headed the same way in the Lord's good time.

"Ah," Slade added, "I wouldn't have anybody think I was in the habit of shafting people who'd done me favors. I don't blame you folks for wiping my memory, but—it wasn't something I'd have talked about anyway."

"There will be some things that will remain," Risa said. She twisted slightly toward the man. Her knee bumped Slade's. When he edged away, she twisted further. "You'll remember meals, probably, though not where you ate them. You'll even remember faces. A memento of . . . us here on Elysium."

The tanker was frowning in concentration. Aloud he said, "The kindness you've done me will be that, Risa. That will stay, I'm sure. I don't forget help I've been given, or who gave it."

"Don, I'm not a child," she said. Her left hand touched the sheet over Slade's thighs, then slipped with a butterfly's delicacy to the man's bare torso.

Slade touched Risa's hand loosely enough for affection but not so loosely that the hand could fumble the way it seemed to want to do. "I know that," the tanker lied. Then he went on fiercely. "And *you* know that I'm not an adult, not like anybody here would recognize. I never will be. *You* know that!"

"Don, that doesn't matter," Risa said. She tugged her hand, away now and not downward. It came free at once.

"Sure it matters, Risa," the tanker replied. "It would matter to you if you saw a friend getting into something that was going to do a lot more harm than good. Wouldn't it?"

Risa sat bolt upright again. "I think that's my decision, isn't it?" she said in a voice harder than any she had used before to Slade. Her garment blurred away from her bosom like shock waves from bullets.

"No, Risa, it's not," Slade said gently. "Not unless I'm—do you have dogs, here? Domestic animals of some sort, anyway. Not unless I'm an animal. If I'm a human being, then it does matter. *That's* your decision, Risa. Am I a human being, to you?"

The girl burst into tears.

Slade wrapped her to his chest, safely now and a little sorry of that fact, but. . . .

"I didn't mean," Risa gurgled. "I just didn't want you to, to leave and—"

"I'm not going to forget," Slade whispered to the soft, curly hair. "Anything that leaves me mind enough to remember meals is going to let me remember you saving my life. And . . . you being you. You being here makes it a better universe, Risa. And I'll know that too."

Risa straightened, sniffled, and stood up. "I—" she began. Then she said, "You've been good for us here on Elysium, Don. It doesn't usually happen, but I think . . . it might be that if you went traveling again, after you've settled your business on Tethys, that you could find your way here again. I'd be a little older then, of course."

Risa turned and walked out of the room. She closed the door softly behind her.

Blood and Martyrs, Slade thought. Sixteen going on forty. . . . And here he was, forty himself and that a miracle the way he'd lived. He had been going to lay back on Tethys, he'd told himself that. But Tom with his chest split open and Marilee calling for help, well. . . . Marilee knew the sort of help you got from Hammer's Slammers. She knew what to expect from Don Slade when she told him there was trouble.

And if they were no more than fancies in a madman's skull, Tom and Marilee and the others—then they were Don Slade's fancies. Maybe there would be a chance to settle down afterwards, if he lived to be forty-one.

Blood and Martyrs. Slade was smiling as he drifted off to sleep again.

In a room not far from Slade's, Nan and Onander held one another. The man was weeping softly.

CHAPTER TWENTY-TWO

Dawn awakened him with her rosy fingers.

The air was brisk enough to be comfortable, and it had enough of a salt tang to remind Slade of home. He stretched in bed—and found himself lying on gravel instead of a mattress.

"Where in the *Hell* am I?" the big man grunted. But the real Hell of it was, he knew the answer before he voiced the question. What he did not know was *how* he had come to lie behind a spaceport warehouse on Tethys.

"Via," Slade said in wonderment. He was wearing boots and a two-piece work-suit of neutral gray, not livery. There was a hand-scrip in one pocket. It held about a month's pay for a laborer in both Tethian currency and in crystalline Frisian talers. There were identity cards as well, three of them in three different names . . . and one of them the card Don Slade would have carried had he stayed on Tethys and succeeded to the Slade Councilorship.

The last thing Slade remembered clearly was boarding a lifeboat on Terzia. That boat sure as blazes had not landed him here . . . but the only other thing in his mind was a girl's face, elfin cute and smiling beneath a tumble of red curls.

The tanker remembered what the phantoms of his mind had told him aboard the Alayan ship, also. He scraped a small hole in the gravel and hid within it the card in his own name and one of the others as well. He kept only the one calling him Donald Holt. Into the same small hiding place he dropped the seal ring from his hand.

178

The ring was unremarkable till its weight indicated that it was of projectile-grade osmium. It would look precisely the same in a bath of molten steel. It was the only thing Slade had kept with him from the day he lifted from Tethys as a Slammers recruit.

He filled in the hole with a gentle motion of his boot sole and noted the number of paces from it to the corner of the warehouse as he walked away.

Somebody had wished him well; the nondescript clothing and the false indentities were proof of that. The memory of the red-haired girl followed Slade, but he could not get a grip on the thought. "I sold my clock, I sold my reel . . ." the tanker sang to himself. But this Johnnie had come back from soldiering. . . .

A train of low-boys were emptying at the front of the warehouse. The foreman of the crew glanced at Slade sharply. The big man was not one of the warehouse team, however, and therefore not worth worrying about. Slade noted that the foreman and the truck drivers all seemed to be in red-piped clothing suggesting Dyson livery. The low-ranking cargo-handlers wore plain gray.

"To buy my love a sword of steel . . ." the castaway murmured as he smiled. He wiped his palms on his thighs.

It was still home. The sky to the west was the right pale gray with its hint of violet. The air had the odors of childhood, though they were over-printed here by ozone from landing thrusters. Slade had never spent much time at the Port when he was growing up, though it existed as an enclave in the family estates. A neutral enclave, administered by a board appointed by the Council as a whole. Now everyone with rank seemed to claim allegiance to the Dysons. Welladay. . . .

It was a city, now, the spaceport. There had been houses for the permanent staff and their families, a few hundred households at the time Slade had left. From the look of the barracks—some of the buildings very new, still under construction—there were many times that number present now.

Of greater concern were the shanties spreading beyond the formal buildings. Some of them seemed to be rigged out for enter-tainment of one sort or the other. Certainly they did not house workers. Men and women lounged among the shanties now, while the bustle of business continued on the field.

There were three huge starships down and a number of intra-system ferries and tenders. One of the latter had landed recently enough that steam was venting from its hull as the thrusters cooled. The cargo bay was still closed, but a handful of passengers had disembarked. Humans were always fringe cargo, save for the occasional new settlement—and, more often, the transport of a mercenary regiment.

Nothing like that here. Most of the passengers were entering a large air car in Krueger colors. They seemed to be a honeymoon couple and their servants, returned now with subdued expressions. Slade had never thought that the uncertainties of a long journey were a good way to begin married life; but then, he had never been married.

There was one man apart from the Krueger party. He was talking to the driver of a utility van outside the port office as Slade approached. Though the man's back was to the tanker, Slade could hear him saying, " . . . to Slade House?"

"Much in the way of luggage, then?" the driver asked.

"Pardon me, master," said Don Slade as he stepped almost between the two men, "but I couldn't help—*Blood and Martyrs!*"

"Came to look for you, my man," said Danny Pritchard with a slow, tight grin.

The driver was blinking from one ex-soldier to the other. Pritchard touched Slade's jaw to silence him and said to the driver, "A standard cubic-meter case is all. In the office. And an extra—"

"Thirty libra," Slade said, cued without either partner's conscious awareness of the question.

"—if you fetch it to the truck yourself."

The driver shrugged. He took the scribbled claim check and sauntered into the building.

"Been back long?" Pritchard asked as the two men sized each other up.

Danny looked a little more gray than Slade had remembered him. Fit, though, the Lord knew. Slade's exercises had not included

walking. He was sure that even the kilometer he had just strolled
through the Port village had raised blisters on his right sole and heel.
"I don't think so," he said aloud. "Say, did you have anything to do
with that?"

"With how you left Terzia, you mean?" Pritchard asked.

"No, I—oh, never mind," the tanker replied. "There's other
things to worry about now, I guess."

His friend frowned and nodded his head. "Look," said
Pritchard, "how much do you know about what's going on here the
last while? Anything?"

"Is my brother dead?" Slade asked.

Pritchard nodded.

"Yeah," Slade muttered, aloud but to the part of his mind which
believed in Hell. "Well," he continued, "I guess I'm not color-blind."
He nodded toward a Port official in full Dyson livery, calling orders
to a gang of laborers. "I suppose there's some things to straighten
out back at the House, too."

"Don, I don't know how bad it is," said Danny Pritchard. "But it
seemed like I ought to take a look. With the Colonel's blessing."

"I'm not asking anybody in to fight my fights," Slade said
sharply.

"And I'm not offering to," Pritchard snapped back. "I'd have
thought you'd seen enough with the Slammers to know that
blowing people away's a curst poor way to settle things anyway—
unless you figure to get them all. How many people do you think
you and I can kill, Don?"

"Via, I'm sorry," the big man said. He chuckled. Clasping his
comrade on the shoulder very lightly, he went on. "You know the
only thing I was ever fit for was line command. Got any bright ideas,
staff mogul?"

"Yeah," said Pritchard. "Got the idea that you lie low for a couple
days instead of barging right into things. The Council's going to
meet at Slade House, you know?"

"Are they now?" said the tanker. He squeezed the knuckles of his
right hand between his lips. "Look," he went on, "have your driver
drop me at one of the processing plants on the way. Number Six,

that's the oldest one and it's close to the House. Nobody ever went hungry if he stopped by one of our plants when *I* was a kid."

"All righty!" called the driver as he wheeled out a plain, rectangular case. "Luggage it is."

Slade and Pritchard moved to either side to help shift the case to the end-bars to which it would be strapped. "You fellows figured out where you're going yet?"

Don Slade laughed. "In the short term, at least," he said. His muscles bunched as he slid the heavy case into position. "In the short term."

CHAPTER TWENTY-THREE

The steel door of the food-processing plant was not only unlocked but ajar. "Hello the house!" Slade called as he swung the door fully open. He waited outside for a further moment. The air car had already disappeared into the eastern sky. The sea sounded a dense background, loud without being obtrusive. The gasp of the pumps within the long, concrete building was by contrast relatively mild.

"Hello there," Slade called again as he stepped inside. He closed the door behind him.

There was a door to the right which would lead to living quarters for the crew during their month-long tours. Beside it was a bright alcove glassed off from the rest of the pump room, the foreman's office. The multiple vision blocks within flashed their images to one another with no human to watch them. Tubing and crates moving beneath the tubing on conveyors covered the long, left-hand wall. There was a slideway leading from the office to the bright splotch which was the open, seaward end of the building.

As Slade watched, a blur grew against the brightness. It accelerated toward him. When the blur slowed to a brutally-sudden stop, it took on shape: a slide bucket holding a hard-looking man in faded Slade coveralls. The rocket gun he rested on his right thigh happened to be aimed squarely at the intruder's chest.

"And just what might *your* business be, buddy?" the man asked Slade. He was not young, but his voice quivered as little as did the gun he held.

"My name's, Don Holt," Slade said with only a moment's hesitation to remember it. "I was hoping you might have some work for me." The fact that the foreman was leaving the office empty to check the lines implied the crew was short, but Slade would have said the same thing in any case.

The man in Slade livery snorted. "I'm the foreman, my name's Pretorius," he said. "And I guess that means you're looking for a meal. Well, I guess we can find you that, sure." He swung his legs out of the bucket and stepped toward Slade. His weapon was now aimed at the roof.

The tanker frowned. "Guess I could use some food, sure," he said. "But I haven't forgot how to catch that for myself, either. I said, I'm looking for work."

"Are you?" said Pretorius without inflexion. "You'd be from around here, then?"

"Been a while, though," said Slade in elliptical agreement. "When I was a kid, I thought all mercenaries got rich. I spent the past twenty years proving I was wrong and a curst fool." He smiled in near humor, then touched his left earlobe. It was a half centimeter shorter than the right one which had not been fried by a power-gun.

Pretorius dipped his gun momentarily, like the neck of a bird bending to drink. He arrested the motion before it was an actual threat, but there was no particular warmth in his voice as he said, "Is that a fact? Then I'd think you'd have found work at the Port, boyo. And just maybe you did, hey? And they sent you here to see what you could learn."

"Could be I got an offer," Slade said. "Could be I didn't like the color of suit they were going to have me wear, too. Look, if I'm unwelcome here, I'll just walk on out. My daddy ran a catcher boat from South Three until a knife-jaw got him. I guess I can find some kin down that way if a strong back don't interest you." He turned away from Pretorius and the gun.

"Blazes, man," the foreman called. "Don't leave me short-handed as I am."

Slade looked back at the foreman. Pretorius was holding out his weapon by the balance. "Here," the older man went on. "You know how to use one of these?"

Slade frowned. "Guess I can learn," he said.

Powerguns would have been useless against the sub-surface life forms that were the bane of processing plants. Instead the crews used short-barreled rocket guns like this one. They fired low-velocity missiles which were unaffected by the media through which they lanced toward their targets. The bursting charge was much bulkier than a powergun wafer liberating comparable energy; but the charges went off in their targets, not on the surface of the sea.

"Come on, then," the foreman said. He pointed to the second slide-bucket. "We've got a ten-meter wriggler giving fits on section two. Isn't big enough to take a nip out of the line, but it keeps tripping the alarm. Come on—you want to learn, I'll teach you."

And what have we got here?" asked the leader of the men who strolled toward Danny Pritchard as the air car took off again.

Pritchard looked them up and down with a lack of expression which was itself significant. All but one of the four men wore belt knives. The leader instead toyed with a nunchaku, a pair of short flails chained together at the slim ends. None of them wore guns, which had been for decades proscribed on the Council Islands of Tethys save for certain jobs and locations. That scarcely made Danny safe at this moment.

The men were among those who had been lounging against the shading wall of the courtyard when Pritchard arrived. There were a score of others in various liveries present, but no one seemed to pay any attention to what was going on. The leader of the men moving in on the visitor wore Slade Blue defaced with a crimson stripe down either leg. The other three were Dyson retainers in full scarlet.

"Friend of the family," Danny Pritchard called cheerfully. He sidled away from his luggage so that it did not block him if he had to jump back suddenly. Hidden at the small of the ex-soldier's back was a glass-barreled powergun. He would use it if he had to—but the illegal weapon's single charge would still leave three opponents. "I'm here to visit the Widow Slade, at her request. You're of the House?"

The man with the nunchaku flipped his weapon out toward Pritchard's trunk. The lid clacked as the further baton touched it. "Can't have any contraband coming in here," the man said. "Think we'll check it right here."

"What the *hell's* going on here?" demanded a voice shrill with tension.

Men who had been covertly watching as the visitor was baited now glanced up in open surprise. The four men who had approached Pritchard now fanned away as if Hammer's man could be safely ignored if they were willing to leave him alone. Not the smartest possible assumption; but they were not pros, only bullies, and not the cleverest bullies Danny Pritchard had met in his career either.

The man who had shouted from the House doorway was young and thin. Pritchard had seen a cube of Marilee—as she was— Dorcas. The youth's features were a near double for those of the woman twenty years before.

It was an open question how Teddy had expected to stop the trouble if his righteous indignation were not enough. The fat old man a step behind him and to the right had a notion of his own, however. The old man's gun-hand was hidden within his loose-fitting jacket.

"Checking for contraband, Master Teddy," said the man with the nunchaku. The weapon twitched in his hand like the tail of a cat which lay otherwise motionless.

"Durotige," said the old man behind Edward Slade, "get your butt out of here. Out of the yard. *Now.*"

"You don't scare me, Blegan!" snarled Durotige.

"Good," said the old man, oblivious to his presumptive master. "Because you'll try something if I don't scare you, Durotige."

"Time'll come, old man," said Durotige. His words were bluster, however—as Blegan's had not been. The man in crimson over blue spun on his heel and marched toward the gate. Its hinges were rusty but they squealed open when Durotige tugged with the fear of death behind him. The trio who had supported him drifted away as well, though they pointedly did not walk toward the gate.

Edward Slade joined the visitor. The young man glanced angrily about the yard at the liverymen who had not intervened in the trouble. They were now insouciantly directed on their own affairs again. "Sir, I apologize for the boors you've met in my House," Teddy said. Someone chuckled from behind a car at the words. "Leave the trunk. I'll have Housemen bring it in."

"No problem," said Danny Pritchard as he swung the gear handle from one corner of the trunk. He began spinning the handle with an ease that belied the trunk's weight. Coon Blegan had grimaced when his master spoke of leaving the trunk. The old servant knew as Pritchard did himself that if left unguarded, the luggage would surely be ransacked.

Wheels lowered from the four corners, jacking the trunk up by smooth degrees. Powered units were simpler while they worked; but they stopped working when your traps were off-loaded into a swamp, or somebody turned a valve that flooded the cargo bay with nascent chlorine. Most mercs got along, as Pritchard did, with muscle-powered come-alongs for their hold baggage.

This time the trunk held clothing along with a submachine gun, three spare barrels, a thousand rounds of ammunition, and a suit of body armor. Pritchard had not been going to leave it in the court-yard if the only alternative had been to lift the full hundred and eighty kilos on his back.

The one-time officer extended the lever into a T-handled tow bar. "Shall we?" he suggested to the others.

But as Danny followed Blegan and young Slade, he swept his eyes around the courtyard. It was filled with men and equipment and arrogance. Pritchard had been a staff officer for a decade and Hammer's heir apparent for over a year. It was still easy to recall the days when he had been only a blower captain himself. The days in which Danny Pritchard's decisions involved no more than how to kill the most men in the shortest time.

*

CHAPTER TWENTY-FOUR

"And with one shot he kills it!" said Pretorius to the men who shared the dinner table with him and Slade. "Bam! Right into the gill chamber."

Chesson and Leaf, the other two members of the crew, smiled. The men maintained the filter lines; programmed the extrusion circuits depending on what the filters were bringing in; and more than occasionally disposed of the larger forms of sea-life when the rhythm and scent of the filters drew beasts to the station.

On Tethys, as almost universally on water oceans, the vegetation was mostly one-celled and the herbivores scarcely more complex. Virtually every life form big enough to be seen with the naked eye was carnivorous. Those carnivores ranged very much larger indeed, and not all of the Tethian varieties were toothless filter-feeders like the largest whales of Earth.

"Look," said Slade in more embarrassment than pride at the subject, "it was one shot after the beggar surfaced; but it was three before that had missed him under water. Don't know about you, Piet, but I was getting a mite nervous about a five-round clip and no reload."

"You'll get used to the angles, Soldier," Leaf said. He waved a rock-cruncher limb with a flag of muscle dangling from the joint. "I remember when the shells didn't have guidance units and you had to allow for deflection as well as refraction."

"Via, but it's been a long time since I ate one of these," said Slade as he forked another mouthful of cruncher himself. He wanted to change the subject; and besides, what he was saying was no more than the truth. "My old man always said nobody eats like a Councilor except the men who fish for the Councilor."

"I tell you, Soldier," said Chesson morosely. He was the youngest of the four by a decade; an eel-like, sharp-faced man. "You're eating a curst sight better than anybody's sending to Slade House this month past."

Leaf and Pretorius looked askance at their fellow, but Chesson plowed on bitterly. "Nobody minds sending a prime catch to the master, do they? Always been proud to, we have. Master Thomas knew he'd never had a better crew than the boys at Station Six. Isn't that so?"

Chesson glared around the table. The others nodded. "But there's no bloody good to that now, is there? Master Teddy can't take care of himself, much less us, and the Mistress—well, she's got some choice as to where she wants to sell herself, and no curst other choice in the world. That's a fact."

"Dyson, I suppose?" Slade said as if he were still concentrating on his meal.

For a moment, the only sound was that of the equipment washing itself down in the pump room. The filter lines were flushed and closed down at night. There was no safe or practical way to police them after dark. Temporarily-increased production would not make up for the certain damage when adult orcs or knife-jaws decided to make a meal of the lines.

Pretorius said, "No, it's not just him." The foreman took a second helping of potatoes in white sauce. "It's the whole Council, all forty of them."

"Thirty-nine," Leaf corrected.

"Whatever," the foreman snapped. More soberly, he continued. "Took 'em all together. Could easy enough have let Master Teddy take the Council seat when Master Thomas was killed. But no, set up a guardianship—the boy's nineteen! Via! I was captain of a catcher boat when I was nineteen. And then they hand the guardianship to Dyson, and every bloody thing to bloody Dyson."

"Bastard squeezes his people," said Chesson as he glared at his plate. "They say, blazes, what's it matter who sits on his butt in the House? You see them maybe twice in your life, so who cares what all they do to each other? But it's not true. If this was a Dyson plant—" he waved around the room and toward the packaging units beyond the wall—"there'd be a guard sitting with us to make sure we ate common rations. And none of the equipment out there'd have been replaced in thirty years."

Slade looked at the hard, weather-stained faces around the table. "Never heard much good about the Dysons myself," he said. He was trying to control the shudder of anger that swept him as he thought of the past. "But that strikes me as crazy. Bad business, let alone being a son of a bitch. I may not've run a Council House—" barely true—"but I don't guess it's a lot different from a company of mercs. You don't have to spring for every bit of hardware comes on the market. But if you run your plant down, buy junk or don't replace it, you aren't competing anymore."

Slade smiled, an expression as grim as anything anger had brought to the faces of the other three men. "Of course," the tanker concluded, "the business I was in you got your ass blown away too. I guess that's different from sea products."

"Might be a change Tethys'd be better off seeing," said Chesson. He gave a black look at the rocket guns racked by the door, ready in an emergency.

"Folks aren't bastards because that's profitable," said Pretorius, "though they may tell themselves that's why. They're bastards because they were born that way. And—" he looked around challengingly— "as long as I've lived, I don't know of anybody who was better off for being a bastard in the long run."

"Nor me," echoed Leaf. Even Chesson nodded agreement, though there was nothing in the younger man's face to suggest that he fully understood his foreman's point.

"So sure," Pretorius continued, "Dyson isn't a businessman the like of any Slade right back to the Settlement—and it isn't that the Slades couldn't show a hard hand when the need was."

Nods all around, Don Slade joining the others. His lips were stiff and his face still.

"But Dyson has the Council," said Pretorius, "and I suppose that means he has us in a few days or so. After all, who is there to stop him?"

"Who indeed?" muttered Don Slade as he clenched his great right hand.

"Well, Major Pritchard," said Marilee Slade, "Coon Blegan— you've met him, my son's . . . companion—"

"Nothing wrong with the word bodyguard," said Danny Pritchard mildly. He had seated himself when the woman offered him a chair, but she continued to pace the Trophy Room. Even flat-footed, she was taller than he was anyway.

"The word implies that we need bodyguards," Marilee said. "That Tethys is no longer a civilized world." When Pritchard made no response but a smile, the woman continued. "At any rate, Coon says I should hire your Colonel Hammer to clear undesirable elements off Tethys. I suppose you agree with that?"

She was not really hostile toward *him,* Danny decided. She was just very frustrated in general. Very possibly Marilee had watched his arrival through the window now behind her, and her subconscious preferred to over-compensate for the embarrassment she must feel.

Aloud Pritchard said, "Well, I might disagree on moral grounds if I thought it would work, ah, madam. But since I never *have* known it to work in circumstances like yours on Tethys, I'll pretend to be a practical man and disagree on practical terms instead."

The tall woman paused in mid-stride as her brain correlated the words her ears had heard a moment before. She looked at the man who lounged at ease, smiling at her. "Major—" she began in a tone more diffident than that of her angry assurance an instant previous.

"Please," said Danny Pritchard. "That was Alois' little joke, I'm sure, when he announced I was coming. Mister Pritchard. Or Danny, which I'd prefer. But I'm not a soldier anymore."

Marilee sat down with the abruptness of a gun returning to battery. She laughed as she looked out the window through which she could see nothing but sky from her present low angle. "Well," she said, "Danny, I suppose you'd better explain that. I hadn't expected to hear from a mercenary that force doesn't accomplish anything."

"Ex-mercenary," Pritchard corrected. The smile was back. "And force accomplishes a lot of things. They just aren't the ones you want here. Bring in the Slammers and we kick ass for as long as you pay us. Six months, a year. And we kick ass even if the other side brings in mercs of their own—which they'll do—but that's not a problem, not if you've got us." Unit pride lasted even after the unit's work became a matter of distaste. Pride beamed now from Danny Pritchard's face, and his hand caressed a tank that only his mind could see.

"So," the man went on. He got up without thinking about the action because he was focused on plans, on possibilities. "There's what? Three hundred thousand people on Tethys?"

Marilee's eyes narrowed. "On the Council Islands, about. There's a lot more in little holdings on the unclaimed islands, but I don't think anyone can be sure of numbers."

"So," Pritchard repeated. The word was his equivalent of the Enter key when his mind was computing possibilities. "You want to kill fifty kay? Fifty thousand people, let's remember they're people for the moment."

"I don't *want* to kill anybody!" the woman snapped. She swung abruptly to her feet again. Her boots rapped on the inlaid floor over which her visitor's heels had glided unheard. "I don't even want to kill Bev Dyson. I grew up with him, after all, I . . . maybe he did kill my husband. But I don't want to know that for sure. And I don't want *him* killed."

"You see," said Danny Pritchard, as if he had not heard his companion expose a part of herself that she had not known existed, "if we go in quick and dirty, the only way that has a prayer of working is if we get them all. If we get everybody who opposes you, everybody related to them, everybody who called them master—everybody."

"They aren't all dangerous!" Marilee shouted. She turned to the wall of trophies and went on in nearly as loud a voice. "They aren't any of them dangerous, except maybe a few. What are you talking about?" She spun back to Pritchard.

The ex-soldier nodded in agreement. "They're not dangerous now, but they will be after the killing starts. Believe me—" he raised a hand to forestall another protest— "I've seen it often enough. Not all of them, but one in ten, one in a hundred. One in a thousand's enough when he blasts your car down over the ocean a year from now. You'll see. It changes people, the killing does. Once it starts, there's no way to stop it but all the way to the end. If you figure to still live here on Tethys."

"M—Danny!" the woman said. "I told you, I don't *want* killing. Why do you keep saying that?"

"What do you think the Slammers do, milady?" asked Danny Pritchard. His grin was wide as a demon's, as cruel as the muzzle of the guns he remembered using so well. "Work magic? We kill, and we're good at it, *bloody* good. You call the Slammers in to solve your problems here and you'll be able to cover the Port with the corpses. I guarantee it. I've *done* it, milady. In my time."

He was still grinning. Marilee Slade gasped and turned away. The blast-scarred skull of a knife-jaw was on the wall behind her. The yellowing skull was two meters along the line of the teeth, a record even for the days of the Settlement when the creature had savaged a guard tower and three men. For a moment, the knife-jaw looked less ruthless than did the man who had seemed so mild until he began describing options.

"All right, Mister Pritchard," Marilee said to her clenched hands. "My son says we're better off letting the law take its course, even when that course is against us. I—I don't think I believe that. I *know* Tom's death wasn't, wasn't chance. But I didn't mean to bring in an army, either, even without what you just said. I suppose we'll let Bev have his way, then, and—hope for the best."

She shook herself. "I'm sorry," she said. "I didn't mean to be ungracious. Will you have refreshments? A stim cone?" She stepped toward the refrigerated cart resting against a sidewall.

"No, I'm fine," said Danny Pritchard. His face had loosened from its rictus. Now he sat again in the chair from which thought had propelled him. "You see," he continued mildly, "using the Slammers on your problem is like settling a tank on a nut to crack it. I . . . I'm not the sort to say, roll over and play dead to injustice. Even when injustice has the law behind it. You were hoping Don would come home. It's for him—and for me and for the Colonel, there's a lot of us who owe Don—it's for him I came here. We pay our debts. But what did *you* have in mind for him, for your— brother-in-law?"

Marilee continued to face her visitor. Her hand crept up unconsciously to caress the trophy skull above her. The cranium between the two eyesockets had been punched away by the shot which killed the creature. It had been a 10 cm bolt from a gun like those on the drones in the courtyard, anti-tank weapons really and the only medicine that could dependably put paid to the monsters which disputed the Settlement. Nothing like them threatened the Council Islands anymore. The beasts bred and hunted elsewhere, now, the progeny of the creatures which had survived. Natural selection had proved to the most savage natives of Tethys that Man was still more savage.

Marilee thought of herself and of her son. The awareness was not a happy one.

"I thought perhaps if they saw him," the tall woman said aloud. She was trying to find words to answer a question she had herself avoided asking. "I thought, they can ignore me, ignore Teddy. They could even ignore Tom because he was too *good,* too curst good to treat them the way his grandfather would have done. Maybe even his father."

Marilee took her hand from the skull and laced her fingers together. She bent them back against one another fiercely. "But they couldn't ignore Don, could they? And besides . . ." she added, her eyes drawn to the window but her mind drifting far beyond the present, "I never really wanted him to leave. Whatever I said."

"Well, knowing Don," said Danny Pritchard from his chair, "I'd expect him back just about any time now."

"He mustn't come now," the woman blurted. "It's too late. The Council's committed. They'd *kill* him."

"*They* would?" said Danny Pritchard. "Those down in the yard?" The professional began to laugh. "They'll learn something about status in Hell if they try, milady. They will that."

CHAPTER TWENTY-FIVE

The slideway rose and fell like a tank racing over broken ground. Danny Pritchard had only a plastic bucket and not the hundred-odd tons of tank armor between him and danger, however.

The sea lifted and ebbed beneath him at no fixed period; or rather, at a period set by as many variables as a sun-spot sequence, theoretically calculable but for human practice lost in uncertainty. The water was a lucent gray-green, metallic. In it moved blurs of other colors, jetsam sucked from the current to be filtered and compacted by type in the tubes running back to the building on the shore.

The concentration of microlife and the leakage of juices from the processing drew larger beasts upstream. They could be seen playing as black shadows about the tubing—two meters long, three meters; one of them five meters at least, Danny would swear. It looked as slippery as a flame and as ravenous. No danger to the filter lines, perhaps; but sure death to any landsman who slipped from the bucket into the water.

Don Slade looked up, mildly startled as the bucket slid to a halt at his guard station. The rails and the catwalk supporting them stretched further out to the posts manned by Chesson and Leaf. Each of the men were responsible for five hundred meters of line. Slade had been bending over the rail. He held a rocket gun in his right hand as if it were a giant pistol. In Slade's left, when he straightened so that it could be seen, was a length of twelve-centimeter tubing. He had been prodding it down into the water.

"Hey, snake," Slade called cheerfully. "Come watch me improve my technique." The tanker bent over the rail again.

Pritchard walked carefully to the bigger man. The filter lines, with the platforms and slideway above them, did not attempt to remain rigid in the sea. Strong as the lines were, the sea was stronger. If the apparatus did not give and flow with the moods of the water, the water would smash it with the casual ease of a vandal with a shop window. Knowing the necessity for flexibility did not prevent the motion from making Danny Pritchard queasy. "All right, trooper," the Adjutant said as he joined Slade at the rail. "What've you got—Via!"

The thing that twisted up through the water had a long nose-spike and ragged teeth the color of blood. Like a trap slamming, it struck the tube Slade used as a lure. The tube sprang upward. It was almost wrenched from Slade's grip. At the surface of the water, refraction bent the white tubing sharply. A meter below that hinge, the jaws were grinding the tough plastic into drifting motes.

Slade fired. When the shell struck it the sea fountained, reaching for the gun muzzle with lambent clarity. Then the water boiled red as the charge blew apart the carnivore's head. The nose-spike and part of the upper jaw lifted from the explosion, then splashed back into the water.

The creature's body began to drift, still writhing, beneath the filter line. Part of the cloud of blood preceding the carcass had been sucked into the line already with the plankton.

Slade pulled up his ragged-ended lure. "You see," he said, "I know where the end of the tube is." He tapped the plastic with the muzzle of his gun. "So I shoot for that, where I *feel* the tube is, and that teaches me how much to hold off when there's only what I can see the next time."

"They hit on this?" Danny asked, tapping the white plastic. He had expected the tube to have a soft, greasy feel, but it rang like steel beneath his fingernail. This was pressure tubing for repairs to the compaction segment.

"They do when I wire some meat onto it," the tanker said with a grin. "Hungry as some of those beggars act, they might anyway. Shows you what greed gets you.

"And—" his face cooled—"that brings us to the question of Bev Dyson, doesn't it? If they say anything as bad about him at the House as they do down here, then I regret nobody called me home before. I started a job near thirty years ago with a wrench, and it sounded like it's past time to finish it."

Pritchard stretched. He laced his fingers behind his back and lifted his arms as high as he could. With his eyes closed against the hugeness of the sea, the lift and fall of the platform was even soothing. "I'm the honored visitor touring the estate," he said while still bent forward. "Your sister-in-law loaned me a car." Pritchard straightened and looked at his big friend squarely. "Tough lady, but she needs help. What she doesn't need is you barging in and getting your ass blown away, snake."

"I said you were in charge, Danny," Slade said mildly. The big man scanned the sensor read-outs on his board. One of them was flickering orange, a beast rippling to and from a distant portion of filter line, nothing to be concerned about as yet. Slade's fingers pulled a rocket from a bandolier loop and slid it into the loading gate of the weapon. "Tell me what you think needs doing, and I'll see about getting it done."

"There's a Council meeting in two days," said Pritchard. "They're gathering in person at the House, the whole Council. Going to decide on the guardianship of your nephew Teddy."

"Council's in Dyson's pocket," Slade said without emotion. He nodded toward the station, though two of the men were actually downline of Slade's post. "What the crew here says is just what I saw myself. The Port's supposed to be neutral ground. Dyson put his own men in and my brother—"

Slade's big hand squeezed fiercely on the alloy barrel of his gun—"let him do it, the. . . . Well. So now they're all afraid to burp for fear their cargo'll get looted or deep-sixed, inbound and out both. He's got the votes he needs, just like he did on that stupid business of me being the real heir. Cop!"

Danny looked at the bigger man sharply. "You could be, you

know," Pritchard said. "Marilee swears that your brother told her that the night your father died. That your father had whispered it to him, just at the end."

"And *I* swear, my friend," replied Don Slade, "that it's cop even if it's true. Look, what do seventeen minutes one way or the other matter, for running this, running *Tethys*—that's what we Slades have done for six generations, Council be damned. You think if I'd really wanted it, that I'd have let a few minutes stand in the way? Blood and Martyrs, snake, *you* know me better than that!"

Pritchard laughed. "Well, you were younger, then," he said.

Slade grinned back. "Yeah, and meaner'n a knife-jaw, my friend. Via, remember that bar on Emporion? The bouncer thought I was just blowing air till my tank came through the wall!"

Both men laughed and linked arms. "Well," said Pritchard, "let's say you rode in to the House on a supply truck tomorrow. I've seen what you looked like before you left Tethys: hair to your belt. I'm willing to bet that without that and the beard, maybe a little dye and editing, there's nobody you'll see who's going to recognize you this long after. Not if you got through the Port. Now, there's likely to be a problem in the yard itself, but I think . . ."

Danny Pritchard continued to talk in a calm, professional voice while the big man beside him nodded. Overhead, fairy skimmers folded their gossamer wings and dived into the rich sea life around the platform.

Slade simply noted their delicate motions. He knew that he could handle moving targets without any need to practice on these.

CHAPTER TWENTY-SIX

Fadel Buckalew, a Steward's Assistant, drove his provisions truck with a hard-handed determination. He managed to ground the steel skirts jarringly on the shingle a number of times, though without achieving more than a moderate speed. Slade had never claimed to be much of a driver himself, but at least the tanker did not regard air cushion vehicles with an angry hostility the way the young Houseman did.

"So," Buckalew said, "old Piet tells me you met the Mad Dog and that's why he's sending you to the House. That a fact?"

"Something close," said the tanker. He knew that Pretorius had never referred to his "Master Donald" as Mad Dog Slade. "Came in on the same ship as a visitor to the House, guy named Pritchard. In Transit I'd mentioned meeting a Captain Slade of Hammer's Regiment on his way back to Tethys himself. When Pritchard got to the House and heard how things were, he thought I ought to go tell the Mistress my story. The foreman thought so too."

The truck ground its left side against the rocks beneath the layer of creeping native vegetation. Though some of the nastier forms of sea life bred on Tethys' scattered islands, there was nothing native to the land which was significantly developed, even the plants. Terran vegetation had been imported, but it grew over the rocky soil only where encouraged: around the manors of the Councilors, and in small plots, among the dwellings of lesser folk.

The sea supplied roughage as it did protein through processing plants like the one Slade was leaving. When people grew vegetables, it was for the sake of luxury or whim, not need. The grass plots, though, served a need: that of Earth-evolved humans to see something green that was not synthetic nor the sea's metallic choice of dress for the moment.

"Well, it's none of my business," the Houseman said, "but if I was you, I'd go back to sucking seawater. Not that *I* would," he added hastily as he realized that he had just suggested a position of basic labor was not beneath him.

"But I mean," Buckalew went on, "you're safe back there—" He gestured. The truck slewed and grated. "But if you go up to the House, meddling with Council affairs, well . . . the Mistress may be glad to see you, I don't say she wouldn't be. But there's some wouldn't, and you'll meet them before you do her."

"Yeah," said Slade, "I was kind of hoping you might drop me around in back."

Slade was uncomfortable with the conversation and with his outfit. The Station Six crew had been adamant that nobody in coveralls would be allowed into Slade House now unless the Mistress led them in by the hand. Master Thomas had been a stickler for proprieties, Pretorius said. Chesson was young, but even he could remember the free and easy days when labor was nothing to be ashamed of and working for the Slades was all you needed to talk to the Councilor.

Don's father had not been a gun-toting brawler like his own progenitor, a throwback to the harsh days of the Settlement. Neither, however, had he stood on ceremony with those who served him. The tanker found it interesting that his brother had insisted on such punctillio, when according to that code—and his own belief—he had no right to be called Councilor at all.

Well, people did strange things, and tanks did strange things. Don Slade had learned to deal with some of the strangeness without bothering himself too much with causes.

Dealing with the problem meant, in this case, wearing the non-service clothes Danny Pritchard sent along for Slade to wear. The tunic was russet, with puffy sleeves gathered at the wrists. It was big enough for Slade's shoulders and would have held two of him at the waist. The slacks were doe-skin, again ample in the waist and thighs—but so tight when his calf muscles bulged that the tanker had considered slitting them up from the cuffs.

Slade wore the boots he had awakened with at the Port. They fit; and he might soon have need for footwork.

Buckalew had taken his time about answering his passenger's implied question. "Well, I tell you," the Houseman said with a side-long glance which shifted the truck, "I'm sorry, and you not used to the House and all . . . but it'd be worth my teeth at the best if I got smart about where I pulled in. Especially with the load I'm carrying from your buddies in Six."

"What's in the load?" Slade asked in surprise.

"Nothing, that's what's in the bloody load!" the Houseman snapped. "Cans of process, that's what we've got. Via! I know and everybody at the House knows that they're bringing in crunchers and that they're taking heart fillets out of duopods—all the good stuff, just like always. But what do they send *me* back with? Process! Compressed protein. Compressed flotsam! One of these days a load of boys from the House is going to come see your buddies, and they're going to wish they'd changed their ways before."

"Well, I don't know," said the tanker without emphasis. "I'd say the crew at Six would be easier folks to talk to than to threaten. True of a lot of people, of course. Been reminding myself of that for going on twenty years."

"You see how it is," said Buckalew. He waved—Slade cringed and the truck rasped—toward the tall outline of the House on the horizon. "I'm in enough trouble, coming back with nothing but turtle cop. If I drop you at Service, they'll be sure I off-loaded anything worth eating there too. You see."

"They will," the tanker repeated. He flexed his fingers, one hand against the other. "Well, I guess I'll see pretty soon."

"Come on, Bucky," crackled the voice through the dash speaker. There was a rush of static or laughter. The voice then continued, "We know it's you, but come on up where we can watch."

The Houseman was shivering. The truck hovered at idle, millimeters off the ground. Its cab was pointed at the closed gate in the three-meter wall.

Buckalew touched the key of the microphone/speaker, a bolt-on set not integral with the vehicle. "Master Hensen," Buckalew said, "you know I'm not . . . could you maybe let me in by the gate this once? You know I don't. . . ."

Buckalew let his thumb slip from the key. The speaker roared, "Get your butt up here, goon, or we'll come and find you!"

"They make you jump the wall to get in?" Slade asked.

Vehicles built for use on Tethys normally had enough extra fan capacity to fly without depending on ground effect, the bubble of air trapped between the ground and the vehicle's skirts. Otherwise they could not be driven over Tethys' omnipresent seas without the likelihood of disastrous attack by the larger predators. The supply truck was heavily laden, however. The ride from Station Six had made it clear that the Assistant Steward did not have the greater skills needed to safely lift the truck from its cushion.

"Well . . ." muttered Buckalew.

"Via, man," Slade said, speaking the obvious. "You'll kill us both if you try that!"

Buckalew nodded miserably as he fed power to the fans. "I know," he said. "I've been buying my way off these runs till today." The truck took a tentative hop and yawed its left front into the gravel.

Slade closed the throttles. His hand gripped the knobs and slid them back as if the Houseman were not trying to fight the pressure. "Get out," Slade said. His voice was thick and irregular, like bubbles boiling through tar.

"Come on, Bucky, we're *waiting* for you," the speaker called.

"W-what?" Buckalew whimpered.

"Get *out!*" Slade repeated. "I'm taking this mother in!"

The tanker reached past Buckalew for the door, unlatched it, and thrust the Houseman out of the cab. Slade moved his own big body under the controls. The speaker started to make another demand. Slade's right forearm crumpled the box into hissing somnolence.

Throttles, attitude adjustments. The Houseman was backing away from the vehicle with a frightened look on his face. Slade dialed up the thrust. Fan pitch and nacelle attitude were not crucial safety factors when operating by ground effect, because the air cushion balanced irregularities and averaged the total power. On true lift, however, the fans required individual settings unless the load were perfectly balanced. This truckload of supplies assuredly was not balanced.

Slade boosted ten centimeters on instinct, over-corrected for a bump on the tail skirt, and lifted over the wall in a curve that was graceful but considerably faster than he had intended. Slade wasn't much of a driver, that was the Lord's simple truth, but he was the right man at the controls just now.

"All right, Bucky!" crowed the loud-hailer on the helmet of a man in crimson. There were dozens of men in the courtyard, backed cautiously against the walls and the line of parked air cars to watch the show. Most of the observers were clapping, though the sound of that and their hooting was lost in the rush of the fans at high load. Slade had neither the time nor the inclination to check the varied liveries below, but there was one man in Slade blue—with a slash of crimson down either leg.

The tanker was even with the upper windows of the House and the Council Hall. His truck was quivering in polarized reflection to either side. The man with the loud-hailer was against the House door, where an armored drone protected him to either side; a pity, but—

"Well, come *on,* Bucky," the loud-hailer called. "All you've got left's the easy part, right? Chop your throttle and I promise you'll come down!"

"Right, fella," Slade muttered as he cut power fifteen percent to the four front fans and cocked the left rear nacelle to the side. Adrenalin made the tanker's arms tremble, and his mind was icy with rage.

The truck slid down a column of thrust. Its rear end was slewing around a pivot point just forward of the cab. Slade could still not hear the hangers-on nor could he see the men among the parked air cars as the truck rotated down toward them with the majesty of Juggernaut's Carriage. The drooping left skirt caught first with a ping and a shudder. Then the whole laden back end crashed along the line of cars.

The lightly-built luxury vehicles disintegrated at the impact. The truck's skirts were steel, flexible only at the edges. They were meant for the sort of rough work on the shingle that Buckalew had been giving them an hour before.

At the end of the line of cars, Slade twitched up his throttles and hopped awkwardly aloft again. The crumpled back end of the truck brushed the corner of the House as it turned. He shouldn't have been greedy about the last car or two . . . but it was with less damage than Slade had expected that he thumped the truck down at last in the center of the courtyard. One of the fans was singing where its blades touched a twisted duct.

Slade shut off all power. He felt for the moment—only the moment, and he knew that—as if he too had been shut down after a successful operation.

There were blue and orange flickers in the shadows which the lowering sun cast across the courtyard. Electrical fires had started in several of the mangled vehicles. With his fans shut off, the tanker could hear the screams of the men pinched and battered when the cars slid from the metal-rending impact of the truck.

There were screams of rage as well, from those who did not have their injuries to occupy them. The Dyson minion with the loud-hailer had lost his helmet and was cowering against the door. A group of men were rushing toward the truck from the other side, however. Three of them wore knives and Dyson livery. The fourth was the one Danny had warned about, Durotige, though his nunchaku was hidden for the moment beneath the tail of his blue tunic. Durotige was a big man and hugely aroused at the moment.

"The Lord eat your *eyes*, Buckalew!" Durotige shouted through the dust which still cavorted around the truck. "Or I will!"

Slade opened the cab door before the other men could reach it. He stood on the entry step, gaining from it a height advantage he would not otherwise have had over the turncoat. "Buckalew's not here," Slade said. "You want to eat *my* eyes, friend?"

In Slade's right hand was a length of control rod, half a meter of chrome steel brought from the Station. It rang as he slapped it against his left palm.

The four men pulled up very abruptly. One of them made a motion toward his knife. He thought the better of it.

Durotige did not lose his mental balance for more than a second or two. "Sure, you're tough with that in your hands," the turncoat said. "But you're not man enough to fight me without it, are you?"

It was a dangerous gamble . . . but the situation was dangerous any way you sliced it, and that was nothing new to Slade.

"Just you and me?" the tanker asked. He waved the rod in a glittering arc, taking in the men with Durotige and the others moving from cover now that the danger of the truck had passed. "And you don't pull a knife?"

"Hey, buddy," called someone in green and lemon yellow, "you're in enough trouble already. Don't get your head bashed besides."

A pair of Dyson retainers from the clot around Durotige moved in on the man who had spoken. He backed, but not quickly enough to keep the men in crimson from seizing him from either side. One of them snarled, "Butt *out,* fishbrain," and punched the speaker in the ribs.

"Just you and me," Durotige promised loudly. He spread his arms wide and waved his bare hands toward Slade. "And with nothing we don't carry right now—soon as you throw down that rod. Just what we stand in. Guess you've got a few years on me, but you look fit enough. Anyhow, it was your idea."

Slade smiled. He rolled the rod back and forth on his palm for a moment. Then he slipped it behind him, onto the seat as he stepped down from the truck. "You're on," Slade said, knowing that in this instant all four of them might pile on him to wash his life away in the dust with their knives and their numbers.

The House door was spilling out far more people than had been in the courtyard when the truck set down. Not liverymen alone, but Councilors, at least a dozen of them. The Council Members were notable for their studied avoidance of any form of dress that might be taken for livery. House colors were for retainers. Many Councilors affected ancient formal wear: stark blacks and whites, and starkly-uncomfortable cuts.

The shattered vehicles drew some of the attention, but that would keep. The two big men now moving from threats to action focused the eyes of both Councilors and retainers.

The Dyson men did not jump Slade with Durotige. They hopped away, well aware of the amount of area which the nunchaku commanded. One of the liverymen guffawed.

Durotige backed from Slade's advance also. He obviously wanted his victim to be too far from the rod to recover it when he learned how he had been tricked.

Just for a moment, Slade thought that his opponent really might intend to settle matters with his fists. Then Durotige reached back, under the flapping tail of his tunic, and slid out his linked flails with the air of a successful conjuror. "Just what we stand in," he repeated. The Dyson retainers cackled in glee at a safe distance, though they were closer to the action than were the other spectators.

"Why Durotige," Slade said. "You didn't *tell* me about the numbchucks."

Durotige blinked as he realized that his opponent knew his name. Before all the implications of that could penetrate, Slade threw himself into a broad imitation of a karate stance.

The tanker's views on personal combat were those he had heard from his grandfather thirty-odd years earlier. You don't hit a man with your bare hand unless you're naked and they've nailed your feet to the ground. No one in the crowd knew that, however, least of all Durotige. The turncoat grinned and moved in with his weapon flickering.

For the benefit of his audience, Durotige executed a series of passes back and forth between his straddled legs. The nunchaku shifted, spinning, from hand to hand in perfect rhythm. It was the sort of nonsense that could have cost Durotige his weapon . . . except that the men in crimson were ready to toss it back should a slip of the hand send it skittering loose.

Slade shouted, "Hai!" and stamped his right foot. It was simply an effort to end his opponent's posturing. The tanker carried his hands up, with the fingers extended as if they were capable of smashing bricks. He had sometimes vaguely wished that he did have the training for formal unarmed combat, but it had never been worth his time. There were sledge hammers for smashing bricks, and for more serious matters—

Durotige made his move. His right hand fed the nunchaku behind his back and over his left shoulder where the left hand took it. Instead of executing another shimmering bit of jugglery, the turncoat lashed out in an overarm cut at Slade's skull. He held one wooden flail by the base. The slashing attack extended the paired flails the length of both and of Durotige's long left arm. It was virtually too fast for Slade to have dodged, had he wanted to.

Instead, the tanker blocked the whirring club with his right forearm.

The blow cracked like lightning close enough to touch. The outer flail rebounded as it was supposed to do. Because the link was not rigid, none of the shock was transmitted to the hand in which Durotige held his weapon.

The turncoat smiled in the certainty that he had shattered his opponent's arm. The sound had been wrong, but there was no time now for nuances, the blow *had* to have been effective. Durotige recovered and struck precisely the same swinging blow again.

The pain of Slade's radius splintered among the blood and soft tissues should have left the tanker open for the follow-up, despite its lack of finesse. Slade was grinning. Durotige noticed that only as the nunchaku cracked again on the right forearm which reflex should have protected at any cost after it was broken.

Slade's left hand caught Durotige's and clamped it firmly to the baton it held. The tanker's snatching motion had started as the nunchaku swung. The motion did not disintegrate in pain as expected when the second blow landed. The turncoat found himself held, face to face with his opponent. The flails dangled uselessly beside them.

Grinning like Heilgate, Don Slade swung his right forearm as if it were a club. Durotige caught the blow with his own free hand. The hand-bones crackled. All the strength went out of the turncoat's arm. The blow, only partially blocked, chunked against his skull. Durotige sagged forward with a bloody welt across his left temple.

Slade's grip would not let the turncoat fall. The tanker hit him again, still with the forearm and not a fist. Durotige's skull rang like an imploding vacuum-bottle. Slade thrust his opponent away to fall, the body liquid, the head staining the dust.

With a quick motion, Don Slade retrieved the nunchaku which had fallen with their owner. None of the onlookers had moved closer when the fight climaxed. The nearest faces, those of the Dyson men, gaped in amazement. To Slade's hormone-hopping glance, the men were little more than pale blurs on crimson blurs, the status they would retain until they moved toward him themselves.

The tanker gripped the base of a flail in either hand. He twisted the weapon against itself so that the three links of chain were taut. "Well?" said Slade. His voice echoed despite the size of the courtyard. "Who's next?"

Using torsion to do what no human muscles, not even his own, could do in a straight pull, Slade parted the flails and hurled them in opposite directions. One of them clacked above the door of the House.

"Bring that man to me," ordered a cold voice from the silence. Lights pinned Slade, though they were not really necessary in the present dusk.

Slade turned. Time had not robbed Beverly Dyson's voice of its familiarity, nor of the swelling rage that it fed in Slade's belly.

Councilor Dyson and a trio of liverymen had come from the Council Hall. To see the fight from that angle, the quartet had to walk around the truck grounded in the middle of the yard. Two of the retainers now flared handlights at Slade from ten meters away. Sidescatter showed that the third liveryman gripped a case. Not even the most ignorant could imagine the case held an information system and not a gun. Dyson himself was behind the lights and shrouded by their glare. He was a slim figure, as cool as his voice.

Slade's right sleeve was torn from the blows it had taken and returned. He jerked the dangling fabric free with his left hand. The length of pressure tubing which covered the right forearm gleamed in the strong lights. There was a smear of blood near the wrist, but the nunchaku had not marked the rigid plastic. A single toothmark winked just above the line at which the tanker had cut the section from his lure.

"I said *bring him,*" Beverly Dyson repeated in a voice with more life than before. Slade, who was expecting the next words to call a spray of gunfire, was amazed to hear the Councilor continue, "Don't worry, my good man. I have an offer for you."

"No," said Slade. He turned quickly, smoothly, a shark twisting against a fool who would grasp its tail.

The gunman might be ordered to fire or might not. It did not matter whether Slade faced the blast. The men who had accompanied Durotige were two paces closer, now. Their confidence had been in their master's promise of good treatment, not in their own numbers. Now they scuttled back so quickly that one stumbled on Durotige's outflung hand. The turncoat still lay in the dust. He was breathing stertorously. Blood oozed from his matted scalp, his nose, and his left ear.

"No," repeated a clear voice. Slade's own refusal had been the rumble of a beast. It had been intelligible only by its tone and the right fist clenched to grip the armoring tube.

A party of four was striding from the House. The lights now silhouetting Slade fell brightly across the newcomers. Marilee was half a step in front. Her face was as firm and clear as the denial she had just spoken. She was not the girl Slade had left on his brother's arm at the Port, but she was perfectly the woman from his dream of Hell.

The youth must be Teddy. He walked to one side, tight where his mother was whip-supple. Danny Pritchard was on the woman's other side, with Coon Blegan beside him. Blegan pushed away one

of the crimson toughs who had not moved in time; but it was Danny
Pritchard who carried the submachine gun.

He did not attempt to hide the weapon. Pritchard's index finger
lay beside the trigger guard, not in it. To Slade's practiced eye, that
was sure proof that no bluff was intended. There was one up the
spout, and the safety was off.

Dyson's men might carry guns: despite the law, and as a symbol
that their power was beyond the law. The Slammers used their guns
to kill, with a frequency no one could keep track of, and with an
effectiveness that Danny Pritchard himself would as soon have
forgotten.

"This man came as a visitor to my House," said Marilee in the
same clear voice as before. She spoke toward Dyson but loudly
enough that every one in the courtyard could hear her. "I won't have
him harassed."

The woman stepped past the tanker to one side while Pritchard
passed to the other. The principle, not the individual, was first in her
mind.

And dear Lord, did *none* of Slade's closest acquaintances
recognize him after twenty hard years?

"That man has a gun," said Councilor Dyson in genuine surprise.

Slade turned to watch the confrontation of which he was no
longer a part. Dyson was pointing to Danny's weapon. The
Councilor himself had not moved, but his three retainers were
edging backward so that light played across their master as well as
themselves.

"And his clothes aren't red," retorted Marilee. "What's the
matter, Bev?"

"In the future, no trucks will land in this courtyard," said Teddy.
His voice was high and on the edge of control, but it was a man's
voice for all that. "It's dangerous. And anybody interfering with
trucks unloading properly will be expelled from the Estate. Do you
hear?"

"Put that away!" Dyson rasped to his liveryman, the one who
had half opened the case holding his own gun. "And put those curst
lights off!" the Councilor added as angrily to the other pair.

Dusk was darkness in the aftereffect of the glare. Dyson stepped forward, beyond his men but not so close to those facing him that he could be thought to be holding a normal conversation. "I don't know what you think you're about, Marilee," the Councilor said, "but it won't work in the Hall. Do you understand? There will be no guns in the Hall. None!"

"The Hall is the Council's business, Dyson," the woman replied. Her words cut through the twilight like lyre notes. "The House is mine. You and your rubbish are not to enter the House again. Good evening." Her heel and toe gouged the dust as she turned. "Gentlemen," she added cooly, "let us go inside."

The rank that Marilee had led to the confrontation returned as a file behind her to the House. Slade was the last man. He fought the impulse to throw back his shoulders as if better to absorb the shots that might still arrive.

Slade had found a good group of people back here.

CHAPTER TWENTY-SEVEN

The interior of Slade House had shrunk in the years he had been away. He would not have expected that. When Don Slade left Tethys, he had his full growth; but he had long been divorced from the life of the House in which he lived. The memories that lived when the earth spouted around him and the sky screamed hellfire were those of his childhood.

In memory the corridors were high and dimmed by mystery, not neglect. Rooms built to house the warriors of the Settlement now stored mementos of that harsh, vivid time. And through all the memories blazed the figure of Slade's grandfather, Devil Don, the Old Man; the craggy, powerful model for Slade's life.

The Old Man had surrendered the administrative duties of House and planet to his son as soon as the son could handle them. But while the duties had been his, the Old Man had performed them with the fierce skill he displayed whenever he forced himself into a business that he hated. In retirement, he fished and hunted across the seas of Tethys, brawling with men half his age. And he carried with him the grandson who bore his name, and whom he swore had been minted from the same die as himself.

The odd thing was that as Don grew older, he resembled his grandfather in no physical respect but his size . . . and for all that, the Old Man was right, was dead right. To copy his grandfather, Don let his hair and beard grow—into a black mass as different from the Old Man's white, silken locks as could be imagined. Brother Thomas cut his own fair hair short, but only surgery could have kept every acquaintance from remarking that he looked just like the Old Man.

As the party turned up the helical staircase just within the entrance, Coon Blegan paused to speak to the doorkeeper. "If you had any guts," Blegan whispered—Slade could hear him, but Teddy and surely Marilee could not—"you might even be good for something."

"Up yours, old man," said the natty-looking doorkeeper. He gestured with his shock rod, real as well as symbolic power.

Slade reached from behind and plucked the shock rod away. It was a baton of thumb-thick plastic half a meter long. Electrodes winked at either end. The doorkeeper yelped and tried to snatch the instrument back. Slade's left arm blocked the servant with no more effort than a wall would have displayed.

The doorkeeper's kiosk was cast concrete like the rest of the House's construction. Slade held the baton at its balance with equal portions extending to the thumb-side and heel-side of his hand. He punched upward toward the corner of the kiosk doorway, where the integral post and lintel met. The two ends of the baton took the impact. The instrument crunched into halves.

The tanker handed the pieces back to the doorkeeper with a courteous nod. "Yours, I believe, sir," he said.

Coon Blegan watched with a look of surmise that Slade had not meant to arouse. Pritchard had paused partway up the stairs, just in sight. Waiting, his weapon was unobtrusively at his side.

Most of those drawn into the courtyard were still there. They were fulminating over the damage to their vehicles or gazing with secret delight at the wreckage of some rival's car. The few who trooped babbling back within the House passed the tableau without noticing it. Even Slade's arm could have been a handshake from the angle past his body.

The doorkeeper took his baton back with a look of amazement as silent as the deftness with which it had been stripped from him. Slade gestured to Blegan. The old retainer grinned and proceeded up the stairs. The tanker followed, without a look back at the open-mouthed doorkeeper.

This was the family staircase. The door from it to the second floor on which the guests were lodged was locked. Slade had spent very little time in the family apartments on the third floor in the last years of his youth on Tethys. The tanker subconsciously expected changes. There were none, none he recognized, save for the size.

The staircase debouched into a walled entryway with a door to the corridor serving the remainder of the floor and a separate door to the Trophy Room which engrossed the quarter of the floor facing the courtyard and the Council Hall beyond.

Teddy was holding the Trophy Room door for Danny Pritchard. From within the room, Marilee said, "Mister Pritchard, Danny. I appreciate your presence tonight and the risk you ran. You were invaluable."

Danny did not move forward. When Slade reached the top of the stairs, he could see that the woman stood not beside the doorway but within it to block passage. "But you'll understand that I want to speak alone to the man who met my—brother-in-law returning."

"Of course," Danny said with a neutral smile. "I'll feel better for a hot bath after all that." He turned. When his back was to the mother and son, he winked at Slade.

"I'll stay, though," Teddy was saying. The anteroom was crowded. Slade and Blegan were big men, Pritchard not a small one. All of them were trying to keep a courteous distance from the family quarrel brewing.

"No, Edward," Marilee said. The edge in her voice was slight, but it was still out of line with anything which was overtly going on. "You have your duties. I'm sure many of our guests will be demanding compensation for damaged vehicles."

"Yes, I'll take care of that," the youth said with a dismissing gesture, "but Mother—"

"Teddy!"

Teddy's head jerked back as the tone slapped him. "Yes, Mother," he said in a subdued voice. "I'll be down in the Audience Room if you need me."

He squeezed past the big men at the stair head without noticing them as individuals.

So softly that even Slade could barely hear him, Blegan whispered in the tanker's ear, "I'm a fat old man, friend. But I wouldn't want anything to happen to the Mistress." Then the retainer turned to follow Teddy down the stairs.

Pritchard was already gone, toward his own suite among the family rooms. "Come here, Mister Holt," said Marilee as she stepped aside.

The Trophy Room had been intended as a museum of human valor rather than of the dangerous sea life of Tethys. The result had made it both. Because the only light in the room at present was the red glow through the west window, the skulls merged with their own shadows. That did not matter to Slade. He could have drawn every piece from memory, have labeled it, positioned it on the wall of his mind. Slade was a child again, walking softly in front of romance.

The glow-strip under the big window was not bright, but its light shocked Slade out of his reverie. His hand was extended, almost touching one of a pair of screw holes. They were below the level at which most of the trophies were mounted. The holes had been filled, and in the ebbing twilight they should have been invisible.

"Yes, there used to be another one there," said Marilee with detachment. She seated herself in the chair from which she had switched on the light. "A larval argus. My husband had it removed. He said it didn't fit with the others, only a larva."

"Yes," said Don Slade. "Not a—thing worthy of a hunter." He had squeezed shut his eyes, but that did not help. The pressure of the eyelids and muscles only forced the welling tears up faster.

"It wasn't exactly a hunting trophy," the woman said to Slade's back. "My brother-in-law—Captain Slade—was eating lunch with his grandfather on one of the islands in the Random Star. The argus must have just hatched. It crawled out and stabbed the Old Man in the small of the back. He just happened to be there, you see, but the defensive spines are quite dangerous. They paralyzed him."

"Yes, the spines can be nasty," said Slade thickly to the wall.

It had been a meter long and gleaming with the pearly iridescence of the eggshell still dragging behind it. Its eyes were broad patches on the exoskeleton, the color of fresh bruises. The spines along the lower edge of its carapace squirmed like a thorn hedge in a windstorm. Most of them were dripping yellow with venom, but some already were smeared with the Old Man's blood . . .

"Don killed it with his hands," the woman was saying. "He pulled it off his grandfather and pounded it to death on the ground. For weeks after that, they thought he might lose both his arms from what the spines did to him. He was seven years old, then."

"Yes," Slade repeated, "the spines can be nasty." He turned away very slowly. His face was under control again. The left shoulder of his tunic was damp where it had hunched to mop away the tear which had escaped. Not for a husk of lacquered chitin, and not for Slade's past youth. For the Old Man, who had mounted the larva with his own hands and, stiff himself with the aftereffects of the venom, had carried his delirious grandson into the Trophy Room to see it. "You wanted to question me, Mistress," said Don Slade.

"Sit down, Holt," the woman said with a brusque gesture. "I'm told that you've seen Captain Slade more recently than Mister Pritchard has."

Slade moved to the indicated bench. It was a low one at a discreet two meters from the seated woman. "Yes, Mistress," he said. "He was on Desmo, landed there from an Alayan ship."

"The same Alayan ship that brought you and Mister Pritchard to Tethys?" the woman interjected.

Slade looked up sharply. The trophy wall had stunned him into a quiescent state which fit very well the persona of a laborer in private conference with one of the planet's great. The question brought the tanker to alertness again. He had not known that Danny had been carried by the Alayans. "Yes, Mistress," Slade said. "That is—they don't land, you know. Tenders carry you to orbit. I suppose it was the same ship. Ah, Captain Slade had business on Desmo, seeing to some of his men. But he told me he'd be home soon and—look me up.

"He was really looking forward to getting home," the tanker added softly. His left hand was absently working loose the tubing from his right arm. The sawn edges were sharp enough to have cut his skin near the elbow, and the battering given and received by the armor had despite its protection caused the tissues to swell.

"I suppose," said Marilee in a tone that supposed nothing, "that Captain Slade will have a family by this time. From what I recall of his youth, presumably he will have a harem. I don't suppose local strictures on marriage apply to off-planet mercenaries, even when there are such—strictures."

The tubing slid loose. Slade extended his right hand with thumb and little fingers touching so that they would not catch the front edges of the plastic. The air was thrilling on the film of sweat and sweat-thinned blood.

"There's mercs who settle, and mercs who move," Slade said with his head lowered. "The Slammers moved. Nobody could afford to keep them long enough for it to be the other way."

He turned the length of tubing, looking at it from one angle and then another to have some ostensible focus for his eyes. "You don't carry women along unless they're part of the unit. There aren't so many of them, and fewer still who'd be interested in a man. I didn't notice anybody traveling with Captain Slade."

The tanker risked a glance toward his hostess. She met his eyes abruptly, but it was not his face at which she had been staring.

Slade looked down again and cursed. He twisted his bloody right arm so that its underside was no longer in the light. Beneath the stains and slickness were still the scars the argus had left on a child. The skin had stretched and filled with muscle over the years, but the unpigmented keloids would remain till the grave. Slade licked his lips and said to the woman, "You wanted your brother-in-law to come home, Mistress."

"No!" said Marilee. She had been leaning forward. Now she thrust herself against the back of her chair. "I wanted him, and that may have been a mistake even then. But I don't want Don to come home now. It's too late. They'd only kill him."

"They're trash, Mistress," said the tanker. The emotion in his quiet voice was not anger. "You can't live, worrying about trash."

"My husband was a good man," said Marilee, "a *good* man—"

"I know that."

"—but he let Beverly Dyson build his organization for two years. All very careful, taking over the Port that was too much work for any of the other board members to bother about. Loans to some, help of other kinds and blackmail besides to some who needed more than money."

The woman swept to her feet again. She stood like a warrior queen. Her voice rolled out in challenge. "All very quiet, Mister— Holt—and none of the thugs, the gunmen, till all that had been taken care of. But the thugs are here, they killed Tom. And they'll kill anybody else who threatens Dyson's plans, I see that now."

"Look," said Slade as he stood also. Half his mind would have taken him nearer to the woman, but instead he walked back toward the trophy wall. They were part of what had forged him, those monsters; and beyond that, he felt a certain kinship with what they represented. "You knew that—Mistress," he said, "when you called your brother-in-law home. Nothing's changed, except your nerve's giving out. And it's not your nerve that matters when h-he gets home."

"That's not *true* about nothing changing!" the woman cried. She raised both hands. "It was a chance for the Council to back a strong leader against Bev Dyson. All right, not Teddy . . . and not me either, some of them because they're fools and some because they didn't see the skills for this—kind of business—in my background. Man or woman. But I thought somebody they *could* respect, and somebody who *could* organize them, lead them—Bev doesn't have any army, and all the Council together could muster enough men to, to get him away. I thought they'd all jump at the chance not to be bullied by Bev Dyson, but . . ."

Marilee sagged in on herself without completing the thought.

The flaring pectoral fins of the orc had been razor sharp when Don Slade first grew tall enough to touch them gingerly. That edge had long been worn round as awe was slowly replaced by ritual. Slade touched a fin now. A part of him visualized the creature alive, forty meters of it spiraling up toward the platform on which the Old Man waited with a rocket gun.

Memory of his grandfather was by no means out of place to

current needs. "And Councilor Dorcas, your brother?" asked Slade as his hand caressed the deadly fin.

"The present Councilor is my nephew, I'm afraid," said the woman. She paced to the window. Through it now gleamed only the lights of those trying to deal with the wreckage in the courtyard. As generally on Tethys, the haze of clouds blocked any but the brightest stars.

"He's even younger than Teddy—isn't that amusing?" Marilee continued. "But well-advised, I gather. The vote to put the Slade Estate in guardianship was unanimous. I don't expect there to be much change tomorrow when the Council determines who the actual guardian should be.

"So you see," the tall woman continued as she faced her visitor again, "why I no longer believe that any possible rallying point would make—" she sniffed— "men out of the Councilors. Except perhaps for me to retain a mercenary regiment. I was almost willing to consider that course, until I talked to Mister Pritchard the other day. I will die before I bring that to Tethys. I will die."

"Yeah," said Don Slade to the window. "Well." Seconds after she thought he was finished, the tanker continued. "I suppose the Old Man's room's been cleaned out years since. I mean, Counc—"

"I know who the Old Man was," the woman said. "Even during Council sessions, there has been space to spare in this House since it ceased to be a barracks. My husband would never enter—his grandfather's room, Holt, but he never permitted anyone else to enter it either. Would you like to, to . . . ?"

"Yes, Mistress," said Slade. "Very much."

Slade stretched. The muscles that rippled across his arms and shoulders gave the lie to his dyed, razor-thinned hair.

"And—" nervous again, but soft as she paused—"you'll be staying tonight in the House?"

The tanker shrugged. He touched the orc again. "I'll get back to Number Six, Mistress. It'll cause less trouble. If you can arrange transportation when you get someone to let me into the Old Man's room? I doubt the truck I came in will run me back." Slade's smile was as bleak and distant as that of the orc.

"Of course," said Marilee. Her voice was normal, but it sounded thin in her own ears as her world shrank down to a point. "I suppose you can understand why Don can't appear now?"

The man did not speak. He stood before the trophies. He looked as massive and powerful and inert as a stalled ox.

"Perhaps," Marilee went on, "things might change. Soon. And it will be safe for Captain Slade to return to Tethys."

"Tethys won't be safe for *any* man, or a woman," said the tanker flatly, "until there's enough men or women—to make it safe. I've heard what I need to hear, Mistress."

Marilee turned and bent over the chair-arm controls. She gave quick orders to the Under-Steward on call. Then, in a clear voice, she said to the man behind her, "That will be all, then, Holt."

Only when the door closed solidly did Marilee open her eyes again. She felt as if the maelstrom had just swept past her last hope of survival.

CHAPTER TWENTY-EIGHT

The pumps were already sluicing the lines again in start-up mode, testing the system for leaks which had opened during the hours of darkness. Their *hoosh* announced Slade as he entered the crew area, then closed the door behind him.

"Hey, it's Soldier," called Chesson as Leaf was saying, "Via! Look how he's togged out!" Slade wore a Steward's tunic, blue-green with silver piping. It fit him no worse than the garment he had worn to the House.

"Fried potatoes with your breakfast?" asked Pretorius. He shook the skillet.

"Via, yes," Slade said as he sat down beside the fourth chair at the table. He took the plate the foreman handed him. Raw fries, nothing processed about them, gleamed beside a filet of shallotte or some similar fish. "You guys teaching potatoes to swim, then?" the tanker asked. There was certainly no garden plot at the station, swept as it was by tides on an average of once a month.

"My wife grows them," said Chesson as he took another mouthful. "Well, we both do every other month when I'm off, but I can't take much credit."

"No trouble at the House, then?" Leaf asked.

"Yeah, what did the Mistress say?" Chesson added as he recollected the circumstances in which the big man had ridden off in the truck.

"Let the man eat his breakfast," said Pretorius. He took his own place at the table. Even in the foreman's eyes, however, were questions dancing to be answered.

"There was a bit of trouble," Slade said. Instead of eating, he eased his chair back and looked across the other three men. "Nothing that couldn't be handled. What happens this afternoon, though, that's going to be harder. They're going to give Bev Dyson guardianship of the Slade Estate."

Unexpectedly Leaf said, "I wasn't but a boy, not so much as Chessie's age." Chesson, who was a good thirty years old, bridled but did not interrupt. "The storm of 161 it was, the Great Storm. You remember that, Piet?"

Pretorius shrugged. "Before my time," he said.

Leaf nodded as if to pump up his memory. "There was never anything to match it," the old man said. "Fifteen days of wind and waves. There wasn't a let-up till the end. The eye missed Main Island altogether, just curled through us like the blade of a circle saw. But you know, lads—it did pass. Master Teddy is of age in two years?"

Chesson and the foreman were nodding slowly in agreement. Slade said, "If Bev Dyson takes over—" he raised his left hand, palm up and fingers extended— "in six months, Teddy will be in a fish's belly." The hand clenched with the suddenness of jaws snapping.

The three other men looked at Slade, at the fist and at the face set as hard as that fist. "This planet's been run a certain way since the Settlement," the tanker said. "Some mightn't like it, but it seemed to suit most pretty well. If Dyson takes over, the system isn't going to change, not really . . . but the way it's applied won't ever be the same. The Council Islands'll toe the line set from the Main, from Slade House or Paraclete, whichever Bev decides should be his capital."

Slade's voice was getting louder, but he did not move from his chair. "Councilors won't decide anything but who they screw on a given night. And all right, that doesn't bother you or me either. But the rock-hoppers, the independants, they'll all be pulled in and settled if they'll come—or hunted down if they won't, you *know* Bev Dyson. And when there's nowhere to run, he'll start squeezing every laborer on Tethys . . . and he'll squeeze you the worst, my friends, because he hates every soul and thing that ever wore Slade Blue."

The clenched fist opened again as if it bore the future on a platter.

Pretorius shook his head with a look of sad wonder. "*I* can't leave, Holt," he said. "Maybe you can go back as a mercenary, but they wouldn't have me at my age. And I wouldn't have them! This is the life I want, right here. And if that means Dyson and all the things that *Dyson* means, then it'll have to be that way."

"It's not what Mistress Slade wants," said the tanker softly.

"It's not what *we* want," Chesson burst out, "but what bloody difference does that make?"

"A good question," said Slade. He grinned as the pieces came together, working his fingers closed again without haste. "You know, I used to wonder why the Old Man put us so heavy into food production. There's ten stations just about like this one, right?"

"Sure, but that's business," said Leaf, watching Slade with puzzlement.

The tanker nodded. "Business, sure," he agreed. "The Slades feed most of the planet from these stations. But there's a lot more profit to cost of plant and maintenance in mining operations, which is why we've pretty well got food stations to ourselves. Right?"

The crewmen gaped or frowned. The economics of the situation had never consciously affected them. They were Slade retainers, and they did the jobs their forebears had done before them.

"Right," said Slade gently. "So what's the difference between mining and food extraction? *Besides* what you're trying to bring out of the sea?"

Pretorius saw where the conversation was directed. He said, "No."

The others looked at him. The foreman nodded to the weapons racked beside the doorway. "The mining rigs have guards, too. Any time you work men near the sea, you need sensors and guards."

"Right again," said Slade. It was good to be sure he could trust the men he was with. Trust them to think as well as act. "But a manganese dredge doesn't bring them halfway around the planet the way the juice does from your rig, does it? How many critters—how many monsters, they'd call them back at the House—have you put down, Piet?" He gestured. "Leaf? Chessie?"

Chesson snorted. "I remember my first, though not real well," he said. "It was when Pops was on this rig, so I must have been maybe five. He let me pull the trigger when a networm surfaced right under the platform."

"All right, friends," said the tanker as he rose to his feet. He stood, arms akimbo, facing the crewmen. "This isn't your job or that of the crews off-duty and at the other stations. But if it isn't done by you, it won't be done at all. For yourselves, and for the Mistress— and for Master Teddy, who can just maybe set things straight again, like they were when I was a kid. If he just gets a chance and a little help. Are you up to it?"

The pumps gentled the silence with their background of *hoosh, hoosh.* At last Pretorius spoke. "It's us you'll want to call the others, I suppose, Soldier?"

CHAPTER TWENTY-NINE

"Mark," said Beverly Dyson to key his throat mike. "Subiyaga, be *very* careful with that one. Take the detector down to aluminum spray if you have to to make sure he doesn't have a throwaway derringer. Mark."

"Mark," said the civilian-suited specialist responsible for the detection unit. "Yes, milord." Subiyaga nodded toward Councilor Dyson, halfway across the courtyard on the roof of his van. Dyson had moved the vehicle ostentatiously into the courtyard the night before when he was ordered out of Slade House.

A squad of Dyson retainers had been told off specifically to support Subiyaga. Besides them, representatives of five other Council Islands observed the detector. Coon Blegan glowered at the equipment on behalf of the Slades. The newness and tailoring of Blegan's blue livery could not disguise the old man's paunch; but the pistol beneath his left arm was to be surmised rather than seen with clarity. Whatever might be the instructions other Councilors had given their observers, it was quite certain that Blegan would object forcefully if anything irregular occurred during the weapons checks.

Councilor Dyson did not care. He and those of his retainers whom he chose to bring within the Hall would submit to the same careful vetting as the others. For this mercenary from Friesland, however, the search had to be extraordinary.

"Bastard," Dyson whispered. The three men of his personal staff

226

stood behind him on the van roof. They looked sidelong at one another in concern.

Ten Dyson retainers were playing music opposite the detection station. Danny Pritchard did not recognize their wind instruments. Allowing for local conventions, Pritchard did not think the musicians were particularly skillful, either. Certainly the pair of Slade Housemen who accompanied Pritchard to the Hall did not seem to appreciate the music any better than did the ex-mercenary.

In all likelihood, the musicians were there to divert attention from the indignity of search; for even Councilors and their families had to go through the detection loop.

As Danny stepped into the loop, he smiled at Subiyaga. The specialist's brief conversation with his master was easy enough to guess, though Pritchard had heard neither end of it. Subiyaga let the unit run its pre-programmed settings without result. Then he began to punch additional commands into the cabinet.

Pritchard watched the apparatus with professional interest. The unit was considerably bulkier than the best of Hammer's similar equipment, but it appeared to be fully as capable once it was set up. The subject within the ground loop was a dancing outline on the screen. A line swept up the image, then down again, for as long as it took the cabinet to run its program. The color of the sweep varied according to the element which was to be detected on a given pass.

Danny had deliberately worn a suit scintillant with fine wire to determine how sensitive the apparatus might be. The threads of stabilized aluminum remained on screen as an orange glow across his image after one of the sweeps. The circuitry of his stylus, his mastoid implant, and the heavy remote unit at his belt, were separate blotches. Their greenish tinge on the screen reflected the close mixture of metals within the electronic mechanisms.

Nowhere on the screen was there evidence of iridium; or significant amounts of iron; or a cylindrical blur of metal deposited to mirror a glass weapons-tube.

Subiyaga ignored Pritchard's stylus. "Mark," he said, so that his master could hear the details. "Sir, what is this, please?" The specialist pointed to a blotch on the screen, but his eyes were on the back of Pritchard's jaw which the blotch indicated.

"That's an implanted radio link," the ex-mercenary replied. He tapped the spot with his forefinger. "Keyed to a base unit, it's very useful. On Tethys, of course—" the smile became momentarily carnivorous— "and without the Regiment, it serves no function. Except to fill the hole cut in the bone to hold it."

"And—" the specialist began, his finger sliding to the lower blotch.

"And this is a remote unit that *does* function on Tethys," Pritchard said, almost anticipating the question. He spoke with the cool good-nature he generally maintained around things wearing crimson. "It's linked to the Port, where a message capsule is already cleared for Friesland. Colonel Hammer wished to be informed immediately if anything untoward occurred during today's deliberations."

He turned. The clothing Pritchard now wore was nothing like the battle-dress he had doffed for good, two years before. No one could look at him at that moment, however, and doubt his military background. "Do you object to Colonel Hammer having that full report?"

"Mark," said Subiyaga, clearing his link.

The man who met Danny's eyes from the van across the court-yard spoke briefly, sharply.

"No, Mister Pritchard," said the specialist to the ex-soldier's back. "We have no objection. You may enter the Hall, sir."

"I appreciate your courtesy," said Pritchard as he faced the specialist again. Danny's eyes swept like gunsights across the retainers, noting their stance, their alertness; where they set or carried the gun cases which were their badges and power. "And in thanking you," Pritchard went on, "I speak for Colonel Hammer."

Pritchard strode toward the massive doors of the Hall. The Councilors and attendants whom the delay had forced to queue now began passing through the checkpoint as well.

Councilor Dyson stared at the empty doorway for some seconds after Hammer's man had passed through it.

✳ ✳ ✳

"Mother!" said Edward Slade when he saw how Marilee was dressed. "It's—you know you can't wear blue, they'll say you look like a servant!"

His mother snorted. Teddy blushed at the patent absurdity of what he had just said.

Marilee's garment flowed from a loose-fitting stasis to follow its wearer's movements with its own slow grace. The garment's color was indeed blue, Slade Blue, but pulses moved up it with the inexorable polish of color in heat-treated steel. The pulses did not, however, so much change the color of the fabric as the saturation of that color. Marilee could no more have been mistaken for a servant than Slade House could have been mistaken for a mining station.

"Besides," the woman said, amplifying the rebuke she had not needed to voice, "there won't be any servants with us. Though—" a wrinkle flitted across her face as she recalled— "I did send two Housemen with Danny since he wanted to enter the Hall early. I suppose they may stay."

"Mother," the youth repeated, this time in irritation rather than surprise.

Teddy himself was a stiff ensemble in black and white. From his outfit, he might have stepped from a subordinate position in Late-Nineteenth Century diplomacy. Housemen in fresh livery glanced from one to another behind the youth, wondering how Marilee's statement would affect them. "I realize how you must feel," Teddy said without even considering whether his words had meaning or were merely sounds, "but we mustn't give in to frustration. We're Slades, and even if we're beaten we mustn't slink away into a corner. That is, I—"

Teddy's breath caught and strangled the next words in his throat.

That was by no means soon enough, but it halted the arm Marilee had raised to slap her son. The tall woman's face was white with blotches as the muscles drew back over her bones, "Will you say I am no Slade, *boy?*" she whispered. Her right arm slipped forward so that the fingers of her left hand could knead some of the tension out of it. "I was a Slade before you were conceived, Edward. Don't you ever forget it. *Ever.*"

She looked back at the servants. "Get out of here!" she shouted.

The Housemen scattered down the corridor. There were more of them than Marilee had realized, at least a dozen.

"Edward, come in here for a moment," the woman said. Her voice trembled around expended emotion. Mother and son had been standing near the door to the Trophy Room. Now she opened the door and waved the nervous youth within.

The corridor had skylights and, along the baseboards, glow-strips. The Trophy Room's great window was vivid with ambient light and the sun reflected from the facade of the Hall. Marilee could have chosen to polarize the glazed expanse, but she did not. The light bathed her, and the warmth massaged the shuddering from her muscles.

Marilee looked at her son. He braced himself defiantly, but she was no longer angry. She had assumed that Teddy did not know how soon he was going to die, to be killed like his father. Now Marilee realized that the youth was not a fool and not too young to recognize that Beverly Dyson had made murder an instrument of policy. Edward was keeping up the appearances of the world in which his father had raised him to believe. The youth did so for the same reason that a drowning man finally breathes the water that will kill him: there is nothing else to do.

"Edward," Marilee said slowly, "I decided—about the Housemen—when we were discussing who we should put at the checkpoint to make sure that everyone was checked even if they wore red."

Her son nodded. He was relieved but still uncertain about his mother's change of tone. "Coon Blegan," he said.

"Yes, Coon," Marilee agreed. "Because there was no other member of this House we could really trust with that duty."

The woman sighed and put a hand on her son's clasped hands. "Something went wrong, Edward," she said. "Somewhere along the line. I think my husband would have been good for Tethys if he had been allowed to be. But not for Slade House."

Her voice rose. "Three times as many servants here as when I was married, and only one holdover that we can trust with our lives. That shouldn't be. All the bowing and sharp dress in the world doesn't make up for that, does it?"

Teddy squeezed his mother's hand. He took a deep breath. "I'm sorry, Mother," he said. He was neither willing nor fully able to state the subject of his apology. "We'll have to do something about the Housemen. As soon as we—can." It would not be their House after the Council met, as surely as the seas washed the shores. "But for now, I think we had best get to the Hall. We are Slades."

They walked formally, arm in arm, the few steps to the door. Edward then preceded his mother down the narrow, tightly-coiled staircase. His head was high, and his pace was as measured as if he had scores of attendants.

Marilee was close to tears, though there was nothing in her quizzical expression to suggest that. Perhaps if he ran? Fled Tethys, became—became a mercenary soldier, with his uncle easing his way in that alien culture, watching over him. And then in a few years, when it was safe to come home—

Don was right. It would never again be safe on Tethys.

As her feet patted against the stair treads, Marilee's face drew itself into a smile as taut as a tetanic rictus. Each tap of sole on stone put her and the House and the planet twenty centimeters closer to disaster. She should have hired the Slammers, curse the expense in all its meanings.

Dear Lord, she should not have ordered away Don Slade. Not now.

And not twenty years before, either.

CHAPTER THIRTY

The doors of the Hall were four meters high and proof against more than storms when they were closed and locked from the inside. The trunions on which they swung inward ran in trackways grooved into the base slab. Open, the doors gaped as wide as they rose in the concrete facade. For the symmetry of the occasion, the leaves were fully open now; but a solid line of Dyson retainers across the threshold made sure that none of those entering failed to go through the security check first.

Two of the red-clad men had stepped aside with perfunctory smiles. Councilor Roosevelt, his wife, and fourteen assorted members of his family and staff were passing into the Hall. The youngest child made a curious attempt to pat a crimson trouser leg. His nurse snatched him back immediately. The adults of the entourage preferred to act as if the guards did not exist.

At least that rascal Dyson had shown the decency to leave his squad unarmed. The remainder—almost fifty—of his men in the courtyard flaunted their cased guns with a particular relish this afternoon. The deliberations of the Council would be sealed by custom against interference; but there was only the single exit from the Hall.

"Passage, gentlemen," said a voice from within the door alcove. The guards were bored and unprepared for someone who wanted to leave at this moment.

"I said," snarled Danny Pritchard, "get your butts out of the way, turtleheads!"

The line clotted as Dyson's men wheeled to face the ex-mercenary. Those in the queue waiting to be checked began craning their necks to see what had happened. The music tangled to a momentary halt before the leader of the musicians snapped his group back to attention with a nervous look toward Beverly Dyson. The musicians were supposed to cover, not join, awkward incidents of this sort.

Danny Pritchard stood with a sneer and his fists on his hip bones. He was not a scarred tough like many of the men he now faced; but he was a commander glaring at men who knew they were only vessels of power. The guards would be discarded without hesitation if they overstepped bounds of which they were only hazily aware.

"Subiyaga! Via!" shouted the leader of the squad on the threshold. Subiyaga was not even in the blurred chain of command, but he was the only one present with a link to the source of power. "Are we supposed to let people out?"

"Blood, McKinney!" Subiyaga said. "Are you crazy? Of course they can get out. What do you think you're doing?"

"Let him go! Let him go!" the shaken squad leader said. His men were already reacting like dollops of a fruit hit by a projectile. They were not there to alienate Councilors whom Dyson wished for the time to coddle.

Danny Pritchard strolled out with a nod toward the specialist. The guards at the detection cabinet had fumbled with their cases during the tension. It was only now, however, that they saw who the source of the incident had been.

"Hey!" called Ahwas, the leader of that armed group. "Mister! You got to go through the loop again before you go back inside!"

The man from Friesland grinned broadly. "I hear you talking," he said. He continued to walk toward the House from which he had come so recently.

Subiyaga watched him walk away. The specialist's face was troubled, but he could not be quite certain of what he saw.

The courtyard was not particularly hot. The bright sun which had been a caress in the Trophy Room was here a slap in the face.

Perhaps that was because of the way the light danced with such frequency from crimson livery. There were numerous groups led by Councilors at one stage or another of their progress to the Hall. Even so, Dyson's retainers seemed omnipresent. The man himself stood on his van ten meters away, as if he were on a reviewing stand.

Marilee paused in the doorway. Behind the Slades, Councilor Picolo squeaked as her way was blocked by her hostess and son. Marilee murmured an apology to her, one of only two women who were Council members in their own right. As Marilee did so, she drew her son into the shade of one of the armored drones flanking the doorway. She needed to take stock.

"Mistress, I was told to escort you into the Hall," said the man who had waited patiently beside the same drone. "Told by Mister Pritchard."

His livery had blended well enough with the blue shade; and until he spoke he had been as motionless as the 10 cm gun above him. For that matter, Don Slade was no longer the flamboyant hell-raiser who had left Tethys twenty years before. Like the gun-drone, he was scarred and stolid now; but not to be ignored.

"You fool, you *mustn't* be here!" the woman said in a voice that was as much a curse as a whisper.

"Mistress," said the big man calmly. "I'm going inside as your escort. Nothing you say will have any effect except to call attention to—us."

"Mother, he *should* go," interjected Edward. "You said we had no one except Coon we could trust. Well, this man, this Holt, proved yesterday that he wasn't afraid of Dyson or Dyson's men. Didn't he?"

"T—," Marilee began. Then, "Edward, there are things you can't . . ." She paused again when she realized that this was neither the time nor the place to explain. Anyway, the explanation would not matter in any real sense.

Not when Don Slade said, "I *will* enter the Hall this day, Mistress." One did not have to know the big man as Marilee Dorcas had known him to realize that he would do just what he said, though it killed him. As this time it surely would.

"I think," said Marilee carefully, "that Mister Pritchard's own presence within the Hall will prevent anything—untoward. I—truly appreciate the solicitude, Holt, but I don't think it's wise under the circumstances."

She and her son could almost pass for sister and brother, Slade thought. His dry mouth made it hard for him to speak. He felt as if he were strapped in and waiting for insertion, desperately afraid as always. To those who heard him, his slow speech was only obsequious. Possibly Edward thought the speech was a symptom of a slow mind, the sort of mind that befitted a powerful body as his father might have said.

"Mistress," Slade explained, "Major Pritchard had other business to attend. He's left the Hall, and he's told me to accompany you." When the woman hesitated with her mouth open but the words not quite ready to come out, Slade added, "We're all adults, you know. We can't live any lives but our own."

"What?" said Edward.

"All right, Holt," Marilee said crisply, unemotionally. "You will follow us at two paces, and you will not speak unless spoken to."

"Yes, Mistress," the big man said. The bill of the cap he wore nodded submissively.

"Come along, then, Edward," the woman said. There were only a few people waiting yet to be passed through the check point. "It's almost 1500 . . . and I very much doubt they'll delay the door closing because we aren't yet present."

She glanced up as they began walking toward the Hall. "Of course," she added dryly, "we can be sure the doors will remain open until the President of the Council deigns to enter."

The man behind her kept his face blank, but Marilee's expression at that moment would have very well fit Mad Dog Slade.

"Them," said one of the men standing behind Beverly Dyson.

The comment had been as much as anything an attempt to drag a reaction, even a rebuke for speaking, from the Councilor. Dyson had not spoken for the past quarter hour, as the queue shortened and more and more people waited within the Hall for his coming triumph. Presidency of the Council was nothing. The Slade Estate was and always had been Tethys itself.

Dyson was erect behind the rail on the van's roof. He had intended to move the vehicle into the courtyard at this time even if—the Widow Slade—had not ordered him out of the House the night before. Now he rotated his head very slightly to watch the trio striding toward the Hall . . . the youth fashionably archaic, the other pair in Slade Blue.

As Councilor Dyson wore crimson.

She understood, the bitch. What it meant to be a Council family, to share Main Island with the Slades, to be as wealthy as the Slades—and to be ignored, whenever a difference arose, because you were *not* Slade. Ever since the Settlement.

Until now.

"The big one," said the retainer. "He's the one . . ."

"Baucom," whispered Beverly Slade as his eyes tracked those crossing beneath him, "shut up or I'll have you killed."

It could not be. Every man aboard every ship which landed was checked. Whether they were passengers or crew, whether they planned to disembark on Tethys or were only staging through. The gunman, Pritchard; *he* had been noted. A mercenary, very likely a courier from the Mad Dog. But not the man himself, not by a half.

Don Slade had not come home. There was no such money in the galaxy that would preserve the man who took it to hide Slade on Tethys from Beverly Dyson. Everybody on Tethys knew that. And Slade, even the madman Dyson knew him for, was as sure of that as were any of the guards searching incoming starships. Don Slade would never even try to walk on Tethys.

And yet—

More or less audibly, the Councilor said, "I can't remember his face." The men behind him strained to catch the words, but the words would have meant nothing without a context thirty years in their master's past. "I hadn't realized that. When I try to remember his face, I see the wrench instead and I see the wrench when I look at that—"

Dyson broke off. He had not realized that he was speaking

aloud. "Baucom," he said. The brief tremor in his voice sounded dangerous to the men who stiffened to attention.

"Sir?" said Baucom. His eyes were wide, but he was deliberately staring past the Councilor.

"I was going to use the radio," Dyson said, again fully composed, "but I will not. That man, the large one."

"Sir." Marilee Slade had passed through the detection loop without incident. Her son was preparing to follow with an expression of cool indifference.

"I want you," the Councilor continued, "to take the squad leader—it's Ahwas, isn't it? At the cabinet?"

"Yes, sir."

"Take him aside before you join us in us in the Hall. Tell him that when that man comes out again, after the Council meeting or before, he is to be shot. Immediately. Is that understood?

There was nothing in the Councilor's voice which permitted any question. "Yes, *sir,*" said Baucom.

As if he were a machine switching frequencies, Beverly Dyson said, "Mark. Subiyaga, I want that man with the Slades checked the same way you did the mercenary. Mark."

The specialist looked up and bowed toward the van. In Dyson's ear, his voice said. "Yes sir, I'm already doing that. There don't seem to be any weapons, but he has the same kind of communications device in his jawbone as the other one did."

The man, the Slade retainer—if he were a retainer—stood in the loop with his back to Dyson. He seemed to be oblivious of the hushed conversation of which he was the subject.

"Mark," said the Councilor. "Very good, Subiyaga. Carry on. Mark."

Dyson turned to face the trio accompanying him. "When they kill that one, Baucom," he said, "they are to avoid injury to Mistress Slade and her son if possible." He paused. In a measured voice, he continued, "I expect that mercenary gunman, Pritchard, to come out of the House carrying his weapon. If he is present when the—other—is killed, I want him treated the same way. Ahwas can pass the word among the other squads."

"Yes, sir," Baucom repeated. He was terrified that his master was about to add some final order which would be suicide for the retainer to execute personally. An order to personally provoke a confrontation with Blegan, for instance, to get the old gunman out of the way as well.

But instead, Dyson said mildly. "They think to threaten me with some jumped up mercenary twenty Transit minutes away. Not here. Not on my world."

Then he added, "Come. It's time for us to open the meeting." Lithely, the Councilor swung down the ladder to the ground.

CHAPTER THIRTY-ONE

The door leaves rang heavily against their stops. Then the crossbar slotted home with a sharper note, and the tension in the courtyard was released. The Council might think it was separating itself from external distractions. Those outside knew that they were temporarily preserved from the screwy whims of their employers.

All but a handful of the men in the courtyard wore crimson.

One of the exceptions was a kitchen assistant. He trotted from the House carrying on a yoke a pair of large insulated canisters. It was food and drink for the musicians. Their leader, Codell, had shown the foresight to lay on the refreshments ahead of time. There was no question of the musicians relaxing in the vans outside the walls which acted as barracks for most of Dyson's men. They were still on duty. They had put up their instruments and were openly belting on the sidearms which were to be part of their regalia henceforward.

Ahwas took off his gold-billed cap and wiped his forehead with his sleeve. The sound the gunman made reminded Subiyaga of the gurgle of recovery following a near drowning.

The guard leader looked around him. His own men were already uncasing their submachine guns. Ahwas nodded approval. He motioned Subiyaga nearer to him and whispered, "You keep an eye on things here, huh? You saw Baucom give the word to me? Right from the top, that was. I got to go *talk* to some people."

The specialist grimaced. "Via," he said, "your goons aren't any business of mine. Do what you please, but leave me out of it."

Four of the men who had formally observed the checkpoint were now clustered a little apart. They were talking while their eyes roved nervously. None of them seemed disposed to notice the guns appearing all around them.

When the Hall closed behind Councilor Dyson, Coon Blegan stalked lumpily away from the detection cabinet. He stood now by the shaded south wall of the yard, not far from the outside gate. His arms were crossed and the sole of his right boot was planted against the wall at knee level. The old man was a brooding threat which drew Ahwas' eyes even though whispers could not carry that far.

"Well," the guard leader said.

Subiyaga had begun disassembling and packing his rig. The specialist had served on a dozen planets with as many different varieties of security forces. That gave him a professional familiarity with weapons. The ignorance of many of the liverymen around him was appalling. The sooner he had his equipment packed and had carried it out of this courtyard, the happier he would be. Incompetence could make the enclosure a killing ground, even without the orders Ahwas seemed so proud to be passing on.

"Blood! Look at that!" the guard leader said. In case his tone were not demanding enough, he snatched at Subiyaga's sleeve to turn him toward the House.

The specialist bit back a curse as one of the sideplates rattled out of the groove in which he had just inserted it. Nervous fools with guns were dangerous enough without having their emotional temperature raised still further. "Well, I see him," Subiyaga said. "The mercenary, Pritchard. And if he's got a gun, it isn't anything as big as the one he backed you boys down with the other night."

"Don't matter," muttered Ahwas, "don't matter cop. We got him this time."

The guard set his cap in place firmly. He began trotting toward Dyson's van. There the liverymen who had blocked the Hall doorway were being issued their own automatic weapons.

Subiyaga paused for a further moment to watch Pritchard. The ex-mercenary had climbed onto the deck of one of the drones. He was relaxed, his arm resting loosely on the gun tube. Hard to tell his expression at the distance, but it did not seem to be too concerned. Too bad. Subiyaga liked to work with other professionals, but this time the few such around were all on the other side.

The detection loop was held rigid and a finger's breadth above the ground by its own internal charge. Subiyaga reversed the polarity with a pop. The loop collapsed. He began to reel it in. One thing Subiyaga had seen for sure: Pritchard still wore his remote unit, the one Subiyaga had thought he must have left behind in the Hall.

Or another one, of course; but why would the mercenary have carried two identical commo units to Tethys?

Ballenger was in charge of the van. He also acted as Councilor Dyson's steward when the Councilor was traveling. The pudgy man considered himself a cut above Ahwas and the other gunmen, though Dyson had never formalized lines of authority. Everyone in crimson livery was *Dyson's* subordinate. The Councilor believed that lack of certainty beyond that fact kept his retainers nervous and alert. It also made it unlikely that Dyson's men would make any major decision without personally clearing it with their master, which suited his style very well.

The ten-meter van looked larger from the outside than it was within, what with the drive units, the equipment that made it the Councilor's command station—and especially because of the squad of armed liverymen now babbling in the main room.

"You have no business here!" cried Ballenger in a powerful voice. It was a surprise coming from a small man who looked soft from any angle. "Take your—" he made shooing motions with the backs of both hands, trying to dismiss the submachine guns he had just been required to issue— "things and get back where you belong. I don't know *what* the Councilor is going to say when he sees the filth you've tracked into his compartment."

"Via, that's easy for *you* to say, piggy," said Ahwas, still puffed with the orders he had delivered to the chief of the other squad. "*We've* got to blast that merc and the other just as soon as they come out of the meeting."

"Right when the doors open, Rag?" the other leader asked. He was toying with the safety of his own weapon in a way which would have terrified anyone in the van with better sense.

"Well, I . . ." Ahwas began.

"Of course not, you buffoons!" snapped Ballenger. "Is this Slade going to be the first person out the door?" Several guards frowned in an attempt to answer the question. "Of *course* not!" the steward repeated in fury. "So if you shoot this one when the doors open, you'll warn the other, won't you? *Won't you?* So wait till the other one comes out of the Hall, then kill them *both.*"

Ballenger paused, breathing hard.

"Right, that's just what the master told me to have done," Ahwas lied. He took off his cap and wiped his face again, darkening the bright scarlet with his sweat.

"Sir," called the driver who monitored the instruments from the cab. "There's a couple supply trucks coming in.

"That's correct," the steward said primly. "There's to be a celebration banquet in Slade House this evening. They'll be bringing additional specialties."

The armed liverymen were beginning to file out of the van. Ahwas watched them with a glum expression. "Won't help us a bit, though, will it?" he said. "Now that we aren't allowed in the House anymore."

Ballenger opened his mouth in an amazement that was only partially feigned. "That isn't a *problem* anymore, don't you see?" he said to the guard. "After the meeting, *we* own Slade House. We own *Tetkys.* In just a few hours."

He continued to shake his head in wonder as the last of the gunmen trooped out of the van.

CHAPTER THIRTY-TWO

Even the Hall had shrunk, thought Don Slade. That was not because of how he had grown since his memories of the building, but rather because of what he had seen on other worlds.

The Council Hall was a ferro-concrete A-frame thirty meters to the roof peak and a full hundred meters along that beam. It had been designed to hold the original population of Tethys—had done so for a day and two nights during the Swarm of Year Three. The Hall remained the planet's largest building now because it was an anachronism—and in his youth, Slade had found very little use for anachronisms.

Communications among the estates scattered across the planet were excellent and trustworthy. Physical assembly of the Council was needless. Because it was also relatively dangerous, the practice had been abandoned by the time the twins were born. Slade's father had reinstituted the practice on an occasional, ceremonial basis. Tom had apparently amplified ceremonies for his own reasons. The Council, with increasingly little of substance to debate after the life and death decisions of the first generations, was willing and more to fall in with the practice.

Beverly Dyson would have seen to it that this occasion was face to face, no matter what had been the practice of the immediate past. His triumph demanded that.

"Mistress," said a Slade Houseman. He bowed low as he never would have done under other circumstances.

Don's father had filled the great room with auditorium-style seating at an expense the Old Man had sneered at. All that was gone, now. It had been replaced with wooden benches and wood-paneled enclosures to waist height. The panels separated the areas assigned to the various Council Islands, formalizing a practice which had some historical support.

The wood, however, was a matter of insanity rather than nostalgia. What Tom—it must have been Tom—was thinking about was wholly beyond his twin. The only trees on Tethys were those carefully nurtured from imported stock, and the gravelly soil tended to stunt even those. Every scrap of these fittings must have been shipped from off-world. Gold would have been cheaper. Sea-mining at least produced an indigenous supply of gold.

As the Houseman straightened, he swung inward the low gate of the enclosure and collided with his fellow. This was not the sort of thing they had practiced often enough to get right. The whole business was a little pathetic. The Slade enclosure would have seated two hundred. The five of them were lost in it.

Some of the other Councilors had as many as forty in their present entourage, but even those enclosures looked empty. The day for which the Council Hall was built would never return. If Don Slade had more affection for the old barn than he ever in youth had thought probable, it was because he now realized that he too belonged in the Settlement, two centuries before his birth.

The Houseman looked askance at Slade when he followed Edward and Marilee into the enclosure. The big man smiled at the liveried pair and asked, "I believe you boys have something for me? Major Pritchard left it with you."

Marilee looked back to see why Slade was not immediately behind her. The servants had started to whisper to one another. One promptly turned to the woman and said, "Mistress, your guest left a, an object with us which this—person—says is for him."

"Well then, *give it* to him," Marilee replied in a venemous tone. It was the first evidence Slade had seen that she was tight as a cocked pistol herself, ready to blast petty officiousness for fear of the real dangers that had drawn her so taut.

The Housemen scrambled to obey. They collided once more and almost got into a tug of war over the remote unit, hidden under one of the empty benches.

Marilee looked puzzled. The object was nothing she recognized. Edward was not so much bored as anesthetized by—fear was too blunt a word, but fear would do to describe the emotion.

"Yeah . . ." the big man said, "thanks."

His head still felt light, airy, as he hooked the unit onto his belt. There was a surge of warmth also, however. Slade had grasped a floating spar; and while that did not itself preserve him from the maelstrom, it at least made preservation conceivable. He was beaming as he sat beside Marilee on the front bench of the enclosure, facing the podium across another low wooden barrier.

"What is that?" the woman whispered. "Holt?"

"Oh," said Slade. "A, well, commo unit, you'd say."

He could have carried the remote unit into the Hall himself; it was genuinely no more of a weapon than was his mastoid implant. It was barely possible that somebody would have recognized the object, however. If there were trouble, it was best that Danny be the one to field it. His status as representative of Friesland did not give him total immunity, but it would carry him further than anything Don Slade had to offer.

The doors shut with the solidity of a natural force. A riffle of air was driven before them into the Hall.

Whispering by less than a thousand people could no more fill the Hall than sunlight could fill a bucket. Still, hushed voices hissed and quivered between the slanted concrete slabs which were roof and walls in one. Through the whispers rapped the boot heels, Beverly Dyson's and those of the three men in lock step a pace behind him. A squad of crimson liverymen guarded the doors they had just closed from the inside. Twenty more men rose to their feet in the Dyson enclosure. These retainers were unarmed, at least in so far as the detection cabinet had shown; but they were scarred, solid men.

When Dyson's own men stood, there was a hasty clatter throughout the Hall. Rising for the President had been no part of the plan. The Council was by history a gathering of equals—in form.

But no one wanted to be the last to honor Beverly Dyson, especially when the toughs in the Dyson enclosure were turning to stare back into the Hall.

The two Slade Housemen popped to their feet from where they sat by the central aisle. Marilee held to an icy indifference. Her eyes were on the podium and the President's chair only two meters in front of her. Edward caught the movement, however. His face blotched angrily and he started to lunge toward the servants.

Don Slade touched the youth's shoulder and held him down without effort. Slade was smiling at the Housemen. One of them glanced around surreptitiously. He saw the smile and edged back onto his bench. The first servant tugged at his fellow's sleeve. The other man looked back in surprise. He also sagged as if shot, just as Dyson strode down the aisle past him.

Slade released his nephew.

Someone began to clap. The sound was nervous in the great building. Dyson's liverymen did not take it up, and the attempt collapsed save for its rustling echoes.

Beverly Dyson mounted the four steps onto the podium with stiff-backed grace. It was four paces more to the President's chair, off-set as it was to the Dyson side of the aisle. The three liverymen of the Councilor's personal staff looked clumsy by contrast as they followed their master onto the podium. They arranged themselves behind the chair, standing formally as they had before on the roof of the van.

A handsome bastard, Slade thought as he watched his enemy sit down. Cold as iced steel, but with the sort of slim good looks that aged better than fuller features did.

Dear Lord, who stood with our forefathers through storm and beasts, be with us now.

Beverly Dyson laid the commo-control board across the arms of his chair. He touched a switch, his own, the red one second from the upper left corner of the forty possibilities. Staring past the Slades and out over the Hall like a hawk sighting prey, he said, "As President, I call to order the Council of Tethys in this, its third formal meeting in the two-hundred and twelfth year of settlement."

Dyson's voice rang out through over a hundred speakers mounted overhead on the sloping walls. The lag between the nearest speaker and those further away created a dynamic echo throughout the Hall. Because the units were in phase, however, the result was clearly audible and not cacaphonous.

"The business before this Council today," the man in crimson continued, "is the choice of guardian for the Slade heir until his majority. No other business will be considered at this time."

It was one of the paradoxes of formal Council meetings that the Hall was too big for face to face contact and hugely too big for unaided speech. When they were scattered across the planet, the Councilors could see each other and speak simultaneously, using satellite relays and large split screens. In the Hall, Councilors could only be glimpsed when they chose to rise. All discussion was channelled through the board in the President's lap, which in turn fed the speakers overhead. Marilee and the thirty-eight Councilors, all but Dyson himself, held short batons. Thumbing the end of a baton would set a corresponding switch in the President's array alight. Not until the President threw that switch, however, would the baton glow and the Councilor's words be broadcast to the Hall. There was one exception to that general rule.

"I will now entertain a motion on the stated question," said Beverly Dyson. His words marched through the Hall with the sonorous majesty of a coronation parade.

Marilee was furiously pressing her baton. Dyson looked directly at her for the first time since he entered the Hall. He smiled and said, "The chair recognizes Councilor Hauksbee."

Clipped to the left epaulette of Slade's tunic was what looked like a standard microphone/loud-speaker, the sort of miniature unit issued to troops where the expense of mastoid implants was not justified. It had a simple mechanical key which Slade clicked home as he stood.

Who the hell did they think had *built* this place, anyway? Dysons?

"By custom of this Hall," the tanker said, "the first speaker on any question is a Slade. That's what my grandfather taught, and I never heard anybody call the Old Man a liar."

His voice rolled through the building. There was no immediate consternation, for the audience expected words. The import of the words which came was not immediately absorbed. The Old Man had liked hardware. He never presided over a meeting in the Hall, but it was with glee that he had demonstrated to young Donald the override which locked out the commo-control board. The override had still been in the Old Man's room, waiting for Don's need with the pair of remote units.

Somewhere toward the back of the Hall, Councibr Hauksbee's unaided voice was being swallowed by the space around it. Beverly Dyson was stabbing at the control board. His expression was one of furious incredulity.

Slade swung over the waist-high panel before him. He cocked his right knee, then, and mounted the low podium without bothering with the steps.

The Hall came alive with nervous exclamations, but the big man rode them down with the amplifiers as he said, "Today I'm the first speaker. And if there's anybody out there who hasn't guessed by now—I'm Don Slade, and I've come here to get justice for my nephew Edward." He paused. Very faintly through the facade of the Hall came the sound of what was happening in the courtyard.

CHAPTER THIRTY-THREE

"Hey, what'd those trucks do?" demanded one of Ahwas' men. "Give us the slip and go round the back way?"

"Bloody well better have," said another with a nod back toward the north wall of the courtyard. The wrecked cars had been removed, but the gravel was still enlivened by scorch marks and bright debris. The van had been parked outside the complex until the present dawn. It was easy enough to imagine the effect another out-of-control supply truck could have on Dyson's expensive scarlet vehicle.

The gate squealed inward before the cab of a truck. The leaves scraped as the vehicle edged them open, but that did no apparent harm to the battered skirts.

"Thought those gates were supposed to be locked," muttered Ahwas.

He wished the Master would give an order about this.

Danny Pritchard's mouth was filled with a dry vileness, as if someone had stuffed a used tennis ball into it. He was too old for this. He had been a *curst* fool to give up the body armor which alone had been his chance of living through the next hour. He was a tanker, by the Lord, and he went into the battle wearing only tinsel that would burn like a torch when he was killed!

Blood and Martyrs. Dyson's liverymen were in scattered clumps across the enclosure. They were either still gossiping among themselves or watching a second truck follow the first through the gate. They knew the meeting would last a minimum of two hours. The only business had been transacted months before, and the formalization required only minutes. All the Councilors would speak, however, both to praise Beverly Dyson out of fear and to hear the sound of their own voices in public.

There were forty-five Dyson liverymen in sight, plus one or more additional within the van to Pritchard's left front. The five observers were still loosely grouped where the detection cabinet had been set up. The specialist was wheeling his gear toward Slade House at something more than a normal pace.

There was Coon Blegan; and Danny Pritchard; and the Lord be *praised!* men in blue coveralls were climbing out of the back of the leading truck as it halted near the gate!

No rest for the wicked. Danny gripped the safety switch at the back of the gun housing. He swung it live in a hundred and eighty-degree arc. The drone quivered in a puff of dust and gravel as its systems came up. Pebbles pinged the skirt of its mate across the doorway. No one noticed because of the commotion at the gate.

Pritchard stepped away from the quivering drone. It was already beginning to drift because its drive fans were out of alignment. A bit of rock spanged from the second drone and rapped Pritchard's instep. He ignored it as he jumped to the second drone's back deck and threw its safety also. Then he dropped to the ground again as the air around the House doorway filled with grit and the sound of fans.

Somebody had noticed after all. Subiyaga flattened himself beside his equipment, twenty meters short of the House and safety. Pritchard did not have to see the specialist's expression to know it for one he had worn himself often enough, when it was about to drop in the pot and you could only hope the splash would miss you.

Both supply trucks were disgorging men, dozens of them. Each man gripped the bulky rocket gun of his trade. Liverymen who had started toward the trucks in curiosity now scrambled away. Submachine guns were being pointed from all around the yard.

When the drones were switched on, Danny Pritchard had no

reason to stand in the open. He gripped the yoke handles of the remote unit, knowing that the hologram display it threw up for his eyes would be the same whether he stood in the courtyard or behind the concrete facade of the House.

But what the Hell. The drone to his right moved as he twisted the controls. The orange pipper on the display skidded across a monochrome landscape to its target. Don Slade was home, but a lot of Danny Pritchard was home again also.

Ballenger flung open the side door of the van. "Hey!" he cried. His loud-hailer had a remote link and belt hooks, but he had not taken time to arrange them. "You *fishermen,*" his voice boomed.

"Get those filthy trucks out of here at once! Don't you realize that the Council will be processing through here in—"

The anti-tank gun on Pritchard's drone ripped the van the long way.

The cyan flash was narrow and intense, but its reflection seemed to fill every angle of the yard. The high-intensity 10 cm gun could knock out the heaviest tanks. On Tethys, it had been used for single-shot kills on creatures large enough to be mistaken for islands when glimpsed from the air. Like any powergun, it liberated most of its energy on the initial impact, but the charge was heavy enough that a hole puffed in the back wall of the van even as the cab exploded in the flames of its own vaporized components. The fireball pitched Ballenger onto the shingle. The skin of the Steward's back was unharmed, but his hair and livery were afire.

"Now listen up," roared the loudspeakers on the drone. The vehicle slid away from the spot in which it had been parked for a generation. There were occasional sparks where the left skirt continued to drag the gravel. "All Dyson servants, drop your guns. You will not be hurt. Drop your guns at once."

Several cases of ammunition in the van went off. Seams leaked blue-green light for an instant as the walls bulged. Then the rear of the vehicle sucked itself flat so abruptly that even the fire in the cab was beaten down for a moment. Subiyaga swore and began to scuttle toward the moaning steward.

The gun drone pivoted on its axis. "You will not be hurt," the loudspeakers repeated dissonantly.

The muzzle of the cannon glowed white. Heat waves above the barrel rippled the image of Slade House. The station crewmen were as surprised by the steel monster as were the Dyson retainers they had come to fight. The blue-suited crewmen were moving cautiously to keep the supply trucks between them and the drone.

As the gun rotated past him, Ahwas saw the ex-mercenary standing fifty meters away in the entryway of Slade House. Ahwas did not recognize Pritchard's voice through the drone's cracked amplification, nor was he fully aware of what Pritchard was doing. Still, he knew enough, and cowardice was not one of the guard leader's failings. Ahwas lifted his submachine gun and thumbed off the safety.

Coon Blegan fired twice from the gate leaf against which he braced his pistol. The second round was from training, not present need, because the first had blasted Ahwas' cap and skull. The head shots were deliberate because the submachine gun was already aimed.

Ahwas spun. His weapon raked the House facade. The window of the Trophy Room dissolved into hair-fine slivers that winked and danced in a cloud drifting down on the courtyard.

"Dyson servants, drop your weapons!" the drone snarled as it threw itself sideways at the pace of a fast walk. The dragging skirt bumped against Ahwas' body, then lurched over and through it. "You will not get another warning! Slade men, prepare to gather up the weapons."

Men were throwing down their automatic weapons. One guard stripped off his crimson tunic and flung it away as well. Like sheep, others began to pull off their livery also. Crewmen strode forward with burgeoning enthusiasm, slapping at one another with weathered hands as their nervousness dissipated.

Then the second drone, the one Danny Pritchard did not control, pulled away from the doorway. A frozen bearing screamed as it galled its shaft, but the heavy vehicle continued to gather speed. Subiyaga was trying to carry the injured steward to a place of relative safety beside the House. The drone swivelled around them, dragging its skirts instead through the molten wreckage of the van. As the drone continued, a trail of blazing plastic followed it toward the armored doors of the Hall.

"This man is an imposter!" Councilor Dyson shouted in a voice that only the handful nearest him could hear over the pandemonium in the Hall.

Slade turned. "Bev," he said, "you know me." He gestured with his left hand, palm down and fingers splayed. Again his amplified voice rocked through the high-pitched clamor. "But there doesn't have to be any trouble."

Dyson flung away the useless control board as he jumped from the chair. "Get him!" he screamed as he backed through his retainers. "Get him!"

Baucom hesitated, then lunged as the big tanker glanced down at the remote unit he gripped with both hands. Slade slammed his left elbow into Baucom's chest, hurling the liveryman back with cracked ribs. His fellows grabbed Slade from either side.

Instead of leaping to the podium himself, Edward Slade caught the nearer liveryman by the ankles and jerked. The man squawked as he fell, banging the point of a hip on the edge of the podium.

Marilee chopped at the liveryman's eyes with the top of her baton. "Come *on* you bastards!" she screamed at the Slade Housemen. She had no leisure to notice that one of the frightened servants actually did clamber onto the podium to face the score of men swarming from the Dyson enclosure.

Slade kneed the third of his immediate attackers in the groin, then shrugged loose from the crumpling man. He looked up from the hologram display. Beverly Dyson was five meters away, flattened against the outside wall. His hands were raised against the wrench which shimmered in his memory. Slade grinned and squeezed the trigger built into the right handle of his remote unit.

The doors of the Hall rang like a god's anvil when the ten-centimeter bolt struck.

The doors were built to be proof against the largest and most vicious monsters that Tethys spawned, but it was only the thickness of the crossbar which kept the anti-tank round from penetrating the Hall as a jet of directed energy. Instead, the great room lighted with a white flash that painted sharp shadows across the wall beyond the podium. Blazing steel and a plasma that had been steel bulged across the squad of Dyson retainers still hesitating near the doors where they were stationed. None of them had time to scream as they shrivelled.

"Don't *move!*" shouted Slade and the speakers as the echoes crashed.

Half the crossbar still sagged against the door beneath the glowing cavity in the center where the leaves met. The other half had been ripped from its bracket by the gout of gaseous metal. The powergun bolt had no kinetic energy of its own, but its impact created enormous secondary kinetic effects.

"Don't move!" Slade repeated, wheeling on the Dyson liverymen whose rush the flash and blast had frozen. The armored drone Slade controlled slammed against the doors, breaking the fresh welds which sealed the panels when the bar was shot away. The doors recoiled open. The fighting vehicle waddled into the Hall.

Husks of liverymen near the door powdered as the skirts touched them. They whipped around the drone as bitter smoke.

The aisle was wide enough for the drone's deliberate passage, but the long-ignored running gear required more than an inertial guidance mechanism to keep the brute in a straight line. When Slade looked up from his display, the drone's back end swung enough to splinter panels of the Hauksbee enclosure. Not, perhaps, the least fortunate of accidents.

"All of you, back out of here," Slade ordered. He gestured with the remote unit toward the red-suited retainers who now cowered at the edge of the podium or just beneath it. The drone had no turret. The whole vehicle rotated in the aisle to enforce Slade's will with the muzzle of the gun.

A number of the liverymen were ducking so that they could no longer see Slade. It was a common misconception. Its converse made drones difficult to manipulate. Slade's own line of sight did not control the cannon's fire. The pipper on the remote display did, and its sending unit was part of the gun mount. Slade and Pritchard had decades of experience guiding heavy armor with no view but that from remote pick-ups. Handling the drones was second nature for them, as it would have been to a settler of the first generation.

Edward Slade stood to his uncle's left, Marilee to Don's right. The Houseman who had jumped to the podium was now standing upright and wondering what to do with his hands. Dyson retainers slunk away from him and from the podium. The broad lighting strips in the roof still seemed dim after the fireball which had blasted clear the doors.

"This isn't a place for people anymore," said Don. The drone slid to the end of the aisle. He grounded the vehicle there, almost touching the podium. Its armored skirts sang and sparked as they settled on the concrete. "We'll go outside—Via, we'll go to the, there's room for forty in the Trophy Room and we can talk—"

"Don!" screamed the woman to his right.

Edward was fast, very fast for a youth with neither training nor experience. He jumped toward Dyson. But Don Slade was the pro, the Mad Dog, and he was fast enough to catch his nephew by the arm and fling him out of the killing zone.

Beverly Dyson was still backed against the wall three meters away, but his hands no longer covered his face. He aimed a glass derringer, the only metal in it the atom's thickness which mirrored the interior of the barrel.

Not a military weapon at all, Slade thought fleetingly, but neither is a man a tank. Aloud, forgetting the link that threw his voice out over the speakers, he said, "Go ahead, Bev. I don't think you've got the guts."

Slade's last thought before the derringer fired was how the Hell had he mistaken Dyson for a handsome man. The face glaring over the muzzle could have come from deep wat—

The bolt made a light popping sound in the air and a crash like breaking glass when it struck the middle of Slade's chest. The big man staggered backward. There were screams from several points in the Hall, though why, one more shooting on *this* day . . . ?

Dyson tossed the gun away like a man snapping a spider from his hand. The discharged piece was too hot to hold. It clattered against the wall and back to the podium.

A plate-sized patch had been burned from the center of Slade's tunic. Its edges were still asmolder. The breastplate of the ceramic armor beneath the tunic was blackened. Crinkle marks at the center of the pattern indicated that the plate would have to be replaced. It had been degraded to uselessness in absorbing the single bolt.

Guess I owe Danny for a chicken suit, Slade thought as he raised the President's chair in one hand. His laughter boomed out over the speakers and he added aloud, "And my life . . ." No one in the Hall understood the words, but by that point no one particularly expected to.

The chair was wooden, like the benches, and probably as uncomfortable for all its smooth curves. It weighed fifteen kilos, a clumsy bludgeon but a massive one. Slade poised it overhead. "Thirty years, Bev, hasn't it been?" he said.

Councilor Dyson turned to the wall. He began trying to claw and bite through the concrete.

Marilee touched Slade's shoulder, the left one, the one that held the chair poised. "Don," she said very softly. "No."

"He's faking that," said Slade and the speakers.

There was blood where Dyson's fingers scratched. The sound of his teeth on the age-darkened concrete was more hideous than a scream.

Slade turned. He tried to set the chair down gently, but his muscles failed him and let it crash to the podium. "Dear Lord," he said. "Dear Lord."

Men and women had already begun to move toward the door. They stepped gingerly or with the set expressions of feigned ignorance as they crunched through what had been the guards. Already the shadows of armed men waiting in the courtyard darkened the doorway. Councilors and their vari-colored retainers paused, trapped between death and uncertainty.

"Go on out," Slade called. "You won't be harmed. No one will be harmed. We're men here on Tethys, not animals."

Beside Slade, Beverly Dyson mewled against the wall he was beginning to scar.

CHAPTER THIRTY-FOUR

"I'll have the Trophy Room readied," Marilee said. She took a deep breath in reaction to the past minutes. Even on this end of the Hall, the air was bitter with ozone and sweetened by death. "The House doors have probably been locked," she added wryly. "I don't doubt you can get in, but . . ."

Slade let the remote unit fall, as if his right arm no longer had strength for its burden. He clicked off the speaker control pinned to his left shoulder as well. "Yeah," he said. "I'll—be along. Have to take care . . ." His voice trailed off as he glanced back at Dyson.

"That's all right," said Edward unexpectedly. The youth had a long pressure-cut on his forehead. Both sleeves of his morning coat had ripped loose at the armpits. "You two—" He pointed at the pair of Dyson liverymen trying to creep off the podium. "Yes, you— Baucom, isn't it? Get back here and restrain the Councilor. We'll take him to the House medicomp. He needs treatment."

Edward turned to his mother and uncle. Marilee nodded very briskly. She scrambled off the podium and over the silent gun drone as quickly as she could. She wanted to prevent the fact that she was crying from being obvious to her son, no longer a boy.

The Houseman who had joined her on the podium now looked around. "I'm coming, Mistress," he called loudly as he bolted after the woman.

You never know, thought Slade as he walked slowly up the long aisle. You never know about other people, and you never know about yourself. Don Slade was anything on Tethys now that he wanted to be . . .

Many of the spectators in the Hall were only now beginning to leave. Shock and fright had kept them hunched behind partitions that would have been of no more account than farts in whirlwind, had the fighting really rolled their way. Now these folk ducked back out of the aisle or scudded ahead of Slade's progress with fearful looks behind them.

Home? Blood and Martyrs! But that would pass, and Don Slade was home indeed.

"I was getting ready to come look for you," said Danny Pritchard. The ex-mercenary lounged again beside the gun of his fighting vehicle. This time it was parked beside the shattered doors to the Hall, as still as it had been when day broke. "Marilee said you'd be along, though, so I figured I could wait."

He slid off the drone. "Here," he said, holding out one of the submachine guns gathered from Dyson's thugs. "You might want this."

Slade took the weapon, checking the load and safety by instinct. He gazed around the courtyard. The pool of orange flames and bubbling smoke took a moment to connect with Dyson's van. There didn't appear to have been the carnage he had feared and expected, though.

There was a crowd of what had surely been Dyson's guards in a corner between the House and the enclosure wall. Most of them had lost their livery as well as their weapons for some reason. Fishermen were pointing guns at their captives from the ground and from the roofs of the supply trucks. There would probably be accidents, but Slade was not disposed to worry about the despondent liverymen at this moment.

Chesson, atop one of the trucks, waved and shouted when Slade appeared from the building. "We got 'em, Soldier," he called gleefully.

"Just a little longer," the tanker shouted back. "By the Lord, it won't be forgotten."

"You know, Danny," Slade said to his companion, "I don't think I want this after all. Not right now." He handed back the gun he was holding. A stream of people was passing across the courtyard from the Hall, but only Council members seemed to be entering the House. Marilee had matters under control there already.

"Let's go talk to some people about the Slade Estate," said the big man mildly. "And about Tethys, I do suppose."

Together, the ex-mercenaries began walking toward the House. Danny Pritchard still cradled the automatic weapon.

"Everyone's gone upstairs, D-don," said Marilee from the bottom of the staircase. The name had come so smoothly from her memory that she stumbled when she paused to consider what she was saying.

Slade smiled. "I thought at least a few of the Councilors'd figure the going was good," he said. "Marilee."

"They may be afraid of what you've got to say," noted Danny Pritchard from the political background which had absorbed him since Hammer took Friesland. "But they're going to be a lot more afraid of not being there when you say it."

He chuckled. In a different persona he added, "Want some company while you talk?" Pritchard did not have to gesture with the gun to make his meaning clear.

Slade punched him gently on the arm. "Hey," the big man said, "that's *my* line. I think—" He paused, then went on. "Upstairs I've got to handle myself. I'm the guy who's going to live here, right?"

Pritchard grinned. "Via, you're learning," he said approvingly. "Come back to Friesland and I'll find you a job in Admin. Hang in there, snake. I'm going to organize some of those people—" he gestured in the general direction of the hidden prisoners— "into a clean-up crew. Crispy critters are likely to offend the tender sensibilities of your peers."

Whistling, Hammer's heir strolled back toward the courtyard. Slade watched him for a moment. Then the big man cleared his throat and offered his crooked elbow to Marilee. "Shall we?" he said.

The woman's mouth quirked in a fashion that could have broadened into a smile. "The stairs are a little tight, aren't they?"

"Via, has it been so long?" Slade said with a chuckle that loosened his muscles and his taut, turbid mind. "Come on, my dear." His arm looped out to circle Marilee's waist. It was, he thought as they climbed in step made awkward by the wedgeshaped treads, a very long time. And it felt as good now as ever it had.

CHAPTER THIRTY-FIVE

Every Council member was standing, though there were seats enough in the Trophy Room for at least half of them.

The room's width between the trophy wall and the shot-out window was enough to keep the gathering from being cramped. No one wanted to be in the front, however. As a result, the Councilors were strung out along the window transom as if awaiting a firing party. Their faces bore out that suggestion, Slade thought as he strode to the center of the room.

"All right, now everybody move closer," Slade said. He raised his voice of necessity but avoided harsh modulations. "We're going to talk like human beings, that's all."

He had done this job before, many times before. Every time his troops set up in a populated area, the local leaders had to be called together. Frightened; the timid ones sure they were about to be shot, the smart ones aware that they *could* be shot at the mercenary's whim, whatever might be the orders of a distant headquarters. These faces were the same, though Slade recognized at least a dozen of them from his childhood.

The Councilors moved in from either end. Most of them shuffled, but two or three stepped firmly and kept their shoulders squared. Jose Hauksbee was one—still short, still pudgy, but willing to meet Slade's eyes. Dyson had not chosen a sycophant, then, to move his triumph but rather a true ally or a foe, now broken to obedience.

"I returned from fighting," the big tanker said as sullen faces waited in a shallow arc around him. When he swayed, he could feel the skull of the knife-jaw at his shoulders and the warmth of Marilee beside him again. "What happened today I regret, it's not what I came home to do. I didn't come back to run the Slade Estate, either."

He paused and emphasized his words by staring at the men and women around him. "That was for my brother," he went on, "and it'll be for his son . . . but right now, because you've decided Edward should have a guardian for the next two years, I think it might be a good idea it you appointed me."

There was a hiss of conversation with one clear voice wondering, "Where *is* the boy, then?"

"I move," cried a Councilor whom Slade did not recognize, "that Donald Slade be confirmed by acclamation as Councilor and heir of his father in accordance with evidence presented at our last meeting." The man who spoke was old and slender with dissipation rather than health. His teeth were perfect. Only the way his face moved when he grinned suggested they were rotten.

"No!" Don Slade was shouting. Marilee's fingers were tight on his left arm. What he heard was a nightmare, a demon repeating words that Slade himself had spoken only in his own mind, over and over as he paced through the courtyard he had won by force of arms. "No, I don't—say that. Guardian for my nephew Edward, Councilor and heir of the Slade Estate. To his majority. That, Via, only that."

"So moved," said Councilor Hauksbee, "by acclamation." He continued to meet Slade's eyes.

There was a rattle of agreement and clapping, even some cheers. If there had been a formal second, it was lost in the noise . . . as the problem would be lost in the formal record.

"One other thing," said Slade, raising his voice over the babble that followed the action. "There's some problems at the Port. If you'll give me six months and a free hand, there won't be problems anymore."

"So moved!" cried the Councilor who had earlier tried to make Slade Councilor in his own right.

"Wait a minute!" the big man added as concern again blanked

the faces of many of those around him. "The Port is an enclave, not part of the Slade Estate. Nothing's changing except that *everybody's* goods are going to be moving through again without screwing around." Slade raised his hands to keep the silence while his words marshalled themselves. "I don't want what you have. I don't even want what Dyson has. His estate will pass by law, wherever. But I'm Don Slade, people. What *I* have, I hold!"

The hush that followed was broken by Hauksbee's dry voice saying, "I second the motion of Councilor Gardiner."

The rattle of agreement which followed was again whole-hearted.

Slade put his arm around the woman beside him. "That's all I have to say," he remarked. The relief and elation he felt softened his voice. "I suppose whatever arrangements were planned for after the meeting are still on."

There were a half dozen cheers. Councilors surged forward to clasp the hand of the man from whom they had edged in terror moments before. Through the chorus of flattery and congratulation, Slade alone really noticed what Councilor Hauksbee was shouting. "Wait a minute!" the tanker roared. He raised his hands again. "Wait a minute!"

Hauksbee had not stepped forward, though he had been the nearest to Slade of the Councilors when the meeting began. With the background noise low enough for everyone now to hear him, Hauksbee said, "What happens to Dyson, Councilor Slade? What happens to the people who supported him? I was nominating him as guardian, you know."

And by the Lord! Dyson hadn't picked a coward for that task, Slade thought. Aloud the big man said, "Bev goes into exile. He can't be here and me be safe, it's that simple. Or any of you safe either."

Slade glanced sternly around the gathering. "Most of the servants he'd gathered up, they'll go too. Lot of them aren't from Tethys to begin with, and we sure as hell don't need them around. For the rest—"

There was a collective intake of breath from the Council. Even Hauksbee swallowed as he tried not to look away from the tanker.

"For the rest, I'm not asking questions and I'm not listening to tales. We've all done things in our past we don't want to be reminded of. Forget about—Via, the past twenty years on Tethys, if you like. I will."

"Why of course—" and "I always said the Slades—" were the only phrases the tanker could hear clearly in the sycophantic chorus. Hauksbee pursed his lips and nodded acceptance, not joy.

"Jose, all of you!" Slade said, using his voice to hammer its own path of silence. Men were grasping his hands. He did not snatch them away, but the slighter fingers fell away from Slade's scarred, powerful ones as he spoke.

"I'm not a saint," Slade went on in the new silence. "I've done terrible things." He swallowed.

Only a few of the faces turned toward Slade understood the sort of things he meant. The profession of slaughter, like others, has its arcana. No one could doubt Slade's sincerity when he went on. "I don't need to lie, people. If somebody's going to be shot, I'll tell you. Bev isn't, and neither are his boys."

There was another roar and surge of agreement. This time Slade responded to every hand, every enthusiastic greeting with the comment, "I appreciate that. You'll want to get down to your people right away and explain that the trouble's over."

He himself was walking slowly toward the door. Marilee paced just ahead of the tanker to boost Councilors to escape velocity with her own handshake and grim smile. *She* had not promised to forget.

Councilor Hauksbee was the last. "I owe you an apology, Mister Slade," the pudgy man said. He extended his hand but did not snatch at Slade's the way so many others had done.

"It was Don when we were kids, Jose," Slade said with a smile. They had not been friends, but each boy for his own reasons had a circle of enemies which often overlapped. "And you needn't apologize for honesty. Not anymore."

The handshake was a little more than formal. The trio poised by the door out of the room. "Not for being honest," Hauksbee said, "but for assummg you weren't. I—just wanted to be sure of the rules."

Slade nodded. His hand was now touching Marilee's again. "There's an Alayan ship in orbit," he said to Hauksbee. "The—Bev and the rest, they'll go aboard. Some may be released on Friesland, if Danny and the Colonel think they'd be useful. Most'll stay with the Alayans for—use." The tanker cleared his throat. How in the *hell* had the Alayans known there would be a cargo for them on Tethys? "They won't be mistreated, but they won't leave the ship."

"We'll talk later," Hauksbee said as he stepped through the door. When he was already out of sight of the anteroom, he called back, "I'm glad you've come home, Don."

"Are *you* glad, Don?" Marilee asked coolly. She stepped to the door to close it. She did not move back into his waiting arms.

"I came home because I wanted to be on Tethys," Slade said. He spoke as he would have walked through a minefield, slowly and with the greatest care. "For various reasons. And if you mean 'glad I came just now'—yeah, I suppose I am. Somebody needed to put things straight. I guess it's worked out as well as anybody was going to make it."

"Guns do make it easier to run things, don't they?" the woman said in the same brittle tone. She began to walk back along the trophy wall, skirting the man as she passed him.

"Listen, curse it!" Slade said. He paced behind the woman, fists clenched, the image of a carnivore at heel. "The guns were there before I was born. The only difference now is there's a *man* behind them again. I'm not going to melt down those gun-trucks, but they'll stay parked till they rust away for anything I do in the next two years."

Marilee spun. "Can I believe that?" she snapped. Her blue gown had not torn in the fighting, but there was a bruise showing already on her left cheekbone.

"Anything we've got left is an administrative problem," Slade said quietly. "I'm not real good at those, but I know how to recognize people who are. You don't use guns to solve admin problems."

He took a deep breath that trembled with the emotion he was trying to keep out of his voice. "But there's gun problems too, Marilee. Don't ever forget it. And don't blame me for seeing that there are."

She moved slightly, away from the wall. He saw the trophy that her body had screened as they walked back from the door. The argus larva was no more than the length of Slade's adult arm, but its spines still bristled with the vicious intensity of life. Old Man Slade had replaced each one of those which the boy's bare hands had shattered.

"I don't blame you," said Marilee as she extended her arms. "Welcome home, Don."

AFTERWORD:
where I get my ideas

If you decide to write about far-famed Achilles,
make him active, hot-tempered, inexorable, and
fierce; let him deny that laws were made for him,
let him think his sword rules all.
—Horace, *The Art of Poetry* (lines 120–2)

My undergraduate double major was history and Latin, and I continued to take Latin courses while I was in law school in a laughable attempt to stay sane. Reading Latin centers me. (Note "laughable" in the previous sentence.)

A story doesn't depend on the language in which it's told, and a story that's been around for several thousand years is likely to be a very good story. While rereading *The Odyssey* (in translation; Ben Jonson would be even more slighting about my Greek than he was about Shakespeare's) I remarked to a friend that the story would make an excellent Western.

And as I said that, a light dawned: *The Odyssey* would make a heck of a space opera as well, though translating Homer's story to an SF idiom would take some subtlety if I were to avoid being absurd. For example, I couldn't just have my hero land on a planet of one-eyed giants who shut him and his crew in a cave. But what about an automated city that . . . ?

I did a precis of *The Odyssey* and plotted my story around that armature, focusing always on situations that would serve the same structural purposes that Homer had achieved in his medium. Then I wrote *Cross the Stars*.

By the way, the Cyclopes appear twice in *The Odyssey*: once in direct conflict with Odysseus (which everybody remembers) and once as the creatures whose savage attacks drove the Phaecians out of their original home. If you've just finished reading *Cross the Stars*, you may recall a passing reference to giant one-eyed mutants. The latter, like the local creature called the argus and other asides in my novel, is homage to the man/men/woman who wrote *The Odyssey*; and who is, for my money, the greatest literary genius of all time.

As I was writing *Cross the Stars* I commented to the same friend that while *The Odyssey* translated easily to other media, *The Iliad* (perhaps an even greater achievement) was too fixed in its own cultural idiom to be used the way I did the other. For a long time I believed that meant I couldn't use *The Iliad* at all in my fiction.

One day I was rereading Horace's *Ars Poetica* and came to the quotation I've translated as the epigraph to this essay. Homer is the only source for the character of Achilles (which Horace summarizes with his usual succinct brilliance), but the *character* can have a life outside the cultural confines of *The Iliad*. There are and always have been men (and here I mean "male human beings") like Achilles; Alexander the Great made a conscious attempt to model his life on the character (and succeeded, in my opinion, only too well).

So I thought about the problem for a long while, then wrote *The Warrior*. I set the piece (a short novel) in the Hammer universe, as I had *Cross the Stars* before it, but *The Warrior* was straight military—as surely as *The Iliad* is. I used the milieu of modern warfare, of tanks rather than armored spearmen, and the background has no connection with the Siege of Troy.

But remember, Homer didn't say he was writing about the Siege of Troy: *I sing the wrath of Achilles. . . .*

Not all of my plots come from classical (or even historical) sources, but most of them do. That's not only because of my personal taste, but because I believe (with Shakespeare) that literature which survives the buffeting of time is worth a second or thirty-second look.

I opened with a quote from Horace. I'll close with another one: *I have builded a monument more lasting than bronze. . . .* Horace did; and Homer did, and Apollonius did, and so many others did. I'm proud to be able occasionally to stand on their magnificent structures.

—Dave Drake
Chatham County, NC

THE VOYAGE

DEDICATION

To Clyde and Carlie Howard

Because they're friends—
and in hope that it was worth the wait.

ACKNOWLEDGMENTS

It's amazing the number of people who helped me on this one. As I edited my manuscript, I kept noticing places where a friend had been of direct assistance (and there were others that I don't recall, I'm sure).

Among the folks I owe on this one are Dan Breen, Sandra Miesel, John Rieber and Kent Williams, Mark Van Name, Allyn Vogel, Clyde and Carlie Howard, and my wife Jo. As I said, there were others as well.

I owe a particular debt to Tom Doherty. Not because he bought the book (which I appreciate, but somebody was going to buy it) but rather because he saved me from myself when the size of the project became clear to me.

It's good to have friends.

CONTENTS

TELARIA

As Ned Slade walked toward the dockyard building with the HEADQUARTERS—PANCAHTE EXPEDITION sign on the door, a line of six human males and a squat, shaggy alien from Racontis jogged past.

"You wonder why I'm a private," the leader sang.

"And why I sleep in the ditch," sang-wheezed the remaining joggers in several keys. The Racontid had a clear, carrying voice which would better have suited an angel than a creature which could pull a strong man apart with its bare hands.

A metal saw shrilled within the starship in the adjacent frames, overwhelming the song. Ned's mind supplied the words anyway: *"It's not because I'm stupid, but I just don't want to be rich . . ."*

The door was ajar. Ned knocked, but he couldn't hear the rap of his own knuckles over the saw, so he let himself in.

"Shut the curst thing!" ordered the man at the electronic desk, cupping a palm over his telephone handset. He was paunchy and at least sixty standard years old. "I can't hear myself think!"

As he spoke, the saw blade coasted back to silence. The fellow at the desk returned to his call. The rangy, somewhat younger man leaning against the office wall prevented Ned from swinging the door to. "Leave it, kid," the man said. "I like the ventilation."

Ned looked from one stranger to the other. Neither of them paid him any attention. "No," the older man said into his handset, "I'm Adjutant Tadziki, but it will *not* help if you call back when

Captain Doormann is here. She's already made her decision on a supplier."

Tadziki looked like a bureaucrat. The other fellow wore a stone-pattern camouflaged jumpsuit with WARSON, T over the left breast pocket. Ned didn't recognize the uniform, but Warson was as obviously a soldier as the men and the Racontid jogging around the starship outside were. Warson continued to gaze out the window, singing under his breath, *I could've been a general and send out folks to die . . .*"

"No," said the adjutant, "since she'll be eating the rations herself, your offer of saving three-hundredths per kilo isn't very important to her—and it *bloody* well isn't important to me!"

"*But the sort of things a general does,*" Ned murmured, watching the soldier, "*they make me want to cry.*"

Warson turned sharply. "You know the song?" he asked.

Tadziki slammed down the handset. "Fucking idiot!" he said.

"Yeah, but in an armored unit it's '*You ask why I'm a trooper,*'" Ned said. "That's the way I learned it."

"Where?" Tadziki asked. "And for that matter, who the hell are you?"

"On Nieuw Friesland," Ned said. "In the Frisian Defense Forces. I'm Reserve Ensign Slade, but I'm from Tethys originally."

"Slade?" Warson said in amazement. "You're *Don* Slade? Via, you can't be!"

Ned's lips tightened. "You're thinking of my uncle," he said stiffly. "I'm not Don Slade, no."

The voices of the jogging troops became faintly louder. They were making circuits around the vessel under construction. Warson nodded disdainfully toward the window and said, "Herne Lordling's got us doing an hour's run each day to shape us up. They're singing that to piss him off."

"Lordling's a general?" Ned asked.

"He was a colonel," Warson said. "He's a pissant, is what he really is. Sure you want to join a rinky-dink outfit being run by a pissant, kid?"

"Lordling isn't running anything," Tadziki said sharply. "Captain Doormann gave the order, and she gives all the orders."

He suddenly smiled. "Via, Toll," he added, patting his gut. "I'm twenty years older than you and I'd never run across a *room* before this stuff started. It's still a good idea."

"*I could have been a colonel,*" the joggers chorused, "*but there it is again . . .*"

"I want to join the Pancahte Expedition, yeah," Ned said, handing an identification chip across the desk to the adjutant. "Whoever's running it."

"We're pretty full up," Warson said without emotion. He could have been commenting on the color of the Telarian sky, pale white with faint gray streaks.

"*The plush seats colonels sit on, they tickle my sensitive skin . . .*"

"The captain makes all those decisions, Toll," said the adjutant as he watched the data his desk summoned from Ned's ID. "Especially those decisions."

"I never met your uncle," Toll Warson said, eyeing Ned with quiet speculation. His look was that of a man who had absolutely nothing to prove—but who would be willing to prove it any way, anytime, anywhere, if somebody pushed him a little too far.

Ned recognized the expression well. He'd seen it often enough in his uncle's eyes.

The door to the inner room opened. A man in fluorescent, extremely expensive clothing looked out and said, "Did you say Lissea had . . . ?" He seemed to be about Ned's age, twenty-four years standard. A quick glance around the outer office, empty save for the three men, ended his question.

Tadziki answered it anyway. "Sorry, Master Doormann," he said. "I'm sure she's coming, but I'm afraid she must still be in the armaments warehouse with Herne."

The young man grimaced in embarrassment and disappeared behind the closed door again.

"Lucas Doormann," Tadziki explained in a low voice. "He's son of Doormann Trading's president—that's Karel Doormann—but he's not a bad kid. He's trying to help, anyway, when his father would sooner slit all our throats."

"Didn't have balls enough to volunteer to come along, though," Warson said, again without emotional loading.

"Via, Toll, would you want him?" Tadziki demanded. "He *maybe* knows not to stand at the small end of a gun."

Warson shrugged. "Different question," he said.

The phone rang. Tadziki winced. "Toll," he said, "how about you play adjutant for half an hour and I take Slade here over the *Swift?* Right?"

Warson's smile was as blocky as ice crumpling across a river in spring. He reached for the handset. "You bet," he said. "Does that mean I get all the rake-off from suppliers, too?"

Tadziki hooked a finger to lead Ned out of the office. "Try anything funny," he growled, "and you'll save the Pancahtans the trouble of shooting you."

Warson laughed as he picked up the phone. Ned heard him say, "Pancahte Expedition, the Lord Almighty speaking."

The adjutant paused outside the office and looked up at the vessel in the frames. She was small as starships went, but her forty meters of length made her look enormous by comparison with the fusion-powered tanks Ned had learned to operate and deploy on Friesland.

"What do you know about this operation, kid?" Tadziki asked.

"I know," Ned said carefully, "that I prefer to be called Slade, or Ned, or dickhead . . . sir."

Tadziki raised an eyebrow. "Touchy, are we?" he asked.

Ned smiled. "Nope. When I get to be somebody, maybe I'll get touchy, too. But since it was you I was talking to, I thought I'd mention it."

"Yeah, don't say anything to Toll Warson that he's likely to take wrong," Tadziki agreed. "Do you know about him?"

Ned shook his head.

"Well, this is just a story," Tadziki said. "A rumor. You know, stories get twisted a lot in the telling."

". . . *could've been an officer,*" sang the joggers as they rounded the nose of the vessel. They moved at a modest pace, but one that would carry them seven or eight kilometers in an hour if they kept it up. The Racontid ran splay-legged, like a wolverine on its hind legs.

"*But I was just too smart . . .*"

"Seems Toll and his brother Deke had a problem with a battalion commander on Stanway a few years back," Tadziki said.

"*They stripped away my rank tabs . . .*"

"One night the CO pushed the switch to close up his command car—"

"*When they saw me walk and fart!*"

"—and the fusion bottle vented into the vehicle's interior," Tadziki said. He cleared his throat. "Toll and Deke turned out to have deserted a few hours before, hopping two separate freighters off-planet. Some people suggested there might have been a connection."

He nodded to the boarding bridge to the hatch amidships. "Let's go aboard."

They walked in single file, the adjutant leading. Power cables and high-pressure lines snaked up the bridge and into the ship, narrowing the track.

"He looks like the kind who'd play hardball," Ned said with deliberate calm, "Toll Warson does. But that's what I'd expect from people who'd—respond to Lissea Doormann's offer."

Tadziki laughed harshly as he ducked to enter the vessel. He would have cleared the transom anyway, unlike Ned who was taller by fifteen centimeters. "You don't know the half of it, Slade," he said. "The battalion commander was their own brother. Half-brother."

The inner face of the airlock projected a meter into the vessel. Tadziki gestured around the vessel's main bay, crowded now by workmen in protective gear operating welders and less identifiable tools. "Welcome to the *Swift,* trooper," the adjutant said. "If you decide to go through with your application, and if you're picked, she'll be your home for the next long while."

Tadziki looked at Ned. "Maybe the rest of your life."

"It'll do," Ned said. "Anyway, it's roomier than a tank."

The bay was filled with bunks stacked two-high on either side of a central aisle. The pairs were set with a respectable space open between them, because they gimballed in three axes to act as acceleration couches. That meant there was no storage within the bay except for the narrow drawer beneath each mattress.

There were two navigation consoles forward, still part of the open bay. Astern were two partitioned cubicles and, against the heavy bulkhead separating the bay from the engine compartment, an alcove holding a commode. Workmen were installing a folding, door to screen the commode.

"That was my idea," Tadziki explained with a glance toward the alcove. "Lissea said she didn't need special favors. I told her she might think she was just one of the guys, but things were going to be tense enough without her dropping her trousers in front of everybody on a regular basis."

Ned nodded to show he was listening while he scanned the confusion to count places. There were sixteen bunks, plus the pair of navigation couches and the private cubicles for— presumably—the captain and adjutant. It was possible but very unlikely that there were bunks in the engine compartment as well.

"Twenty places," Tadziki said in confirmation. "Six of them for ship's crew—sailors. A few of the others can double in brass. I can."

He looked sharply at Ned. "I gather from the curriculum in your ID you know something about ships yourself?"

Ned shrugged. "I've had a course in basic navigation," he agreed. "In a pinch, I'd be better than punching in coordinates blind, I suppose. And fusion bottles are pretty much the same, tanks or starships."

The saw began to shriek again as a workman shortened the mounting stanchion of the pair of bunks which had to clear the airlock's encroachment. The sound was painful. Despite the tool's suction hood, chips of hot steel sprayed about the bay.

Ned backed out onto the boarding bridge a moment before the adjutant gestured him to do so. When the workman shut the saw down, Ned said, "I was at home in Slade House on Tethys when Captain Doormann's message came. That's all I know about the expedition—that Lissea Doormann's preparing to visit the Lost Colony of Pancahte with a picked crew."

"And," Tadziki said, nodding but smiling slightly as well, "that she invited Captain Donald Slade to accompany her."

"She could do worse than take Uncle Don," Ned said crisply. "She could do worse than take me, too."

An air-wrench began to pound within the *Swift*'s bay. Tadziki motioned Ned to follow him back down the boarding bridge, sauntering this time.

"Telaria's pretty much a family concern," the adjutant explained. "The Doormann family. There's a planetary assembly here at Landfall City, but the real decisions get made at the Doormann estate just outside the town proper."

He nodded vaguely northward.

"Okay," Ned said to show that he understood the situation—as he certainly did. Many of the less populous (and not necessarily less advanced) human worlds were run by a family or a tight-knit oligarchy. On Tethys, the Slade family had been preeminent since the planet was settled centuries before.

"Twenty-odd years ago, there was a flash meeting of the Doormann Trading board while the president, Grey Doormann, was on a junket off-system on Dell," Tadziki said. "Grey's half-brother Karel replaced him as president. The genetic access codes to Doormann Trading facilities and data banks were reset to deny Grey entry."

The joggers had finished their exercise and were straggling toward the two-story prefab beside the office building. None of the men were less than ten years older than Ned. They moved with the heavy grace of male lions.

"Okay," Ned repeated. Power was a commodity always in short supply. The events Tadziki had described were thoroughly civilized. On some worlds, a similar transfer would have been conducted by hirelings like Toll Warson and Don Slade, late of Hammer's Slammers.

The adjutant paused at the base of the boarding bridge and looked out across the dockyard. A mobile crane squealed as its boom lowered a drive motor into place. A dirigible carried a slingload of hull plates slowly across the sky to a freighter being constructed at the opposite end of the complex. The thrum of nacelle-mounted props provided a bass line to the yard's higher-pitched activities.

"Karel didn't know Grey's wife had just borne a daughter, though," Tadziki said. "They left the baby on Dell to be raised by a couple there they trusted. The parents came back and lived in a private bungalow here on the Doormann estate, as quiet as church mice."

"Lissea Doormann was the daughter?" Ned said, again to show that he followed.

"You bet," Tadziki agreed. "She had the genes, and there wasn't a specific block on her code . . . so six months ago, she waltzed into the middle of a board meeting to demand a seat and control of her branch of the family's stock. Grey had left Karel with a proxy when he went dicking off to Dell. Lissea claimed to revoke it as assignee of her father's interest."

He shook his head and smiled. "I'd have liked to been at that meeting," he added.

Ned frowned. "Weren't there human guards?" he asked.

"Close to a thousand of them," the adjutant said. "I've seen base camps in war zones that weren't near as well defended as the Doormann estate. But she *was* a Doormann, an unarmed woman. The guards didn't realize just who she was, but they curst well knew that if she was a family member, she could have them flayed if they were uppity enough to lay a hand on her."

Ned grinned and looked back at the *Swift*. "The prodigal daughter returns," he murmured. "It sure proves the expedition's leader has guts."

While the commercial liner that brought him to Telaria landed, Ned had watched the displays. The hectares of open area north of Landfall City proper (strip development surrounded it on all sides) must be the Doormann estate rather than a large public park as he'd assumed. There was a tall central spire and scores of smaller buildings scattered over the grounds.

"Oh, she's got guts, all right," Tadziki said. "Brains, too. Lissea's foster father had her trained as an electronics engineer, and she's a good one. I doubt there was ever anything Lissea really cared about besides booting her uncle out of the presidency, but she's an asset to the expedition as an engineer, believe me."

"*Why* an expedition to Pancahte?" Ned prompted.

"The short answer," Tadziki said, "is that seventy years ago one Lendell Doormann embezzled a large sum from Doormann Trading and fled, it's rumored, to Pancahte. Now, what Karel might have done if he'd had Lissea alone is one thing, but at a board meeting where everybody present was her relative as well as his, well they weren't going to just call in the guards. So Karel came up with a compromise."

Ned pursed his lips. "Lissea recovers the missing assets from Pancahte, in exchange for which, Karel doesn't challenge her right to vote her father's stock."

"When she returns," Tadziki agreed. "Which Karel doesn't think she's going to do." He gave Ned a rock-hard smile. Ned was suddenly aware that Tadziki deserved to be adjutant of a force comprised of men like Toll Warson. "Me," Tadziki said, "I'm betting on the lady. I'm betting my life."

A limousine drove through the dockyard gates. Men in blue uniforms on three-wheelers escorted the car before and behind. The guards carried iridium-barreled powerguns like those of President Hammer's forces on Nieuw Friesland.

Ned thought of the veterans of Hammer's mercenary regiment whom he'd met, men and women whose scars were as often behind their eyes as on their skin. Veterans like Don Slade.

The guards looked like puppies.

The limousine drew up in front of the office. A big man jumped from one side of the vehicle and strode quickly around the back toward the other door. He wore a holstered pistol and battledress which blurred chameleonlike to match its surroundings.

"Herne Lordling," Tadziki murmured. He walked toward the office with Ned a half-step behind. "Who—whatever he likes to think—reports to the captain the same as does every other member of the crew."

The limousine's other door opened from the inside before

Lordling reached it. A slim dark woman got out and started directly for the office. Lordling fell into step, but there was no suggestion that the woman would have waited if he had lagged behind.

"Time to introduce you to Captain Lissea Doormann," Tadziki said. He smiled. "Ned."

Lucas Doormann stood in the doorway to the inner office, saying, "Lissea, I'm glad to—"

Toll Warson had a broad grin on his face. He held the telephone handset out at arm's length. The gabble from whoever was at the other end of line was an insectile chirping.

"Toll, where's Tad—" Lissea Doormann said before she turned in response to the gesture of Warson's free hand. Herne Lordling bumped into her, then jumped back and was blocked by Ned Slade's forearm—outstretched instinctively to keep the big ex-colonel from crushing Tadziki against the door-jamb.

"Sorry, s—," Ned began.

Lordling cocked his fist. He was as tall as Ned and bulkier; not in the least soft, but no man of fifty was likely to be in the shape Ned was no matter how he pushed his body.

On the other hand, Lordling carried a gun.

Tadziki laid his palm across Lordling's knuckles. "Do you have business in my office, Herne?" he asked coolly. "Because I do, and brawling isn't part of it."

"Lucas, I'm terribly sorry," Lissea said with at least a pretense of sincerity. Up close, she had a sparkling hardness that belied her slight build.

She pressed Lucas' right hand in both of her own, then spun to take in the situation in the outer doorway. "Herne, *will* you stop pretending you're my shadow. Tadziki, where have you been? Herne says the arsenal's trying to fob us off with over-aged powergun ammunition!"

"The invoice is for lots manufactured within the past three years, Captain," Tadziki said. "Well within usage parameters."

"That's not what's set aside for us in the arsenal," Lordling snapped.

"I don't have any control over the arsenal's procedures, Herne," the adjutant said with a politeness so icy it burned. "I *do* have control over what we receive aboard the *Swift* per invoice, and I assure you that I will continue doing my job in that respect. As no doubt you will have opportunities to do your job after we're under way."

Toll Warson chuckled. If there could have been any sound more offensive than Tadziki's tone, Warson's laughter was it. Ned noticed that Warson had dropped the telephone and was holding instead a paperweight, a kilogram lump of meteoritic iron which his callused palm nearly swallowed.

"*Stop* this," Lissea said crisply. "Toll, you're not needed here. Herne, neither are you. Tadziki, I'll expect you to double-check the ammunition before it comes aboard."

The adjutant nodded. "Yes ma'am," he said, gesturing toward Ned with a cupped hand as he spoke. "I was just showing the *Swift* to a potential recruit for the expedition here."

"*Blood,* Tadziki!" said Herne Lordling. Neither he nor Watson seemed in any hurry to leave the office. He looked at Ned and added, "The Pancahte Expedition's by invitation only, kid. Go back home till you grow up."

"My name's Slade," Ned said in a voice as thin and clear as a glass razor. "I came in response to the courier Captain Doormann sent to Tethys."

His eyes were on Lordling, but the older man was a mass rather than a person. If the mass shifted significantly, if the hands moved or the legs, Ned would strike first for the throat and then—

"You're Don Slade?" Lordling said in amazement.

"His uncle didn't choose to accept the invitation," Tadziki interjected smoothly. "Ensign Slade here did. He's a graduate of the Frisian Military Academy and he's served with the planetary forces in pacification work."

"The Pancahte Expedition isn't for just anybody, Slade," Lucas Doormann said. The young noble wasn't actively hostile, but he *was* glad to find someone in the gathering whom he could patronize safely the way he could most of the civilians of his acquaintance.

Lissea looked at her cousin. "He isn't just anybody," she said. "He's Don Slade's nephew."

"I'm Edward Slade," Ned said, more sharply than he'd intended.

Lissea eyed Ned with the cold speculation of a shopper choosing one mango from a tray of forty. He stood at attention. Nobody spoke for a moment.

She grimaced and glanced over at her adjutant. "We've filled nineteen, haven't we, Tadziki?"

"Yessir, but—"

Lissea's focus hadn't left Ned when she asked for affirmation of what she knew already. "Sorry, Master Slade," she said. "We'll keep your name on the list if you like, but I can't hold out much—"

"As a matter of fact, Captain," Tadziki said, "I want to talk to you about the ship's internal layout. I don't think I should have a private compartment—or a single bunk."

"How many tankers do you have in the troops you've signed on, ma'am?" Ned asked. His eyes were front and level, focused on a strand that wind had lifted from Lissea's near skullcap of short black hair.

"We don't have any tanks either, Slade," Lissea said in puzzlement at the pointless question.

"And your enemies, ma'am?" Ned said. "You're sure they don't have tanks?"

Toll Warson chuckled again, softly this time. "Nice shot, kid," he murmured.

"We don't know a great deal about conditions on Pancahte," Lissea Doormann said coolly. A smile touched her lips, slight, but the first sign of good humor Ned had seen her express. The stress on a young woman welding together men like these would be greater than that of anything Ned could imagine attempting.

"As a matter of fact," she continued, the smile flicking off and on with the suddenness of a serpent's tongue, "we know bugger-all about Pancahte, which is why it's called the Lost Colony."

She looked at her adjutant. "Tadziki, if you're so sure you want to berth in the open bay, give the orders. We'll decide what to do with the space later."

"Lissea, what do you think you're doing?" Herne Lordling

demanded. "He's an *applicant*. He hasn't even passed the physical and the proficiency testing!"

Toll Warson gave Ned a speculative look, appraising him from a viewpoint quite different from the parameters against which Lissea had measured the potential recruit moments before. "I can run him through that now if you like, ma'am," he offered.

"No," Lissea said crisply. "Perhaps when we get back. Lucas?"

The nobleman, seemingly forgotten during a discussion of which he understood enough to be concerned, brightened.

"There's no problem getting Slade into the laboratory with us, is there?" Lissea said. "He has an Academy background which I think might be useful." She looked at Tadziki. "Whether or not we accept him for the expedition itself."

"Well, I—" Lucas Doormann said.

He was speaking to Lissea's back, because she'd already started out of the office. "Come along, Slade," she ordered without looking around. "You can tell us about yourself in the car."

Ned bowed to Lucas, then gestured the nobleman to precede him through the door.

"I will *not* have some kid who doesn't know his ass from a hole in the ground endangering the lives of everybody on the expedition, Lissea!" Lordling said.

Lissea, as petite as the sharp steel tip of a push dagger, turned in the hazy sunlight. "That's fine, Herne," she said. "Neither would I, so we don't have a problem."

The limousine's door was still open. She hopped in. As Lucas Doormann went around to the other side, Lissea slid over on the soft lip of the seat and motioned Ned to sit beside her.

In the office, Toll Warson was chuckling again.

The limousine had no windows, but the interior of the armored passenger compartment was covered with vision screens. The view was a little grainy, and primary colors didn't match perfectly from one panel to the next; but Ned's interest wasn't in Telarian scenery anyway.

"Why's Tadziki in your court, Slade?" Lissea asked bluntly. Her body swayed as the driver pulled a hard turn to point the limo toward the dockyard gate.

Ned locked his left hand against the panel separating the passengers from the driver's compartment; his right gripped the plush seat in determination not to slide into the diminutive woman. "Ma'am," he said, "I'm curst if I know. He read the file out of my ID, but I won't pretend I'm, well—"

Dry land on Tethys was scattered among thousands of islands and islets; aircars capable of free flight were the standard means of transport. The ride of this limousine, bonded to the ground by elastic metal tires, had a disquieting solidity.

Ned shrugged. "Look, I've been shot at, and I've shot back. But I won't pretend that I'm my uncle Don."

Lucas Doormann leaned forward to look at Ned. "Not yet, at least," Lucas said.

They were heading north on a high-speed motorway. The escort kept a clear space around the limousine, but traffic wasn't heavy.

"Whatever," Ned said. That was a polite lie. Don Slade had learned a lot of things in twenty years as a mercenary. From what Ned had seen in the brief periods the two of them were alone together, many of those were things neither Ned nor anybody else wanted to know.

Lissea sank back against the seat cushion and crossed her hands behind her neck. "My great-granduncle Lendell Doormann," she said with her eyes closed, "was one of three brothers. He wasn't interested in business—the trading side, that is."

"Or politics," Lucas said. "That's business too, if you're a Doormann."

Ned nodded, though the statement should have been broader. Politics were a part of human life. People who thought they didn't play politics, simply played politics badly.

"Lendell was a scientist," Lissea said. "He was head of research for the company—and good enough to have gotten the position even if he hadn't been family. Nobody paid much attention to what he was doing. He didn't bother his siblings, which permitted them to operate more freely in the real affairs of Doormann Trading."

"They were trying to extend family interests on Dell," Lucas said. "It ended up with the chief planetary administrator being appointed by Doormann Trading."

The limousine swung down an off-ramp framed by a pair of pillboxes. Uniformed guards presented arms as the car thundered past.

"Lendell told his brothers he was on the track of a means of instantaneous transportation," Lissea said. "Distance would no longer exist. They were interested—after all, we *are* an interstellar trading company. But they didn't understand even the first syllables of the explanation Lendell tried to give them. Afterwards, it turned out that Lendell's closest associates in his department didn't understand much more."

"Lendell's personal laboratory was in a sub-basement of the main spire of the estate," Lucas said. "The regular R&D facilities were across town in the spaceport rather than part of the estate. There's sometimes risk during testing, so that was a normal safety precaution."

The limousine slowed, causing the passengers to bob forward. The car was on a viaduct that was about to arch over a wall. Looking down, Ned saw a six-lane highway paralleling the exterior face of the walled enclosure but set back from it by a chain-link fence and twenty meters of coarse vegetation.

The buffer wasn't a landscaping feature. Rather, it was whatever greenery sprang up in a minefield that was occasionally burned off because it couldn't be safely mowed.

The wall was about four meters high. Towers studded the circuit at half-kilometer intervals. Each tower mounted an anti-starship weapon with a bore larger than the twenty-cm main guns of President Hammer's tanks.

Two of the huge guns tracked the limousine as it approached.

"Then the bills started to come due," Lissea said. "They were enormous, for the costs of Lendell's supplies and particularly for the real-time transgalactic conferencing in which he'd indulged to get the information he needed for his obsession."

The limousine stopped. A pair of guards bent to check the

identification of the driver. Because the receptors feeding the "windows" of the passenger compartment were on the vehicle's exterior, the driver him/herself remained invisible.

"The ultimate total," Lucas said, "was nearly thirty percent of Doormann Trading's book value. The bills were years coming in. Lendell's personal holdings wouldn't have covered a fifth of the amount."

The limousine eased down the inner slope of the viaduct, leaving the escort of three-wheelers behind. They were headed at a sedate pace toward the gleaming spire which dominated the enclave of manicured vegetation and low, classically styled buildings nestled against rolling hills.

"He'd hocused the data banks, of course," Lissea said. "Even given his name and position, it was a brilliant job and completely secondary to his real purpose, building his . . . his . . ."

The spire was a cone with fluted exterior walls. The shallow flutes twisted slowly, describing one full revolution by the time they rose to the top of the building.

The limousine pulled up in front of the entrance. Armed guards sprang to attention. Civilian underlings, chatting as they exited the lobby, quieted and scurried respectfully aside as they noticed the vehicle. A young woman carrying an infant to show to her coworkers turned her back and cooed to hush the child.

"Matter transmitter," Lucas supplied.

"No," Lissea said, shaking her head fiercely. "That's making an assumption that I can't justify from the evidence."

She leaned across Ned's body—her touch was startlingly warm—and pressed a latch invisible to him until the door opened and the screen blanked. Ned got out quickly. Lissea followed, and Lucas trotted around the car from the opposite side to follow them.

The civilians who'd been walking toward the bronze-and-crystal entrance before the limo arrived held chip-implanted IDs with which to trip the electronic latches under the watchful eyes of the guards. The clear panels slid aside for Lucas and Lissea automatically. Ned and the two nobles strode inside together through a detector frame.

The lobby was floored in metamorphic stone which held tiny speckles of pure red against swirling gray shades. It reminded Ned of a starscape seen from high orbit. The joints indicated that each slab was over three meters wide and longer still.

Civilians inside had seen Lucas coming through the crystal. They crowded to the sides of the lobby. Lucas nodded to an elderly man in an expensively conservative suit; the fellow bobbed a near bow and said, "Master Lucas!"

One of the bank of elevators facing the front doors opened. The babble of its passengers stilled into silence, relieved by coughs and nervous shuffling. The people caught in the elevator cage were afraid to stay or move in any direction lest whatever they did seem disrespectful.

Tethys had never been like this. Never. But Ned's stomach turned at memory of the rank he'd taken for granted at home.

On Telaria, Edward Slade was nothing . . . and at the moment he preferred it that way.

"May we use this elevator please," Lucas Doormann said to the open cage, pleasant enough but with no more question in his words than the owner of a dog has when trying to silence the beast. The occupants scattered like roaches from a light.

Lucas got in and brushed button S3 with his fingertip. He didn't bother to check whether or not his companions were clear of the door.

Ned noticed with amusement how much the young nobleman's attitude had changed since he regained his home ground. It was a compliment to Lucas' intelligence, or at least to his instincts. His diffidence among the mercenaries meant he realized men like Warson or Lordling might shoot him out of hand, whatever his wealth or lineage.

"What *is* known," Lissea resumed, as the cage dropped swiftly, "is that when the family realized Lendell was linked to the problem—"

"They didn't know the extent of the problem," Lucas said. "They didn't dream of the real extent."

"—his brothers called on him in his personal laboratory with an escort."

The elevator slowed, then settled with a lurch. Sub-basement 3 wasn't a common destination. The door opened on a lobby, brightly lighted but broken into aisles by stacks of hardboard boxes. Lucas led the way to the left.

"As they entered the lab . . ." Lissea said.

They came to a metal-finished door. A kiosk of structural plastic, clearly an add-on, stood adjacent. Someone was snoring inside. Legs, clad in a gray uniform, projected from the open door of the kiosk along a bench made of storage boxes.

"Open up there!" Lucas shouted in a blaze of real anger. "At once!"

The legs thrashed. A man bolted upright so that his head was visible through the kiosk's front window. Then he fell off whatever he'd been lying on. "Look," he whined as he clambered to his feet, "if you were in such a bloody hurry, you could've called, couldn't you?"

He tapped the one-piece phone scabbed to the side of his kiosk, bent, and hacked to clear his throat of phlegm. He was middle-aged, wispily balding, and soft rather than fat. His face was pockmarked, and stains of some sort marked the front of his rumpled gray uniform. The name-tape read PLATT.

When Platt's eyes focused, he recognized Lucas Doormann. He gasped and bowed, furtively wiping drool from his receding chin. "Master!" He mumbled to the floor. "I've served your family all my life. I assure—"

"Just open the curst laboratory, man!" Lissea snapped disgustedly.

In any hierarchical system, there were going to be people on the bottom. The attendant at a doorway nobody used was about as low a rung as there was. It still wasn't pretty to watch.

Platt stumbled to the shining door and held his card to the center of the panel. He was more awkward than usual because of his determination to stare fixedly at the floor. "No disrespect, master," he mumbled. "Didn't imagine it was *you*, master."

The trio strode past him, controlling varying emotions. Ned's stomach turned because he was part of a social continuum that included persons like Platt.

When the door opened fully, lights came on within the laboratory. It was a big room, ten meters by thirty. The illumination by hundreds, *thousands,* of microminiature point sources was harsh, brilliant, and shadowless. For the first time, Ned got a sense of Lendell Doormann as a person—

And a very strange person he must have been.

"Is that the—" Lissea began, walking toward the dais at the far end of the room.

"Yes," said Lucas. "That's where the—the capsule was when Lendell's brothers arrived to confront him."

The laboratory was divided into specialties. Burners, sinks, and piping so clear that only the haze of decades gave it form, stood cheek by jowl with a computer console feeding a holographic display meters in diameter. An intricate test pattern ran on the display.

Ned hadn't realized that such a unit had been available anywhere seventy years before. He could only guess what resolution and computing power like that must have cost at the time.

Lissea stopped short of the empty dais. Twelve black pentagonal mirrors stood on thin wands to focus into the air above the horizontal surface. The inner surfaces were slightly concave, distorting their images of Lissea oddly. Her reflections looked as though she was drowning in tannin-rich jungle pools.

"When his brothers and the guards entered this room," she said, "Lendell was about to enter the capsule that stood here. It was described variously as egg-shaped and as a sphere compressed in the middle. There were recording devices, both as part of the laboratory equipment and in the helmets of the guards, but the shape of the device seems to vary in those images also."

"The capsule was two meters high," Lucas said. "Lendell wasn't tall, about a meter seventy. The witnesses could judge the capsule's height against his."

The air in the laboratory was dry and as dead to the nostrils as a mouthful of cotton. Ned could hear both his companions perfectly, though he still stood near the door and the two of them had advanced some distance within the room.

"They yelled at him to stop," Lissea said, running her palm a few centimeters above the surface of the dais. "No one threatened him. He was a Doormann, after all, no matter what he might have done. He looked back and called something. There was a crackling or perhaps roaring in the air, so no one could hear the words."

"One of the guards thought Lendell said, 'You'll understand in a moment,'" Lucas said. "But he wasn't sure."

"Lendell closed the capsule over himself," Lissea said. "It was split vertically in halves, and there was nothing, or at least very little inside it. But when it closed, everything on the platform vanished."

"Was there a sound?" Ned asked. "A pop, an implosion?"

Lissea turned and shrugged. "Nobody heard it," she said. "Nobody would have heard it with the noise as loud as they said it was."

"That was the transformers," Lucas said. "One of the staff from the normal R&D facility was summoned to turn them off. It turned out that Lendell had routed all the generating capacity of the *planetary* grid to his equipment for his final experiment. The spire itself was the only building on Telaria to have mains power until the transformers were disconnected."

"I thought. . ." Ned said, ". . . that Lendell fled with something. From what you say, he simply spent the money, wasted it. He didn't take it with him to wherever he went."

"My father thinks that the money wasn't wholly wasted," said Lucas, "if we find and can duplicate the capsule. Lendell's research was the bulk of the sunk costs. The incremental expense of building and operating the device might prove practical for certain purposes if in fact it did instantly transport Lendell to Pancahte."

Lissea nodded slowly, though Ned wasn't sure that it was a gesture of agreement. "Rumors came back, years after the event, that Lendell Doormann had landed on Pancahte and was living there. His siblings were still in control of the company. They'd just managed to rebuild from the financial damage Lendell had done Doormann Trading. They forbade any public mention of his name."

"They said Lendell was insane," Lucas said. "They were right, of course."

"There was never any direct trade between Telaria and

Pancahte," Lissea said. "Pancahte is nearly thirty Transit hours away." Her figure, by tradition, ignored the set-up time which, depending on circumstances and the available computing power, increased elapsed time by up to three orders of magnitude.

"And it was beyond the Sole Solution," Lucas said. "A generation ago, that closed. At any rate, there's been no contact with Pancahte for at least that long."

Under normal circumstances, there was a practically infinite number of routes by which to reach any point from any other point through Transit space. There were a few anomalies. The most extreme of these was the Sole Solution, which was just that: a single point in the sidereal universe through which a vessel had to pass in order to reach certain other destinations. Pancahte was one of the worlds in that twisted gut of spacetime, the Pocket.

"Ah, Captain Doormann?" Ned asked. He didn't know how to address the person he hoped to serve under. It was very little consolation that, judging from the varieties of 'sir,' 'ma'am,' and 'Lissea,' nobody else in the expedition was sure either.

"Yes, Via, go ahead," she snapped. "*Captain Doormann*" *was a bad choice.*

"What is it you came to the laboratory to learn, sir?" Ned said.

"What have you learned here, Slade?" she countered. "Anything at all?"

"I learned something about Lendell Doormann," Ned said. He didn't know what she wanted to hear, so he told her the truth. "I learned that he was very sure of himself, and that he knew something. But I'm not at all sure he was right about what he thought he knew."

"He was insane!" Lucas repeated, as if the statement had any relevance to the subject under discussion.

Lissea smiled speculatively at Ned. "Do you think we should be going to Pancahte, Slade?" she asked.

"You should, sir," he replied. "Because that's how you'll get the place here that you ought to have."

He smiled back. Something in his expression surprised both his companions. "And I should," he continued, "because I volunteered to do just that."

Lissea barked a laugh. "Let's get back to the office," she said as she strode toward Ned and the doorway. "I'll tell Warson to run you through our tests."

Because of the omnidirectional lighting, she seemed a beautiful hologram rather than flesh as she approached. "If you pass them, Slade," she said, "you can call me Lissea."

Male twins in gray battledress walked toward the warehouse converted into a gym and target range as Ned and Toll Warson left it. The strangers were in their thirties, but Ned had first guessed they were considerably younger. They were slightly built, with fine blond hair and complexions of pinkish good health.

"Got a newbie there, Toll?" one of them called cheerfully. There was a scar across his temple, barely visible through the pale hair. Close up, neither of the men was quite as boyishly open as the image he obviously chose to project.

"He's passed the physical, anyway," Warson said. "Not a terrible score, either." He grinned and added, "He could give points to Cuh'nel Lordling, for one."

"I'm not long out of the Academy," Ned said, not sorry for the implied praise. "And, ah, Master Lordling has a few years on me as well."

"Captain Doormann seems to be going for experience," said one of the twins. Ned didn't know enough to guess whether or not there was a comment beneath the surface of the words.

Ned was taking deep but controlled breaths. Warson's run-through had been brutally complete. It was nothing Ned wasn't used to, though when the veteran had activated a series of pop-up targets while Ned rappelled, Ned had almost broken his neck.

He'd gotten two of the four targets with his submachine gun. "Them others would've toasted your ass, kid," Warson said with a chuckle. "Either get better, or don't get into a spot like that without backup. Right?"

"Yessir."

"Louis"—said Warson, gesturing to the twin with the hidden scar—"and Eugene Boxall. They're from Wimbledon."

"Ah," Ned said, giving the Boxalls his sharper attention.

"Yep," said Louis, "that's us."

Except that it *wasn't* Louis who finished the statement; it was his brother Eugene. The twins had traded places instantaneously and without any motion Ned could observe. Alternatively, the keloid on Louis' scalp had vanished and an identical scar had appeared across his brother's temple.

"Wimbledon teleports," Eugene said. "The future of the human race in two extraordinarily handsome packages."

"Well, on a good day, two," Louis said. *And they'd switched back again.* "Though I think *my* profile is a little more regally superior."

The twins were flushed and sweating beneath their grins, though they kept the strain out of their voices.

"They're the best," Toll Warson said with personal pride.

"So we are," Eugene agreed, his tone still light but with a dead-serious under layer to the words. "The best teleports on Wimbledon, the best in the universe."

Wimbledon was a perfectly normal world, lighted by a K-type sun through a moderately dense atmosphere. Ambient radiation on the surface was lower than that of Earth and well beneath the norm of the planets humans had settled during the expansion.

For no reason anyone could explain, a significant proportion of children born in the Wimbledon Colony were able to teleport. The talent wouldn't make buses obsolete: thirty centimeters was a good jump, and fifteen meters was a remarkable one; but very few walls are more than thirty centimeters thick. Teleportation had its uses in military as well as civilian life

"They tested out all right, too," Warson said. "Most ways. If one of them starts shooting, though, I suggest you stand in front of the target."

"We're lulling you into a false sense of security," Louis scoffed.

He fingered the fabric of Ned's khaki coveralls, a pair he'd left the patches on. "Hammer's Slammers, eh?" Louis said.

"I'm a reserve ensign in the Frisian Defense Forces," Ned said.

"The Slammers were formally dissolved after Colonel Hammer returned home and became president. They, ah . . . There's still a social organization of that name."

"And your name?" asked Eugene.

"Sorry," Ned said. He offered his hand. He was embarrassed. He hadn't wanted to butt into a discussion among veterans. "I'm Edward Slade. Ned."

"Slade?" said Louis, shaking Ned's hand in turn. "You wouldn't have been on Crater?"

"That was my Uncle Don," Ned said.

"There was a Slade got across the Kingston Gorge," Eugene explained to Toll Warson, "to call in fire missions on the Corwinite positions. They'd wanted a cousin of ours to jump it, but it was twelve *klicks.*"

"Even the highlands of Crater are muggy," Louis said. "You can't live down in the valleys without an environmental suit, and that would have showed up like a turd on the breakfast table to Corwin's sensors."

"Uncle Don said that he'd have sweat his bones out on Crater," Ned said, "except the air was so saturated that just breathing replaced your fluid loss."

Don Slade talked frequently about the things he'd seen—climates, geography, life forms. He didn't talk about the things he'd been doing against those exotic backgrounds, though. At least not to his nephew.

"Let's get you back to the office, kid," Warson said. "I got a date in town in an hour, if I can get somebody to advance me a little money."

"Glad to have you aboard, Slade," Eugene said as the brothers entered the gym.

"I'm not aboard yet," Ned called over his shoulder.

"Tsk," said Warson. "Worried 'cause Lordling doesn't like you? Don't be. Tadziki's worth two of him."

"Well, it's the captain's decision," Ned murmured, trying to avoid getting his hopes up.

The road between the converted warehouse and the expedition

office was concrete, but the expansion joints and cracks in the slabs sprouted clumps of dense vegetation. The foliage was dark green with brownish veins. It seemed lusher than that of plants growing in the unkempt grounds to either side.

"To tell the truth," Warson said, "I sometimes think Tadziki's worth two of most folks. He doesn't know the same stuff as the rest of us. But he knows his stuff."

Ned glanced at his companion. It would be very easy to discount Toll Warson as being an extremely competent thug. Ned wondered how many people had died over the years because they made that misestimate.

They entered the office. Tadziki sat at his desk, saying to the big man bent over a document, "You may have to wait more than an hour for the captain, Master Jones."

"Blood and martyrs!" Toll Warson shouted. "What in *hell* are you doing here?"

"Signing up," said the stranger as he turned. "Via, I should've known you'd be here, squirmed into some cushy wormhole, I suppose."

He grinned at Tadziki. "I don't guess I can be Jones anymore, huh?" he said. Despite the nonchalant tone, there was an edge of concern in his voice.

"You can be anybody you please, Master Warson," the adjutant replied. "But the authorities on Telaria aren't looking for you."

Ned backed into a corner, staying out of the way. Toll Warson turned to him and said, "This is my brother Deke, kid. Haven't seen him in—Via, we're both getting old, Deke."

"Edward Slade, sir," Ned said. He held himself at attention. "Ned."

"Don't 'sir' me, Slade," Deke Warson grumbled. He was a centimeter shorter than Toll and perhaps a year or two younger. Kinship showed in the brothers' eyes rather than in their faces.

Deke looked at Toll and raised an eyebrow.

"His uncle," Toll said. "Remember Sangre Christi?"

"I remember being glad I got out with my ass in one piece," Deke replied. "I still think that was doing pretty good."

"Tadziki?" Toll said. "There's going to be a problem if I take Deke off for a drink and to catch up with things?"

"No problem with his application," Tadziki said. "He was an invitee, though I don't think the courier ever caught up with him."

"I been keeping a low profile," Deke muttered. "There was a little trouble after Stanway, too."

"If the two of you get drunk and tear up the center of Landfall City," the adjutant continued, "then you better hope they don't jug you for longer than three days. That's when we do the test lift—"

He nodded out the open door toward the *Swift*. Workmen were beginning to dismantle the external supports.

"—and if that goes right, it's off to Pancahte twelve hours later."

The brothers left the office arm in arm. Ned expected them to collide with both jambs of the narrow doorway, but they separated like a dance team, with Toll preceding.

Deke turned and offered Tadziki a loose salute. It could have been read as mocking, but Ned didn't think it was. There were soldiers—warriors, really—whose distaste for authority was so ingrained that it was difficult for them to offer respect even when they knew it was due.

"I, ah . . ." Ned said. "Ah, should I wait for the captain, sir?"

"Tadziki'll do fine, Ned," the adjutant said, leaning back in his chair to stretch. "And you don't have to wait unless you want to."

"I suppose she won't make a decision about a place for me until Toll gives her a formal report that I passed?" Ned said. He hadn't been able to relax more than to an at-ease posture even now that he was alone with Tadziki in the office.

Tadziki laughed. "Sit down, curse it, you make me tired to watch you!" he said. "And as for a report—if Toll Warson didn't think you were safe backing him up, he'd have told you to get your ass off-planet in the next sixty minutes. If you were smart, you'd have known he meant it."

"Oh, I'm smart enough not to think Toll's bluffing if he says something . . ." Ned said as he lowered himself into the visitors' chair. "I, ah—"

He met Tadziki's eyes. "It's down to her decision, then?" he said.

Tadziki smiled. "She made her decision when she sent you off with Toll. Via, kid, nobody thought one of Hammer's boys couldn't handle the gym. Ned."

Ned relaxed. His body was cold. He'd sweated like a pig as Toll put him through his paces, and the air temperature was cool enough to bite as it dried him. Only now did he notice.

"I, ah . . ." he said, "I wasn't sure."

"That's good," Tadziki said with a nod. "But everybody else was. Go clean up and—well, there's nothing on till the official banquet two nights forward. Let off some steam in town if you like. Do you need an advance on your pay?"

"Huh?" Ned said. "Oh, no thank you, I'm fine." His personal fortune would suffice to purchase a starship larger than the *Swift*, if it came to that. Tethys was a prosperous world, and generations of Slades had displayed businesslike competence in whatever they were doing.

He started to rise, but then settled back onto the edge of the chair. "I want to thank you for going to bat for me the way you did, sir," he said. "But I'd like to know why you did."

Tadziki shrugged. "Does it matter?" he asked.

"It might," Ned said.

"It hadn't anything to do with your uncle," Tadziki said. When Ned heard the words, he felt himself relax again.

"Although," Tadziki continued, "I don't suppose Don Slade would have let you come if he hadn't thought you could stand the gaff. That counts for a certain amount. But mostly it was your background."

"My background?" Ned said in amazement. He slid against the back of the chair.

"Yeah, I figured that'd surprise you," the adjutant said with a laugh. "Look, Ned. You've met some of the crew and I'll tell you, the rest are pretty much the same. What do they all have in common?"

"They're the best there are," Ned said. "They're—professionals that other professionals talk about. They're—"

He shrugged. There was nothing more to say.

"They're people who've been in just about every tight spot there is," Tadziki said, "and got out of it alive. There'll be more combat experience lifting in the *Swift* than there is in most battalions."

"Sir," Ned said, "I've got the Academy, but that's nothing compared to what any of the others has *done*. And a year of pacification."

Tadziki nodded. "Don't knock a formal education, Ned," he said. "There are things you take for granted that Toll Warson wouldn't understand if they bit him on the ass. *Or* Colonel Lordling. But that's . . . It's not that simple."

He opened his hands on the desk and stared at them. Ned noticed there were pads of yellowish callus at the bases of the fingers.

"I guess," Tadziki said, "I thought it might be useful to have somebody along who *didn't* know the answers already, so maybe he could look at the problem instead. Somebody besides me, I mean."

He grinned ruefully at Ned. "And maybe it could be handy if somebody else's idea of an answer wasn't necessarily to blow the problem away."

Ned laughed and stood up. He reached across the desk to shake the adjutant's hand. "I'll go shower and change into civvies," he said. "Hey, do you ever get some time off, Tadziki?"

"A little, I guess," Tadziki said.

"When I'm fit to associate with something besides a billy goat," Ned called from the door, "I'll drop back by. Maybe you can show me a bit of the town tonight."

The banquet was held in the Acme, the finest hotel in Landfall City. It was scheduled for 1700 hours the day before launch. Ned arrived fifteen minutes early.

He wasn't afraid of the expedition's dangers. Socially, though, he felt as empty as if he were leaping into a pit with no lights and no bottom.

"Yes sir?" said a bellhop, blinking at the formal suit Ned wore for the occasion.

Nobles on Tethys went for florid effects. In this case, gold lace overlay fabric which fluoresced red or blue depending on the direction of the light. Whatever the bellhop thought about Ned's taste, the range of his net worth wasn't in question.

"The Pancahte Expedition banquet," Ned said. "Mistress Doormann's party."

"Of course, sir," the bellhop said, even more surprised than he'd been by the suit. "The penthouse that will be. Ah—would you like me to guide you?"

"No problem," Ned said, striding toward the elevators. Tadziki had muttered that Ned could wear "any curst thing" to the banquet as he typed with both hands and the phone cradled between his ear and shoulder. From the bellhop's reaction, formal wear hadn't been the overwhelming choice among the crewmen.

In the past two days Ned had met more than half the expedition members and had at least seen most of the others. He hadn't noticed any hostility toward him—but he'd effectively been ignored.

The rest of the crew pretty much knew, or at least knew of, one another. There were cliques and in some cases mutual antipathies, but members of the *Swift*'s complement didn't disregard their companions—with the exception of Ned Slade, who might have been a plank of the barracks' flooring.

Ned had better sense than to force his company on the adjutant this close to launch. When they found a good restaurant two nights before, Ned had pumped Tadziki for details about the expedition. The exchange was a mutual pleasure, since Tadziki was glad to offer information which he had to know and most of the crew didn't care about.

Since then, however, the adjutant was swamped with work. Ned didn't know the system or personalities well enough to be more help than hindrance, so he'd kept clear.

Under other circumstances, Toll Warson might have taken Ned under his wing, but he and Deke had vanished completely when they left the expedition office the morning they'd met. No news wasn't the worst possible news: there hadn't been any calls from the Telarian police regarding the pair.

"Room for one more?" Tadziki called from the lobby as the elevator door closed behind Ned.

Ned hit the DOOR OPEN button rather than grabbing the leading edge with his hand. Elevators at the Academy were built like firedoors and airlocks, without safety switches. It was a case where the wrong civilian reflex could get you killed in combat, so the Academy made sure the reflex was modified before cadets graduated.

Tadziki slipped into the cage and whistled. "My lord," he said, "you're beautiful! What're you doing after dinner tonight, gorgeous?"

Ned laughed. "Thought I'd cruise some navy bars and get pin money for the expedition," he said. "Via, Tadziki, you told me to wear anything, and I've always been told you can't overdress."

Tadziki wore a fawn-colored dress uniform with a white ascot. Ned didn't recognize either the uniform nor the epaulet insignia. He did note that there were four rows of medal ribbons, and that the ribbons were of slightly different heights—implying service under several flags.

The adjutant followed the flick of Ned's eyes. "I kept busy," he said, "but back where I was, it only got exciting when somebody screwed up."

"Sure," said Ned. He'd had a logistics instructor who'd used almost the same phrase; Major Kline. Besides the stories going around the Academy to make the statement a lie, there was the fact that Major Kline's legs had been burned off just above the knees.

Even before the door opened when the elevator stopped at P, the floor above 14, they could hear the sound of voices. Three attendants, a man and two young women in black-and-white uniforms, stared toward the dining room so fixedly that they jumped when Tadziki brushed one as he got out.

It wasn't a riot, not yet; but the party was well under way.

"*Very* sorry, gentlemen!" a female attendant said. "We'll take your weapons here, please."

The other woman stepped behind a counter. The man took his position at the controls of an extremely sophisticated security frame at the entrance to the dining room.

"What?" said Ned.

"Lissea thought it would be a good idea if everybody left their hardware outside the banquet," Tadziki explained nonchalantly. He handed the counter attendant a small pistol from his breast pocket. It had almost no barrel and a grip shaped like a teardrop.

"If there's a real problem tonight," he went on, reaching beneath his right coattail, "we can escort the parties to the barracks separately. That'll help some to keep the bloodshed down."

He gave the girl a thin, 10-cm rod which looked to Ned like a folding cutting-bar. She tagged both weapons and opened the lid of the counter.

"Blood and martyrs!" Ned said as he looked inside. The tagged weapons the woman had collected ranged from a pair of spiked knuckle-dusters to—

"What's that?" Ned said. He pointed to the fat, meter-long tube fed from a box magazine large enough to hold women's shoes. Its buttstock was curved horizontally to be braced against the chest rather than a shoulder.

Tadziki leaned over his shoulder. "Oh, the rocket gun," he said. "That would be Raff's, I suppose."

"The Racontid," Ned said/asked, knowing that Tadziki would correct him if he'd guessed wrong. The recoil of a closed-tube, all-burned-on-launch rocket would be brutally punishing for even big men.

Though there were a number of other projectile weapons, most of the guns in the collection were service pistols chambered for the standard 1-cm powergun wafer. The details of the guns and their associated carrying rigs varied considerably.

The half dozen needle stunners didn't necessarily imply that some of the crewmen were more squeamish than the rest. Though the stunners were small and highly concealable, the fluctuating current from their bipolar needles could sometimes bring down a target from neural lock-up faster than blowing the heart out would manage.

As for cutting implements—both the powered and non-powered varieties—the counter held a stock sufficient to begin clearance of a major forest.

"A lot of that's for show," Tadziki explained. "They knew they'd be disarmed at the door. I doubt most of the crew packs this kind of hardware on a normal liberty."

He stepped into the security frame. The mechanism chuckled; the attendant watching the screen nodded approvingly. Ned started through behind the adjutant.

"Sir!" called the woman behind the counter. "Please leave your weapons here."

Ned looked over his shoulder at her. "I'm not carrying any weapons," he said.

He walked through the frame. The male attendant shrugged and nodded to his companions.

"I don't need a gun to prove I'm a man," Ned muttered to Tadziki as they entered the dining room together.

The adjutant smiled. "It must have been interesting," he said, "growing up around a certified hero like your uncle."

Two elevators opened simultaneously. The Warson brothers were among the efflux, talking loudly about a woman. Presumably a woman.

Most of the *Swift*'s complement was already in the hemispherical dining room. The men seemed to have made the accurate assumption that there'd be something to drink ahead of time, and that perhaps somebody else would pay for it. A handful of them sat at tables while the rest were bellied up to the bar erected along the flat wall.

The room's outer wall and ceiling were glazed, looking northward over the city. The blur of light in the distance was the wall surrounding the Doormann estate, illuminated for security.

"Uncle Don wasn't around at all till six years ago," Ned said, looking at Telaria but remembering the roiling seascape of his home. "After he came back to Tethys, he got me a place in the Academy—"

He looked sharply at Tadziki. "I asked him to," he said. "It was my idea."

Tadziki nodded expressionlessly. They remained standing just within the doorway. "Hey, Tadziki!" called a ship's crewman named Moiseyev from the bar. "Come buy me a drink!"

"So I haven't seen him much since then either," Ned continued.

"Some, when I was home on leave. He's . . . I think my mother's good for him. I think he talks to her, but I don't know."

"I met your uncle once," Tadziki said. "We were on the same side, more or less." His voice, lost in the past as surely as Ned's had been, snapped the younger man back to the present.

The Warson brothers, Herne Lordling, and Lissea Doormann close behind, entered the dining room. Toll put his heavy hands on a shoulder each of Ned and the adjutant and moved the men apart. "Make way for a man who's dying of thirst!" he boomed.

A chime rang. Even the men at the bar turned toward Lissea. She lowered the finger-sized wand that combined a number of functions, including recorder and communicator, along with providing an attention signal.

"If all you gentlemen will find places," she said, "I personally haven't had a chance all day to eat."

The room was arranged with three round six-person tables in an arc that followed that of the glass wall, and a small rectangular table with three chairs on the chord. The places at the small table were marked RESERVED with gilt cards.

The crowd came away from the bar like a slow-motion avalanche: one man, three, and the remainder of them together. Ned walked around the rectangular table; Tadziki put his hand on the back of one of the reserved chairs.

Deke Warson took the reserved chair on the end opposite the adjutant.

"That's my seat, soldier," said Herne Lordling.

Deke looked Lordling up and down. "Was it, buddy?" he said. "Well, you're a clever boy. I'm sure you'll find just as nice a one over by the wall."

"Listen you!" Lordling said. Lissea said something also, but her words were drowned in the rumble of men shouting.

Toll Warson stepped in front of his brother. He put his right arm around Deke's neck in what was either an embrace or a wrestling hold, as needs required. He fished for Deke's bunched fist with his free hand.

Tadziki touched Lordling's left arm. Lordling tried to swat him off. Ned came around the other side of the table. He grabbed Lordling by the right wrist and right elbow. Lordling tensed, swore—and stopped the motion he'd almost attempted when he realized that Ned not only *could* break his arm but that the younger man was preparing to do just that.

"*Will* you stop this nonsense!" Lissea said.

Tadziki reached back with his left hand. His right continued to touch Lordling's arm and he didn't look away from Lordling's face. He picked up the card from the seat he'd taken and said, "Deke. Here's a place for you."

Deke Warson stared in the direction of the card for a moment before his eyes focused on it. He relaxed, pulled himself away from his brother, and walked around the front of the table to the seat Tadziki offered.

The adjutant let go of Herne Lordling. Ned stepped backward and only then released his own grip. There was a possibility that Lordling was going to lash out as soon as he was free. Ned couldn't prevent that, but he sure didn't intend to make it easy.

Both Lordling and Deke Warson sat down. Lissea remained standing between them until they were firmly settled. She didn't look in the direction of either man. There was a general scuffle of boots and chair-legs as the rest of the company found places.

"Blood and *martyrs*," Ned muttered. There were patches of sweat at the throat and armpits of his dazzling suit.

Tadziki put a hand on Ned's shoulder and guided him to one side of the center table. There weren't two empty places together anywhere in the room. Tadziki gestured curtly toward a man to move him. The startled crewman obeyed.

"As cramped as we're going to be for the next howeverlong," the adjutant said, "I don't think we need to push togetherness right now."

It was going to be a long voyage, in more ways than one.

Lissea seated herself decorously after everyone else. She gave a regal nod toward the service alcove.

Waiters, having clustered nervously at the threatened riot, began to bring the meal in.

The Boxall brothers were at the table Tadziki had chosen, along with Raff and a ship's crewman named Westerbeke. The other five ship's personnel were together at a side table— with Toll Warson, who'd taken the seat without being in the least interested in who else might be at the table.

Toll might have traded with Westerbeke in a friendly fashion; and again, he might not, which wasn't something anybody in his right mind wanted to chance. Westerbeke looked as lonely as Ned had felt before Tadziki joined him.

Lissea seemed not lonely but alone, putting food in her mouth and chewing distractedly. Her clothes were resolutely civilian, though a great deal more subdued than Ned's: dark gray trousers, a jerkin of a slightly paler shade, and a thin tabard with diagonal black-and-bronze striping. Herne Lordling spoke to her a number of times, but Ned didn't see the woman respond.

"What's Lordling's position, then?" Ned asked Tadziki in something between a low voice and a whisper.

"Military advisor, I suppose," the adjutant explained. "Formally, he doesn't have a position—Lissea likes to have everyone reporting directly to her. But Herne had a lot to do with the list of invitees and the—the tactical planning, I suppose you'd say. He has a deserved reputation."

Tadziki took a sip of water and looked out the glass wall, ending the discussion.

As waiters removed the salad, somebody tugged the puff of fabric on Ned's sleeve. He turned in his chair. The man seated at his back on the next table said, "Hey, you're Slade, aren't you? I'm Paetz, Josie Paetz. I guess we're the up-and-comers here, huh?"

"Right, I'm Ned Slade," Ned said and shook hands. Paetz was big, red-haired, and as hard as a bodybuilder between contests. He looked much sharper-edged than other crewmen because he was so much younger: certainly younger than Ned, and possibly less than twenty standard years.

"Tell the truth," Paetz continued, "from your rep, I thought you had a few more years on you too. The time you took a platoon through the sewers on Spiegelglas, wasn't that—"

"My uncle Don," Ned said. He should have known. Waiters maneuvered awkwardly around the tables to avoid stepping between the two mercenaries. If Paetz even noticed that, it didn't embarrass him the way it did Ned.

"Oh, I got it!" Paetz said happily. "I thought, you know—for somebody like you to have that much a jump on me, I thought you must be really something. But you're just out to get a rep, same as me. Well, we'll see how it goes, won't we, buddy?"

"You bet," Ned murmured, but Paetz had already scrunched his chair back around to his own table.

"The man next to him is Yazov," Tadziki explained quietly, "his father's half-brother, born on the wrong side of the bedclothes. We invited the father, who's Primate of Tristibrand. He let Josie come, and sent Yazov to keep an eye on him."

He took a forkful of pilaf. "They should be valuable additions to the company. In different ways."

"Josie isn't . . ." Ned said, ". . . one of the people you pushed as having open minds, I would judge."

"Sometimes you simply have to charge straight uphill into a gun position," Tadziki said. "Then it's nice if you've got people along who think that's a good idea."

The food was excellent in a neutral sort of way, without anything Ned perceived as Telarian national character. The hotel catered to off-planet traders and perhaps to Telarians who wanted to emphasize their cosmopolitan background.

Few of the mercenaries cared about what they were eating one way or the other. If they'd been told they were to skin rats and eat them raw, nine out of ten would have done so, if only to prove they were as tough as their fellow crewmen.

Raff shoveled through a vegetarian meal as if he were filling sandbags. The Racontid held his knife and fork in four-fingered hands. His retractile claws provided delicate manipulation when required. He showed some interest in the texture of his food, but none whatever in its flavor.

Tadziki and the Boxalls were discussing a mercenary Ned didn't know, an invitee who'd been shot by his lover as he prepared to board ship for Telaria. For a time, Ned simply ate morosely. Then out of fellow-feeling he asked Westerbeke about the *Swift*'s systems.

The crewman responded enthusiastically. The degree of detail Westerbeke offered strained the bounds of Ned's training, but he could catch enough of the meaning to nod intelligently. The capsule reading was that the *Swift* wasn't a large vessel, but she was as solidly built as any hull of her displacement. Furthermore, her major systems were redundant and better-shielded than those of many warships.

The discussion made both Ned and Westerbeke more at home at the banquet, and the details made Ned more comfortable about the voyage itself. Whatever Karel Doormann hoped would result from the expedition, Doormann Trading was sparing no reasonable expense in the outfitting.

The same was true with the complement. They were all good men, and all clearly fit despite the emphasis on experience over youth. Though tough, they weren't a gang of cutthroats either. Uncle Don would have been right at home among them.

A realization struck Ned as he viewed the assembled crew. "Tadziki," he said, "we're all males, aren't we? Except for Lissea, I mean."

"Yeah, that was a decision she made herself, though Herne and I both would have argued for it if it had come up," Tadziki said. "It's pretty tight quarters, and for a long time."

"There's Raff," Louis Boxall suggested. "You're not male, are you, buddy?"

The Racontid laughed like millstones rubbing. "It doesn't signify," he—she?—said. "You humans don't have a transfer sex."

Raff lifted his fruit cup and licked it clean with a single swipe of his broad tongue. Waiters were removing the last of the dishes. The Racontid took a lily from the table's centerpiece and began thoughtfully to munch the fleshy stem.

Lissea stood up. She looked lost and frail.

"Gentlemen," she said. The room quieted. "Fellow crewmen! We're here together for our last night in safety until we've managed to retrieve the device in which my great-granduncle fled Telaria.

Perhaps our last night in safety before we disappear forever into myth and the fading memories of our loved ones."

"Don't you worry yourself, Lissea!" said Herne Lordling. There was a half-filled whiskey glass at his place, but the volume and slight slurring of his words showed that this drink was the most recent of many. "You've got me along. Everything's going to work out just fine."

"Seems to me," snarled Deke Warson, leaning to peer past Lissea, "that being a pansy colonel doesn't make you an authority on much of anything except covering your ass, Lordling!"

Lissea thrust a hand out to either side, trying to cover both men's eyes with her fingers. "Stop this at once!" she said.

Tadziki stood up. "Captain?" he said calmly. "I wonder if you'd let me bring everyone up to speed on the plans thus far? Then they can ask questions if they have any."

Ned, who'd been poised to back the adjutant in a physical confrontation, settled in his chair again. The emotional temperature of the room dropped to normal as a result of Tadziki's tone and the volume he'd managed to project without seeming to shout.

"Yes," Lissea said. "Yes, that's a very good idea."

She reseated herself, a supple movement which her outstretched arms turned into a dance step. Only when she was down did she lower her hands and nod at the adjutant to begin.

"The first portion of our voyage will be relatively straightforward," Tadziki said. He moved from one side of Ned's chair to the other so that he could face all the personnel except the trio at the small table behind him. "We won't be putting in to major ports, however. We're an armed expedition. Entry checks and quarantines on highly developed worlds would add months to what's already going to be a lengthy process."

"Hey, I'll give up my gun if you'll land on a place with decent nightlife," said a mercenary named Ingried.

"Don't worry, Ingried," Harlow called back loudly. "There'll be sheep-farmers who'll set you up with company just as pretty as what *I've* seen you with on leave."

Everybody laughed, Ingried included.

"The major question mark involves the Sole Solution," Tadziki continued when the laughter died down. "Very little has been heard from beyond it over the past generation. There've been rumors that it closed, or that it's being held by a military force that won't permit anyone through that point."

"Can we go around?" asked Yazov. Ship's crewmen chortled at the soldier's ignorance, though not to the point of openly insulting a man who'd made killing his business for thirty years.

"So far," the adjutant continued calmly, "the only person who's managed to do that is Lendell Doormann, and that's a matter of rumor rather than certainty also. But let me emphasize: I'm speaking of information available on Telaria. When we're nearer the Sole Solution, there'll be hard facts and we'll be able to refine our plans."

Tadziki cleared his throat, then sipped from the glass of hot, tart Telarian chocolate which a waiter had left at his place. "I won't claim that our information on intermediate stops is perfect either," he said. "Because we'll be touching down on minor planets, our pilotry data is likely to be out-of-date or simply wrong.

"But that doesn't matter. That doesn't matter because of *you*. You're picked men, the best there are in the human universe." His voice was growing louder, and the syllables he hit for emphasis resounded like drumbeats. "With all of us working together, there are no emergencies, no unexpected dangers that we won't be able to wriggle out of or *smash* our way through!"

"That's sure the bloody truth!" shouted Toll Warson.

Cries ranging from *"You bet!"* to *"Yee-ha!"* chimed agreement.

"And when we return," Tadziki continued, thundering over the happy assent, "we'll have more than the capsule we've been sent for. We'll have a name that nobody will ever forget. For every one of us here, there'll be a thousand others out there—"

He made a broad sweep of his extended arm, indicating the night sky beyond the glazing.

"—telling people that *they* were aboard the *Swift* too. But they weren't because they weren't good enough. *We* are good enough, and we're going to see this business through whatever it takes!"

The cheers overwhelmed even Tadziki's booming voice. Ned shouted as enthusiastically as the rest, though a part of him marveled at the expert way the adjutant had used a tense situation to weld the crew into a unity of purpose which might well last till success or disaster.

Tadziki turned, gestured to Lissea, and sat down with his arm still pointing.

Lissea rose again. She held a glass of amber wine which she extended toward her gathered subordinates. "Gentlemen," she called without any remaining indecision. "I give you ourselves and the *Swift*. May we be worthy of our triumph!"

The waiters looked on from the edges of the room, like humans watching a ritual being performed by great, bellowing cats.

The man was young, fit-looking, and above average height. His hair was light brown, almost blond at the roots, and he wore loose khaki clothing.

He stood alone in the crowd which waited for Lissea Doormann and her escort to enter the *Swift* for liftoff.

"It's so big!" said a young Telarian woman in a sundress with a cape of blue gauze over her shoulders. "I thought it was just a little boat."

Her beefy escort chuckled knowingly. "It's a *star* ship, Elora," he said. He waved at the vessel a hundred meters away. "As starships go, it's a small one. And for the distance they say they're going, it's tiny. Too small. They don't have a prayer of making it back."

The *Swift* wore a coat of black, nonreflective paint which showed orange-peel rippling from the stresses of the shakedown run the previous day. There were striations in a reticular pattern where the plates joined, but the crewmen who magna-fluxed the seams after landing had found no sign of cracks. The plates dovetailed before being welded. Repair would be difficult in any-thing less than a major dockyard, but the interlocked hull had enormous strength.

The *Swift* lay on its side like a huge cigar. The central airlock was closed, but the three-meter boarding-ramp hatch, forward on the port side, was lowered. It provided a good view of the vessel's bustling interior.

A man with a case of instruments and tools knelt on the ramp, adjusting the flexible metal gasket. Beyond him, two more crewmen shouted at one another, each waving a pack that bristled with weapons. The personnel were garbed in the battledress of their various former units, but all now wore a shoulder patch with the new insignia of the Pancahte Expedition: a red phoenix displayed on a golden field.

"Is that Colonel Lordling?" Elora asked, pointing indiscriminately to the pair arguing.

"No, no," said an older woman the crowd pressed against Elora's other shoulder. "Those are the Warson brothers. They've each killed *hundreds* of people."

The pair are Bonilla and Dewey, thought the man in khaki. *They are ship's crewmen. They both know which end of the gun makes the noise, but they aren't killers by temperament.*

The rear of the crowd gave a wordless murmur. Someone called, "They're coming!" over the general noise.

The *Swift* set down on an open cell of the starport when she returned from testing. The crowd of thousands that gathered to watch her lift for Pancahte came from all over Telaria and even beyond. Independent news associations recorded events from the roof of the terminal building. They would sell copies to the crewmen's home worlds and to planets settled enough to have a market for vicarious adventure.

Scores of green-clad police patrolled the lines marking the safe separation from the vessel's drive motors. The police used their shock rods freely to reinforce the warning of the yellow paint, but pressure from behind still edged the crowd forward. A police lieutenant spoke angrily into her lapel mike as she scanned the sky.

Three large aircars rumbled low overhead and settled in the cleared area around the vessel. The hot breeze from their ducted fans buffeted the crowd. Elora's cape lifted from her shoulders. The man behind her caught the garment's hem and held it safe, unnoticed, until the cars had shut down.

"Oh!" cried a woman. "I've got something in my eye!"

Blue-uniformed Doormann Trading security guards hopped from the rear of the aircars. There were forty or fifty troops in each vehicle.

Instead of shock batons, the new arrivals carried powerguns: slung submachine guns in the case of enlisted men, holstered pistols for officers and noncoms. The *Swift*'s hatch filled quietly with men as the presence of armed troops drew the attention of the mercenary crew.

The police lieutenant undipped the loud-hailer from her harness. "Stand aside!" she called, her voice turned into a raspy howl by amplification. "Make way for the honorable Lucas and Lissea Doormann!"

The company of security guards linked arms and struck the crowd as a wedge. An officer with his pistol drawn walked just behind the point of his burly men, shouting for them to put their backs into it. Civilians stumbled aside, crying out in surprise and anger.

"Go it, mob!" cheered a mercenary. *Josie Paetz,* thought the lone man. "Go it, cops!"

The guards shoved directly past the man in khaki. He concentrated on keeping his footing and moving the citizens behind him back without starting the sort of surging panic that could get people trampled to death.

Paetz wore two pistols, one high on his right hip and the other in a cross-draw holster on his left. He also cradled a submachine gun at port arms. His burly uncle Yazov looked on from behind the young gunman with a tolerant smile.

"Move it, move it, move it!" shouted the officer commanding the guards. He was close enough that the lone man could have reached across the line of blue uniforms and touched the fellow—

—crushed his throat—

—grabbed a handful of the hair curling out beneath the helmet, jerking the head backward hard enough to—

"Hey!" said a guard in horror.

The man in khaki blinked in surprise. He looked at the guard he'd been staring *through* with an expression that he wouldn't consciously have worn.

"Sorry, buddy," he called. The guard was already gone, swept past on the current of blue uniforms which hosed a path into the spectators. Another company was carrying out a similar maneuver from the back of the crowd. The forces met midway, then squeezed outward to widen the opening.

"Look at them!" said Elora's companion. "Here they come! They're coming right past us!"

A pair of three-wheelers drove at a walking pace between the lines of guards. The vehicles were *en echelon* because the cleared way wasn't quite wide enough for them to proceed side by side. Behind them came an open-topped limousine.

The anger building in manhandled spectators evaporated when the victims realized that they had the best view of the celebrities. Cursing guards flung their weight outward to counteract the nearest civilians' tendency to lean toward the oncoming limousine.

"Lissea! Lissea!"

"Oh!" said the woman on the other side of Elora. "They're too beautiful to die!"

"She sure is!" Elora's companion said, mistaking the object of— his mother's? his mother-in-law's?—enthusiasm.

The limousine was a three-axle model. The driver was covered by a polarized hemisphere in front, so that he or she wouldn't detract from the attention focused on the passengers.

Lissea Doormann rode in the backseat with her cousin Lucas beside her. He was dressed in a blue suit that might almost have been a uniform, while Lissea wore coveralls whose fabric, as lustrous and colorful as a peacock's tail, belied the utilitarian lines. She smiled tautly and waved, though her eyes didn't appear to focus on her enthusiastic surroundings.

Her right shoulder bore the same phoenix patch as did the other members' of the expedition.

Lucas was regal and perhaps a degree, self-satisfied. The fact that Lissea was getting such a send-off had to be his doing, in spite of his father.

Lissea's parents, Grey and Duenya Doormann, sat in jump seats facing the younger pair. Grey looked bewildered. Lissea's mother was crying. She dabbed alternately at her eyes and her sniffling nose. Her lace handkerchief was too delicate to be of much use for either purpose.

The Warson brothers, Herne Lordling, and Raff sat on the limo's body with their legs down inside the passenger compartment. They carried powerguns (in the Racontid's case, a rocket launcher) ready in their hands. The gun muzzles were lifted slightly and the butts were cradled rather than shouldered, but the mercenaries' readiness to use their weapons was beyond question.

"Beautiful!" repeated the older woman.

Elora nodded in agreement, though it wasn't really true. Lordling had the sort of beefy good looks that might have been "beautiful" when he was twenty years younger. The Warsons shared a craggy roughness that couldn't have passed for beauty even without the scars—the cut quirking Toll's lip, the burned speckles on Deke's right cheek. As easily claim Raff was beautiful, or that a wolverine was.

What Lissea's escort had was an aura of raw male aggression. The same was true of the rest of the *Swift*'s complement: they were men that no woman would overlook, though many would react with horror and loathing to what they read on the mercenaries' faces.

Elora's companion grimaced as Deke Warson's eyes fell across him. The mercenary wasn't threatening, just alert to possibilities for trouble. The civilian glanced away and didn't look back until the limousine had passed.

"They could cut their way through anybody, that lot," he muttered to Elora. "It's not enemies they have to worry about, just space itself. Space is too big for them, though."

Does he really imagine that twenty gunmen, no matter how skilled and brave—but courage has rarely been a short-term survival characteristic—could overwhelm all human opposition? thought the man in khaki. *Shoot it out with a column of tanks? Dance through an artillery stonk?*

Perhaps he does. He is a civilian, after all.

The limousine's driver made his vehicle pirouette, to bring it broadside to the end of the boarding ramp. Lucas Doormann got out and offered his arm to Lissea. Herne Lordling stepped from his perch in front of the young noble, then moved backward as though Lucas didn't exist.

Lissea handed her parents out of the limousine, ignoring both men. She hugged first her father, then her mother. The older woman suddenly twisted away in a fresh onset of grief.

With a final wave to the spectators, Lissea turned and walked up the ramp. The crowd cheered with the mindless abandon of a flock of birds.

The man in khaki sighed. He shook the microchip-keyed ID card he wore on a lanyard around his neck out from under his tunic.

"Excuse me," he said to the man in front of him. "Excuse me," he repeated a little louder, gripping the man's shoulder and easing him aside despite the fellow's instinctive resistance.

"Hey!" said the civilian in surprise, but he'd seen enough of the stranger's expression not to make a problem of it.

"Who is he, Chechin?" Elora asked in a voice whose emotional loading shifted from anger to interest in those few syllables.

"You can't—" a security guard began.

"I can," the lone man said, waving his ID in a short arc to call attention to it.

"Oh," said the guard. "Ah . . ."

"I'll duck under," the man said. He did so as the guards to either side, their arms still linked, squeezed as far apart as they could.

The four mercenaries of Lissea's escort formed an outward-facing line across the bottom of the ramp. When their captain entered the ship, they turned together and sauntered up behind her. Lucas Doormann stood with his feet spread and his hands clasped behind him, looking up at the *Swift*.

The man in khaki strode toward the vessel with his ID raised in his right hand. His left hand was ostentatiously spread at his side. He had to stutter-step to avoid the three-wheelers as they spun to get in front of the limousine, preparing to lead it back with Lucas.

The police lieutenant opened her mouth to shout. She turned aside when she recognized the card's phoenix blazon.

Machinery on the *Swift* gave a high-pressure moan. Lucas Doormann turned and almost collided with the man approaching from the crowd. "Slade?" he said. "What are you doing here?"

"A fair question," Ned replied. The boarding ramp was starting to rise. He hopped to the end of it and trotted into the hull of the starship. The ramp continued to grind its way closed.

"Twenty-one and all told," Tadziki said to his multifunction baton. He smiled at Ned. "I wasn't sure you were coming."

Ned shrugged. "I signed on," he said.

The vessel's interior was bedlam. Everyone *knew* how tight space would be, and the men were experienced veterans who'd often subsisted on the minimum or even less than that. Nevertheless, last-minute additions to personal belongings brought the total to half again or even double the limits Tadziki had set. It would take an hour to make the *Swift* shipshape enough to lift off safely.

Ned noted that his bunk astern was covered with gear. He laughed. None of it was his own.

"I just thought," he said to the adjutant, "that maybe I could understand what we were doing better if I looked at it like an outsider. So I was playing spectator."

"Westerbeke," Tadziki ordered, speaking into his baton. His thumb switched his booming voice through the speakers fore and aft in the bay. "Open the ramp again."

The crewman in one of the navigation consoles forward obeyed. The noise of men arguing over volume and location continued. Lissea Doormann stood in the center of the bay. Her blue-green-golden coveralls blazed like metal burning, but her face was white and silent.

Smiling coldly, Tadziki dialed a feedback loop into the speaker system. When the painful squeal died away, everyone in the bay was silent.

"Captain," Tadziki said with a nod toward Lissea, "do I have your permission to handle this?"

"Go ahead." Her voice was crisp but detached.

Tadziki smiled again. "Gentlemen," he said, "we'll all take the next fifteen minutes to separate our personal belongings into two piles. At the end of that time, the captain and I will inspect them. The pile of your choice will be tossed onto the concrete for the locals to fight over."

The adjutant's pause didn't invite comment. There were a few vague murmurs, not directed at him.

"If it turns out that both of an individual's piles are still in excess of the volume limits you were provided, then *both* piles go," Tadziki continued. "If the individual objects, his shipmates will send him out along with his gear. Any questions?"

"There will be no questions," Lissea Doormann said.

Toll Warson laughed. "Hey Cuh'nel Lordling," he said, "somebody's gonna set up a regular grocery store with what you leave behind, aren't they?"

Herne Lordling was red-faced. "No questions," he said in a clipped voice.

"Go to it, boys," Tadziki said with a nod. Mercenaries turned to their rucksacks and footlockers. Many of them began to hurl the excess directly out the three-meter hatchway.

Lissea offered her adjutant a slight smile. Tadziki leaned close so that he could speak without shouting and said, "They wouldn't be the men we want if they didn't push, ma'am. This isn't a problem."

He turned to Ned. "How about you, Slade?" he asked.

"I'm under the limit," Ned said. He grinned in a way that made the adjutant remember Slade's uncle. "I'm going to take some pleasure in clearing my bunk, though, if the dick-head who piled stuff there doesn't do it for me."

"You said you wanted to figure out what we were doing," Tadziki said. "Did you?"

Lissea drifted close enough to listen, though her unfocused eyes denied she was taking part in the conversation. The three of them were the only ones aboard the *Swift* who didn't have to comb through their personal belongings.

"I don't have a clue," Ned said. He looked at the men around him.

"These guys don't have a thing in the world to prove to anybody. They've done it all, one time or another. And here they are to do it again."

He nodded out toward the spectators behind the police line. "They think we're a bunch of heroes going to certain death," he said, his tone deliberately mocking.

"And you?" said Tadziki.

"I don't think I'm going to die," Ned replied. "And I *sure* as hell don't think I'm a hero."

"Are you sure you want to be here?" Lissea said unexpectedly.

Ned looked at her. "I'm an adult," he said. "And I'm here. So this must be what I want to do."

He laughed with real humor. "But I'm curst if I could tell you why," he admitted.

Tadziki put his hand on Ned's shoulder. "Let's go clear your bunk off," he said. "Next stop is Ajax Four, and that's a long cursed way to travel standing up."

AJAX FOUR

A yellow-gray plume to eastward streaked the intense blue of Ajax Four's sky. A similar trail a hundred kilometers north marked a second volcano. Droplets of spume blowing inland from the surf popped and sizzled on the barren, sun-cracked rocks.

"Fuckin' wonderful," muttered Deke Warson. "Hey, Tadziki! I'm going to fire my travel agent."

Ned opened the front of his tunic and shrugged to loosen the fabric where sweat had glued it to his skin. He felt good. Better than he'd felt since he'd last been home on Tethys.

Ajax Four wasn't a seaworld like Tethys, but the *Swift* had landed on the shore a few klicks south of Quantock, one of the planet's larger human settlements. The air was clean, and a storm had passed recently enough to give it the familiar tang of ozone.

Ajax Four wasn't home, but it reminded Ned of home; and that was a good thing just now.

The *Swift* had set down in a scallop several hundred meters across. Originally the landing site had been a miniature crater, but the sea had carved away the western third of the cone.

Lava within the volcano's channel had cooled into a basalt plug far sturdier than the cone of compacted ash. The plug provided the *Swift* with a surface as solid as Landfall City's concrete spaceport. At low tide the basalt would be a shelf well above the sea, but at the moment surf pounded its edge.

Herne Lordling had ordered six men to string a line of medium-distance sensors around the crater's lip, thirty to forty meters above the plug. Because the soft rock was weather-checked, the inner wall wasn't as difficult to climb as it appeared to be from a distance. The exterior of the cone would actually be a more difficult proposition. A climber's weight would crumble the slope into gravel with neither handholds nor footholds.

A team of ship's crewmen had unslung the pair of air-cushion mini-jeeps from the blister on the *Swift's* hull astern. The jeeps would only carry two people apiece, so most of the personnel would have to hike or borrow vehicles from the colonists if they wanted to leave the vessel.

"*Sir, I still can't raise the settlement,*" Dewey reported. "*Over.*"

He was using the general push rather than a command channel, so everyone could hear him through their commo helmets. With the exception of Dewey, whose duties kept him in the navigational console, the whole complement was outside on this, the *Swift's* first landfall since Telaria. Everyone wore his helmet visor down and polarized against the brilliant sunlight doubled by reflection from the rocks.

"*All right, Dewey,*" Lissea replied. "*Have one of the teams on the ridge relay the call. Use Yazov. He'll know what to do. Out.*"

Ned knelt and peered into a crack deep enough that spray or possibly ground water kept the interior damp. He locked his visor out of the way for a better view. There was a smudge of green against the rock. "Hey, Tadziki," he called. "Plant life!"

"It's not the plants that worry me, Slade," the adjutant said as he wandered over, faceless behind his visor. "It's the Spiders and the big nasty guns they're supposed to carry."

"Wouldn't mind having something to shoot," Deke Warson said idly. "It'd make a change."

Lissea walked over to the adjutant. "Tadziki!" she demanded. "There was no place nearer to Quantock?"

"We could have tried landing in the settlement itself," Tadziki said calmly. "The settlers here have a great deal of trouble with pirates and the interloping traders who sell weapons to the Spiders. I was concerned that if they saw an unexpected vessel coming in to land, they might shoot first and ask questions later."

Lissea raised her visor and rubbed her face with her palm. "Sorry," she said. "I feel like a fish in a barrel in this place. I—"

"Sir, I've got them on Channel Seven!" Dewey reported. *"Do you want me to patch them directly to you? Over."*

"No, hold them for a moment," Lissea replied as she strode back up the ramp. *"I'll take it at the console. Out."*

Apart from algal smudges like the one Ned had noticed, the only land-dwelling life form on Ajax Four when humans arrived was a creature whose males averaged three meters tall and a hundred and fifty kilograms. They were bipedal but four-armed. The colonists called them Spiders, though they were warm-blooded and had internal skeletons.

The Spiders ranged the interior in bands of a dozen or so individuals, living on creatures teeming in the freshwater lakes and streams. They were relentlessly hostile to the colonists, which wouldn't have made any difference—had the Spiders not also been highly intelligent.

Humans settled Ajax Four with two separate commercial purposes. The ocean provided protein, some of it of luxury quality, and algal carbohydrates which could be processed into basic food-stuffs. Oceanic aquatic fed the colonies from the beginning. It now provided most of their export earnings as well.

According to the original plan, analgesics processed from several varieties of freshwater coral would in a few years pay back the cost of settling Ajax Four. Thereafter the colonists should have become as wealthy as the citizens of *any* human planet. When Spiders with weapons made of seashells and obsidian had attacked settler foraging parties, the humans' guns cut the aliens down without loss.

Human interlopers landed on Ajax Four to scoop up coral and flee before the settlers could stop them. The Spiders traded with the interlopers instead of fighting them: traded coral for guns, and used the guns to bloodily ambush the next group of colonists who had ventured into the interior.

Since that day, the interior hadn't been safe for the colonists. They swept the vicinity of their settlements in large parties, killing the Spiders they found and accepting the inevitable sniping casualties as a cost of remaining on Ajax Four. Though the Spiders held the interior, they rarely ventured against the sensors and heavy weapons which protected the coastal settlements.

The parties' *modus vivendi* wasn't perfect, but life was rarely perfect. Since the situation hadn't changed significantly in a hundred years, it had to be considered an acceptable one.

Lissea stepped out onto the ramp. *"Captain to crew,"* she called on the general push. *"There's a party coming along the coast from Quantock. The settlement's control center has told them we aren't hostile, so they won't be shooting. Don't let's us have any problems either. Out."*

Ned looked in the direction of Quantock. Surf had battered the volcanic rock into a cornice, which except at the very highest tides, overhung a narrow shingle beach. Air-cushion and perhaps tracked vehicles could drive along the shore, though to Ned that didn't seem a safe way to approach an armed enemy. Perhaps the locals had hoped to take the presumed interlopers unaware, but that was a very risky bet.

For want of anything better to do, Ned walked toward the edge of the crater, where the settlers would be appearing. His submachine gun flopped against his right hip, so he tightened the sling. His bare forearm brushed the iridium barrel. The metal was searingly hot. Ned yelped and rubbed the red splotch which would shortly be a blister.

"What's the matter?" Lissea Doormann asked.

Ned jerked his head around. She was only a half-step from him. A commo helmet's ear-pieces cut off enough of the wearer's peripheral vision to hide nearby objects surprisingly.

"Lissea, where are you going?" Herne Lordling shouted from the hatchway.

"To make sure the first person to greet the welcoming committee isn't shooting!" Lissea called back.

"I just burned myself on my gunbarrel," Ned muttered in embarrassment. "Sorry, I didn't know you were there."

"Company coming!" Josie Paetz called in a clear, terrible voice. He stood on a ledge just below the crater rim. His submachine gun was pointed in the direction of the beach, and he was sighting along the barrel.

"*Captain to crew!*" Lissea said. "*Everybody take your hands off your weapons. Now!*"

She deliberately lifted her empty hands in the air with her elbows at shoulder height. Ned started to do the same then realized he'd feel like an idiot. He crossed his hands behind his back instead.

An air-cushion truck of 5-tonne or greater payload whuffled into sight. Its skirts cast up spray on one side while the other ricocheted pebbles between the cliff and the vehicle's own flank. A civilian manned the tribarrel on the truck cab's ring mount, while other armed men—no women that Ned could see—peered over the front of the cargo box.

The tribarrel's gunner waved enthusiastically at Ned and Lissea. He was shouting something, probably a greeting, but the truck's roaring lift fans overwhelmed the words.

Though the fellow clearly wasn't hostile, it didn't occur to him to point his weapon up at a safe angle. Stupid mistakes had probably killed as many people over the years as aimed shots.

The vehicle slowed but didn't stop. Ned hopped out of the way, touching Lissea's arm to bring her with him. There was a second truck behind the first, and the vehicles had to get onto the basalt plug to be out of the surf. The first pulled far enough forward to let its companion past; then they both shut down. Though the surf instantly filled the relative silence, it was now possible to talk again.

The gunner slid down into the truck cab, opened the passenger door, and jumped to the ground. He was thirty or so, a handsome man with tawny hair and shoulders broad enough to make his waist look falsely narrow.

"Hello there, welcome to Quantock!" he called, waving his right arm like a semaphore. "I'm Jon Watford, the governor here, and I can't *tell* you how happy my wife's going to be to meet another woman from off-planet! Who's in charge?"

The truck tailgates banged down and the remainder of the locals began to get out. The insides of the cargo boxes were armored with thin concrete slabs, sandwiched three-deep to give protection against multiple hits. It struck Ned as a reasonably effective makeshift.

The men were a heavily armed militia instead of a trained military force. They carried a variety of weapons, with powerguns in the majority.

Nothing is ideal under all circumstances, but powerguns were more effective over a wide range of conditions than any alternative Ned knew of. Ajax Four had to be tied firmly into the interstellar trade network in order to be able to buy and maintain hardware so sophisticated. Of course, a gun is only as good as the gunman using it. Most of the Quantock contingent looked at least reasonably competent.

The truck bodies bore cratered splash marks from where they'd been struck by powergun bolts. As the *Swift*'s pilotry data indicated, the Spiders too were involved in interstellar trade.

"Very glad to meet you, Governor Watford," Lissea said. She extended her hand. "I'm Captain Doormann, Lissea—"

"You're in command, then?" Watford said in something between interest and amazement. He shook Lissea's hand.

Militiamen traded glances with the *Swift*'s complement. The locals were obviously taken aback by their heavily armed visitors, but they didn't seem really concerned. There were fifty-odd Quantock militiamen. They didn't have enough experience of real warfare to realize that the dozen expert killers surrounding them could have blown them to sausage before the victims could fire a shot in reply.

"Yes," Lissea said crisply. "I'm on a . . . an embassy to Pancahte. We're prepared for trouble on some of the wilder worlds, of course, but I assure you all we ask of you is the opportunity to purchase supplies at market value. We won't impose on Quantock in any way."

"Sure wouldn't mind having a decent meal, though," said Toll Warson, who'd drifted up behind Lissea.

"You'll have every facility we can provide!" said Watford. "Why, Mellie would never forgive me if I didn't bring you—and your crew, of course—to the settlement for a feast. Do come back with us. We've got room in the trucks if you don't mind squeezing a bit."

Lissea turned and looked at Tadziki. He shrugged and said, "I don't see why not. We'll leave an anchor watch, of course, but now that the sensors are in place, four men ought to be plenty."

"Might even be a woman or two looking for company," Deke Warson said to his brother in a tone of consideration.

"Warson—both of you," Lissea said as though Deke's words had thrown a switch in her tongue. "You'll provide the anchor watch with Ingried and—someone from the ship's crew . . ."

"Bonilla," Tadziki suggested.

"Right, Bonilla," Lissea said. "*If* I feel like it, you'll be relieved at around midnight. The rest of you, get aboard the trucks."

As Ned climbed into a truck box, using the latch of the tailgate as a step, he heard Toll Warson say, "You know, brother, you always did have more mouth than sense."

Jon Watford drove the leading truck and carried Lissea in the cab with him. The previous driver stood in the center of the bench seat to crew the tribarrel. There was no gun-shield. Even if there had been, the gunner's lower extremities were exposed through the windshield.

The tide was going out, exposing enough dry land for the trucks to start back without adding to the spume. The cargo boxes were comfortably roomy for thirty-odd men on a three-klick excursion, though Ned sure wasn't going to stay aboard if shooting started.

"Do you have much trouble with the Spiders this close to the settlement?" he asked the local who was pressed against his right side. Like Ned, the man carried a submachine gun—which might even have been of Telarian manufacture.

"What?" the fellow said. "Spiders? No, no. We sweep the coast every couple months. They keep out of our way."

The deck appeared to be sheet metal. Ned toed it with his boot and grimaced when his suspicions were borne out. An air-cushion vehicle wasn't likely to set off a mine by direct pressure, but that wouldn't save this truck from a command-detonated or rod-fused mine. There ought to be floor protection—and not concrete, which would shatter into deadly shrapnel in the initial shock wave.

Tadziki, on Ned's left, noticed Ned's examination. The adjutant clung to the side of the truck with his right hand to steady himself.

He raised the other hand and ostentatiously crossed his fingers while giving Ned a wry smile.

Ned looked down at the beach. Weed and occasional lumps that could be either animal or vegetable splotched the shingle, but there were relatively few signs of life. The broken tuff was too loose to anchor the shellfish and other sessile life-forms which would have populated a more resistant shore. One blob of protoplasm a meter in diameter was surrounded by hand-sized things which waved forelegs as the truck bellowed past.

When the trucks got to the fortified settlement, Ned might check the shore life more closely for old times' sake, but the Spiders weren't going to spring an ambush from the surf. Ned turned, leaning his back against the side of the truck so that he could view the corniche. He wished he'd worn body armor, to spread the jolts to his rib cage as well as for protection.

The cliffs generally ranged two to five meters above the beach's high-tide mark. One tongue of particularly refractory rock thrust so far west that the trucks had to drive around in a vast explosion of spray. Rainbows ringed the vehicles, and the salty mist cooled Ned's lungs refreshingly.

The trucks' ground pressure was too high for them to skim the wave-tops as lighter air-cushion vehicles could have done. The headland would be dangerous during the journey from Quantock at high tide.

A number of gravel-bottomed ravines drove deep into the interior. They were dry now, but they certainly held raging torrents when they carried storm water, to the sea. The barren, rocky soil would do nothing to slow runoff.

The gullies were an obvious means of approach for Spiders who wished to reach the seacoast while remaining below the horizon of active sensing devices. The colonists probably planted passive sound and motion sensors in the low spots, but such gear would take a beating during every downpour.

There was nothing sexy or exciting about the business of maintaining detection apparatus. Ned doubted whether the colonists had the discipline to keep it up as religiously as safety required.

The colonist manning the cab's tribarrel raised his muzzles to a forty-five-degree angle and ripped off a burst. The cyan bolts were nearly the same hue as the sky, but their brilliance—pure energy instead of merely the diffraction of sunlight—made them stand out like pearls against linen.

All eight mercenaries in the leading truck—and probably the contingent in the second vehicle also—had their weapons raised and off safe. Lissea poked her semiautomatic 2-cm shoulder weapon out of the cab, searching for a target like the rest of them. The colonists were grinning.

The man beside Ned leaned over and shouted, "We're just letting them know in Quantock that we're back. Nothing to get concerned about."

To underscore his words, he aimed his submachine gun skyward and fired half a magazine. The pistol-caliber bolts were pale compared to the tribarrel's heavy charges. Empties spun from the ejection port, disks of half-molten plastic matrix whose burden of copper atoms had been converted to energy in the weapon's chamber. The hot plastic reeked, and ozone from the discharges bit the air.

"I prefer flares," Tadziki said with a cold disdain which probably passed right by the local.

"I told you, the Spiders don't come around here," the militiaman said.

Watford drove the truck up a concrete ramp and down into a vast polder whose floor was below water level at high tide. A seawall, anchored at either end on the cliff face, looped far into the ocean. Within the protected area were a series of square-edged ponds, some of them greenish or maroon from the crops grown there. Several hundred buildings sheltered beneath the corniche.

The polder was defended from enemies as well as the sea. Every hundred meters along the seawall and on the corniche across the chord was a fully enclosed turret. For weather protection, the weapons remained masked until use. From the size and design, Ned judged that each emplacement held a tribarrel in a fully automated or remotely controlled mounting.

People stepped outdoors as the trucks pulled up in front of the long building in the center of town. The sign over the main doors read CIVIC HALL.

The hall was a two-story structure ornamented with whimsically angled 'exposed beams' painted white against the pale blue of the rest of the facade. The whole Quantock community was decorated in pastels, and most of the residences had window boxes or planted borders.

Watford got out of the cab and started around the front of the vehicle. Herne Lordling leaped over the side and executed a perfect landing fall, but neither man was quick enough to beat Lissea to her own door handle.

Watford put his arm around the woman who ran up to greet him and said, "Mellie, let me introduce you to Captain Lissea Doormann, who commands the *Swift*. Lissea, this is Mellie Watford. Mellie came to Quantock as factor for a Xiphian import-export combine. She's the finest import *ever* to Ajax Four."

"We've been married a week," Mellie said. She looked down and blushed at her husband's flattery, but Ned noticed that her left hand squeezed Jon's hip firmly before she transferred her attention to Lissea.

The two women could have passed for sisters. Both were petite with dark short hair and a sort of elfin vivacity. Only in their present garments did they differ strikingly: Mellie wore a peach-colored frock, similar to those of the other women in the crowd, while Lissea was in gray utilities over which she'd slung a bandolier of reloads for her 2-cm powergun.

The sun hung low on the seawall. Its glow further softened the colors of the buildings, blending them with the ruddy tuff of the cliff face.

"I'm not really, ah, dressed for a banquet," Lissea said.

Ned exchanged bland glances with Tadziki. The captain, who led a score of the most deadly men in the galaxy, was embarrassed at not having a party dress.

"Come on home with me," Mellie said. "I'm sure I've got something to fit you." She caught Lissea's hand and tugged her unresisting toward a fuchsia house next door to the civic building. "I can't tell you how nice it is to meet another woman from off-planet, not that there's anything . . ."

Jon Watford glanced after the women, then returned his attention to the remaining locals and visitors. "Well, gentlemen," he said generally toward the mercenaries, "I think maybe a drink or three would be a good way to break the ice and start the celebration. Any takers?"

"*Yee-ha!*" somebody shouted. Ned wasn't sure who the enthusiast was, but a good hundred throats took up the call as the crowd surged toward the broad doors of the hall.

Six hours later, the gathering was a good-natured success. That surprised and pleased Ned, and it must have absolutely delighted Tadziki. Individual members of the *Swift's* complement talked, in the center of large groups of locals like the grit at the core of pearls. The mercenaries were able to boast in a way they'd never have dared do among their own kind—and the listeners loved it.

The funny thing was that so far as Ned could tell, about half the stories were true and the others were fantasy. The fantasies were generally less amazing than the unvarnished accounts— which were sometimes told by the same man.

A number of the mercs had gone off with local women. That didn't seem to have caused any problems. Dewey had gone off with a local man, which *would* cause problems when Bonilla heard about it, but for the moment, Bonilla was safe aboard the *Swift*.

"Can I bring you anything?" asked a voice at Ned's elbow. "Another drink?"

He turned to Jon Watford. "No, I'm not that much of a drinker," he said. "I'm just looking at your chart here."

The two-by-two-meter hologram on one of the room's short walls was a 5000:1 relief map of Quantock and the terrain inland of the settlement. By manipulating the controls at the bottom of the frame, Ned found he could shift the alignment from vertical to a silhouette at any plane in the coverage area, and could decrease the scale to as low as 100:1.

"You know," said Watford thoughtfully, "I don't believe I've looked at this in the past ten years. We're pretty much focused on the sea here in Quantock. That's true everywhere on Ajax Four. But a map of wave-tops isn't much of a decoration, is it?" He chuckled.

"Has there been any attempt to, well, make peace with the indigs?" Ned asked.

"What?" said Watford.

"The indigenes," Ned said. "The Spiders."

"The Spiders aren't indigenous to Ajax Four!" Watford said with unexpected vehemence. "They're aliens, just as sure as men are, and there's curst good evidence that we were here first!"

"Oh," Ned said as his mind worked. "I didn't know that."

"There's no other land-dwelling life-forms bigger than algae," Watford said. "Do you mean to tell me that the Spiders evolved directly from algae?"

"No, I see your point," Ned said.

He pursed his lips. He wasn't looking for a fight, but he *was* curious, and if he'd liked the experience of being steamrollered in an argument, he wouldn't be the type to volunteer for the Pancahte Expedition.

"Thing is," he continued mildly, "I had the impression the Spiders didn't have any technology of their own. Not starships, anyway."

"Look," Watford said. He was getting red-faced. Ned recalled that it wasn't only mercenaries who'd been having a good deal to drink this night. "We've got *every* right to be on this planet. And I'll tell you another cursed thing: they aren't really intelligent, the Spiders aren't. They're really just animals with a talent for mimicking human beings."

"I see your point," Ned said, as though Watford hadn't made two mutually exclusive points. "You know, maybe I'll have another drink after all. What's good here?"

The funny thing was that this sort of philosophical problem concerned only decent people raised in civilized surroundings. Ned doubted that any two members of the *Swift*'s complement besides himself would even bother talking about the rights of indigenous aliens. As for the right of survival of a life-form, human or otherwise, with hostile intentions—

Pacifists didn't enter the Frisian Military Academy.

Watford cleared his throat in embarrassment. "Oh," he said. "Well, we've got a couple of good wines, but if you're willing to—"

"*Attention,*" called a voice so distorted by the hall's multiple loudspeakers that Ned didn't recognize Tadziki for a moment. The adjutant stood on the dais opposite the main doors with a microphone in his hand. "*Sorry, ladies and gentlemen, but there's some ship's business to take care of. Yazov, Paetz, Westerbeke, and Raff— you're next on the rota, and it's time to relieve the anchor watch. Our hosts are loaning us a truck, so you don't have to walk.*"

"Hey, the party's just getting started," Josie Paetz called, though he didn't look that disgruntled. The young mercenary did everything with verve, but only the prospect of combat really excited him.

Lissea stepped to the dais. She wore a tawny dress with gold polka dots. Her hand extended back toward Mellie Watford to show that she wasn't abandoning the woman who'd been her companion throughout the evening. Because the mike was live, Lissea's murmured "*Westerbeke went off with a girl. . .*" crackled through the speakers.

Ned strode toward the dais. "I'll go, Tadziki," he said.

Tadziki switched off the mike. "I want a ship's crewman, Ned," he said.

"I'm good enough for government work," Ned said. "Besides, I'm sober."

Tadziki looked at Lissea. She gave him a brief nod.

"Right," said the adjutant. "Governor, you offered us a vehicle?"

Watford had followed Ned to the dais. "Sure, no problem," he said. "Would you like one of our people to drive?"

"I'd just as soon drive it myself," Ned said before the adjutant could answer. "Got anything smaller than those behemoths you brought us here in, though?"

"Sure we do," Watford said. "Just come along with me."

The *Swift*'s complement had piled their weapons on a table near the door. The locals didn't care if their visitors were armed, but Lissea did. Watford waited while the mercenaries rummaged for

their equipment, then led them outside and down a ramp to the
garage beneath the building.

Ned paused a moment and studied the unfamiliar stars. He'd
spent five years on Nieuw Friesland without getting used to those
constellations, but recently he'd found the night sky of Tethys
looked distorted also.

"You coming, Slade?" Josie Paetz called up the ramp.

"You bet," Ned said. He wondered whether or not there was a
place in the universe where Edward Slade belonged.

The forty-some vehicles in the basement garage ranged from
five-tonne trucks down to one-man skimmers. All were battery-
powered, but two large repair vans were equipped with liquid-fueled
generators as well.

The patrol radius of the heavily laden trucks would be a hundred
klicks or less without a recharge. That didn't strike Ned as far enough.

Jon Watford leaned over the driver's side of the open utility
vehicle he'd offered the mercs. "Here's the power switch," he said,
pointing.

Ned flipped it up. The instrument panel lighted. There were a
dozen individual gauges rather than a combiner screen.

"Fan switches—"

There were four of them. Ned snapped them individually,
watching the dials as he did so. An unexpectedly high drain might
indicate a short in one of the drive motors.

"And the collective," Watford continued, touching the control
yoke. "You've handled hovercraft, I trust? With this broken lava, we
don't have much use for wheels."

"I've handled hovercraft," Ned agreed. *Up to and including
170-tonne supertanks, any one of which could turn Quantock into
glowing slag in three seconds flat.*

"Can we get this show on the road?" Josie Paetz demanded
from the other front seat. "Curst if I don't start walking pretty
quick."

The truck had seats for six people in pairs, but the two rear
benches could be folded flat for cargo space. Yazov sat behind his

young charge, while Raff sprawled on the rear bench with his rocket launcher pointed straight up like a flagpole. If Raff were human, Ned would guess he was three sheets to the wind, but from what he'd seen at the party, the Racontid stuck to water.

"What I figure to do," Ned said mildly, "is learn about the equipment before I take us all out in it."

He tapped a gauge. The needle didn't move. "This says we're at sixty-two percent charge," he said. "How long has it been charging?"

Watford grimaced. "It ought to have a few cells replaced," he said. "Don't worry, though, it'll get you to the ship and bring your friends back. And don't worry about the ground. We're at low tide now, so you'll have a couple hundred meters of beach to run on."

"All right," Ned said. He engaged the fans and felt the truck shiver like butter sliced onto a hot grill.

He backed into the central aisle and spun to face the entrance. The vehicle responded nimbly. Ned had forgotten how much handier an air-cushion vehicle was when the driver didn't have to contend with tonnes of armored inertia. "See you in the morning," he called over his shoulder to Watford as he accelerated out of the garage.

"Aren't you going to turn on your headlights, hotshot?" Josie Paetz asked. He reached over to the marked switch on the dashboard.

Ned raised his knee to block the younger man's hand. "No," he said, "I'm going to use moonlight. The big one's just above the horizon, but that'll do better than advertising us to anybody who wants an easy target."

Paetz sniffed and settled back in his seat. "Maybe *you're* easy," he said, but he didn't press the matter. His uncle eased slightly.

Ned took the utility vehicle up the ramp over the seawall. The salt breeze felt good and the moonlight was, as he'd expected, adequate without enhancement. Switching his visor to light-amplification mode would rob him of depth perception.

He felt himself relax. This was a nice, easy job to focus him after a social evening in which he felt uncomfortable.

Powerguns threw cyan lightning across the sky southward.

"The ship's being attacked!" Josie Paetz said. "Let's get 'em!"

"Wait for bloody support!" Yazov boomed. Several men, mercs to a near certainty, sprang out the doors of the Civic Hall with guns in their hands. The truck dipped down the outer ramp, cutting off the view of Quantock in the driving mirrors; but the *Swift's* whole complement would be armed and on its way in a minute or less. The community militia would follow.

Raff said nothing. His rocket launcher's heavy bolt clanged to chamber a round.

"Hang on!" Ned cried. He turned the truck hard left, up a broad gully instead of due south along the shoreline. When he was sure of the surface he pushed the collective forward, feeding more power to the fans.

"What the fuck are you doing?" Paetz screamed. He pointed. "The shooting's *there*, by the ship!"

"And that's where we're going," Ned said, "only not by the bloody front door. If you do your job as well as I do mine, sonny, then we're going to come through this just fine."

That was a crazy thing to say to the young killer, but the only sane response to combat is to avoid it. If you head toward the guns in a plastic-bodied truck, then your sanity isn't even in question.

At high speed, the truck bounced on its flexible skirts. Rocks, stream-sorted to the size of a man's fist, whopped toward the walls of the ravine. The shielded nacelles kept gravel out of the fan blades. The vehicle could move with three fans instead of four, but it would lose speed and agility. Climbing the gully wall would be a bitch even with full power.

Yazov leaned forward. "There's a lot of wasteland out here," he said in Ned's ear. His voice sounded calm.

"It's okay," Ned said, shouting as he had to do to be heard while facing front. "I'd been looking at a map. I'm going to take us back from the southeast."

The ravine kinked through ninety degrees or so for the third time since Ned had turned into it. The change was due to a dike of harder rock that pinched the gully. It made the sides steeper as well. He should have thought of that when he'd decided to climb back to the surface here.

"Hang on!" he repeated. He banked up the outside of the curve and gunned the fans. His three passengers threw their combined weight to the right without being told. Raff's snarls might have been Racontid curses. Paetz and Yazov were certainly cursing.

Centrifugal force lifted the vehicle over the lip of rock. They'd been millimeters from turning turtle and landing upside down in the ravine, but only horseshoes and hand grenades . . .

The terrain was corrugated. Tubes of lava a meter or two in diameter had hardened alongside one another in past ages. An over-burden of ash had fallen across the denser lava, had been compacted and then swept away by centuries of pounding rain. The present surface was almost impossible to walk over, difficult to traverse even in an air-cushion vehicle, and provided no cover whatever for a man-sized target.

The truck rubbed and pitched. The corrugations were deep enough to spill air from the plenum chamber, so Ned couldn't proceed as fast or as smoothly as he had up the streambed. From what he remembered of the chart, they had about a klick to travel.

"Where are we headed, Slade?" Yazov said. He was using his helmet radio to avoid windrush. The high metallic content of the planet's volcanic rocks absorbed radio signals over very moderate distances, but it wasn't so bad it affected four men sitting within arm's reach of one another.

"There's another ravine," Ned explained. The vehicle bucked high. Ned twisted the bar on the dash which controlled the attitude of the fan nacelles. By angling them vertical, he managed to cushion the truck's impact.

"We'll take it back toward the coast, but south of the ship," he said, wheezing because the shock of landing had jolted him against the yoke. *"They won't expect us from that way."*

Powergun bolts streaked the sky and lit the dark mass of the crater which bowered the *Swift*. More shots reflected from the ground and glowed in the gas vaporized from gouges of rock.

Josie Paetz stood. He presented his submachine gun with both hands instead of clinging to the windshield with one or the other. His body swayed, perfectly in balance despite the truck's violent motion. His eyes scanned the horizon from that slightly higher vantage.

Ned took a hand away from the collective to key his helmet. *"Best we not call attention to ourselves too soon, Paetz,"* he said.

"Fuck off," Paetz shouted.

There was a series of bright red explosions from the battle scene. Raff stroked his rocket launcher and laughed like gears clashing.

A shadow on the ground, streaking lesser shadows. Sooner than he'd—

"Hang—" Ned cried.

They were airborne, dipping into the gully that Ned had thought was just another corrugation until it was *real* close. He spun the yoke and leaned. The truck didn't have an aircar's power-to-weight ratio so it dropped instead of flying, marginally under control.

Paetz fell to his knees and grabbed the windshield. The clear plastic cracked across with the strength of his grip, but he didn't go out. His weapon still pointed forward in the other hand, ready to engage any Spider that showed itself.

It took ten meters before Ned thought he could get the truck stable, twice that before he did. Even then the ravine twisted unexpectedly and he tore off a chunk of front molding. Only the skirts' resilience kept them from worse trouble. Yazov cursed him for a cack-handed fool.

Paetz shot—three bolts so dazzling that Ned's visor blacked out to save his night vision. The object in the gully ahead of them was just an object to Ned, a boulder in the way. Paetz, his faceshield set to thermal imaging, recognized it as a Spider while Ned was trying to maneuver safely around.

The creature lunged upward, screaming like a glacier about to calve icebergs. It had been crouching to aim its own powergun toward the kilometer-distant cone which protected the *Swift*. As the truck howled past the Spider, Yazov shot it with his 2-cm weapon and Raff fired his rocket launcher point-blank.

The rocket motor was of the all-burned-on-launch variety so there was no danger to the shooter from backblast, but the supersonic *crack!* behind Ned's left ear was deafening despite his helmet's protection. The Spider blew apart in a white flash. The warhead's explosion had been lost in the motor roar.

The ravine twisted. Three Spiders hunched like squat bollards across the truck's path. Instinct told Ned to brake by aiming the fan output forward. Training—*when in doubt, gas it*—slammed his throttle to the stop.

It seemed as if the whole world was shooting, but the only gunmen were the three mercs with Ned. Paetz and Yazov hit the right-hand Spider simultaneously, head-shots from the submachine gun while Yazov cratered the creature's chest with a bolt from his heavier weapon.

Recoil from the rocket launcher lifted the nose of the truck. The Racontid had to have muscles like tow cables to be able to accept the shock. The Spider in the center disintegrated. Fragments of its pelvis and torso blew into its fellows like secondary missiles.

The truck hit the left and center Spiders a fraction of a second apart. The gooey corpse Raff had shot swept away the damaged windshield and knocked Josie Paetz backward. The powergun the creature had been carrying in one of its upper hands clattered on the short hood and off the other side of the vehicle. Yazov fired again, twisting backward in his seat, and lit up the third Spider with his bolt.

The Spiders were retreating, running away when they learned that the *Swift's* anchor watch was more of a bite than they could chew. Most of the aliens weren't going to survive to run far, though.

Ned switched on the headlights. A mass of Spiders stood like startled deer, twenty or more. Sweat and weapons gleamed on their dark gray bodies. They'd heard the shooting ahead of them, but they hadn't known how to react, and anyway, there wasn't time.

There wasn't time for the Spiders now, either.

The creatures were so tall that Ned felt he was driving into a grove with arms flailing above him like windswept branches. Paetz, flung into the well between the front and second bench, fired from a sprawling position. Yazov fired, and Raff emptied his magazine with two thunderous blasts so quick that there was barely time for the breech to cycle between the shots.

Ionized air, matrix and propellant residues, and the unforgettable reek of living creatures whose body cavities had explosively emptied, merged in an atmosphere you could cut with a knife. The truck brushed between two Spiders, one of them dying, and hit a third squarely. A headlight shattered. The heavy body skidded over the vehicle and off.

They were around a twitch in the ravine, so slight that it would appear straight to somebody looking at a map. The three-meter walls cut off view of the carnage behind the truck. There was nothing but rock in the headlight beam. Spiders were shrieking. None of them had fired during the momentary contact.

The volume of distant gunfire suddenly increased tenfold. The *Swift* wasn't the focus of the shooting. The rest of the mercenaries and the Quantock militia must have run into another party of Spiders.

The rocket launcher clanged as Raff locked home a fresh magazine. *How he stood the recoil. . .* Josie Paetz was upright, reloading also, and the *shuckclack* directly behind Ned meant that Yazov's 2-cm was ready as well.

"Go on back!" Paetz screamed. "We'll finish them! Go on!"

Ned spun the yoke with his left hand and unslung his submachine gun in his right. He pointed the weapon over where the windshield had been. "You bet your ass!" he said as the truck tore back into conflict.

The Spiders' thin bodies were exaggerated by the great length of their limbs. Their heads were nearly spherical and about the volume of a man's. The eyes were large and slightly bulged, while the mouth was a point-down triangle with teeth on all three flats.

Translucent membranes slipped sideways over the eyes as the glare of the halogen-cycle headlight flashed on them again.

Half a dozen of the Spiders were down. One had lost half its skull to a powergun bolt. Two of its fellows helped the creature stand upright, though it must have been mortally wounded.

Raff put a rocket into the injured Spider. The warhead blew the trio down like pins struck squarely by a bowling ball.

Ned hosed the aliens, keeping his muzzle low. He couldn't hope for accuracy while he drove, but he knew that being shot at didn't help *any* marksman's aim. Besides, he was bound to hit a few of them, trapped in the trough of the ravine.

Paetz fired three-shot bursts, aiming for Spiders' heads and always hitting with at least one of the bolts despite the truck's speed and the slewing turn. His uncle aimed single shots at the center of mass of each target in turn. None of the mercs knew where a Spider's vital organs were—the brain might not even be in the skull—but a 2-cm bolt packed enough energy to cook everything in the torso, and the least Josie's head-shots were going to do was blind the victim.

The Spider who'd been alert enough to aim as the truck came back was Yazov's first victim. Another of the creatures managed to swing his submachine gun to bear. The Spider disintegrated in a mix of powergun bolts and a rocket before it could fire.

Ned humped over a corpse, caromed off the legs of a Spider which stood upright but was missing two arms and the left half of its chest, and spun safely out of the killing zone again.

The iridium barrel of his submachine gun glowed white. He must have sublimed five millimeters from the bore by emptying the magazine on a single trigger-pull. There were times you had to misuse tools, waste them, to get the job done. Tools and men as well sometimes, if you were in command and the devil drove.

He tossed the submachine gun over the side of the truck. He couldn't reload one-handed with the weapon so hot, and the eroded barrel wouldn't be safe for another burst anyway.

Ned rotated the truck on its axis again, scrubbing away velocity between the skirts and the streambed. He switched off the headlight, spun the roller switch above his forehead to change his visor to thermal imaging, and held out his right hand. "Paetz!" he said. "Gimme one of your pistols!"

The butt of a 1-cm service pistol slapped Ned's palm. The weapon was already off safe. He closed his fingers about it and slammed the control yoke to the dashboard again. Stones spewed from beneath the skirts as the truck accelerated under maximum thrust.

They rounded the slight corner. The Spiders were pale wraiths against the relative darkness of rocks which had cooled during the night. Two of the creatures clung to the sides of the ravine, trying to climb, or just desperate to stay upright. A few others knelt or squatted, and limbs thrashed all over the killing ground.

Paetz, Yazov, and Raff blasted the aliens which weren't already flat on the stones. Ned emptied his borrowed pistol, but he didn't think he hit anything useful with it. There was probably nothing useful *to* hit. None of the Spiders had been able to raise a weapon against the mercenaries.

He slowed the truck to a crawl and idled back among the huge corpses. His companions were reloading.

"Wanna take pictures?" Paetz asked.

"No," Ned said. "They aren't going to walk off before daybreak."

He reached over the side of the truck and grabbed a standard-looking submachine gun from a Spider. The creature's arm fell apart under the tug of the sling. Shrapnel from a rocket warhead had shredded the Spider from skull to pelvis.

"Let's go see what happened at the ship," he said. Shooting had died down almost completely. "Besides, there may be some stragglers."

The Spiders hadn't fired a shot at them. Not one single shot.

Raff began to sing in his own language, pounding time on the flooring with the butt of his rocket launcher. His voice sounded like a saw cutting stone.

We are the best, Ned thought. His tunic was soaked with sweat and the fluids with which the Spiders had sprayed him during point-blank kills. *We are the best!*

Crewmen had carried minifloods from the *Swift* to throw blue-white light over the bodies. Elongated shadows made the Spiders look even larger than they were. Most of the creatures had slid to the base of the cone in their death throes, but a few lay nearly at the rim.

"We never killed that many of them," said a marveling colonist.

"I never *saw* this many Spiders!" said Jon Watford. "In thirty-two years, I never saw this many Spiders. You're—"

He turned to Lissea Doormann. "Lissea, you're incredible, you and your men. It'll be a generation before they get up enough strength to be a problem again."

"I'm afraid your dress is a casualty, though, Mellie," Lissea said.

She looked down at herself ruefully. She'd dropped a bandolier over the garment as she left the Civic Hall at a run. A clasp had caught and torn the light fabric. The black smudges were iridium. The metal sublimed from powergun bores as they channeled the enormous energy downrange and redeposited on whatever was closest when the vapor cooled. Lissea's hands and the bare skin of her throat beneath the line of her visor were gray-tinged also.

Mellie, still in her own peach frock, hugged Lissea fiercely. "Don't worry about that!" she said. "What's important is that *you're* all right."

"Silly bastards thought they'd sneak up on us," Deke Warson said. The cloth facing of his hard body armor was abraded. At some point during the night, Deke must have skidded ten or twenty meters on the lava. "Because we didn't shoot the first time one of them poked his head out, they thought we didn't know they were coming."

"If that's what passes for fire discipline on Ajax Four. . ." his brother said. He spoke in Watford's direction, but he didn't raise his voice to emphasize the criticism, ". . . then I'm surprised there's any colonies left."

Virtually the whole Quantock settlement was present *ooh*ing and *aah*ing at the windrow of huge bodies. The trucks that brought the reaction force had returned to ferry civilians. Parents carried babies to see the unique sight.

"And there's more back there along the cliffs," a colonist said. "I don't know how many there must be."

"There were half a dozen Spiders on the corniche," Tadziki said to Ned in a quiet voice. "They were going to ambush whoever came from the settlement."

The older man shook his head at the memory. "It was as though they'd never heard of thermal imaging," he said. "Or maybe they'd just never met humans who could hit anything from a moving vehicle. They scarcely got a shot off, the Spiders."

"They come up two of the gullies south of us and spread all

around," said Harlow, a skeletally thin man whose skin was as pigmentless as an albino's. He had red hair. "We could see them like it was in broad daylight. We just waited till we figured we could make the bag limit."

"Amateurs," Tadziki said as he studied his hands. Like those of the other mercs, they were stained by redeposited metal. "They'll buy guns, but they won't buy support weapons like sensors and night-vision equipment to make the guns effective."

"And they act," Ned said, "as if everybody else did the same thing."

Tadziki smiled. "You all right, then?" he said.

"Sure," Ned said. "I don't know what made me do that. I'm fine."

He and the others, the *team*, reached the *Swift* less than a minute after the first 5-tonne from the settlement arrived. Ned got out of the utility truck, looked around, and vomited in the full glare of headlights.

The truth was, he still felt as though his mind was detached from the body which happened to be occupying the same space. He supposed that would pass. Blood and martyrs! He'd been shot at before, which was more than the Spiders had managed to do.

Mellie was with her husband. Jon gestured animatedly toward the fallen Spiders. Lissea walked over to Ned and the adjutant. "I hear you had some excitement of your own," she said to Ned.

Ned quirked a smile. "Seemed like that at the time," he said. "Seeing this, I don't know that we did so very much, though."

"Hey, don't sell us short!" said Josie Paetz. "We nailed every one we saw, didn't we? Musta been thirty of them, at least."

"We killed twenty-six," Raff said. "We did well, my brothers." The Racontid gave his terrible equivalent of a laugh.

"When they clumped up, Bonilla stomped them with the mortar," Toll Warson said to a crowd of admiring colonists. "Mostly, though, it was shoot and scoot."

He pumped his 2-cm powergun in the air. Civilians laughed and cheered. Ned noted that Toll had also been firing the submachine gun slung across his chest. Its hot barrel had seared a series of indentations in the fabric cover of his body armor.

"And shoot again," his brother said, "while they blew holes in the rock where the first rounds had come from. As if we wouldn't have multiple hides, with all afternoon and nothing else to do."

"You're okay, then?" Lissea said sharply.

"Look, I'm fine!" Ned said. He looked away. "I did my job, all right?"

"He did better than that," Tadziki said. "He's the one who decided on his own hook to cut the Spiders' line of retreat—and did it too."

Yazov turned. He was polishing the film of matrix from the ejection port of his shoulder weapon. "He can drive for me any day. Hey, Slade?"

Ned grinned at the older man. "Hey," he said. "We're a team, right?"

Lissea Doormann squeezed Ned's shoulder. Herne Lordling watched with eyes like gun muzzles. "That's right," she said. "We're a team."

"Well, you've got to spend the night with us at Quantock," Mellie Watford said, linking her arm again with Lissea's. "You should all of you come. You don't need guards anymore."

Ned winced. Some Spiders—probably a few dozen or even scores of them—would have escaped by the other ravine. Making a needless bet on how aliens would react to a disaster was naive and foolish beyond words. *He* didn't like the idea that Quantock was empty at the moment, though the settlement at least had automatic defenses.

Lissea smiled and hugged Mellie. "No," she said, "we'll all stay by the ship tonight. We've got a long way to go, and I don't intend to take risks."

"Well, you'll let us entertain you again tomorrow night, won't you?" Jon Watford said. "A victory celebration, that'll be."

Lissea shook her head crisply. "I'm sorry," she said. "We'll take on food and water from your settlement in the morning, if you'll be so kind; but we lift for Mirandola by noon."

She looked back at the ship, then faced the Quantock governor again.

"We have a mission," she said. Her voice made the night chime.

* * *

Three hours and forty-seven minutes out of Ajax Four, Ingried called from the consumables module, "Hey, why can't I get any water out of this? Hey, Bonilla—what's wrong with the water?"

Dewey, who was at the navigational console instead of Bonilla, called up the proper gauge on his screen. Then he swore and said, "Captain? Captain! The tank's open. We've voided all our fresh water!"

"All right," boomed Herne Lordling as he swung himself out of his bunk. "Who was responsible for filling the tank? That was you, wasn't it, Warson?"

He pointed a big finger at Deke Warson.

Lissea stepped out of her room. The flimsy door was opaque but didn't pretend to soundproofing.

"I'll handle this!" Tadziki said, coming off his bunk also. Ned, who'd been reading a translation of Thucydides, dropped the viewer and jumped down behind the adjutant. The whole crew was on its feet, except for Deke Warson.

"I put *a* load of water aboard, Cuh'nel, sah," said Warson. His bare feet were braced against the stanchions supporting Toll's bunk above him. His hands were behind his head; significantly, Deke's right hand was beneath his pillow as well. "I didn't top off the tank. There was one, maybe two bladders after the one I siphoned aboard."

"That's a curst lie!" Lordling said. "Those were four-thousand-liter bladders, and the one you loaded was the third. The tank only holds twelve kay!"

The tank connections were badly designed. The access plate could be closed over the vent and spout even though the valves weren't screwed down to lock. For that matter, it wouldn't be the first time a seal had failed in service, particularly on a new vessel.

"I'll han—" Tadziki repeated.

"No," said Lissea. She stepped between Lordling and the Warsons. "I will. Dewey, chart a return course to Ajax Four. Westerbeke, oversee him."

Westerbeke had lurched from the commode, pulling his trousers up. He nodded and shuffled forward to the other navigation console.

Lissea looked around at her crew. "Gentlemen," she said, "this isn't a race we're in. Eight hours more or less isn't going to make a difference. But fuck-ups can kill us. Somebody didn't do his job. Somebody else didn't check that the job was done."

She looked at Herne Lordling. "And going off half-cocked isn't going to help a bad situation either. Let's take this as a cheap lesson and not do it again. Any of it."

"It was my fault, Captain," Tadziki said. "I went over the connections before liftoff, but I must have missed that one."

One of the ship's crewmen—Ned thought it was Hatton— had been officially responsible for checking the external seals.

"There's enough blame to go around," Lissea said coldly. "There aren't so many of us aboard that we can afford to trust that somebody else will make sure we all stay alive. It's over for now."

"Sir, we've got the course charted," Westerbeke called from forward.

Lissea turned on her heel. "Then engage it at once," she ordered as she strode back to her tiny compartment.

The *Swift* shuddered into Transit. Ned returned to his bunk. Like Lissea said, eight hours didn't matter a great deal.

The *Swift*'s landing motors converted the rain into visually-opaque steam. The automatic landing system used millimeter-wave radar, so optical visibility wasn't important, but the roiling gray mass on the screen above the navigation consoles didn't do anything for Ned's state of mind. He was nervous. Therefore, he kept his face abnormally calm.

"Touchdown," Westerbeke reported. Ned didn't feel the skids make contact, but the motors shut down an instant later.

"Sir, I still can't raise Quantock," Bonilla said. *"I think it's their equipment, not just the storm and, you know, the planet. Over."*

Everybody was getting up. Lissea and Tadziki walked forward. Ned stayed where he was, near the engine-room bulkhead. Lissea spoke to Bonilla without using helmet commo. Ned caught only the general drift, something about the settlement.

"All right, listen up," Tadziki said loudly. "The following

personnel will put out sensors. Deke Warson, Hatton, Lordling, and myself. Get your wet suits on, boys, because it's raining like a sonuvabitch out there."

Herne Lordling turned toward the adjutant. His face was cold.

"I'll go along too," Toll Warson said. "I gave Deke a hand with the bladder."

Lissea looked at Warson and nodded.

Ned opened the drawer in his bedframe and pulled out the stretchable black overstocking of waterproof fabric. "Sir?" he said. "Tadziki? I'll take one of our jeeps to Quantock and tell them we're back. They can bring us water in the morning."

Somebody started to lower the ramp. Water spewed in as soon as the seal broke, soaking the nearest bunks.

"Close that up!" Tadziki snapped. "We'll use the airlock instead."

"Those robot turrets'll chew you up just as fast as they would a Spider, kid," Deke Warson said. "Better wait till the storm passes and we can get a signal through."

"I'll use laser commo when I get a line of sight," Ned said. He worked his hands through the armholes of the wet suit, then rolled the collar about his neck. He wouldn't bother with the hood. "After that I'll wait till they send somebody out to clear me through."

"It's high tide," Tadziki said. "I don't think it'll be safe along the beach. And anyway, I don't want you going alone."

"Hey, he's looking for a regular bed to sleep in, that's all he's doing," Louis Boxall said.

"And maybe somebody to share it?" his brother offered.

"I'll ride shotgun," Josie Paetz said.

"No, I figured to come back to the ship as soon as I'd delivered the message," Ned said, sweeping his comment across the Boxalls and Tadziki, "so that you know it's been delivered."

Yazov put down the 2-cm barrel he'd been inspecting on his bunk. "I promised your father that I'd stick with you, Josie," he said. "If you go, I go."

"Look, those jeeps won't haul three!" Paetz said. From a deadly gunman he suddenly switched to being a petulant boy of nine or ten.

"Then you stay," his uncle said flatly. "Or you shoot me here."

"Look, I don't really need—" Ned said.

"I'll go with Brother Slade," Raff volunteered. He stood up with his rocket launcher. If the Racontid even had a wet suit, he didn't bother with it.

"I'll go myself," Lissea Doormann said unexpectedly. "I'd like to see Mellie again. And anyway, I should have checked the valves myself."

She grinned wryly at Ned. "Wait a moment while I get my suit," she added.

"I'll take longer than a moment to get the jeep out of external storage," Tadziki grumbled. "Coyne, Harlow, both of you Boxalls— get your suits on. Setting up the jeep's your job."

"Lissea," said Herne Lordling, "I can't permit you to do this!"

Lissea stared at him. Lordling, with one leg into the overstocking, looked so silly that Deke Warson had an excuse for laughing.

"That's right, Herne," she said. "You can't permit me to do anything. Because you work for me, not the other way around!"

She stamped past Ned and tried to slam the door of her room. It wasn't heavy enough to do a good job.

Ned's lips were pursed as he took a bandolier of ammunition from the arms locker. He now carried the submachine gun he'd taken from the dead Spider. It was a perfectly serviceable weapon; and it meant something, to Ned and to his companions.

"Got it!" Louis Boxall shouted as he kicked the main-pin home on the collapsible jeep. "Your chariot awaits, milord Slade."

When the waves withdrew from the shore, the hissing roar muted to the point you could hear the sheets of rain hammering on the *Swift*'s hull. Ned's boots sloshed in a centimeter of water. The storm didn't leave it time to run off the flat, impervious surface of the basalt.

"I'm used to this," he said to Boxall as he got in on the driver's side.

"It rains like this on Tethys?" Lissea said as she scissored her legs over the jeep's right sidewall.

The setup crew trotted back to the airlock. The last man, anonymous in helmet and wet suit, waved.

Ned threw the main switch and checked his gauges. Everything was in the green. "No ma'am," he said. "But I did a lot of diving."

Lissea chuckled. She carried a shoulder weapon slung muzzle-down to keep rain out of the bore.

Ned cleared his throat. "Ah, Lissea," he said. "There's two ways to do this: inland—where there's a couple rivers to cross—and out to sea beyond the surf. I think going out over the breakers is the better idea by far, but—well, I don't think most of the people back aboard would like me taking you that way."

"You're the driver," Lissea said. "I wouldn't be here if I didn't trust you."

Ned engaged the fans and spun them up. The little jeep combined a high power-to-weight ratio with agile handling, making it a delight to drive. It wasn't an aircar, but you could glide three meters for every one you dropped if you knew what you were doing.

"Hang on, then," he said. "The next part's the only tricky bit."

He idled down to the shore. Because the jeep was designed for military use, there was a sleeve between the two seats to clamp the butt of Ned's submachine gun. He'd covered the muzzle with a condom, normal practice and nothing he thought about until Lissea fingered the rubber.

"Good idea," she said.

"It's SOP in the Slammers," Ned said, keeping his voice level.

A major wave hit the lip of basalt and cascaded almost as far as the skids of the *Swift*. Ned eased the yoke forward, building speed gradually to match that of the retreating sea-water. Spray puffed around the vehicle as its skirts rode over rock. When the jeep ran into the open sea, it dipped slightly under its own weight and that of the passengers. The plenum chamber sealed perfectly. The jeep, wallowing like a dory with no rudder, began to move forward.

Ned turned the vehicle's head, fighting the sluggishness of the fluid medium. A wave struck them. The mixture of water and trapped air gurgled into the passenger compartment and down across the plenum chamber. The jeep bucked and bubbled higher, regaining its handling.

Ned goosed the throttles off the back of the wave. The jeep was dancing across the surface of the water when they met the next big comber. They were far enough out now that they could skid across it as a swell rather than a cataclysm.

"Next stop, Quantock!" Ned cried. Seawater streamed out the side-vents. Some rain was falling, but either the storm had slacked off or it wasn't as fierce over the ocean as it had been onshore.

"People pay good money for fun like that," Lissea said, tightening her suit's throat seal with one hand. She was being ironic, but she didn't sound angry until she added, "Just what the hell do you suppose Herne Lordling thinks he's playing at?"

Ned checked his compass direction. To gain a moment's time while he decided whether to answer, he illuminated the map display on the dashboard.

"He thinks," he said, staring far ahead of the vehicle, "that he's in love with you. And he thinks that eventually you'll, ah, fall in love with him."

He felt Lissea's eyes on him. He glanced over to prove that he wasn't avoiding her—as he was—and then focused back on his driving.

"And what do you think, Ned?" the woman asked in an even tone.

Ned looked at her and away. "I think," he said, "that you're just about the most controlled person I've ever met. It'd be a disaster for the expedition if you got together with Lordling—with any of us, but especially with Lordling. So there isn't a snowball's chance in hell of that happening."

He cleared his throat. He was driving with a natural grace. For having fun in a jeep, open water was a better medium even than a rolling meadow. There were no obstacles, and the flowing surface turned every line into a thrilling slalom.

"Why especially Herne?" Lissea asked.

"Because," Ned said, "he isn't smart enough not to get involved in things that he doesn't know anything about. Which means most things."

He didn't know how she was going to take that until she giggled. "He was a colonel, you know," she said.

"Ma'am," Ned said, "my uncle Don would say, 'There's only one Colonel, that's Alois Hammer, and I served with him.'"

"And you can say the same thing, can't you, Ned?" Lissea said.

He looked at her again. Her face in the dashlights was quiet, expectant. "Yes ma'am," he said. "In my own way. Yes, I can say that."

She faced front. "I still prefer 'Lissea,'" she said.

The first cyan ripple of powergun bolts was lost in the occasional cloud-top lightning. Three mortar shells went off, followed by three more, as quickly as the *Swift*'s crew could feed a fresh clip into the 10-cm weapon. The red flashes were unmistakable.

"The ship's being attacked!" Ned said. They were about midway on an arc between the *Swift* and Quantock, almost a kilometer out to sea. He started to swing the jeep's bow shoreward.

Lissea prodded at switches on her commo helmet. Persistent static swamped any attempted radio communication. She snarled, "Bloody hell! They could be on Telaria for any good I'm able to do to raise them."

Ned reached down with his right hand and worked his submachine gun's charging handle. "I'll drop you at the settlement," he said.

"Like hell you will," Lissea said. "You'll bring us around the back of the Spiders and we'll light them up, just like you would if it was Paetz with you."

"Lissea . . ." Ned said. The ravines would be gushing torrents now, but the jeep was handy enough to breast them. The very violence of the run-off would conceal the little vehicle and smother the fan's noise signature.

"And don't tell me I can't shoot like Josie Paetz!" Lissea said as she chambered a round into her 2-cm weapon. "Neither can you!"

"Yes, ma'am," Ned said. He concentrated on his driving.

All hell was breaking out around the partly crumbled cinder cone. The attackers were using at least one tribarrel. Chunks of the crater's rim dissolved.

Where the chosen ravine—now river—met the ocean, the water boiled like soup left on too high a fire, but there was no current since flow and counterflow balanced. Ned brought his speed up.

The Jeep's skirts dabbed at surges, causing the vehicle to pitch and yaw. He couldn't anticipate the fiercely pulsing water. The barren rocks upstream sped the runoff, but at least Ned didn't have to worry about meeting a tree-trunk rolling in the flood.

The mortar landed another triple hammerblow. Blue-and-orange flames flashed skyward in response to the shellbursts. A ripping sound indicated a powerful electrical current was shorting across the wet ground.

"That's—" Lissea said.

"Blood and martyrs!" Ned shouted, hauling on the yoke. He leaned almost across his passenger's lap to tighten the jeep's swerve away from the sudden obstacle.

Ned was using thermal imaging rather than the vehicle's central headlight in order to achieve surprise. The river was a black mirror, sharply in contrast to the banks even though the bordering stone had been drenched by the storm.

He *knew* there would be no obstructions. Therefore he almost ran into the scissors bridge lying low across the stream, even though the stark lines of the structure were as obvious as blood on a sheet.

They bumped up over the bank of the stream. The air-cushion jeep didn't have a ground vehicle's advantage of using friction to scrub off momentum, but the lack of running gear made it very light. They skidded across the side of the approach ramp, close to the end, low, and not fast enough to rip the skirts off.

"Via," Lissea said, "the Spiders don't have gear like that. The settlers thought the *Swift* was a smuggler. They've attacked us."

"Yeah, that's what it looks like," Ned said softly.

The tribarrel had been silenced. Richly saturated bolts from the *Swift*'s defenders ripped and played across the landscape.

"Stop here," Lissea ordered. "I'll use modulated laser."

Ned skidded the jeep to a halt. He left the fans at idle, though he was ready to shut them off if Lissea demanded that. The slight vibration wouldn't significantly affect communication, but using tight-beam laser without a clear receptor was a frustrating business. It was still raining, though maybe not enough to matter.

"Doormann to *Swift,*" Lissea said. Ned, breathing hard through his open mouth, marveled at how calm Lissea kept her voice. She'd focused her faceshield's pipper on the rim of the cinder cone. The miniature laser was mounted over her right ear, with the pickup tube right above it. "Cease firing immediately. You are shooting at Quantock settlers."

The transmission was invisible and inaudible unless it painted a tuned receptor. Three quick bolts proved at least somebody hadn't gotten the word.

"Doormann to *Swift,*" Lissea repeated. "Cease firing immediately. These are our friends."

A 2-cm powergun could claw a satellite from orbit through a normal-density atmosphere like that of Ajax Four. Powerguns were line-of-sight weapons, but the laser communicator was line-of-sight also. A single bolt reflected from the cloud base. It had been aimed southward from the cone. No further shots followed.

Lissea slumped back in her seat. "I think that's got it," she said. "Whoever caught my transmission passed it on by helmet radio. Curse this planet!" She lifted her visor and rubbed her face with her hands.

"What do you want to do now?" Ned asked. He was half-inclined to suggest that they keep out of everybody's way until daybreak. There'd been a number of hideous mistakes already this night, but there was plenty of scope for another one.

Lissea nodded forward. "Head for the *Swift,*" she said. "We've got to see how much damage has been done."

"Yes, ma'am," he said.

Ned lifted the jeep and started south, keeping his speed down to twenty-five to thirty kilometers per hour. That was plenty fast enough for the fractured terrain. The dead weren't going anywhere, and the wounded would be getting what was available in terms of help already. *Curse this planet!*

He heard something ahead of them. For a moment Ned thought

of another tumbling watercourse; then he recognized the intake roar of big lift fans.

"Lissea?" he said. He grounded the jeep. "I think we're about to run into the locals."

"Via!" she said as she reached over his right knee to turn on the headlight. "Let them know we're here, then!"

A huge truck grunted over an intervening ridge of hexagonal crystals. The jeep's headlight caught it squarely. There were a dozen or so settlers in the box. As one, they ducked beneath their concrete armor. The survivors were utterly cowed by the mauling they'd taken from the *Swift*'s professionals.

"We're surrounded!" cried the man at the cab-roof tribarrel. He'd been staring back toward the cinder cone until the light fell across him. His radio collar was compatible with the mercenaries' commo helmets.

The truck slewed to a halt as the driver threw himself on the cab floor.

"Jon, it's me, Lissea!" Lissea cried. She stood up in her seat.

"Fight, you cowards, or we've had it!" Jon Watford screamed as he swung his tribarrel toward the jeep.

"Jon!"

Ned's burst hit the settlers' leader four times in the upper chest and throat. Ned's visor blanked the core of the flashes, leaving only shimmering cyan haloes.

Watford recoiled against the back of the hatch ring. He still held the tribarrel's grips. Ned raised his point of aim. This time only two of the bolts hit, but even the pistol-caliber rounds were enough to rupture Watford's cranial vault.

"Cease fire!" Lissea Doormann ordered. *"All units cease fire!"*

A safety device in the truck switched off the fans after ten seconds of unattended operation. Cooling metal clicked and pinged.

Ned leaned over the side of the jeep. He managed to raise his faceshield before he vomited.

"We saw the ship land," the settler said. His eyes were closed, and he couldn't have been really conscious with the amount of painblockers in him as Tadziki worked on the stump of his right leg. "We thought, 'They took care of the Spiders but we'll show we can handle smugglers the same way ourselves.' We were—we wanted to show the women what *we* could do."

"There, that's as much as I can do," Tadziki said. He stood up. "Keep him warm, don't let him go into shock, that's as much as anybody can do now."

Two colonists edged past the adjutant and put the wounded man on a stretcher. They were careful but not very adept at their task.

The surviving 5-tonne—mortar shells had left the other a burned-out wreck—was full of corpses. The wounded were moved to smaller vehicles and taken back to Quantock. The settlement's doctor was one of the fatalities, but medical personnel were flying in from other colonies.

"You know whose fault it is?" Deke Warson shouted. He pointed to a colonist. "It's you people's fault! What did you expect when you started shooting at us?"

The colonist bunched his fists and started for Warson. Toll grabbed his brother. Ned caught the settler and twisted both wrists back behind the fellow's back.

"He doesn't know what he's saying," Ned said. "He's as spooked as you are."

"Buddy," Toll Warson said, "there's no such thing as friendly fire." The big merc spoke loudly, but he wasn't looking at anyone in particular. "I'm sorry as hell, but that's the way it is."

Mellie Watford stood beside the five-tonne's open tailgate. She wore a waterproof cape over a lacy nightdress, and she had house slippers on.

Lissea tried to put an arm around her. Mellie shook herself violently, as though she'd been drenched in ice water. She began to cry, for the first time since a courier had summoned ambulance vans from Quantock and the women came with them.

"They *shot* at us," Deke Warson said. His voice was almost a whimper. "What the hell did they expect?"

"Ah, Mistress Watford?" one of the colonists said. "We're ready to start back now."

"Tadziki," Lissea Doormann said crisply. "I want the desaliniza-tion gear set up tonight. We'll lift for Mirandola as soon as we've filled our fresh-water tank."

"What the hell did they expect. . ."

MIRANDOLA

The foliage ranged from azure to maroon, spreading broadly from squat tree-trunks. Ned had been raised on a planet where vegetation was sparse and thin-stemmed, so Mirandola's forests struck him as strange; but the landscape was very beautiful in its own way.

"I don't see why the settlers are so shirty about us keeping our distance," Herne Lordling grumbled. "If we were pirates, it wouldn't help them a bit to tell us to stay away, would it? Anyway, most little colonies, they're glad of some company."

"Go around the left side of this tree," Tadziki said. "It's only another fifty meters."

The adjutant was directing the five personnel who hauled a 10-cm hosepipe to a spring-fed stream to replenish the water tank. Four more men paralleled the fatigue party at some distance in the woods: pickets, in case Mirandola turned out to have dangers the pilotry data had ignored.

The hose was flexible, but it had to be stiff-walled so as not to collapse under the suction of the *Swift*'s pump. Even though the direction was basically downhill and the hose didn't bind on the surface of fallen leaves, the team doing the work mostly staggered forward with their heads down.

"I didn't even know there was a permanent settlement on Mirandola," said Louis Boxall. "It was just a stopover point from anything I'd heard, though . . ."

He looked around

". . . it seems a pleasant enough place."

"There's nothing on file about them," Tadziki said. "Judging from orbital imaging, there's only forty-odd houses and some fields that don't look very extensive."

"Maybe they got spooked when they heard about Ajax Four," Dcke Warson said.

"That's enough of that!" Lissea snapped. "Why they don't want company is their own business. We could go all the way to Pancahte on stored rations, and we can get our own water easily."

Carrying the hose required strength and weight. Lissea, though fit, couldn't compare to any of her subordinates in either aspect. She was present now because the morning the *Swift* lifted from Ajax Four the second time, she had insisted on being added to the duty roster.

She ignored Tadziki and Lordling when they told her— correctly—that her business should be with matters more important than guard-mount and fatigues. Military structures don't function as democracies, and pretending otherwise is counterproductive.

Lissea turned her head to the side and added sharply, "It's just as well that we don't have to waste time socializing, anyway."

If the captain chose to feel responsible for a tragedy that was none of her doing, Ned thought, then it was just as well that her self-punishment be limited to a few blisters. People had a right to manage their own souls, however foolish the means chosen might appear to other people.

"Here we go," said Tadziki. "Now, don't let's break our necks in the last three steps."

The loam gave way to rocks, polished and slick with moss. Ned, at the end of the line, prepared to brace himself in case anyone ahead of him slipped.

"*Captain,*" the commo helmets reported in Bonilla's voice, "*the colonists say they changed their mind. They want a meeting with you. The lady calling, she sounds scared to death. Just you come and one other, she says. Over.*"

"Well, they can curst well wait till we get this intake set!" Lissea snarled. Her boot-heels were bedded firmly in the wet ground. "*Out!*"

Tadziki scrambled down the bank and checked the position of the filter head. He glanced back up the pipe. His expression might have been innocent, but Lissea took it as a smirk.

"Don't you patronize me, Tadziki!" she said. "I knew you were right to begin with. Okay?"

"Slade," the adjutant called. "Set a clamp to the tree beside you, will you? That ought to keep the line from lashing when we fire up the pump."

Ned flipped a coil of cargo tape around a tree bole fifty centimeters thick. He wrapped the coil around the pipe and itself, then cut the section while Deke held the ends in place. Ned touched the piece with the electrodes in back of the tape dispenser. The calibrated current induced changes in the tape's polymer chains, bonding them to one another at the molecular level. Overall length shrank by ten percent, snugging the line firmly to the tree. Waste products driven off in the process had a faint fruity odor.

Warson stepped away, brushing together his hands in satisfaction. "Let's go home, right?" he said.

Lordling tried to help Lissea up the slope. She was closer to the top than he was. She allowed the contact, but her expression made the pointlessness of it clear.

"Tadziki," she said in a clear voice, "take me off the rota from here on out."

"Yes, sir," the adjutant said.

Lissea looked around at the men with her. "Boys," she said, "you're going to have to do the heavy stuff without me. I've got to handle deeply important discussions. With dick-heads who can't make up their minds whether they want to see us or not!"

"There may be some risk involved in meeting these people, Lissea," said Herne Lordling. "I think I'd better handle it."

"I'll handle it, Herne," Lissea said in a tired voice. "I trust my diplomacy farther than I do yours."

Creatures flew and jumped about the high tree-limbs, rattling the foliage. One of them, hidden but apparently able to see, chittered down at Ned like a high-speed relay. It sounded quizzical and not unfriendly.

"They may figure to take you hostage, Lissea," Lordling said.

"Deke," Lissea said, "if I'm taken hostage by these people, I want you to get me out dead or alive. If I'm dead, I want you to kill every one of them. Think you can handle that?"

"Yes, ma'am."

Lissea looked at Lordling. Ned, watching out of the corners of his eyes, was glad the expression wasn't directed at him. "I guess that problem's taken care of, Herne," she said. "I trust you'll be able to carry out the duties that Deke assigns you."

"Lissea. . ." Lordling said. He sounded as if he were being strangled.

The *Swift* had crushed the clearing in which it landed to double the original size. The boarding ramp was clear, and off-duty crewmen were stringing hammocks from trees. If the weather held, they'd be able to sleep outside the vessel's metal walls tonight.

"Do you want a driver, Lissea?" Ned said with his eyes straight ahead of him. They hadn't spoken, she and he, since the last night on Ajax Four.

"Yes, I want you to drive me, Slade," Lissea said coolly. "I need a driver I can trust."

"I'll put on clean utilities, then," Ned said, in a similarly neutral voice. "We'll want to impress the locals."

Also, he'd clip a third magazine pouch onto his equipment belt. Just in case.

Ned's first impression of the community was its neatness. The houses arranged along the central street were built of native products, generally wood. Most had porches and many had floral plantings, sometimes within little fenced enclosures. The street had a surface of crushed stone stabilized with yellowish gum that Ned assumed was of vegetable rather than of mineral origin.

Not a soul was visible. A caged bird sang within a house whose windows were open. There were slatted blinds but no screens, though Ned had already killed a biting gnat. Mirandola had been a stopover point for starships for so long that it was inevitable some human parasites would have found a home.

"That must be the community building," Lissea said, pointing to the single-story structure forming the bar across the far end of the street. Artificial light gleamed through the open windows.

"Let's hope they all walked," Ned said as he pulled up in front of the building. He'd seen only a few parked vehicles, although there was a charging post beside every house. He didn't know where the community's generator was; the distribution lines were underground. A single fusion bottle the size of a tank's power supply would be ample for the residents' probable needs.

The wooden double doors opened as Ned shut down the jeep. A middle-aged woman called, "Please come in, gentlemen. We're waiting for you."

"I've been called worse," Lissea muttered. She sounded detached, a sign Ned knew by now to read as nervousness. She carried her usual 2-cm weapon. She'd slung it muzzle-down, perhaps to appear less threatening.

The disquieting thing about the town was that it would have been normal on a civilized planet—and this was a frontier.

"My goodness," said the woman as Lissea walked into the building a step ahead of her escort. "You're a woman!"

"Do you have a problem with that?" Lissea snapped. "You wanted the commander and I'm the commander, Captain Lissea Doormann."

She stared around the gathering. "You're all women!"

Fluorescents in wall sconces added to the daylight in the big single room. The fixtures had paper shades which gave the effect of cressets. There were about a hundred people present, sitting on wooden benches. The furniture could be folded and added to the pile of similar benches against the back wall. The ages present ranged from early teens to quite old, but there were no young children.

And no men, as Lissea said.

"Yes," said the woman who'd greeted them at the door. "Ah, I'm Arlette Wiklander, and we've agreed that I'll conduct this meeting. That's what we'd like to discuss with you. Ah, will you come sit down?"

Arlette gestured the outsiders toward a pair of chairs set to face the benches. She touched Lissea's sleeve. Lissea twitched the cloth away.

"Let me understand this," Lissea said. There was no sign of an amplifier in the room, so she spoke in a deliberately loud, cold voice. "You're telling me that your community has no males in it?"

"No, no!" said a younger, hard-looking woman in the front row. "We just didn't think they ought to be around for this. *They* didn't think they ought to be around."

"Talia, let *me* handle the discussion," Arlette said. To Lissea she added, "Please won't you sit down. This is extremely difficult for us. Please, Captain, ah, Doormann."

Lissea sat down carefully. The iridium muzzle of her weapon clunked against the chairseat. Ned took the other chair, his face as blank as he could make it. Arlette returned to an empty space on the front bench, between Talia and a younger blonde woman.

"You see, the case is," Arlette said, "that Liberty has a problem."

"We named the colony Liberty," Talia added.

"We've been here five standard years almost," said a girl in the second row, probably the youngest person present.

"*Please!*" Wiklander said. The room hushed.

"We came here from Stadtler's Reach," Arlette continued. "There had been political difficulties—"

"It was a coup, pure and simple!" Talia said. Her left hand gripped Arlette's right as she spoke. "The legal government was forced out by thugs on the basis of a referendum they trumped up!"

"Be that as it may," Arlette said firmly. "A number of us believed it would be better to leave Stadtler's Reach and found a new colony on Mirandola. The new government—"

"Thugs!"

"—was willing to support us in the endeavor, for their own reasons and in exchange for clear title to the property we left behind."

Ned looked slowly around the room. Some of the women refused to meet his eyes, angry or embarrassed depending on their temperament. Others were speculative or more actively interested than even that.

The latter expressions were of the sort he'd noted often enough on the faces of soldiers on leave as they prepared to hit the Strip. He'd rarely seen a woman's eyes with that particular blend of lust and intention, though.

The blonde in the front row looked anxious but determined.

"We knew we couldn't go back to the government later," Arlette said, "so we made sure we got everything we thought we might possibly need from the initial bargaining sessions. We have medical facilities every bit as advanced as those we were leaving behind. We were people of, well, influence. Power."

"Where are your men?" Lissea demanded.

"I'm getting to that!"

Arlette cleared her throat. "Please," she muttered softly, then raised her eyes to Lissea's again. "We were inoculated against diseases which might transfer to humans from the Mirandolan biosphere. That's quite possible, especially at the viral level."

"They did it deliberately," Talia snarled. "They were afraid we'd reproduce."

"No!" Arlette said. "I believe—Sean believes, and he's the medical researcher, Talia—that it was an accident. If it had been a deliberate plot, they would have attacked female fertility."

She looked from Lissea to Ned. "Instead," she continued in a voice combed to the bone by control, "the inoculations appear to have rendered every male in the community sterile. The situation might be reversible with the resources of Stadtler's Reach tackling the problem, but the government has ignored our pleas."

"Oh," Lissea said. "Oh."

Ned glanced at her. Lissea couldn't have been more stonily embarrassed if all her clothing had vanished.

"Therefore . . ." Arlette said. She faced Lissea, but her eyes weren't focused. The expressions of the two women were mirror images of one another. ". . . we were hoping that your crew might be able to help our colony. The male members of your crew."

"We're equipped to set up a sperm bank," called an older woman in the back. "There needn't be any . . . any contact."

Lissea rose to her feet. "No," she said.

Other women got up, scuffling the benches, but Arlette Wiklander remained seated. Her extended arms gestured down Talia and the softly attractive blonde on her other side. Ned didn't move either.

"Wait!" Lissea continued. She held her arm out, palm foremost. "You'll get your genes. But you'll have to pay for them."

She surveyed the room again. "I can't demand that my crew masturbate in bags for you. I wouldn't if I could. If you want sperm, you'll have to collect them in the old-fashioned way. Whatever sort of medical procedures you indulge in then is your own affair."

The blonde beside Arlette gave a smile, half real and half sad. "Live cover or nothing," she said. "Well, we expected that."

"Yes," said Arlette to her hands as she folded them again in her lap. "Well, Captain Doormann, I've drawn up a series of—guidelines. Which I hope will be acceptable."

She removed her hologram projector from its belt sheath and switched it on. Some of the women who'd risen were seating themselves again, trying to be unobtrusive about it.

"Wait," said Ned. He hadn't spoken since he entered the building, and his voice was much louder than he'd intended. Everyone stared at him, Lissea included. "Where *are* your men?"

Arlette nodded heavily three times. "We had a town meeting last night, as soon as we knew a ship had landed. We—all of us—decided it would be best if the men camped ten kilometers outside Liberty for as long as you stay. When your ship leaves, it'll be—as if it never was. We're a small community. We can't afford to have . . ."

"Memories," said the blonde beside her.

Arlette cleared her throat. "Now, about the guidelines . . ." she said.

"They're coming!" Westerbeke called from a navigation chair. Liberty was three klicks away, but the *Swift*'s sensor suite registered the vehicles as soon as they switched on. Half the men rushed toward the boarding ramp.

"Wait!" said Lissea Doormann. "Everybody back inside. I have things to say to you."

She pushed through her crew and turned, facing them from the bottom of the ramp. Ned was at the back of the crowd. He put his boot on a bunk's footboard and raised himself so that he could see as well as hear Lissea.

"You may have heard," she said, "that the citizens have agreed among themselves that everyone is available to any crew member who wants to date her."

"You bet your ass!" somebody said.

"Hey, that's a thought!" another replied.

"Shut up, curse you!" Lissea's face had gone from white to flushed. Men's heads jerked back.

"What I'm telling you is this," Lissea resumed in mechanically calm tones. " 'No means no.' Maybe she thinks you're ugly, maybe she thinks you've got the brains of a sea urchin—maybe she's really got a headache. No means no!"

She glared across the men generally, then focused for a moment on Ned. He met her eyes, but he swallowed as soon as she'd looked away.

"There's plenty of pussy out there for every one of you," Lissea continued coldly. "Nobody's going to have to date the five-fingered widow tonight. But if anybody pushes in where he isn't wanted—*for any curst reason!*—I'll leave him behind to explain himself to the colony's menfolk when they return. Is that clearly understood?"

"I'm bloody well a believer!" Deke Warson said, and he sounded as if he meant it.

It was dusk. The lights of wheeled vehicles from the community glittered among the trees.

Lissea shuddered. She suddenly looked very small. "All right, boys," she said, "have a good time. If anything breaks, Raff or me'll give a buzz through the external speakers of your commo helmets, but you can pretty well expect to be clear till ten hundred hours tomorrow."

"*Bless them all,*" Harlow sang. "*Bless the fat and the short and the tall . . .*"

The first vehicle pulled up at the base of the ramp. It was a tractor pulling a twin-axle flatbed trailer. A cab-over pickup truck followed, and there were two or three similarly utilitarian vehicles behind those.

Men piled onto the trailer. Toll Warson got up on the tow bar and began chatting with the driver.

Dewey and Bonilla headed for the pickup. "Hey, Dewey!" Westerbeke called. "Why're you going along?"

"Hey, I've got nothing against women!" Dewey replied.

"*I* haven't had anything against a woman in seventeen years," Bonilla said. "But that doesn't mean I'm going to turn down a chance at booze and a cooked dinner."

The tractor pulled around to circle back. The motor had a heavy flywheel/armature to prevent it from stalling in a muddy field. It thrummed with a deep bass note.

"Lissea," said Herne Lordling. "I want you to understand that I'm doing this only—"

"Get aboard, Herne," Lissea said tiredly. She turned her back on the scene.

The pickup drove away with a full load. A jeep and another pickup took its place. Herne got into the jeep beside the driver. The Boxall brothers took the back pair of seats.

Arlette Wiklander drove the second pickup. She looked at Ned and said, "Are you the last, then?"

He nodded. "I guess," he said. "I wasn't sure, but I guess I am."

He put a boot on the side-step and lifted himself into the back instead of riding in the cab with the driver. "Ready when you are," he said.

Arlette turned sharply. The headlights flashed and flickered from the tree-trunks. Ned looked over his shoulder. Lissea was watching him. Her face was without expression.

The clear sky above Liberty was bright in comparison to the forest canopy, but at ground level the truck's headlights slashed visible objects from a mass of blurred shadow.

Many of the houses had their porch lights on. In a few cases, mostly at the end of the street near the community building where the tractor-trailer was parked, the exterior bulbs were switched off but light glowed through heavy curtains.

Several houses were dark and shuttered; but as Lissea had said, there were still plenty of willing takers for the *Swift*'s small crew.

Toll Warson stood on the porch of a house with blue trim. He was turning to leave. When he saw Ned in the back of the pickup, he called, "Hey Slade! This one says she's waiting for you. Shag her twice for me, okay, handsome?"

Warson waved cheerfully as he walked toward the house next door. The brothers had bragged that they were going to fuck their way up one side of the street and down the other, but that was just the friendly exaggeration of men old enough to wonder secretly about their performance.

Arlette slowed the truck to a crawl. "Ah—sir?" she called out the side window. "Shall I stop?"

"Yes ma'am," Ned said. *May as well.* "Please."

He hopped down from the bed and dusted his palms against his utility trousers. There was a pistol in the right cargo pocket, not obvious to an outsider but a massive iridium pendulum every time his thigh swung.

He didn't imagine the weapon would serve any practical purpose. It was a security blanket in a situation that confused Ned more than it seemed to affect the other mercs.

"Her name's Sarah," Arlette said quietly. "She sat beside me when we met with you and Captain Doormann."

The blonde, then.

"I'm the community's doctor," Arlette said. "Well, Sean and I, though the hands-on side never appealed to him." She looked down the street. Most of the mercenaries had disappeared within houses by now. "I'm going to be busy tonight."

Ned walked up the three steps to the porch. The door was already open halfway. Behind him, Arlette drove off in the truck. As Ned raised his hand to knock on the jamb, Sarah appeared in the opening and swung the door wide.

"Will you come in please, Master Slade?" she offered. "I was hoping you might. . ."

Sarah's dress was a lustrous beige synthetic, probably one of the cellulose-based polyesters. The cutwork collar was handmade but not particularly expert. She moved with a doelike grace and beauty.

How did she learn my name? Maybe from Toll Warson?

He stepped into a parlor furnished with a sofa and three chairs, all very solidly made from wood with stuffed cushions. Though they were all of similar design, the sofa's cabinetry was of a much higher order than that of the smaller pieces. The differences probably indicated the learning curve of a white-collar professional finding a new niche in the colony.

The shaft of the floor lamp was a column of three coaxial helices. It was an amazing piece of lathework which would have commanded a high price on any planet with a leisure class.

Sarah closed and barred the door; there was no key lock. The windows were already curtained.

"I'm Ned," he said. "And Dr. Wiklander said that your name is Sarah?"

Sarah looked up in startlement. "She told you that? Ah—but yes, I'm Sarah. I, ah . . ."

She looked away. The parlor filled the front of the house. Behind it was a kitchen/dining room with separate doorways from the parlor into either half, and a staircase to the second floor.

"I've made supper, it's a game stew and vegetables or there's cold ham if you'd like it," she said in a quick voice like a typist keying. "And I have drinks, it's all local but I've bought some whiskey from Juergen that's supposed to be very—"

"Sarah."

"—good!"

Ned put his hands on the woman's biceps, just touching her, until she raised her eyes to meet his. She giggled.

"Look," he said, "dinner later would be very nice. But you're nervous and I'm nervous. Either I ought to leave, which wouldn't be my first choice. Or we ought to make love."

"You're direct," she said. "That makes it easier."

She stepped away from Ned and turned off the lamp. The kitchen was still lighted. When Sarah came back, she pressed her body close and kissed him. He turned slightly to prevent her from noticing the pistol. He undid one of the front buttons of the dress. She wore no undergarments above the waist.

Sarah's breasts were fuller than he'd expected beneath the slick, stiff fabric. Ned took off his commo helmet with his free hand and tossed it onto the shadowed sofa.

"Upstairs," she said. She giggled again. "Maybe on the sofa later, if you like."

She drew him after her up the narrow staircase. The open jalousies let in moonlight, though the sun was fully down. The upper story was a single room, narrowed by the roof's pitch. The bed stood in the center, with storage chests lining the long sides.

Sarah turned at the head of the stairs. She kissed Ned again as he stood on the step below her. He slipped her puffed sleeves further down her arms to bare her breasts, then kissed them.

"Most of the colony came as couples," she said, playing with his hair. "I was . . . Sean and Arlette are my parents. I married Charles here in Liberty."

She twisted back into the room proper and began undoing the rest of her buttons. Ned took off his tunic. He slit open the pressure seal of his utility trousers with an index finger, then realized that he needed to take off his boots first. He undid them, glad of the semi-darkness because he felt as clumsy as a mule in ballet class. After you knew somebody a while, you didn't think about that sort of thing anymore; but he never would know Sarah better than he would this night.

He lowered the trousers carefully to keep the pistol from banging against the wooden floor.

"Come," Sarah said, sitting on the edge of the bed and drawing him over on her as he knelt to kiss her, "later we can . . ."

Somebody began hammering on the front door.

"What?" said Sarah as she sat bolt upright.

"It's one of the guys who forgot the ground rules," Ned said grimly, feeling for his trousers. He took the pistol from the cargo pocket and held the garment as a shield in front of him and the weapon. "I'll go talk to him."

His penis had shrunk to the size of his thumb. He wished he had time to put the trousers on. They wouldn't stop a determined mosquito, much less a powergun bolt, but they'd make him *feel* less vulnerable.

He didn't recall ever having been this murderously angry before in his life.

"Sarah, you whore!" the man on the porch shouted. "Open the door! I know you're in there!"

"Good lord!" she said. "It's Charles. It's my husband."

Oh boy.

"Look, I've got to go down to him," Sarah said pleadingly.

"Lord, yes!" he agreed as he stuffed the pistol back in his pocket. He began pulling the trousers on. He'd stopped using underpants when he noticed that none of the *Swift*'s veterans wore them.

Sarah took a robe from the rack beside the mirror-topped dresser and wrapped it around her. She padded quickly down the steps, still barefoot. "Charles!" she called. "I'm coming."

Ned grabbed his socks and boots. The tunic could wait, but he wanted his boots on no matter which way the next few moments went.

The door bar slid back on its staples. The man's voice boomed again, though it quickly sank to noise rather than words Ned could understand. Charles was either drunk or so angry that he slurred his syllables. Sarah's voice lilted like a descant above the deeper sound. The parlor light went on.

Ned donned his tunic, but he didn't bother to squeeze the seam shut. He stepped to the big window at the end of the room opposite the dresser. The glazed sashes were already latched open. The jalousies were mounted on dowels, not cords, but he could swing the whole set out of the way.

The stairs creaked behind him. He turned, stepped away from the window that would have backlit him, and reached into his pocket.

"'Ned?" Sarah whispered from the doorway. She was tugging the robe close about her with both hands.

"Right," he said, also pitching his voice too low to be heard on the ground floor. "Look, I was just about to leave."

"Oh, Lord, I'm so sorry," she said. She stepped toward him, then stopped and convulsively smoothed the patterned bedspread where their bodies had disturbed it. "You can come down the stairs. Charles is in the kitchen. I'm so sorry, but I think you'd better leave."

"No problem," Ned said. He pulled the jalousies back from the window ledge and looked down. Less than three meters, and smooth sod to land on. He'd had to jump farther in training while wearing a full infantry kit.

"I hope it works out for you all," he said as he swung himself from the window. Sarah started toward him again, perhaps to kiss him good-bye, but he deliberately let himself drop before she reached him. The wooden slats clattered against the sash.

An easy fall. The physical one, at any rate.

Though the ground-floor windows were curtained, Ned ducked low as he rounded the house. A high-wheeled utility vehicle pulled into the yard, but Charles hadn't stopped to connect it to the charging post.

The parlor was dark again, perhaps to provide privacy for Ned leaving. It was a useful reminder that when reason fought with emotion, the smart money was on emotion to win.

A pickup accelerated down the street from the community building. Ned stepped off the pavement—the small community didn't have sidewalks—but the vehicle pulled up beside him.

"Is there a problem?" Arlette Wiklander asked. "I heard shouting."

Ned squatted to put his face on a level with hers, so that he didn't have to speak loudly. "No problem," he said. "Ah—the lady's husband seems to have had second thoughts, but it's no problem."

Arlette winced. "I see," she said. "Ah . . . There are other, ah, houses."

Ned looked down the street. Several mercenaries were walking from house to house already. Like the arsenal disgorged at the banquet on Telaria, it was a form of boasting; but the weapons the crew carried to the banquet had been real also.

"No, ma'am," Ned said. "That's all right. I'd appreciate it if you gave me a lift back to the ship, though. Or—"

"Master Slade, I'm very sorry," Arlette said. Her intonation was almost precisely that of her daughter. "Of course I'll take you back, if that's what you want."

"Bloody hell!" Ned said. "I've left my helmet in there, on the sofa!"

Arlette shut down the truck and got out. "I'll take care of it," she said.

Ned stayed by the vehicle. He didn't hide, but he was ten meters from the door and as much out of the way as he could be. Arlette marched up on the porch, knocked hard, and called, "Sarah, it's your mother. Would you come to the door, please?"

The panel jerked open. The man who stood in the doorway said, "Couldn't wait to come laugh, could you, bitch?"

"Charles, I need to talk to Sarah for a moment," Arlette said. "Then I'll get back to my other business."

"Sure you will, *Mother* dear," he snarled. "You didn't want her to marry me from the beginning, did you?"

Charles was tall but stooped. He looked down as he fumbled with his belt. His bald scalp gleamed in the light from the houses across the street.

"Charles, let me see what Mother needs," Sarah said softly from within the parlor.

Charles turned his head. He hadn't hooked his belt properly. When he took his hands away, his trousers dropped around his ankles with a loud *thunk!* against the board flooring.

He bent down and came up, not with the garment but with a pistol.

"You think it's fucking hilarious that I'm not any kind of man, don't you, *Mother?*" he shouted.

Sarah grabbed her husband's arm from behind. He shrugged violently and threw her away from him. His right forearm was vertical. The gun muzzle pointed skyward.

"That has nothing to do with being a man, Charles," Arlette said in a calm voice. "And we've always wanted the best for you and Sarah."

Part of Ned's mind wondered at her control. He'd drawn his

own powergun, but he kept it out of sight at his side. He wasn't a good snap-shot, not good enough to trust himself in this light and the two women in the line of fire. He didn't dare aim now, though, for fear of precipitating the violence.

"Charles . . ." from within the room.

"Sure you did," Charles sneered. "You and dear Sean, such *sensitive* people. I'm sure it really pains you that your son-in-law can't get it up!"

He put the muzzle of the gun against his temple. Arlette reached for him. He fired. The red flash ignited wisps of Charles' remaining hair as the bullet kicked his head sideways.

He fell onto the porch. Sarah screamed. Charles' heels drummed against the boards and his throat gurgled, "K-k-k . . ." The sounds weren't an attempt at words, just the result of chest convulsions forcing air through the dying man's windpipe.

Both women knelt over Charles. Mercenaries and some locals poked their heads out of windows, wondering whether they might have heard a door slam closed.

Ned thrust his pistol back into his pocket. He got into the truck and switched the motors on. "I'm going back to the ship," he called generally to the night. "The truck will be there."

He still didn't have his commo helmet. He wasn't about to go back for it now, though.

Lissea was sitting on the ramp when Ned parked the truck. She drank from a tumbler. Only the cockpit lights were on, so the illumination spilling from the broad hatch was soft and diffuse.

Ned got out of the vehicle. "There was a problem in town," he said carefully.

Lissea nodded. "All taken care of," she said. "Arlette Wiklander radioed us."

She tapped the ramp with her fingertips, indicating a place for Ned at arm's length from her. "Want something to drink?"

"I'm fine," he said. He sat down. He supposed he was fine. His blood and brains weren't sprayed across a doorjamb, at any rate.

Lissea drank from her tumbler, looking out into the night. "Arlette says nobody blames you," she said.

Ned laughed. "I don't blame myself," he said. "I'll take responsibility for what I've done, but that whole business was somebody else's problem."

He stopped talking, because he could hear his voice start to rise.

"Arlette said the husband had had more than his share of problems in the past," Lissea said to the night. "He was a good deal older than the girl. The . . . It was the sort of thing Arlette had worried about happening years ago. The sort of thing."

The communications suite crackled. Lissea turned her head alertly, but Raff handled the query himself. Night creatures trilled.

"Do you ever think about what makes somebody a man, Lissea?" Ned said.

She frowned. "As in 'human being,'" she said, "or as in 'male human being'?"

"Not exactly." Lissea's tumbler was three-quarters full. "Can I have a sip of that?"

She handed it over. She was drinking water laced with something tart.

"You know," Ned said, "man—as opposed to wimp or pussy or whathaveyou."

Lissea laughed harshly. "Having doubts, Slade?" she asked.

"Not really."

"Well, don't," she said. "You became a fully certificated Man the moment I signed you on for this expedition. Is that why you volunteered?"

He shrugged. "I don't know," he said honestly. "I'd like to think there was more to being a man than that. I'd like to think there was more to it than being able to get my dick hard, too, though that isn't something I worry about either."

Lissea held a mouthful of water for a moment, then swallowed it. "My parents think I want to be a man myself," she said. Neither of them looked at the other. "My mother, especially. She's wrong."

She turned fiercely toward Ned. "I only want what's mine!" she said. "Do you have to be a man to get what's due you?"

"You shouldn't have to be," he said. He sniffed or laughed. "A lot of things shouldn't be the way they are, though."

"Don't I know it," Lissea muttered. She drank the tumbler down to the last two fingers of its contents, then offered it again to Ned. He finished it.

"Arlette says," Lissea said in the direction of the trees, "that her daughter Sarah is in a pretty bad way. She could use some company just now. I said I'd see what I could do when you got back to the ship."

Ned looked at her. "I . . ." he said. "I didn't want to make a bad situation worse."

"That's always a possibility," Lissea said. She stood up. "You're the man on the ground. I won't second-guess your decision."

Ned stood up also. He felt colder than the night. The radio inside the *Swift* was live again.

"Captain?" Raff called.

"In a moment, Raff," Lissea said. She looked at Ned. He stood below her on the ramp, so their faces were level. Very much as . . .

"Well?" she demanded.

"I left my commo helmet back in Liberty," he said. "I'll go get it now. I'll probably return with the other personnel in the morning."

Lissea nodded crisply. "As you wish," she said.

He looked away but didn't move. "It's Paixhans' Node for our next landfall, Tadziki was saying?"

"That's right. It's a long run, but nothing that should present real problems. We should be able to update our data on the Sole Solution there."

"Right," Ned said. He reached into his pocket and brought out the pistol. "Will you stick this back in the arms locker for me?" he said. "I don't know why I brought it in the first place."

Lissea took the weapon and nodded again.

Ned glanced in the rearview mirror as he drove away. Lissea still stood in the middle of the hatchway, silhouetted stiffly against the soft light.

PAIXHANS' NODE

Pilotry data indicated the airlock/decontamination chamber of the Paixhans' Node Station could accommodate two suited humans at a time. There was nothing about the landscape to attract strollers, so the *Swift*'s complement left the vessel in pairs at the three-minute intervals the entry process required. Ned accompanied Louis Boxall near the end of the slow parade.

"I think," Boxall said, "that my ancestors must have had Paixhans' Node in mind when they wrote about Hell. Sang about Hell."

Ned looked around him. The atmosphere was breathable, as close to Earth Normal as, for example, that of Tethys. The communications station which the Bonding Authority maintained here filtered and heated the air to one hundred fifty degrees Celsius to kill possible spores, but there was no need to supplement the atmosphere to keep the station personnel alive.

The station person, actually.

Apart from that, however, Paixhans' Node was dank, wretched, and purulent with life—all of which was fungoid. Water condensed from the air, dripping over every surface. Sheets and shelves and hummocks of fungus grew, rotted to slime, and were then devoured by their kin.

The highest life-forms, the Nodals, were human-sized and ambulatory. They had a certain curving grace, like that of a fuselage area-ruled for supersonic operation. The Nodals crawled a millimeter at a time as though they were osmosing across the surface of the rocks. The contact patch served also for ingestion, absorbing all the stationary fungus in the Nodals' path.

The Nodals were the closest thing to beauty on a world with a saturated atmosphere and a sky that glowed white at all times from the light of billions of stars. They were also the only real danger here, not for themselves but because of the spores which ejected from the core of a ripe Nodal.

"Hell's supposed to be hot and fiery," Ned said. He picked his way carefully across the slippery rocks. The *Swift* had put down half a klick from the station because the ground closer to it was too broken to be a safe landing site. It didn't make a great footpath, either.

"Not on the Karelian Peninsula," Louis said. He gestured. "This would do fine."

They used their external helmet speakers to talk. Normally when personnel wore protective suits, they spoke through radio intercoms. On Paixhans' Node, electrooptical radiation from everywhere in the Milky Way galaxy converged at the apparent distance of forty-one light-minutes. Ordinary communications gear was swamped to uselessness; though for properly filtered apparatus, the unique conditions were of enormous value.

The Bonding Authority was the lubricant that made the interstellar trade in mercenary companies work. The Authority guaranteed the table of organization and equipment of mercenary units to the parties who wished to hire them, and guaranteed to the mercenaries that they would be paid per contract.

For the Bonding Authority to function efficiently, it needed something as close as possible to real-time communications across the galaxy. The communications station on Paixhans' Node acted as a transceiver serving the Authority and, at considerable fees, the needs of other users.

"Well," said Ned, "I won't tell you your ancestors were wrong."

Their path would take them within arm's length of a Nodal. It swayed gently to a rhythm beyond human comprehension. The creature's upper portions swelled slightly from a pinched waist.

Bubble-like vacuoles as well as chips of solid color were visible beneath the translucent skin. The axial core had a pale yellow tinge.

"Via!" Boxall swore. "Don't touch it or you might set it off."

"They've got to be as bright as tractor enamel before they're really ready to burst," Ned said. He angled well away from the Nodal nonetheless. "That's what the pilotry data says."

"The pilotry data isn't going to be dissolved from inside if a spore lands on it," Boxall said. He laughed sharply. "Come to think, I guess it might. But it wouldn't care the way I do."

They were nearing the station. It was a hemisphere over a hundred meters in diameter. Antennas of complex shape festooned the dome and were planted in farms some distance away.

"I hear," Boxall said after a moment, "that you might know something about the guy who mans the station. Gresham?"

Ned nodded, though he wasn't sure how visible the action was beneath his suit. "I made something of a study of it," he said. "Of him."

There was a lot of information on Friesland, in the Slammers' archives. Uncle Don had never said anything about it, except that he'd seen the prettiest sunset of his life once on Taprobane.

"Gresham worked for the Bonding Authority," Ned said. "He was a field agent, new to the job. He talked too much. At least that was what prisoners said later."

"He was bribed?" Boxall asked.

"No, he just talked. While he was inventorying mercs hired by the Congressional side on Taprobane, he let out that while there was supposed to have been a battalion of Slammers' tanks landed in the capital to support the Presidential party and secure the spaceport, it was really only two infantry companies."

The external speaker distorted Boxall's whistle. "So the Congressional party took the spaceport," he said.

"Nope," Ned Slade said coldly. He'd watched images of the battle, mostly recovered from the helmet recorders of dead troopers. "But they sure-hell tried. And it wasn't cheap to stop them, even for the survivors."

They'd reached the dome. Close up, the structure loomed over them. Water condensing on the curved sides dripped down in sheets of gelatinous fungus—orange and saffron and a hundred shades of brown.

The light above the airlock blinked from red to green. Boxall pressed the latch button.

"Afterwards," Ned said, "there were discussions between the regiment—"

"Colonel Hammer?"

Ned nodded. "Colonel Hammer. And the Bonding Authority. Everybody knew what Gresham had done, but all the evidence was secondhand. Handing Gresham over to the Slammers for execution would compromise the Authority's prestige and neutrality. That was what the higher echelons felt, at any rate."

The airlock door slid abruptly into the side of the dome. The chamber within was a meter square. The walls were glassy and faceted internally.

"What they did," Ned said, "the Authority did, was to offer Gresham a contract. So long as he worked for the Authority, his life was safe. Not even Hammer's Slammers were willing to murder an Authority employee."

The door slammed home with the enthusiasm of a guillotine's blade. Ned's visor went opaque for protection. Infrared light bathed the men from all six surfaces of the chamber. Ned bumped his companion as they both turned slowly, sure that the light cleansed every crevice of their suits.

"And then they transferred Gresham here, to Paixhans' Node," Ned said. "For as long as he lived. Seventeen years so far."

His visor cleared. An instant later, the lock's inner door shot open. Ned and his companion stepped into the foyer where empty suits stood or lay on the concrete floor. The air was muggy.

They stripped off their own suits and followed the sound of voices down a hall to a large room with equipment built to waist level around all the walls. Surfaces above the electronic consoles were of a gleaming white material that cleaned itself.

Most of the *Swift*'s complement stood and looked with neither comprehension nor particular interest at the equipment surrounding them. The Warson brothers squatted before a console. They weren't touching the access plate in the front, but they were *pointedly* not touching the access plate. The fragments Ned heard of their low-voiced discussion were surprisingly technical.

"Look, Master Gresham," Lissea said in the tone of someone forced to argue with a senile relative, "that's between you and your employers. We're perfectly willing to pay you—we'll pay you in rations, if that's what you'd like. But—"

"It wouldn't do any good," said the man to whom she spoke. He hunched in the room's sole chair, a black structure which appeared to have been scooped from an egg. Its flat base quivered nervously at the floor, like a drop of water on a sea of mercury.

Gresham was sallow. His bones stuck out, and there were sores on his elbows and wrists.

"Master Gresham," Tadziki said calmly. "We can't afford to offend the Bonding Authority. All we're asking from you is information on the Sole Solution."

"On Alliance and Affray, you mean," Gresham said. As he spoke, Ned noticed that the man's teeth were black stumps. "On the Twin Planets."

Gresham grinned with something approaching animation. "But you don't know that. Yet. I'll tell you everything you want to know. But you have to stop whoever's stealing my food."

"We'll give you food!" Lissea repeated.

"It won't help!" Gresham cried. He tried to get up from the chair, but he couldn't summon the strength. He began to cry. Through the blubbering, he mumbled, "I have to eat the fungus. The rations dispenser drops a meal for me. And they steal it! They steal it! I have to eat what I gather outside or I'd die."

In a tiny voice he added, "I want to die. I can tell you anything about anything in the galaxy. But I want to die."

"Well, that could be arranged," said Josie Paetz.

Yazov gripped his nephew's jaw between his thumb and forefinger. "Don't speak like that!" he said. "He's a Bonding Authority employee. If he wants to die, then he can kill himself!"

Yazov released Paetz as though he was flinging away a bloody bandage. The younger man was white-faced. He swallowed before he holstered the pistol which he'd thrust into his uncle's belly.

"Who steals the food?" Lissea asked. She seemed to have swept frustration out of her mind. "Not the Nodals, surely."

"Who else is there?" Herne Lordling asked.

"I don't know," Gresham said. "I'll show you, though. It's almost time."

Gresham snuffled loudly to clear his nose. He seemed almost oblivious of the presence of other human beings. Resupply ships would arrive on an annual, or at most, a semiannual schedule. The number of other vessels which touched down on Paixhans' Node must be very small.

"Time for what?" Coyne asked. Everybody ignored him.

Gresham got up from his chair and stepped to the hallway door. He walked like an old man, his head down and his legs shuffling forward mechanically. Though he couldn't have been much over fifty years old, deficiencies caused by a diet of local produce had aged and weakened him. He was lucky to be alive.

Or perhaps not.

Across the foyer from the control room was a chamber one meter by ten, with a high ceiling. The long wall facing the foyer was of a gleaming, glassy material like that which lined the airlock. There was a niche at waist height in the center of it.

"A Type Seven-Six Hundred Rations Dispenser," Tadziki said approvingly. "Or maybe a Seven-Eight Hundred—it's a matter of storage capacity, and I can't be sure how deep the room is. It's a bulletproof design. Trust the Authority to buy the best."

"What *is* it?" Ingried said peevishly.

"When somebody's alone in a station like this," the adjutant explained, "you don't want to leave all the rations under his control. People get funny. A dispenser like this provides his meals one at a time, so that he doesn't decide to make a bonfire of a six-months' supply when he's having a bad time one night."

"This poor bastard's had a bad time longer 'n that," somebody muttered.

A chime sounded softly in the bowels of the mechanism. A sealed carton about thirty by thirty by ten centimeters in size dropped into the niche. Gresham reached out as if to take it.

"As if," because after seventeen years he certainly knew it was going to vanish again, as it did.

"*Via! Bloody hell! Blood and martyrs!*" across the semicircle of mercenaries standing behind Gresham. He turned, looking almost pleased.

"Stop that happening," he said, "and I'll help you. I'll *save* you; I know how. You can't give me my freedom, but let me eat food again."

Lissea looked at Tadziki. He pursed his lips and said, "There's the question of your employer's intention in this matter—"

"No," Gresham said. He fumbled carefully in a breast pocket of his coveralls and brought out a folded sheet of hard copy between two fingers. He handed it to Tadziki.

Tadziki opened the document. "'Inspection of the Type Seven-Six Hundred dispenser by manufacturer's representatives indicates the unit is in proper working order,'" he said/read aloud. "'This office will not authorize further off-site repair expenditures. If station personnel desire, they may procure local support and charge back costs within Guidelines Bee Three three-nine-four to Bee Four ought-ought-seven inclusive.'"

Gresham began to cry again. "Sixteen years ago they sent that," he said. "They don't care if I starve so long as they can *say* they stood up to Colonel Hammer!"

"Seventeen years seems a pretty long time," Lissea said doubtfully.

"It's that much longer than some eighty poor bastards got on Taprobane," Deke Warson said in a voice that could mill corn. Ned wasn't the only member of the company who knew why Gresham had been exiled to this planet-sized dungeon.

"Which brings up the other question," the adjutant went on. "I think we can presume the problem with the food—whatever—isn't the Authority's doing, though it doesn't appear to bother them a great deal. I suspect that—President now, isn't it?—Hammer might still be displeased by meddling with what he considers his business."

Lissea looked puzzled. "Surely that's no concern of ours, is it?" she asked.

The Boxall brothers had been talking in low tones ever since the meal container vanished. Now Louis looked up and said, "If it's a choice of the Bonding Authority or Colonel Hammer wanting my hide, I guess I'd choose Hammer. But believe me, Gene and me aren't going to fix this if Hammer *is* involved."

"You can fix it?" Tadziki said sharply.

"We might be able to do some good," Eugene said in the tone of someone making a promise with everything but the form of the words.

"But not if it pisses off Hammer," Louis repeated. "Sure, it's a big universe, but I don't want to spend the rest of my life looking over my shoulder."

"I think I can clear things," Ned said. His hands were trembling, but he kept his voice steady.

"You, Slade?" Herne Lordling sneered. "You're going to use your vast influence as a reserve ensign to bring President Hammer around?"

"Herne!" Lissea said.

"Slade?" said Gresham. "You're *Slade?*"

"You're thinking of Uncle Don," Ned said to Gresham. He looked at Lordling. "I don't have any influence with President Hammer," he said. "I saw him once on a reviewing stand, that's all. But my uncle commanded the regiment's initial force on Taprobane."

"You're Slade," Gresham whispered. He reached toward Ned but his hand paused a centimeter away, shaking violently.

Ned gripped Gresham's hand. "I'll need to send a real-time message to Nieuw Friesland."

His eyes focused on Lissea. "I'll pay for it personally," he added.

She shook her head. "It's an expedition expense," she said.

Gresham began to giggle hysterically. Ned had to hold the older man to keep him from falling.

At last Gresham got control of himself again. "I've been here for seventeen years," he said. "They pay me well—there's a hardship allowance. And there's nothing for me to buy. *I'll* pay for the cursed message!"

They walked back into the control room. Ned and Tadziki supported Gresham; Ned thought of offering to carry the man but decided it might be an insult.

Gresham unlocked a keyboard. A holographic screen sprang to life above the console. He typed in his access code, summoned a directory for Nieuw Friesland, and added an address to the transmission. He seemed both expert and much stronger while he worked.

He lurched out of the chair. "There," he said to Ned. "Go ahead. When you're done, hit SEND."

Ned sat down, paused, and began by typing his serial number. He heard his fellows whispering behind him. The two men who'd come from the ship most recently hushed as others filled them in on events in the dome.

Letters of gray light formed in the hologram field:

RESERVE ENSIGN SLADE, E., WISHES TO INFORM PRESIDENT HAMMER THAT HE PROPOSES ON HIS SOLE RESPONSIBILITY TO CORRECT AN ANOMALY IN THE FOOD DISTRIBUTION SYSTEM OF THE BONDING AUTHORITY STATION ON PAIXHANS' NODE. THIS ACTION WILL TAKE PLACE IN THREE STANDARD HOURS FROM SLUG TIME. OUT.

"How do you walk with balls that big, kid?" Toll Warson asked in a friendly tone.

Ned tried to get up from the chair. The first time, his legs failed to support him and he fell back.

"So now we wait three hours," Tadziki said in a neutral voice.

"Captain," Louis Boxall said, "we'll need some apparatus to make this work. Can you give us a hand with the shopwork? You're the best hand with the hardware on the *Swift*."

"I'm not sure I'm willing to go through with this, Tadziki," Lissea said. Her eyes were on Ned.

"It's my responsibility!" Ned shouted. "You will *not* interfere with matters that are my responsibility!"

Men looked away. "Touchy little feller, ain't he?" Deke Warson murmured to the ceiling.

"All right, Boxall," Lissea said. "Come back to the ship with me and we'll build your apparatus."

"We can only clear one suit at a time with the hand sterilizer, ma'am," Eugene said doubtfully. "Should we wait a couple minutes, Lou and I?"

"No, you can curst well stand outside the ship while I clear through the airlock!" Lissea replied as she stamped into the foyer. "This is your idea!"

To Ned's surprise but perhaps not to Tadziki's, there was a reply. Gresham's console logged it in eighty-eight minutes after Ned had sent the query on its forty-one-minute route to Nieuw Friesland. Hard copy scrolled from the printer, but the assembled men read the message from the screen:

INFORMATION NOTED. IF YOU'RE WILLING TO ANSWER TO YOUR UNCLE, THERE'S NOTHING USEFUL I COULD SAY. HAMMER.

Herne Lordling swore under his breath.

Ned said, "My uncle Don understands what it's like."

He spoke loudly but without a specific listener in mind. His mind was a collage of memories, views of a big man with a smiling mouth and eyes that could drill an anvil.

"He won't second-guess the man on the ground."

Gresham was crying.

Save for the anchor watch, the *Swift's* complement was assembled in the station foyer. It was a change of scenery from the interior of the vessel, though a sterile one. Paixhans' Node wasn't a world which encouraged spacers to sightsee during their stopovers.

"Ten minutes till the next feeding, then?" Tadziki said after glancing at the clock above the door to the supply alcove.

Gresham nodded sluggishly. He'd eaten a ration bar from the

Swift. It was the closest thing he'd had to a balanced diet since a similar offering from the most recent supply ship months before.

The station ran on Zulu Time: a twenty-four hour clock based on that of Earth at the Greenwich Meridian. It was as good a choice as any, since planetary rotation didn't affect the bright skies and the personnel weren't expected to go outside often anyway.

The inner lock cycled to admit the Boxall brothers and Lissea. The three of them had squeezed into the decontamination chamber together.

"That's not safe," Gresham complained. "You might miss a spore—"

Lissea opened her helmet. "Shut up, Gresham," she said.

Ned looked away from her.

"Well, I suppose if you're careful . . ." Gresham mumbled.

"We got it done," Eugene Boxall said. "Are we in time?"

Tadziki shrugged. "Eight minutes," he said. "Then twelve hours to the next, ah, load."

"Plenty of time," said Louis. *"Plenty* of time."

He opened the front of his pressure suit and held out the egg-shaped case he'd carried inside the garment. "We're going to need one of you to go along with us," he continued. "Slade, that's you if you're up to it."

Ned reached for the egg. "You bet," he said.

Herne Lordling snatched the object from Boxall's hand. "Negative," he said. *"I'll* go."

Eugene dropped his suit on the floor of the foyer. "Look, Lordling," he said. "This isn't about shooting. This *particularly* isn't about shooting."

"Give him the scrambler, Herne," Lissea said. "Ned was my recommendation for the job."

Lordling glared at the Boxalls, then Lissea. He refused to look at Ned, and he continued to hold the object. Without speaking to one another, the Warsons shifted in concert to put themselves at two corners of an isosceles triangle with Lordling the third point. If shooting started, the brothers wouldn't be in one another's line of fire.

"We're not," Tadziki said, "in that much of a hurry." He stepped forward so that he was between Lordling and the Warsons, looking from Deke to Toll and back with a glum expression.

"Take the curst thing!" Lordling said. He thrust the object out to the side, not so much handing it to Ned as dissociating himself from what happened to it.

The egg was heavy. Within the clear plastic case, Ned could see a power supply and what he thought was an oscillator.

"Whoever's taking the food," Eugene resumed, "he's got to be a Wimbledon teleport like ourselves. Now I know, five meters is usually good distance and here we're maybe talking thousands of parsecs."

"But this is the Node," his twin said, taking up the theme. "We figure he could be coming from anywhere, anywhere in the galaxy. In and out like a pop-up target."

"Fine, but why?" Toll Warson asked.

Lissea looked at Gresham coldly. "I assume because somebody paid him to make this gentleman's life a little more miserable," she said. "But not to kill him."

"You see what we meant about Colonel Hammer," Louis said. "Seventeen years means a long memory."

"We don't want the guy killed," Eugene said. "Not if there's any other way. He's just doing his job."

Harlow laughed. "I've killed lots of people who was just doing their job," he said. "Via, I killed plenty who just happened to be standing on the wrong piece of real estate. We all of us have."

He looked around the band of mercenaries, inviting argument.

"Wimbledon isn't a very big place," Louis said. When his face flushed, the scar on his temple stood out more sharply. "We're doing this our way or not at all."

"I said that Ned," Lissea said, "could be trusted not to shoot unless there was no other choice."

Ned dabbed his lips with his tongue. "Thank you, Lissea," he said.

"We're going to carry you with us," Eugene said to Ned.

"You can do that?" Westerbeke demanded. "Carry stuff with you when you teleport?"

"It's a lot harder to jump out of your clothes than it is to wear them with you," Louis said. "Likewise the bubble of air around you."

"Him, he's heavy enough to be a problem," Eugene said with a nod toward Ned. "But we're good."

"Via, we're the best!"

The twins looked scarcely teenaged in their glow of anticipation. They knew as surely as everyone else in the company did that there were stronger men and better shots on every side of them now—but this was *their* skill, and there was nobody like them in the galaxy.

"When he comes, we follow him," Eugene continued. "We don't know where that'll be. Anywhere in the galaxy, like I say. When we get there, you trigger this."

His index finger indicated the thumb switch on top of the egg in Ned's hand.

"It's an RF scrambler," Louis explained. "It'll disorient any teleport within maybe five meters of it. Us included, that's the problem."

"Optical would work as well as radio frequency," Eugene said, "but we don't know where we're going. It has to function if he's turned away or there's a wall between us or something."

"Via! I forgot the tape," Louis said. "Did you bring the tape?"

"*I* brought the tape," said Lissea. She handed Ned a roll of black, 75-mm tape. The adhesive was alcohol-soluble, but you could lift the bow of a tank on a properly rigged cable of the stuff.

"When we get there," Eugene repeated, "you trigger the scrambler. The guy'll probably fall down."

"We'll sure fall down," Louis said. "It's like having the worst headache ever in your life."

His twin shrugged. "It stops when the oscillator stops," he said. "But *don't* turn it off till you've got his eyes bandaged with the tape. Otherwise he'll likely jump again, and maybe we won't be ready to follow."

"One minute," said Tadziki.

Ned had come to the station unarmed. Lissea held out to him the submachine gun she'd brought on this trip from the *Swift*.

"I don't think I'll need this," Ned said.

"The teleport should be helpless," Lissea said, "but he may not be alone wherever he comes out. Take it."

Eugene Boxall shrugged. "Hey look," he said. "We don't want anybody croaking us while the scrambler's on, either. Do what you've got to do."

"Nearing time!" Tadziki said sharply.

Ned slung the submachine gun over his shoulder and stuck his right arm through the spool of tape. The twins gripped his wrists firmly, as if they were preparing for a trapeze act.

A chime sounded in the dispenser. The meal packet landed in the niche with a *choonk*—

Ned's mind everted in a blaze of dazzling light.

The room was sunlit through a netlike screen across one whole wall. The Boxalls gripped Ned's wrists crushingly. The figure directly in front of the mercenaries was turning as Ned's thumb mashed down the scrambler switch.

The stranger, a woman with long, curling hair, flung up her hands with a cry of pain. Louis Boxall collapsed like a steer in the abattoir, but Eugene thrashed wildly and continued to hold Ned.

The switch had a detent to lock it until a second thrust released the spring. Ned dropped the unit. It bounced on a floor covered with long, meter-wide rugs laid edgewise and overlapping by half their width. He used both hands to break Eugene's grip, then turned his attention to the woman.

She was short, young, and strikingly beautiful in a smooth-skinned, plumpish style. The scrambler's invisible impact had driven her to her knees. Her eyes were closed, and she squeezed her temples with clenched fists while she made cackling sounds.

Ned yanked the roll of tape off his arm. He stretched a length, slapped it over the woman's eyes, and knocked her hands aside so that he could complete the loop around her head.

The submachine gun swung like a heavy pendulum, getting in his way. He set it on the floor with hasty care—there was one up the spout, and *no* safety could be trusted absolutely— before he finished the job of blindfolding the woman.

Breathing hard, more from stress than actual exertion, Ned looked for the scrambler. It had rolled beneath the legs of an intricate brass floorlamp. Ned poked the switch again to release it.

This was a *very* nice room, tasteful as well as expensively decorated. The window overlooked a parklike city from thirty stories up. The glazed surface curved to include half the ceiling as well, showing that this was the penthouse. The long wall opposite displayed two large abstracts, coolly precise, which flanked a curtained doorway. There was relatively little furniture, but pillows heaped against the short walls would serve as chairs or couches.

Louis Boxall raised himself to a squat. "Lord, Lord," he muttered. "Did anybody get the number of the truck that hit me?"

"Hey, it's a girl," Eugene said with considerably more animation. He still lay on the rugs, but his eyes were open and turned toward the captive. She was beginning to stir also.

"Rise and shine, troopers," Ned said. "I've done my part. The rest is up to you."

A man walked through the curtained doorway. "Tanya?" he said. His face blurred in surprise at the scene. He reached into the pocket of his flaring jacket.

Instead of snatching the submachine gun, Ned grabbed a double handful of a rug. He yanked at it, thrusting off with his legs as well as using his upper body to pull.

The newcomer's feet flew up. His arms flailed and the back of his head clunked into the wall. A needle stunner flew from his hand into a corner of the room.

"Father?" the girl called. She jumped to her feet, her face terrified beneath the band of tape. "*Father!*"

"He's all right!" Ned said as he grabbed the man. He pulled the man's jacket down to bind his arms while he was still logy, then checked the pockets for further weapons. There were none. The fellow's hair was coarse and black, but by the looks of his facial wrinkles he was probably in his sixties.

"Father?"

"Who are you?" the man asked.

"Hold him," Ned said, swinging the stranger toward Louis. He scooped up the submachine gun and quickly checked the remainder of the suite. There were two large bedrooms, two baths, and a fully equipped kitchen/dining room. No one else was present, and the exterior door was secured with a 5-cm steel bar as well as a pair of electronic locks.

Ned walked back into the living room. "All clear," he said. He tossed Eugene a bottle of clear liquor.

"Meet the Glieres, Slade," Louis said. "Oleg, and his daughter, Tanya. We're just explaining to them that their contract with Colonel Hammer is now at an end."

Eugene wetted the tip of the neckerchief he wore over his tunic with the liquor. It had a minty odor. He dabbed alcohol onto the tape, starting at the woman's hairline. Oleg watched nervously. There obviously wasn't any fight in him.

"Where are we, anyway?" Ned asked, looking out the window. It was a lovely city, wherever it was.

"Wonderland," Tanya said. She had a throaty, attractive voice that fit her physical person. "In the Trigeminid Cluster."

Ned shrugged. He'd never heard of the place—which implied that Wonderland had never been a market for mercenary soldiers, an even better recommendation than the broad swathes of landscaping among the buildings below.

"I . . ." Oleg said. He looked as though he wanted to sit down but didn't dare to. Louis gestured him toward a pile of pillows. "We'll of course do what you say. But I hope Colonel Hammer won't be offended."

"Oh," Ned said, rummaging in his breast pocket. He came out with two flimsies: the hard copies of his message to Friesland and Hammer's reply. He handed them to Gliere, who read, then reread the documents to be sure of their meaning.

Eugene lifted the cargo tape from Tanya's eyes. She had remained perfectly still during the process, but now she shuddered and said, "Oh thank God, thank God. I was *blind.*"

"We needed to talk with you," Eugene said, "so that, you know, it could stop with talking."

Louis took the liquor bottle from his brother and swigged it. "I don't know about you," he said, "but my head feels like somebody's been using it for a rabbit hutch."

"You're from Wimbledon too?" Tanya asked.

"Where else?" Eugene said. He loosened the last tag of adhesive and dropped the blindfold onto the floor. "You've both been doing this, then?"

"I don't jump very well anymore," Oleg said. "My age, you know."

A muscle in Louis' cheek quivered. Nobody likes to be reminded that he will inevitably grow too old to perform his specialty.

"Tanya has taken over the duties this past five years," Oleg went on, "so that we didn't lose the retainer."

"We don't need the money!" his daughter said sharply. "My paintings already earn more than this *theft* does." She looked from Louis to Eugene and patted her disarranged hair. "I'm glad it's over."

"It's got to be," Eugene said. He offered the bottle to Tanya, then drank after her. The twins' eyes were approving.

"Do you suppose we could get back to Paixhans' Node?" Ned said. "They're going to be wondering about things until we report."

"Slave driver," Louis said. He bent and scooped up the meal container Tanya had dropped when the pursuit arrived. "Look, though," he said, glancing between the Glieres, "I'll be back to visit, if you don't have objections."

"*We'll* be back," Eugene added. He put his boot on the scrambler and crushed it, despite the layers of carpet beneath the object. "We don't meet many of our sort off Wimbledon."

"*We,*" Tanya Gliere said, "would like that."

Half a dozen of the mercenaries in the foyer were singing "Sam Hall," entranced with the acoustics of the room and the long corridors curving off it. Deke Warson reached into the guts of the ration dispenser and shouted over the racket, "Who wants a . . ." He paused to rip open the meal packet. "Roast duckling!"

"Warson, both of you!" Tadziki ordered. "Go easy on the food. Remember it'll be two months before the next supply ship."

Deke and Toll had opened the loading gate of the dispenser so quickly and easily that Ned didn't imagine the resupply crew could have beaten their time. Whether or not the two *had* rigged their brother's vehicle to blow up, they certainly had the expertise to do so.

"My Nellie's down below all dressed in blue."

"I assure you, Master Gresham," Lissea said, "that we'll leave ration packets to make up for those we're consuming tonight. I can't pretend the quality will be up to those the Authority supplies, though."

"Says my Nellie dressed in blue—"

Gresham laughed so hard that he began to hiccup. "Oh, Mistress Doormann," he said. "Oh, Mistress Doormann, there's always the fungus outside."

"—now I know that you'll be true—"

He'd eaten half a packet of spiced meatloaf, then had promptly vomited the whole contents of his stomach back up. Now he wore a fresh uniform and picked carefully at the remainder of the meal.

"Yes I know that you'll be true, goddam your eyes!"

Tadziki looked from the cheerful mercenaries to Gresham. "You agree that we've carried out our part of the bargain, I trust? Then it's time for you to do your part."

Gresham and the *Swift*'s complement ate at tables and benches built from maintenance stores: plating, tubes, and boxes that could be used to repair the antennas outside and the electronic modules within the dome. Minor tasks were a part of Gresham's duties, while larger ones—a tower which collapsed in a storm, for example—had to wait for the supply ship to arrive.

Gresham blinked as the adjutant spoke. He started to rise immediately, mumbling, "Of course, of course—"

He was trying to lever himself up from the table, but his wrist buckled. Ned grabbed the frail civilian before he fell facedown in the meatloaf.

Lissea looked fiercely at Tadziki. "I don't think we need be in *that* much of a hurry," she said.

The Boxall brothers stepped into the makeshift banquet hall, carrying a case of bottles between them. They set the load down on the concrete.

"Hey, come and have dinner!" Deke Warson called from the dispenser. He reached down for another pair of meals.

"Have a good trip!" Louis replied. The twins vanished in the same eyeblink.

Everyone looking in the teleports' direction fell silent. Ned and Tadziki both jumped to their feet, but Lissea beat them to the case of bottles.

There was a note on it, folded into a fan. She opened it. "Shut up, you lot!" Tadziki ordered.

"*'Dear Captain,'*" Lissea read aloud. "*'We're going to leave you here. Hope you think we were worth our rations, and you can keep the pay.'*"

She looked up. "They both signed it," she added.

"Deserters!" Herne Lordling said.

The adjutant lifted a bottle from its foam cocoon. "Iron Star Liquors," he said, reading the label. He shook the clear liquor.

"It's mint-flavored," Ned said. *And it cleaned the adhesive off cargo tape about as quickly as industrial alcohol could.*

Lissea looked at Ned and raised an eyebrow.

"They made a friend on Wonderland," he said. He didn't have any idea of what domestic arrangements on Wimbledon were like. "I guess they figured they . . . Well, I don't know how long it'd take to get to the Trigeminid Cluster in normal fashion."

Lissea shrugged. "They earned their keep," she said. She tossed a bottle to Toll Warson, another to Westerbeke in the center of the singers, and a third to Coyne at the far table.

Noisy enthusiasm echoed around the foyer.

Lissca looked at Ned. "And so did you," she added in a barely audible tone.

"There's been no astrophysical change in the Sole Solution," Gresham said from the console attached to a projection screen. "The change—the problem preventing normal navigation—was wholly political."

The station administrator was a different man since the thefts of his food were ended. He hadn't regained his physical health from a few normal meals; in some ways, long-term deficiencies had damaged him beyond complete recovery. Mentally, however, Gresham was free of the strain that had hagridden him over his years of exile. He spoke distinctly and with obvious command of his material.

"The Twin Worlds," he continued, "Alliance and Affray, are close enough to the Sole Solution through Transit space that they are virtually a part of the anomaly. A generation ago, the Twin Worlds completed the cooperative project that had absorbed a significant portion of their planetary output for nearly twenty standard years."

A torus bloomed in the center of the holographic projection. The object had no scale, no apparent size. Gresham worked a detached control wand with a cold smile on his face, focusing the image on half the screen down to increasingly small portions of the doughnut displayed in full beside it.

"Blood and martyrs!" said Westerbeke. "How big *is* the fucker?"

"There are occupied satellites of considerably smaller diameter," Gresham said with cold amusement. "It doesn't have a name. Technically, it's Twin Worlds Naval Unit One. They call it the Dreadnought."

The small-scale image focused on a weapons blister from which three tubes projected. *A tribarrel,* Ned thought; until the scale shrank still further and he saw that the specks on the outside of the turret were men. *The guns must have bores of nearly a meter.*

"But what do they do with it?" Lissea asked. "You could never invade a planet with that."

All of the ship's crewmen—save Dewey, on anchor watch—were in the station's control room. Some of the other off-duty mercenaries hadn't bothered to come. They didn't regard navigation as anything to concern them. Even on a planet as boring as Paixhans' Node, they preferred to play cards and drink the remainder of the Boxalls' parting gift.

"The Dreadnought was built to control trade through the Sole Solution," Gresham said. "To end all trade except for what was carried on Twin Worlds hulls. They require merchants to land on either Alliance or Affray and to transfer their cargo to local vessels."

"Will they sell ships to outsiders?" Tadziki asked.

"No," Gresham said. "Nor, if you were considering it, would they permit you to reflag the *Swift* as a Twin Worlds vessel."

"I suppose they charge monopoly rates for their services?" Ned said. The point didn't matter since Lissea wasn't about to leave the *Swift* behind, but it showed that he was awake.

"Of course," Gresham agreed. "Since the Dreadnought has been operating, the value of trade through the Sole Solution has dropped to five percent of the previous annual total. This has hurt many planets, particularly those of the Pocket. The situation is satisfactory to the Twin Worlds themselves because *their* combined planetary income has increased markedly."

"Why doesn't somebody do something about it?" Toll Warson asked.

His voice wasn't quite as relaxed as he had wanted it to sound. The Warsons were as close to being functioning anarchists as anyone Ned had met. The notion of imposed authority was genuinely offensive to them. That they'd spent all their lives in the rigid hierarchies of military systems implied an insane dichotomy.

It also implied they'd been very good to have survived this long, but that was true of almost everybody aboard the *Swift*. By now, everybody. Even Ned Slade.

"Economics," Lissea said before Gresham could answer. "There are planets and planetary combines which could take this *thing* out of play."

She gestured at the hologram. The scale had shrunk to show that the Dreadnought did mount tribarrels. The installations on the main battery turrets looked as though they had been planted on flat steel plains.

"But a fleet that could accomplish that would take years to build, decades. Nobody with the resources had a good enough reason to employ them for the purpose."

"Precisely," Gresham said, a teacher approving his student's answer. It was hard to equate this man with the whimpering wreck who'd greeted the *Swift* on its arrival.

"We'll come back to the problem," Gresham continued. He

blanked the display. "Now, as to a rest-and-resupply point on this side of the Sole Solution, you'll land at Burr-Detlingen."

"Will we, now?" Deke Warson murmured.

The screen panned across a gullied plain with little vegetation. There were occasional human-built structures, all of them in ruins.

"There's no settled agriculture," Gresham said. "No human society since the wars, really. The atmosphere is ideal, and you'll be able to replenish your water supply from wells. Do you have equipment for processing raw biomass into edibles?"

"No," Tadziki said. "That'd be too bulky for a ship of the *Swift's* size."

"Well, you should be able to shoot animals for fresh meat," Gresham said. The image slid across a family of rangy herbivores, perhaps originally sheep or goats of Earth stock.

"On the other side of the Sole Solution," Gresham said as he blanked the display again, "is Buin. I can't really recommend it as a stopover, however. I think you'd be better off to continue to one of the developed worlds further into the Pocket."

"We'll need copies of all your navigational data for the Pocket," Lissea said.

"We've already downloaded it into the *Swift,*" Westerbeke assured her.

"All right," Lissea said. "I want to avoid developed worlds wherever possible."

"And there's the time factor," Tadziki said. "The nearest alternative landing point is another five days beyond Buin."

"Bugger *that* for a lark," a mercenary muttered. Under weigh, the *Swift* differed from a prison by having far less available space for those enclosed.

"Yes," Gresham said tartly. "The problem with Buin is the autochthonal race."

The display flopped from a pale white glow to the image of a gray-skinned creature beside a scale in decimeters. The Buinite was about two meters tall, within the human range, but its legs were only half the length of its arms and torso. The jaw was square, with powerful teeth bared in a snarl. One big hand carried a stone. Ned couldn't tell from the image whether the stone had been shaped or not.

"They don't look like much of a problem," Harlow said. "Nothing a shot or two won't cure."

"Individually, you're correct," Gresham said with no hint of agreement. "The autochthones' technology doesn't go beyond stakes and rocks—"

The hologram shifted to a panorama. Buin was rocky, and the vegetation tended toward blues and grays rather than green. A band of twenty or so autochthones was scattered across the field of view, turning over stones and sometimes probing holes with simple tools. They wore no clothing, though some of the medium-sized adults slung food objects on cords across their shoulders.

"Nor have they traded with travelers to gain modern weapons," Gresham continued.

"Do they have anything to trade?" Ned asked.

"Not really," Gresham said, "but the question doesn't arise. The autochthones invariably kill everyone who lands on their planet, unless he escapes immediately."

"I'd like to see them try *that*," Herne Lordling said. For once, the muttered chorus of other mercenaries was fully in support of his comment.

"You will, sir," Gresham said. "You assuredly will, if you land on Buin."

He switched the image to an overhead view of a mound. Vegetation hadn't started to claim the raw earth mixed with boulders the size of cottages.

"Artificial?" Lissea said.

"Yes," said Gresham. "And at the bottom of it, there's a starship, the *Beverly*. Autochthones damaged her engines with thrown rocks—"

The hologram switched to a Buinite stretching his left arm out behind him, then snapping forward like a sprung bear trap. The stone that shot from his hand sailed a hundred, perhaps a hundred and fifty meters in a flat arc before it hit the ground. Ned judged that the projectile weighed about as much as a man's head.

"And then they buried her, as you see," Gresham said. "Don't confuse intelligence with technology, mistress and gentlemen."

"Twenty of them did that?" Toll Warson wondered aloud.

"Probably two thousand," Gresham said. "Perhaps twenty thousand. Male Buinites concentrate on any ship that lands, like white cells on a source of infection. They appear to be telepathic. They are careless of their individual lives, and they are utterly committed to destroying the intruders."

He cleared his throat. "There have been cases where a vessel was undermined rather than being overwhelmed by advancing siege ramps," he added.

"But they *are* intelligent," Lissea said musingly.

"Clearly," Gresham agreed.

"That will help," Lissea said. "I'll want full data on the Buinites, physical and psychological. I assume that's available?"

Gresham looked surprised. "Why, yes," he said. "Everything is available here, in a manner of speaking. But I strongly recommend—"

"Before we worry about Buin," Tadziki interrupted, "we've got to get through the Sole Solution. Now, either it *isn't* the only way into the Pocket through Transit space;—"

"It is," Gresham said, nodding vigorously.

"—or we've got a real problem," the adjutant continued. "I don't see any way in hell that we can get past that Dreadnought in the time it'll take to recalibrate for the next Transit."

"We bloody well aren't going to fight it," Deke Warson agreed.

"There is, I believe, a way," Gresham said. He was smiling. "I've had a great deal of time to consider the matter."

His expression didn't look sane. Ned supposed that nobody exiled to Paixhans' Node could remain sane.

"Your *Swift* has a lifeboat with stardrive, I presume," Gresham continued.

"Yes," Lissea said.

"Then this is how you will proceed . . ."

BURR-DETLINGEN

Ned carried the submachine gun in his hands, not slung. The sky of Burr-Detlingen was white with occasional hints of blue, darkening now toward the east. The sun was just above the horizon, though in these latitudes full darkness would be some while to come.

It was still no time, and certainly no place, for Tadziki to be off wandering alone.

"Tadziki!" Ned called toward the masses of iridium armor, polished to a soft patina by windblown grit. "Hey, Tadziki! Anybody home?"

The *Swift* was a kilometer to the south. Ned had been on the crew that had reopened the well from which the vessel was now replenishing its water supplies. The thousand-meter shaft, a relic of human civilization on Burr-Detlingen, had been partly choked with sand.

Four of the men had gone off in the jeeps, to hunt for meat and for the fun of it. Bonilla, deck watch at the navigation console, told Ned that the adjutant had taken a walk toward the vast boneyard of military equipment near the landing site.

There was enough wind to scour away sound as well as all the paint and insignia from the shot-out vehicles. A yellow haze on the northern horizon indicated a storm sweeping across the badlands. If it changed direction—and who knew what the weather patterns of this place were?—getting back to the *Swift* would be a bigger problem than a dry walk.

"Tad—" Ned called. A figure stepped away from the bulk of a vehicle. Ned presented his weapon, then lifted it when he recognized Tadziki.

"Hey, I was looking for you," he said. "You, ah . . . Your helmet radio?"

"Sorry, I didn't mean to bother anybody," the adjutant said. He touched a switch on the side of his helmet. "I set it to ignore non-emergency calls. Even I ought to have a few hours off, eh?"

"Via, I'm sorry," Ned said. "I was—well, not worried, but there's supposed to be bands of locals running around. I just thought I'd, you know, make sure everything was okay."

The tank directly before him had been hit three times by kinetic energy shot. Two of the rounds had failed to penetrate but the projectiles had blasted deep pits in the tank's frontal slope. The sides of the craters were plated a purple that the sunset darkened.

The third shot had punched through the side of the turret. The interior of the tank burned out with such violence that the thirty-plus-tonne turret had lifted from its ring and resettled at a skew angle before being welded to the hull.

"The locals aren't any threat," Tadziki said. "They've sunk so far that it's hard to imagine them as being human. Sometimes passing ships capture them as slaves. Sometimes they're shot. Just for the fun of it, you see."

He spoke without emphasis, and his eyes held a blank fatigue that Ned didn't like to see—see in anybody, and Tadziki was by now a friend.

"That wasn't in the pilotry data," Ned said carefully. Tadziki carried a ration pack and a condensing canteen, but he appeared to be unarmed.

Either there was more in Ned's expression than he thought there was, or the two men were linked to a degree beyond that of physical communication. Tadziki reached into a breast pocket and pulled out a needle stunner.

"I suppose I'm making a statement, Slade," he said, "but I'm not trying to commit suicide."

Ned smiled. "Well, you can never tell," he said lightly.

"Come on and take a look at this," Tadziki said. He waved at the vast junkyard, armored bulwarks squatting in mounds of fine sand. "It's an interesting experience."

They walked past a command car whose fusion bottle had failed. The gush of plasma had not only eviscerated the vehicle, it had sucked the relatively thin armor inward so that the wreck looked like crumpled foil.

"This is my second trip to Burr-Detlingen," the adjutant said.

Ned looked at him sharply.

"No, no," Tadziki explained. "Not during the fighting—that was nearly a century ago. A cartel on Thunderhead got the notion of salvaging the equipment here. I was part of the team they sent to assay the possibilities."

Three armored personnel carriers were lined up nose to tail. Each had taken a powergun bolt through the center of its broadside. All the vehicles' plane surfaces were bulged convex by internal explosions.

"Salvage this?" Ned said.

"Yeah, well, they hadn't seen it," Tadziki explained. "They'd just heard about all the high-quality equipment abandoned here with nobody to claim it. We spent a week on the survey without finding a single piece that was worth more than metal value."

"Metal value" meant "worth dirt." Every planetary system had an asteroid belt which sorted metals in pure form and rich alloys, ready for the taking. Only colonies which had lost the ability to travel in space placed a premium on metal.

Tadziki climbed the bow slope of a tank and onto the turret. Ned followed him onto the artificial hillock. The barrel of the main gun had been shot out so badly that there was no way to tell from the cone-shaped remnant what the bore's original diameter had been.

"This is where the final battle of the war was fought, did you know?" Tadziki said. He gestured again at the field of gigantic litter

"Really?" said Ned. "I would have thought it was just a salvage yard."

"They fought with spears and clubs," Tadziki explained. "One side built rock walls between the carcasses of the vehicles and used them for fortifications."

He pointed.

Ned could see signs of artifice, now that they were pointed out to him. "The other side attacked them. Nobody won, of course."

"I think it was a religious war," Ned said. He looked down. Sand had eroded the join between the hatch cover and the coaming into a deep, thumb-thick gully. He couldn't see any sign of battle damage to the tank, however. "We studied one of the battles at the Academy. In Intermediate Tactics class, I think."

"It was excellent equipment!" Tadziki said angrily. He stamped his foot on the turret roof. It was like hitting a boulder: the armor was too thick to bell at the impact. "There isn't one planet in a thousand today who could build or afford to buy hardware like this."

"Yeah," Ned agreed as he surveyed the hectares of sophisticated equipment. "I was wondering about that myself. This isn't exactly a land flowing with milk and honey."

The sun was down, though the sky still looked bright. "You know," he said. "It wouldn't be a bad idea for us to be getting back to the *Swift*, whether or not the locals are a problem."

"They grew citrus fruit," Tadziki said. He showed no signs of planning to leave the graveyard. "Lemons in particular—Terran lemons naturalized here. They had a unique flavor. Burr-Detlingen exported fruit all over the galaxy."

Ned looked around. Except for the vicinity of the *Swift*, nothing in the landscape moved but what the wind blew.

"Any of the groves left in driving distance?" he asked. "If we have to wait here three days before trying the Sole Solution, maybe we could get a jeep."

"There's nothing left," the adjutant said. "They weren't groves; they were individual trees in walls to keep the wind from stripping them. The walls became pillboxes, and of course the irrigation system was destroyed early on. There's nothing left that anyone would want to have."

It was becoming appreciably darker. Well, the charge-coupled devices in their helmet visors could increase ambient light by three orders of magnitude. Lack of depth perception wasn't a problem in terrain this barren.

"I'd never have come back here if there'd been a choice," Tadziki said. "There wasn't a choice: no planet close enough for us to launch the lifeboat into the Sole Solution in a single Transit."

Everybody had moods. Tadziki was under greater stress than anybody on the expedition except Lissea herself. Maybe more than Lissea, even, because the adjutant had enough experience to know how bad it could get.

Ned reached down and twisted the hatch's undogging lever. To his surprise, it rotated smoothly. "You couldn't have checked all these vehicles in a week," he said as he lifted the hatch open.

The stench hit them like a battering ram. The tank hadn't been opened in the century since it had been destroyed. The crewman who died lifting his hands toward the inner hatch release had mummified. His teeth were a polished yellow against the coarser saffron skin. The eyes had sunken in, but they were still open.

And the stench . . .

The two men tumbled down the sides of the tank as if a grenade had burst between them. Ned wheezed and gagged. He closed his eyes for a moment, then found that it was better if something other than memory provided his mind with images.

"Why do men go for soldiers?" Tadziki shouted. They were walking back toward the *Swift,* wallowing in sand which had drifted around the skirts of the vehicles. "Do they believe in *that?* Is that what they want?"

It was too dark to see clearly unaided, but Ned didn't want to shut his visor. Concussion from a large mine could have killed the tank crew, crushing their internal organs without penetrating the hull of their vehicle.

"It's not that simple," he said.

"On the contrary, boy," Tadziki said. "It's *exactly* that simple."

After a moment, he reached out and gripped Ned's shoulder. "I'm sorry," he said.

Ned reached up and squeezed the adjutant's hand against him. "No sweat," he said. He looked back at the armored wasteland, tombstones for a whole planet. "I'm sorry too," he added.

THE
SOLE SOLUTION

"Stand by for Transit," Westerbeke announced.

Lissea was at the backup console, though Ned doubted she'd had much more navigational experience than he'd had. She was nervous, just like the rest of them. If she wanted to be in position to see disaster instantly, then nobody aboard could deny her the right.

"Via," said Ingried plaintively. "The worst it can be is they tell us we're bad boys to try to run the Solution, and they make us land on Alliance. Right? Maybe we get fined."

"The *worst* it can be," Yazov said in a harsh, no-nonsense voice, "is that they figure out we're the ones that tried to kill them all, and then they torture us to death. Maybe the same way that we tried to do them."

"*Shut up, both of you,*" Tadziki said, using the vessel's PA system.

"Transit."

Ned felt the flip-flop passage from one bubble universe to another with wholly different physical laws, then back again to the first. He deliberately prevented himself from gripping his bunk rails fiercely. Part of his mind *felt* that could help him against a bolt of plasma devouring the entire vessel.

"No sign of the Dreadnought," Westerbeke said. "*No* sign of the Dreadnought, but there's our lifeboat."

"Boys, I think we did it!" Lissea cried.

She adjusted the holographic display at her console, projecting the view at maximum enlargement. The lifeboat the *Swift* had launched from orbit above Burr-Detlingen hung in vacuum; there was nothing material within a light-month of the Sole Solution.

Men cheered and swung out of their bunks—Ned as quickly as any of the others. The *Swift* had the traditional 1-g way on, so there was considerable risk if the vessel made another Transit while the complement was out of its couches. Fifteen minutes was as fast as the AI could recalibrate, though; and anyway, it was worth a bruise or even broken bones to release the tension of the last few hours.

"Here, I've got the data dump," Lissea said. She touched her controls. The starscape shifted to a recording made inside the lifeboat during its unpiloted Transit into the Sole Solution. Initially, that meant the holographic display was a pulsing purple, the closest the equipment could come to reproducing the absolute lightlessness within the little vessel.

"*Unidentified ship,*" snapped a transmission-modulated laser rather than a radio, judging from the static-free reception. "*Heave to immediately. This is Twin Worlds Naval Unit One. You will not get another warning. Over.*"

The lifeboat's interior lights went on at full intensity. The six Nodals within were of an unhealthy translucence from days of lightlessness. Their flesh, yellow and pustulant, began to firm up visibly under the illumination.

"*This is trading vessel* Southshields *out of Nowotny,*" the lifeboat's AI replied on cue. "*We are heaving to. We have a load of cacao and worked bronze only. What's the trouble? Over.*"

The voice from the Dreadnought laughed harshly. "*No problem at all, Southshields,*" it said. "*We'll just confiscate your ship and cargo for entering closed territory of the Twin Worlds. Unless you try to get away, in which case we'll blast you to vacuum, and that won't be a problem either.*"

"Southshields, *stand by to be boarded,*" another voice interjected.

The lifeboat's navigation display was crude, and the images were further degraded by copying and retransmission from the internal camera. The Dreadnought was visible as a vast doughnut, but the catcher boat launched from it was no more than an approaching quiver of light.

The Nodals were becoming active now that the lights were on. At this final stage of their breeding process, their bases remained fixed. Ripples like slow tides worked up their swaying bodies. The yellow tinge of the creatures' flesh became brighter and more saturated.

The lifeboat's hull thumped, then rang metallically as the lip of a boarding tube clamped around the hatch. The boat didn't have an airlock—most low-end cargo vessels didn't. The catcher vessel was equipped to board without putting the Twin Worlds crew to the discomfort of suiting up.

A Nodal's skin ripped from top to bottom as if a seam had given out under pressure. Yellow spores exploded in a haze that hid the interior for a moment. The spores began to settle on all the surfaces of the vessel.

The hatch opened. Spores swirled in the air currents.

A burly man with a fat-muzzled pistol stood framed by the coaming. He wore an airpack but not a pressure suit. Behind him stretched the boarding tube to his own vessel. The tube's reinforcing helix acted as a light guide, illuminating the pathway.

A second Nodal ruptured.

The Twin Worlder's scream was loud despite being muffled by the airpack. He opened fire with his pistol, the worst thing he could have done—

Though at this point, there wasn't anything he could have done that wouldn't have been disastrous.

The weapon fired charges of airfoils shaped to spread from the muzzle into a broad, short-range killing pattern. They sliced the remaining Nodals into geysers of spores, seconds or minutes before the creatures would have opened naturally.

The atmosphere of the cabin was yellow mud. As the air cleared, the camera showed that tendrils of spores had followed the panicked Twin Worlder back down the boarding tube. Thousands—*millions*—of them clung to the man's flesh and clothing.

"Good enough!" Deke Warson cried. The *Swift*'s bay was alive with glee. "That'll teach the bastards!" several men shouted at once.

"What they should do," Tadziki said, "is to blow themselves up right now. It's the only way."

"Nobody wants to die," Ned said from beside him.

"They're going to die, quickly and certainly," the adjutant said. He sounded detached, as though he were assessing the state of play in a bridge rubber. "Not quickly enough, though. There's no cure for the spores once they've infected a human. Cauterizing heat, that's all, heat beyond what flesh can stand. UV and hard radiation simply stimulate growth."

"I think," Toll Warson said, "that this calls for a party!"

Lissea got up from the console. Men clapped her on the back as she walked down the aisle. "Yes," she said. "We can break out a double liquor ration. Herne, you're in charge of dispensing it."

The boarding tube ripped as the catcher vessel powered up without going through the time-consuming procedures to release it. Automatic systems within the device immediately clamped it shut at the break. Vacuum wouldn't have affected the spores one way or another, but the lifeboat's navigational equipment depended on an atmosphere to reveal its holographic images.

Most of the men ignored the display as soon as Lissea ordered a liquor distribution. Westerbeke, on duty while the AI calculated the next Transit, glanced toward the hologram occasionally. Mostly he watched his fellows queued before Lordling at the liquor cabinet.

The fleck of the catcher vessel merged again with the shape of Twin Worlds Naval Unit One. "They wanted medical help," Tadziki mused aloud. He still stood at Ned's elbow. "People don't like to believe how serious a crisis is at first."

"If they'd reported the situation," Ned said, "they'd never have been allowed to dock. But they should have had the balls to report anyway!"

The adjutant shrugged. "They aren't fighting men," he said. "They just happened to have a job on a warship so powerful that it could never be used. They didn't *believe*, none of them, that they'd ever be in a life or death situation."

"Oh, dear, what can the matter be?" Coyne sang, waving a tumbler of ruddy brandy in the air.

"Shut the fuck up!" Harlow said. "You got a voice to scare crows."

"And the Dreadnought left station," Ned said. "They went back to the Twin Worlds, I suppose? One or the other of them."

"Seven old maids, locked in the lavat'ry," Coyne and Yazov continued.

"Who's got the dice? Shmuel, you've got dice, right?"

Tadziki nodded. "Presumably," he said. "There's really nowhere else they might have gone. They may not be planning to land."

"They were there from Sunday to Saturday," crewmen sang. Several of them had surprisingly good voices. *"Nobody knew they were there!"*

"They can't land the Dreadnought," Ned said. "But no matter what, some of them'll get down in gigs and catcher boats. And some of those will already be infected."

"Yes," Tadziki said. "That's what I think too. Now I'm going to have a drink."

Ned walked to his bunk. The bow and center of the bay were a party room, but the back was empty.

He didn't want his liquor ration. He could trade it to somebody, but there wasn't anything else Ned wanted, either. Nothing that a human being could give him, anyway.

Ned picked up the microchip reader. He still had Thucydides loaded. The author's introduction claimed he was writing a paradigm for human behavior. The work itself was an account of two powerful nations lurching toward mutual destruction; not inevitably, but with absolute certainty nonetheless.

Lissea retched behind her thin door panel.

Ned got up. He dampened a towel at the water dispenser, then gently tried Lissea's door.

It was locked. He glanced toward the bow. The party went on merrily. Lordling and the Warson brothers were singing with linked arms.

Ned took a finger-sized probe from his equipment belt and

tried the lock. The telltale on the probe's back flicked from red to green in less than a second. The latch wasn't much of a challenge to equipment and training by which Ned could bypass the security devices on a tank.

He checked the party again, then slipped into Lissea's compartment with the wet towel. The door closed behind him as part of the same motion.

She'd been sick into a bag. She looked up, her eyes red and furious.

"Brought you a towel," he said, turning his back as he thrust it toward her.

"Yeah, I see that you did," Lissea said. She didn't shout or curse, as he'd expected and as he knew he deserved. Her voice was husky, burned raw by stomach acid. She took the towel from his hand.

"Go on, sit down," she said. "Want a drink?"

Ned sat down on the end of the bunk. The bulkheads provided privacy but actually reduced Lissea's apparent space, because they cut her off from the volume of the bay.

"No thanks," Ned said.

"I do," Lissea said. The locker beneath her bunk was of double depth. She leaned over, opened it, and took out a bottle with conifers on the label.

"Wood alcohol," she said. "That's a joke, boy. It's what we brew on Dell." She drank directly from the bottle. The towel lay crumpled at her feet.

A craps game competed with the singers in the bay. From what Ned could tell, there might have been two songs going on at the same time.

"They don't know what they've done, do they?" Lissea said brightly. "What we've all done, I should say, shouldn't I?"

"They know," Ned said. "They've killed the crew of the Dreadnought, however many thousands of people that was."

"And how many people on the Twin Worlds?" Lissea said. She flung the bottle down. The container bounced, spilling liquor from the mouth, but didn't break. "And to the next planet and the one after that, and the one after *that*."

Ned set the bottle upright. The stopper was still in Lissea's hand. He didn't ask for it.

"No," he said. "On the Twin Worlds, maybe. One or the other of them. But there's no place except Paixhans' Node where Nodals can get the permanent illumination they need to thrive. Maybe a few of them will get to the fruiting stage. But not many, and none beyond one or two generations."

"I'm supposed to feel good that I've only killed thousands, not millions?" she said. "Is that it?"

"You knew," Ned said coldly, "what was going to happen when you made the decision to proceed. The only way this wouldn't have been the result is if the plan had failed—and we all died instead, most likely."

"All right, Slade, you've—"

"No!" Ned said. "Nothing's changed. *Don't* second-guess yourself. We all knew what we were doing and we did it. Now we're going to go on. And there'll be some hard choices to make later, too. We *know* that."

Lissea laughed. "You haven't told me that they were evil bastards and no better than pirates," she said. "Do you want to tell me that, too?"

"What's done is done," Ned said softly. "If you don't like the way things look from this side, then pick another route the next time."

He thumbed toward the bulkhead and the noise beyond it. "Most of the people here, they've got a lot less trouble with what happened than they would've with getting greased themselves." He grinned. "Which is why you hired us, I suspect."

Lissea chuckled again, this time with more humor. She picked up the bottle. "Want a drink?" she offered again.

"No, thanks though."

She stoppered the bottle. "Thanks, Ned," she said. "Let's us go join the party now. I wouldn't want anybody to get the wrong impression."

There might have been a speculative tone behind her words; but Ned was a man, and he knew that men thought that way.

BUIN

"*We're still getting signals from the crashed vessel's crew,*" Bonilla reported from the backup console. Westerbeke always had the con in tight situations, and powered flight through Buin's atmosphere was certainly that. "*The survivors have abandoned their ship and headed for high ground. They say they can't hold out much longer. Over.*"

Buffeting made all objects within the *Swift* rattle, adding considerable noise to the wind-roar through the thick hull. All personnel were in their bunks, wearing body armor and festooned with weapons and equipment.

Ned was dry-mouthed. He'd never before had this long to expect certain combat.

"*Lissea, the indigs'll be concentrated on the downed ship,*" Herne Lordling said. His helmet gave him the ability to enter the command net rather than simply listen to Channel 1 traffic, the way other personnel did. "*We shouldn't land within fifty klicks of them. Let the fools get themselves out of their jam. Over.*"

Ned suspected Lordling spoke for most of the complement. The *Swift* wasn't crewed by Good Samaritans, and this looked like a dicey business at best. The crewmen of the vessel that had either crashed or foolishly landed on Buin—it wasn't clear which—were in desperate straits, but that wasn't a problem the Warsons, for example, felt they were being paid to solve.

Ned was green enough, he supposed—soft enough—to be

willing to help. He just didn't see there was a thing in hell he could do.

"*Westerbeke*," snapped Lissea's voice, "*land us as planned if the site is clear. Lordling, you have your orders.*"

"*All personnel prepare for landing,*" Westerbeke ordered. The pilot sounded cool, almost bored.

The boom of the jets segued into a ringing *blammm!* as Westerbeke or the ship's AI doubled the number of lit nozzles and shifted the direction of thrust. Flat clamps held Ned to his bunk when inertia tried to shift him first forward, then up.

Reflected exhaust hammered the *Swift*, a warning that the vessel was within meters of the ground. The touchdown itself was accompanied by a series of raps on the lower hull.

Ned's first thought was that the Buinites were already attacking. Tadziki, who was importing visuals from the navigational console to his visor, said, "*Loose gravel, boys. It's all right.*"

The main hatch began to open an instant before the jets shut off and the couch clamps released. Mercenaries swung from their bunks with a long crash of boots against the decking. The ramp was only halfway down when Herne Lordling's four-man team pounded across it and leaped to the ground. The second team was a stride behind them; Ned and Lissea were half of the third.

It must have rained recently. The brush was alive with yellow, white, and orange flowers which almost hid the cooler-colored foliage that Gresham's holograms had led Ned to expect. Between bushes scattered at several-meter intervals, the stony soil had a white crust that could be either salt or lichen.

The *Swift*'s external cargo blisters were already open. The Warson brothers had lifted out one of the jeeps and were reaching for the other. Ned didn't recall having ever before seen such a casual expression of strength.

He unlocked the fan nacelles of the first jeep and levered them up into operating position. Somebody fired from the other side of the vessel. The plasma discharges sizzled through the commo helmet an instant before the sonic hiss-*crack!*

Crewmen with bundles of poles, wire, and directional mines

staggered through the brush under guard of their fellows with weapons ready. Three men remained aboard the *Swift:* Westerbeke and Petit, at the navigational and engine-room consoles respectively, and Tadziki—against his will—to take charge of the vessel if things went badly wrong. The adjutant stood in the center of the main hatchway with a 2-cm powergun ready.

The *Swift*'s upper hull was the best vantage point for a kilometer in any direction. The two-man crew who'd set up the tribarrel there cried out. They pointed over the jeeps toward vegetation lining an underground watercourse; then cut a long burst loose. Cyan bolts blew stems upward in a haze of soapy black flames.

Lissea lurched into the jeep with the device she'd built in the *Swift*'s maintenance shop. The electronics chassis mounted three separate lenses on the front, with a shoulder stock and a clumsy-looking handgrip underneath. From the way Lissea struggled, the apparatus must weigh twenty kilos.

"Are you ready?" Lissea shouted as Ned dropped into the seat beside her. She glanced around at the other jeep. "Is everybody ready?"

"Let's get 'em," Deke Warson said with his hands on the driver's yoke. His brother lifted the muzzle of his 2-cm powergun slightly. He'd slung an identical weapon across his chest. This wouldn't be a good time to have to clear a jam.

Three Buinites ran from the shelter of a flat-topped tree half a kilometer away. A merc guarding the wiring party fired and spun the middle indig. The remaining pair dropped flat, then rose again together. A storm of cyan bolts devoured them before they could release the stones their arms were cocked to throw.

"Get a move on, Slade!" Lissea shouted, though the only delay had been that of the fans accelerating the loaded jeep after Ned shoved his controls forward.

By plan, Ned's jeep—Lissea's jeep—was to lead. Ned was pretty sure that the actual reason he was a nose ahead of the Warsons as they raced toward the knoll just within the gap in the new-strung wire was that the brothers and their equipment were that much heavier than the load Ned's vehicle had to carry.

The crews had laid a conductive net as fine as spider silk between posts at hundred-meter intervals. The wires weren't so much material presence as scatterings of sunlight. They sagged at some points and were twisted around brush.

With luck, the net would provide a stable base for the minutes Lissea needed to carry out her plans.

The rocky knoll was the only high ground—three meters above its surroundings, putting it above the treetops—in the vicinity. The tribarrel on the ship fired a long planned burst, blasting the site clear of vegetation. Ned steered by memory, because he wouldn't be able to see the rise until it was right on top of him.

Somewhere a Buinite hit the net. Electricity from the nuclear batteries in the nearest post coursed through the creature in a long, drawn-out thunderclap. Cross-wires were insulated from one another, guaranteeing a current path whether or not the victim was grounded.

A dozen more Buinites reprised their dead fellow's actions within the next ten seconds. None of the victims screamed.

The roots of bushes held soil together, forming squat plateaus like the drums carnivores perch on in a circus act. Ned skidded between a pair of the short columns. He wasn't driving a tank, though with a load like this the little jeep handled as sluggishly as a tank did. He had to go around things, not over them, and there wasn't any protection for when—

A submachine gun and three or four 2-cm weapons opened up. They were a good distance away and hidden by the brush. Somebody shouted.

"Up here!" Lissea called, but Ned was already steering to hit the rise bow-on. If he tried to climb the knoll at a slant, the loaded jeep might turn turtle. Ash and bits of charred brushwood sprayed from beneath the skirts, but the plasma-lit fires were barely smoldering.

Ned halted, spinning the jeep to put its bow inward again. The braking force threw them against the seatbacks rather than forward toward the windscreen. He unslung his submachine gun and glanced to the right, toward where the commotion was occurring.

The Buinites had rolled a mass of brush into a fascine four meters in diameter and twenty meters across. The crude construction rocked across the landscape like a bad clockwork toy. Powergun bolts lit the face of it, shattering stems without penetrating.

When green, the local vegetation didn't burn hot enough to sustain combustion. Veils of dirty smoke swathed the fascine, but the autochthones protected behind it continued to advance the cylinder unhindered.

Ten Buinites trotted toward the knoll. Deke and Toll Warson opened fire from beside Ned and Lissea. Their single aimed shots cracked as quickly as those of an automatic weapon.

"Don't shoot, you bastards!" Lissea screamed.

Autochthones spun in cyan flashes. The survivors dropped to cover.

A Buinite jumped upright. He was a hundred meters away. Lissea's device hummed, bathing the autochthone and a one-hundred-twenty-degree swath of the landscape in pulsing light.

The creature's whole body snapped forward like the arm of a ballista. The Warsons fired together. The autochthone's head and upper thorax gouted blood and fierce blue light, disintegrating under twin megajoule impacts.

"Don't—" Lissea said as she thumbed a dial to a higher setting. Three more Buinites stood, arched, and blew apart as the device in the captain's arms hummed uselessly. The last of the creatures died with four bolts from Ned's submachine gun flashing across the gray chest.

All the Buinites were down, but more rushed from concealment. They'd reacted instantly to the *Swift*'s arrival. Their speed and organization was remarkable, even granting the previous shipwreck had concentrated them only a klick away.

Lissea adjusted the frequency of her device again. The Warsons waited, and Ned waited. Heat waves trembled above the iridium barrels of their powerguns.

The Buinite fascine staggered under the impact of four rocket shells from the Racontid's launcher. The cylinder, brush bound with branches, ruptured and spread like a jellyfish cast onto hot sand.

Powergun bolts released their energy on the first solid object they intersected. They could only claw the outside of the fascine. Raff had adjusted the fusing to burst the warheads of his projectile weapon a tenth of a second after impact. The charges went off deep inside the tight-wrapped brushwood, ripping it apart from within.

There were at least forty autochthones behind the fascine, protected by the cylinder's bulk as they pushed it toward the vessel. Crumpled, the loosened pile still provided cover from ground level, but the men atop the *Swift* had a better angle.

The tribarrel ripped a bloody swath through the Buinites. As survivors rose to scamper away, individual marksmen knocked them down with stark flashes.

An autochthone threw a rock more than one hundred fifty meters to the knoll. The missile thumped down in a cloud of ash between the two jeeps.

Then a group of a dozen or so approached by short rushes, two or three moving at a time. As each team lurched forward, occasionally dabbing their hands down as they moved, the rest crouched and waited. The Buinites were obviously preparing to loose a shower of stones together while the gunmen focused on the party making the rush.

A Buinite cocked his arm back.

"Next one's *mine*, ma'am!" Deke Warson cried.

Lissea triggered her device on the new setting. The Buinite preparing to throw and his crouching fellows all collapsed limply as if shot through the brain stem. The three running autochthones weren't affected. They hunched as they scampered, so they hadn't been looking in the direction of the device.

Lissea held her finger down. The runners flopped to cover, peered upward, and sprawled mindlessly in turn.

"Go!" Lissea ordered as Ned shifted power to his fans.

"*Yee-ha!*" Deke Warson cried as he did the same, guiding the yoke with his knees while he kept the powergun's shimmering muzzle aimed toward the fallen Buinites. He'd have to take the controls normally in a moment . . . or maybe he wouldn't—the

Warsons were good, *everybody* aboard the *Swift* was good, incredibly good at what they did.

By itself, that would just have increased the cost the autochthones incurred when they—crushed, buried, destroyed—the *Swift*. Lissea's nerve scrambler emitted a pattern of light on the critical frequency on which the Buinites' central nervous system operated.

The scrambler's broad-angle effect would not be enough to stop such dedicated creatures either. In a short time, they would find a way to overcome it.

The jeeps bumped awkwardly across the remainder of the knoll, spitting out bits of charred brush. The downslope gave the little vehicles a gravity boost. Ned's controls felt lively for the first time since they'd gotten the jeep operating this morning.

The wiring crew had left a gap two meters wide in front of the knoll. Harlow stood behind the self-setting post at one side of it, looking outward.

A Buinite who wasn't part of the previous squads rose from cover with a rock in his hand. Lissea swung her heavy scrambler toward him.

Toll Warson's bolt blew the autochthone's arm off. The limb, still gripping its fistful of basalt, spun in one direction while the torso contra-rotated more slowly in the other. A splash of greenish, copper-based blood dissipated in the air between them.

"We've got enough down now," Lissea muttered to Ned. "If they'll stay down."

"So far, so good," Ned said as he lunged back. He used his weight as well as the nacelle angle to help the jeep clear a jut of harder rock running unexpectedly above the scree to either side.

"It took me three *tries* to get the frequency!" Lissea said. "*A* frequency. It may not give us ten minutes; they may be hopping up right when we get to them!"

"Then we'll put them down again, won't we?" Ned said, guiding the jeep around the stump of a tree, blown apart in smoldering needles where a plasma bolt had struck it. The first of the catatonic autochthones lay just beyond. The others of the creature's—squad? family?—sprawled back over a distance of fifty meters.

"Jump!" Ned ordered as he slowed. "I'll take the other end!"

They hadn't discussed procedures at this stage, because they hadn't known how the comatose victims would be arrayed. Lissea didn't argue: Ned was right, Ned was driving, and anyway, there was no time to argue.

She rolled out of the vehicle, dropping the scrambler onto the seat as she left it. She managed to keep her feet despite the jeep's forward motion.

Ned accelerated again toward the middle of the straggling line.

Two more fascines rolled toward the *Swift* from opposite sides of the perimeter. The rocket gun hammered again. Raff was beside the tribarrel on top of the vessel now, so that he could swing his rocket gun in any direction.

The mortar, set up near the *Swift*'s ramp, fired a ranging shot. Using the high-angle weapon hadn't been part of the plan, but the crew hadn't expected the autochthones to concentrate and to deploy siege equipment so quickly. Pretechnological, *hell!* If the Buinites were hunter-gatherers, it was because they wanted to be hunter-gatherers.

And the *Swift* would leave them to run their planet the way they wanted to; but first the crew needed water and a break, and that meant discussions with the Buinites on the terms that the Buinites understood.

Two mortar shells burst with pops rather than bangs, ejecting submunitions to cover a wider area than individual blasts could do.

A moment later, the bomblets detonated with a sound like the snarl of a huge cat. If Tadziki had placed his rounds correctly, the autochthones behind one or both the fascines were now flayed corpses.

Killing them wasn't enough unless every male autochthone on the planet could be killed. Killing and the nerve scrambler were only the preliminary parts of Captain Doormann's plan. Lissea was just as good at *her* job as the men she commanded were at theirs.

Ned stopped the jeep by venting the plenum chamber while the fans continued to run. He jumped out, leaving the vehicle howling. Shutting down would save power, but battery life wasn't likely to be a problem. Ned might not have a lot of time to spin the fans up to operating speed when he wanted to leave.

He wanted to leave now, but he had a job to do.

The submachine gun banged against his breastplate. He ignored it: the Warsons were providing cover. Ned drew the knife from the sheath outside his right boot and knelt beside a Buinite.

The creature lay on its back. Its mouth gaped. Oils blasted from the vegetation by powergun bolts had a strong, spicy odor. Perhaps that was why Ned's eyes started to water.

The Buinite's muscles were lax. Ned spread the short legs apart and went in with the knife, following his instructions precisely. A bone held the penis semierect at all times. The gonads were internal, but they bulged the flesh of the buttocks obviously. The scales there were white and finer than the mottled gray which covered other parts of the autochthone's body.

The knife was a weapon, not a tool. Its straight, twenty-centimeter blade was double-edged and narrow; not ideal for gelding, but it served well enough.

Ned stabbed, twisted as if he were coring an apple, and pulled the knife away. The ugly gouge filled with blood smearing over the lips of the cut. The excised organs hung by tags of skin. The Buinite remained flaccid, breathing in shallow gusts through its open mouth.

Ned ran to the next victim. If this were a commercial operation rather than punishment and a warning, he would have some means of cauterizing the terrible wounds. The fighting knife was razor-sharp, with an edge of collapsed matter which would stay sharp despite brutal use. It severed the arteries so cleanly that the cut ends shrank closed, leaking relatively little blood.

Not perfect, but good enough. Ned stabbed, twisted, and moved on. The third Buinite slicked nictitating membranes sideways across its eyes as the knife slipped in. The scrambler's effects were beginning to wear off.

Another victim, this one humped on his face. The limbs splayed as Ned tried to operate from behind, so the knife cut an accidental collop from the autochthone's thigh. Ned botched the job, leaving the parts still attached but so hideously mutilated that they would never heal normally. He wondered if microorganisms on Buin carried the equivalent of gangrene.

The autochthones were beginning to move. One of those Lissea had gelded moaned loudly.

Ned's right boot slipped on a stone because the sole was bloody. His arms were sticky green to the elbows. His knife stabbed and turned, this time completing the operation perfectly even though the Buinite tried to rise to its hands and knees while he cut.

Ned wished he were dead rather than doing this.

The next autochthone turned its head as he approached. The creature's eyes were still mindless.

Guns fired. The tribarrel swept very close and the Warsons let off aimed shots as steady as metronome strokes. A bolt struck an active Buinite so close by that its body fluids sprayed Ned.

Ned wished he were dead, but he had a job to do. He knocked the autochthone unconscious with the butt of his knife, then used the point and edge with practiced skill before he got up; there were no more victims to be mutilated and he hurled the knife into the brush with as much strength as his arm retained.

"Ned, come on for the *Lord's* sake!" someone was shouting— Lissea, as she struggled to lift the nerve scrambler with hands as bloody as Ned's own. He ran for the jeep thirty meters away.

Toll Warson stood on the seat of the other vehicle. He aimed at Ned and bellowed, "Ge' *down!*"

Ned dropped, twisting his face back. He saw an autochthone standing by the body of his mutilated fellow. The stone the creature had already thrown exploded in a cyan dazzle because Toll had shot the missile first. The second bolt, quick as a finger twitch, hit the base of the Buinite's neck and blew the head off in a high arc that looked like a planned effect.

Maybe it was. Toll was very good, and Ned Slade was good enough to have done his job without the slightest hesitation because he had his orders and it had to be done.

Ned got into the jeep and slammed the vents closed. The Buinites' blood was tacky, so his hands wouldn't slip on the controls. He spun the vehicle. Lissea was saying something, mumbling. He couldn't understand her and he didn't much care whether the words were directed to him.

Harlow had already withdrawn. Two Buinites lay outside the wire, shot dead, and three others hung on the gossamer. The limbs in contact were burned to husks of carbon by the amperage which coursed through the net's seeming delicacy. Ned drove past. He was controlling his speed carefully. If he let instinct slam the yoke to the dash, the jeep would pogo on the rough terrain and lower the actual speed over distance.

He skirted the knoll. They didn't need to look for anything; they'd seen and done all that was required. The Warsons followed, Toll facing the rear and his brother driving with one hand while the other held his 2-cm weapon ready.

Deke fired once, shattering a stump that could have been an indig but wasn't. He hit it squarely though the bolt snapped close past the lead jeep in order to find the target.

Huge hollow explosions hammered the air from the other side of the vessel. The crew had set a thin belt of directional mines midway between the *Swift* and the wire to gain additional time for the withdrawal. The mines were going off now, blasting cones of shot outward toward the Buinites.

Ned had hoped—they'd all hoped—that the shock of mangled bodies would cause later waves of autochthones to pause. Nobody who'd seen the Buinites in action still believed that was a realistic likelihood. It was going to be close, one way or the other.

The *Swift* quivered on its lift engines. Two men carried a third into the vessel while six or eight mercenaries fired from the hatchway. More directional mines detonated, a multiple stroke like thunder glancing from all the sides of heaven.

"Drive straight aboard!" Lissea cried, twisting backward in her seat with her powergun gripped in her bloody hands. She didn't fire—the other jeep was right behind them.

Ned didn't back off the throttle until his skirts brushed the ramp; judging the slope would brake them enough to keep control. He popped the vents and let inertia fling them into the bay as the skirts sagged with a great sigh.

Ned hadn't thought there was enough room for the jeep, but there was—barely. Hands gripped him and yanked him out of the vehicle, out of the way. His boots tangled with the jeep's sidepanel and he flopped clumsily in the aisle, on top of the reeking mortar tube.

The interior was a chaos of men and weapons. The tribarrel lay across somebody's bunk. The shimmering barrels had cooled themselves by melting the synthetic bedding into a cocoon about the iridium. It would take hours to chip and polish the gunk out of the workings so that the weapon could function again.

"Leave it!" Lissea screamed from the hatchway as Deke Warson drove the other jeep up the ramp. "Leave it!"

Men were firing past the brothers. Ned could see Buinites running from the shelter of trees, rocks in their hands. He tried to clear his submachine gun but the sling caught in the mortar's elevating screw.

The Warsons jumped from either side of their vehicle as though they were making a combat drop. "*Leave*—" Lissea cried, but they grabbed handholds meant for two men per side and lifted the jeep with the fans still howling in the nacelles.

Josie Paetz fired his pistol. A stone slammed Toll in the back, ricocheting upward from his body armor and taking his helmet off. He grunted, then regained his balance. The Warsons threw their jeep on top of Lissea's, trusting everybody else to get out of the way in time or take the consequences.

Rocks clanged on the *Swift*'s hull. She was already lifting with a tremendous roar: cargo blisters open, ramp down, and Moiseyev— his right cheek bruised and bloody—gripping Deke Warson's arm, the only thing keeping the big mercenary from tumbling out as a final missile dropped onto the surface of Buin.

Despite the windrush and buffeting, the hatch closed in ninety seconds. That was nearly up to the best speed the hydraulic jacks could have managed ahead of a normal liftoff. The bay was thunderous hell as Westerbeke carried out his instructions: one low orbit and back to the point of departure.

Ned stood still-faced beside somebody's bunk. He'd washed the blood from his skin though not his memory. Lissea was near the ramp. They'd cleared the hatchway by hauling the jeeps down the aisles on their sides. The heavy weaponry that should have been stowed in the external blisters with the vehicles lay on bunks. Nobody was pretending to bother with normal landing procedures on this one.

Ned gripped the bedframe as though his hands were cast around it. Hatton chortled something to him, looked at the younger man's face, and began talking to Yazov instead.

They couldn't go any distance from Buin like this. Even if the water held out, the weeks of Transit and recalibration before the *Swift* reached Pancahte would drive everybody aboard mad. At worst they'd have to touch down to hurl out the jeeps and heavy equipment if there wasn't time to stow the gear properly.

"Captain, there's movement at the site," Westerbeke warned. *"There's indigs all over the ground where we landed the first time! Over."*

"Set down on the knoll," Lissea ordered. *"Be ready to make a touch-and-go if we need to. Out."*

"The locals'll ring us if they've got a problem," one of the mercenaries shouted. Other men laughed. Either they were genuinely unconcerned that the rocks clanging against the hull would smash an engine nozzle, or they were determined to give a carefree impression.

Ned latched his faceshield down and thumbed the rotary switch on the lower edge till it gave him visuals from the navigational console. He normally didn't like to do that because when the visor was opaque to the outside world, it made him feel as if he were trapped in somebody's fantasy. Right now, he could use fantasy.

The directional mines had blown great wedges out of the landscape so that the *Swift*'s former landing site seemed ringed by pointers. Smoke drifted downwind from one of the abandoned fascines. Tadziki had fired a charger of incendiary shells from the mortar. He hoped that the flames would prevent fresh autochthones from replacing the team pushing the fascine, as would happen if he'd used normal antipersonnel bomblets.

Buinites were all over the site, like bees preparing to swarm. In pairs and quartets they carried away the bodies of fellows who'd been killed while attacking the *Swift*. The fenceline, still deadly despite the scores of victims it had claimed, was buried under a mound of brush—further proof that the autochthones could respond effectively to the starfarers' technology.

The vessel roared with braking effort as it settled toward the knoll. Buinites turned their long-jawed faces upward to watch.

"*Adjutant to crew,*" Tadziki said. "*I won't—repeat, will not—open the ramp until I'm sure we're staying, so don't be in a hurry. Out.*"

Scattering rocks, ash, and brushwood, the *Swift* landed where Ned and Lissea had waited for their victims to come to them. The knoll wasn't big enough for the vessel's length: bow, stern, and even the tips of the landing skids overhung the outcrop.

Tadziki, at the backup console, set the visuals to magnify two autochthones carrying a headless corpse, and behind them, a third living Buinite with a smashed arm. The injury was the result of a mine blast, not a powergun's concentrated hellfire. The creatures stared at the *Swift*. Their eyes quivered as the vessel shuddered to stasis with the ground.

Moving with the unified precision of a flock of birds, the three living Buinites turned and loped off through the brush. The corpse lay where it fell. The wounded autochthone spurned the body with his clawed foot as he ran.

Tadziki pulled back on the image area. Buinites fled the *Swift*'s return on all sides. They ran *away* rather than toward anything: every figure in the sensors' quick panorama was vectored directly outward from the vessel, like chaff driven by a bomb's shockwave. The autochthones threw down whatever they'd been holding in the moments before they recognized the *Swift* as the same vessel that had landed an hour and a half before.

Those who were missing a leg hopped. Those who had lost both legs dragged themselves by hands and elbows. *Away.*

Westerbeke shut the engines off. Hissing gases and the ping of metal parts filled the *Swift* with their relative silence.

"*Master Tadziki,*" Lissea said, "*you may open the hatch. I believe the locals have decided to leave us alone from here on out.*"

Tadziki didn't hit the hatch switch instantly. "*Adjutant to crew,*" he ordered, using the PA system rather than radio. "*Starboard watch stays with the ship to clear and stow cargo. Toll, you're in charge. Out.*"

The ramp began to whine open. Lissea turned in the hatchway and called, "Don't stow the jeeps. We'll need them to check out the people from that other ship. Are we still getting calls from them?"

Westerbeke peered past the back of his couch. "Negative," he said. "Nothing since they reported they were leaving the wreck."

"Well, maybe they abandoned the commo gear for its weight," Lissea said. She hopped gracefully through the hatch ahead of the mercenaries.

They might well have pushed her if she'd delayed much longer. Nobody wanted to be trapped within the vessel's bay in its present condition.

Ned was the last of the port watch to disembark. The duty crew had already begun to clear the bay of damaged and temporarily stored equipment. One bunk was ruined. The sooner the stink of its melted bedding was removed from the closed atmosphere, the better for the *Swift*'s complement.

Lissea walked downslope to where the autochthones were gelded. Herne Lordling was beside her, ordering her to be more careful. Several other mercs accompanied them with fingers on their triggers. Ned fell in behind them.

Tadziki was still aboard, keeping watch on the surrounding terrain. It was difficult to see any distance in this flat, brush-speckled landscape, but the *Swift*'s sensor suite could identify individual Buinites up to a kilometer away. The party would meet no hidden threats.

Ned's eyes felt hot and gritty, and his skin prickled. He didn't remember these trees with yellow seedpods among their thorns, but the whorls of lighter soil indicated the jeeps' air cushions had swept the rocks here.

The leaders came to the nearest of the mutilated victims. He—

it—was alive and sitting up. The stone he'd been carrying when the scrambler anesthetized him lay at the creature's side, but there was no sign of intelligence in the dull eyes.

"Bloody hell, Lissea!" Lordling said with what was, for him, restraint. "Not a very neat piece of work, was it?"

"It did the job, Herne," Lissea replied in a brittle voice. "I said I would do what was necessary to make the autochthones leave us alone while we restocked and rested."

"It wouldn't have done any good to neuter them with a jolt of radiation, Lordling," Ned said. He'd heard other men speak in the tone he was using now, but he'd never imagined he would join their number. "We didn't dare be neat. They had to know instantly that they'd been emasculated, that any of them who fought *us* would either die or be emasculated."

"They don't mind dying," Lissea said. "That we knew. But they couldn't be sure."

She walked on. The mercs following her skirted the first victim gingerly, staring with sick fascination at the creature's bloody groin. The Buinite had no expression at all; nor did Ned as he brushed past.

The second Buinite was dead—not from the knife wound or from shock, but because the creature had begun to chew off its limbs when it awakened. Its powerful teeth had crushed through both arms at the elbow joint and were working on the right knee when blood loss accomplished the desired purpose.

"I think we've seen enough," Lissea said. She turned and started back toward the *Swift* without seeming to look at her companions. "Slade, take the jeeps and three men. See what you can learn about the castaways. Tadziki will download navigational data to your helmet."

"Yes ma'am." He'd take Raff, and the Warsons would drive. *Good men to have at your back in a tight place . . .*

Herne Lordling's lips pursed. He glanced at Ned, then sidelong back toward Lissea. "The locals may not have run far," he said. "There could be an ambush."

"I figured to carry the scrambler myself," Ned said before Lissea could speak. "And I'll replace the knife I lost. We'll be all right."

The look on Lordling's face as he stared at Ned was one of pure loathing. That was fair enough, because it only mirrored the way Ned felt about himself. But he would do what had to be done.

"Think your little toy's going to scare all the locals away from us, then?" Deke Warson asked as he guided the lead jeep expertly with his left hand alone. He held the butt of his 2-cm weapon against the crook of his right elbow instead of trusting it to the sling or the clamp beside his seat.

"No," Ned said. "It was for use in case the *Swift* herself didn't scare them out of our way. As she fortunately seems to have done."

Each jeep left behind it a plume of dust high enough to call autochthones from klicks distant if they wanted to come. Behind Ned, Toll kept the second vehicle slightly to port, the upwind side, instead of tracking his brother precisely.

"Via, boy," Deke said. "I swapped barrels on the old girl here"— the muzzle of his weapon nodded—"and I'm ready for a little action."

Some of the trees rose from ten or a dozen separate trunks, individually no more than wrist-thick, on a common root system. Often the lower branches appeared to have been browsed off so that the surviving foliage formed a bell like the cap of a mushroom. Ned knew nothing about local life-forms except for the Buinites themselves.

"Deke," he said, "you're welcome to all the kind of action Lissea and I had on the first touchdown. If the locals come round again, we'll be reinforcing that lesson the same way."

Ned's submachine gun was slung. The nerve scrambler filled his arms, and he was using the lower half of his visor as a remote display for the *Swift*'s sensors. He wanted all the warning he could get if there were autochthones in their neighborhood.

Warson chuckled. "It's not like they're human, boy," he said. "Even if they was, what happens to the other guy don't matter."

They passed a fresh cairn at the base of a thorn-spiked tree. The stones in this region of Buin oxidized to a purplish color when exposed to air for a time, but the undersides remained yellow-gray. The cairn melded the colors into a soft pattern like that of a rag rug.

"We're on the right track," Deke said, pointing.

"A local marker?" Ned asked. The drivers were navigating by means of a map projected onto their visors, a twenty-percent mask through which they could view the actual terrain. Under other circumstances, Ned would have checked the heading, but he had to concentrate on the autochthones—

And the chance of Deke Warson getting lost because he misread a chart wasn't worth worrying about.

"Naw, I figure there's some poor turd from the wreck smashed to jelly down there," Deke said. "The locals, they don't do a job halfway."

There was approval in his voice.

"Rescue party?" said a voice on Channel 12. That wasn't a push the expedition normally used, but the commo helmet scanned all available frequencies and cued the transmission. *"We see your dust. Are you a rescue party? We are the survivors of yacht* Blaze. *Ah, over?"*

Half a klick away, basalt in the form of hexagonal pillars cropped out ten to twenty meters high above the scrub. Broken columns lay jumbled below. Sunlight reflected from the pinnacle, a space of no more than a hundred square meters.

"Telarian vessel Swift *to survivors,"* Ned replied. *"Yes, we're a rescue party, but we're not going up there to meet you. Come on down. The locals have cleared out. Over."*

"How'd they get up there to begin with?" Deke said.

Ned cranked his visor to plus-six magnification. The angle wasn't very good. Three human figures waved furiously toward the jeeps.

"Looks like an aircar," he said. "Pull up here. If we get any closer to the rocks, we won't be able to see the people."

"Rescue party, are you sure the nonhumans are gone?" the voice asked. *"Our car has been damaged and we won't be able to get back to safety again."* A pause. *"Over."*

"We're here, aren't we?" Deke Warson interjected. *"Come on,*

buddy. If you don't want to spend the rest of your lives on a rock spike, you better come down and let us escort you to the ship. Fucking out."

He looked at Ned and grinned through the faint haze of topo map on his visor. "Somebody scared like that, don't screw around with them. Slap 'em up alongside the head if you're close enough, or anyway don't give them a choice."

The grin became broader. "Or we could just leave them," he added. "It's not like we've got a lot of extra room about the *Swift*."

"Blaze *to rescue party*," the voice said. *"We're coming down. Out."*

Ned cleared his visor to watch without magnification or a clutter of overlays. The figures got into the aircar. The vehicle lurched over the edge with only marginal control. The lower surfaces had been hammered by thrown rocks. One of the four nacelles—providing enough power for the car to fly rather than merely skim in ground effect—had been smashed out of its housing.

"Five to three they don't make it!" Toll called from the second jeep.

"You're on in Telarian thalers!" Deke called back.

The car did make it, though it rotated twice on its vertical axis before the driver brought it to a skidding halt in front of the jeeps. The occupants were male. One of them had his left arm bound to his chest by bandages torn from what had been the tunic of his white uniform. The survivors carried carbines, but they didn't look as though they were practiced gunmen.

The aircar's driver got out. Ned swung from the jeep to meet him. The stranger was young, with dark hair and a large, gangling frame. Instead of a uniform, he wore a robe that billowed freely when he moved but tailored itself to his body when he was at rest.

"I'm Carron Del Vore," he said, extending his hand to Ned. "I—we—we're very glad to see you. More glad than I can say."

He looked worn to the bone. Nobody had bothered to inform the castaways of Lissea's plan before the *Swift* lifted off again. They must have felt as though their guts were being dragged up to orbit on the same vapor trail.

"Edward Slade," Ned said. "Ned. I believe you sailed out of Pancahte?"

Carron smiled wryly. "Yes, we're from Pancahte," he said. "As a matter of fact, my father is Treasurer Lon Del Vore."

When he saw that the term and name meant nothing to Ned, he added, "That is, he's the ruler of the planet."

Buin's atmosphere was clear, so the stars gleamed from it like the lights of plankton feeding at night in one of Tethys' crystal atolls. In the background, the *Swift*'s drill sighed softly as it cut its way to a deep aquifer.

"Yes, certainly Lendell Doormann came to Pancahte," said Carron Del Vore. "I've seen him myself, when I was very young. Walking into Astragal, up the old road from Hammerhead Lake to talk to my grandfather."

The crew had spread a tarpaulin of monomolecular film from the *Swift* as shelter, though there seemed no threat of rain. The thin sheet hazed but did not hide the stars when Ned looked up through it.

They'd replaced the wire perimeter and directional mines as well. Buin wasn't a place to take chances.

"Maybe he's still alive," Carron said. "Though . . . it isn't clear that he was ever present *physically*."

The Pancahtan noble sat on the ramp. Lissea and Herne Lordling knelt before him, and the remainder of the *Swift*'s complement lounged on the ground further back to listen. The mercenaries were interested not only because this was a break from the boredom of Transit, but also because Carron was speaking about Pancahte, the expedition's goal.

One of the yacht's other survivors was present for the company. The third lay anesthetized on a bunk while the vessel's medical computer repaired injuries from the rock that had broken his arm and several ribs.

A stone had dished in the skull of the last of the common sailors who'd escaped with Carron in the aircar. As Deke surmised, his body was beneath the fresh cairn.

Ned squatted at the rear of the gathering, beyond the edge of the tarp. He felt alone, dissociated even from himself. Part of his soul refused to believe that he was the person who had gelded Buinite warriors and who was coldly prepared to repeat the process if the needs of the expedition required.

"Present on Pancahte?" Lissea asked.

Tadziki knelt down beside Ned in the clear darkness. Insects or the equivalent burred around the light, but none of the local forms seemed disposed to regard humans as a food source. "Good work today, Ned," the adjutant murmured.

"No, in the Treasurer's Palace, I mean," Carron explained. "Lendell Doormann seemed to walk normally, but his feet weren't always quite on the ground. A little above or below, especially when the footing was irregular. Nobody mentioned it, at least in my hearing. Perhaps my grandfather knew more; he and Lendell often talked privately. But my grandfather died twenty years ago, and Lendell appeared for the last time months before that."

"But the ship that Lendell arrived in," Lordling said, "is *that* still around? That's what we've come for."

"Thanks," Ned whispered to Tadziki. "I wish I felt better about it, though."

"When you start feeling good about that sort of duty," Tadziki said, "I won't want to know you. But it had to be done."

"Is it a ship?" Carron said. "We always called it 'the capsule.' It's a tiny little thing, scarcely more than a coffin. Yes, it's still there. Not that anyone really sees it, except through long lenses. You see, the area five kilometers around Hammerhead Lake in all directions is patrolled by tanks. Two of them. They don't let anyone any closer than that."

Several men spoke at once. Lissea touched the key on the side of her commo helmet and murmured something to Dewey, on duty at the console. An air-projection hologram bloomed above the Pancahtan's head. Details were less sharp than those of an image on a proper screen, but the display was big enough that everyone present could see it.

Carron looked up. "Yes, that's one of the tanks," he said. "They were on Pancahte before the settlers landed there five hundred years ago—that's standard years. There are other artifacts from that time, too. I was on my way to Affray to see whether there are any leavings from the . . . the earlier race there, or whether Pancahte is unique."

Tadziki leaned close to Ned and said, "He had quite a library with him. Lissea converted one of our readers to project the chips."

"He might better have grabbed another box of ammo when he ditched from the yacht," Ned whispered back.

As he spoke, however, he knew he was wrong. The Pancahtan castaways couldn't have survived more than a few hours had the *Swift* not rescued them. A few hundred rounds more or less wouldn't have made any difference. Carron was a scholar, and he had chosen to save his research materials rather than leaving them to be flattened beneath the hammering stone weapons of the autochthones.

"Looks man-made to me," Lordling said. "*How* old do you claim it is?"

"Older than the colony," Carron repeated. "More than five hundred standard years."

"Balls," said Lordling. "Pancahte was a first-dispersion colony, right after humans learned to use Transit space. Nobody sneaked in there first and left a couple tanks."

"Parallel evolution works with machines as well as with life-forms, Herne," Lissea said. "Until the laws of physics change, equipment that does the same job is likely to look pretty much the same."

"It's not just the tanks," Carron said without apparent anger. "There are structures on the near peninsula of Hammerhead Lake that are equally old."

Lissea handed him a control wand. Carron twitched it, displayed an index, and summoned an image that seemed to be from an orbital camera. Though the Telarian equipment was unfamiliar at least in detail, Carron used it with the skill of an expert.

The map first established scale by including a community of ten thousand or so residents at the bottom of the image. At the top of the frame was a sparkle of water more than a kilometer through the long axis. It was clearly artificial, consisting of two perfectly circular lobes joined by a narrow band of water.

"Below is Astragal," Carron said. "That's the capital of Pancahte. And this—"

The image focused on the body of water. Scores of other pools and lakes dotted the landscape, but none were so large or so regular in outline.

"—is Hammerhead Lake."

A pair of pentagonal structures stood on the lower peninsula. Fat spits of land almost joined to separate the lake into two round ponds. As the scale shrank, Ned used shadows to give the buildings a third dimension. They were low and had inner courtyards of the same five-sided shape. One building was slightly larger than the other, but even so it was only twenty meters or so across.

"What are those pentagons?" Lissea asked.

"Nobody knows," Carron replied. "Nobody can inspect them because of the tanks. They shoot at aircraft as well as ground vehicles. These images were made from orbit."

"I don't see why," Deke Warson said, "if these tanks are so much in your way, that nobody's done something about them. I might volunteer for the job myself, if we're going to be there on Pancahte awhile."

"They aren't particularly in the way, sir," Carron said. He continued to lower the scale of the display. One of the pentagonal buildings swelled and would soon fill the image area.

Deke's voice was thick with the sneering superiority of an expert speaking to someone who hadn't dealt with a problem the expert viewed as simple. Carron Del Vore responded with an aristocrat's clipped disdain for a member of the lower classes who was getting uppity. That was an aspect of the Pancahtan's character which Ned hadn't seen before.

Toll Warson grinned at his brother. It was hard to tell just what his expression meant.

"There," Carron said, pleasantly informative again. "In the center of the courtyard."

He played with the control wand for a moment. A red caret sprang into the center of the holographic image and blipped toward a round object. "This is the capsule which brought Lendell Doormann to Pancahte. It isn't really big enough for a ship, is it? And it certainly couldn't hold enough food and water for the fifty years he visited Astragal, but he never took anything while he was with us."

Men looked at one another. Nobody spoke for a time.

"I want to see that tank again," Deke said in a colorless voice.

"Yes, all right," Lissea said. "If you would, Master Del Vore?"

"Of course," he replied. "But I would prefer to be called Carron by one of your rank, mistress."

The display flipped back in three quick stages to a close-up of the tank. The vehicle was low-slung. It had a turret and a single slim weapon almost as long as the chassis. No antennas, sensors, or other excrescences beyond the weapon marred the smoothly curving lines.

There was no evident drive mechanism. The hull seemed to glide a few centimeters above the ground. Where the terrain was sandy, the vehicle left whorls on the surface as it passed, but the weight wasn't supported by an air cushion as were the supertanks on which Ned had trained.

"What kind of armor does that have?" somebody demanded. Ned's mouth was already open to ask the same question.

"We don't know," Carron said. "Neither projectile nor directed energy weapons have any effect on the tanks. I should rather say, no effect save to stir the tanks up. When they're attacked, they respond by destroying all artificial devices within their line of sight—rather than limiting themselves to their normal radius. That means among other things that they knock down all communications satellites serving the capital."

"What's its power source?" somebody asked. "Five hundred years is a lot of power."

Simultaneously, Lissea said, "Do you know how the gun operates? It's an energy weapon, I presume?"

"This was recorded a century ago, when a member of the

Treasurer's Guard decided to prove he was a better man than his rival for the same woman," Carron said. "We don't have satellite views, for obvious reasons."

The image had been recorded at night, from ground level. Buildings in the foreground suggested it had been taken from Astragal itself. There was a great deal of ground fog.

A ribbon of light wavered across the sky. It seemed smoky and insubstantial. "The discharge," Carron explained, "if that's what it was, didn't give off energy. What you're seeing is a reflection of external sources, stars and the lights of Astragal itself."

"Reflection in the *air?*" said Herne Lordling.

"No," Carron said. "The effect occurred in hard vacuum as well. At the far end of the beam, a communications satellite vanished into itself. That's as accurate as anyone was able to describe the result."

He surveyed the mercenaries, a sea of faces lit gray by scatter from the hologram display. "And no," he added, "we don't have any idea what the vehicles use as a power source. Only that it seems inexhaustible."

"We . . ." Lissea said. "Ah, as Herne said a moment ago—"

And had no business saying, but what was done, was done—

"We've come to retrieve the device by which my great-granduncle traveled to Pancahte. It wasn't his to take away the way he did. I've been sent to your planet by the proper owners in order to retrieve it."

"I don't see that that's possible," Carron said. "Because of the tanks, of course. But I don't really see my father approving a . . . ah, strangers coming to Pancahte and taking something."

"It's no bloody use to him, is it?" Deke Warson said.

"I'm afraid that Lon's attitude is if something is valuable to anyone, it's valuable to him," Carron said. "He's not a charitable man. Nor a kindly one."

Lissea cleared her throat. The streak of frozen destruction in the screen above her was a stark prop. "Perhaps," she said, "he'll be moved to a friendlier state of mind by the fact we've rescued his son and heir."

"What?" Carron said. "Oh, I'm not his heir. That's my brother

Ayven. Frankly, I doubt that even Ayven's life would affect my father's actions very much, and I don't know that Ayven would want it any other way. They're very much alike—hard-handed men both of them."

He touched the display control and projected instead a landscape of fog and bright, glowing streaks of lava. The view was twilit, though Ned realized after a moment that the point of light at zenith was the system's sun.

Much of the sky was filled with the great ruddy arc of a planet. Pancahte was the moon of a gas giant rather than a planet in solar orbit. The regular shapes in the middle distance were buildings, or at least man-made objects.

"Madame Captain, gentlemen . . ." Carron said. "Meeting you was a great day for a person of my interests. On Pancahte, there's very little interest in artifacts of the Old Race. Not among the general populace, and certainly not within my family."

"You'll help us with your father?" Lissea asked.

"Well," Carron said. "I'm sure I can show you the collection of Old Race artifacts in the Treasurer's Palace. The only collection on Pancahte, really. I doubt if anyone but me has viewed it in my lifetime. And a few kilometers from Astragal, there's a dwelling of some sort, a bunker, that I believe was built by the Old Race. I'll take you there. It isn't dangerous, the way the tanks are dangerous."

"What do you expect in exchange for helping us?" Herne Lordling demanded harshly.

"Herne," Lissea said.

"Besides expecting you to save my life again at some future date, you mean?" Carron said ironically. "All right, then."

He stood up. He gestured with the wand, flicking off the display so that it didn't detract attention from him.

"Note that all my life I've worked to understand the artifacts of the Old Race," Carron said, arms akimbo. He was a handsome man in his way, though in the company of these killers he looked like a plaster cherub. "Note, *sir,* that my present journey was to Affray, to see whether the Twin Worlds have Old Race vestiges also."

"Look, buddy," Herne Lordling said. "Don't use that tone with *me.*" He started to rise. Lissea gripped his biceps firmly and held him down.

"You asked the question, Lordling," said Deke Warson. "Hear him out."

"Note," Carron continued in a ringing voice, "that if you are able to avoid or deactivate the Old Race tanks I will gain information about them that no one in five centuries has had. So it's purely out of self-interest that I'm willing to help you, sir. You can rest easy on that score."

The Warson brothers started the laughter, but much of the company immediately joined in.

"On the other hand," Carron said, lapsing into what seemed to be his normal manner, that of a subordinate briefing superiors, "I can't offer you much hope of being allowed to remove the capsule or even being allowed to try. My father simply wouldn't permit that. He's quite capable of killing me out of hand if he feels I'm pressing him excessively."

Lissea stood up. "I'll want to discuss the situation on Pancahte with you in detail," she said. "We'll use the navigational consoles and their displays."

"Of course, Lissea," Carron said.

"I'll come too," said Herne Lordling. "This is military planning."

"I trust not," Lissea said, though there was little enough trust in her voice.

She stepped into the vessel's bay, between Carron and Lordling. Mercenaries stood up, brushing their elbows and trousers and stretching.

"I'd best get in there also," Tadziki said without enthusiasm. He looked at Ned and added, "It doesn't appear that we're much closer to Lissea achieving her goal than we were on Telaria."

Ned shrugged. "If I'd known what we were really getting into," he said, "I wouldn't have bet there was a snowball's chance in hell that we'd get as far as we have already."

"If you'd known," Tadziki said. "Understood, that is. Would you have still come on the expedition?"

Ned laughed. "I suppose so," he said. He looked at himself in the mirror of his mind.

"The person I am *now* would have come anyway," he said.

Tadziki walked up the ramp to join Lissea in the nose of the vessel. Ned watched him, thinking about changes that had occurred since he'd signed aboard on Telaria. He wondered what his kin would think of him at home on Tethys.

And he wondered if he'd live long enough to get there.

PANCAHTE

Pancahte was as grim a world as Ned had ever seen. The primary's bloody light filled the sky, and the atmosphere was thick with mist and the reeking effluvia of volcanoes. For all that, the temperature was in the middle of the range Ned found comfortable, and the *Swift*'s sensors said that it wasn't actively dangerous to breathe the air.

The sailor with the broken arm waited until the boarding ramp clunked solidly into the crushed stone surface of the spaceport. He took two steps forward, then ran the rest of the way and threw himself on the ground mumbling prayers.

The other Pancahtan sailor moved with the same initial hesitation. A squad of guards wearing powered body armor began to approach the *Swift*. A woman holding an infant pressed past them. She and the sailor embraced fiercely. Other civilians,·mostly women, scuttled around the guards also. They stopped in frozen dismay when they realized that no more of the yacht's crewmen were disembarking from the rescue vessel.

"We radioed from orbit," Ned muttered. "Why did they have to come? They knew there wasn't going to be anything for them."

"It's no skin off our backs," Deke Warson answered, curious at the younger man's concern.

"I'd rather lose some skin," Ned said, "than be reminded about Buin."

Deke laughed.

The spaceport was designed like a pie. Blast walls divided a circle into sixty wedges, only half of which were in immediate use. The administrative buildings were in the center. Rows of rectangular structures to the south of the circular landing area contained the shops and warehouses.

The guards walked toward the *Swift* from the terminal. Their suits were bright with plating and inlays, though Ned presumed the equipment was functional also. The men's only weaponry was that which was integral with their armor.

The powered suits struck Ned as a clumsy sort of arrangement—overly complicated and hard to adapt to unexpected conditions. The armor might stop a single 2-cm bolt, but it was unlikely to protect against two—or against a well-aimed burst from Ned's submachine gun. Still, like anything else in life, proper equipment was mostly a matter of what you'd gotten used to.

Lissea stood beside Carron Del Vore in the center of the hatchway. Tadziki and Herne Lordling flanked them. The rest of the *Swift*'s complement waited behind the leaders, wearing their best uniforms and carrying only minimal armament.

The gold-helmeted leader of the guards stopped before Carron, raised his faceshield, and said, "Prince Carron, your father welcomes you on your return to Pancahte. We have transportation to the palace for you."

Carron nodded. "Very good," he said. "I'll be taking Captain Doormann, my rescuer, with me to the palace. She has business with the Treasurer."

The guard's body was hidden beneath the powered armor, but his face gave its equivalent of a shrug. "Sorry sir," the man said. "We don't have any orders about that."

Carron's jaw set fiercely. "You've got orders now," he said. "You've got my orders."

"The car won't handle the weight," another guard volunteered to his chief. Ned couldn't be sure if Pancahtan etiquette was always so loose, or whether Carron's father and brother were so public in treating him as the family idiot that the guards too had picked up the habit. "We'll have to leave Herget behind to get off the ground, like enough."

"Then two of you will stay behind!" Carron snapped. "Do you think I'm in danger of attack on my way to the palace? You—" he pointed to the man who had just spoken "—and *you*—" to the guard beside him with green-anodized diamonds decorating his suit "—stay behind! Walk back!"

The guards were obviously startled by Carron's anger—or his willingness to express it. How much did Lissea's presence have to do with what was apparently a change? "Well, I suppose . . ." the leader said.

"Captain," Carron said, offering Lissea his arm.

Lissea laid her hand in the crook of Carron's arm, but she turned to her men instead of stepping off with the Pancahtan.

"Their armor empty weighs as much as a grown man," she said. "If two of them stay behind, four of us can ride. Tadziki, Slade— come along with me. Herne, you're in charge of the ship till I get back. Break out the jeeps, and I'll see about arranging to replenish our stores."

"Yes, of course," Carron agreed. "You should be accompanied by your chiefs. Your rank requires it."

"Hey Slade-chiefy," Deke said in a loud whisper as Ned stepped through the front rank of men, "see if your chiefness can score us something better than water to drink, hey?"

"This isn't my idea!" Ned snapped back. Except for the stares of his fellows—Herne Lordling's eyes could have drilled holes in rock—he was both pleased and proud to be chosen.

The guards fell in to either side of the contingent from the *Swift*. The powered armor moved with heavy deliberation as though the men were golems. The suits' right wrists were thickened by what Ned surmised was the magazine for the coil gun firing along the back of the palm. A laser tube on the left hand was connected to the power supply which bulged the buttocks of the suit.

"It's through there, in the admin parking area," the leader muttered, pointing. He frowned as he studied Carron, both irritated and concerned by the young prince's assertiveness. "The car, I mean."

Twenty-odd civilians watched Carron go past. Some of them

were crying. A young boy tugged on a woman's waistband and repeated, "Where's daddy? Where's *daddy?*"

Ned avoided eye contact with them, the widows, orphans, and bereaved parents. He'd never seen the *Blaze,* so he had no idea how many crewman the yacht had carried. More than would ever come home, certainly.

The knife grated on bone as he cut too deeply into the Buinite's crotch. He twisted the blade—

Tadziki gripped Ned's hand. "What's wrong?" the adjutant demanded. "Why are you smiling like that?"

"Sorry," Ned muttered. He didn't want to think that way. There were things you had to do—but if you started to justify them, you were lost to anything Ned wanted to recognize as humanity.

The port buildings were of stone construction rather than the concrete or synthetics Ned would have expected. The blocks were ashlars, square-cornered, but the outer faces had been left rough and the courses were of varied heights.

The finish and functioning of Pancahtan powered armor, and the ships docked at neighboring landings, looked to be of excellent quality, so the rusticated architecture was a matter of taste rather than ability. Ned found the juxtaposition of high technology and studied clumsiness to be unpleasant; but again, style was what you were accustomed to.

A few spectators watched from behind the rails of upper-level walkways or through the gap at the inner end of the blast walls while they took breaks. Maintenance and service trucks howled across the spaceport on normal errands. All the vehicles were hovercraft, even a heavy crane that Ned would have expected to be mounted on treads.

Ned tapped the armored shoulder of the nearest guard. The man looked at him in surprise and almost missed a step. Servo lag in the suit's driving "muscles" meant that you had to take care when changing speed or direction. The armor's massive inertia could spill you along the ground like an unguided projectile in the original direction of movement.

"Do you have wheeled vehicles?" Ned asked. "All I see are air cushions."

"Huh?" said the guard.

Carron looked back at Ned. "There's too much vulcanism and earthquakes for roads," he said. "Induced by the primary, of course."

He nodded upward toward the ruddy hugeness of the gas giant which Pancahte orbited.

"The buildings are on skids," Carron added, "with integral fusion bottles for power. Other structures—"

He gestured toward the blast walls. Ned now noticed that the repaired stretches, differing slightly in the color and surface treatment of the concrete, were more extensive than the normal frequency of landing accidents would account for.

"It's simpler to rebuild when they're knocked down."

It was easy to spot the vehicle they were headed for in the parking area. All but a handful of the forty-odd cars and light vans were hovercraft. The exceptions were a few aircars, whose lift-to-weight ratio permitted them to fly rather than merely to float on a cushion of air trapped beneath them by their skirts. Most of the latter were delicate vehicles like the one Carron had carried on his yacht.

The only exception was truck-sized and armored. The roof and sides were folded back, displaying spartan accommodations and surprisingly little carrying capacity. Most of the bulk was given over to the drive fans and the fusion power-plant that fed them.

Lissea stopped and looked at the sky, arms akimbo. "Does it ever get brighter than this?" she asked. "I mean, is this daylight?"

"Well, yes," Carron said. "It's daylight, I mean."

He looked upward also. Somewhere in the port a starship was testing its engines. A plume of steam rising from geysers at the edge of the port drifted across the parking lot, almost hiding the members of the party from one another.

Carron's voice continued, "It's really—well, it's bright enough to see by easily. The primary provides quite a lot of energy, particularly in the infrared range, so we're always comfortable on Pancahte."

"I'd think people would go mad in these conditions," Lissea said. "Even after, what, twenty, twenty-five generations?"

Carron cleared his throat. The band of steam drifted on, dispersing slowly in the red-lit air. "Well, there are social problems, I'll admit, at full primary," he said. "Suicide, domestic violence . . . Sometimes more serious outbreaks. We tend to live in communities on Pancahte rather than in isolated houses, even though most dwellings are self-sufficient."

His face was set firmly again. He crooked his finger in a peremptory fashion to Lissea and resumed walking toward the vehicle to catch up with the guards who waited two paces ahead. "Sometimes we visit, well, brighter worlds. But very few Pancahtans leave permanently. It—the world—it's our home."

Ned looked up at the primary also. The planet's mottled red appearance was no more than a mixture of methane and scores of other gases, not a promise of blood and flame. . . .

But all the male civilians he'd seen on Pancahte, workmen and lounging spectators alike, went armed. Even Carron wore a pistol, a jeweled projectile weapon scarcely larger than a needle stunner.

The knives and guns were simply parts of their dress, like the vivid neckerchiefs they affected. The choice of weapons as fashion accessories said even more about Pancahtan society than Carron's halting defense of it had done.

The guards had a quick argument among themselves at the aircar. Two of the men stepped aside.

Carron pointed to a different pair. "I said that *you* two would walk!" he said. "If you forget my orders once more, you needn't bother returning to the palace at all because you won't have a post there."

The guards glanced at one another in rekindled surprise. "Yessir," mumbled the two Carron had indicated, who weren't the ones culled on the basis of seniority. The man wearing the diamond-pattern decorations even bowed before he backed out of the way.

Lissea looked at Carron. With only an eye-blink's delay to suggest that she'd hesitated, she said, "Will you hand me in, then, Carron?"

"Milady," Carron said with nervous smile. He bowed low and offered Lissea the support she claimed as right rather than need. The primary's light accentuated his flush.

Lissea stepped lithely into the big aircar, her fingertips barely resting on Carron's. The open cabin contained six oversized bucket seats arranged in pairs. The backs of the forward four were fitted with jump seats. Lissea sat on the edge of a bucket seat and patted the expanse of padding beside her. "Room enough for two, Carron," she said archly.

Tadziki took the other bucket seat of the center pair. His lips were pursed. Ned avoided meeting the adjutant's eyes as he got into the vehicle, and he particularly avoided looking at Lissea and Carron. Squatting in the gap between the two forward seats, he looked out over the raised windscreen.

It wasn't that he didn't know what was going on. It was just that he didn't much like it.

Guards got in. The weight of their armor rocked the aircar on its stubby oleo suspension struts. The remaining pair trudged toward a terminal building, to cadge a ride or call for another vehicle.

The Treasurer's Palace was ten klicks away, on the north side of Astragal. Walking that far in powered suits would bruise the wearers as badly as a kick-boxing tournament. Ned wasn't sure the suits' powerpacks would handle the drain, though that depended on how good Pancahtan technology was. From what he'd seen, it was pretty respectable.

"Now, the bunker—I call it a bunker, but you'll be able to judge for yourself—is only two kilometers from the port, due east," Carron said, answering a question of Lissea's about Old Race sites. It wasn't what most people would call a romantic discussion, but it was the subject nearest to the Pancahtan prince's heart.

Carron didn't have much power in his own family. That would have been obvious even if he hadn't said as much himself. If Carron was the only help the expedition had on the planet, the *moon,* then they might as well have stayed home.

The car lifted, wobbled queasily as the automatic control system found balance, and flew out of the lot. The vehicle accelerated slowly because of its load.

The guards locked their faceshields down. They were probably talking by radio. Ned's commo helmet could access the conversation—signals intelligence was a skill the Academy taught with almost as much emphasis as marksmanship. He didn't care, though. Right now he didn't care about anything that he had any business thinking about

Tadziki tapped Ned's elbow and pointed down at the port. The car had risen to fifty meters, giving the occupants a good view of the other vessels present. There were a dozen or more large freighters and double that number of smaller vessels, lighters and yachts presumably similar to the one in which Carron had been wrecked on Buin.

Tadziki indicated the three obvious warships, each of five to seven hundred tonnes. They were streamlined for operations within atmospheres; one, slightly the largest, had bulges which held retractable wings for better control. Shuttered turrets for the energy weapons and missile launchers were faired into the hull.

The ships would be formidable opponents for vessels of their own class. The *Swift* was designed for exploration, not war. Any one of the Pancahtan ships could eat it for breakfast.

The car flew over the city of Astragal. Buildings were low and relatively small, though grouped structures formed some sizable factory complexes.

Lines of trees bordered and frequently divided broad roadways. The grounds in which structures stood were generally landscaped as well. Pancahtan foliage was dark, ranging from deep magenta to black.

The buildings were skewed in respect to one another and to the streets. The straight lines of one house were never quite parallel to those of its neighbors. It was that slight wrongness, rather than the occasional major break where a road axis leaped three meters along a diagonal, which most impressed the lower levels of Ned's consciousness. He found Astragal profoundly depressing, even without the fog drifting across the landscape and the yellow-red glow of lava in the near distance.

Lissea and Carron talked loudly on the seat behind him. That didn't help his mood. He couldn't make out words over the windrush.

They were nearing the largest single building Ned had seen on

Pancahte, though the suggestion of unity was deceptive on closer look. The structure was really four separate buildings arranged as the corners of a rectangle. The curtain walls connecting the blocks showed signs of frequent repair. The inner courtyard was a formal garden in which numerous people paced or waited near doorways.

The aircar's driver adjusted his fans to nearly vertical and let air resistance brake the vehicle. He angled toward a landing area of crushed rock beside one of the corner buildings, rather than toward the larger lot serving the gated entrance in a wall.

Ned noticed a double-row missile launcher tracking the vehicle from the top of the structure. When the aircar dipped below the cornice and out of the missiles' swept area, it was still in the sights of two guards at the entrance.

The guards' weapons were unfamiliar to Ned. They seemed to be single-shot powerguns with an enormous bore, 10-cm or so. Perhaps the mass of the powered armor permitted the guards to handle weapons whose recoil would ordinarily have required vehicular mounting.

Carron claimed Pancahte had a unitary government which dated back to the colony's foundation, but this certainly wasn't a peaceful world. Well, that needn't matter to Ned. He wasn't going to stay here any length of time, at least if he survived.

The driver shut off the fans, stood up, and shouted, "Prince Carron Del Vore and companions!" toward the entrance guards, using a loudspeaker built into his powered suit.

The guards didn't respond. More particularly, they didn't lower the fat energy weapons, one of which was pointed squarely at Ned's chest. The mirror-surfaced door opened in response to an unseen controller.

"Captain Doormann," Carron said formally as he extended his hand to Lissea. "Permit me to lead you into the presence of my father, the Treasurer."

Ned and Tadziki pressed back so that the two leaders could step between them and out of the aircar. The adjutant looked up at the walls: concrete cast with engaged columns between pairs of round-topped windows. "Looks sturdy enough," he said.

"It's old," Ned said. "When they built the spaceport buildings, they used stone. This place dates from before they had much time for frills."

They hopped down to follow Lissea and Carron inside. The aircar took off again behind them. The entrance guards had put up their weapons. They now looked like grotesque statues, men modeled from clay by a child.

The interior of the building was a single large room with a seven-meter ceiling and walls covered with vast murals. There were hundreds of people present: guards, clerks, officials, and petitioners. Everyone but the guards in powered armor seemed to be talking simultaneously, creating bedlam.

The twelve floor-to-ceiling pillars weren't structural—the coffered concrete vault was self-supporting. Rather, the columns were giant light fixtures, and their white radiance lifted Ned's spirits the instant he entered the room.

The throne room, near enough. The burly man sitting on a dais opposite the door must be Lon Del Vore. He was framed by the double line of columns. Guards stood before the dais with the integral weapons in their forearms pointing outward.

The guards weren't really protection. Every civilian present, including the visitors, wore a holstered pistol. A good gunman could draw and fire before the armored men could react. Ned knew that as a pistolero he was at the low end of the *Swift*'s complement, but he was confident he could assassinate the Treasurer if it came down to cases. Lon's willingness to expose himself in this fashion was a comment on his physical courage.

Three men were on the dais with Lon, standing rather than seated. Two of them were old. They dressed in bunchy dark fabrics and used small electronic desks that looked like pedestals.

The third man was small, blond-haired, and about thirty standard years of age. By looking carefully Ned could see that the blond man, Lon, and Carron all had similar features, though their body types could not have been more varied. *Ayven Del Vore, the Treasurer's heir—and from the look of him, a very hard man despite his slight build.*

Lon's chair was ornate and decorated with hunting scenes in blue enamel, but there was a keypad built into one arm and a hologram projector in the other. As one of the older men spoke earnestly, the air in front of the Treasurer quivered with images which couldn't be viewed from the rear of the coincidence pattern. The holograms distorted his face with shifting colored veils.

At Lon's feet lay a carnivore of a type depicted frequently in the room's murals. It was four-legged and rangy, so that it would weigh less than a man of similar torso length. The claws on the forepaws were fifty to eighty centimeters long. Too big to retract, the claws pivoted up so that they curved against the ankle joint with their needle points forward.

The beast had a hooked beak, though its body was covered with brown fur worn down to calloused skin over the joints. When Ned first noticed the creature, it was lying on its back to scratch itself under the chin with a dewclaw that could have disemboweled an ox. Though one of the guards stood with his laser focused on the beast at all times, the Treasurer's choice of a pet also indicated his contempt for personal danger.

An usher whose blue robe fluoresced in vertical lines stepped close to Carron. They exchanged details in tones lost in the surrounding babble.

The official turned and strode down the aisle with his arms akimbo, shouting "Make way!" as he advanced. His chest and elbows thrust people aside to create a zone in which Carron with Lissea, then Ned and Tadziki behind them, could walk without themselves bulling through the crowd.

Ayven glanced at his brother without interest, but his eyes lingered on the *Swift*'s three personnel. Ayven wore a big-bore powergun in a shoulder holster. The rig was out of the way during normal activities but was almost as accessible as a hip carry should need arise.

Carron's brother was the first Pancahtan Ned had seen who looked as though he might have earned a place on the *Swift*. From the way Ayven watched Ned and Tadziki, Ned suspected Ayven was making a similar assessment of the visitors.

"Prince Carron Del Vore and companions!" the usher bawled, his face centimeters short of the guards at the foot of the dais.

Lon shut off the holographic screen which had blurred his face till that moment. He was balding and heavier than he probably wished to be, but he remained a powerful man with features that could have been chipped from stone.

"You're back soon, aren't you?" he said. He spoke over the ambient noise without giving the impression he was shouting the way the usher had done. "Thought better of that nonsense, have you?"

"We landed on Buin, Father, because the auxiliary power unit was overheating," Carron said. His voice sounded brittle in contrast to that of the Treasurer. "By great good fortune, Captain Doormann of Telaria and her vessel arrived on Buin at the same time. She and her crew were able to rescue me and the survivors of my yacht from the natives, who would otherwise have infallibly slain us all."

"Lost the ship, did you, brother?" Ayven said. He didn't sneer, exactly. Rather, he displayed the sort of amused contempt a man might for the mess a puppy had made in someone else's house. "Well, I suppose you could have gotten into worse trouble if you'd been fooling around here. I've always been afraid you were going to manage to destroy the satellite ring with your nonsense."

"Go on, boy, introduce your friends," Lon said. "I'm going to be up half the night with this curst redevelopment scheme for the Foundation District as it is, so I don't have a lot of time to waste."

"Sir," Carron said with spots of color on his cheekbones, "permit me to introduce Mistress Lissea Doormann, captain of the vessel *Swift* out of Telaria. These are two of her officers, Masters Tadziki and Slade."

"Where's Telaria?" Ayven asked sharply.

Lissea stepped forward. She didn't shove Carron aside, but her hand on his shoulder urged him to leave her in charge. "Telaria is a world well outside the Pocket, sir," she said.

"Impossible!" Lon said. "The Twin Worlders don't let any ships through the Sole Solution. Unless—*Telaria*, you said?"

"The Twin Worlders don't command the Sole Solution anymore, sir," Lissea said. "But if you think you recognize the name, you probably do. Lendell Doormann was my great-granduncle, and it's to retrieve the capsule that he stole from Telaria that I've come here."

"You *fought* your way through the Sole Solution?" Ayven said in wonder.

Other conversations hushed throughout the hall, though the shuffle and rustling of bodies continued to create background noise like that of distant surf. The carnivore on the dais stared at Lissea. Its eyes had horizontally slitted pupils and golden irises.

"The Twin Worlds will not be interdicting the Sole Solution in the future," Lissea said. "There was no fighting involved. We've come to Pancahte in peace, and with the intention of bringing your world and mine into closer relations."

Ayven knelt beside the chair and used the keypad. A miniature image trembled before him, unreadable to the visitors.

"Don't talk nonsense," Lon said with a quick wave of his hand. "Telaria's half a galaxy away. What I want to know is how you got past the Dreadnought."

Telling him wouldn't do Lissea's cause any good. If the Treasurer learned the expedition had been willing to use biological warfare against whole planets, he was very likely to forestall a similar attack with a quick massacre.

"The Twin Worlds ended the blockade by their own decision," Lissea lied. "The Dreadnought wasn't on station when the *Swift* reached the Sole Solution."

We wouldn't land Nodals on a world as dark as Pancahte. They wouldn't ripen here.

"So you're diplomats, are you?" Ayven said as he stood again. The image he'd summoned from Pancahte's data net sprang to large size and rotated toward the audience. It was a view, possibly real-time, of the *Swift* with members of her complement amusing themselves around her in the landing area:

Yazov threw gravel up in the air, several bits at a time. Josie Paetz blasted the pebbles with his pistols, trading weapons between his right and left hand after every shot like a juggler. Other men watched, cheered, and occasionally fired shoulder weapons.

The Warsons squatted in the shelter of the hull with a box between them for a table. They were playing cards and occasionally swigging directly from a carafe. The ship's liquor supply was supposedly locked up in the absence of the captain and adjutant, but Ned had already seen what the brothers could do to electronic security.

Even so, it would have been a placid enough tableau, except that Deke and Toll between them carried enough hardware to arm a squad. Ned knew the Warsons well enough by now to read the seemingly aimless glances they gave their surroundings. They were hoping somebody would view their feigned nonchalance as an opportunity to attack.

Herne Lordling stepped to the middle of the hatchway. He yelled at the shooters. The projected display didn't include an audio track. Josie fired one more round and turned insolently. The breeches of his pistols were locked back, empty. A gray mist of matrix residue streamed from them as air cooled the bores.

Herne turned toward the recording instrument and shouted again. He outstretched his left arm, pointing with the index and middle fingers together. His right hand hovered over the grip of his holstered pistol—

The image quickly jumped away, then ended.

"Diplomats?" Ayven repeated. He laughed.

Ned made a decision because he'd noticed that besides Lissea, there were only two women in the big room. He didn't have time to discuss the matter with his captain.

"Sir, if we were only diplomats," he said as he stepped forward, "we wouldn't have survived to rescue your son."

The analytical part of his mind noted approvingly that his voice rang across the hall like the note of a bar of good steel.

"I'm Slade, nephew of the Slade of Tethys." The nouns wouldn't mean anything here, but the statement's form would. "The other members of Mistress Doormann's company are of similar rank on their own worlds. We come to you in peace, aiding a worthy lady to redress the wrong done by a kinsman of hers."

Ned was glad that he couldn't see Lissea's face as he spoke, but they both knew by now that the way forward needn't be a pleasant one. Twenty gunmen couldn't gain Lissea's ends by main force, so they had to adapt themselves to circumstances.

Lon Del Vore straightened in his chair; Ayven's stance became a challenge. For all that, the two men relaxed somewhat, because *this* was a situation they understood.

"I'd say that after seventy years," Lon said, "that this capsule you claim is forfeit to the state of Pancahte for nonpayment of personal property taxes."

His face broke into a smile like a landslip. "But if you choose to contest ownership, you can apply for appointment of three assessors under our laws. With right of appeal to the Treasurer."

"We're of course willing to pay for your help," Tadziki offered quickly. "In currency, if you will, or in our labor. The matter is a moral obligation for our mistress, you see."

Ned risked a glance back at Lissea. She stood with her lips composed, her hands folded demurely before her, and hellfire glaring from her dark eyes.

"There's no more possibility of bank transfers between our planets than there is of trade," Lon said irritably. "And as for labor— the men of Pancahte can arrange their own disputes without need of diplomats of your sort."

"It's moot anyway," said Ayven. Behind the mocking smile, his mind had given the question serious consideration. "The capsule is on Hammerhead Lake. Nobody can get close to it without being fried."

"Father!" Carron said. Ned started. He'd forgotten that Carron still stood just behind him. "Seventy years ago, a Doormann reached Hammerhead Lake despite the tanks. Perhaps now another member of the family can do the same and teach us how to do so. That would be of enormous value."

"Value to boys who don't have anything better to do than play with old junk, maybe," Ayven snapped. "No value to Pancahte, that we should turn over property on the say-so of a woman who claims a relative of hers stole it."

The carnivore became restive. It got to its feet, turned toward

Lon, and made a mewling sound. Lon rubbed the beast's throat with the toe of his boot, calming it again.

"You offer labor," he said, speaking toward Tadziki. "Well and good. I'll make you a proposition. The tanks—I suppose my son has told you about them?"

"Yes I have," Carron said crisply.

"The tanks kill a certain amount of livestock and a few careless people every year," Lon continued. "They're an irritation. If you can destroy them, then I'll let you have the capsule you claim."

"Or you can leave Pancahte immediately," Ayven said, "with as much help from me and the Treasurer's Guard as it takes to shift you."

"Yes, I accept," Lissea said. "I'll need a few days to prepare for the operation, however."

"Three days, then," Lon said. Ned stepped sideways to remove himself from the discussion. "But if you think you're going to look the tanks over from close up—well, their weapons don't leave enough to require burial, so it's no concern of mine."

"I'll order supplies to be sent to the *Swift* to replenish her stores," Carron said.

"*Will* you, brother?" said Ayven.

"They rescued me and my men at considerable personal risk," Carron said with a cold power that his voice hadn't held before in this audience hall. "They fed us during the journey. I don't believe the state of Pancahte is so poor that we can't show such persons hospitality."

Lon grimaced. He pointed to one of the old men on the dais. "Make it so," he said.

Returning his gaze to Lissea, he went on. "Three days. Or you leave Pancahte and return at your peril."

Lissea nodded with cold contempt and turned on her heel.

Carron started to go out with her. "Not you, son," Lon said. "You've trespassed long enough on our visitors' hospitality. From now on you'll leave them strictly alone."

Carron blinked like a burglar caught in the act.

Tadziki tapped Ned's wrist, then nodded toward the official

on the dais. "I'll stay back a time," he whispered. "Take care of Lissea."

Everyone in the room watched Ned trotting to catch Lissea before she left the room. He supposed it was his imagination that he could actually feel the carnivore's eyes on him.

The view of the audience with Lon Del Vore and Ayven was an amalgam of the recordings Lissea's helmet and Ned's had made. As a result, the hologram played back by the *Swift*'s equipment differed subtly from Ned's memory. That disturbed him, as did watching himself on a tightrope between the Pancahtans and Lissea—without the adrenaline rush that had carried him through the event itself.

"Those *bastards*," Herne Lordling said, facing the projection from the bottom of the ramp. The *Swift*'s entire complement, save Tadziki—who was still in town—and the man on instrument watch, sat or squatted before the hatchway to watch.

The image of the door swelled on the display until the hologram dissolved. The crew had rigged translucent tarpaulins between the ship and the blast walls as protection against both the elements and Pancahtan eyes. The filmy sheets were sullen with the primary's shadowless light.

"It's their planet," Lissea said. "They've agreed to let us proceed, which is as much as we could ask for."

Her voice was emotionless. She was so angry that she'd shut down to keep from exploding, but Ned wasn't sure Lordling realized that.

Herne stared at Lissea. "But their *attitude*, woman!" he said. "They're sneering at us! These hicks are sneering at *us.*"

"I'm not unfamiliar with the experience of being patronized by my inferiors, Herne," Lissea said coolly. "Let's get on to the problem at hand."

A ship lifted from across the circular port. There was a quick shock as the engines came up to full power, then a sustained roar which faded slowly as the vessel rose into the thinner layers of the atmosphere. The ship was a big freighter. Pancahte had an extensive trade network among the worlds of the Pocket.

"They don't believe we can really evade—overcome, whatever—the tanks," Ned said while the rumbling continued. "If we accomplish that, we may still have difficulty getting the Treasurer to honor his agreement. He wasn't just joking when he let us know that he personally is the highest law on the . . . the world."

"What somebody ought to do is to give that Treasurer a third eye-socket," Lordling said. "And that somebody just might be me."

"And what would that gain us, Herne?" Lissea snapped.

"It'd gain us the bastard being dead!" Lordling said. "Look, Lissea, you can't let pissants think they can push you around. It's—well, you'll have to take my word for it."

"No, I won't have to do that, *Master* Lordling," Lissea said. "Because *I'm* in charge." She pointed toward the hatchway. "Go relieve Harlow on the console. Now!"

Lordling looked amazed. He didn't move. Ned leaned forward, his eyes on Lissea. He reached across her and put fingertips on Lordling's knee.

She grimaced. "No, cancel that order," she said. "But Herne, stop acting like an idiot."

"The capsule's not so big that we'll have trouble handling it," Toll Warson said. "I can borrow a van easy enough to hold it. What we ought to do is make a quick snatch and run before Del Vore has second thoughts."

"Steal one of the trucks right out there?" Petit asked, nodding in the direction of the terminal parking area.

"No, no," Toll said. "Via, off a street. We just went through the lot to check out door and power locks. It won't be a problem."

"What about the tanks?" Ned asked.

"Some people like to think tanks can stand up to anything an infantryman can dish out," Deke Warson said, loud enough to focus attention on him. He was at the back of the audience, where Ned couldn't have seen him without standing up. "The tanks *I've* run into, that's not the way it is. I'm willing to bet these are no different."

"Worst case," Toll said, "we take out the running gear and then keep clear of the guns. Our Carron may be a very bright lad, but he's sure no soldier."

Toll met Ned's eyes with a degree of amusement, though without malice. By this point he respected Ned, but he still felt there was a lot the boy had to learn.

Which was true. But the Old Race tanks, which glided above the ground without any visible running gear, were as new to the Warsons as they were to Ned. And the Warsons couldn't accept that. . . .

"*Captain, there's a truck seems to be heading for us,*" Harlow warned. "*They come from town and turned through the terminal. Over.*"

Everybody moved, fast but smoothly. Deke Warson twitched aside an edge of the tarp to look around it. His 2-cm weapon was muzzle-up in his hand, though hidden to the oncoming vehicle.

Josie Paetz climbed the three-meter blast wall with a short run and a boot-sole partway up to boost his head over the lip, pushing the top sheet out of the way. He clung there one-handed. Unlike Deke, he didn't have the least hesitation about presenting the pistol in his right hand.

"It's Tadziki," Deke reported in a tone of disappointment.

"*Adjutant to* Swift!" Tadziki rasped over the general push. "*Blood and martyrs, you curst fools! Don't be pointing guns at me unless you want to eat them! Out!*"

Paetz dropped down from his perch. "Talks big for an old guy," he muttered.

Yazov cuffed him. Paetz grunted and turned his back on his uncle.

The vehicle was a hovercraft with an open box rated for a tonne of cargo. The fans would lift all the men you could cram onto the vehicle, but if there were more than a dozen they would have to be good friends. A similar truck had carried Lissea and Ned back from the palace. Tadziki had relayed their request for transport to the Pancahtan official with whom he was discussing the expedition's supply requirements.

The adjutant was driving this one. No one else was in the vehicle. Mercenaries held the side tarps out of the way, but the overhead sheets bellied down dangerously in the suction before

Tadziki pulled up beside the *Swift* and shut the fans down. He got out, looking worn and angry.

"I held a meeting to discuss what our next move ought to be," Lissea said by way of greeting.

"Did you come up with any good ideas?" Tadziki asked. It disturbed Ned to hear the adjutant's tone, though sneering irony was common enough among other members of the expedition.

"Take out the tanks and take off with the goods before the authorities know what's happened," Toll Warson said, agreeably enough. You had to look carefully in the odd light to note the slight frown indicating that he, too, was concerned by Tadziki's uncharacteristic display of irritation.

Lissea touched Tadziki's hand. "No, we didn't," she said. "Should you and I go inside and discuss privately what you've learned at the palace?"

Tadziki looked at her. "Bloody hell," he said. "I'm sorry. Yeah, maybe we ought to talk, just you and me."

He rapped the side of the truck. "We've got this on loan for while we're on the ground here. Yazov, take three men at any time past oh-five-thirty standard and pick up our supplies. I've got the coordinates downloaded, it's a warehouse on the west of the city. You can drive a hovercraft?"

"Yeah, I can drive one," Yazov said. "But you know, I think if you've got something to say that concerns all our asses, it'd be nice if all of us heard about it."

"Anybody tell you this was a democracy?" Herne Lordling snapped.

"Nobody told me I was cannon fodder, either," Yazov said.

He put his arm out to his side, so that it lay across the chest of his nephew. Josie Paetz wore the kind of smile Ned had seen on his face once before, when they prepared for the second pass through the Spiders on Ajax Four. If Yazov held a grenade with the pin pulled, his gesture couldn't have been more threatening.

"Guys," Lissea said, stepping between the men. She sounded like the boy the whale flopped on. "Guys? Let's all sit down, all right?"

She shook her head. "You know, if I had it to do over, I'd take a female crew." She smiled, still tired but no longer looking frustrated. "Except if I'd done that, none of these Pancahtan bastards would do anything but pat me on the head and tell me to go off and be a good girl. Eh, Ned?"

He grinned back. "Hey, the universe wasn't created on *my* watch," he said.

Tension eased. Ned lowered himself onto the gravel by crossing his ankles and sitting straight down. Other men followed his lead with more or less effort, depending on the technique they chose and how flexible their joints were.

A nearby ship ran up its engines, but that was apparently only a test rather than preparation for immediate takeoff. The port quieted enough for normal speech again.

"All 'right, Tadziki," Lissea said calmly. "Tell us what you've learned."

The adjutant began. "Though the Treasurer ordered Carron to keep away from us . . ." He was seated beside Lissea on the ramp, so he would have had to turn his head to meet her eyes. He did not do so. ". . . he, the boy, wants to meet with you secretly at the Old Race site he mentioned. The bunker. He's given me the coordinates."

"That makes sense," Lissea said. "What's your opinion?"

Tadziki nodded twice, as though he had to jog the data loose within his mind. "I think," he said toward the men seated before him, "that Carron is interested in more than the technology, Captain. But I don't see any choice other than you meeting him. Going up against those tanks unaided is like stepping out a window in the dark. It might be survivable, but the chances are against it."

"You want her to be a whore, is that it?" Herne Lordling said. He didn't jump to his feet, but that might have been because Toll Warson sat beside him with a hand poised to grab Lordling's belt. "Go on, Tadziki, say it: you want her to fuck this boy on the off chance that he knows something useful!"

"No," the adjutant said tersely, "I do not want that."

"Not that it matters a curse what anybody else wants on that subject," Lissea said, cool as winter dawn. "How soon is he willing to meet?"

Ned expected silent anger from Lissea like that which she displayed when he interrupted to save the audience with Lon Del Vore. Instead, Lissea seemed to have stated a simple truth, that the subject was one on which she would make the decisions without consultation.

Tadziki undipped a control wand from his breast pocket and brought the hologram display live. A topo map formed in the air. "He wants the meeting at Hour Nineteen local. That's in three hours twenty-two minutes standard. Here."

A red spot glowed on the map. "And here we are."

Lissea looked at Lordling. "The jeeps are ready to roll?" she said.

"Yes, ma'am," Herne replied in a husky voice. "But look. *Lissea*. There needs to be ten of us with you in case it's a trap."

Lissea made a moue with her lips and shook her head. "Herne—" she said.

"I'm not claiming the boy's deliberately setting you up," Lordling continued. The harsh timbre of his voice indicated he was conceding Carron's goodwill from policy rather than belief. "But his brother and father, *they* may be using the boy for bait. The rest of the unit stays aboard the *Swift* with engines hot, so—"

"*Stop*, Herne," Lissea said. A Warson chuckled.

She looked at Tadziki. "What're our chances if the locals launch an attack on us here in port?" she asked.

"None," Tadziki said. He looked around the gathering, not so much inviting comment as projecting his flat certainty. "They'd have casualties. Worse casualties than they'd probably expect. But there's no question of the outcome."

None of the mercenaries spoke. A few of them avoided the adjutant's eyes, but they couldn't argue with the assessment. As Yazov had said earlier, they hadn't joined the expedition to become cannon fodder.

"Right," Lissea said. "If I go with a mob behind me, it'll destroy any chance of empathy with Carron. So I'll go alone."

"Empathy?" Deke Warson called from the back of the group. "Gee, I never heard it called that before. I should've stayed in school longer, huh?"

Everybody laughed. Almost everybody. Herne Lordling got to his feet and walked stiffly up the ramp. "I'll relieve Harlow on watch," he said hoarsely.

"It might," Ned said, looking toward the triple-headed hologram projector within the vessel's bay, "be desirable for you to have a, you know, driver, a radio watch along, though. If you're going to be down in a bunker that may be shielded."

He felt Lissea's head turn. He lowered his eyes and met hers. "Yes," she said crisply. "That's a good idea. Slade, you'll drive me."

She got to her feet. Others followed. "I'm going to change my uniform. Tadziki, do we have enough water for a shower before the locals come through with resupply?"

Tadziki nodded. "I'll rig shelter and a hose on the other side of the ship," he said. "Warson, both of you. Westerbeke, Paetz. Get out another tarp, some high-pressure tubing for a frame, and the welder. I'll be along in a moment to supervise you."

Lissea entered the *Swift*. The meeting broke into half a dozen separate conversations. Some of the men were speculating on their chances of leave in Astragal and the possible opportunities there.

Tadziki gestured Ned toward him. The men stood shoulder to shoulder. Their heads were turned toward but not *to* one another. They stared at the gravel.

"That was a good idea about you going along," the adjutant said. "But you'll make sure that the principals have privacy for their discussions, won't you?"

"I'm not a kid, Tadziki," Ned said. He sounded angrier than he'd intended to let out. "And I won't be a third wheel, no."

He stamped back aboard the vessel. Before he drove off tonight, he wanted to check his submachine gun and ammo bandolier again.

"Half a klick to the bunker now," Lissea said, the first words that had passed between her and Ned since they drove away from the *Swift*.

Most of the trees had spongy, pillarlike trunks only six to ten meters high. The black-red fronds grew out in a full circle from each peak like a vertical fountain spraying. There were exceptions that spiked up twenty meters and more but didn't have branches at all. Their trunks were slender cones covered with a fur of russet needles.

Bits of plant matter danced from beneath the jeep's skirts, though Ned kept his speed down. "Keep an eye out," he said. "I'm busy not running into a tree."

The primary had set beneath the curve of Pancahte, but the sun was up in the east. The star was a Type K4 whose light was balanced toward the red also, but it seemed white by contrast to the glow of the near-stellar primary. Pale sunlight flickered through the forest's veiling fronds.

"I'm going to go back with Lendell's capsule, Ned," Lissea said quietly. "And I'm going to take my place on the board of Doormann Trading."

"You bet," Ned said. "And we're here to help you do that."

"There," Lissea said, pointing to a delicate four-place air-car like the one which the Pancahtan yacht had carried. She'd held her 2-cm weapon on her lap during the ride. Now she thrust its butt into the socket beside her seat.

Carron Del Vore stood up in the waiting vehicle. He was alone. Ned swung the jeep in so that Lissea was on the Pancahtan's side.

"Did we mistake the time, Carron?" she asked. Her helmet sensors would have noted the heat and sonic signatures of the aircar's passage if it had arrived any time in the past five minutes.

"Oh, no, Lissea," he said. "I was—well, I thought I'd get here early to mark the spot. It's hard to find if you're not familiar."

He stumbled getting out of the aircar. Lissea waited a beat, then raised her hand so that he could help her from the hovercraft.

They were in a forested valley. To either side, the ground had cracked open millennia before and oozed lava into parallel basalt ridges a kilometer apart.

The *Swift*'s navigational system plotted a route from the spaceport using satellite charts which Carron provided. The necessary data was then dumped into Ned's and Lissea's helmets. There was no more chance of them missing the bunker than there was of them missing the floor if they rolled out of bed.

But then, Carron's nervous anticipation didn't have a lot to do with Old Race artifacts. Despite his rank—and he wasn't a bad-looking guy—he must not have known many women.

There weren't many women like Lissea Doormann.

Ned stepped around his side of the jeep. His right arm cocked back so that his hand could rest lightly on the butt of the sub-machine gun, slung with the muzzle forward.

The vehicles were parked in a perfectly circular clearing, obviously artificial. Ned lifted his visor with his left hand. He no longer needed the line projected onto the inner surface to give him a vector to their goal.

Ned laughed without humor. Lissea and Carron looked at him. "Um?" Lissea said

"We got here," Ned said. The bunker was the physical location at which the two principals hoped to reach their separate goals.

"Yes, I haven't been here in years myself," Carron said. The center of the clearing was sunken. He reached down for the hasp which barely projected from the leaf mold. When Carron straightened, a flat, rectangular plate, about a meter by two, pivoted upward with him. It spilled soil and debris to the sides.

Carron moved without effort. The plate was over a hundred centimeters thick and burdened with a considerable accumulation of dirt and decaying fronds, so the hasp must merely trigger a powered opening mechanism.

Ned touched Carron's wrist with his left hand. "Let me take a look, if you will," Ned said with no hint of question. He grinned. "I'm expendable. Then I'll come back up here and keep out of the way."

"I'll determine where you'll go and when, Slade," Lissea said in a thin voice.

He looked at her. She nodded toward the opening. Now that she'd greeted Carron peacefully, she'd taken her heavy powergun back from the jeep's clamp. She held the weapon ready.

"Really, there's never anyone here," Carron said plaintively.

Steps led from the above-ground shadows to darkness. The staircase had no handrails.

Ned twisted a lightball clipped to his belt, breaking the partition between the chemicals so that they bloomed into white effulgence. He pulled the ball free and lobbed it one-handed into the bunker. It clattered around the interior. The bioluminescent compound would gleam with cold radiance for an hour or so, depending on the ambient temperature.

Ned walked deliberately down the first five steps. They were of some cast material with a nonslip surface on the treads. The material sounded brittle beneath his boots, like thermoplastic, but it showed no signs of wear.

The interior, which unfolded as Ned stepped downward, was light gray. There was nothing visible except dirt that had fallen in when the hatch opened.

Ned suddenly jumped to the floor and spun behind the submachine gun's muzzle.

"There's really no one here," Carron repeated. He was right, and Ned felt slightly more of an idiot than he had before.

"Looks good to me," he said with false nonchalance. He started up the steps. Lissea, descending, waved him back down again. She'd slung her powergun and carried in her left hand the heavy testing kit she'd brought from the *Swift*.

"There were no artifacts at all in the bunker?" she asked Carron over her shoulder.

"The bunker itself is an artifact," he corrected her. "When I first located it—from records in the palace library—the hatch was open and the cavity was half filled. Mostly leaves and branches, of course. At some point the settlers must have used it for storage and perhaps living quarters, though."

He waved a hand around the circular interior. "I had the contents cleaned out and sifted. There were some interesting items from the early settlement period—some objects that must have traveled from Earth herself, five hundred years ago. But the settlers *found* the bunker here, they didn't build it. And there's no sign of whoever did build it."

The bunker was about ten meters in diameter. Floor, walls, and ceiling appeared to have been cast in one piece with the staircase.

Ned picked up the lightball and set it on a tread at the height of his chin, so that it illuminated an arc of wall evenly.

"What are these?" Lissea asked, touching the wall beside a spot of regular shallow, four-millimeter holes in the material. "Ventilation?" There was a sparse horizontal row of similar markings, midway between floor and ceiling.

"No," Carron said. "There's a gas exchange system within the wall's microstructure. If we could determine how that worked, it would be—"

He lifted his hands in frustration—"of incalculable value. I think the holes may be data-transmission points and I even manufactured square wave guides to fit them. It would make a . . . a *burp* at me. But I haven't been able to get a response."

He looked around and added peevishly, "I should have brought ch-chairs. There's nothing to sit on."

Lissea brushed the comment away. "I've sat on worse than a clean floor," she muttered. She bent close to the hole, then knelt and opened her case.

Carron noticed Ned's eyes counting holes. "There's ten of them," Carron said. "Every ninety-seven centimeters around the circumference. Almost ninety-seven centimeters."

"If the ventilation system works and the door mechanism works," Lissea said as she chose a cylindrical device from her case, "then the powerplant's still in operation. The place should be capable of doing whatever it was built to do."

She looked at Carron. "Square wave guides. You brought some, didn't you? Where are they?"

He blinked in surprise at her tone. Carron might have been used to being ignored, but he didn't expect to be spoken to as if he were a servant.

"Yes, why I did," he said. He opened the lid of his large belt pack, flopped the front down into a tray, and took two square tubes from pockets within. The pack was a small toolkit rather than a normal wallet of personal belongings.

"I'll go up to the surface," Ned said quietly.

"Yes, do," Lissea said. She didn't look up as she spoke. She'd taken another tool from her case and was cutting at the end of a wave guide with a tiny keening noise. "Both of you go up, will you? I don't know how long this is going to take."

Ned turned without speaking and climbed the stairs, two steps at a time. He heard Carron's feet behind him. The staircase, though apparently flimsy, didn't spring or sway under foot.

By the time he stepped over the lightball, his head was above ground again. It felt good.

Carron snicked closed the catch of his belt pack, rotating so that a spear of sunlight illuminated the task. He avoided eye contact with Ned.

The immediate forest held nothing of interest on any of the spectra Ned's helmet could receive and analyze. He squatted to watch through the hatchway as Lissea worked. Carron moved a little farther back in the clearing so that he too could see without rubbing shoulders with Ned.

Lissea had broken her case into three separate trays which she'd laid out to her right side. She used the floor in front of her as a worktable, picking up and putting down items with precise movements. A lamp extending from one tray threw an oval of intense light across the floor. Occasionally a welding head sparkled viciously.

Ned had seen Lissea perform as the female captain of a band of hard-bitten, intensely *masculine* men. She'd done a good job, a remarkable job; but that was all on-the-job training. This was the first time Ned had seen Lissea doing the sort of engineering task for which she'd been formally educated.

Repeatedly, Lissea held a device against the wall, touched a switch, and went back to work. She was proceeding by trial and error, but there was no waste motion whatever. Each action was calculated to determine a particular question, yes or no, and thus take another step toward the goal.

"She must be incredibly brave, isn't she?" Carron said quietly.

Another step toward *Lissea's* goal.

Ned gave Carron a friendly but neutral smile. "You bet," he said. "In some ways, I don't think I've ever met anybody braver."

Because she had something to lose. There were no cowards aboard the *Swift*, but most of the men knew they'd be doing this or some equivalent of this until the law of averages caught up with them.

"Aside from being brilliant, that is," Carron added hastily. "I've been . . . consumed with the Old Race since—well, since I can remember thinking. And she dives in with a plan only minutes after she gets here!"

"A lot of times it's having a fresh perspective," Ned said dryly. Pancahte wasn't the sticks, exactly, but the whole Pocket would have been a backwater even without the Twin Worlds strangling access. "But I agree: Lissea is brilliant."

He waited a beat to add, "Besides being beautiful, of course."

Carron grimaced as though by forcing his face into a tight rictus he could keep from blushing. He couldn't. "Ah, yes," he said, staring toward a tree ten meters away, "I think she's very attractive too."

Ned looked down at Lissea again. He couldn't really see much of her at this angle. She'd lowered her faceshield to protect her against flying chips and actinic radiation from the welding.

What he saw when he looked at her was the image his mind painted. That was more than a trim body and precise features, though it included those aspects. He wouldn't define Lissea Doormann as being the ideal of physical beauty . . . but beauty wasn't solely or even primarily physical.

And yes, she was beautiful.

"I suppose that she . . ." Carron said. "Does she have a protector?"

Ned looked at the tree on which Carron's eyes were focused. It was one of the tall cones. Tiny blue flowers grew among the shaggy needles. "She's got twenty of us," Ned said with unintended harshness. "Well, eighteen, now. But if you mean—"

He fixed Carron with his gaze and waited for the Pancahtan to meet his eyes before he continued. "—is she involved with anybody, no, I don't think she is. Certainly not anybody aboard the *Swift*."

Carron nodded and let out a breath that he might not have been aware he was holding. He opened his mouth to say something noncommittal.

The bunker roared.

The interior was a hazy ambience rather than clear air and pale walls. Glare quivered through the mass like lightning across cloudtops. The bioluminescent globe had faded to a shadow of itself.

Carron started to jump down the hatch. Ned grabbed him across the waist left-handed and flung him back. Lissea might be trying to run up the stairs.

"It's all right!" she shouted as thunder coalesced around her. "I've gotten it to work!"

Ned dropped into the bunker in three strides, judging where the treads were by memory. He held his submachine gun like a heavy pistol so that his left hand was free to take the shock if he slipped.

His soles hit the floor. He reached out for Lissea. She was there, her shoulder warm through the tunic and her hand reaching up to clasp Ned's.

The wall before them erupted in a massive bombardment taking place on a horizon kilometers away. White, red, and yellow light gouted, and the air shook with repeated concussions.

The image vanished rather than faded. On the opposite side of the room, blue light limned a gigantic structure composed of pentagonal facets. Either the object was hanging in space or it was so huge that the supporting surface was beyond the image focus. Bits of the ship/building hived off as bands of non-light struck and scattered and collapsed in searing bolts which flashed from corners of the pentagons.

As suddenly as the conflicting images had appeared, the circular wall cleared again. The air still had a shimmering materiality: the lightball glowed as if it stood behind a dozen insect screens.

Ned couldn't be sure where the air stopped and the wall began. He didn't reach out, because he wasn't sure what his hand would touch—or whether it would touch anything.

Carron Del Vore stood with them. His eyes brushed Ned's with a cold lack of expression. Ned took his hand away from Lissea and stepped to the side.

"I loaded a vocabulary cartridge and told the system to switch on," Lissea said to the men. The room hissed with sound that was barely noticeable until someone tried to speak over it. "There weren't any input devices, so it's likely the system was voice-actuated. But it had to recognize my words as data, so I made a core load through a guide hole."

"Ready for instructions," a voice said from the whole circumference of the bunker at once.

"Well, I'll be hanged," Ned said. "You mean it's a data bank with no security gate controlling access?"

"You loaded a vocabulary?" Carron said. "But how did that help? How did it translate the words into information it could process?"

Lissea squeezed Carron's hand. Ned looked at his feet. He'd flipped over one of the trays when he leaped into the bunker. Now that the light was steady, Ned bent and concentrated on picking up tools he'd scattered.

"A seven-hundred-thousand-word vocabulary of Trade and Standard English," Lissea said, "is enough self-consistent information to provide its own code—for a sufficiently powerful processor. This one was."

Presumably the bunker didn't care where the controller was facing, but human beings like to act as if there were a point of focus. She turned to the wall again. "There are two tanks defending a perimeter around Hammerhead Lake, fifteen kilometers north of Astragal," she said. "How can the tanks be shut down or destroyed?"

"Define Hammerhead Lake or Astragal," the environment said.

"I'll handle it," Carron said with matter-of-fact firmness. He took the control wand from Lissea's breast pocket without bothering to ask. "Project a relief map of the ten thousand hectares of surface centered on this bunker."

Carron was taking charge rather than begging a favor. Ned had noted the dichotomy in the young noble's personality before.

The interior of the bunker changed. Ned felt an instant of vertigo. A vast map curved into view some meters beyond where the wall should have been. Either the illusion of flying tricked the balance canals in his ears, or for a moment gravity had shifted and he was looking straight down at Pancahte itself.

A flat, palm-sized disk from Lissea's toolcase hung in the air, attached to nothingness by one of the wave guides Carron had provided. She hadn't removed the device after she dumped data into the vast bank encircling them. Ned wondered what storage method the builders had used, and how long ago they had lived.

Carron adjusted the wand's lens into a needle of light. "This location," he said, flicking the beam around the easily recognizable dumbbell silhouette. There was no sign of Astragal or any human construction on the projected map.

"Do the tanks you're concerned with look like this?" the bunker asked.

The image of an object with twenty pentagonal sides appeared. The topographic map was still there. The projections neither masked nor intersected one another even though they should have been occupying the same points of space.

The tank, if it was a tank, had no weapons or other bulges to mark its flat sides. The vehicle rotated like an ill-made wheel across waste terrain, leaving cracked indentations on the surface. Broken rock spewed out whenever a corner bit. The vehicle looked like nothing Ned had ever seen in his life.

"No," Carron said. "It's a . . . there's a hull and on top a—"

Another vehicle replaced the first against the same setting. The change was so complete and sudden that Ned wasn't aware of any point of transition. This tank was identical to those whose images Carron had showed them on Buin, except that the details were precise, down to splotches of tarnish on the flanks. There was either a persistent highlight or an emitter on the gun mantle.

"Yes," said Carron. "Like that. How can we get past them safely?"

"Describe the behavior of the tanks," the bunker directed.

Ned was beginning to get used to the omnipresence of the voice. What he still found disquieting was the background vibration. The longer he listened to it, the more it sounded like a battle of enormous scale going on in the far distance.

"They circle the lake," Carron said. "They shoot at anyone or thing that comes within six kilometers of it."

"They've been operating for at least five hundred years," Ned added.

Perhaps the hum was merely the operating frequency of the vastly complex computer in which they stood. Or again, Ned might be reading his own fears into random images which the system displayed as it booted. . . .

But he didn't believe that.

"The tanks are on autopatrol," the bunker said. The system's designers had made no effort to humanize the voice. The words were dead and *wrong* without a tone of satisfaction to accompany them. "They can be disarmed by anyone they've been programmed to recognize as friendly."

Ned and Lissea exchanged glances—she frowning, he with lips pursed in consideration.

"It is unlikely after five hundred years," the bunker continued, "whether standard or local, that anyone from the contemporary population would remain alive. Did you have another type of year in mind?"

"No," said Carron tightly.

"Then the only way the tanks can be disarmed is through the use of a standard key," the bunker said. "This is a standard key."

A flat, square object some sixty millimeters per side appeared in front of Lissea and the two men. It had a wristband, though Ned thought the object was too large to be comfortable when worn that way. There were no distinguishing marks on the smooth gray surface.

The third image appeared with/over the topo map and the vision of the tank maneuvering across rocky terrain. The combined views were simultaneously clearer than any one of them should have been, no matter what distance from which they were seen. The bunker's display certainly wasn't holographic, and Ned now wondered whether it had any presence in the physical universe whatever.

"All right," Lissea said. "That's how the tanks can be disarmed. Now, how can they be destroyed?"

"The tanks can be destroyed by the application of sufficient energy," the bunker said. "The flux required is of stellar magnitude.

Nothing within the information you have provided me suggests that you have knowledge of the principles necessary to apply such volumes of energy."

Ned didn't look at his companions. He was also only marginally aware of the map, tank, and key before him. The rumble of warfare, cataclysmic and unimaginably distant in time, filled him like flame in the nozzle of a rocket.

"I've seen a . . . a key like that," Carron said. "My father has one in the collection of Old Race artifacts in the palace."

"You've *got* one?" Lissea said. "Wonderful! When can you bring it to me?"

"The top lifts up," Carron said, gesturing toward the display. "There's points marked on the inner surface. When you touch them, light flashes from the back of the lid."

The bunker changed the image as Carron spoke. The lid raised ninety degrees; the view rotated to show ten unfamiliar symbols arranged in pyramid fashion with a solid bar across the bottom. The image turned again. The raised back emitted pulses modulated in both time and hue—spectrum—across the entire surface.

"Carron," Lissea said. "You have the key. Our lives depend on it, *my* life. When can you bring it to me?"

"Lissea," the Pancahtan said, "*I* don't have the key, and my father does. I can ask him to loan it to you; I'll do that—"

"A little thing like that?" Ned interrupted harshly. "You say nobody ever looks at the artifacts and your *father* certainly doesn't care. He'll never miss it!"

"He'll see you use it, though!" Carron said. "You can't hide *that.* He'll see and he'll understand, and then he'll have me killed. Probably kill me himself. You don't *know* Lon!"

Ned turned his back to the Pancahtan.

"If you ask your father to let me use the key," Lissea said, ticking off probabilities without particular emphasis, "then he'll know its significance—guess, at any rate. After that, you won't be able to remove the key yourself."

Carron nodded miserably.

"I don't think there's any likelihood of his agreeing to your request," Lissea continued. "Especially since he's ordered you to keep away from me and the expedition members in general. Is that correct?"

"I don't know," Carron said, knotting his fingers together before him. "Yes, I suppose so. Yes."

Lissea nodded, her eyes empty. "Yes," she said, "that's what I thought."

She shrugged. Her visage and stance shifted with the movement, becoming as hard and brilliant as an oxy-hydrogen flame. "Slade," she said, "go back to the jeep and monitor radio traffic. Don't disturb me unless there's an attack on the *Swift*."

"Yessir," Ned said. He turned to the steps, putting his left hand on an upper tread to guide him in the surreal half-light.

"I'm going to get additional information on these keys," Lissea said in a brittle voice. "Perhaps we can build one from equipment aboard the *Swift*."

Perhaps pigs can fly. Perhaps the lion will lie down with the lamb.

"And Slade?" Lissea called. "Close the hatch behind you, will you?"

"Yessir."

Echoes of fire and bloodshed reverberated, in the bunker and in Ned's mind.

The sun had set while the three of them were in the bunker. The primary had not yet risen.

Given the size of Lon Del Vore's pet, the variety of life in the forests of Pancahte shouldn't have surprised Ned as much as it did. He sat with his back to a tree-trunk at the edge of the clearing, as still as a sniper: watching, listening, trying not to think.

The largest creature of this night was a snuffling omnivore the size of a raccoon. Its long snout delicately skimmed the leaf mold. When scent located a target, one or both of the creature's thumb-claws swept sideways and down. Each stroke was as quick and startling as the snap of a spring trap.

In the air, other hunters patrolled. Small, scale-winged creatures drove ceaseless spirals and figure-eights across the clearing, sucking gulletfuls of the chitinous insect-equivalents that chose the open space in which to dance and mate.

Twice while Ned waited, a hook-beaked flyer stooped from its vantage point on the peak of a cone tree. Both times the killer smashed an insectivore to the ground, pivoted on one wing, and snatched its prey back up to its eyrie. The flight was a single complex curve, executed as smoothly as a sailor ties a familiar knot.

With magnification at ten-power and his helmet's microprocessor sharpening the infrared images, Ned watched the killer shred its prey. The victim's skin and wings, stripped away by tiny cuts of the beak, fell to the floor of the clearing in tatters before the creature bolted the remainder whole.

Ned watched; and, despite himself, thought.

The hatch opened partway. The bunker was silent. The system's own illumination had shut down, and the lightball was by now only a flicker of gray.

Lissea held the hatch vertical. It shielded her from the vehicles, though Ned had a perfect view of his companions from the edge of the clearing. She bent down, kissed Carron as he stood two steps below her, and then shook free of his would-be embrace.

She flung the hatch fully open and called exultantly, "All right, Slade. We're ready to go. Fire 'em up!"

"You've got interesting bird life here, Del Vore," Ned said easily as he rose to his feet. "Do you call them birds, though?"

He rolled the switch over his visor to restore an unmagnified field of view, though he left the receptors on thermal imaging.

Carron tripped on the last step and almost dropped Lissea's toolbox. Lissea continued to walk to the jeep. She neither paused nor looked back.

"I can take that," Ned said, reaching for the toolbox and removing it from Carron's grip.

"Ah, yes, we say birds," Carron said, but Ned was already striding for the hovercraft behind Lissea. "I, ah—Lissea, I'll be there."

She was in the driver's seat. "I'll take us back," she explained as Ned settled the case carefully into the small luggage trough behind them. "I like to drive, sometimes."

Carron had jumped into his vehicle. The aircar spun its fans up loudly, howling before Carron suddenly coarsened the blade angle. The car jumped vertically and bobbled as the AI kept it balanced with difficulty. Carron waved over the side as he flew out of the clearing, fifty meters high and rising.

"Not a natural driver," Lissea said mildly as she engaged the jeep's fans. "But he's going to steal the key we need from the collection in the palace."

"I thought he might," Ned said. He removed his commo helmet and massaged his temples with his eyes closed.

"The bunker provided full instructions as to how to use the key," Lissea said. "There's a virtually infinite number of settings, but only three standard ones. The bunker thinks that in these circumstances the people who set the tanks on auto-patrol would have used a standard setting."

What circumstances are these? Ned thought, but he didn't say that aloud. Instead he said, "Carron seems a nice fellow. Certainly bright enough. Seems a bit, you know . . . young for his age."

"Slade," Lissea said without looking away from her driving, "drop it. Now."

A lot of us guys are young for our age.

There was a party going on around the *Swift* when Lissea pulled up.

The wedge-shaped landing site was big enough to hold a freighter forty times larger than the expedition's craft. Shelters of canvas, wood, and plastic sheeting had sprung up in the vacant area between the blast walls. Ned wasn't sure the light structures would survive a large vessel landing in one of the immediately neighboring berths, but the spaceport authorities were routing traffic to the opposite side of the field for now.

The Pancahtan official with whom Tadziki negotiated had been willing to find accommodations for the crew within Astragal. Tadziki refused the offer because he wanted to keep the men close by the vessel, but he'd parlayed it into supplies with which the crew could build their own quarters.

With the supplies and privacy had come local companionship. Privacy wasn't, as Ned remembered from field service, an absolute requirement.

"I figured on the merchants," Lissea said to Ned. "But I didn't expect so many women."

"The men did," Ned said. "Wonder what they're using for money, though?"

"Let's hope nobody's managed to trade the main engines for a piece," Lissea muttered as she shut the jeep down.

The *Swift*'s boarding ramp was raised. Deke Warson sat cross-legged in the open airlock with a 2-cm weapon across his lap.

A redhead with blonde highlights and more drink in her than she had clothes on tried to climb over Deke. He turned her around with a gentleness that belied the strength he applied as he set her back on the gravel. "I come off watch in forty-three minutes, sister," he said affectionately. "I'll look you up then, okay?"

Deke noticed the jeep and waved. "Hey, Cap'n!" he said. "Don't you got your suit on inside out?"

"Aw, I never get classy women," Toll Warson called from a bench at the table set up along one blast wall. "The ones I meet never bother to take their clothes off."

Men cheered and catcalled. Herne Lordling wasn't visible. Tadziki appeared at the hatchway behind Deke, wearing a reserved smile.

"Hey, what do you mean?" cried the woman seated beside Toll. Ned wasn't sure how serious she was. "I'm classy, honey. *I'll* take my clothes off!"

She started to roll her tube-top down over a bosom that looked outsized even on a torso which no one would have described as slim. Toll laughed and stopped the woman by gripping her hands and burying his face between her breasts.

Lissea stood up. She stepped from the driver's seat to the jeep's slight hood, a framework joining the two forward fan wells.

"Ned," she ordered, "blip the siren."

Still-faced, Ned leaned over and obeyed. He kept his finger on the button for three seconds, letting the signal wind to the point at which everyone in the encampment could hear it.

The locals—whores, gamblers, and the tradesmen who provided food and drink—blatted in surprise. The *Swift*'s mercenaries didn't speak. Breechblocks clashed as men made sure their weapons were charged before they lunged from their shelters. Some of the mercs appeared undressed, but none of them were unarmed.

"Crew meeting in the *Swift* in one—that's figures one—minute," Lissea shouted. "All personnel need to be present; nobody else will be."

Lissea looked around at her crewmen. "I'll keep it short, gentlemen," she added. "Then you can get back to what you were doing. Sorry."

She hopped down from her perch and strode to the airlock so swiftly that Deke had to hop to clear her path. Ned followed, wearing a cold grin. "Game point to the lady, Toll," he called over his shoulder as he entered the *Swift*.

Tadziki, careful as always, had kept a four-man watch. The vessel could take off at a moment's notice. Ned was the next man aboard. He squatted in front of the navigational consoles. They'd been rotated rearward for the moment. Dewey reclined in one, the adjutant in the other.

Lissea stood between the consoles with the control wand in her hand, watching her crewmen come through the airlock in various states of dress and drunkenness. Her face was unreadable.

Deke Warson cycled the hatch closed behind his brother, who lurched aboard carrying Coyne over his shoulder. "Forty-seven seconds!" Deke announced.

"Gentlemen," Lissea said. She didn't use the internal PA system. Men held their breath or shielded their open mouths with their hands.

"The operation will proceed tomorrow morning," she continued. "I'll have a device that will freeze the operations of one tank at a time. Cause the tank to pause, that is. Somebody has to enter each tank to shut it down."

"Who's in charge of the attack?" Herne Lordling asked from the back of the gathering. He'd been drinking, maybe more than most of the crew, but he held himself straight as a gunbarrel. He spoke in a truculent tone.

"I'm in charge, Herne," Lissea said. "I'll be operating the key, the device. I've had training regarding the device—"

A few minutes with a nonphysical simulacrum in the bunker.

"—and anyway, it's my line of work. For the first phase, all I need from most of you gentlemen is the absolute certainty that you won't try to get involved in the operation. In particular, that you not shoot at the tanks. If anybody shoots, the tanks switch from standby to attack mode. The key won't affect them in attack mode, and they'll quite certainly kill me. Does everybody understand that? *Clearly?*"

"What the hell did we come for, then?" Harlow muttered. Tadziki looked at him hard, but the mercenary sounded puzzled rather than angry.

Lissea raised a data disk fitted with a wave guide like the one with which she'd entered the bunker's memory. "The key works on one tank at a time. Then somebody has to enter the unit and load its internal computer with a language chip so that it can understand commands. The bunker, the Old Race system that provided the information, tailored a pair of language chips so that the less powerful computers aboard the tanks will be able to convert the data."

"Sounds like a job for me, Cap'n," Deke Warson said. Because he'd been on watch, his information-processing faculties were a hair sharper than those of his brother who'd been drinking.

"What?" said Herne Lordling. "No, that's my job!"

"I'm not ready for comment, yet," Lissea said harshly. "While my subordinate shuts down the first tank, I'll pause the second and shut it down myself. *Then* and *only* then, the rest of you will be responsible for proceeding to the lakeside complex, removing the capsule, and bringing it aboard the *Swift.*"

"We'll have to move quickly, before the Treasurer decides to go back on his word and stop us," Tadziki said from the console. "But if we enter the patrolled area while the tanks are still operating, we blow the operation sky-high. Timing is critically important."

Lissea looked across the crowd to the Warsons. "Deke," she said, "Toll—there may be electronic locks on the buildings. I expect the two of you to get our people inside. Do you think you'll be able to open up an unknown system?"

Toll Warson raised his closed right hand. "Like a fish, Captain," he said. As he spoke, a shimmering blade snicked from between his fingers and snicked back.

"Worst case," Westerbeke volunteered, "we go over the roof into the courtyard and hump the curst thing out on our backs. Shouldn't be a big problem."

Other men nodded.

"Captain," Tadziki said, "I recommend that Slade act as your subordinate for the disarming process. He won't be necessary for moving the capsule. And he's got experience with tanks besides."

Tadziki's gaze was bland. Ned knew that Lissea and her adjutant hadn't had time to set this up since she'd returned from the bunker.

Lissea looked down at Ned as though the suggestion was a surprise to her. "Yes, all right," she said. "That's the way we'll do it. Herne, you'll command the anchor watch, and Tadziki will be in charge of retrieving the capsule. Any questions?"

"Wait a minute," Lordling said. "*Wait* a minute!"

"If there are no further questions," Lissea said, switching to the vessel's PA system to overwhelm the babble, "you can go back to your recreation."

"Curfew is in four hours standard," the adjutant added, rising to his feet. "We've got work to do in the morning."

"Wait a minute!" Lordling repeated.

"Shut up, you dickhead!" Josie Paetz snarled. "Uncle and me got a girl *good* and ready about the time we got called away!"

"Dismissed," Lissea said. Deke hit the ramp switch to empty the vessel fast. There'd be no problem with locals boarding while the herd of mercenaries thundered in the opposite direction.

"Slade," Lissea said, speaking unamplified again, "you and I will need to go over familiarization procedures for the tanks. I've brought data from the bunker in holographic form."

"Yessir," Ned said as he stood up. He kneaded the long muscles of his thighs. It felt like it'd been a long day, but he hadn't done anything yet. "Yes, Lissea. I'm looking forward to that."

✳ ✳ ✳

The sun and the primary were near opposite horizons. Ned, at the controls of one jeep, watched the faint double shadow they cast around the *Swift.*

A Pancahtan driver pulled up in an empty 1-tonne truck and got out. He waved gaily toward the mercenaries as he joined the spectators clogging the terminal area.

This was the most exciting event on Pancahte in decades. People from all across the world had turned out to watch it.

Yazov's five-man team leaped aboard the second of the trucks Pancahte was loaning the expedition for transport. Deke Warson and his team were on the vehicle Tadziki had borrowed the day before, while the adjutant himself manned a powerful sensor suite on a jeep with Toll Warson driving.

"Ready when you are, Cap 'n," Deke reported.

"Let's do it," Lissea said.

Ned twisted the throttle to three-quarters power and tilted his yoke forward to follow at a comfortable ten-meter separation behind the jeep Toll drove. The borrowed hovercraft slid in behind the jeeps with their fans bellowing. A single truck could have carried all ten men, but not ten men and the capsule they meant to return with.

The crowd cheered. Hovercraft and a few aircars paralleled the expedition as Toll swung east to skirt Astragal. Streamers flew from the vehicles, and many of the brightly caparisoned passengers waved enthusiastically.

Ned hadn't expected the locals to be supporting Lissea. In all likelihood they were just cheering for the excitement. A public execution would have done as well.

That might be next.

Crops grew in vast fields illuminated by tethered balloons which emitted light at the high-energy end of the spectrum that the Earth-derived vegetation required. Local plants couldn't supply human nutritional needs, though Pancahte's animal life was fully edible.

"How do you like being star turn at the circus?" Lissea asked.

Their commo helmets clicked—leakage from the microwave

links transmitting power from each field's fusion plant to the balloons. Ordinary pole-mounted lights would be toppled within days by Pancahte's seismic activity.

"Let's see how the performance goes," Ned said. "Just now, I'm thinking farming—*that's* a worthy occupation."

She laughed, squeezed his biceps without looking at him, and went back to studying the minute projection of a tank's interior on her visor.

Ned hadn't carried his submachine gun. There wouldn't be room for the weapon within the fighting compartment of the Old Race tank which the bunker had displayed. There shouldn't be need of the weapon—any weapon—if it came to that; but Ned had stuck a pistol in the right breast pocket of his tunic. It only weighed a kilo, and it didn't cramp his movements.

A quartet of big aircars loaded with members of the Treasurer's Guard in powered armor fell in behind the expedition. A few of the civilian vehicles sheered off, and the enthusiasm of the remaining spectators was noticeably muted.

"*Adjutant to captain,*" Tadziki reported from the lead jeep. "*There's quite a reception committee waiting for us three klicks ahead, just short of the start point. Over.*"

"*Noted,*" Lissea replied. "*As we expected. Captain out.*"

She glanced over at Ned. "Usually about half the men carry submachine guns," she said. "Today everybody's got a two-centimeter instead. What do you think?"

Ned smiled. The big shoulder weapons were medicine for powered armor.

"I think you hired the best there is, Lissea," he said. There was a trill in his voice that surprised him. Adrenaline was already making his muscles shiver, bucking against the limited movements that driving a jeep permitted. "My money's on the visitors if something pops."

"I'll have the balls of any of my people who starts it," Lissea muttered; which was a way of saying the same thing: that both of them expected to survive, and *that* was an irrational attitude if Ned had ever heard one.

The lead jeep carried a portable sensor suite nearly comparable to the unit built into the *Swift*. Toll would halt on high ground outside the tanks' patrol area. Tadziki would monitor the sensors, providing remote data to Ned's and Lissea's commo helmets on call—and, in an emergency, without being asked. The need to judge when to interrupt somebody in a life-threatening situation was the reason Tadziki and not another crew member was in charge of the equipment.

The country south and east of Astragal was flat between volcanic dikes and had good soil. Where the ground hadn't been cleared for agriculture, it was covered by native forests.

North of the city, the land became broken and sandy. Trees dwindled to stunted individuals spaced ten or twenty meters apart, then were replaced by a species of ground cover that was so pervasive as to constitute a virtual monoculture.

Purple-black leaves spread from spiky centers like lengths of carpet. They completely hid the soil. Where the skirts of the lead jeep bruised a track across them, the leaves curled up and exuded a spicy fragrance. Droplets of condensed dew glittered among the undersurface hairs.

Ned worked cautiously over a jumble of rocks that were almost big enough to force him to take the jeep around. "There's the welcoming committee," Lissea said. She was able to watch the horizon while the driver's attention was focused just ahead of the flexible skirts.

Thousands of Pancahtans waited near a ridge of rock or hard-packed sand. The civilians wore the bright garments that most on this dismal world affected, but there were over a hundred guards in powered armor as well.

Toll Warson curved his jeep off to the left, heading for a single gigantic boulder which had collected a ramp of sand up its lee side. Topo maps showed the boulder was the best nearby vantage point. It provided a view across to the other side of Hammerhead Lake.

Lissea and Ned might have used the Pancahtans' own satellite imagery. Neither of them wanted to trust the goodwill of the Treasurer, who was at best a very doubtful neutral.

The ridgeline and the reverse slope were in the area which the tanks defended. Ned would enter while terrain blocked both tanks' line-of-sight weapons, but there'd be no chance of withdrawing over the crest once he'd committed. The ridge was quite literally a deadline.

He drove toward the array of Pancahtan troops. Lon Del Vore and Ayven wore gold and silver armor respectively. Their faceshields were raised. The powered suits were so brightly polished that reflections turned their surfaces into a harlequin montage.

"Pretty little peacocks, aren't they?" Lissea murmured, but that was probably bravado. She knew as well as Ned did that mirrored metal would scatter much of the effect of a powergun bolt.

Lon, Ayven, and the six guards closest to them sat on two-place aircars with spindly fuselages. The fan nacelles were mounted on outriggers. There was a small cab to protect each fabric-uniformed driver, but the soldier behind him had only a saddle and footboards.

The six cars lifted in unison and flew toward the jeep in two parallel lines. Ned slowed without orders. He heard the note of the trucks behind him change as the mercs driving flared to either side, ready to spread their troops in a line abreast if shooting started.

The aircars roared down. Each pivoted on its vertical axis like members of a drill team. The Treasurer was showing off the proficiency of his troops; but no argument, they *were* proficient.

Lon flew at ground level to the right of the jeep; Ayven, to the left. They'd closed their faceshields. "*I want you to know,* Captain *Doormann,*" Lon's amplified voice boomed, "*that I'm aware you came to Pancahte to scout us for pirates. Well, your plan won't work. Off-world thugs will get no more from us than enough ground to scatter their ashes!*"

Lissea touched a switch on her commo helmet. "*Sir,*" she said on a push the locals had used in the past, "*we came in peace and we hope to go in peace. All we want from Pancahte is the loot my kinsman stole—and that on the terms you set, after we first disarm the tanks which have heretofore interdicted this portion of your planet. Over.*"

The lines of aircars accelerated away in a pair of fishhook curves without further comment. They stayed low. The powerful downdraft of their fans flung long leaves about like sheets flapping from the line on a windy day.

Carron pulled out of the mass of armored men in an even smaller vehicle, a one-man hovercraft. It swayed and hopped across irregularities hidden beneath the vegetation. Lon bellowed something from his aircar, but he didn't attempt to intercept his son.

Ned slowed the jeep as Carron brought his vehicle in close on the passenger side. "Stop us here," Lissea ordered, adding a hand signal in case her soft words were lost in the intake rush. Ned eased them down gradually, so as not to surprise either Carron or the vehicles following.

Carron reached over and gripped the side of the jeep. He'd taken off his jacket and held it crumpled in his hand. "Lissea," he said, "I've thought it over. Lon will kill me—*kill* me when he learns that I've taken the key."

"Carron, my life depends of you keeping your word," Lissea said. There was a hint of desperation in her voice. Ned didn't know how much of it was assumed—for the purpose of convincing a needed supporter who'd gotten cold feet at something beyond the last minute.

"I'm going to keep my word," Carron said, "but you've got to help me. Lissea, *do* you love me like you said?"

Ned's eyes studied the ridgeline ahead of them. His skin prickled as if it was being rubbed with a wet sponge.

"Yes I do, darling," Lissea said with soft certainty. "I never dreamed I'd meet a man who shared my own soul so completely."

"Then take me away with you!" Carron said. "That's the only way I'll be safe. We can stay on the Twin Worlds and study how the capsule functions!"

"All right, Carron," Lissea said. "If that's what you want, I'll take you away with me. I love you, darling."

"Oh, Lissea . . ." Carron said. He straightened, balancing again on his vehicle, and sped back toward his armored kinsmen.

His jacket was still draped over side of the jeep. Lissea felt the fabric, then reached into a side pocket. "It's here," she said.

She looked at Ned.

He shrugged. "Whenever you want to, Lissea," he heard his voice say.

"Then let's do it," she replied, rocking forward and back as Ned shunted power again to the fans.

Ned keyed his helmet's Channel 3, a link to Tadziki that not even Lissea could enter. Channel 2 was reserved for her and the adjutant. "Give me three-position topo"—his jeep and both tanks—"on the left half of my visor, fifty-percent mask," he ordered.

The vehicles—red, orange, and the white jeep—appeared against a sepia-toned terrain map through which Ned's immediate surroundings were still visible. He had full binocular vision, though the map was a hazy intrusion on the landscape.

Lissea sat in a state of apparent repose. She'd strapped the key onto her left wrist; its lid was closed. She showed no signs of impatience, though the jeep idled when she had given the order to execute. The operation wouldn't begin until Ned was good and ready to commit.

"Mask the beaten zones in blue and yellow," Ned said.

Tadziki's response was only a heartbeat behind the last syllable of Ned's command. The beaten zones, portions of the terrain on which the tanks' weapons could bear, appeared as irregular, ever-changing blotches across the map display. Where both weapons bore, the colors merged into bright green.

Because the tanks were moving, the beaten zones varied from one moment to the next depending on where the vehicles were in regard to the broken terrain. Tongues of rock, boulders higher than the gunmount, and the slopes when a tank cruised along a swale—all reduced the area the weapons covered. By the same token, a tank that crested a ridge could suddenly sweep twice the ground it had a moment before.

The tanks were moving slowly, about—

"Eighteen kay-pee-aitch," Lissea said, as though she'd been reading Ned's mind.

"Any data on what their maximum speed is?" Ned asked as he watched the soft lights and waited to move—another thirty seconds unless the tanks reacted before then. . . .

"No," said Lissea. "A lot faster than this, though."

"That we can count on," Ned murmured as he slid his throttle and yoke forward.

He leaned slightly as he steered for one of the ten-meter gaps between civilian vehicles and the central mass of armored soldiers. He wanted an angle on the slope ahead, anyway

"Go get 'em, Cap'n!" a mercenary shouted. Curst if a few of the Pancahtans didn't cheer as well.

It didn't matter. Nothing mattered but washes of blue-and-yellow light, and the white point accelerating toward them.

At the base of the ridge, air bleeding from the jeep's plenum chamber made leaves hump and flail. Some of the foliage slapped the skirts angrily.

Ned brought his speed up. The sand higher on the slope wasn't as well compacted. A few of the spike-cored plants had taken root, but they were small and their leaves were mere tendrils. The jeep spat them away in clouds of sand drifting downslope. It wasn't a good surface even for an air-cushion vehicle, but the jeep was light enough to maintain the momentum it had gained in its running start.

"They're reacting," Lissea said, a trifle louder than the howling fans required.

"Roger."

Ned and Lissea had considered timing their intrusion so that the tanks would be at the east and west limits of the patrol area when the jeep entered the zone from the south. They'd thought the better of it when they realized that would leave them facing both tanks simultaneously, with only a single key to disarm the pair of them.

Instead, one tank was on the far side of Hammerhead Lake. The other, though within a klick of where the jeep would appear on the ridgeline, was in a channel. The surface rock had cracked and been wedged farther apart by lava that hardened into basalt at the base of the trough. For the ten or fifteen seconds the tank was in the narrow passage, its long gun could only bear frontwards.

The ridge was a spit of red sandstone too dense for the roots of normal plants to find purchase. Lichens marked the surface in concentric rings of varied hue, often brightly metallic.

"Hang on!" Ned cried, though he scarcely had to. The jeep whooped onto the crest, bounced, and skidded down the reverse slope with gravity speeding its progress.

The more distant tank was marked orange on the display and its beaten zone was blue. It was accelerating but continuing to follow its previous patrol track. That was good. Ned had been afraid—and he'd seen the thought in Lissea's eyes, though neither of them had mentioned it—that the tanks might be able to cross the lake in an emergency rather than going around it.

The nearer tank stopped on a dime and backed, instead of proceeding to the far end of the channel it had entered. The turret rotated as soon as the sandstone walls permitted it to do so.

On Ned's visor, the yellow mask of the killing zone washed down from the ridge crest, pursuing the white dot but not quite catching it before the howling jeep hurtled into a meter-deep gully as planned. Ned and Lissea shrieked triumphantly though the shock slammed them bruisingly forward.

Ned dumped the plenum chamber. He and Lissea dived from the jeep to opposite sides. They and the vehicle were now safe until the tanks approached from one end of the gully or the other.

As they would surely do.

Lissea raised the lid of her key and touched markings on the formerly covered surface. Ned crouched against the wall of the gully, watching a schematic of his life or death played out on his visor against a background of grainy stone. The plot of the gully was a brown streak across the yellow of the beaten zone.

The red dot wobbled toward the gully. Topography prevented the tank from describing a perfectly straight line. Lissea took a deep breath, touched a point on the key, and raised the device over the rim of the gully. The Old Race vehicle didn't fire at her, but neither did it slow its advance.

Ned took the pistol out of his shirt pocket. It was something to do with his hands, as useful as whittling though no more so. Lissea lowered her device and punched another set of points, numbers, onto the markings.

The tank was two hundred meters away. In a moment, the

vehicle's path would intersect the ravine and its weapon would rip across the intruders. A roar like the crackling of water poured into boiling grease accompanied the tank.

Lissea raised the key again. Light from the lid flickered over Ned's face for an instant.

The crackling stopped. The red dot on Ned's visor halted, and the ground shook as the vehicle dropped.

Ned jumped up. The second tank was moving fast, but it'd be out of sight for another minute, perhaps a minute and a half. "Come on!" he shouted as he climbed behind the yoke of the jeep.

Lissea swung herself doubtfully into the vehicle. She held her left arm toward the tank and braced the wrist with the other hand. "Careful!" she said. "If you jar me out of line with this thing, they won't find enough of us to bury."

"Via, they won't come looking!" Ned said. He slammed closed the shutters and used the bounce of the plenum chamber filling abruptly to lift them over the lip of the ravine. Lissea's upright torso dipped and bobbed, but her arm remained pointed like a tank's stabilized main gun.

The gun of the Old Race tank was at a safe forty-five-degree angle; the turret was aligned fore and aft. The vehicle rested on the ground rather than drifting above it.

The smoothly curved tank was only six meters long and three meters in maximum breadth and height, but it must have weighed at least a hundred tonnes. Its weight had shattered the rock beneath in a pattern of radial cracks.

Ned pulled around to the rear of the vehicle where the hatch was supposed to be. Lissea pivoted on the seat beside him, pointing the key over his head. He vented the plenum chamber and leaped out as the jeep skidded to a halt.

The surface of the tank had an opalescent shimmer like that of black pearl, irrespective of light from the sun or the primary. There was a sharp tang to the air, not ozone. Ned sneezed, then sneezed again.

According to the images the Old Race bunker supplied, a hasp on the rear of the tank would raise the hatch. There was no hasp on the glowing surface before him.

Ned opened his mouth to call for help. Nobody knew any more about the situation than he did. He patted the curved smoothness in hopes of finding a hidden mark or indentation.

There wasn't any mark, but an oval portion of the armor slid within itself when Ned touched it.

"Get on with it!" Lissea cried. "The other one's going to be on top of us!"

Ned flipped up his visor, then tossed the whole commo helmet to the ground. He slid feet-first into the tank. It fitted him more like a garment than a hundred-tonne machine.

A dull red lightbar glowed across the upper front of the cockpit. Except for that, the interior was as featureless as the inside of an eggshell. None of the controls or displays the bunker had briefed him to expect were present. This tank was similar to the bunker's examples, but it was a later model.

"Ned, for the *Lord's* sake!" Lissea screamed.

The bunker said the controls were smoothly rounded knobs on the dashboard. Ned visualized their location, then set his hands where they should have been.

The jeep exploded in actinic brilliance that flooded through the open hatch. The gun of the oncoming tank seemed to fold matter inward along the path of its discharge.

"*Ned—*"

So she was all right, keeping the first tank between her and the weapon of the second, and the knobs *were* there; the controls sprang up beneath his palms, molding themselves to the shape of Ned's hands. Gunnery on the right, movement on the left.

The hatch behind him closed with such silent precision that Ned was aware only of the silence that now wrapped him. A panoramic display that gave the impression of sunlit solidity surrounded him. The other tank rippled forward, proceeding like a well-found ship over rough seas.

Ned was supposed to insert the language chip as soon as he got aboard, then shut the tank's systems down by verbal command. Instead, he pressed up and left on the gunnery control. The knob remained fixed. A white targeting circle slid down across the panorama. The displays didn't move, but the walls of the turret slid behind them as silent as quicksilver. He twisted the unmoving knob counterclockwise, tightening the circle to a white dot at the base of the other tank's gun mantle.

The oncoming tank halted and crunched into the ground. The long-barreled weapon that had been questing for Lissea rose to its safe setting. She jogged around the bow of Ned's tank, holding the other vehicle in the key's calming transmission.

Ned let his breath out. He must have dropped his pistol in the ravine or the jeep. He didn't have it now.

He took his left hand from the unseen control and fished the language chip from his right breast pocket. The square, four-millimeter input point in the center of the dash had appeared when the systems came live. Ned inserted the wave guide and switched the chip to dump to the vehicle's computer. He didn't suppose it was necessary, but it was what they'd planned to do.

"Go to standby," Ned ordered.

The panoramic display vanished, leaving only the lightbar and cool gray surfaces. The turret aligned itself. Probably the gun rose to a nonthreatening slant as well, but Ned couldn't tell from where he was. The dash ejected the data disk and the input hole blanked over.

The hatch behind Ned opened again, to his sudden relief. He'd had a momentary vision of his body entombed in an armored coffin no one could breach. Perhaps Lissea would drape a banner reading MISSION ACCOMPLISHED on the tank . . . except that she'd be trapped forever in the other vehicle, wouldn't she?

Ned levered himself backward through the hatch. His arm muscles wobbled in reaction to the hormones that he'd finally burned away. He wondered if the Old Race crewmen had helpers or special equipment to ease the job of boarding and evacuating their vehicles.

Lissea crawled from the other tank. She looked as wrung-out as Ned felt, but he noticed that she'd brought her data disk out. He hadn't bothered to pick his up.

The tanks were dull. They looked like clay mock-ups rather than the glowing, vibrant terrors they'd been moments before. Ned ran his hand curiously over the flank of his unit. The surface felt vaguely warm.

A wave of vehicles swept toward the tanks across the previously forbidden area. The three hovercraft holding the *Swift*'s personnel were in the lead. Lissea spoke into her commo helmet's internal microphone.

Ned walked over to pick up his own helmet. His legs were unsteady for the first few steps.

The jeep Ned and Lissea had ridden smoldered in a tiny knot that couldn't have contained more than a tenth of the mass the vehicle had had in the instant before the tank weapon had hit it. But all's well that ends well. . . .

Yazov's truck and the jeep carrying Tadziki and Toll Warson pulled up beside the tanks. Scores of vehicles filled with Pancahtan civilians rocked along behind them.

Deke Warson waved from the cab of the other one-tonne without taking his eyes off the terrain in front of him. He kept going toward the lakeside buildings. The hovercraft was moving fast for the conditions, but Ned noted Deke made constant minute corrections to his vehicle's course and speed. He was driving with ten-tenths concentration, not simply barreling straight ahead.

Lon Del Vore and most of his troops advanced only to the ridge marking the area which the tanks had interdicted. Ayven, however, in company with another two-place aircar and a pair of the larger vehicles loaded with six of the Treasurer's Guards apiece, sailed along fifty meters up and that far behind Deke's truck.

Though the aircars could easily have passed the air-cushion vehicle, Ayven and his troops instead matched speed. They followed like a pack of hunting dogs running down an antelope.

The four mercenaries in the back of Deke's truck eyed their escort with a deceptive nonchalance. Each man rode with a hand on the grip of his weapon and the muzzle cradled in the crook of the opposite arm. If trouble started, the sky would rain powered armor and bits of blasted aircars in a fraction of a second.

Lon's silver-armored son certainly knew that, so he wasn't planning to start trouble.

Toll skidded to a halt. Tadziki lifted himself from the jeep one-handed before the skirts had braked to a complete halt. With his boot-soles as fulcrum, the adjutant used momentum to swing his body upright from the carefully chosen angle at which he'd left the vehicle. Whatever Tadziki's claims to have been strictly a non-combatant, the guy who performed that maneuver without falling on his ass had made more than his share of hot insertions.

"Slade, are you all right?" he demanded. "What happened to your helmet?"

The ground shook, though not as fiercely as some of the shocks Ned had already felt on Pancahte. The tanks jiggled, grinding the rock beneath them into gravel of a smaller size. The trembling impacts sounded like heavy machinery working—as, in a manner of speaking, it was.

"I took it off," Ned said. "It's like wearing a glove inside those things."

He stepped toward the back of Yazov's truck. Josie Paetz reached down to help him board.

"Tadziki, Warson," Lissea said brusquely, "go on with Yazov. Slade, we'll take the jeep."

Toll rose from the driver's seat as though he'd expected the order. Maybe he had; Ned certainly hadn't.

Half the civilian spectators followed Ayven at a respectful distance. The others were circling or had parked near the tanks.

Carron broke through the pack and drove straight to where Lissea stood. His one-man hovercraft had a narrow footprint and a proportionately high center of gravity with a man aboard. It wasn't a good choice for terrain so rough. Plant juices staining Carron's cheek and right sleeve suggested that he'd managed to low-side when the little vehicle went over.

"Lissea!" he said. "Remember your promise. You're going to take me along?"

Toll Warson withdrew his head from the hatch of the nearer tank. "Sure doesn't look like much," he said. Ned looked at him sharply.

"If you're going to come," Lissea said, "then *get* moving. We're heading for the lake."

She took the Old Race artifact from her wrist and tossed it to Carron as she got into the jeep. He squawked and caught it.

The sensor suite bulged from the luggage trough and added nearly fifty kilos to the jeep's burden. If the loaded vehicle could carry the two big mercenaries, it ought to manage one man and a small woman, though.

"Bloody hell, Slade, drive!" she said. "Do you need an engraved invitation?"

Ned fumbled clumsily with the controls for a further instant before he got them sorted out. Toll had feathered the fans as he cut power, while Ned always left the blade angle coarse. The fans sang as Ned pushed the throttle forward, but it wasn't until he changed the unexpected setting that the jeep lurched ahead.

The ground trembled again, without violence but continuing over a thirty-second interval. Ned wondered whether the crust of Pancahte was setting up for a major displacement. Worse come to worst, open country like this was as good a place as any in which to ride out an earthquake.

"But Lissea?" Carron called.

Pancahtan aircars marked the position of the leading truck like vultures following a dying horse. Yazov put his boot to the firewall as soon as Lissea implied he was clear to follow Deke's truck. Tadziki and Toll Warson boarded the 1-tonne on the fly, drawn onto the bed by the men already there.

Ned slid the jeep's throttle to the stop also. He could adjust his speed by tweaking blade pitch and the angle of his fan nacelles, lifting high enough that the skirts spilled air when he needed to slow. The battery temperature gauge began to rise with the constant high-rate discharge, but that was nothing to worry about.

Some of the hurry was justified. Lissea was in command, so she ought to be present when her personnel reached the capsule. Less creditably, a part of Ned had no intention of losing a race to Yazov in a locally built truck.

Least creditable of all, Ned wanted to leave Carron Del Vore as far behind as possible. That was petty, but Ned didn't claim to be perfect

On smooth stretches, the 1-tonne might have had a speed advantage, but on this terrain the jeep's agility put it ahead early and kept it there. A bulge in a spreading leaf might be no more than a kink of growth, but it might as easily conceal a boulder big enough to rip the skirts off a hovercraft. The two mercenary-driven vehicles skidded and wove about the potential hazards.

Pancahtans took chances in an attempt to keep up with the *Swift*'s experts. Some of the locals flew up, flailing as their vehicles cartwheeled and scattered bits of bodywork across the landscape.

The peninsula was nearly three hundred meters long. Some of the civilian craft had stopped or were idling at the near end. Because all the Pancahtans were looking in the other direction, dicing between the vehicles brought shouts of anger and surprise. When the jeep's skirts brushed an enclosed sedan, the civilian driver reached out to shake his fist—

And almost lost it when the 1-tonne blasted by, thirty meters behind. Several men in the box of Yazov's truck kept their weapons pointed while Josie Paetz jeered and pumped his right index finger through his left fist.

On both sides of the peninsula, Hammerhead Lake danced in vertical spikes. The jeep's air cushion and the howl of its fans masked the vibrations agitating the water. Ned wished he'd learned more about the amplitude of the quakes to be expected on Pancahte.

The buildings and vehicles at the end of the peninsula were fifty meters ahead. "Hang on!" he ordered.

The nacelles were in the full-aft position to provide maximum forward thrust. Rather than reverse their angle with the wand on the left side of the control column, Ned spun his yoke to pivot the jeep at the same time he dumped the plenum chamber.

The combination of active and passive braking slowed the vehicle from seventy kilometers per hour to a dead stop in less than twenty meters—excellent performance for a hovercraft. Besides, deceleration stresses pushed Ned and his passenger comfortably into their seatbacks instead of trying to bounce them off the dashboard.

Ned added a bit of tricky reverse steering to fishtail the jeep between the big Pancahtan aircars. Guards with their face-shields raised gaped at the exhibition.

Ned hadn't thought about Lissea since he had got the jeep under weigh. His attention had been limited to the potential threats and potential obstacles in all directions of his vehicle. Now he looked at his commander in sudden trepidation—*the sedan their skirts had brushed, that was on Lissea's side.*

She was smiling and relaxed. "Not bad," she said as she scissored her legs over the sidepanel. "Not bad at all."

Via, they'd both been tight as cocked pistols when they got into the jeep. The fast ride had let out tensions. The business with the tanks was more like waiting for the guillotine to drop.

Deke Warson knelt beside the circular door of the nearest building. "Knelt" was the operative word: the opening was only a meter-fifty in diameter, and the wall from soil to roof was less than two meters high. A sunken floor could explain the outside height, but the door was presumably sized to its builders.

Who were unlikely to have been human—though the Old Race tanks had to be crewed by beings the size and shape of men. As Ned had said, the tank fit him like a glove.

Three Pancahtan soldiers stood in line abreast on either side of Ayven in his silver armor. They watched the mercenaries involved with the building five meters in front of them.

A severe shock—the first Ned had noticed during this spasm—rocked the site. One of the armored men fell down. He jumped upright again and backed into his proper space. Hammerhead Lake was beginning to boil.

"Got it!" Deke shouted, oblivious to external events while he concentrated on the lock. A kit of delicate electronic tools lay open beside his right boot. The circular doorpanel rotated outward and up from a hinge concealed at the two-o'clock position.

Harlow and Raff jumped onto the roof from the inner court-yard. "No problem!" Harlow called. "We can just lift it over."

Lissea slipped between Pancahtan guards. Ned followed a pace behind her. As a reflex, he put his hand on one man's shoulder.

That was a waste of effort. The fellow didn't feel the contact. When he lurched, startled by Lissea's sudden appearance before him, he knocked Ned into his fellow. It was like jumping between moving buses: nothing an unaided human did was going to affect his mechanical neighbors.

"Like hell we're going to lift the sucker!" Deke called as he squatted in the low entrance with his 2-cm weapon pointing forward. "We're going to take it right through this door I got open!"

"Shut up, Deke," Tadziki ordered. "We're going to do exactly what the lady behind you says we're going to do. Now, get out of her way!"

Deke glanced over his shoulder in surprise. "Sorry, Cap'n," he muttered.

He hunched quickly through the opening instead of hopping aside. Lissea followed. Ned gestured Tadziki to go through behind her, then gripped the roof's coping with both hands. Harlow reached down to help. Ned got his boot over the edge unaided and straightened again on top.

Ned wasn't claustrophobic. After his moment of fear in the Old Race tank though, he didn't feel an immediate need to enter another strait enclosure.

Like the Old Race bunker, this building appeared to have been cast in one piece. The roof was unmarked by antennas, ventilators, or support devices of any sort.

The walls of the inner court were pentagonal and parallel to those of the exterior. The enclosed area was about five meters wide. Flanked by Harlow and Raff, Ned reached the inner edge just as Deke Warson led Lissea into the courtyard on her hands and knees.

Raff spun twice, aiming his rocket gun at what turned out to be nothing—smoke or the brightwork of a civilian vehicle catching the late sun. His disquiet bothered Ned. The Racontid generally seemed as imperturable as a rock.

"See, it's just a little thing," Deke said. "We'll get it through the doors easy." He gestured to the capsule as though it was his sole gift to Lissea.

The ground shook again, violently. The building moved as a

piece, but Ned noticed the ancient structure fifty meters away was dancing to a slightly different rhythm. He bent to rest the tips of his left fingers on the roof to keep from falling.

A crevice opened beneath a Pançahtan hovercraft, then slammed shut again to pinch the flexible skirt. The occupants bailed out, bawling in surprise. This couldn't be a common occurrence, even for Pancahte.

Hammerhead Lake shuddered. Great bubbles of steam burst in a warm haze that drifted over the buildings.

Carron Del Vore was in the courtyard with Lissea and six of the mercenaries. Toll Warson waited at the outside entrance, his weapon held across his chest as if idly.

Several of Ayven's companions had fallen because of the most recent shock. The Treasurer's son remained upright. The primary washed the left side of his powered armor blood red.

"Lissea?" Ned called. "Better move it out. I don't like the look of the lake."

He gestured. She couldn't see the lake's surface, but the plume of steam must by now be visible from the courtyard.

"What do you figure's going on, Master Slade?" Harlow muttered. He was as nervous as Raff, or he wouldn't have asked the question in a fashion that tacitly granted Ned officer status.

Lissea gave a curt order and pointed at the capsule.

"Lava must've entered the water channel feeding the lake," Ned said. "We're going to have a geyser or worse any minute now."

The capsule rested on an integral ring base. Four of the mercenaries gripped the ovoid and tilted it end-on so that they could manhandle it through the doors. It was heavy but not too heavy to carry.

Carron reached between two of the men. He touched what must have been a latch because the whole upper surface of the capsule pivoted upward. Deke Warson cursed and bobbed his head as the top opened toward him.

Inside the capsule was the wizened yellow mummy of a man. They'd found not only Lendell Doormann's capsule, but the desiccated remains of Lendell Doormann as well.

"All right, let's get it moving," Lissea ordered. She slammed the capsule closed again. "We can look at all that later."

Her voice sounded thin against the background rumble of Hammerhead Lake. Ned wished he had a gun, even if it was no more than the pistol he'd lost while deactivating the tanks.

Feeding the capsule through the doorway was a two-man job. Deke took the front of the load; Coyne, who was bigger than he was strong but was strong nonetheless, took the back.

Lissea was talking to Tadziki and Carron. The men bent with their heads cocked to hear her over the voice of Pancahte.

"Come on," Ned muttered to Harlow and Raff. "We can help out front when they get it clear."

The other men in the courtyard couldn't get through the doorway while the capsule blocked it. Dewey looked up and called to the trio on the roof, "There's nothing but dust inside. What do you suppose this place is? It's *old.*"

Ned nodded. All they could prove was that the bunker, the tanks, and these very different buildings predated the settlement of Pancahte five hundred years before. His instinct told him that they were at least an order of magnitude more ancient yet; which of course was impossible, if the Old Race was really human.

If humans had evolved on Earth.

"Let's go," he repeated to his companions. He crossed the roof in quick strides. The land shuddered in an undertone. The vibration wasn't immediately dangerous, but it seemed even more menacing that the fierce jolts of moments before.

"Toll, we're coming," he called and dropped down beside Warson.

Toll grinned sidelong at him. "Our friends there are getting nervous," he said with a nod toward the guards in powered armor. Ground shocks had kinked the parade-ground line. Even Ayven stood skewed a little from his original stance.

"They're not the only ones," Ned said.

Deke backed through the doorway, cursing the load and the building's architect. He kept his end of the capsule centered perfectly in the circular opening. Ned stepped in beside him. There were no handholds on the top end of the ovoid, so it was a matter of balancing the weight on spread hands. A patina roughened the capsule's metal surface enough for a decent grip.

Raff and Harlow took opposite sides in the middle. More men spilled through the doorway behind Coyne, but there was no need for them now.

Toll Warson walked to the bearers' right front like a guide dog. He waved with his left hand to Ayven Del Vore. "Give us a hand, then," he warned. "Or get out of the way."

"What is it?" Ayven said. His voice was harsh and metallic through the suit's amplifier, but even so it sounded weak beside the crust's groans.

"Show him what it is!" Carron said, stepping between the capsule and the line of guards. "Set it down for a moment so that my brother can see exactly what he's trying to steal."

"Yes, do that," Lissea said.

"I represent the government of Pancahte!" Ayven rasped. *"I have a right to know what strangers are trying to take from our world!"*

The mercenaries lowered carefully. The ovoid wasn't intended to rest on its side. Ned stuck the reinforced toe of one of his boots out to cushion the capsule from ground shocks. The adjutant muttered an order to Coyne, who did the same on the reciprocal point.

"Blood and martyrs!" Josie Paetz said. Hot water slopped over the shoreline and swept across the rock.

When the wave withdrew, it left a slime of mineral salts. The water lapped one of the Pancahtan guards to the ankles of his armored boots. He backed farther away, staring at the lake's roiling surface.

Carron worked the capsule's latch again and drew the lid open. Ayven started back, throwing a hand up reflexively to shield his armored face.

"It's a coffin, brother dear!" Carron cried. "Do you begrudge Captain Doormann the corpse of her great-granduncle? Do you?"

The two-place aircar which Ayven had ridden jiggled on the ground. The driver looked nervously out of his cab. The similar vehicle whose soldier passenger was still astride the saddle now hovered twenty centimeters above the rock.

Ayven spun on his heel. His armored foot struck sparks from the rock. "*Go on back to Astragal,*" his amplified voice commanded. "*The body you can have, but the capsule my father will decide on.*"

The men lifted. Lissea stepped close to Ned to swing the lid down with her extended arm. The Pancahtan guards stepped dashingly out of the way. Had they never seen a dead man before?

Though the remains of Lendell Doormann had an eerie look to them. It wasn't that the wizened corpse seemed alive: the rings of blue-gray fungus on the sallow skin belied that notion. Rather, it seemed that the body had been dead and mummifying in the sealed capsule for the entire time since Doormann vanished from Telaria—despite the fact that he had carried on intercourse with the Pancahtans for another fifty years yet.

A double wave broke over the margins of Hammerhead Lake. The pulses washed across the peninsula from three directions. "Bloody *fucking* hell," Deke muttered, stepping through water as high as his boot tops with the same mechanical precision that he had maintained when the surface was dry.

Yazov was already in the open cab of the nearer 1-tonne, though it wasn't the vehicle he'd driven to the site. The hovercraft's flexible skirts dampened the quick choppy motions of the ground into longer-period motions. The truck surged and fell slowly. By contrast, the two big aircars of the guards hopped and chattered despite the shock absorbers in their landing struts.

The mercenaries handed the capsule to their fellows waiting on the bed of the 1-tonne. "Tilt it back on its base," Lissea ordered.

"And two of you hold it there," Tadziki added as he helped lift the ovoid straight himself. "Paetz and Ingried."

Ned's helmet hissed, static leaking from a nearby transmission. Ayven had given an order to his men, who stamped toward the six-place aircar. One of the guards slipped on yellow-white froth that had been left when the waves receded. He hit the rock like a load of old iron.

A shock knocked down almost all of the people standing on the peninsula, Ned among them. The open door of the pentagonal building flapped with the violence of the quake. Hinges which had survived centuries and perhaps millennia snapped off. The panel clanged down on edge and hopped around an inward-leaning circle until it fell flat.

Hammerhead Lake belched again. Because of the steam, Ned thought another wave was oozing over the shore.

Yazov ran up his fans. Air spewed from beneath the truck's skirts. Ned stepped back, peering toward the lake.

"Get going!" Lissea ordered. Her shout was barely audible. Carron was at her side, looking concerned but not frightened.

Yazov pulled the 1-tonne in a tight turn. Mercenaries on the truck bed braced themselves against the capsule to steady it.

It wasn't a wave. It wasn't a geyser either, though steam and water roaring a hundred meters high made it look as though it might be.

Ned ran toward the parked jeep. He keyed the general push on his helmet radio and shouted, "Don't anybody shoot! This is Slade! Don't anybody shoot or we're all dead!"

The thing rising from the lake was faceted and huge, towering a hundred meters above the shoreline before anyone could be sure it was a solid presence. Its bulk walled the three sides of the peninsula into what had been Hammerhead Lake. The lake was the pit which had held the thing, and the thing filled that kilometers-long cavity as a foot does its sock.

The thing was a starship, a pair of dodecahedral masses joined at the center by a pentagonal bar. Though three hundred meters long and nearly as thick from base to peak, the bar looked tiny compared to the twelve-faceted balls it joined together. Lightning flashed from one lobe to the other. The enveloping steam flickered like a fluorescent tube warming up.

"Don't anybody shoot! Don't shoot!"

Beside Ned, the guard riding the two-place aircar twitched forward the fat-bored powergun slung across his back. He aimed upward at a forty-five-degree angle and fired. The concussion knocked Ned down again.

Recoil from the big weapon made the struts of the hovering aircar tap down. It slid back toward the larger unit with six guards aboard.

A spark snapped from one of the starship's triple angles. The shooter's head and helmet vanished in liquid fire. The guard toppled backwards out of his saddle. The large aircar behind him exploded, punched through by a five-sided beam that expanded during its passage.

The vehicle doubled in on itself. Men in powered armor tumbled to either side. Four of them were uninjured, but the two on the center seats had lost everything between waist and knees. Rock beyond the collapsing aircar gouted up as lava, twenty meters high, spraying as far as the civilians at the base of the peninsula.

The driver grounded his vehicle, jumped from his cab, and collided with Ned. The Pancahtan ran blindly toward Hammerhead Lake, and the starship still rising from it.

Ned grabbed the handhold on his side of the small aircar's cab. There was a folding step, but he couldn't flip it down with his boot toe and he didn't dare risk taking his hands off the grip while the driverless vehicle slid sideways.

Something whanged off the opposite side of the cab, a fan-flung pebble or a bullet loosed wildly by a man trying to fight the terrors in his head. The aircar pivoted in a half circle as Ned pushed it in his desperate attempts to board. He finally got his leg over the frame connecting the cab to the rear saddle, then dragged himself through the cab's side door.

The starship continued to rise. The upper angles of the lobes were lost in haze and lightning half a kilometer high, but the lower surfaces were still within the margin of the pit. Twice sparks licked away swatches of rocky landscape. The discharges might have been retribution on human gunmen, though there was no evidence left in the bubbling lava.

Ned had never driven a Pancahtan aircar before, but there were only so many ways to arrange the controls of a vehicle meant for general use. He checked for the throttle and found it as an up-and-down motion of the control column. He lifted, spun, and hauled back on the wheel. The car rose to ten meters in a climbing turn, accelerating above the ground traffic as Ned drove toward the deactivated tanks.

The Old Race hadn't left the tanks to keep later humans away from Hammerhead Lake. The tanks had held something else down in that pit. It was up to Ned to undo his mistake of an hour before.

If it was possible to undo the mistake now.

Pancahtan hovercraft tore across the ground like windblown scud. They dragged humps and tangles through the vegetation to mark their passage.

Ned had lost his commo helmet when he'd struggled aboard the aircar. He didn't know what was happening to the rest of the *Swift's* complement, didn't know if any of the others were alive, and that couldn't matter now.

He didn't know if Lissea was alive.

The tanks were where he and Lissea had deactivated them a hundred meters apart, skewed and lonely on the purple-smeared landscape. Ned brought the aircar down hard and too fast. He was ham-fisted in reaction to the second adrenaline rush in an hour. The skids banged to the stops of their oleo suspension, then bounced him up and sideways.

Ned didn't have the right reflexes for this particular vehicle. He tilted the column against the direction of bounce, but he must have managed to lift the throttle also. Increased power to the fans flipped the vehicle to the ground on its back. Momentum then rolled it upright again.

The cab was dished in, wedging the driver's door. Ned put his boot-heel to the latch, smashing the panel outward as violently as if a shell had hit it. He was all right. He'd clamped his legs beneath the seat frame to keep from rattling around the cab like the pea in a whistle. He'd feel it in his calf muscles in twelve hours or so, but he was fine for now.

And now might be all there would ever be for Edward Slade.

He ran toward the tank. The hatch was open as he'd left it. The massive vehicle quivered in response to high-frequency shocks pulsing through Pancahte's crust.

The alien starship had risen completely above ground. The lower surfaces appeared to rest in a pillow of steam bloodied by the light of the primary. Beams sprang from a high point on either bell. Their tracks looked as if matter had been pressed flat in their path and twisted.

Ned grabbed the edges of the tank's hatch to support himself. Previous blows by the starship had been quick, snapping sparks. These beams differed in type and intensity. They augered south, beyond the visible horizon. The beams had no identifiable color, but they throbbed dazzlingly bright on a world where ruddy light muted all other brightness.

The horizon swelled into a bubble glowing with the colors of a fire opal, as furious as the heart of a star. The Old Race bunker. The starship was attacking the Old Race bunker.

Ned squirmed feet-first into the Old Race tank. The bubble at the point of the intersecting beams burst skyward like a lanced boil, spewing plasma and vaporized rock into Pancahte's stratosphere. The whole sky shimmered, white at the core of the jet and a rainbow of diffracted hues shimmering outward from that center.

Ned gripped the dashboard. The controls shaped themselves to his palms; the visual panorama sprang into razor-sharp life. The hatch thudded closed behind his head an instant before the shock of the bunker's destruction reached him through the rocks of the crust.

The landscape hunched upward in spreading compression waves, then collapsed in the rarefactions that followed. The Old Race tank had lifted on its propulsion system when the controls came live. Even so it pitched like a great turtle coming ashore. The atmospheric shock seconds later was mild by comparison, though it must have been equivalent to that of a nuclear explosion at a comparable distance.

Despite Pancahtan construction methods, there couldn't have been a building undamaged in Astragal. As for the *Swift*—

The *Swift* would have to wait. Ned focused his targeting circle on the center of one of the alien starship's huge lobes.

He pressed his right thumb down. The springiness of the tank's controls shifted to something dead and dry, like old concrete. The panoramic screen didn't blank, but the real-time visuals switched to icons: the starship was a red Crosshatch, while the Pancahtan landscape became a sweep of tan polygons over which skittered blue blobs in place of the hovercraft fleeing from the peninsula.

The white targeting circle had vanished from the new display. The dull lightbar across the front of the fighting compartment shifted through bright red to orange.

The display returned to normal visuals. The tank gave a great lurch upward. The controls were live again, but the beam of the tank's weapon ripped a hole almost vertically into the sky, above the starship even though the vast construct continued to rise.

The rear hull of the tank had sunk turret-deep in lava so hot the rock curled in a rolling boil. When the propulsion system came on again, the tank sprayed upward to hover above the dense liquid as if it were still solid rock.

The starship lashed out again with the paired beams that had destroyed the Old Race bunker. The other tank was at the beams' coruscant point of intersection. The vehicle tilted, sinking into the molten rock as Ned's own tank had done a moment before.

The other tank's gun had sheared a collop out of one of the starship's lobes. Ned lowered his targeting circle to the upper edge of the pentagonal tube joining the bells. He cut downward.

The bar across the front of the tank bathed him in lambent yellow light verging toward green. The starship rotated around the vertical center of the tube. Ned's beam pared metal away from the alien construct like whiskers rising from the workpiece on a lathe.

The controls went dead; the display returned to icons. The second Old Race tank became a white star that dominated the dull landscape around it.

The color of Ned's lightbar rose from bright green to blue. His hands had a leprous cast. He thought of the fungus on Lendell Doormann's face. He licked his lips, but his tongue was dry as well.

The visuals returned, flaring. The pool of lava encircling Ned's tank was white and meters deep, but his massive vehicle broached like a huge sea beast. The magma was unable to harm the tank so long as the vehicle's defensive systems had power, but if the rock hardened it would entomb Ned until the stars grew cold.

The other tank fired also, its beam a chain of hammered light. The starship's lobes had separated and were drifting downward in reciprocal arcs.

Ned focused his targeting circle on the lower edge of a bell. He held his gun steady as gravity dragged the ship fragment through his beam. Fiery streamers sparkled from the point of contact, twisting like octopus arms. They gouged away more of the ship's structure wherever they curled back against it.

The lightbar was vivid indigo, except where patches were beginning to sink into violet and blackness.

The other tank shot at the same lobe as Ned. An irregular wedge peeled away from the great dodecahedron and smashed into the ground an instant before the mass from which it had separated did. Sparks gouted skyward like kilotons of thermite burning. The sparks enveloped the larger portion as it fell into them, warping the hull plates inward.

The tank's hatch shot open behind Ned. *"Eject at once!"* cried a voice that rasped directly on the human's lizard brain. *"This vehicle will terminate in ten seconds!"*

Ned had concentrated on gunnery, ignoring the movement controls because his tank could neither pursue nor flee from the starship lowering in the heavens. Now, the lava that glowed beyond the hatch was a ram battering the back of Ned's neck. He spun the live but unmoving knob within his left hand. The tank rotated on its axis, swinging the rear opening away from the pool of bubbling rock. Ned heaved himself clear.

The remaining lobe of the starship hit the ground kilometers away a few seconds after its sectioned fellow had struck. The glare was a sparking echo to the southern aurora where plasma from the bunker's destruction cooled and dissipated in a broad cloud.

Ned lay on sand and broken rock. The vegetation that had covered the ground was dead. Leaves were seared to a brown tracery of veins which themselves crumbled at the touch of Ned's hand.

Heat hammered Ned every time his heart beat. He stayed low,

but sulphurous gases from the melted rock made his throat burn and his eyes water. He began to crawl toward where the other Old Race tank had been.

The vehicles rotted like sodium in an acid atmosphere. Bits scaled away from armor that had withstood forces that devoured living rock.

The groundshocks had ceased when the alien starship rose fully clear of its pit. The pop and crackle of huge explosions scattered the remaining wreckage, but that was a mild substitute. Occasionally a fireball sailed thousands of meters in the air, burning itself out to fall as ashes.

A breeze blew from the south to feed the flames of the starship's immolation. The air was fierce and dry, but cooling. Ned rose to his hands and feet, then stood upright.

Lissea was staggering toward him. She'd somehow lost the trousers of her utility uniform, and her right arm bled where the tunic sleeve was torn—

But she was alive, they were both alive, and the distant flames laughed as they cleansed Pancahte of the gigantic star-ship which had laired so long in its crust.

Light flickered from a dozen places on the horizon, as bright in total as the half-risen primary. A vehicle was coming toward Ned and Lissea from the east. Ned couldn't make out what it was.

"I saw you go off," Lissea croaked. "I . . . First I thought you were running away."

"I wasn't running away," Ned said. His voice sounded as though he'd had his throat polished with a wire brush.

Lissea nodded. "I know that. How long do you suppose it's been there, waiting?"

Ned looked toward the broad expanse of the starship's crash and shrugged. The white sparkle was dimmer than it had been initially, but parts of the mass would burn for days. "I don't want to think about it," he said. "If there was one, there could be others—here, maybe anywhere. *We* couldn't have done anything to stop it."

"No, I don't guess we could," Lissea agreed. She still wore her commo helmet. She adjusted the magnification control on her visor and said, "Carron's returning to pick us up. He brought me to the tanks when I realized what you were doing, but he had to get clear of the area at once. The car was no protection."

"*Carron* brought you here?" Ned said in amazement.

The aircar was a big, six-place unit like the ones that had carried sections of the Treasurer's Guard. It was the surviving member of the pair that had accompanied Ayven. Carron brought it down twenty meters from Ned and Lissea. The stubby landing legs skidded on the rock, striking sparks.

"Yes—Carron," Lissea repeated. She and Ned jogged drunkenly toward the aircar. Carron might have landed closer—but he might have put it down on top of them if he'd tried. The Treasurer's younger son hadn't become a better driver in the past hour. After Ned's own "landing" in the smaller car, he was willing to be charitable.

The sky toward Astragal glowed. Parts of the city were afire.

"Do you want to drive?" Carron shouted as Lissea climbed into the car. He didn't take his hands off the controls to help her. The fans buzzed angrily because of his unintended inputs. "If you want, you can drive, either of you!"

"Not in the shape we're in!" Lissea said. "Get us to the *Swift* as fast as you can."

She threw herself onto the other forward seat. Ned squatted behind and between the pair. Lissea seemed oblivious of the fact that the tail of her utility jacket barely covered her—lacy, black—underwear. An explosion had partly stripped her without taking either her boots or her commo helmet

Carron lifted the big aircar to fifty meters and pointed it south. As soon as it was airborne, the vehicle's automatic controls took over, leveling and smoothing the flight. Ned hadn't realized how much the car's nervous hopping on the ground had irritated him until the motion stopped.

"How did you get this car?" Ned asked. "The guards didn't just let you have it, did they?"

"I EMPed them," Carron said. The smooth ride of the vehicle's own systems had calmed him also. He gestured toward the large attaché case lying in the midsection of the car beside Ned. "A cold electromagnetic pulse to freeze their armor. The powered suits have some shielding, but I scaled my generator to overcome it at short range."

At the end of the gesture, Carron put his hand on Lissea's bare thigh. She laid her own hand on top of his.

They passed an overturned civilian hovercraft. The survivors waved furiously. Carron ignored them. They'd probably be as safe where they were as they would in ravaged Astragal.

"I thought Ayven might have his men arrest me," Carron continued. "For the, you know, the key. I couldn't shoot my way through them, but a pulse that burned out the circuits of their suits all at once . . . So I carried a generator with me today. And I used it on the guards because I knew we couldn't get clear of that *thing* in a ground vehicle."

Carron was talking to Lissea. Ned avoided looking directly at the other man and calling attention to himself.

That Carron was technically capable of preparing such a plan shouldn't have been a surprise. He clearly wasn't stupid, and he was well enough versed in electronics to discuss the subject with Lissea, who was expert by galactic standards.

That Carron was ruthless enough to carry out the plan in the fashion described, leaving six men to die because he'd fried their circuitry and turned their powered armor into steel strait-jackets—

Maybe that shouldn't have been a surprise either. He *was* Lon Del Vore's son and Ayven's brother.

The car reached the northern outskirts of Astragal. They'd risen to a hundred meters, high enough to get a broad view of the chaos occurring in the city.

A series of parallel cracks arced through the developed area, about a kilometer apart. Extended, they would form circles centered on the site of the Old Race bunker.

When the bunker's defenses failed, the shock was sudden and from virtually a point source. At its highest amplitude, the wave front created stresses beyond the elastic limits of the rock on which Astragal was built. Everything along those points on the radius of expansion had been shattered to rubble.

People huddled in the streets, looking up at the aircar. Fires burned in many places, ignited by internal damage to the structures or by blazing matter slung from the bunker site. There was neither water nor the coordination necessary to extinguish the fires, so the situation was rapidly getting out of control.

"Lissea," Ned said, "the spaceport was closer to ground zero than the city was."

"Do you think I don't know that?" she snapped.

Carron, struck by the tone though the words weren't directed at him, snatched his hand away from Lissea's thigh.

He gestured again toward his case. "I brought an alternate routing out of the Pocket," he said. "The navigational logs of the original settlers are in the palace library. I've gone through them, looking for information on the Old Race. If we try to go back through the Sole Solution, I'm afraid my father will hunt us down."

"There isn't any other way into the Pocket," Lissea said querulously. "That's *why* it's the Sole Solution."

Ned raised himself, gripping the seat backs for support against the one-hundred-fifty-kilometer-per-hour windrush. He squinted toward their destination. The spaceport seemed in relatively good condition, though ships lay like jackstraws rather than in neat, gleaming radii pointing toward the terminal buildings at the hub.

A large freighter lay on its side. The gray smoke leaking from ruptures in the hull plating was the only sign of movement about the vessel.

"There's only one way *in*," Carron corrected. "But there's another way out. And I've brought the navigational data."

"Blood and martyrs, man!" Ned snarled. "That's the ship! Don't fly us off into the desert!"

"Oh!" Carron blurted. He'd set the course when they lifted from the battle site, but he'd forgotten to take the car off automatic pilot. Now he shoved the column forward and banked around the vessel he'd overflown.

Both 1-tonne hovercraft were parked in what had been the *Swift*'s landing segment. The blast walls had collapsed into twisted ribbons; one of the borrowed trucks lay beneath concrete and strands of wire reinforcement—the remains of the nearer wall.

The vessel herself was undamaged, though she now rested on the ruins of the other wall.

"They lifted off!" Lissea said. "Thank the Lord, somebody had sense enough to get them airborne before the worst of the shock-waves hit."

"Score one for Herne," Ned said, though he was by no means sure Lordling was responsible for the decision. Westerbeke and Petit were on anchor watch as well. Ned disliked the ex-colonel so much that he forced himself to give the man his due and more whenever he had to speak of him.

Pancahtans had waved at the aircar or merely stared apatheti-cally as it flew overhead. The men crouching in the rubble about the *Swift* watched the vehicle through the sights of their powerguns. At least some of them had their fingers on the triggers.

Carron was too focused on his landing to notice the overt threat, but Lissea keyed her commo helmet. *"Captain to* Swift *personnel,"* she said. *"Don't shoot; I'm in the approaching aircar. Over."*

Ned noticed that she didn't sound angry, just fatigued. He was suddenly tired also. He could melt onto his bunk now, no matter what was happening around him.

Carron landed in two bounces, the second of which put the car's legs into the jumble of the blast wall and almost overset the vehicle. The *Swift*'s ramp was raised but not quite closed. It began to lower again as Tadziki and Herne Lordling sprang out of the narrow airlock.

"Are we prepared to lift?" Lissea demanded as those men and other mercenaries ran toward the aircar. She started to get out but stumbled because her legs didn't want to support her.

"Lissea, what happened to your clothes?" Lordling demanded. He kept her from falling, then picked her up bodily despite her struggles.

"We're ready, but we don't have clearance to lift," Tadziki said.

"We were hovering, but the tower threatened to turn the port's defensive batteries on us if we didn't set down."

"Herne, curse you for a fool!" Lissea snarled. "Put me *down!*"

"I can take care of that," Carron said as he hefted his case out of the vehicle. "We've got to leave at once, before Lon is able to take control again. He won't let us go."

"Tadziki, help him," Lissea said, nodding toward Carron. "He'll need access to the navigational system. Make sure he gets it."

The adjutant put his hand on Carron's shoulder to guide rather than force his attention toward the *Swift*'s landing ramp. "Yes, we've got to hurry!" Carron agreed.

"I'm going to take a party to the terminal building and clear it out," Lordling announced. "Yazov, Paetz, Warson—yes, you—Harlow . . ."

"No, no, I can take care of the tower," Carron called as he shambled up the ramp. Tadziki's hand was out to help with the case of heavy equipment, but Carron didn't appear to notice the offer. "Don't worry about that."

"*Captain to* Swift *personnel,*" Lissea ordered. "*Everybody board ASAP. I want to be able to lift the instant we get clearance. Over.*"

"A mother-huge rock hit us aft, Captain," Dewey reported. "It smashed hell out of the lifeboat bay. We were going to put the capsule there, but it's all bunged in."

They'd gotten back with the cursed thing, then. Ned had almost forgotten that the expedition's purpose was to retrieve the capsule.

"Lissea, you can't trust that pissant!" Lordling said. "Come on, boys, let's take care of this. It's not far enough to drive."

"Sounds to me like mutiny, Herne," Toll Warson called from the left side of the airlock hatch. He was right-handed, and only his right arm and eye were visible beyond the hull metal. His brother squatted behind the lowered ramp with his submachine gun in his hands.

"*I* think it's a pretty bloody good idea!" Josie Paetz said loudly. He put his hands on his hips and turned to face around the whole assemblage.

"It is not a good idea, nephew," Yazov said. He stepped chest to chest with Paetz and grabbed the younger man's wrists when he tried to pull away. "It is *not* a good idea to side with a fool against your commanding officer."

A warehouse of flammables blew up on the outskirts of Astragal. There was a bubble of liquid orange, followed by another on a slightly different center. The third blast hurled entire drums hundreds of meters in the air. Some of them fell into the city proper.

"Let's get aboard, Herne," Lissea said. She put her hand on Lordling's shoulder. He shook her off.

"Carron's got a pretty good track record thus far, Herne," Ned said. The *whoomp* of the third explosion hit the port area hard enough to shake the crumbled blast walls into lower piles. "He—"

Lordling punched him in the face.

Ned fell onto his back and elbows. He wasn't sure what had happened. He was dizzy, and hot prickles spreading from his mouth and nose made his vision pulse between color and black-and-white.

Herne Lordling turned on his heel and stamped up the boarding ramp, his back as straight as the rope holding a hanged man.

Lissea holstered her pistol before she bent to help Ned rise. "Are you all right?" she asked. "Your lip's cut."

It wasn't the punch, it was everything else that had happened. Ned felt sick to his stomach, but that passed a moment after he stood upright again.

"Let's get aboard the ship," he said, leaning on Lissea's arm. Men stood close, ready to help but unwilling to interfere until asked to. Their gun muzzles were vertical. "We've got to get out of this place."

A plume of smoke curled up like an auger from the site of the warehouse explosions. The light of the primary tinged it dirty gray. Filth and blood, that was all that remained on Pancahte since the expedition had arrived.

Tadziki met them at the top of the ramp. "He's loading a new navigational program into the data base," he announced without preamble. "Del Vore, I mean. Do you want us to use it when we lift? Westerbeke sounds doubtful."

"Yes," Lissea said. "Yes, I suppose he's right. He ought to know what his father's like. It's best we avoid the risks when we can."

Ned grabbed the frame of the nearest bunk and transferred his weight to it. The troops who'd been outside the *Swift* clomped up the ramp, trying not to jostle their captain and adjutant.

Westerbeke came aft to join the officers. Lissea glared angrily past him, but the pilot had left Bonilla in the console beside Carron. Bonilla was competent and anyway, they couldn't lift until things were sorted out further.

"Captain," Westerbeke said, "that course the kid's loaded, the system rejects it as outside parameters. We'll have to override the system to use it."

"You *can* override the system?" Lissea said.

"Ned," Tadziki said in an undertone, "get aft to the medicomp and tell Deke to take care of the swelling and abrasion. If you let it go and it gets infected, you'll be out for the next week."

"Yeah, I can, but it may Transit us off to West Bumfuck with no way to get back," the pilot explained. "It's a big universe. If we don't have reference points, our chances of getting any bloody where are less than zip."

"I'll do that," Ned murmured. He made no attempt to let go of the bunk.

The ramp rose with the last man, Josie Paetz, still on it. Paetz backed aboard, watching for an excuse to shoot until the rising slope forced him down to the deck proper.

The capsule was secured in the center aisle, where they'd heaved the jeeps during the first hurried getaway from Buin. Lendell Doormann's creation wasn't quite as much in the way, but neither did the capsule improve traffic flow within the small vessel.

"Two, maybe all three of those Pancahtan warships are operable despite the commotion," Tadziki reported unasked. "They'll take a while—a day or so unless they're kept on hot standby—to load supplies and get the crews aboard."

"We'll chance the new course," Lissea decided aloud. In deliberate echo she added, "Carron's got a pretty good track record so far." She gave Ned a lopsided grin. "Get forward to the controls, Westerbeke. You'll take us up when I tell you to."

The tannoys rasped, "—*not lift off! I repeat, Telarian vessel*

Swift, *you do not have permission to lift off. If you lift, you will be*
destroyed! Over."

Bonilla peered around the enveloping back of his seat, waiting for
orders. He'd patched the transmission into the PA system in order to
get his superiors' attention. The tower must have noticed that the
Swift's crew had come aboard and the ship was buttoning up.

Westerbeke hastened forward, shoving past men trying to sort
their gear and to understand the situation. Carron stood. "It's
ready!" he called. "I'm ready to shut down the tower."

Lissea keyed her helmet to access the ship's external commo
system. "Swift *to Astragal Tower,*" she said. *"We hear and understand.*
We're just checking airtightness following hull damage. Swift *out.*"

She glanced at Tadziki. "We *are* airtight, aren't we? How much
damage do we have?"

The adjutant shrugged. "Nothing we can't fix at the first layover,"
he said. "Some leakage, yes, but nothing that would keep me on
Pancahte."

"All personnel in place for liftoff!" Lissea ordered. The tannoys
thundered her words an instant out of synch with her lips. "Carron,
when Westerbeke tells you, shut down the tower."

Ned stepped down the aisle to where the capsule was stored. He
paused for a moment. Raff picked him up bodily and handed him
over the obstruction to Yazov on the other side.

"How's he going to fix the tower?" Josie Paetz demanded from
his uncle's side. "Is he going to blow it up?"

"My guess is he's going to send a shutdown signal to the
terminal's powerplant," Ned replied. "But I didn't ask. Maybe he *will*
blow them up. He's capable of it."

The part of his mind that answered the question floated some
distance above the body it putatively occupied. Though Lissea's
voice was strong and controlled, her face looked as though she'd
been dragged from the same coffin as her great-granduncle.

Ned pulled himself onto his berth and closed his eyes. He felt
the paired bunks sway as the adjutant got into the lower unit.

Ned lifted himself onto an elbow and looked around. "Hey
Tadziki," he said. "Where *are* we going then? I didn't ask."

"Wasatch 1029," Tadziki said. He sounded tired as well. The past several hours hadn't been a rest cure for anybody. "It's a listed planet, not that there's anything there according to the pilotry data. We'll have to hope our—Master Del Vore is correct about the routing."

The *Swift* shook herself. Westerbeke was clearing the fuel feeds before he applied full power.

"*Tower to Telarian vessel* Swift!" the PA system snarled. An image of the terminal complex filled the main screen forward. Smoke from the overturned freighter drifted past the buildings, and there seemed to be a fire in the parking area as well. "*You have been warned for the last time! A detachment of the Treasurer's G—*"

The Pancahtan voice crackled silent. All the terminal's lighted windows went dark.

"Lift off!" warned Westerbeke, and the *Swift* began to rise on full power.

WASATCH 1029

Wasatch 1029 was brilliant in the blue sky of its human-habitable planet. The air was like summer in the mid-latitudes of Tethys, though the vagrant breezes didn't leave a taste of salt on Ned's lips to make him feel completely at home.

"Blood and *martyrs,*" Deke Warson snarled. "This place gives me the creeps."

A saw screamed on the other side of the vessel. Three men under Tadziki were cutting and welding plastic sheet-stock into a casket for Lendell Doormann.

Lissea and Carron Del Vore had spent the uneventful Transit from Pancahte studying the circuitry beneath the capsule's outer plating. They wanted to remove interior plates as well, but not even the *Swift*'s hard-bitten complement was willing to share their limited interior accommodations with a grinning mummy.

Deke struck viciously with his gun butt at what Ned called a plant for the lack of a better word. A gnarled bloom the size of a man's fist grew on a meter-long stalk. Its form was as insubstantial as patterns of dust motes dancing in sunlight, but the shape retained itself until the plastic butt smashed through it. Bits of bloom, vaguely russet, drifted away in the air and settled slowly.

"Look at that!" Deke said. "How does that happen? What if we're *breathing* them?"

Ned looked down. His boots and those of the rest of the *Swift*'s personnel had crushed other, infinitely varied "plants" into the soil around the vessel. It was inevitable and no different than what would have happened on a planet whose vegetation was more similar to that of Earth. The fragility of the trampled forms made the destruction seem worse, though.

He ought to be used to destruction by now.

"It's no problem, Deke," Ned said aloud. "You breathe microbes and bits of plant life on every planet you've ever been on. This place isn't dangerous."

He looked at the sunlit hills. He didn't suppose he'd ever see the planet again after the *Swift* lifted for Kazan. "It's clean here. I like it. Especially since Pancahte."

"If you like this place. . ." Warson said as he turned away. He swatted at another bloom, scattering it like a bomb blast. ". . . then you're fucking nuts!"

The *Swift* would leave Wasatch in a day or two, carrying Lendell Doormann's casket in the external lifeboat bay. Toll Warson and another team were repairing damage caused by a hundred-kilo chunk of lava. The impact had sprung plates and probably would have smashed the lifeboat if the *Swift* still carried one.

The hilltops were forested with larger versions of the plants here in the valley. The planet had animal life as well, though none of the reported larger forms had appeared since the *Swift* landed.

Some of the men compared the local life-forms to jellyfish, but the creatures were really more similar to ripples in a running stream. A ripple is a disruption to a fluid's smooth flow. It remains essentially unchanged so long as the flow maintains, even though the molecules forming its pattern shift rapidly and constantly. Life here imposed its patterns on the environment as surely as hidden rocks did on the water of a stream.

Half the men aboard the *Swift* hated Wasatch as much as Deke did. The other half relaxed for the first time since they'd lifted from Telaria, and neither party could imagine why the others felt the way they did. Funny to think that people similar in many ways would react so differently to a planet: rock and air and water. It was a mistake to believe every ruthless killer was the same. . . .

Lissea loved Wasatch. She and Carron had wandered off

together, taking a break from their concentrated examination of the capsule. The ground would be pleasantly warm on the south slopes.

Herne Lordling came out of the hatchway and stood on the ramp, looking around. He didn't carry a tumbler, but he'd been drinking. Like Ned, he was off duty at the moment, and he had a right to his liquor ration.

"You," he called. "Slade."

The men nearby grew quiet. Moiseyev, on top of the vessel, slid down the opposite side to where Tadziki was.

"Got a problem with me, Herne?" Ned asked. His upper lip began to itch, though during Transit the medicomp had repaired the damage the punch had done. The physical damage.

"No problem," Lordling said. His face was flushed. Ned couldn't read his expression, but anger and embarrassment were both part of it. "I just want you and me to talk. We can take the jeep."

"Take the jeep where, Herne?" Tadziki asked as he walked around the stern of the vessel. His casket-builders, Raff among them, sauntered along behind him. Unlike Ned, they were all armed.

Lordling turned. "Just out a ways," he said. He wiped his mouth with the back of his hand as if to scrub away a bad taste. "Look, I want to talk to Slade, that's all. Do you have a problem with that?"

"I don't have a problem with it," Ned said. "But I'll drive. And we're not heading east."

"I don't give a fuck where we go!" Lordling said. "I just want to get away from this place, all right?"

The adjutant nodded slowly. "Sure, Herne," he said. "That's all right. But don't get out of helmet range—"

About two klicks with the *Swift* in a valley and no repeaters setup—

"—and be back in an hour. We might need a jeep for something, and we've only got the one now."

Lordling jumped from the ramp without responding and strode to the little hovercraft waiting by the bow blister.

"Hey, kid?" Deke Warson called.

Ned looked up. Deke held his 2-cm weapon by the balance. He pitched it muzzle-up to Ned, who caught the heavy weapon.

"He won't need that!" Herne Lordling said from the passenger seat of the jeep.

"That's good, Herne," Warson replied. "Because it'd be really too bad if he did."

Lordling faced front. Ned got in, stuck the borrowed weapon in the butt sock, and switched on.

"Where do you want to go, then?" he asked quietly. The inner muscles of his forearms were quivering in hormonal expectation. Herne was the bigger man by twenty kilos and not much of it was fat, but the day Ned couldn't handle somebody twice his age—Well, he wasn't worried.

"Just get the fuck out of here!" Lordling snapped. He shook himself. "Look, Slade, I don't want to fight. Okay?"

Ned engaged the fans and pulled away from the vessel. "That's your choice, Lordling," he said, making an effort to prevent his tone from turning the statement into a challenge.

He headed west, because the sun was already in the tops of the tall trees there, and because Lissea and Carron had gone east. He hoped he'd be able to drive between the insubstantial trunks rather than tearing a swath through them.

"Look, Slade, I wanted to talk to you because I think you respect Lissea," Lordling blurted. "Those other bastards, all they care about in a woman is her cunt and if she gives good head."

"We're not on a church outing, Herne," Ned said carefully. "If Lissea doesn't mind people treating her like one of the guys, then I don't see where the problem is. It's not as though anybody's made trouble about taking orders from a woman." *Except maybe you.*

"It's not that!" Lordling said. "It's what she's doing with this pissant she's brought along. That's got to stop, and if she doesn't see it, somebody's got to stop it for her."

Ned drove through a band of brush several meters tall. The branches spread into bell-shaped tips, like morning-glory flowers, from which dangled veils of fronds. The shapes were immeasurably more delicate than could have been achieved by denser matter which had to support its structure physically.

The jeep tore the bushes like violet fog. Ned thought the air was suddenly cool, but his mind could have been playing tricks on him.

"Herne," he said as if each word were a cartridge he was loading in preparation for a duel. "I don't think Lissea's private life is any business of ours."

"Look, Slade," Lordling said hoarsely. His big hands knotted on the jeep's dashboard and his eyes were straight ahead. "I'm not saying a woman ought to be alone, it's not like that. But this *puppy*. She's wasting herself just to look at him!"

The jeep was among the tall trees. They grew more like coral branching in a fluid medium than internally supported plants. The bases were a meter or two across, but vast pastel arrays lifted to spread and ramify over hundreds of square meters at their tops.

Driving through the forest was like entering a cathedral with groined vaults. The sound of the jeep's fans was an intrusion.

"Herne . . ." Ned said. He stopped, because he didn't know how to continue.

"Well say it, then!" Lordling snapped. "Are you just like the rest? I tell you, Lissea's *different*."

Ned saw a patch of direct sunlight and steered for it He couldn't talk while he was driving, not about this. His hands were sweaty, and his muscles jumped as they had before the firefight on Ajax Four.

"She's different, we're all different, Herne," he said. He'd been all right because he hadn't let himself think about it, he was good at not thinking about things, but Lordling wouldn't leave it at that. "It's our job to leave her alone!"

Full sun struck them on a tongue of rock which stabbed into the next valley. Ned reversed his nacelles quickly and dumped the plenum chamber. The jeep stopped a few meters from the edge of a seventy-degree escarpment.

The immediate slopes were covered by the big trees, but the valley floor was open. On it were hundreds of golden puff-balls the size of Terran hippopotami. Some of them drifted against the wind. Ned had found the animal life of Wasatch.

Ned stepped from the jeep, staring across the valley. He thrust his hands into his side pockets. "Look, I don't much like the guy," he said, "but I don't have to. He got us out of a couple tight places. I could say, 'Lissea pays her debts,' and that'd be enough."

"That's how a *whore* pays her debts!" Lordling said. "She's not a whore!"

The golden creatures were nearly globular. They began to move as a group up the valley's western slope. As the herbivores moved, three streaks of silvery translucence shifted from among the golden creatures to space themselves along the eastern edge of the herd.

"She's a person," Ned said. The silvery figures were more than three meters tall, slim and as supple as willow wands. "She's got a lot in common with Del Vore—"

"She's got nothing in common with him!"

Ned turned. "They're of the same *class,*" he said harshly. "They've both been stepped on by their families. They're both engineers. Grow bloody up, Herne! He didn't hypnotize her, he didn't hold a gun to her head. She's doing what she wants to do!"

Lordling looked around for something to hit. He took a step toward a tree, thought the better of it, and kicked the jeep's skirts as hard as he could. His boot rebounded and spun him halfway around.

Ned faced the valley again. The distant crest was unforested. Sunset turned the herbivores into disks of molten gold as they eased out of sight. The silver figures moved slowly up the hillside after their charges, staying always between the herd and the watching humans.

"I thought," Lordling muttered, "that if we arranged it together . . . I thought you'd understand."

"I understand," Ned said. I *understand that I'd like to stick a pistol in Carron Del Vore's mouth. I'd like to make him bite on it before I pulled the trigger.* "If I thought he had to be killed, I'd kill him myself and not worry about what happened next. But it's her choice. It's Lissea's choice."

Lordling muttered something, probably a curse. "Let's go back, then. I was wrong about you."

"In a moment," Ned said.

The herbivores had vanished. The silvery figures stood on the far crest with the low sun behind them. Ned bowed toward them, as though he were greeting Councillors of Tethys at a formal gathering.

One after another, the shimmering silver creatures bowed also. Then they drifted out of sight.

"Now we'll go," Ned said.

He felt calm. It had been a long time since he last felt calm.

KAZAN

Westerbeke was at one of the aft-rotated navigational consoles; Lissea was in the other. Facing the seats and the projected display was the rest of what had become the *Swift*'s command group: Tadziki, Herne Lordling, Carron, and Edward Slade.

Kazan, their planned layover, was the blue-green ball forming a backdrop to the defensive satellite on which the *Swift*'s sensor inputs were focused. Ned wasn't good at keeping his face blank, but the others didn't look happy at what they saw on the display either.

"Intercourse with this world has been proscribed by the Sextile Alliance," the tannoys said, broadcasting the warning from the satellite by modulated laser. *"Vessels which approach within one light-minute will be destroyed if they attempt to leave the proscribed region again. Vessels which attack a satellite of the defensive cluster will be destroyed. There are no exceptions. Intercourse—"*

Lissea touched a switch and shut off the sound. The remainder of the crew, watching over the shoulders of the command group, muttered and argued among themselves. Their lives were at risk also. Though none of them expected their opinions to affect the captain's decision, they *had* opinions.

The satellite was one of a quartet forming a tetrahedron to enclose Kazan. Each satellite contained enough directed energy and missile weapons to ravage a continent.

"After two hundred years," Herne Lordling said without enthusiasm, "the systems may have broken down."

"The sensors and commo haven't," Westerbeke said. "Look, I don't like this. We can hold out till Celandine."

Several of the men behind Ned growled.

"If we don't land here," Tadziki said, "then I advise sequestering all the weapons. It won't do a great deal of good, of course, as there's no one aboard who isn't capable of killing with his bare hands."

The *Swift*'s complement had accumulated gear at every layover, and the initial tight stowage of Telaria had long since gone by the boards. Boxes, bags, and bottles covered bunks and the spaces between them. The interior fittings themselves had never recovered from damage inflicted during the panicked rush from Buin.

Partially dismantled for examination, Lendell Doormann's capsule blocked the aisle even more thoroughly than it had when the crew brought it aboard. The ship stank like a pigshed despite constant filtering by the environmental system.

Tempers were short. As Tadziki had implied, lethally short.

"We'll proceed," said Lissea, "on the assumption that we're going to land." She smiled coldly. "Landing's easy, after all. The trick will be lifting off again."

Kazan was a jungle planet with a considerable resource base. The colony's population was split between a ruling oligarchy and— the ninety-eight percent remaining—workers whose very lives were forfeit at the oligarchs' whim.

None of that would have been a matter of concern off Kazan, were it not that the oligarchs visualized themselves as rulers of a multi-planet empire as well. Manpower was no problem for them. Just as European colonizers had conquered Africa with native African troops, and millennia earlier Spartan nobles had gone to war accompanied by ten times their number in armed slaves, so the underclass of Kazan fought with a merc leavening of oligarch officers.

Three times Kazan attacked its neighbors—and was driven back, but at the cost of enormous disruption to the victimized planets. After the third time, the six worlds under potential threat had banded together to end the problem once and for all.

Cities could be bombed, but the oligarchs had dispersed their industry widely. Invading the planet was out of the question. The population of Kazan would inevitably outnumber whatever ground forces could be transported across interstellar space, and none of the Alliance's planners had had the stomach for guerrilla warfare in a jungle against a fanatical foe.

So the Alliance had opted for quarantine instead. It cut Kazan off from the rest of the universe with a constellation of unmanned satellites, programmed to destroy any vessel that attempted to leave the planet.

That had been two hundred years before. No one knew what Kazan was like now, but the planet was still the only charted layover point between Wasatch 1029 and Celandine. Given the conditions aboard the *Swift*, the risk was one the complement was willing to accept—if they could avoid the defensive satellites.

"We can enter the satellite's control system through the communications channels," Carron said. He stood with his heels twenty centimeters apart, toes splayed outward, and his hands crossed behind his back. "When we have gotten access, we need only to exempt ourselves from the parameters of ships to be attacked."

"If it were that easy, somebody would have tried it before now," Herne Lordling said, glaring at the Pancahtan.

"The satellites were built two centuries ago," Lissea said. "The *Swift*'s systems are Telarian state of the art *today*. We have more processing power than the Alliance's engineers dreamed of—or Kazan's."

"They don't *have* a commo system," Westerbeke said. "What they've got is a warning beacon, but you can't talk *back* to the satellites. There's no way in like that."

"They have sensors, though," Ned said. "They have to, for targeting. There's a channel to their control system that way. It ought to be possible."

Lissea looked sideways at Westerbeke, then across the display to the four men standing in front of her. "All right," she said. "That should be possible. Are we agreed?"

Westerbeke grimaced. The others nodded, even Lordling.

Lissea nodded also. "Agreed, then. Carron, Ned—the next step is up to us, I believe. We need to find both an access channel and the codes with which to insert our requirements in the satellite's data base."

She frowned. "Will one satellite be enough, or will we have to deal with the entire constellation?"

"If we remove one satellite from the array," Tadziki said, "it leaves a gap through which we can exit the planet if we're careful."

He looked at Westerbeke.

"Oh, we'll be careful," the pilot said. "Don't worry about my end of this. But you'd better be right about making friends with their AI. The first we'll know if you screw up is the fifty-centimeter bolt ripping us inside out."

After seven hours thirty-two minutes, Ned made the last keystroke and rocked back from his cross-legged sitting position to lie on the deck. The other two team members were slumped in the navigational couches.

"'*She has wrapped it in her kerchief, she has cast it in the sea,*'" Ned quoted in a loud voice to the ceiling. "'*Says sink ye, swim ye, bonnie wee babe, you'll get no more of me!*'"

"What the hell's that?" Herne Lordling growled. He and Tadziki sat on the lower forward bunks, by their presence closing access to the team working at the computer stations in the bow.

"It's an old song about a woman who found a way out of her problem," Ned said. "Her name was Mary Hamilton, and they hanged her. Hung her?"

He closed his eyes, then quickly opened them again. When Ned's eyes were shut, his brain pulsed with the sine curves that they'd been using as code analogues. Yellow and blue—green for a match, but always with tiny spikes of yellow and blue to mar the chain. Not much of a difference, but a man with a bullet hole through the forehead isn't much different from a living man—to look at.

"Have you gotten us clearance to land, then, Lissea?" Tadziki said. "To lift off again, that is."

"Yes," said Carron.

"No," said Lissea a half-beat later.

Ned lifted himself onto his elbow. Lissea and Carron raised themselves on the couches and looked at one another.

"Well, it's the same thing," Carron said to her. "Just as good."

"Just as good *isn't* the same thing," Lissea said tartly. They were all frazzled by the project. The rest of the crew, left twiddling their thumbs while the experts worked to enter the satellite's control system, probably wasn't in a much better humor.

"Instead of fucking around," Deke Warson asked in a voice as soft as a snake crossing a bedsheet, "would somebody like to explain what's going on?"

"The folks who built the satellite, may they rot in Hell," Ned said without turning his head, "designed two separate systems. One collects and analyzes sensor data."

"Tracking and targeting," Lissea said. "That's the system we can access."

"And when it's done," Ned resumed, "it hands the data over to a wholly separate chain which makes the decision to fire. The second system is a closed loop and we can't touch it."

"Can you adjust the sensors to feed improper range and course information to the gunnery control?" Westerbeke suggested.

Carron waved his hand to brush the suggestion away. "That wouldn't do any good," he said. "It's self-correcting. The second salvo will be on top of us if the first one isn't. I came up with a solution: change the firing order of the batteries that engage us."

"What the hell does that mean?" Josie Paetz growled.

"Hey, Slade?" said Toll Warson.

Ned lurched upright again and swung to look at the gathered crew. The men were drawn and angry. Several of them were playing with weapons.

"Yeah, Toll?"

"This going to work?"

"You bet your ass," Ned said. He smiled coldly.

Warson smiled back. Between them, it must have looked like feeding time in the lion house. "Cap'n," Toll said to Lissea, "if we're going to go, let's go. Sitting around like this just makes it worse, it always does."

There was a rumble of assent from the crew. Herne Lordling turned and glared a challenge to Lissea.

"Yes," she said, "all right. Westerbeke, take the helm again. Carron, go to your bunk. The same with the rest of you. We'll transit within the proscribed area, between the satellite and the planetary surface. Is that understood?"

Carron rose, but the arc of men watching and listening didn't break up for him to pass them to what had been Louis Boxall's bunk.

"What happens then?" Herne Lordling asked.

"Then there's a choice," Lissea replied in a cool tone that ignored the fact her orders were being disregarded for the moment. "Either we land on Kazan, or we make an immediate attempt to lift out of the gravity well. The choice, which is *mine,* is that we lift. That we know immediately whether or not we've gimmicked the satellite sufficiently to keep us alive."

Westerbeke laughed grimly as he pushed past Carron. "No, ma'am," he said as he seated himself and began setting up the Transit parameters. "We only know if it *did* work. Otherwise, we don't know any bloody thing at all."

Deke Warson stretched and sauntered back toward his bunk. "You know," he said, "nobody'd ever believe it if I was to die in bed. . . ."

                                        .

They came out of Transit within the orbits of the constellation of satellites, nearly into the upper reaches of Kazan's atmosphere. The planet more than filled the frame of the main display forward. Ned switched his visor to accept a close-up view of Satellite III, the nearest of the array, instead.

At standby, the satellites were spheres overlaid with smooth bulges. That shape changed in the view Ned watched.

The *Swift's* systems chuckled and groaned. The navigational computer was updating the vessel's real position against the one it had calculated before Transit. Even after so short a hop, less than three light-minutes, the calculations required for another Transit would take the better part of an hour.

The preliminaries to Transit would require minor attitude

adjustments to align the vessel perfectly with the gravitational field. At the point the *Swift* began making those adjustments, Satellite III would convert the vessel to an expanding fireball.

Because the *Swift* had entered the proscribed region, Satellite III unmasked the batteries that would be required if the interloper attempted to leave. Covering plates opened so that missile carousels could extend. Turrets rotated and their shutters withdrew to expose the huge powerguns within—50-cm, Westerbeke had guessed. The weapons were at least that big.

Westerbeke wasn't going to Transit away from Kazan. All he had to do to trigger the satellite's response was to trip the main engines for a second or two to raise the *Swift* into a higher orbit.

"*Stand by for acceleration,*" Westerbeke warned. Then, muttered but still on intercom, "*If we had a lifeboat, we could use it for the guinea pig.*"

"*We have used the lifeboat for other necessary purposes, Master Westerbeke,*" Tadziki said in a voice colder than Satellite III's unfired cannon. "*Get on with your duties. Now!*"

The engines snarled, thrusting Ned against the contoured cushions of his bunk.

The image of Satellite III rotated and began to expand. There was a blue flash, copper ions from ten or more big-bore powerguns firing simultaneously—

Into the shutters that protected the weapons from cosmic dust and radiation. A moment later, missiles launched from within closed batteries ruptured the structure still further. Though the warheads didn't have time to arm, rocket exhaust had the effect of explosives when vented within the satellite.

"*Good* fucking job, Slade!" Deke Warson shouted down the bay.

"Wasn't my idea," Ned called back. "Thank Prince Carron."

They—Lissea and Carron, but particularly Ned, because he was the one who was familiar with weapons systems—had switched Satellite III's firing order. Instead of the guns and missiles prepared for use, the firing signal had gone to batteries that didn't bear on the *Swift* and therefore hadn't been deployed.

The control system would have corrected the error with its

second salvo—if there had been anything left of system or satellite after the first.

The explosions that vaporized half the structure provided a violent thrust to spin the remainder around the center of mass. Satellite III ripped into three large chunks, a spray of fragments, and a cloud of gas and plasma. Centrifugal force flung the portions apart in a glowing, glittering starburst.

"Take us in closer for reconnaissance, Master Westerbeke," Lissea ordered from the backup console. *"I don't think we need to worry about the defensive cordon when we're ready to leave."*

Men cheered from their bunks. There was still the situation on Kazan to worry about, but when Coyne shouted, "I'm going to find me a girl with tits so big I'd smother if she got on top of me!" he was voicing the optimism of most of the complement.

"Prepare for—" Westerbeke began.

The *Swift* shuddered.

"What the hell was that?" Bonilla said, his voice high in the sudden silence.

"That was the satellite," Lissea said in cool assurance. *"We were close enough to feel the gas ball from the explosion. Gentlemen, prepare for acceleration as we drop into a lower orbit to choose a landing site. Captain out."*

As the engines fired, Ned switched on the remote image on his visor. Kazan rushed up at him, a green surface that took on form and texture with the passing seconds.

From a reconnaissance orbit, the trees looked like the tops of green thunderclouds, surging with death and rage.

On the second orbital pass, Lissea switched the imaging system to ground-penetrating radar. It quickly limned the geometric outlines of a city hidden from optical scanners by the vegetation. There was a circular crater in the center of the thirty-hectare sprawl.

"Did the Alliance bomb Kazan?" Ned wondered aloud. "There isn't any record of that in the pilotry data. Just that they'd built the satellite array."

While the *Swift* was in unpowered orbit, he didn't need to use his commo helmet to speak. Tadziki could answer or not, as he saw fit.

"There wouldn't necessarily be a record," Tadziki replied. He sounded vaguely doubtful also. "Our data base was assembled on Telaria, after all; and in a war, not everything gets reported."

He paused. "It may be that the damage occurred after the quarantine, though. It's unlikely that a society like the one described became peaceful when it was forced in on itself."

The damage—the bomb damage, nothing else could have caused it—hadn't been repaired.

"*All right, pilot,*" Lissea ordered. She used the general channel so that everyone aboard would be clear about the intended course of events. "*Set us down on the outskirts of that settled area on the next pass. Adjutant, prepare a security detail for following the landing. Over.*"

"*Roger,*" Tadziki rasped. "*Yazov and Paetz, you Warsons, Harlow and Coyne, and I'll take Slade for the fourth team. Locations as marked on your visors—*"

The adjutant overrode Ned's visor display and those of the others. A schematic of the *Swift* and four points at some distance from the vessel appeared against a neutral background. The dot at the bow pulsed, indicating the location Ned would share with Tadziki.

"*That's a hundred meters out, not a cordon and not an ambush, just listening posts. Remaining personnel form a reaction group under Lordling's tactical control. Out.*"

"*Adjutant,*" Lissea said. "*I don't want you running out into the jungle like that. Choose somebody else for that slot. Over.*"

"*Captain,*" Tadziki said, "*you have full authority to remove me from my position and make any assignments you please. Adjutant over.*"

One or both of the Warsons chuckled. Ned himself grinned.

"*Assignments confirmed,*" Lissea said in a flat voice. "*Prepare for braking. Captain ou—*"

The final consonant was smothered by the roar of the engines dropping the *Swift* finally toward the planetary surface.

❊ ❊ ❊

At the hatchway, Herne Lordling handed a man-pack sensor to the low man of each outpost team. Ned took his, paused while Tadziki lifted the unit onto him, and grunted as he trotted down the ramp.

Twenty kilos of electronics, plus the submachine gun, two bandoliers, helmet and body armor, equipment belt with tools and medical kit, ration pack, and two-liter condensing canteen. The ground at the base of the ramp smoked, and the leaf mold had burned to carbon dust in the exhaust.

The buttress roots of great trees were festooned with vines and epiphytes beyond the ellipse the *Swift* had cleared for itself to land. The debris rotting on the forest floor was dusted with fungus and pale-leafed saplings that would die soon unless something ripped a hole in the canopy so that light could reach them.

Ned's load made him waddle in the soft soil. He had outfitted himself this way even though they wouldn't be so far away that he couldn't hit the *Swift* with a thrown pebble, if it weren't for the trees in between.

Raff was on the *Swift's* upper deck, carrying the tribarrel as well as his rocket launcher. Dewey and Hatton clambered up the external ladder with the weapon's base and two canisters of ammunition. Three steps beyond the edge of the exhaust-seared clearing, Ned couldn't see them or the ship. Voices were muted, and though metal clanged, the direction even of audible sounds was uncertain.

Tadziki led. Both men carried cutting bars, but they didn't need to hack their way. Ned stumbled twice on surface roots, and once the loop of a heavy vine rapped his helmet hard enough to stagger him, but there was no close-woven ground cover to turn travel into an exercise in carpentry.

There was no sign of Kazan's human colonists, either.

"Here," the adjutant said, dropping to one knee where the leaf mold humped above a long, linear mound. Trees, spaced so closely that their roots formed knotted handshakes on the ground, cut optical sightlines down to a few meters, but the electronic sensors wouldn't care.

Tadziki was breathing hard, though he didn't have the additional burden of the sensor pack. Instead of reporting verbally, he broke squelch twice with his helmet radio, indicating that Team Two was in position.

The adjutant must be nervous. Ned sure was. The sweat wicking through his utilities beneath his body armor was only partly the result of heavy work in a hot, saturated atmosphere. He hit his pack's cross-strap release buckle, then helped set the sensor unit up on its own short legs.

Ned eyed the green/green-brown/green-black/chartreuse surroundings with his submachine gun ready to fire. The pack's built-in screen defaulted to LIFE FORMS/50K+, but Tadziki shifted it through the alternative readouts one by one.

"Well, I'll be hanged!" Tadziki said. He sounded surprised, not concerned.

Ned grinned. "So it tells fortunes? What else d'ya see?"

He glanced down at the unit. The built-in screen wasn't strictly necessary since the data were transmitted to the base unit in the *Swift,* but people in an observation post like to know what's going on around them too.

Tadziki used the tip of his cutting bar as a trowel, curling plant debris off the mound where he'd been sitting. He didn't turn on the tool's vibrating blade.

The display, set to neutron-emission patterns, showed the ground plan of a built-up area. Nothing but trees and lesser vegetation appeared to Ned's naked eyes. He scraped at the mound with the edge of his boot.

Tadziki reached down, grunted, and came up with a squared stone which dripped dirt and pink worms. The upper surfaces of the stone were scorched, and the bits of remaining mortar were calcined from heat.

"There's a whole foundation down here," Tadziki said. He dropped the stone and worked out another. "Building burned and the foundation knocked over with hammers and prybars."

"The bomb blast," Ned suggested. "They were using nukes. The background radiation's still five times what it ought to be here."

"Negative," Tadziki said. "Wrecking bars." He pointed to the parallel chips from one edge of the ashlar; upward pressure had flaked the stone away.

Ned looked to where his boot had scored the leaf mold. A jagged spike of bone stuck up from between jumbled stones. Ned levered one of the blocks away with his heel and pulled the yellowish shaft free. The other joint was intact.

"Human arm," he said.

"Thigh bone," Tadziki corrected. "A child's."

Ned put the bone down gently in the hole from which he had drawn it. He switched the sensor display to the default setting again.

"Like Burr-Detlingen," he said. He tried to imagine what the city had looked like before men bombed it, burned it, and pulled down the very stones of its foundations. Not even an archaeologist could tell without first clearing the jungle which had recovered the site.

"Not like Burr-Detlingen," Tadziki said. "On Burr-Detlingen, they fought like cats, tearing each other's throats out."

"What would you call this place, then?" Ned asked. He watched the screen out of the corner of his eye. Its pink field would ripple with interference patterns if an animal entered its hundred, hundred-and-fifty-meter range. The sensor's shielded back prevented it from registering the outpost crew.

Tadziki brushed his hands together, then wiped the remainder of the clinging dirt off on his trousers. "This was a cancer," he said softly. "The people of Kazan were sheep, and their rulers were cancers that they wouldn't cut out. They obeyed until they'd destroyed everything. At the end, I suppose the oligarchs died too, but by then it was too late."

"Why in hell did they want to do *this?*" Ned demanded. "The rulers, I mean?"

"In Hell, yes," Tadziki said, "Because they were insane, I suppose. And because, instead of rebelling, people took their madmen's orders right down to the end, until there was nothing left. If people will take crazy orders, there's always somebody to give those orders."

His mouth quirked in something that could have been described as a smile. "Maybe the people were afraid to fight them, maybe they were just conditioned for too long to obey. Either way, they're all dead now."

A broad-bodied worm or caterpillar crawled over the leaf mold, oblivious to the humans. The creature was brilliantly scarlet and covered with fine hairs. It was as long as Ned's foot. He shifted cautiously to avoid coming in contact with something so obviously poisonous.

"What's the answer, then?" he asked. "Fight the crazies or knuckle under to them, you're saying it comes to the same thing in the end?"

"Sometimes there aren't any answers," the adjutant said. "No good ones, at any rate."

He braced his palms against a tree-trunk and stretched until he'd bowed his back into a reverse curve. The muzzle of his slung submachine gun knocked against the pulpy bark. "I needed to get out of the ship," he said.

Ripples shimmered across the sensor screen, but the source that caused them didn't appear as a point on the display. Something of large or moderate size had walked through the jungle, roughly paralleling the edge of the coverage area.

Ned relaxed again. "What," he said, looking at the older man, "do you think about Lissea and Carron?"

Tadziki laughed. "I'm impressed by your subtlety," he said.

Ned gave him a hard grin. "I thought of saying, 'Lissea and the new fellow seem to work well together,'" he said. "But you're going to know what I mean, so instead of pretending to manipulate you, I just asked."

Tadziki nodded. "So you did," he said. "What I think is . . ."

He looked at Ned, assessing him, and resumed. "Lissea needs somebody. For 'release,' however you want to phrase it. Del Vore's an outsider. She can—deal with him without causing the problems there'd been if she chose anybody from the crew. The real crew."

"Sort of what I thought," Ned said, turning to face the jungle. Voices hooted in the near distance. He thought they might be birds, though he hadn't seen any flying creatures here, even at the invertebrate level.

"I don't think," Tadziki continued calmly, "that Del Vore would be Lissea's first choice under other circumstances. The situation could change when we get back to Telaria and Lissea takes her place on the board."

"Dream on!" Ned said.

"Umm?"

Ned looked at the adjutant. "They aren't going to give her a seat," Ned explained. "Tadziki, this sort of politics I know—I've *seen.* I saw it when my uncle Don came home to Tethys."

"What *will* happen, then?" Tadziki said. "Assuming we get back."

"Oh, yes, assuming that," Ned said. Politics were part of the Academy's curriculum, because the politicians make the decision to hire and release the mercenaries who are the final arbiters of right.

"What I think," he continued, unconsciously aping the adjutant's delivery of moments before, "is that when Lissea returns with the capsule instead of dying conveniently out of sight as her relatives had intended . . . I think they'll give her a further runaround."

The muscles of his face set in planes that made him look wholly different, and not entirely human. "Then I think she'll stop playing the game by their rules. And play by ours."

"Outpost Two," warned the *Swift* in Lissea's voice. *"There's a group of creatures approaching your location. They may be the local inhabitants, over."*

He and Tadziki had forgotten the screen as they talked. Black ripples streamed back from eight—no, seven points advancing toward the outpost. The thickness of the ripple was related to the size of the creature being sensed, while the angle of the V indicated the speed at which it was moving. These were broad and shallow, suggesting creatures at the upper human parameter sauntering very slowly through the jungle . . . or creeping forward to attack.

Tadziki keyed his helmet. *"Roger, we're observing,"* he said. *"Two out."*

Ned heard the hooting again, coming from their front. He checked the loaded-chamber indicator on his submachine gun's receiver, switched the weapon off safe, and slipped three meters away from Tadziki to crouch in the gray folds of a buttress root. He silently adjusted his helmet to echo the sensor data as minute points in the upper left-hand quadrant of his visor. He needed to know where the intruders were, but not at the cost of degrading his ability to see and shoot.

Brush crackled. Voices hooted to one another. If this was a hunting or war party, the members had terrible noise discipline. That didn't mean they *weren't* hunting. The local prey might have dull senses by human standards.

The midmost of the seven dots was ahead of its companions. The creature it indicated must be very close to—

Hairy hands gripped a fan of leaves two meters from Ned and tore them away. The creature reached for a vermilion fruit swelling against the uncovered tree-trunk an instant before it saw Ned staring through his gunsight.

The creature weighed in the order of two hundred kilograms. It was covered with delicate blond fur, all but the face, which was bare and human. Its blue eyes flashed fully open as the creature leaped onto its hind legs and fluted a mellifluous challenge with its long arms spread wide.

Ned didn't move. His weapon was aimed between the creature's nipples. He wasn't sure that the submachine gun's 1-cm charges could stop an animal so large if it rushed him.

It was male. Its pubic triangle was marked by darker fur.

Wild crashing sounded in the forest beyond. The dots indicating the remainder of the pack, or family, rocked back the way they had come.

The creature facing Ned dropped to its knuckles and hooted angrily again. Ned didn't move. The creature turned suddenly and vanished into the forest. After a moment, Ned let out his breath and stood up.

He keyed his helmet. "*Two-two to base,*" he reported. "*All clear. Just local apes. Over.*"

"*Roger,*" Lissea said. "*Base out.*"

He returned to sensor pack. Tadziki was still there, his submachine gun ready.

"You saw what it was?" Tadziki asked.

"Yeah."

"There aren't any indigenous apes on Kazan," Tadziki said quietly.

"There are now," Ned said. He thought of the radiation readings, at this site and the Lord knew what in other flattened cities.

The *Swift*'s drill whined, beginning to pierce the laterite in search of water for the vessel's tanks. The next layover— Celandine—was a highly developed planet. It would feel strange to resupply through normal commercial channels.

Tadziki keyed his helmet and said, "*Adjutant to outposts. Things seem pretty quiet. Each post can release one man at the senior's choice. The other fellow will be relieved in two hours. Out.*"

He looked at Ned. Ned shook his head. He didn't want to go back to the ship any more than the adjutant himself seemed to want to.

Ned squatted down. "Hey, Tadziki?" he said.

"Umm?"

"About Lissea and Carron, what you said?"

"Yeah."

"Sometimes there aren't any good answers," Ned said. His smile was as humorless as a knife blade.

CELANDINE

Île de Rameau on Celandine was the busiest spaceport in a trading cluster of twenty worlds. The sound of ships taking off and landing was a constant rumble through the roof and walls of the closed dock in which the Port Authority's tugs had lodged the *Swift*.

The dock could easily have held a freighter of one hundred thousand tonnes or a score of smaller vessels. The *Swift* was alone; the two robot tugs had returned to orbit before the clamshell roof closed again.

The members of the Pancahte Expedition watched the main forward display tautly. Six Celandine officials drove an open vehicle through a small side door and across the dock's scarred floor toward the *Swift*. The locals chatted to one another.

"They've got guns," Josie Paetz said.

"Two of them are cops, an escort," Ned answered loudly before anyone ratcheted the mercs' nervousness up another notch. "The pair in back have enough braid between them to sell brass for a sideline. That kind of rank doesn't show up if they're expecting a firelight."

"Wish I had a gun," Deke Warson muttered in frustrated wistfulness.

"When I decide to declare war on a planet this size, Warson," Lissea snapped, "you'll be the first one I'll tell."

All the weapons aboard the *Swift* were in closed containers. Not concealed, not even locked away, most of them: there was no way the *Swift* could pretend here to be a peaceful freighter. Tadziki had insisted, however, that none of the crew be openly armed when they greeted the Celandine authorities.

The adjutant's belief that they had to tread lightly was supported by the way the authorities sequestered the *Swift* in a closed dock and ordered the crew to stay buttoned up until further instructions. None of the mercenaries argued the point, but nobody was happy about it either.

Everyone but the driver, one of the policemen, got out of the vehicle. An official in civilian clothes put the end of a contact transducer against the airlock and spoke into it. *"Inspection team coming aboard,"* the *Swift*'s hull announced. *"You may open your hatches now."*

Tadziki opened the main boarding ramp. As the hydraulics whined, Toll Warson said in a lilting voice, "We've come this far with no problems, boys. Let's get the rest of the way back, all right?"

Ned couldn't tell whether or not "with no problems" was meant to be ironic.

Echoes from other spacecraft made the huge hangar rumble like a seashore. The most richly decorated Celandine official raised his voice with familiar unconcern as he and his fellows walked up the ramp, roaring, "I'm Port Commander Flamond and I want you lot to understand two things right off!"

Flamond glared at Lissea and her crew, drawn up two abreast in the aisle on either side of the head of the ramp. Ned and Tadziki headed one rank. Ned hoped that none of the mercenaries behind him were going to catcall in response to Flamond's bluster.

"First," Flamond said. He seemed to have decided Tadziki rather than Lissea, who was on the other side of the aisle, was captain. *"I'm* in charge of Île de Rameau Spaceport. I don't look kindly on anything or anybody who makes my life difficult."

Tadziki nodded. His expression was open, solemn—that of a responsible man agreeing with another responsible man. The lower-ranking Celandine officials looked around the *Swift* with interest, surprise, and—in the case of the armed policeman—obvious concern.

"Second," Flamond said, "there's three warships from Pancahte docked here since two tennights."

Carron stood beside Lissea. His mouth opened in horror. Ned's stomach dropped through the deck plates, and his hands began to tremble.

"They've put in a claim for return of this vessel and crew to answer charges on Pancahte," Flamond continued, "so you people are *already* causing me difficulties."

"Commander Flamond," Lissea said, "I'm Captain Doormann—"

The port commander turned to face her.

"—of the *Swift*. We're registered on Telaria and I'm on the board of Doormann Trading there. The Pancahtans have no right to detain my ship. If they believe they have a claim, they can prosecute it in our courts."

"Which," Tadziki interjected, "are a great deal more fair than the mixture of piracy and imbecility to which we were subjected on Pancahte."

Flamond looked from Lissea to the adjutant and back. He smiled, in a manner of speaking. "Are you telling me that I don't have the authority to hand you over to the Pancahtans, Captain?" he asked softly.

"No sir," Lissea said. "Celandine is a major commercial power, just as Telaria is. You have your law codes, and if they require you to . . . hand us over to murderous pirates, you most certainly have the authority. As well as the power. But I would be surprised to learn that Celandine's codes contained such a provision."

"What's she saying?" Josie Paetz whispered loudly to his uncle. Yazov, standing directly behind Lissea, put a stiff index finger to Paetz' lips. From his expression, he was willing for it to be a pistol.

Flamond guffawed. "Good, good, you understand the position, then," he said. "Which that Del Vore from Pancahte doesn't seem to. He keeps claiming that our laws don't hold for a prince of Pancahte."

He eyed the assembled mercenaries. "I told him that our guns held him, if it came to that. The same holds true for your lot, Doormann. Squashing you like a bug would solve my difficulties quite nicely. Give me half an excuse and that's just what I'll do. *Do* you understand?"

Somebody in a rank behind Ned started to speak. Somebody else had sense enough to elbow the troublemaker hard.

"Yes sir," Lissea said quietly. "We were hoping to water and resupply here for the last leg of our journey back to Telaria. If circumstances make that impossible, we of course understand."

She cleared her throat and lowered her eyes. "We only ask that you hold the Pancahtans here for a few days. To do otherwise would be to turn us over to pirates."

The two civilian officials behind Flamond whispered to one another. The subordinate military officer joined the conversation after a moment.

"That's what you request," Flamond said harshly. "*This* is what you'll get. First, your vessel can resupply here in normal fashion. I will add that although you'll be charged for the use of a bonded hangar—"

He moved his head in a quick upward jerk, indicating the structure which enclosed the *Swift*.

"—you're not being charged the additional costs you've imposed on my operations by the fact I can't permit other vessels to share Hangar Thirty-nine with you. Under the circumstances."

Lissea nodded contritely.

"Second," Flamond continued, "you have five days from now to leave Celandine. If you don't leave, you will be expelled. And I assure you, armed resistance would be most unwise."

The other military officer nodded grimly.

"Third," said Flamond, "no weapons will be taken out of or into this hangar. There will be a police detachment to enforce this prohibition at Entrance Five—"

He thumbed back toward the open doorway through which his vehicle had driven.

"—which will be the only entrance unsealed during the time you're here."

"We understand," Lissea said, nodding again.

"Fourth and finally," Flamond said, "all the same regulations apply to the Pancahtan contingent, who are *also* in a bonded hangar. The deadline for leaving Celandine is the same for both parties. And it *will* be enforced."

"What the hell's he expect us to do, then?" Coyne demanded. "Just shoot ourselves?"

Lissea turned her head. "Herne," she called in a cold, deadly voice to Lordling, who stood at the end of the formation, directly behind Coyne. "The next time someone speaks out of turn, silence him."

Flamond raised an eyebrow at the tone. "As a matter of fact," he said to Lissea, "what I hope and expect you'll do is to negotiate a mutually acceptable compromise with this Del Vore."

Carron winced at the repeated name. Flamond ignored him to continue. "From discussions with the Pancahtans, I have reason to believe they might be satisfied with less than their stated demands. To that end—"

He beckoned forward one of the civilians, a squat man in his fifties who carried a briefcase of naturally striped leather.

"—since it will lessen my difficulties, I'm putting Master Nivelle at your mutual services. He's head of the commercial mediation staff here at the Port Authority."

Nivelle made a bow of middling depth. "Mistress Captain," he said without a trace of irony, "I'm looking forward to working with you. If you have a few minutes after Commander Flamond finishes, I can suggest some neutral venues for meetings with the Pancahtan parties."

The mediator stepped back. Flamond nodded crisply.

"Yes," he said, "well, I'm almost finished."

He looked hard at one half of the *Swift*'s complement, then the other. "I need hardly mention that in addition to regulations specific to the present situation, Celandine has normal civil and criminal codes, all provisions of which will be enforced by the proper authorities."

Deke Warson grinned at Flamond from over Carron's shoulder. Toll nudged his brother warily.

"Apart from that," the port commander continued, "Île de Rameau Spaceport averages a hundred and thirty-one movements per day. We get all kinds here, even your kind. So long as you keep your public behavior within reason, I think you'll find that our community can supply any kind of entertainment you're able to pay for. That's all."

Nivelle said, "I'll wait for you at the entrance, Mistress Doormann. I realize you may want to discuss matters among yourselves in private for a few minutes—but only a few minutes, I trust."

Flamond nodded curtly. He turned on his heel and marched back to his car, followed by his entourage. Tadziki raised the ramp behind them.

The mercenary ranks dissolved into babble. Over the ruck of voices Westerbeke said, "Well, that lets us know where *we* stand!"

By chance, Ned's eyes met those of Carron Del Vore as he looked away from Lissea. He realized from Carron's blank tenseness that the Pancahtan noble *didn't* know where *he* stood.

"No one leaves here until I release you or Tadziki does," Lissea said to the mercenaries standing formally at ease in one of the Hotel Massenet's three bars, rented for the afternoon. "Colonel Lordling is in charge."

"The drinks are on the expedition account," Tadziki interjected, "but I suggest you recall that we may be leaving very curst fast when we go."

Eyes flicked from captain to adjutant. The bartender watched with his lips pursed and his hands spread on the bar's polished granite surface.

"Lissea, I ought to be upstairs with you," Herne Lordling said. There was more despair than bluster in his voice.

"This is where I need you, Herne," Lissea said crisply. "I can handle a negotiation, and I've got Tadziki and Slade to help with the technical presentation."

"And," Deke Warson cooed, "she's got the princey along for swank."

Men laughed. Herne Lordling flushed, and Lissea trained eyes as hard and gray as the bar-top on Warson.

Deke looked away. "Sorry, ma'am," Toll said.

Yazov and Paetz were on anchor watch. The rest of the

complement had come with the negotiators to the Massenet. There wasn't any reason to keep specialists from the navigation and powerplant side on duty, since the *Swift* couldn't lift off until the authorities opened the hangar roof. Flamond *was* in charge, there were no two ways about it.

"I'll give you men a full report after the meeting," Lissea said. "I know you're nervous, but there's nothing here that I can't work through if you'll remain patient and keep the lid on. That's all for now."

She turned and strode from the closed bar. Tadziki was at her side, Ned behind them, and Carron Del Vore scrambled to join the movement that had caught him unawares.

"Why's she think we're nervous?" Ingried asked as the mercenaries surged toward the bar.

The Massenet was a dockside hotel, but it catered to ships' officers and wealthy transients. The lobby staff included a discreet security presence to prohibit roistering crewmen, and the internal decor was expensively florid. The capitals of the square stone pillars supporting the double staircase were flanged outward to form bases for lions holding coats of arms; crystal electroliers glittered down on the lobby.

Though the Massenet was decorated in classic fashion, there was nothing antique in its operations. The molded ceilings themselves glowed to supplement the electroliers with soft, shadowless illumination. Movement between floors was by means of modern demand-actuated lift- and drop-shafts rather than elevators (or the staircases, which were kept for show).

There were about a dozen non-uniformed people in the lobby. The couple checking out were probably civilians, but the rest were divided between hotel security and plainclothed governmental types.

Nivelle had known what he was doing when he chose the venue for negotiations. Seeing the security presence made Ned feel calmer. The *Swift*'s personnel weren't going to get into a bloody war with Pancahtans here in the hotel while the expedition's cooler members negotiated in the roof garden.

Delegation of tasks among expedition personnel was *ad hoc,* but by now areas of specialization were pretty obvious. Ned's job included worrying about possibilities that gunmen—better gunmen—would have laughed away.

Carron looked at the heavyset Celandine personnel with their good clothes and eyes like trip-hammers. He wrung his hands.

Lissea stepped to the liftshaft and reached for the call button. Ned blocked her hand and said, "Captain? Let me lead."

"He's correct," Tadziki said. "I'll bring up the rear."

"This isn't a combat patrol!" Lissea said, but she let Ned take her place on the lift disk.

"Not if we handle it right," Tadziki murmured.

Ned held the attaché case close to his chest and poked the R button. The lift mechanism judged its moment, then rotated the meter-diameter disk on which Ned stood into the shaft and raised him in a single smooth motion.

At the top of the shaft, the disk rotated outward again and deposited Ned in a kiosk in the roof garden. He stepped out, meeting the professional smile of another security man whose briefcase certainly did *not* contain electronic files and a hologram projector as Ned's did.

"They're waiting in the gazebo, sir," the Celandine said with a nod.

The gazebo was a substantial building, a heavy roof on tile-covered columns with couches to hold thirty-odd visitors in comfort. Several security men faced outward from beyond the low hedge encircling the structure. Nivelle and half a dozen brightly garbed Pancahtans led by Ayven Del Vore were seated at a round table in the center.

The liftshaft shunted Lissea onto the roof. Ned nodded acknowledgment and led the way toward the gazebo.

The walkways were tiled in a herringbone of green and white that *clock*ed beneath their boots. Ned glanced at the flowering shrubs bordering the path and said, "A pretty blue, aren't they?"

"Slade, don't be an idiot!" Lissea replied.

He grinned toward a fountain. Fish of an unfamiliar breed, almost as clear as the plashing water, curvetted among lilies and snapped insects out of the air.

Ned felt loose and positive. For a moment he didn't understand why. Then he realized that he knew he was physically safe in the midst of such tight security. It was the first time his unconscious had been sure of that since the *Swift* lifted from Telaria.

Of course, there wouldn't be any safety at all in four and a half days if they blew this meeting.

The liftshaft sighed open again. Ayven stood up and very deliberately spat onto the tiles at the gazebo's threshold. "Good afternoon, brother!" he called. "*So* glad to meet you on Celandine. For a time I thought perhaps I'd miscalculated."

"Good afternoon, Ayven," Carron answered calmly. "I would just as soon have left you to your interests on Pancahte while I live my own life in the wider universe."

Ned had been doubtful about bringing Carron to the meeting— not that anybody'd asked his opinion. Even if Carron kept his temper (and so far, so good), his presence was likely to have a bad effect on his brother. He suspected the reason Lissea brought Carron was that she didn't want to risk leaving him in the company of the mercenaries when she wasn't there to protect him.

Ned put his case down on the table and opened it. From what he could tell, the Pancahtans accompanying Ayven were simply muscle, soldiers who were uncomfortable without their powered armor. Their suits would be aboard the vessels—and completely useless to them here under Celandine supervision or if the Pancahtan squadron ran down the *Swift* in space later.

The mediator rose and offered his hand to Lissea. "Glad to see you again, Captain Doormann," he said. He was a cultured man, but in his way just as tough as any of the security personnel standing quietly in the background. "And this would be Carron Del Vore, one of the bones of contention?"

"Master Nivelle," Lissea said, shaking hands. She nodded to Ayven. "Prince Ayven. But as for Carron here, he's a free citizen— of Pancahte, as it chances—and not an object to be bargained."

"He's a traitor," Ayven said flatly. "We want *him,* and we want the capsule you stole. When those two items have been turned over, we'll permit the rest of you to go where you please, *despite* the damage you did to Astragal."

"Succinctly put," Nivelle said. "But may we all sit down, please? There's less chance for actions being misunderstood if—"

"I'll stand!" Ayven said.

Lissea pulled her chair out and seated herself. Ned, Tadziki, and—a half-beat later—Carron followed her lead.

"Master Del Vore," the mediator replied, "I would be most appreciative if you would sit down as I requested you do."

It occurred to Ned that Nivelle considered his position here to be as much arbitrator as mediator, and that the Celandine certainly had the force to back up his will. Ayven must have realized that too, because he suddenly dropped back into his seat beside Nivelle.

• The prince was an extraordinarily handsome man. The flush on his cheeks complemented his blond hair.

"Master Slade," Lissea said in the tense silence, "will you run the first set of clips, please?"

Ned switched on the hologram projector in his briefcase.

"This was assembled," Lissea explained to Nivelle and the Pancahtans as the equipment warmed up, "from the helmet recorders we normally wear—and wore throughout our stay on Pancahte. The full texts from which the clips were taken are available, sir—"

She nodded to Nivelle—

"—Should there be any question about the authenticity of the excerpts."

A view of the throne room in Astragal hung above the center of the table:

"The tanks—" Lon Del Vore's image boomed from his throne, while the image of Ayven stood beside him and nodded agreement "—they're an irritation. If you can destroy them, then I'll let you have the capsule you claim."

"Yes, I accept," said an image of Lissea in profile, viewed from the recording lenses in Ned's helmet.

The view cut quickly to a figure—Ned, though the view was from behind and the resolution wasn't very good— running toward one of the Old Race tanks. The figure patted at the concealed latchplate and the hatch opened to him.

From the recording, it looked as though Ned had known what he was doing. His guts knotted as he watched the scene, recalling how utterly lost and alone he'd been at that moment.

The view shifted again: Ned, helmetless, staggered toward the viewpoint against a landscape of magma and hellfire. In the background was the tank he had abandoned in the last seconds of its existence. Armor slumped, and the gun's long barrel hung askew because the mantlet could no longer support the weight.

The image panned too fast for good resolution. The recording viewpoint, Lissea, looked back over her shoulder. The tank she had crewed against the alien starship was dissolving in a pool of yellow-white rock.

The demonstration clip ended with a silent pop of light. Ned switched off the projector.

"Fulfillment of the agreement is the basis on which we removed the capsule," Lissea said. "Although the capsule is itself Telarian property. As a matter of fact, it was the coffin of my great-granduncle. We carried out the Pancahtan terms to the letter. *Despite* the fact that the Treasurer and his son here concealed the existence of—"

"We concealed nothing!" Ayven shouted as he jumped halfway from his seat.

A burly Celandine put a hand on the prince's shoulder and pushed him straight back down. Two soldiers started to rise and thought better of it when they noticed the guns pointed by other security men.

Nivelle's mouth curved in a smile that didn't reach his eyes.

"Thank you for your forbearance, Master Del Vore," he said softly. "Let me remind you all that my instructions from the port commander are to remove this problem by any means within the laws of Celandine. The force that will be used to suppress, for example, the felony of assault and battery would achieve Commander Flamond's desires."

He looked from the Pancahtans to Lissea. "*Will* be used," he repeated. "And as for you, Mistress Doormann . . . I would appreciate it if you avoided the use of loaded terms yourself. They won't advance the discussion."

Lissea nodded. "I'm sorry, sir," she said, sounding like a good actress pretending to be contrite. "I might better have said that disabling the tanks as requested brought my crew and myself into dangers that we had no reason to expect."

Ned's fingers moved, cuing another chip while he continued to watch the eyes of the Pancahtan contingent.

"That ship was your doing!" Ayven snapped. "You used it to cover your escape with what you'd stolen—and with my brother who helped you steal it."

Ned switched on the projector. The image began with the dumbbell-shaped starship, half-risen from the shaft in which it had laired for centuries or millennia. Tiny figures of men ran toward their vehicles. The gigantic ship continued to rise.

The notion that the starship was somehow a ruse of Lissea's was so ludicrous that even the careful Nivelle smiled. Aloud he said, "I think we can dismiss that, Prince Ayven, since you've already stated that you're willing to forego damages caused during the incident in question. And—"

His tone hardened, though the mediator hadn't raised his voice at any point in the proceedings. Ned switched off the projected image.

"—it appears to me that Captain Doormann has made an unanswerably strong case for her continued possession of the capsule. That leaves the other point."

Nivelle eyed Carron with the expression of an inspector viewing a quarter of beef. "The request for extradition of your brother here."

"No doubt Celandine honors the principle of asylum?" Lissea said coolly.

"Celandine has enough problems of its own without our feeling the need to import troublemakers from outside the polity," Nivelle replied. "We certainly do *not* grant asylum."

He turned like a bullfighter between two animals to face Ayven again. "Nor, I might add, do we extradite to other states as a matter of right."

Ayven's face had remained set in anger during the exchange. The smiles of several of his subordinates wilted like frost-killed flowers.

"What Celandine *will* do," Nivelle continued, "is to view evidence presented by the state desiring extradition, and to make a binding decision whether or not to extradite. What evidence can you provide, Prince Ayven?"

"He stole a thing, a device, from our father," Ayven said, coldly precise. "I saw him give it to her."

He glared at Lissea. "That was why the tanks didn't kill her: that theft. Carron is a traitor and has been *convicted* as a traitor on Pancahte." He nodded, terminating his statement.

The trial Lon gave his younger son had probably taken all of thirty seconds, Ned thought.

Carron stared at Lissea. He reached sideways to take her hand. She twitched it away without looking at him.

"Yes, that could constitute a serious charge," Neville said. He tapped Ned's briefcase with the tip of his index finger. "But what *evidence* do you have, Prince Ayven?"

Tadziki drew Carron close to him and whispered into the younger man's ear. Lissea continued to watch Ayven and the mediator, as though no one else in the open room existed.

Ayven flushed again. "It didn't occur to me," he said, clipping his words in his cold rage, "that I would be treated with such disrespect by *bureaucrats.*"

Nivelle nodded calmly, protected from insult by consciousness of his absolute authority. From what Ned had seen of Celandine thus far, it was a place with common-sense rules and very good people enforcing them.

"However," Ayven continued, "we have recordings just like they do."

He flicked his chin in the direction of Ned and the hologram projector. "I watched Carron hand over the device, and my suit recorded it. The recording itself is on Pancahte, but you have my word of honor that it exists."

Nivelle nodded again. "Mistress," he said, "gentlemen, I'm going to propose a course of events. You'll have time to consider it, the remainder of the five days. And while I can't compel agreement—"

He smiled to underscore the patent lie.

"—if one party agrees and the other does not, it's likely to affect Commander Flamond's further actions. Is that understood?"

"Get on with it," Carron Del Vore rasped. His fingertips were pressed tightly together, and his eyes were on the center of the large table.

"First," Nivelle said, "the capsule in question remains the property of Captain Doormann."

He looked at Ayven. "'If you wish to press your claim for it, you may do so through the judicial system of Telaria."

"Go on," Ayven said, his voice a near echo of his brother's.

"Second," Nivelle continued, facing Lissea. "Carron Del Vore will remain on Celandine at his own expense for five tennights to permit the Pancahtan authorities to provide evidence substantiating their demand for extradition."

"No!" said Carron. Tadziki dragged him back down into his seat before a Celandine security man did.

"If evidence isn't forthcoming within that period," Nivelle continued, "or I deem the evidence insufficient for the purpose offered, Master Del Vore will be free to go or stay as he desires. If, however, Pancahte meets its burden of proof—"

He smiled again. "—in my sole estimation . . . then Master Del Vore will be handed over to the Pancahtan authorities."

"Lissea," Carron cried, "you can't let them *do* this to me! I—"

Lissea turned like a weasel striking. "Carron," she said, "if you can inform me on how your situation would be improved if the *Swift* and everyone aboard her were blasted to plasma, then do so. Otherwise, please *shut* your mouth!"

Carron swallowed.

Lissea stood up slowly and easily. The mediator wagged a finger to warn off his security men before one of them reacted. "Master Nivelle," she said, "I'll take your suggested procedure under advisement. I'll have a response for you shortly, certainly before the deadline."

Nivelle nodded. "I understand that you'll want to consider the matter privately, mistress," he said. "But as you no doubt realize, the matter is absorbing Celandine state resources to very little state benefit, so a prompt response would be appreciated."

Lissea walked out of the gazebo. The three men got up and followed. Tadziki gripped Carron's shoulder in what could have been a comforting gesture.

The Pancahtans scraped back their chairs. "I'd appreciate it if you gentlemen stayed with me a few minutes," Nivelle said with his normal bland insistence.

Tadziki put Carron into the dropshaft, then took the next disk himself. As Ned waited with Lissea, he heard Ayven Del Vore snarl, "I suppose you think you've got me over a barrel, don't you?"

Lissea stepped off.

"Yes, Prince Ayven, I do," the mediator agreed. "But it doesn't affect my judgment on what would be a fair result."

The mechanism swung Ned into the dropshaft. He didn't know that he'd want to live on Celandine. But he respected the people who did.

Lissea and Tadziki, with Carron between them, were already striding to the temporarily private bar. Mercenaries cheered as Lissea opened the door. The sound was so viciously bloodthirsty that several of the security men in the lobby reached beneath their tunics.

Ned smiled with cold reassurance. "Not a problem," he murmured to the nearest Celandine. "They're just happy." He closed the door behind him.

Lissea waved a hand for silence, but the men had already quieted. They weren't tense, exactly, but none of them were so drunk that they didn't realize the importance of the meeting that had just concluded.

"Gentlemen," she said, "Tadziki has booked a corridor of rooms for you at the Sedan House a block west of here. Anybody who wants to stay at the Massenet is welcome to do so, but I believe the comfort range of the Sedan House is more in keeping with your requirements."

"They'll cater liquor and girls at the Sedan," Tadziki amplified. "Or you can bring your own."

"That's *my* requirement!" Deke Warson shouted.

"We'll continue with two-man anchor watches," Lissea said. "Westerbeke and Slade, you're on in an hour and a half. You'll be relieved in another eight hours, but if you've got anything urgent I suggest you take care of it fast."

Ned met her eyes without comment.

"I've got some decisions to make," Lissea continued, "and I'm going to make them alone. I don't want to be disturbed, and I *won't* be disturbed. Do you all understand?"

"I understand I'm going to be too busy to worry about anything but where my prick is in about three seconds flat," Westerbeke muttered, shaking his head with irritation at where his name appeared on the duty roster.

"Tadziki, do you have anything further?" Lissea asked.

"Toll and Deke, I need to speak with you," the adjutant said. "Nothing beyond that."

"Dismissed, then," Lissea said. She turned. Ned opened the door for her.

Carron Del Vore caught up with her in the lobby as the mercenaries spilled out, heading for the street door. "Lissea—" he cried.

"Carron," she said as Ned and, from within the bar, Tadziki and the Warsons watched, "if you lay a hand on me, I'll turn you over to Nivelle right now. I doubt he's left the building yet. Is that what you want?"

"But—"

"*Is that what you want?*"

Carron walked toward the street door. He hunched as if he'd recently had an abdominal operation.

Ned left the Hotel Massenet through the door at the far side of the lobby. He thought he'd have a drink, but not here.

Part of Ned didn't like what he'd just seen done to Carron Del Vore. That same part didn't like the other part of Edward Slade's mind, grinning gleefully to have watched Carron's humiliation.

Josie Paetz waited with Yazov just inside the entrance to Hangar 39. They wore their commo helmets and there was no access to the *Swift* except past them, but it seemed to Ned that the two men were jumping the gun on their liberty a little.

Paetz regretfully unfastened the pistol belt with twin right-hand holsters and handed it to Ned. "See you, then," he said. He seemed keyed up—and happier than prospects for a drink and a woman would have made him. "Lay it on my bunk, okay?"

The heavy door was beginning to close. Paetz jumped out to avoid pushing the call button so that the police guards outside would open the hangar again. Yazov followed.

Ned opened his mouth to say that one of the pair ought to wait until Westerbeke arrived to fill the minimal anchor watch. He suppressed the words. There was no real risk and anyway, Paetz and Yazov weren't going to pay the least attention.

Westerbeke and Carron Del Vore leaped into the dock an instant before the door slammed.

Westerbeke looked at the gunbelt Ned held. He raised an eyebrow. "Expecting trouble?" he asked.

Ned shrugged. "They're Paetz's," he explained. "In his terms, he's just thinking positively."

He thought about the attitude of the men he'd just relieved and added, "They were acting . . . as if they expected to land hot. Does that mean anything to you?"

Westerbeke looked in the direction Paetz and his uncle had gone, though there was a massive door panel between them by now. He shrugged in turn and said, "Tadziki called them after he'd grabbed Deke and Toll. Maybe they've got something up, but they haven't told me—"

He grinned brightly. "Which suits *me* just fine. I pilot space-ships. I always figured 'When bullets fly, I don't,' was a curst good rule to live by."

Ned didn't comment, but he remembered Westerbeke's flawless extraction from Buin and his landing at the same point an orbit later. Like many (though not all) other members of the *Swift*'s complement, the pilot chose to downplay his accomplishments rather than boasting.

"Westerbeke," Carron said, intruding with the air of a man committing to a high dive. "I'll take your watch. You can go back and . . . and—whatever you want to do. I need to talk to Slade."

"I don't think—" Ned began with a frown.

"You know, *that* suits me too," Westerbeke said. He reached for the call button.

Ned caught the pilot's hand. "I don't—" he repeated.

"Slade," Carron said, "I *need* to talk with you. It's critically important. All of our lives are at stake."

Westerbeke's eyes bounced from one man to the other. The pilot looked more entertained than concerned.

Ned scowled, then came to terms with his own jumpiness. There was no way into Hangar 39 except at the will of Celandine spaceport police; and if he couldn't handle Carron Del Vore by himself, then he deserved whatever happened to him.

"All right," he said, pushing the call button for Westerbeke. It was mildly amusing to note that he'd assumed control, and that neither of the other men had attempted to argue with the assumption.

He looked Carron over without affection. "You're here for the full eight hours, *Prince,*" he said. "You don't get another chance to change your mind."

The door rumbled open. Outside, artificial lights supplemented the rosy sunset. A policeman stood beside the weapons detector with his pistol drawn. Westerbeke gave Ned a three-fingered salute and sauntered out for renewed liberty.

An armored conduit snaked across the concrete between the *Swift* and a junction box near the door. The walls were thick enough to swallow radio and microwave signals. The vessel had to be patched into the planetary system in order to communicate beyond Hangar 39.

Ned waved the Pancahtan toward the *Swift* ahead of him. "What is it, then?" he demanded. "That you need to say to me?"

"You know that my brother can't be trusted, don't you?" Carron said.

"I think that a number of people in your family," Ned said, "feel they have a right to do anything they bloody well please." Until he heard the venom with which he spoke, he hadn't realized how much he hated Carron.

Ned's tone didn't seem to concern or even affect the Pancahtan. "If you turn me over to Ayven," Carron said as they walked up the boarding ramp together, "he'll still hunt down your ship and destroy it. You made fools of him and my father. We made fools of them. They'll never forgive us."

"I don't make those decisions," Ned said, being deliberately obtuse.

The interior of the *Swift* looked even more like an animal's lair now that Ned had spent the past eight hours in civilized surroundings. It was filthy, it stank, and the disorder was more akin to a heap of rotting vegetation than it was to living quarters. It would take days to clean and disinfect the ship when they returned to Telaria, if and when . . .

"I've come to you," Carron said, "because you're intelligent enough to understand what I'm saying."

He stood in the central aisle, staring aft toward the capsule. Half the external panels had been removed, exposing circuitry.

Carron's back was to Ned. "Also," he continued, "because you will keep your word to me. The others, any of them—"

He turned to face Ned. His expression was cold and imperious, that of a king greeting his conqueror.

"—would promise but would betray me; though it will be all your lives unless you accept my plan."

"Do you think I wouldn't lie to you?" Ned wondered aloud.

"You will do what you think is necessary," Carron said flatly. "I accept that. But I trust your honor as well as your capacity to see where necessity lies. Even Tadziki—"

He shook his head angrily, the sort of motion a man with his hands full makes to shoo a fly.

Josie Paetz slept in the top bunk, now vacant, forward on the port side. The cellular blanket was twisted in a heap, and the replaceable sheet which covered the acceleration cushion was gray with dirt. Ned put the gunbelt on the integral pillow and sat down at one of the navigational consoles.

"What about Lissea?" he said to the forward bulkhead.

"I've come to you, Slade," Carron said.

In sudden anger, the Pancahtan continued, "Doesn't it mean anything to you, all I've sacrificed? You'd have failed, *died,* on Pancahte a dozen different times if it weren't for me! And what I'm doing now, it's the only way for you to survive again! Do you *want* to die?"

Ned rotated the console, facing it aft toward Carron. "Not a lot, no," he said. "Tell me your plan, then."

Carron nodded. "Yes," he said. "The only way the *Swift* will be able to reach your home—be able to leave Celandine's space, even—is if my brother is aboard. My father's ships won't destroy us if Ayven is our hostage."

"Go on," Ned said, resisting the impulse to sneer. Carron had been consistently right in his assumptions, particularly those involving the behavior of his father and brother.

"He'll come to you," Carron said. "Here, to the ship, where you can capture him. If you offer him what he wants."

Ned looked at Carron coldly. The Pancahtan stood in the aisle with his arms akimbo, smiling slightly.

"You," Ned said. "You as his prisoner."

Carron nodded. "That's correct," he said. "Me as his prisoner."

There was fear in the young Pancahtan's eyes, but the smile didn't leave his lips.

Herne Lordling hadn't been too drunk to function since a three-day family celebration when he turned twelve, but he was nonetheless carrying a load as he walked up to the sidewalk from a sub-level bar. He didn't remember that there'd been steps when he entered, but he negotiated them in a satisfactory fashion anyway.

The bar faced the high berm surrounding Île de Rameau Spaceport. A starship rose on a plume of plasma, shaking the night sky with a familiar thunder. Lordling had been in a lot of ports, on a lot of planets. Now he wished he were on another one—and in a universe in which Lissea Doormann had never existed.

The sidewalk was busy. Vehicles ranging from monocycles to a forty-roller containerized-cargo flat snarled slowly along the circumferential road which girdled the port. Lordling swayed. He was considering the alternate possibilities of going upstairs in one of the buildings behind him to find a woman or throwing himself out in front of traffic.

A bright blue bus marked SPACEPORT SHUTTLE pulled in on its programmed circuit. The spiked barriers that kept ordinary traffic from parking in the shuttle stops withdrew before the nose of the bus. Sailors jostled past Lordling to board. The bus attendant watched from his cage in the center of the vehicle.

Lordling squeezed in with the others and presented his credit chip to the reader beside the attendant. One thing about a major port: your money was always good, though they might discount it forty percent from face value depending on how difficult they expected clearance to be.

Lordling didn't care what things cost. All he really wanted was someone to kill. Several choice candidates shuttled back and forth through his mind. It took all the remains of his self-control to keep from grabbing the unknown sailor next to him and squeezing until the man's eyeballs popped out.

He punched two-three-seven-one into the destination panel. It was only after he'd done so that he realized it wasn't the location of the closed hangar which held the *Swift*.

He stepped to one of the benches. It barely had room for a child remaining. Lordling seated himself with a double thrust of his elbows. A fat sailor cursed and stood up. The attendant watched but didn't interfere. Lordling stared at the sailor's face, his puffy neck . . .

The sailor turned his back.

The bus pulled away from the stop. Because the vehicle was full, it left the curb lane and shunted across the circumferential to the next spaceport entrance. The whine of the turbine and the high-frequency clacking of the shuttle's spun-metal tires buzzed Lordling into a haze of alcohol and bloody dreams.

The bus drove a route it chose for itself based on the destination codes loaded by its passengers. The attendant was aboard to summon emergency services if there was a problem among the human cargo, and to report if the vehicle was involved in an accident.

Breakdown codes were, like the actual driving, the responsibility of the shuttle itself.

Ten passengers got off at the first stop, the hiring office in the port's administrative complex. The shuttle moved down the line of docks on an elevated roadway, occasionally pulling into a kiosk to drop or to load passengers. There was little other traffic.

Beneath the roadway were huge conveyors shunting goods unloaded from starships into warehouses or vehicles for ground transportation. When the bus passed over an operating conveyor, the low-pitched rumble jarred Lordling temporarily alert again.

The lights of work crews dotted the landing field. At regular intervals a ship landed or lifted off in overwhelming glare and thunder.

"It's yours, buddy," the attendant said. "Hey! It's yours!"

He reached through the cage and shook Lordling's shoulder. Lordling came alert with a reflex that brought both hands toward the man's throat. The attendant lunged against the back of his tubular cage to get clear.

"*Hey!*" the attendant shouted again, fumbling for the handset of his red emergency phone.

Lordling lurched to his feet. "You shouldn't grab a guy like that," he muttered as he stepped toward the door. It started to close at the end of its programmed cycle, then caught and reopened as the attendant pushed the override button.

Lordling stepped from the shuttle. He was the last of the passengers who'd boarded outside the spaceport, but the vehicle was half-full of sailors headed into the city.

The attendant watched, holding the handset to his mouth until the door closed behind Lordling.

The location sign in the kiosk had been defaced by names and numbers scratched on its surface, but the huge building the stop served had BONDED HANGAR 17 in letters a meter high across the front wall. Lordling walked down the zigzag flight of steps to ground level and started toward the hangar entrance.

He hadn't had a drink for half an hour. That didn't make him sober, but he had enough judgment back to know what he was doing wasn't a good idea. Not enough judgment to prevent him from doing it, though. Anyway, the sort of decisions a professional soldier regularly makes aren't those a civilian would consider sane.

To either side of Hangar 17 were open docks, discharging the cargo of twenty-kiloton freighters along conveyor belts. The stereophonic racket dimmed only when a large vessel took off or landed. Cargo handlers wore helmet lamps to supplement the pole-mounted light banks along the rollerway.

Two men in the green-and-black uniform of Port Authority police watched from their air-cushion van as Lordling approached. One of them got up, yawned, and drew his bell-mouthed pistol. He gestured the mercenary to the detector frame set a meter in front of the closed doorway.

"Through here, buddy," the policeman ordered. He didn't look or sound concerned by the fact Lordling wore stone-pattern utilities rather than the orange-slashed yellow uniform of the Pancahtan naval personnel.

Lordling hesitated. He wasn't stupid, and he'd survived decades in a business where often you get only one mistake.

"Look, pal," the policeman still in the van said, "if you're not going in, piss off! I don't want you hanging around, you understand?"

Anger—at the cop, at life, at a woman who fucked boys but wouldn't give Colonel Herne Lordling the time of day—jolted the mercenary. He stepped through the frame and grasped the latch of the sliding door.

Neither the latch nor the door moved.

"Don't get your bowels in an uproar," the first policeman ordered. "This don't open till we tell it to open."

He turned to his partner. "Is he okay?"

"What the hell's wrong with your back, buddy?" the man at the detector readout within the van demanded. "You got bits of metal all through it!"

Lordling stared through the van's windshield. "Shell fragments," he said. "If it's any of your business."

"Bloody well told it's our business," the policeman said, but he touched a switch anyway.

Servos slid the vehicle-width door slowly sideways against its inertia. The panel was fifteen centimeters thick and far too massive for an unaided man to move. Lordling walked inside.

Though the three Pancahtan vessels within Hangar 17 were individually much larger than the *Swift* in Hangar 39, they were still dwarfed by the vast cavity in which they rested. Inlaid letters on the bow of the nearest announced that it was the *Courageous*. The next over read *Furious,* and Lordling couldn't be sure of the third.

Lordling walked along the side of the closed dock, staying at a considerable distance from the *Courageous*. The vessel had two flat turrets, offset forward to port and aft to starboard. They were faired into the hull and shuttered for the moment. Lordling judged that each could mount a pair of 20-cm power-guns, weapons as heavy as the main gun of the largest armored vehicles.

A team of Pancahtan sailors had removed access plates from the stern of the *Furious*. They were working on the attitude-control motors. There was a man at the foot of each open hatchway. Other yellow-and-orange personnel moved between vessels on their errands, but no one paid any attention to Lordling.

The complements were probably in the order of a hundred men per ship, counting crewmen and soldiers together. As with the *Swift*'s personnel, most of them would be billeted in portside hostelries while the ships were on Celandine.

A belt of linked plates circled the vessel's midpoint. Alternate sections slid sideways so that missles could be launched from the openings. There was a variety of other hatches and blisters as well, some of which housed defensive batteries of rapid-fire powerguns to protect against hostile missiles.

The *Swift* mounted no external armament whatever. If the Pancahtans ran her down in space, as they surely would unless Ayven Del Vore was mollified, the Telarian vessel would provide only target practice—and that not for long. Lissea had to surrender her . . . her *boy*. There was no other survivable choice.

Perhaps Herne Lordling could himself arrange for Carron to wind up in the hands of his brother.

Lordling turned with decision toward the door in the enclosure wall. He was steady on his legs again, and his vision had sharpened through the earlier haze.

The door rumbled open while Lordling was still fifty meters away. He paused, standing close to the grease-speckled wall. A party of Pancahtan sailors entered the hangar, laughing and calling to one another. There were seven of them. When he was sure the last man was inside, Lordling broke into a run. He had to get to the doorway before the servos closed it.

A Pancahtan caught the motion out of the corner of his eye and turned around. "Hey?" he called. "Hey there! Who the hell is that?"

The last of the sailors shifted to put himself in Lordling's path.

"Hey, it's one of—" the Pancahtan shouted. Lordling kicked his knee out from under him and dived through the door an instant before it slammed against the jamb

"Freeze, you!" shouted a policeman as he leveled his gun at Lordling. "*Freeze!*"

An orange light winked within the van, the call signal indicating that someone within the hangar wanted to get out. The second policeman aimed a similar weapon from the van's open window.

"Keep them in there!" Lordling cried as he got to his feet. "There's six of them—they'll kill me if you let them out!"

"Stand in the fucking frame, you bastard!" the first policeman cried. "If you're packing anything now, you're cold meat!"

Lordling backed into the detector frame again. The plasma exhaust of a landing starship reflected from Hangar 17's facade, throwing the mercenary's tortured shadow toward the waiting policeman.

"He's clean!" reported the man in the vehicle. "But you know, I figure if he's one of them Telarians nosing around here, then anything he gets is what he's got coming to him."

He touched a switch. The servos whined, beginning to open the door again.

Lordling ran toward the conveyor serving Dock 18. Pallets supporting huge fusion bottles rumbled down the belt at intervals of five or six minutes. They moved very slowly because of the enormous momentum which would have to be braked before the cranes at the far end could lift the merchandise.

A few cargo handlers stood on catwalks along the conveyor, watching for signs of trouble. There was little they could do if a pallet began to drift. Stopping the belt abruptly would more probably precipitate a crisis than prevent one.

The trestles supporting the conveyor were enclosed in sheet metal to form a long shed. There were doors at fifty-meter intervals, but the first one Lordling came to was closed with a hasp and padlock.

He jogged on to the next. He was breathing through his open mouth. He'd never been a runner, and though adrenaline had burned the alcohol out of his system, it hadn't given him a younger man's wind. The second door was padlocked also.

Lordling glanced over his shoulder. Men in yellow-and-orange uniforms were grouped at the entrance to Hangar 17. Lordling was in the hard shadow cast by light banks on the conveyorway above, but one of the Celandine policemen pointed in the direction he'd run.

Bastard!

The Pancahtans started toward the conveyor. Lordling knew he couldn't outrun them. He stepped back and brought his right foot around in a well-judged crescent kick. The edge of his boot sheared the hasp and sent it whizzing off into darkness with the lock.

Lordling opened the sheet-metal door, slipped in, and tried to pull the panel closed behind him.

It swung ajar, and anyway he couldn't expect to fool the Pancahtans as to where he'd gone.

The interior of the shed was echoing bedlam. Stark, flickering light leaked in through seams between the conveyor and the support structure as the belt material flexed. Flat loops of power cables feeding the rollers' internal motors quivered in the vibration. The piers and trestles were fifty-centimeter I-beams, useless for concealment if any of the sailors pursuing carried lights.

Lordling ran across to the other side of the shed. He'd break out through one of the doors there, wedge it shut from the outside, and climb up to the catwalk while the Pancahtans searched the shed.

From there he would go outward, to the ship that was unloading, rather than directly back to pick up the shuttle.

He ought to be able to find a weapon before he next saw a yellow— There were no doors on the other side of the shed. Access was from one side only.

The door by which Lordling had entered swung back. A handlight swept him and jiggled as the Pancahtan waved his comrades over. . . .

Lordling kicked at the metal siding, trying to find a seam he could break. The sheet belled and fluttered violently. It was too flexible to crack the way he needed it to do if he was going to get out.

All six Pancahtans entered the shed. They were illuminated from above and by side-scatter from the lights two of them held.

The sailors carried crowbars and spanners with shafts a meter long. They'd broken into a toolshed for the conveyor maintenance crews. Lordling wondered if the bastard cop had told them about the shed, also.

He shifted so that he stood a meter in front of one of the support pillars. That would cover his back but still give him room to maneuver.

When a bottle moved down the conveyor overhead the noise in the shed was palpable, and even when the rollers turned without load there was too much noise for voice communication. The Pancahtans fanned out and advanced in the harshly broken light. They stayed in an arc, close enough for mutual support but not so tight that they'd foul one another when they struck. They knew their business.

Lordling braced himself mentally. He could take one down with a spearpoint of stiffened fingers, but the others would be on him before he broke through to the door. Even if he got to the door, he couldn't outrun the sailors; he'd—

The door opened. The Pancahtans, three meters from their prey and preparing for the final rush, didn't notice the men who entered the shed behind them.

Light as white and intense as a stellar corona blasted from the doorway. It threw shadows sharp enough to cut stencils against the metal of the wall behind Lordling. Pancahtans turned.

The shots were silent in the background thunder. Orange muzzle flashes and the bright blue glare of a powergun flickered from the fringes of the main light source. Pancahtans thrashed in their death throes. A fid of hot brains slapped Lordling in the face, hard enough to stagger him.

All the Pancahtans were down. The light switched off. Its absence was as shocking as silence would have been. Lordling was blind, and his ears were numb with thunder.

A shadowy figure stepped close and handed Lordling a commo helmet. He slipped it on. The positive-noise damping was a relief greater than he could have guessed before it occurred.

The unit was set to intercom. *"Hey Paetz,"* Deke Warson crowed. *"You fucked up. This guy's tunic's all over blood. We can't use it."*

"Fuck you, Warson! I shot him in the fucking head, didn't I? How'm I supposed to keep him from bleeding?"

"We've got five, that's enough," said Tadziki. Lordling's retinas had recovered enough for him to recognize his companions: Tadziki, carrying a 30-cm floodlight and its power-pack, Paetz and Yazov, and the Warson brothers. *"Lordling, are you all right?"*

Toll Warson stood in the open doorway with his pistol concealed as he watched for possible intruders. The other four were stripping the dead Pancahtan sailors. Paetz had set his powergun on the concrete beside him. The glowing barrel would have ignited his clothing had he dropped it back in his pocket.

"Yeah, I'm okay," Lordling said. *"That was curst good timing, though. Where'd you get the guns?"*

"I've never been in a port where you couldn't find just about anything you were willing to pay for," the adjutant said. He grunted and straightened his torso so that he could unstrap the heavy light-pack. *"Île de Rameau is no different."*

"Hey, Cuh'nel?" Deke Warson said. He'd taken off his own tunic, mottled in shades of gray, and was pulling on the orange-and-yellow jacket of the headless corpse before him. *"You did just fine. I was going to be the bait, but we saw you and thought we'd use the Big Cheese instead."*

One of the Pancahtans had taken ten or a dozen high-velocity projectiles through the face. The mercenary shooter hadn't trusted an unfamiliar weapon—but it'd worked just fine, and there was a tight pattern of holes in the bloody sheet metal beyond. The Lord only knew where the bullets had wound up.

"You saw them come after me?" Lordling demanded. *"You could've stopped them before?"*

Tadziki was putting on a Pancahtan tunic that was too long for his torso but still tight across the shoulders. *"We couldn't have done anything without the police seeing it until we had some cover,"* he said. *"Herne, since you're here, you can watch our gear. We shouldn't be too long. Don't do anything to attract attention and there should-n't be a problem."*

"What we did, Cuh'nel buddy—" said Deke Warson as he stepped to the doorway to take his brother's place—*"is watch you get off the bus and trot right into the hangar. So we thought we'd wait and see."*

He wore Pancahtan trousers and jacket. A very careful observer might notice that his boots were nonstandard for the uniform.

"You—" Lordling said. He didn't know how to complete the sentence. Instead, he turned and kicked the sheet metal. This time a seam split, letting in a quiver of light from Dock 19's rollerway.

"Look, you can't get into the hangar with those guns!" Lordling said loudly. *"Or do you plan to shoot the cops? Via, that'd send us all for the high jump!"*

Tadziki's trousers didn't fit well either, but at least the jacket's overlap covered the way he'd folded the waistband over his belt rather than cuff the pants' legs. *"Herne,"* he said, *"this one's in the hands of the proper parties. When we're done, you can get back to the* Swift *and sleep it off. Chances are we'll be leaving Celandine very shortly."*

"But what are you going to do?" Lordling demanded.

Tadziki looked over the men he'd brought. All of them wore Pancahtan uniforms. Yazov had slung the jacket over his shoulder to conceal the blood that had speckled the front of it. He wouldn't be the first sailor wearing an undershirt in public while on liberty.

The men laid their bootlegged guns beside the corpses. Tadziki took his helmet off and handed it to Lordling. Lordling took it blindly as the others followed suit.

More cargo rumbled its way cacophonously down the conveyor belt. Tadziki gestured and moved toward the door with three of his disguised men.

Deke Warson cupped his hands between his mouth and Lordling's ear and snouted, "What we're doing is our job, Cuh'nel. Now, you be a good boy while we're gone."

And then Deke too was gone.

The door stayed open as the five men in orange-slashed yellow uniforms entered Hangar 17 one by one, processed through the detector frame by the policemen outside. Deke Warson did a little dance, circling while his feet picked out a surprisingly complicated step. He tried to grab young Josie Paetz, who angrily pushed him away.

The party made for the *Furious,* the midmost of the three Pancahtan vessels, with more deliberation than speed. Deke linked arms with his brother Toll. They did a shuffling two-step across the concrete until they were hushed by Tadziki. The stocky man looked older and perhaps more nearly sober than his companions.

The boarding stairs of the *Furious* were wide enough for two men abreast, but both brothers tried to cram themselves in beside their leader. He turned and growled an order while the two sailors on access duty watched from the top of the stairs.

The Warsons subsided. Tadziki climbed the last two steps. He threw a salute that started crisply and broke off with him staggering against the rail.

"You got the wrong ship, Compeer," one of the on-duty pair observed, reading the name tapes on Tadziki's right breast and around his left sleeve. "The *Glorious* is the next berth over."

He nodded toward the vessel farther from the hangar's entrance.

"Good stuff, boys?" the other on-duty sailor asked with amusement.

"The best fucking stuff I've drunk since the last fucking stuff I've drunk!" Deke Warson said forcefully. He pulled a square-faced bottle of green liquor from a side pocket. The seal was broken, but only a few swigs were gone. He thrust the bottle toward the men on watch. "Here, try some."

As he spoke, Yazov lifted a similar bottle, nearly empty, and raised it to his lips.

"Hey!" Josie Paetz bleated. "Save some for me!"

One of the sailors looked quickly over his shoulder to see if an officer was watching. The ship was almost empty, and the duty officer was probably drunk in his cabin. Ships' crews on Pancahtan vessels were definitely inferior compared to the soldiers of Prince Ayven's entourage. Morale among sailors suffered as a result.

"Naw, we don't—" his partner said.

"The hell we don't!" insisted the first sailor as he took the bottle and opened it. He drank deeply and passed it to his fellow. "Whoo! Where'd you get that stuff, boys?"

"We are here," Tadziki said with a gravity that suggested drunkenness better than if he had staggered, "to pay a debt of honor. Honor! To Charl-charl . . . Charlie!"

"Who the hell is that?" the first sailor said. He reached for the bottle again. Yazov handed his bottle to Paetz and pulled a fresh one out of the opposite pocket.

"Charlie," Toll Warson said. "Charlie is our dear friend. *He* told us that Dolores, the headliner at the Supper Club, made it onstage with a Kephnian Ichneumon."

"We doubted him," Deke said. "Our friend, our friend . . ."

There was a full bottle in the right-side pocket of his jacket. He fumbled at great and confused length in the empty left pocket instead.

"An Ichneumon?" the second sailor repeated. "They're female, though. I mean, the ones that're a meter long, they're female. That's not really a dong."

Josie Paetz spluttered liquor out his nose. Yazov clapped him on the back. "She's queer, then?" Josie giggled. "Dolores is queer?"

"Our good friend Charlie is on duty," Tadziki said. "In our wicked doubt, we bet him that Dolores did *not* make it with a

Kephman Ichneumon, and we were wrong. We are here to pay our debt of honor to Charlie."

He lifted yet another bottle into the air.

The on-duty sailors looked at one another. "Look, you mean Spec One Charolois?" the first one asked. "About fifty, half-bald, and looks like a high wind'd blow him away?"

"That's the very man!" Deke cried. "Our friend Charlie!"

Toll Warson watched the hangar entrance out of the corner of his eye as he waited with a glazed expression on his face. He and his brother were the only ones necessary to this operation, but the others had insisted on coming . . . and Toll was just as glad to have them along. Not that they'd be able to do any real good if it dropped in the pot.

"What would he know about the Supper Club?" the second sailor said, shaking his head. "Charolois's as queer as a three-cornered wheel!"

"Just like Dolores!" Josie Paetz chortled. "Charlie and Dolores, my dearest, dearest . . ."

He looked up. "Hey! Gimme another drink, will you?"

Tadziki pointed to the bottle in the first sailor's hands. "That's yours," he said, "if you let us go see Charlie. Right?"

The sailors exchanged glances again. The second one shrugged. "Yeah, well, keep it down, okay? If he's on board, Charolois ought to be in his cabin forward."

The five men wearing *Glorious* tallies slipped into the *Furious*. Despite the concerns of the men on watch, the strangers were amazingly quiet once they were aboard.

Ayven Del Vore wasn't with the two Pancahtans who entered Hangar 39. The men rolled between them a portable sensor pack, similar to those the *Swift* carried, but even bulkier.

Before the door slammed, Ned glimpsed two more men waiting at the police outpost. They wore the lace and bright fabrics of Pancahte's military nobility. Though the lighting was from behind and above, Ayven's trim figure and ash-blond hair were identification enough.

The Pancahtans approaching with the sensor were tough as well as being big men. Ned waited for them at the top of the boarding ramp.

"I told Prince Ayven to bring only one companion!" he called. "I'm here alone with the prisoner."

One of the soldiers mimed *"Fuck you"* with the index and little fingers of his right hand. "Four's the minimum to drive and control a prisoner, dickhead," he said, "*If* it's you alone, then the prince and Toomey come aboard to collect the dirt. If you don't like the terms, you can stick them up your ass."

The sensor's small wheels balked at the lip of the boarding ramp. The men lifted the unit by the side handles and carried it to the hatchway. From the way they grimaced, the pack must weigh closer to a hundred kilos than fifty, though Ned doubted it was as capable as the Telarian man-packs.

Still, it was as well that Ned had decided not to try concealing additional mercs aboard the *Swift*. The sensor would easily sniff them out.

Ned backed away to let the Pancahtans set up their unit. He wore a 1-cm powergun in a belt holster. "You know if you spend a lot of time dicking around, somebody's going to come back aboard, don't you?" he said harshly.

"Come *here* when there's all Île de Rameau out there?" a soldier sneered. "Sure, buddy. I'm really worried."

"Don't matter if they do," his partner said as he closed a chamber in the side of the sensor to get a baseline reading. "They don't like the deal they're offered, well, I'd just as soon fry the lot of you in orbit."

He grinned at Ned. "You see?"

The hatch through the bulkhead astern of the main bay was open. One of the soldiers stalked down the aisle, climbed around the capsule, and entered the engine compartment.

"It's clear," he announced to his partner. "No sealed containers, not unless they're hiding in the expansion chambers."

"I guess we can risk that," the man at the sensor said. The radiation levels inside a well-used expansion chamber were in the fatal-within-minutes range.

He switched the sensor pack to area sweep, watching the read-outs intently. The unit clicked to itself as it analyzed temperature, carbon dioxide levels, and vibrations down to and including pulse rates.

"Looks good," he said as he straightened to his returning partner. "Nothing but the chump and the package."

He looked at Ned. "Call the gate now, and I'll tell the prince it's clear."

The navigation consoles were rotated to face aft. Carron Del Vore, bound and gagged in the portside acceleration couch, stared wide-eyed as Ned picked up the land-line telephone from between the consoles and handed it to the soldier.

"Boy, you high-class foreigners," the other soldier said, looking around the vessel's interior. "You really know how to live—like pigs!"

Ned sat at the open console. "Do your business and get out," he said. "Then you won't have to worry about how we live."

His voice trembled slightly. That didn't bother him. He was ready to go—good jumpy. His subconscious thought it would be very soon now, and his subconscious was right.

The entrance door opened. The walls of the enclosed hangar damped the spaceport racket, particularly at the higher frequencies. Though the door itself wasn't particularly noisy, it slid open to the accompaniment of metallic cacophony from the wider world.

Ned got up and reached beneath Carron to lift him. "Give me a hand!" he ordered the nearer soldier. "The quicker this is done, the better I like it."

"You're doing fine, dickhead," the soldier said. He squeezed back to let Ned and his burden pass in the aisle.

Ned set Carron down in a sitting posture on the lower bunk facing the hatchway. Ayven and a third Pancahtan soldier strode up the ramp. The outside door slammed closed behind them, returning Hangar 39 to relative silence again. The soldier who'd operated the sensor pack removed a panel on the back of the unit.

Ned nodded toward Carron. "You've got what you came for," he said.

"So we shall," Ayven said. He stepped to his brother and pulled off the gag.

"Ayven!" Carron cried. "They kidnapped me! Thank the Lord you're here to rescue—"

Ayven reached a hand behind him. The soldier at the sensor pack pointed a projectile pistol of Celandine manufacture at Ned. He gave the prince a similar weapon, then held out a third pistol so that the partner who'd helped with the sensor could reach around Ned and take it.

The sensor's necessary shielding provided concealment from the detector frame. The police had either missed one of the compartments in the large unit, or they had simply checked to be sure the sensor functioned—as, of course, it did, whether or not a baseline chamber contained three pistols as well as air.

"Ayven—"

Ayven smacked his brother across the forehead with the butt of his pistol. Carron went glassy-eyed, bounced off the bunk support, and fell backward. There was a bloody streak at the base of his scalp.

"You two," Ayven said. "Get the capsule out. The curst fools have it all in pieces."

"The capsule wasn't part of the deal, Del Vore!" Ned said in a trembling voice.

The soldier behind Ned stepped up close behind and stuck the muzzle of his pistol in Ned's ear. Toomey, who'd arrived with Ayven, leaned forward and drew the powergun from Ned's holster.

"The deal," said Ayven, "is whatever I—" He raised his arm to swing the pistol again, this time at *Ned*. He was smiling, but his face was white with rage.

"—*say* the—"

Ned ducked, kicked Ayven in the crotch, and slammed his left elbow into the stomach of the soldier behind him. The motions weren't quite simultaneous, but they overlapped enough. The Celandine pistol's *whack! whack! whack!* slapped the back of Ned's neck, but the high-velocity bullets ripped trenches in the lining of the ceiling aft.

Ned grabbed the shooter's wrist. Ayven tried to level his gun while his left hand gripped the numb ache in his lower belly. Ned yanked the soldier over his shoulder and knocked the prince down.

Toomey pulled the trigger of Ned's pistol repeatedly. Nothing happened—the weapon wasn't loaded. He thumbed the safety in the opposite direction and tried again. His body blocked the third soldier behind him.

Carron's false bonds draped him loosely. He'd risen to one arm, but his eyes were unfocused. Blood dripped down his right cheek. When he raised his hand to dab at it, he slid off the bunk into the crowded aisle. A needle stunner dropped out of his sleeve.

Ned snatched the pistol he'd clipped beneath the bottom bunk facing the hatchway. Toomey smashed the butt of the unloaded powergun into the left side of Ned's neck.

White pain blasted in concentric circles across Ned's vision. He fired three times into the man who'd struck him, dazzling cyan spikes flaring across the waves of pain. The Pancahtan slumped sideways, gouting blood.

Ned's trigger finger stabbed two bolts more into the man still standing. The soldier's face exploded, ripped apart by flash-heated fluids. The unfired Celandine pistol flew out of his hand.

Ayven and the remaining soldier had gotten untangled. Ned aimed, squeezed, and nothing happened. Jets of liquid nitrogen cooled a powergun's bore after every bolt. Ned had fired so quickly that the plastic matrix of the last round was still fluid when the gas tried to eject it from the chamber. Instead of flying free, the spent matrix formed a stinking goo that jammed the pistol.

Ned threw the powergun at Ayven. Ayven ducked sideways. The other Pancahtan rose to a kneeling position and aimed at Ned. The pistol's smoking muzzle was a meter away as Ned scrabbled for another weapon.

A burst of cyan bolts hit the soldier between the shoulder blades. Exploding steam flung the body forward.

Ned found the needle stunner with which Carron was supposed to surprise his would-be captors. Ayven turned in a half-crouch, aiming back over his shoulder.

The front of the capsule was open. Lissea Doormann stood in it, aiming through the holographic sights of a submachine gun. Heat waves danced around the weapon. The muzzle glowed white from the first long burst.

Ned put needles into Ayven's midback and right shoulder. Lissea fired simultaneously, ripping six or seven rounds all the way up the prince's breastbone. Ayven's chest blew open in a mush of ruptured internal organs.

Carron lay across his brother's feet, pinning them. His eyes were open. What remained of Ayven slumped down on Carron like a scarlet blanket.

Ned tried to pull himself to his feet. His left arm wouldn't obey him. It flopped loose, and that whole side of his torso pulsed with hammerblows of pain. He braced his right shoulder against a bunk support and used his legs to thrust himself upright.

The temperature of the vessel's interior had shot up five degrees Celsius from the released energy. Matrix residues, ozone, and propellant smoke mixed with the stench of men disemboweled and cooked in their own juices.

Lissea put her boot against the side of a dead Pancahtan and tried to push him out of the hatch. The body was freshly dead, as limp as a blood sausage. She held the submachine gun out to her side. The barrel shimmered, cooling slowly in the heated air.

"Carron?" she croaked. She knelt down. "Carron, are you all right?"

He moaned and raised a hand to his head.

Lissea looked at Ned. "Sound recall," she said. The gunshots had half-deafened Ned, giving the words a rasping, tinny sound. "Get everybody back on board soonest. We'll lift in an hour if terminal control will clear us."

"Yeah," Ned said. "Yeah."

He dropped the needle stunner and stuck a projectile pistol through his waistband. He and Carron had put the loose weapons aboard the *Swift* in lockers so that they wouldn't be to hand for the Pancahtans they intended to take hostage. He should have known Ayven wouldn't have come unless he'd figured out how to bring weapons with him.

"Oh, Lord," Ned wheezed. He found the land-line phone and flipped open the protective case.

"The capsule was shielded," Lissea said. She wasn't talking to him, just reviewing the steps that had led to the unacceptable present moment. "I heard you and Carron talking as you came aboard. I didn't trust any of . . . of—with the *Swift* and the capsule. So I waited."

Ned keyed the outside line, keyed a separate code for a commercial paging system that would access the commo helmets of the *Swift*'s personnel, and then typed the recall code: six-six-six.

"I didn't have any choice!" Lissea shouted. Her voice broke with the strain and foul air. She was gripping Carron's left hand. "I *had* to turn him over, didn't I?"

Carron groaned and tried to get up. He didn't seem to be aware of his surroundings.

"There was a choice," Ned said. "We took it, the three of us."

He had a little feeling again in his left arm. He didn't think the collarbone was broken—or his neck, but there'd be time enough for the medicomp to check him later, if there was any time at all.

"We'd better not dispose of the bodies until we're in space," Lissea thought aloud. She stood up abruptly. "It was probably a crime, wasn't it?" She laughed, cackled. "That's a joke! Shooting somebody, a crime."

Ned fumbled the handset. "Lissea," he said, "you'll have to call terminal control. With one hand, I can't manage the phone and access the necessary codes from the data bank."

Carron moaned.

Noise hammered within the enclosed dock as the entrance opened again. Lissea turned, pointing the submachine gun. Ned stumbled to the hatchway over Pancahtan bodies.

The men of the *Swift*'s complement were pouring into the hangar. They couldn't possibly have reacted to the summons so quickly.

The whole crew was present and accounted for, though a few of them were drunk enough to lean on the shoulders of their fellows. Moiseyev and Hatton, the two junior engine-room personnel, carried Petit, their senior.

There were two Pancahtan uniforms in the midst of the loose grouping. The Warson brothers wore them. They did a shuffling dance, arm in arm.

Josie Paetz was the first man up the ramp. "Hey," he said. "*Hey*, not bad!"

Yazov gripped Ayven Del Vore's short hair and tilted the undamaged face to the light. "And I thought *we'd* done something!" he said, shifting an appreciative glance from Lissea to Ned and back.

"Lissea, we've got to get out of here fast," Tadziki said. Westerbeke, looking squeamish, hesitated at the top of the ramp. The adjutant tugged him forward and gave him a push toward the navigation consoles.

Lissea had returned to the phone when she saw the new arrivals were her men rather than Pancahtan reinforcements. She put it down again. "Yes," she said. "They're processing the clearance now. It'll take—"

She shook her head as if to clear it of cobwebs. "I don't know. Half an hour? An hour?"

Herne Lordling tried to put his arms around her. "No!" she screamed. "*No!*" She twisted away hard, her boots slipping in blood.

Ned looked at the Celandine pistol he'd drawn without being conscious of the movement. Tadziki stepped close to him with a concerned expression.

Ned tossed the gun on a bunk. He began to tremble. In a loud voice he said, "We need to get away fast, before the Pancahtans sort out a new leader. They won't dare go home without catching us, but just for the moment they'll be disorganized."

"Everybody get in your couches," Toll Warson boomed. "Don't worry about the mess, we've all smelled worse, haven't we?"

"'Specially Harlow has," Coyne shouted. "Did you see what he was doing to that pig in the Double Star?" Harlow hurled his helmet at Coyne, but it was a good-natured gesture.

"And you're right about the Pancahtans being disorganized," Toll continued with a broad, beaming smile. "When the *Furious* engages the liftoff sequence in her navigational computer, there's going to be a little software glitch."

He waved his hand to the adjutant, as if presenting him to an audience.

"Her fusion bottle," Tadziki said with a smile as cruel as a hyena's, "is going to vent. I don't think *any* of the three ships in Hangar 17 are going to be functional for a very long time."

DELL

The ship landed on Dell as the last sunlight touched the tops of the tall evergreens surrounding Doormann Trading Company Post No. 103. The plasma exhaust threw iridescent highlights across the clearing. Livestock in the corral bellowed.

The factor waited a few moments for the ground to cool, then sauntered out to meet the strangers. The vessel wasn't one of the familiar tramps that shuttled back and forth in the Telaria-Dell trade.

This one had radioed that it was the *Homer,* operating under a Celandine registry, a first for Post No. 103 in the thirty-seven years Jirtle had been factor here. He looked forward to seeing some new faces.

The vessel's boarding ramp lowered smoothly. The *Homer* was quite small, which wasn't unusual; in fact, a large vessel would have been hard put to land in the clearing in front of the post. There wasn't a real spaceport at Post No. 103—or virtually anywhere else on Dell.

Lone entrepreneurs ranged the forests of Dell, culling the products that were worth transporting between stars and bringing them to the nearest Doormann Trading outpost. It was small-scale commerce, but it appealed to those who found cities and governmental restrictions too trammeling.

It appealed to Jirtle and his wife.

Four men stood at the head of the boarding ramp. They wore

body armor and carried stocked powerguns. They looked as stark and terrible as demons.

Jirtle gasped and turned to run. There was no reason for pirates to come *here,* there was nothing worth the time of those engaged in criminal endeavors on an interstellar scale. But they were here. . . .

"Jirtle!" a woman's voice called. "Jirtle, it's me!"

The leaf mat slipped beneath the factor's slippers and threw him down. He fell heavily. He was an old man anyway, gasping with terror and exertion after only a few steps. He couldn't have outrun the pirates, and nobody could outrun a bolt from a power-gun . . .

"Jirtle, it's *me!* Lissea!"

The factor looked over his shoulder. "Lissea?" he said. "*You're* back? Oh, thank the Lord! They'd said you were dead!"

Pots clanged from the summer kitchen behind the post, where Mistress Jirtle was cooking dinner for twenty with the somewhat bemused help of her husband.

Lissea glanced in the direction of the noise. "They were more parents to me than Grey and Duenya, you know," she said affectionately. "I only saw my mother and father one month a year when they were allowed to come to Dell on vacation. The rest of the time, Karel kept my parents on the Doormann estate."

The *Swift's* personnel were gathered in the factory's public room. There was plenty of space on the near side of the counter. In treacle-wax season, as many as a hundred forest scouts might crowd into the post demanding that the Jirtles weigh their gleanings "*now, before these other bastards!*"

"Yes, fine, it's nice you've had this reunion," Herne Lordling said curtly. "But we landed here for information before we made the last leg to Telaria, and I don't like the information we got."

Lissea sat on the factor's counter with her legs dangling down. Carron stood beside her. The rest of the personnel spread in an arc around the walls, bales, and barrels in the public room.

"If the Doormanns believe the story of Lissea's death," Ned said, "then we've got the advantage of surprise. Of course, Karel may have spread the story himself."

Tadziki shook his head and raised his hand to quiet the half dozen men who began talking at once. "I think we can take that as real," he said when he'd gotten silence. "It's too circumstantial to have been entirely invented—all of us dying on Alliance when the Dreadnought landed and the plague broke out there."

He looked at Lissea and added grimly, "Besides, that was the point at which Grey and Duenna Doormann were taken into close custody."

"And we can assume they'll take me in charge also, just as soon as I reappear," Lissea agreed calmly.

"They may *try!*" said Herne Lordling.

"Yes," said Lissea. "Well, I don't think fighting all Telaria is the way to proceed."

"We could do that, you know, ma'am," Toll Warson said quietly.

Everyone looked at him. Half the men present started to speak, mostly protests. Toll, sitting on a bale of lustrous gray furs, waited with a faint smile.

Ned frowned. The Warsons were jokers, but they weren't stupid and they didn't bluster in the least. Toll (and Deke even more so) had the trick of stating something so calmly that nobody would believe him—

And then ramming the statement home to the hilt.

"Wait!" Lissea ordered with her hand raised. "Toll, go on."

"Everybody here's worked in the business," Toll said. "We know folks. Some of us have had rank, some haven't. . ."

He grinned at Herne Lordling.

"But we've all got reputations that'll get us listened to by the folks who've worked with us before."

Toll glanced around the room, then back to Lissea. "We can raise you an army on tick, ma'am," he said, his voice as thin and harsh as the song of a blade on a whetstone. "We can bring you twenty brigades on your promise to pay when the fighting's over. I can, Herne can. If Slade can't bring in the Slammers, then his uncle curst well can!"

He slid off the bale to stand up. The crash of his boots on the puncheon floor drove a period to his words.

"Blood and martyrs, he's right!" Lordling said. "Doormann Trading's enough of a prize to cover the cost, and it *will* cost, but—"

"No," said Lissea, her voice lost in the general babble.

"—it's worth it in the mid- and long-term," Lordling continued enthusiastically.

"Hell, short-term is that we all get chopped when we land on Telaria," Deke Warson said, "Fuck *that* for a lark if you ask me!"

"No," repeated Lissea. "No!"

As the room quieted, she went on, "I didn't come back to wreck Telaria forever. I'll—I'll deal with those who lied to me, who mistreated my parents. But all-out war on Telaria will leave . . ."

She grimaced and didn't finish the sentence. *Burr-Detlingen. Kazan. A hundred other worlds where men had settled.*

"Look, Lissea," Herne Lordling said in the tone of an adult addressing a child, "all of a broken dish is better than no plate at all. And Warson had a point about what's going to happen to us if we land openly on Telaria—"

"I don't think we need be concerned about our safety," Tadziki interjected. "The professionals, that is. As Toll pointed out, we are individually, ah, men of some reputation and authority. I don't believe Karel Doormann will go out of his way to antagonize the sort of persons—"

He smiled coldly

"—who might be offended by our needless murders."

"What do we do then, ma'am?" Deke Warson demanded. As he'd listened to the discussion thus far, he stroked the barrel of his slung powergun. His fingertips had a rainbow sheen from iridium rubbed off onto his skin. "Do you want Karel dead? I can do that, any of us can do that. But that alone won't give you what you want."

He thumbed toward his brother. "Toll's right. You've got to smash the whole system so there's nothing left to argue with you. You need an army behind you if you're going to force your kin to your way of thinking . . . and even then, it'd be better if they were dead. All of them."

He spoke with the persuasive rationality of a specialist advising a professional client. That's what he was. That's what they all were.

"No," Carron said, speaking for the first time since they entered the trading post. "There is a way."

"All right," Toll Warson said. "I'll bite, kid."

Carron stepped forward, so that he stood between Lissea and the men present. She frowned slightly from her perch above him.

"I have been studying Lendell Doormann's device," Carron said, "as you know. I think at this point I understand the principles on which it operates."

Lordling guffawed.

"I can land us on Telaria, kid," Westerbeke said huffily. "With or without tower guidance. *That's* no problem."

Carron shook his head fiercely. "No," he said. "No, the device is necessary, but not as transport, of course." He glared imperiously at the mercenaries, in control, and well aware of it. "We will land openly," he said, "on Telaria . . ."

TELARIA

Two more truckloads of Doormann Trading security personnel pulled up before the *Swift*'s landing site. About half the guards wore body armor over their blue uniforms and carried submachine guns in addition to their sidearms. They looked wide-eyed, and the faces of their officers were set and white.

The scores of city police and Doormann personnel already present were swamped by the civilian crowd including newspeople which had gathered within minutes of the *Swift*'s arrival. Westerbeke had come in under automated control, letting the ship's AI handshake with that of the terminal. No humans were involved in the process until the slim, scarred vessel dropped into view and spectators realized that "*Movement Delta five-five-niner, Telarian registry,*" was the returning Pancahte Expedition.

Ned, Tadziki, and Carron Del Vore stood at the base of the boarding ramp. They wore their "best" static-cleaned clothes; in Ned's case, the uniform that had the fewest tears. Nothing available from clothing stocks on Dell would have been more suitable for present purposes.

Ned's dress clothes were in storage in Landfall City, but he wasn't about to send for them now. His feet were thirty centimeters apart and his arms crossed behind his back as he waited for someone with rank to arrive.

An official car pulled through the crowd, the driver hooting his two-note horn. A man Ned remembered was named Kardon, an assistant port director, got out. He was accompanied by a woman who was probably his superior. A police lieutenant tried to get instructions from the pair as they strode toward Ned. The woman waved him away without bothering to look.

"*Everyone move back-k-k,*" crackled a bullhorn. "*This is a closed area. Everyone moo-*urk!"

Toll Warson led the six-man team opening the *Swift*'s external storage bays and undoing the lashings within. More armed mercenaries stood or squatted in the hatchway, grinning out at the Telarians.

There were three meters of cracked concrete between Ned and the edge of the crowd. Media personnel shouted questions across it, but no one stepped closer. Harlow, at the spade grips of the tribarrel mounted on the upper plating, grinned through his sights as he traversed the weapon slowly across that invisible line on the ground.

"I'm Director Longley," the woman said. "This vessel is quarantined. Take me to Captain Doormann at once."

The director was in her thirties, younger than her male assistant. She radiated an inner intensity. Her voice and manner didn't so much overpower the confusion as much as they rode over it.

"I'm in charge now," Ned said harshly. Out of the corner of his eye he noticed a squad of blue uniforms deploying on the terminal's observation deck. "Captain Doormann's dead, a lot of people are dead. But we brought back the capsule—"

Ned was rigidly focused on the step-by-step accomplishment of his mission. It was a series of hurdles, and it couldn't matter that some of the obstacles might be blood and fire. Part of him wondered, though, what his expression must be to cause Kardon to flinch that way.

"—and we brought Lendell Doormann besides."

"*Got* the fucker!" Deke Warson cried. The crew gave a collective grunt and tipped the large sealed casket out. The plastic box was a clumsy piece of work, but it was as sturdy as befitted the skill of men whose training was in starship repairs rather than cabinetry.

The clear top the crew had added on Dell didn't improve the casket's appearance. Lendell Doormann grinned out at the crowd. He looked like the personification of Death by Plague.

Ned gestured. "As you see. Now, one of you take me at once to the board of Doormann Trading. I need to speak to the board immediately."

There was movement inside the *Swift* as another team carefully walked the capsule up the aisle to the hatchway. Lendell Doormann's device had been returned to its original status, with all the internal and external panels in place. The front of the capsule was open, displaying the empty interior.

"Keep your shirt on, Master . . . Slade," Longley said, reading the faded name tape on Ned's breast. "You've landed without proper authorization, and—"

"Excuse me, Director," Tadziki said, "but we landed normally— as the navigation records will prove."

"You're Tadziki, aren't you?" Longley said, turning her attention to the adjutant. "I've dealt with you before. Well, Master Tadziki, I can tell you right now I don't appreciate you sneaking in on the regular landing pattern this way. *Look* at this chaos!"

She waved her hand at the crowd. "Somebody's likely to be killed in a mess like this!"

As if that triggered a memory, Longley pointed up at Harlow. "And put that cursed cannon away or I'll have you arrested right now! I'll have you all arrested!"

Harlow grinned.

Kardon looked over his shoulder toward the mixture of police, security guards, and civilians. He thrust his way past Carron and started to climb the ladder extended from the *Swift*'s side to access the gun position.

Deke Warson muttered something. Raff slung his rocket gun and grabbed the assistant director by the wrists, plucking him easily from the ladder.

"Kardon, what are you playing at?!" Longley demanded.

The Racontid swung Kardon around, holding him well off the ground. Kardon bleated with rage. Several of the police and guards had drawn their weapons, but their officers were angrily ordering, *"Don't shoot! Don't anybody shoot!"*

"That's enough!" said Tadziki.

Deke Warson slit Kardon's waistband with a knife sharp enough for shaving, then pulled the man's trousers down over his ankles.

"That," Deke said, "is enough."

He nodded to Raff. The Racontid let his victim down. Kardon bent over to grab his pants and tripped. There was laughter, but it was all from mercenaries and civilians.

"Director," Ned said, "you're not a fool, so stop acting like one. If you want real problems, for yourself and for Doormann Trading, then indeed go ahead and arrest these men who have risked their *lives* for Doormann Trading. We are *not* a rabble, mistress! I'm nephew to Slade of Tethys, and my companions are men of rank and power in their individual right!"

"We are here to report, mistress," Tadziki said forcefully. "To report and to be paid under contract. We've suffered enough for Doormann Trading. We don't choose to be chivied by bureaucrats who can't control traffic in their own port!"

A pair of three-wheelers bulled through the crowd, carving a path for the limousine behind them. A video cameraman didn't move out of the way. His bellow of anger turned to fear as an escort vehicle knocked him down from behind.

The trike drove over the man's ankle and crushed part of the tracery of lenses which provided three-dimensionality for the holographic images. The cameraman's producer managed to drag him out of the way of the limousine that was following.

Lucas Doormann opened the door of the limousine and got out. Time constraints and the crush of the crowd prevented the driver from waiting on his master in normal fashion.

"Where's Lissea?" Lucas demanded. His gaze traveled over the *Swift* and those around it.

"Via!" he added with a moue of distaste. "Are all these guns necessary? Put them away, all of you."

He gestured imperiously to a captain wearing a Doormann Trading uniform. "You! There's no need for guns! Put your weapons up at once."

"Captain Doormann is dead, Master Doormann," Ned said as Lucas' eyes returned to him.

"Dead?" Lucas repeated.

Kardon, holding his trousers up with one hand, looked as though he was about to interrupt. Longley shushed him with a curt chop of her hand.

"On Pancahte," Ned said grimly. "We retrieved the capsule, though, and I *must* speak to your board immediately."

"The capsule is an amazing advance over Transit," Carron Del Vore said. "Your ancestor was right, *but,* for two-way traffic the device must—"

"Who is this?" Lucas demanded. Before anyone could answer, he spun on his heel. "Clear the crowd back, can't you?" he shouted toward the red-faced officer who'd been bawling orders to the security personnel. "Blood and martyrs, what *is* this? A circus?"

Longley made a quick decision and stepped away from the discussion. She took a communications wand from her shoulder wallet and began speaking crisp orders. There were by now several hundred blue- and green-uniformed security personnel present. What was lacking was central direction, and Longley could supply that.

"Prince Carron," Tadziki said, "is the heir and emissary of Treasurer Lon Del Vore of Pancahte. He is in addition a respected scientist, who believes it will now be possible to set up instantaneous communications between Telaria and Pancahte."

Lucas' eyes narrowed in surprise. "The lost colony really exists?" he said. He shook his head. "I suppose it must; I . . ."

"I must speak to the board of Doormann Trading," Ned repeated again. "And the capsule should be returned to its original location in Lendell's laboratory."

Ned knew that Lucas was swamped by the situation. The Telarian noble's mind was on a knife-edge, tilting one way and the next without real composure. If nudged successfully, Lucas had the rank and ability to do all the things necessary for the operation to succeed.

"Lendell?" Lucas said. He looked, perhaps for the first time, at the crude casket. "That's Lendell. Good Lord, that *is* Lendell! What happened to him?"

"He never really left Telaria," Carrion said, though "explained" would give too much effect to his words. "Though he couldn't be seen here and he *appeared* to be present on Pancahte. That's why the device must be returned to its original location, as precisely as possible, to permit two-way communication."

"Good *Lord*," Lucas repeated. "And Lissea . . . I didn't think anything would really, would—"

He made a fist and broke off. He stared at his clenched fingers for a moment, then relaxed them and looked up at Ned again.

More police and guards were arriving, but the haste and panic of the early moments were over. The security personnel worked in unison, guided through their in-ear speakers by Longley and her assistant.

The crowd continued to grow as word of the *Swift*'s arrival spread beyond the spaceport boundaries, but nothing was happening to raise the emotional temperature. Harlow tilted the muzzles of the tribarrel skyward, though all the mercs kept watch from beneath easy smiles and gibes to one another.

"I very much regret all of this," Lucas said. "The—Lissea."

He looked at Ned. "Yes," he continued. "An emergency board meeting was called as soon as my father heard of the *Swift*'s arrival. I will take you to the meeting, Master Slade. *If* you're worried about your claims for payment, don't be. I will personally guarantee them."

"Thank you, sir," Ned said, "but it's necessary I report in person to . . . those who sent us to Pancahte."

"And the device?" Carron put in. "This is an advance beyond conception!"

Lucas glanced at the Pancahtan, then back to Ned. "Should he be present at the board meeting?" he asked.

"No," Ned said. "But Prince Carron *should* supervise the place-ment of the capsule back in the laboratory. That isn't the first thing on your mind or on mine, sir, but I have no doubt that he's correct in his valuation of the device."

"All right, then," Lucas muttered. He turned his head. "Director Longley? Director!"

Longley stepped quickly back to Lucas. "Yes sir?" she said. Kardon, still holding his trousers up, continued to oversee the security details.

"How quickly can you get two separate vans here?" Lucas demanded. "I want this object—"

He gestured to the capsule

"—taken to the laboratory in the basement of the Main Spire in the Doormann estate. And I want my . . . my great-granduncle's body taken to the family chapel. That will require cargo handlers as well."

Lucas looked at the mercenaries standing in falsely relaxed postures. "None of these gentlemen," he added, "will be involved in the work."

Longley spoke into her communications wand, then met the young noble's eyes again. "The vehicles and crews will be here within ninety seconds, sir," she said, "or I'll remove a department head. They'll need clearances to enter your family's estate, of course."

Lucas nodded brusquely. "Yes, of course; I'll clear them through. Just get it done and done quickly. It's not seemly to have—"

He looked at the casket and grimaced." Was it really necessary to use a clear top?" he muttered, half under his breath.

"I'll accompany the device," Carron said to the port director. Longley glanced at Lucas.

"Yes, yes!" Lucas said with an irritated wave of his hand.

Doormann looked at Ned again, and his eyes hardened.

"You won't be allowed in the meeting room armed, Master Slade," he said.

"Of course," Ned said with a sniff of surprise. He unlatched his pistol belt and handed the rig, powergun and all, to Tadziki. "On Tethys, it would be an insult to appear armed in public."

The first of two spaceport service vehicles pulled through the gap the police had made in the spectators. Lucas turned and strode toward his limousine.

"Come along, then," he muttered. "They'll be expecting *my* report. Father didn't want me to come."

As he got into the big car, Lucas added, "I just can't believe someone so alive as Lissea . . ."

* * *

"Hey, Tadziki," Deke Warson called from the hatchway. "Master Customs-Agent here says he's maybe going to quit hassling us so we can get our asses out of here."

Tadziki spun his navigation console to face aft. He gestured toward Warson to indicate that he'd heard but continued talking earnestly to someone on the other end of the *Swift*'s external communications link.

The vessel's bay looked more of a wreck than it had at any time since initial liftoff from Buin. Men had sorted their gear, but most of it remained on top of their bunks, and spilling into the aisle. In truth, most personal items had been reduced to trash during the voyage, but the bald willingness to walk away from objects that had been companions for so long was alien to civilian sensibilities.

The men of the *Swift* weren't civilians.

Tadziki finished his conversation and stood up. "There," he said as he picked his way down the aisle to the hatch. "I've got lodging arranged for all who want it at the Clarion House, admission on ID or an expedition patch. And I've got a mobile crane rented. Coordinates to both are downloaded. You say the rigmarole here's taken care of?"

The gray-suited customs supervisor with Warson bridled. "Master Tadziki," he said, "I realize you men have gone through a great deal, but Telaria is civilized and civilization requires rules. I assure you my people and I have made quite extraordinary efforts to clear you immediately."

He looked around with unintended distaste.

"Are we 'go,' then, Tadziki?" Deke Warson asked in a voice that surprised the customs official for its gentleness.

"That's right," the adjutant said.

He stepped to the hatchway and looked out. The security presence had shrunk to about thirty green-uniformed police, but the media were gone and the tension had left the remaining crowd.

The *Swift*'s personnel were drawn up in two lines at the base of the ramp. Three vans rented from a spaceport delivery service waited nearby. The crates in the back of two of the vans were full of weapons and ammunition. Customs officers nearby eyed the vehicles and the mercenaries with disquiet.

"All right, boys," Tadziki called. "Have fun, and if there's a problem you'll find me here."

He gave the troops a palm-out salute. The men returned it in a dozen different styles. None of them were very good at the gesture. In the field, the only purpose of a salute was to target a hated officer for an enemy sniper . . . and these men were more likely to use self-help for even that purpose.

"Dismissed!" called Herne Lordling. The ranks broke up. Men scrambled to the vans. Dewey and Bonilla from navigation, and Petit and Moiseyev from the engine room, boarded the empty vehicle. The rest split among the vans carrying crated weapons.

Deke turned and shook the adjutant's hand. "Hey, good luck," he said. "Sure you wouldn't like a little company?"

Tadziki smiled wanly. "We've gotten this far, haven't we?" he said. "What can happen now?"

Motors revved. Deke ran down the ramp and jumped in through the open back of a van as his brother drove it away.

"I, ah . . ." the customs supervisor said. "Where are they going with all those weapons? I realize that it's technically beyond my competence, but. . ."

Tadziki watched the vehicles until they disappeared around a maintenance building. The mobile crane he'd rented was in a lot on the north edge of the spaceport, convenient to their destination.

"They're going to take them back to the warehouse," Tadziki said at last. "They're Doormann Trading Company property, you realize?"

"Yes, of course," the supervisor said. "Most of them. I'm familiar with the manifest, of course. Some of the serial numbers weren't— but that's not a serious matter. As I said, we had no intention of delaying you gentlemen needlessly. And the individuals' data were in order from your initial entry to Telaria."

He paused. The inspectors under his direction waited on the concrete, murmuring among themselves and glancing at the battered black hull of the *Swift*.

Tadziki stared northward, toward Landfall City and the Doormann family estate beyond it. He blinked and looked at the supervisor again. "Eh?" Tadziki said. "Sorry, did you say something?"

"I notice," the supervisor said, "that your men are still wearing their uniforms?"

"Well, what else do you expect them to wear?" the adjutant snapped. "This wasn't exactly a pleasure cruise, you know, with twelve trunks for every passenger."

He waved toward the rumpled disaster area which the vessel's interior had become.

"Anyway," he continued in a milder voice, "they aren't uniform. Not here. They're battledress from as many different units as there were men aboard. And if you mean the commo helmets—"

Tadziki gave the supervisor a wry grin

"—we're used to using them, you know. I've downloaded routes and locations into the helmet files."

The supervisor nodded. It was all perfectly reasonable, but he felt uncomfortable. This wasn't a standard task. The pilot who was in charge while Tadziki made calls said that one of the Doormann family had cleared through a number of passengers without even registering them. Well, what could you do when your superiors wouldn't let you do your job?

He shook himself back to the present. "I'm sorry, Master Tadziki," he said. "We both have business to attend, I'm sure. I shouldn't be wasting your time."

"All I have to do," Tadziki said, staring out of the hatch, "is to wait. But I'm not in a mood for company right now, that's a fact."

The supervisor stepped down the ramp. "Come on, all of you," he ordered as his subordinates stiffened at his notice. "The *Puritan* landed half an hour ago with seven hundred passengers on board!"

The *Swift*'s adjutant had gone back inside. The supervisor didn't know how the man stood it. The vessel made *him* extremely nervous.

* * *

"Look, I don't know if I ought to be doing this," Platt whined at the door to the basement laboratory.

"Will somebody *please* make a fucking decision?" grated the foreman of the cargo handlers carrying the capsule. The load wasn't exceptionally heavy for the four-man team, but the seedy-looking attendant was obviously capable of dithering for hours.

Carron Del Vore snapped his fingers. "What do you mean you don't *know*, dog?" he demanded. "You've got orders from the chamberlain, haven't you?"

"*All* I got," the attendant said, "is somebody called and said she was the chamberlain. Look, I think you better bring me something in hard copy. I don't know you from Adam and these guys, they don't belong in the spire at *all*."

Platt straightened. He fumblingly tried to return the electronic key to the belt case from which he'd taken it a moment before.

Carron looked at the cargo handlers. "Set that down," he ordered. "On its base, and *carefully*. Then beat this creature unconscious and open the door."

"No!" Platt bleated.

"Suits me," said the foreman. The crew tilted the empty capsule to set it down as Carron ordered.

Though Platt spilled most of the contents of his case onto the floor, he managed to hold on to the key. He pressed it against the lockplate. The cargo handlers started for him an instant before the heavy door began to open.

"No!" Platt said, squeezing himself against the doorjamb and raising thin arms against the threatened blows.

"That's enough," Carron said to the foreman. "Carry the device to the platform at the other end of the room. I'll show you exactly where it goes."

The men sighed and lifted the capsule again. One of them spat on the attendant as they passed him.

"We're going to be on overtime before we get back," the foreman muttered. "And *won't* Kardon tear a strip off me? As if I could do anything about the estate staff getting its finger out of its bum *every* curst door we had to get through."

"Hey, did you see Kardon having to hold his pants up?" another handler said. "Whoo-ee, I'd have liked to see when that happened!"

The carefully positioned lights flooded the lab and everyone in it with their radiance. Carron watched nervously as the crew wound its way between benches and free-standing equipment. For all their nonchalance, the men didn't bang the capsule into anything. Platt peered from the doorway, scowling and rubbing his shoulder as if he'd been punched.

"What is this place, anyway?" a man asked querulously.

"Don't move the mirrors out of alignment!" Carron warned. The crew was edging its way to the dais. It wasn't clear that it would be possible to put the capsule back *without* moving one of the pentagonal black mirrors that ringed the location.

"Don't have kittens!" the foreman snapped. He paused, judging the relative shapes and sizes. "All right, Hoch, let go now."

The man at the base of the capsule with the foreman obediently stepped away. The foreman eased forward, ducking his shoulder. By keeping the device low, he managed to dip it under the narrowest point and then raise it to clear the dais.

"There!" he announced with justifiable pride. He lowered the ring base, and his men lifted together to set the capsule upright.

"We're not done yet," Carron said sharply.

He switched on a measuring device from the kit he'd brought with him from Pancahte. It projected a hologram of the capsule taken at the moment Lendell Doormann vanished from Telaria for the next seventy years and compared the recording with present reality.

"There, you see?" Carron said. "The orange points are out of synchrony. Turn it clockwise ten degrees and move it a centimeter closer to the wall."

Two of the cargo handlers moved to obey. The foreman waved them back. He viewed the image, then spread his arms around the capsule and himself began the minute adjustments.

Carron watched his measurement device tensely. The areas of orange slipped into the cooler end of the spectrum. "That's far enough!" he cried as the foreman's boot scraped the capsule the necessary distance toward the wall. "But keep turning, another degree."

The foreman's face was set. His mouth was open, and he watched the holographic display out of the corner of his eyes. The display wavered into the violet range then back toward indigo. He released the last pressure and stepped away, breathing hard. The main image was violet again.

"There!" he said.

The door of the capsule showed red to orange on the display. It had been closed when Lendell Doormann vanished. The foreman put his hand on the curved panel to swing it shut.

"No!" Carron cried, grabbing the man's arm. "No, don't do that! This is fine, this is perfect the way it is."

The foreman shrugged. "Whatever," he said. He stepped out between two mirrors. "You know," he added, "this is a spooky place."

"It is?" said Carron in puzzlement. "I wouldn't have said so."

The cargo handlers were sauntering back toward the door. "No, I don't guess you would," one of them muttered loud enough to be heard.

Carron walked out of the laboratory behind the crew. The lights cut off automatically. Platt shut the door, avoiding the eyes of the visitors.

Carron paused and looked at the attendant. "I have the phone number of your station," he said. "You or someone else will be present at all times, is that not so?"

"Yeah, it's fucking so," Platt muttered. "Unless somebody gets me up to dick around in the lab again, at least."

"I may be calling soon," Carron said. "You will regret it if you do not carry out to the letter any instructions I may give you."

But the despicable little man would regret it even more if he *did* do as he was told. . . .

The boardroom of Doormann Trading Company was on the top level of the crystal spire in the center of the family estate. It was nearly an hour before the board readmitted Lucas to its presence.

Ned had waited a further hour alone. He paced slowly around the broad walkway which served as an observation deck.

Two guards with submachine guns stood at the ornate bronze doors giving access to the boardroom. There were two more guards at the single elevator which opened onto the observation deck on the opposite side of the circuit. As a further security precaution, before entering the armored boardroom one had to walk all the way around it.

The two guards who'd come up with Lucas Doormann and Ned kept pace behind Ned now. They were bored, but not too bored to remain watchful.

The exterior of the spire was optically pure and had the same refractive index as Telaria's atmosphere. Though the curved, fluted walls were at no point flat, they did not distort the view.

The view was breathtaking. The Doormann estate spread over hectares of rolling hills in every direction. Ned knew from his view out of the limousine that the surface in the frequent glades and bowers was as carefully manicured as that of the surrounding grassy areas.

Buildings in a mix of styles, mostly those of Terra's classical and medieval eras, nestled in swales or sat on hillsides. None of the structures had more than two above-ground stories, though from the traffic in and out, some had extensive basements. The aggregate floorspace of the outbuildings probably totaled as much as that of the central spire, but the careful planners had succeeded in preserving the illusion of agrestic emptiness.

Machines and humans in drab uniforms worked like a stirred-up anthill to keep the grounds pristine. Ned noticed that when people in civilian clothes walked near or paused to view the formal gardens, maintenance personnel moved out of the area so as not to disturb them. Most of those who lived within the estate were the Doormanns' servants and office staff, but even they had the status of minor nobility on Telaria.

One of the buildings on the grounds was the Doormann family chapel. Ned would learn where it was when he needed to; which would be very soon, unless his interview with Karel Doormann proceeded in an unexpectedly reasonable fashion.

The door to the boardroom opened with only the sigh of air and the faint trembling from the electromagnets which supported and moved the massive panel. Ned turned. Lucas Doormann walked out. "Master Slade," he said, "the board is prepared to see you now."

"Yes," said Ned as he stepped forward. The entranceway was constructed on the model of an airlock. An iridium-sheathed panel closed the inner end whenever the main door was open. The designers had taken no chances with a guard going berserk and spraying the boardroom with his submachine gun.

The outer panel slid shut behind Ned and Lucas. Ned felt as if he were riding a monocycle at high speed across glare ice. At any moment he could lose his balance and go flying, and he had no control at all . . .

The inner door snicked upward with the speed of a microtome blade. It was time.

Eight men and three women faced Ned from around the oval central table. There was an empty place for Lucas, who remained at Ned's side.

Karel Doormann was neither the oldest nor the most expensively dressed of the board members, but his dominance would have been obvious even had he not been seated at the head of the table. He watched Ned with the smile of a cat preparing to spring.

"Mesdames and sirs," Ned said, taking off his commo helmet. His voice was clear and cool. He spoke as the peer of any of these folk. "I am here to tell you of a necessary deception. Lissea Doormann is alive on Dell, awaiting the outcome of this meeting."

Karel Doormann's smile broadened. His son made a startled sound. A heavyset man leaned close to the woman beside him to whisper, but both of them kept their eyes on Ned.

"I say 'necessary,'" Ned continued, "because Lissea and yourselves have the same basic desire: to avoid trouble. Had she returned with the *Swift*, an underling might have taken actions that were not in the best interests of Doormann Trading, and which might have prejudiced chances of a beneficial outcome."

"Go on, Master Slade," Karel Doormann said. There was a catch in his voice between words, like the sound of a whisk on stone. "Explain what you consider a beneficial outcome."

"Lissea," Ned said, "Mistress Doormann. Has completed a task that we all know was thought to be impossible. The capsule which she has returned to Telaria has the potential of revolutionizing star travel—and with it the profits of Doormann Trading."

The board members were silent, facing Ned like a pack of dogs about to move in. The table was black and shiny and slightly distorted on top. It had been made from a single slab of volcanic glass—useless as a working surface, but richly evocative of the power of the men and women who sat around it.

"I understand business, mesdames and sirs," Ned said. "I understand politics. I don't ask you to grant Lissea the place she demands out of justice or fairness or any of those other things which are quite properly excluded by the walls of this room."

Lucas Doormann backed a step away. His father, still smiling, nodded to Ned. "Go on," he said.

"What I put to you is this," Ned continued. "Lissea Doormann has displayed the resourcefulness that will make her an invaluable member of this board, and at some future point a worthy leader of it."

He waited, looking down the table at the board members.

"At some future point," Karel Doormann repeated. "I believe our relative's demand was for immediate chairmanship."

He raised an eyebrow.

Ned nodded. "I said I understood politics," he said. "I can't sell what I wouldn't buy, Master Doormann. In your place, I certainly wouldn't buy that."

Karel nodded approvingly. "You know, young man," he said, "there could be a place for you in this organization if you cared to accept one. However."

To this point, the president's tone had been playful, cruelly humorous. Now it became as hard and dry as a windblown steppe.

"First," he said, "this board has no confidence in the willingness of your principal to accept the terms you're offering on her behalf. Your Lissea made it clear from the beginning that she wants *everything.* Her ability to control a band of murderous cutthroats does nothing to dispel our concerns about her future behavior."

Some of the board members glanced at Karel in concern. The president was obviously no more interested in their opinions than he was in the opinions of the obsidian table.

"Second and, I'm afraid, finally, Master Slade," Karel continued, "we expected some such trick as this. As soon as I learned the *Swift* had arrived via Dell, I sent—this board sent—a shipload of company security personnel to that planet. *They will . . .*"

He shrugged, then resumed, "I hate to say this, sir, but your public assertion that Lissea was dead was a bit of good fortune. It will help greatly to avoid future difficulties."

"Father!" Lucas Doormann cried. He started around the table. "Father, you can't *think* of this, of *murder!*"

Karel pointed a warning finger. "Lucas," he said, "stop where you are. Otherwise I'll face the embarrassment of seeing the automatic restraint system act on my offspring."

Father and son glared at one another. Lucas turned and covered his face in his hands.

Karel looked at Ned and raised an eyebrow in prompting.

"Yes," said Ned. "Master Doormann, I very much regret this."

He reverted to at-ease posture with his hands behind him and went on. "Now, sir, what does the board intend for the rest of the crew and myself?"

"Your due," Karel said calmly. "You've accomplished a difficult task for Doormann Trading. You'll be paid according to your contracts, and there'll be an added bonus for success."

Karel pursed his lips as he chose his next words. "I can't imagine that many of your fellows would care to remain on Telaria, nor will they be permitted to do so. Their passage will be paid to their planets of residence and, if they claim no residence, to their planets of origin. Deported, if you will, but certainly not wronged."

He paused. "I will make an exception for you, Master Slade, if you choose."

"No," Ned replied curtly. Braced as he was, his eyes were focused on the wall above the president's head. "I do not so choose."

"I thought as much," Karel said, "though you would have been welcome."

The dry chill returned to his voice. "Let me make the matter very clear to you, Master Slade. This is a Telarian problem. We have no desire to offend you or the other members of your company, but you will *not* interfere in our affairs."

He smiled again. "I know you're intelligent enough to realize that without Lissea's presence as a rallying point, there is no possibility of gathering a coalition to redress what—"

He paused

"—for the sake of argument we may describe as the 'wrong' done her. Some of your fellows may not be as sophisticated. I trust that you'll be able to convince them not to . . . do themselves harm."

Ned nodded. "I'll do what I can," he said tonelessly. He raised his commo helmet and settled it back on his head. "I believe we've said everything that needs to be said," he went on. "With your leave, I'll return to the *Swift* and gather my personal belongings."

"As you choose," said Karel, gesturing toward the doorway behind Ned.

"Lucas," Ned said, "I would appreciate a few words with you outside."

"Did you think I'd stay here?" Lucas snarled. He strode into the anteroom ahead of the mercenary. The stroke of the inner panel closing cut off sight of his father's frown.

"I can't believe this!" Lucas said as the main door opened.

"I can," Ned said. *For my sins, I can.*

The commo helmet was set to the channel linking it with the *Swift,* and locked against all other parties. As Ned stepped out of the shielded boardroom, he faced south and broke squelch twice.

The alarm clanged through the *Swift*'s internal PA system.

Carron Del Vore was straightening the bunks on one side of the aisle. Unlike playing solitaire or staring at the ceiling, it gave him the illusion of accomplishment. He'd worked his way to the third pair, pulling the sheets tight and arranging the jumble of gear and tattered clothing in neat piles at the foot and head respectively. He jumped as if he'd been stabbed in the kidneys.

Tadziki sat at the backup navigational console, facing aft. He was as still as a leopard in ambush. Occasionally in the past twenty minutes he'd blinked his eyes; when the alarm sounded, he blinked them again.

"It's time, then," he said to Carron. "Make the call."

"I think . . ." Carron said. He tried to lick his lips, but his tongue was dry also. ". . . that we ought to wait a, a few minutes."

"No," said Tadziki as he rose to his feet. "We shouldn't. You can either use the console, or the handset—"

He indicated the unit flexed to his console. Its keypad permitted handier access to some planetary communications nets than the voice-driven AIs built into commo helmets did.

"—or a helmet, if you'd be comfortable with that. But it has to be done at once. Preset five."

"Yes, I know it's preset five," Carron said. He flipped up the handset's cover, held the unit to his ear to be sure of the connection, and pressed SYSTEM/FIVE.

The *Swift's* main hatch was open. Sounds of the spaceport rumbled through. At the graving dock nearby, polishing heads howled and paused, then howled again as they cleaned the hull of a freighter.

"I don't like having to do this," Carron said to Tadziki as circuits clicked in his ear. "I know it was my idea. But I don't like it."

"We aren't required to like it," the adjutant said, looking through the Pancahtan and into his own past life. "People depend on us, so we'll do our jobs. Lissea depends on us."

"I know . . ." Carron said.

The paired chimes of the ringing signal rattled silent. *"Yeah?"* a voice croaked. *"Two-two-one, ah . . . Fuck. Two-two-one-four."*

"Platt," Carron said imperiously, "this is Prince Carron Del Vore. You are to go into the laboratory at once and close the door of the device we brought in this afternoon."

"What?" the attendant said. "What?"

"Close the door of the device so that it latches, but don't slam it,"

Carron said. "Otherwise the atmosphere will degrade the interior and cause irreparable harm. And don't touch the mirrors surrounding the installation."

"Look, this isn't my job!" Platt cried. *"I'm not even supposed to go into the lab—I'm just here to watch the door!"*

"Platt," Carron said, as implacable as a priest of the Inquisition, "I will arrive in a few minutes with mercenaries from the Pancahte Expedition. If you have not carried out my instructions to the letter, they will kill you. Hunt you down and kill you, if necessary. Do you understand?"

"Yeah, yeah, I understand," the attendant whined. *"Look, I'm doing it, I'm doing it right now. But I shouldn't have to, you see?"*

Platt broke the connection.

Carron sighed and closed the handset. "The man's scum," he said to Tadziki. "But there must be thousands of people in the building now. We don't have anything so large on Pancahte. So tall, at least. Because of the earthquakes."

Tadziki eased past the younger man and stood in the hatch, looking outward.

"What happens now?" Carron asked. He hadn't been part of the tactical planning from this point on.

"We wait," Tadziki said. "I wait, at least. You might want to get out of the way, hide somewhere in Landfall City. I can arrange credit for you if you don't have any of your own."

Carron stood beside the adjutant. An articulated three-section roadtrain clanked slowly by on steel treads, carrying heavy cargo. Tadziki was looking beyond it, and beyond anything visible.

"You think there's going to be trouble here, then?" Carron asked.

"There's going to be a great deal of confusion," Tadziki said. "If the state organization is good enough, there will certainly be police sent to arrest everyone aboard the *Swift.* I don't expect that. There's a far greater chance of rioters attacking, however."

He smiled wanly at Carron. "Some of the men—men from the ship's crew—didn't choose to be involved further. They'll stay low in their hotel room until the business is done. The combat personnel are where they need to be also. And I'm here, because the potential need for a command post is greater than the risk."

Tadziki's hand gripped the hatch coaming so hard that the veins stood out. His skin blotched white and red because the tense muscles cut off their own blood supply.

"I wouldn't be much good to Herne and the others," he said harshly toward Landfall City. "I'm a fat old man, and I could never hit anybody far enough away that his blood didn't splash me."

Carron looked at Tadziki and swallowed. "Yes," he said. "Well, I think I'll stay here too."

Dockyard machinery screamed like lost souls.

The limousine was parked in front of the building. It was unattended because both the security personnel from the vehicle were escorting Ned.

There were two similar cars whose driver/bodyguards were still present. Most of the board members would have come to the meeting via underground tramlines from their private residences within the estate rather than being driven.

The guards opened both doors of the limo's passenger compartment deferentially. The Telarian noble paused and said to Ned, "Did you really want to speak to me, or . . ."

Ned nodded. "Could we drive slowly around the estate for a moment?" he asked. "Back trails?"

"Yes, of course," Lucas said. He gestured to the man holding his door, the driver. "Go on, then."

Lucas looked drawn. People on the stone-flagged patio fronting the spire watched the tableau sidelong. The armed, uniformed attendants in front of the building were the only ones who felt they could openly stare at the folk who rode in limousines; and that only while Lucas and Ned stepped through the weapons detector that covered the entranceway.

Ned and Lucas got into the car from opposite sides. As soon as the doors *thunk*ed closed, Ned retrieved the needle stunner he'd hidden between the seat cushions during the ride from the spaceport. His body concealed what he was doing from his companion.

"Master Lucas," he said, "I don't like what's going to happen now—"

"You know this is none of my doing!" Lucas burst out. "I—I'll leave home, I won't stay on Telaria even, not after this. But it's already done, Slade. There's nothing I can do now!"

The guards closed themselves into the front with the same solid shocks as those the rear doors had made. Ned's view forward ignored the guards. The limousine pulled away silently, heading down a curving drive.

"I know that, Lucas," Ned said. "That's why I wanted you out of the building. You're not the only innocent person, I realize, but you're the only one I know personally."

"I don't understand," the Telarian said. He frowned as he tried to fit the mercenary's statement into a knowledge base which had no category for it.

Secondary trails within the estate were only wide enough for one car at a time, so there were pull-overs every half kilometer or so. The limo approached one of them. A bank of red and white flowers grew on the left side, with a bower of trees with long flexible tendrils in place of leaves on the right. There were no other persons or vehicles in sight.

"Just a moment," said Ned. He reached forward with his left index finger and touched the switch controlling the armored window between the front and rear compartments.

The driver started slightly at the sound. The guard broke off a comment about the soccer final and twisted to face the men in back. "Yes sir?" he said to Lucas.

"Would you please park here a moment?" Ned said.

Lucas nodded. "Yes, do that," he said. He looked disconcerted. "There's an intercom, you know," he added as the limousine pulled beneath the trees.

Ned shot the guard, then the driver, in the back of the neck with his stunner. The weapon clicked as its barrel coil snapped tiny needles out by electromagnetic repulsion.

The guard went into spastic convulsions while the fluctuating current passed between the opposite poles of the needle in his spine. The driver arched his back and became comatose. His foot slipped off the brake, but the limousine's mass held the vehicle steady against the idling motors.

Lucas screamed and slapped the door latch. Ned grabbed Lucas around the neck left-handed but didn't squeeze.

"Wait!" Ned shouted. "They'll be all right! *Don't* make me hurt you."

The door was ajar. Ned slid sideways, pushing Lucas ahead of him from the vehicle. He continued to hold the Telarian for fear the fool would try to run and he'd have to shoot him down. Needle stunners could do permanent nerve damage or even cause death through syncope. If Ned had wanted *that,* he'd have left the boy in the boardroom with his relatives.

"What are you doing?" Lucas gasped. "You can't get out of here, you know that! Am I a hostage?"

Ned opened the driver's door with the little finger of his right hand. The driver fell to the pavement in catatonic rigidity. His submachine gun and that of his fellow still stood muzzle-up in their boots on the central console.

"You're not a hostage," Ned said. At any moment, somebody might drive up and he'd have to kill them. "Look, this car has an autopilot, doesn't it? Program it to drive to the family chapel."

"But—"

"*Now,* curse you, now!" Ned said. He thrust Lucas' head and torso within the driver's compartment. He was bigger than the Telarian and stronger for his size, but it was the sheer violence of Ned's will that dominated Lucas utterly. The presence of the submachine guns within millimeters of Lucas' hands was no danger.

The Telarian called up a map on the dashboard screen. He touched a point on it without bothering to check the index of coordinates. The mechanism chimed obediently.

The guard thrashed again, then subsided. He'd lost control of his sphincter muscles, voiding his bladder and bowels. Lucas stared at the man in obvious terror.

Lucas withdrew from the car. "You can't get off-planet in your ship," he said to Ned. "The port defenses will destroy it before you're a thousand meters high. And even if you got to Dell, it's too late for Lissea—you *heard* my father!"

"Listen to me," Ned said. "If you're smart, you'll just lie low here for the next while. I don't care what you do, I don't care if you raise an alarm—it won't change anything now. But for your own sake, *don't* go back to the spire."

Ned got into the limo. He dropped the stunner into his pocket— waste not, want not—and charged one of the submachine guns. He looked again at Lucas, still standing frozen above the uniformed driver. "You've been as decent as you know how, Doormann," Ned said. "I wish it didn't have to happen this way."

He engaged the autopilot. The dash beeped at him chidingly: the rear door was open.

Ned crushed his boot down on the throttle pedal. The limousine's metal tires sang, chewing divots from the rubberized road material as they accelerated the heavy vehicle. Inertia slammed the door shut.

Ned lifted his foot and let the car drive itself as he checked the other submachine gun. Lucas stood in the center of the road, staring after the limousine until a curve took the vehicle out of sight.

Platt muttered to himself as he opened the laboratory door. He forgot to squint as he stepped inside, so the sudden harsh illumination slapped his eyes. The fog of fortified wine in his brain ignited in a fireball that made him curse desperately.

After a time, Platt regained enough composure to pick his way through the ranks of equipment with his eyes slitted. There was an unfamiliar humming in the big room, but he couldn't identify the source. Anyway, it might have been the wine.

The capsule squatted on the platform at the end of the lab, as ugly as an egg after hatching. Pareto, the night man, claimed there was a corpse in the thing when they found it, but Platt didn't watch the news himself much.

He didn't trust that bastard Pareto, either. Pareto kept asking for the lousy ten thalers he'd loaned Platt last . . . last—whenever it was.

Platt lurched into one of the mirror stands. It was anchored to the floor. Instead of toppling over, the stand threw the attendant back with the start of a bad bruise. He cursed again, rubbing himself and thinking about the unfairness of life.

The black concave mirror whined shrilly, then slowly returned to synchrony with the others.

Platt touched the door of the capsule, then leaped away. He thought he'd received an electric shock. When he rubbed his fingertips together, he realized that the feeling was simply high-frequency vibration.

Gingerly, he gripped the edge of the door and slammed it with all his strength. Air compressing within the ovoid prevented the *clang!* from being as violent as Platt would have liked.

The humming was louder. It appeared to be coming from around the capsule, rather than from the capsule itself. The attendant turned away and started for the door.

Red light bathed the room. Platt glanced over his shoulder, suddenly afraid to face fully around.

The capsule was glowing. Atoms within its structure were coming into sequence with their selves of seventy years before. The meld was not absolute, but as more and more points achieved unity, they dragged neighboring atoms into self-alignment also. Closing the front of the ovoid started the mass down a one-way road to critical perfection.

The capsule was fire-orange, then yellow. As the blaze verged into white, all trace of physical structure was lost within the radiance.

Platt tried to run. His uniform seared brown and the hair on the back of his head burst into flame. The hum was a roar and the fires of Hell were loose.

All the lights in the laboratory shattered, but their absence was unnoticeable. Platt threw himself behind a massive computer console, unable to hear his own screams. The soundproofing cones in the walls and ceiling sublimed and drifted as black cobwebs in fierce air currents.

Matter attempting to fill the same space as its own earlier/later self became the energy that alone could escape from the catastrophic paradox. Laboratory equipment shattered. Metals and plastics began to burn in temperatures beyond those achieved in the carbon-iron cycle of a dying sun.

Devouring radiance ionized the whole contents of the laboratory into plasma. A spear of light sprang up the long axis of what had been the capsule, piercing the armored ceiling above like an oxygen lance through tissue.

The humans on the floor above didn't have time to scream, nor did those on the floor above them; but the fire screamed like a god of destruction.

A switch on the dashboard could lock the tracks of the mobile crane into linked plates fifty centimeters long to lower the equipment's ground pressure on yielding surfaces. For this concrete roadway Westerbeke, who was driving, left the tracks at maximum flexibility. They sang at high frequency, giving the impression that the 80-tonne crane was moving much faster than its actual forty kilometers per hour.

A car that had been trapped behind the crane for some time managed to get into the center lane. It passed with its horn hooting angrily. Josie Paetz leaned out of the crane operator's cab and screamed, "Fuck you! Just fuck you!" to the vehicle.

Yazov drew him back. The boy had kept his guns hidden, so there was no harm done. "Let him be, Jose," Yazov said. "We'll have something real to do soon enough."

"Amen to that," Deke Warson said. His fingertips caressed a submachine gun beneath the tarp beside him on the crane's back deck. The big construction vehicle was taller than the other traffic, but guards on the wall surrounding the Doormann Estate could still look down on it. For the moment, the guards had nothing better to do.

Raff and Herne Lordling were in the driver's cab with Westerbeke. The rest of the mercenary crew rode on the back of the vehicle. They wore ponchos to conceal their battledress, body armor, and slung weapons.

The team was in position: the crane had been driving along the innermost lane of the highway paralleling the walled estate for the past five kilometers. Until the signal, the mercenaries could only gaze at the wall and the twenty-meter band of wired and mined wasteland protecting the Doormann family's privacy. Occasionally a blue-uniformed guard watched idly from the wall.

Every half kilometer stood another tower mounting a huge anti-starship weapon.

"When are we—" Josie Paetz said.

Something within the estate flashed brightly enough to be seen in the full sunlight.

"Got it!" Josie Paetz screamed, ripping off his poncho. Yazov clutched him. A moment later, Lordling ordered through the commo helmets, *"Don't anybody move! We've got to get closer to the gun tower before we move!"*

"Then get fucking moving," Deke Warson whispered through clenched teeth. Toll looked at him, but Deke was just letting off a touch of the pressure building in the instants before insertion.

When the column of light bloomed within the estate, the crane was nearly midway between a pair of the towers mounting 25-cm weapons. As the treads whined forward, the tower behind the mercenaries dropped out of sight because of the wall's curvature.

A pair of company guards, visible from the waist up, stood on the firing step of the wall outside the approaching tower. They were four meters above the road surface and across the buffer strip. The light from within the estate had broadened into a ball of iridescent rose-petals. The guards, a man and a woman, must have heard a sound inaudible over the singing chatter of the crane's treads, because they turned.

Westerbeke slipped the right-hand set of steering clutches but kept full power to the left track. The crane squealed and executed a right turn, heading directly toward the gun tower.

Westerbeke locked the track plates when he felt soil shift under the crane's weight. A series of antipersonnel mines went off harmlessly beneath the treads, whacking like a string of firecrackers. Dirt and black smoke flew out.

The guards on the wall spun back at the sound of the mines and the clanging treads. At least six of the mercenaries fired simultaneously, blowing the guards' heads and torsos apart in cyan fury.

An antivehicle mine containing at least ten kilos of high explosive went off under the left-hand tread. The track broke and the forward road wheel flew skyward. The men on the rear deck had to grab for handholds when the cab lifted, but Westerbeke kept the crane grinding onward.

The drive sprockets were at the rear. The vehicle held a nearly straight line, though one broken end of the track remained where it was on the ground. The wheels rode off it. Festoons of razor ribbon and vines streamed back from the running gear.

The huge powergun started to depress. The weapon couldn't be aimed low enough to bear on a vehicle already at the base of the tower, and the next gun position in either direction was out of sight. A guard ran from the building, tugging at his holster. Both Warson and Josie Paetz shot the fellow before his hand was fully around the butt of his pistol. The body, headless and eviscerated by the bolts, spun off the firing step like the others.

The crane hit two more big mines, both on the right. The vehicle tilted sideways, then settled back upright on its shattered road-wheels. Westerbeke disengaged the drive train.

Yazov clutched in the crane itself. The vehicle had come close enough that the end of its boom already projected above the wall. Yazov lowered the boom until it—a massive square-section girder—rested on the masonry. He shouted after his nephew, but Paetz was already racing up the boom ahead of the rest of the mercenaries.

The armored hatch in the side of the gun tower was open. A woman in blue was trying to tug it closed. Paetz fired toward the gap as he ran along the girder. His submachine gun put two bolts of the three-round burst into her head.

Paetz jumped to the parapet, then caromed within the tower structure as part of the same motion. A man crouched at a console with a microphone in one hand and a pistol in the other. Paetz fired, and Toll Warson fired his 2-cm weapon from the boom. The Telarian guard's right arm flew from his torso.

Warson's shot singed the hair from the back of Paetz' neck, but it probably saved the younger man's life as well. Even head shots with the submachine gun's lighter bolts might not have been instantly fatal.

A circular metal staircase with an open railing of tubes led up to the gunhouse. A guard hesitated on it, halfway through the opening to the upper chamber.

Paetz emptied the rest of the submachine gun's magazine into the man, igniting his clothing and blowing chunks of the stairway into dazzling sparks. The Telarian slipped down the treads, howling mindlessly and dragging a pink trail of intestine.

The room stank of ozone and burned meat. Paetz ejected the empty magazine and slapped a fresh one home in the well. Toll Warson swept past, aiming his powergun upward but letting his brother lead. Deke carried a submachine gun, and the lighter weapon would be quicker to swing onto targets from uncertain directions. They leaped the dying guard and pounded up the stairs.

There was no one in the gun chamber. Identical chairs and consoles sat right and left of the gun's breech and loading mechanism. They and the weapon rotated together with the floor of the chamber.

Screens above either console provided a three-hundred-and-sixty-degree panorama from the gun tower. Fine orange crosshatching covered the portion of the display showing the estate proper. Lockouts within the control system prevented the gun crew from accidentally aiming their weapon toward the area they were defending.

"We're clear here!" Toll Warson shouted down into the lower chamber. "We'll take care of the rest!"

Deke's miniature toolkit lay on the barbette floor beside him. He'd already removed the plate covering the front of one console.

The screen above Deke showed the spouting geyser of plasma which was devouring the estate's central tower, but he ignored it. He had work to do.

"Look at that!" Westerbeke said as he—last of the mercenaries to leave the mobile crane—jumped down to the wall's firing step. "*Look* at it!"

The clear exterior sheath of the office spire crumbled away, dropping in bits like snowflakes toward the mist of charged ions at the base of the building. The floors and the central support column containing the elevator and utility conduits looked like the remains of a fish after filleting.

The remnant was beginning to waver. Distance silenced the screams of humans who shook from the edges of the structure. Bits of furnishings and partition walls fell with them.

Cars on the six-lane highway slowed and pulled off on the median. Civilians were stopping to watch what they thought was a major accident. Harlow and Coyne eyed the scene. Together they raised their 2-cm weapons and opened fire, raking the soft-skinned vehicles.

Most Telarian cars used ion-transfer membranes to power hub-center electric motors. The fuel cells ruptured in balls of pale hydrogen flame which quickly involved upholstery and plastic body panels.

Survivors ran screaming, some into the path of oncoming vehicles. A tanker of petroleum-based sealant exploded into a huge orange mushroom, raining fire across the entire highway.

Coyne and Harlow crouched on the firing step to reload, then dropped to the mown sward within the estate to join their fellows.

"What the hell do you think you're playing at?" Herne Lordling grumbled.

Harlow grinned. "Just giving the cops something to worry about besides us," he said. "And having a little fun."

A one-lane road ran parallel to the boundary wall, separated by a few meters of grass. At one end it dipped over a hill in a profusion of pink and blue flowers. The moan of a loud klaxon swelled from that direction.

Ten of the mercenaries poised. Lordling gave Paetz and Yazov a two-fingered gesture to watch the wall behind them: guards might approach along the firing step from the neighboring towers.

Westerbeke remained kneeling as he scrolled through the map display on the inner surface of his visor. The team had known neither its destination nor the point at which it would enter the estate, since the latter depended on when the spire's destruction gave them the signal to come over the wall. Westerbeke carried a pistol and a submachine gun, but his prime value in *this* company wasn't his marksmanship.

A three-wheeler carrying two guards and a tribarrel came over the rise at ninety kilometers per hour. Cyan bolts blew the Telarians out of their saddles before they had an inkling of the emergency they'd been summoned to deal with.

The trike lifted and was fully airborne when Raff put a rocket into the center of it. The little vehicle disintegrated in black smoke and bits of metal. Its klaxon cut off with a startled croak.

"Why'd you do that?!" Josie Paetz screamed at Raff. "D'ye want to fucking walk?"

"Paetz, watch your—" Herne Lordling began.

A second trike, running silent twenty meters behind the first, squealed and fishtailed as its driver broke the single rear tire loose in trying to stop. The gunner was desperately swinging his tribarrel toward the wall, but he didn't have a target when Paetz' one-handed burst killed him and his partner.

The three-wheeler twisted broadside and flipped at least a dozen times before it came to rest a hundred and fifty meters down the road. The riders, two of the three wheels, and shards of the instrument console lay scattered at angles to the main track.

"Blood *and* martyrs!" Ingried said in amazement.

"Shall we ride yours, then?" Raff said to Josie Paetz. "But good shooting, very good."

A half-tracked water tanker, marked FIRE and painted red with white stripes, rumbled into sight behind the wrecked three-wheelers. The four-man crew wore fire-retardant suits and helmets with neck flares as protection from falling debris. The driver and one crewman bailed out on the far side of the vehicle.

The truck coasted to a halt. The other man in the cab crawled out the driver's door, but one of the firefighters on the tailboard actually started paying out a hand-line toward the burning wreckage of a trike. When he saw eleven mercenaries in motley battledress running toward him, jingling with weapons, he froze.

None of the mercenaries fired. They jumped aboard the truck, clinging to the handholds above the tailboard and climbing on top of the four-kiloliter watertank.

Westerbeke got behind the wheel and drove the vehicle off. Paetz fired another one-hand burst at the pair of people he glimpsed at the edge of a grove two hundred meters away. They were grounds-maintenance personnel. He killed them both.

The firefighter standing by the road watched his hand-line jounce behind the disappearing truck like a thin white tail.

The limousine brought itself to a perfectly calibrated stop before a gray stone building, Gothic in styling but only seven meters high to its peak over the rose window. A black van, built on the body of a luxury car and polished to a soft gleam, was parked around to the side.

A number of civilians stood in front of the chapel, looking in the direction of what had been the central spire. They were all well dressed—not menials. One of them, a woman, wore clerical robes and collar. They stared in amazement as Ned, in tattered battledress and carrying a pair of submachine guns—one slung, the other in his hands—got out on the driver's side.

Ned's legs were shaky. "Where's Lendell's body?" he demanded in a high-pitched shout. "Where's the coffin?"

Klaxons rose and fell from several places within the Doormann estate. The unsynchronized moans were further distorted by Doppler effect as emergency vehicles sped through the growing chaos.

"Sir?" said the woman in clerical dress. "Sir? Who are you?"

A terrible sound drew Ned's head around despite his focus on the task at hand. The spire had begun to collapse. Because of the building's size, the process went on for more than thirty seconds. It seemed to take minutes.

The release of energy in the sub-basement laboratory had finally dissolved the concrete spine from which the upper floors were cantilevered. A cloud of plasma enveloped the lower hundred meters of the building. Now the upper portion of the structure sank slightly and began to tilt like a top at the end of its rotary motion.

Figures jumped or fell from the visible floors. They disappeared in the boiling ions beneath.

The spine plunged downward at an angle. Stress broke the upper levels apart while the lower portion of the huge structure simply crumbled in a disintegrating bath. The building dropped out of sight a moment before it hit the ground.

Seconds after the impact, dust and smoke sprang skyward in a great, flat-topped pillar that hid and smothered the sea of ions. The crash took ten seconds to arrive at the chapel. It went on for at least that long.

A man in the quiet black garb of an undertaker stared at the destruction. His legs folded beneath him. He knelt and began to pray, moving his lips, as tears rolled down his cheeks.

"The coffin!" Ned snarled. No one looked at him. He ran into the chapel. The swinging butt of one weapon knocked a splinter from the dark wood of the door panel.

The chapel was quiet. There were three closed pews in front for members of the Doormann family and six open rows behind for their retainers. Light streamed through stained-glass windows illustrating Old Testament scenes. The building was bowered in trees. The light—equal to north, south, and through the east-facing rose window over the door—was artificial.

A pair of folding trestles waited before the altar, but the coffin wasn't on them yet. The small door to the side behind the pulpit was open. Ned pushed through it.

He was in what would normally be a changing and storage room for the chapel staff. To the right was a staircase leading up to the choir loft. On the floor, Lendell Doormann grinned from the clear-topped casket the *Swift*'s crew had built on Wasatch 1029 and rebuilt on Dell. Beside the plastic box was a traditional coffin of dark, lustrously rubbed hardwood.

Ned stepped to the casket, looking around for a tool. The female cleric walked into the room. "Sir!" she cried. "You must leave at once!" Two of the undertaker's assistants stood in the doorway behind her, looking doubtful.

The woman grabbed Ned's arm. He pushed her away. A

heavy screwdriver lay on the floor beside the coffin. He bent to pick it up.

"Sir!" the woman shouted. "I'm the Dean of Chapel! What are you doing?"

One of the assistants stepped forward with a set expression on his face. Ned dropped the screwdriver to point his submachine gun.

"Get out, you fuckheads!" he screamed. "Do I have to kill you? Get out!"

The dean got to her feet. "Sir," she said in a trembling voice, "this is sacrilege. You must leave here—"

She extended her hand. Ned took up the slack with his trigger-finger, then raised the muzzle and put a single bolt into the ceiling.

Shattered plaster exploded across the room. The undertaker's assistant grabbed the dean from behind. He dragged her back into the nave as the other assistant jumped out of the way. The three of them were gabbling unintelligibly.

Ned tried to sling the weapon he'd just fired. It clanked against the other submachine gun. He swore and dropped the gun beside him on the floor.

The plastic casket was welded smoothly all around the top. Ned set the screwdriver blade against the seam and slammed the butt of the tool with the heel of his right hand. The blade scrunched in, but only a few centimeters of the weld on either side broke.

A klaxon howled to a halt in front of the chapel. Voices shouted to one another. Ned stretched out his foot and kicked the door shut as he levered the lid upward. More of the weld broke, but the transparent sheet Tadziki had used for the lid was too flexible either to lift away or shatter the way Ned wanted it to do.

He stepped back and brought his boot up hard, smashing his heel into the juncture just beyond where he'd managed to crack the bead. The gray sidepanel broke apart, tags of it still clinging to the clear top.

Ned grabbed the slung submachine gun and aimed toward the doorway. The door flew open. Two security guards burst in, one of them rolling in some desperate vision of how to enter a room safely against an armed man.

Their pistols were drawn. The rolling man fired into the wooden coffin as his partner shot a robe hanging on a peg in the far corner.

Ned hit the standing man twice in the upper chest. The guard's pistol flew out of his hand. His body.fell, its legs tangled with those of the man on the floor. Ned fired a long burst into both guards.

Somebody in the nave screamed.

The guards' uniforms only smoldered, but the hanging robe managed to sustain a low, acrid flame. Smoke and ozone made Ned's eyes water. He stepped over the casket and laid the gun he'd just fired across its top.

The broken sidepanel permitted a two-hand grip on the lid. Ned pulled upward and back with all his strength, ripping the seam apart and flinging the submachine gun against the wall behind him.

Lendell Doormann lay now on his side, disturbed by the violence with which Ned had opened the casket. Ned rolled the body out. It was as light as a foam mannequin. He pulled up the layer of red baize from the stock of trade goods on Dell.

Lissea lay beneath the baize. Her eyes were closed, and her chest did not move.

Ned fumbled an injector out of his belt wallet. Klaxons outside the building were suddenly much louder: the chapel's outer door had opened. He reached over the casket for the gun with which he'd fired the shot into the ceiling. The limo's driver and guard had carried only four spare magazines between them, so he had to watch his ammo expenditure.

Ned aimed the submachine gun at the door with his right hand. Holding the injector against his left palm, he let his fingertips trail along Lissea's shoulder to the skin at the base of her throat. He squeezed down with his thumb, breaking the seal and triggering the injector.

Three Doormann security personnel rushed the door. They wore back-and-breast armor and helmets with faceshields.

Ned knelt behind the casket and blazed the twenty-nine rounds remaining in his magazine into the trio. The tightly grouped bolts chopped the guards apart in thunder and blue glare despite their armor. The Telarians were firing their submachine guns also, but wildly. The third guard shot the woman in front of him several times in the back before Ned killed him.

Ned groped behind him for the other gun he'd brought from the limo. The air was gray and his lungs burned. He supposed that was because of the flames and powergun residues, but maybe the security people had thrown tear gas at him.

Perhaps they hadn't used frag grenades because the body of a Doormann was in the room, but it was equally likely that such equipment wasn't an item of issue for security personnel. They were guards, after all, not combat troops.

Lissea groped at the edge of the casket.

Ned reached beneath Lissea's shoulders with his left arm and lifted her upright. Like her great-granduncle, she seemed almost weightless to Ned's adrenaline-fueled muscles.

"Oh Lord!" Ned gasped. "You're all right! Are you all right?"

Lissea clutched him. "I think you're supposed to kiss me, aren't you, prince?" she murmured.

Effects of the drug and its antidote suddenly washed her face saffron. She leaned out of the coffin and vomited the bile which was the sole content of her stomach.

Pews scraped in the nave. The door between the rooms was ajar. Ned took a chance. He got to his feet and stepped to the hinge side of the inward-opening door.

A whistle blew. Ned reached around the door left-handed and fired a short burst into the nave. Then he put his shoulder and full strength against the panel to slam it shut. A dead guard's foot was in the way. Ned kicked it free, then banged the panel against the jamb.

Bolts from the nave hit the panel, but the wood was heavy and the chapel's architect had added metal straps for the look of it. The security forces carried 1-cm pistols and submachine guns. If a few of them had been issued projectile weapons or even 2-cm powerguns, they'd have blasted through the door and the man behind it; but they weren't expected to fight a full-scale war.

They shouldn't have fucked with Lissea Doormann, then. . . .

"*Ned!*" Lissea screamed.

Smoke and haze swirled as security personnel outside the

building jerked open a door that Ned hadn't noticed because the burning clerical robe hung beside it. The man lunging in hosed the room with his submachine gun, firing blind because his eyes weren't adapted to the smudgy atmosphere.

Ned tried to swing his weapon, but the target was on his left and the submachine gun was still in his left hand. The guard's line of bolts snapped toward him across the partition wall, chest-high.

Two cyan flashes lit the Telarian's faceshield, spraying a mist of vaporized plastic into the man's eyes. His hands flew upward.

Ned shot the guard in the throat and, as the Telarian toppled backward, sprayed the doorway and the further guards clustered there. They fell or scattered. He knelt and replaced his magazine, though there were still a few rounds in the one he dropped into his pocket.

Lissea climbed out of the casket, holding the pistol she'd scooped from the floor where a dying guard flung it. "Stairs!" she cried. "There's stairs behind you!"

"Go!" said Ned. He saw movement through the open doorway and shot, aiming crotch-high in case the guard was in body armor. Return fire chewed the door panel and jamb, but none of the security people outside were willing to rush the scene of sudden carnage again.

Lissea ran to the stairs, bending over as if she were in driving rain. She hesitated once, to tug a submachine gun out of the hands of a fallen guard. His fingers twitched mindlessly for the missing weapon.

Ned backed after her. The *hisscrack!* of bolts wove fiery nets across the changing room. Bits of stone exploded from the walls like shrapnel, stinging and even drawing blood. The door to the nave exploded in a welter of splinters and cyan as a dozen Telarians opened fire on it together.

More klaxons sounded outside the chapel. Many more klaxons.

The firetruck slowed. *"Hold your fire,"* Herne Lordling ordered. *"I'm not going to commit till I know what we're getting into."*

"Who died and made him God?" Josie Paetz muttered, but the

three tense veterans on the tailboard with him were nodding grim agreement to Lordling's words.

There was heavy firing to the front of them, small arms and at least one tribarrel; no high explosive. Rushing into a doubtful situation was a good way to get killed. It wasn't a good way to accomplish anything useful, either, and staying alive was a higher priority of most of the *Swift*'s complement than a grand gesture was. They'd lived to become veterans, after all.

The truck plowed through a bed of white-flowering bushes. The bluff cab crushed the shrubs down, and the tracks supporting the rear of the vehicle chewed up foliage and spat it out behind.

The firetruck hadn't attracted dangerous attention in the midst of so much violence and confusion. Westerbeke was driving a straight vector to the rendezvous point. He didn't want to take chances with a road net designed for scenic vistas rather than high-speed communication.

As a sensible security precaution, there were no openly available maps of the Doormann estate. The team didn't have time or the proper equipment to break into the estate's data base now.

Besides, the data base had probably been housed in the central spire.

In the cab, Lordling called up a chart of recent powergun discharges onto his visor display. The weapons' bursts of ionized copper atoms threw high spikes into the radio-frequency bands. The energy of each discharge was closely uniform within classes of weapon, permitting easy correlation between signal strength and range. Though the sensors built into a commo helmet were rudimentary in comparison to those of dedicated packs, they gave Lordling a fair schematic of the fighting half a klick ahead of the firetruck.

Shots had been fired from thirty-one points during the past five minutes, though some of the locations might have been alternate firing positions for a single weapon. Most of the points formed a pair of inwardly concave arcs a hundred meters apart. A gun or guns were also being fired frequently from the point squarely at the center of the common radii.

"*Set your helmets to receive,*" Lordling ordered. "*Now!*"

Copies of the display Lordling had summoned echoed on the visors of his team, then vanished. The men could recall it from their helmets' data storage if needed.

"*Yazov,*" Lordling continued, "*take four men and jump off in thirty seconds. Leg it into position. Don't start shooting until I give the signal from the other side. And don't forget, they may be getting reinforcements so you need to watch your back. Clear?*"

"*Worry about your end, Herne,*" Yazov said. "*I'll take care of mine. Harlow, Coyne . . . Hatton, I suppose.*" He didn't bother naming his nephew to the team he would lead. "*Execute—now!*"

The five men stepped off the truck's tailboard at the edge of a glade. The trees were forty meters high and waved brilliant streamers into the air to attract winged pollinators. The team quickly melted into the manicured shadows among the trunks.

The firetruck made a sharp turn in order to curve around the firefight. It growled out of sight.

Using hand signals, Yazov sent Harlow and Coyne out on the flanks. He didn't especially trust Hatton, an engine-room crewman, but he supposed the fellow would be all right if they kept an eye on him.

The fire team moved through the glade in line abreast, with a five-meter interval between troopers. Birds twittered invisibly, but the only sign of human beings was a woman's shoe caught in a branch high overhead. It looked badly weathered.

The estate was enormous, and the people working in it were concentrated in a relatively few nodes. With all that was going on, there shouldn't be many strollers out, either.

On the far side of the glade was a narrow path. It appeared to be made of brick laid in a herringbone pattern, but it had a rubbery resilience underfoot. They trotted across it.

The path was bordered by waist-high clumps of pink and magenta flowers, interspersed with saw-edged grasses that shot tufts up six or seven meters tall. Yazov had fought in vegetation like that before. He couldn't imagine anybody having the stuff around if he employed gardeners—or owned a flamethrower.

"Yase, the shooting's died down," Josie called. "What do you think that's because?"

Yazov signaled his nephew angrily to shut up. The kid was good, no question; but he hadn't lived long enough to have good *sense*. Well, that was why Josh Paetz had sent his bastard brother Yazov along with Josie.

They'd come to a two-meter hedge growing along a low stone curb. Yazov signaled Josie to watch their backs: they didn't need a squad of locals jumping them from behind. The rest of the team flattened behind the curb and peered through the scaly lower branches of the hedge.

They were looking into a rectangular garden, fifty meters by one hundred. Walkways from corner to corner and down the long axis met at a stone fountain of four stacked bowls in the middle. Each quadrant had at its center a tree sculpted into a slim green spindle. The trees and stone benches scattered among artistically ragged plantings made it impossible to see everything within the garden from one point, and perhaps even from four points.

Yazov's team was arrayed on a long side of the garden. Within the rectangle and facing in the same direction along the parallel hedge on the far side were eighteen or twenty Doormann security personnel.

The guards had a three-wheeler. They'd parked the vehicle so that a large marble urn gave it a modicum of protection, but no one was crewing the pintle-mounted tribarrel at the moment. Instead, several Telarians crouched behind the trike, muttering over a casualty sprawled in a bed of variegated flowers.

The hedge had sere yellow scars where powergun bolts had pocked it. Portions of the foliage still smoldered. The large scallop which outgoing bolts from the tribarrel had cut was twenty meters from the trike's present position.

Other guards lay tensely prone, well back from the hedge so as not to draw fire. The fighting certainly wasn't over, but no one was shooting at the moment.

The hedge was thorny and impenetrable, at least to anything short of a bulldozer or some minutes' work with a cutting bar. There were arched bowers at each corner, however, giving access to the garden. The terrain on Yazov's side of the barrier was flat, with regular beds of knee-high flowers. They didn't provide any cover, but they were decent concealment.

Yazov keyed his commo helmet. *"Harlow and Coyne, opposite corners,"* he ordered. *"Wait for it. Paetz and I'll drive them to you. Hatton, watch our back. Paetz, take the crew around the tribarrel when you get the signal. Nobody get early or we'll get somebody killed. Move out."*

The end men scuttled into position. Both of them carried 2-cm weapons. At this range and these conditions, Yazov would as soon they had submachine guns, but they were pros. They'd manage.

Hatton faced around with an obvious air of relief. Josie thrust his left hand into the hedge to broaden his viewpoint. Yazov was ready to snap an order, but the younger man was merely eager, not rabid.

Nothing to do now but wait for the signal.

"Yase, why aren't they shooting?" Josie said over the spread-band radio net. *"Why're they just sitting there?"*

"They're waiting for something," Yazov explained. *"And don't ask me what it is because I don't know."*

What Yazov did know was that *"it,"* whatever it was, was nothing he wanted to be around to see. He took four fresh magazines out of their pouches and set them by his left hand, behind the stone curb.

"It would be nice if you got your thumbs out of your ass, Herne," he mouthed, but the thought wasn't even a whisper.

"Go," said the command channel, and Yazov's trigger finger had blasted the head off a Telarian security man before his ears caught the *whop! whop! whop!* of powerguns firing from Lordling's side of the double ambush.

Yazov swung to the next target, a guard lying prone who lifted her head to look at the comrade who'd died a few meters from her. Yazov's bolt converted her startled expression into a cyan flash.

One of the Telarians ministering to the casualty leaped to his feet; his two fellows tried to flatten when the shooting started. All three of them were down now, their limbs thrashing in their death throes. Josie had taken them out in three aimed bursts, though the separation between trigger-pulls was scarcely more than the normal cyclic delay of his submachine gun.

Coyne and Harlow both fired, but Yazov couldn't see their targets through his narrow niche in the hedge. A guard scrambled toward the tribarrel. Josie shot him in the cheek, ear, and temple. The victim's cap flew off and he plowed a furrow through ankle-high flowers with his face.

Yazov dropped his weapon, braced his left hand on the curb, and tugged a fragmentation cluster from its belt carrier. Simultaneous pressure from thumb and fingertips released and armed the weapon. Yazov gave the thumb-switch another poke to change the setting from TIME to AIR BURST, then lofted the bomb high over the hedge. A third squeeze on the thumb toggle would have set the fuse to CONTACT.

A guard, either wild with terror or trusting in his body armor, jumped up in a crouch behind the fountain. He held his submachine gun at waist height.

Harlow and Coyne shot him simultaneously in the torso. The ceramic breastplate shattered like a bomb under the paired 2-cm bolts. The guard's body did a back-flip, flinging his unfired weapon through the spray of the fountain.

The fragmentation cluster popped into three separate bomblets. They burst in red flashes two or three meters above the soil of the garden. Guards leaped up like a covey of birds rising. Five of them died in instantaneous gunfire from the waiting mercenaries.

A surviving guard waved his pistol from a clump of low-growing evergreens. Yazov shot the arm off and, as the screaming Telarian lurched upright, finished the job and the 2-cm weapon's five-round magazine.

Yazov stripped in a fresh clip. Coyne and Harlow stood in plain sight in the archways, raking the guards who cowered among the low plantings. Most of the Telarians were dead already, but the muscle spasms of a beheaded corpse were enough to draw a bolt for insurance.

Josie Paetz got to his feet, wild-eyed with enthusiasm. His submachine gun's iridium barrel glowed white.

"Wait!" Yazov ordered. He was still kneeling. He aimed his powergun at the gnarled base of the hedge plant. Six or eight stems twisted from the sprawling roots.

Yazov fired twice. The plant lifted on a blast of cyan plasma. The soil was moist enough to erupt into a cavity also. Splinters and microshards of terra cotta sprayed out in a circle.

The shrub's fragments fell into the garden, still tangled by thorns and interwoven branches. Josie Paetz leaped through the gap without hesitation, dragging branches with him further into the killing zone.

Yazov reloaded and followed more circumspectly, brushing grit off his faceshield. His mouth smiled, but the expression had nothing to do with what was going on in his mind. "Hatton, you can come on through," he said, "but keep your eyes on the back-trail."

The whole team was in the garden. Coyne stood at the tri-barrel; Harlow checked the mechanism of the Telarian submachine gun in his left hand while he held the shimmering barrel of his 2-cm weapon safely off to the side.

Insects buzzed among the flowers. The firefight had done surprisingly little damage to the plantings, though the stench of the shooting and its results weighted the air worse than the miasma of any swamp.

A guard with no obvious injuries lay spread-eagled near the line Yazov followed across the garden. Blue flowers lapped her cheeks and neck.

Yazov swung his weapon one-handed, like a huge pistol. He fired into her back as he passed. Vaporized fluids turned bit of rib bone into shrapnel. The guard's head and heels lifted waist-high, then flopped again. The point-blank charge had virtually severed the body at its thickest point.

Better safe than sorry.

Yazov knelt at the far hedge. "Coming through!" he bellowed at the top of his lungs. There hadn't been any radio communication with Slade. "Coming through! Coming through!"

His own team was in position. Yazov held the powergun out at arm's length and fired into the root-stem juncture of a plant beyond the one he crouched behind. Powergun bolts had little penetration; the twisted branches and foliage of the hedge provided almost as much protection as a steel wall could have done.

The shrubbery blew apart as before. Splinters blazed, but the raggedly severed ends of the stems themselves were too green to do more than smolder.

There were still occasional shots in the near distance. With luck, that meant Lordling's team was policing up its area too.

"Coming through!" Yazov shouted again. Coyne seemed to think the tribarrel was operable, because he now crouched in the sidecar saddle with his hands on the weapon's double grips.

"Come on then, curse you!" cried a voice too cracked for Yazov to identify the speaker. "And we're bloody glad to see you!"

Yazov risked a glance outward. This side of the garden faced a gray stone building. The facade was shattered by powergun bolts. A limousine and half a dozen emergency vehicles burned in front of the structure, a van of some sort burned around to the right side, and the lower floor of the building itself burned like the box of a wood stove.

The flames had driven Doormann security personnel out of the building. The bodies of at least a dozen guards lay in a straggling windrow where submachine-gun fire had laid them.

Ned Slade dangled Lissea Doormann from the cavity that had been a window on the second floor. She pushed off from the wall so that she landed in the drive, well clear of the black smoke gushing from the doorway. Slade jumped after her. It took him a moment to rise again to a crouch.

Yazov led his men through the hedge. Lordling's team appeared from the woods behind the shattered structure. The firetruck snorted along behind them as Westerbeke steered it between the well-spaced boles.

Lissea helped Slade stand. His commo helmet was skewed sideways. A powergun bolt had grazed it, melting the outer sheathing and shattering the ceramic core. Slade reached down to grab the ammo pouch of a fallen guard. Lissea pulled him upright again. As the rescue team closed in on the couple from both directions, she kissed Slade full on the lips.

"Water!" Ned croaked. "Gimme—"

Three mercenaries thrust their condensing canteens at him. Herne Lordling tried to push the nipple of his canteen between Lissea's lips, like a clumsy father feeding a newborn. She snatched the canteen out of his hands and drank greedily on her own.

"Hey, Harlow," Coyne called. He was astride the driver's saddle of the captured trike, which he'd maneuvered out through the hedge despite the curb. "Come drive this thing and I'll work the tribarrel."

"Have you got transportation?" Lissea asked Yazov.

The skin was peeling over her right cheekbone, and the brows and eyelashes were scorched away. Ned didn't remember how that had happened. It might have been a hostile bolt striking almost too close, but Lissea's own weapon could have done it when a guard lunged unexpectedly up the blazing staircase. The Telarian had grappled Ned from behind and was pushing him toward the window. Lissea leaned close to be sure of her target and fired one round.

"Like hell you'll get me on that!" Harlow said. "If I wanted to die, I'd eat my gun."

"We've got a truck," Lordling said. "Westerbeke's coming in it." He looked drawn. Three of the two-magazine pouches of his bandolier were empty, and the submachine gun he carried now wasn't the weapon he'd had when he left the *Swift*.

"Chicken!" Coyne gibed. "Okay Hatton, *you* drive. And don't give me any lip!"

Hatton looked uncomfortable, but in the midst of a firefight, the big gunman was too high on the pecking order for a ship's crewman to object. Hatton took over the trike's steering chores as Coyne settled behind the tribarrel on the sidecar.

The firetruck pulled up beside the burning building. The troops climbed aboard. Men moved deliberately, as though they had walked forty klicks and knew that the day's work was not yet over.

"Here's a helmet, ma'am," Raff said to Lissea. "It was Ingried's. He bought it back there."

The Racontid had four mutually opposable fingers on each hand. He gestured toward the woods with two of them while the other pair gripped the commo helmet he was offering to Lissea.

"He have any kin?" Ned wondered aloud.

"Get aboard *now* or we'll be telling yours that we left you behind," Herne Lordling snapped.

"We've been lucky," said Yazov. "We've been *bloody* lucky."

The firetruck pulled out. Lissea and Herne were in the cab; Westerbeke drove. Ned hugged his chest close to the chromed vertical rail at the side of the tailboard. If he let himself dangle at arm's length, the first serious turn would send him flying from the vehicle.

Hatton started off leading the firetruck in normal escort fashion, then realized that Westerbeke would be choosing the course. The three-wheeler pulled onto the grassed shoulder to let the bigger vehicle accelerate past.

Coyne waved cheerfully. Ned wasn't sure the trike would even be able to follow on its small wheels if Westerbeke headed through soft terrain, but he didn't have enough energy to worry about that now.

Ned felt cold. His stomach was threatening to vomit up the water he'd drunk moments before. If his commo helmet worked, he could have listened to the chatter among the rest of the team, but he didn't have even that.

Raff, Yazov, and Paetz were on the tailboard with him. The Racontid looked at Ned's submachine gun, then lifted the weapon between paired fingers to stare at it muzzle-on.

Ned looked also. The iridium barrel had sublimed under heavy use until the bore was almost twice its normal diameter.

Ned grimaced and reached for the equipment pouch that should have carried two spare barrels and a barrel spanner. He wasn't wearing the pouch. His present gear was what he'd taken from the limousine's crew. Doormann Trading Company had never dreamed its guards would shoot a barrel out.

Raff grinned with a mouthful of square vegetarian teeth. He offered Ned the 2-cm weapon and bandolier which he wore slung beside his own rocket gun. "Better, yes?" he said.

"Better," Ned agreed. "Ingried's?"

He dropped the burned-out submachine gun onto the tailboard beside him.

"Ingried's," the Racontid confirmed.

The weight of the 2-cm weapon reassured Ned. When he draped the bandolier over his shoulder, it clacked against the pair of submachine gun magazines in the left side-pocket of his tunic. He thought the magazines must be empty or nearly so, but he didn't guess they were doing any harm where they were.

When the terrain rolled, Ned caught glimpses of the gun towers on the perimeter wall. The team was nearing its goal. Westerbeke had been keeping to the roads, perhaps in consideration of the men on the three-wheeler.

The firetruck approached a replica of a Greek temple on the crest of a barely perceptible knoll. The reliefs on the triangular pediment were painted in primary colors, with red and blue predominating. The stone of the structure itself was stained a creamy off-white.

Civilians stood on the temple porch, staring at the vehicles and the gang aboard them. The Telarians didn't appreciate that the mercenaries were really exactly what they looked like, a band of heavily armed pirates, murderous and as deadly as so many live grenades.

Coyne stood on his footboards and doffed his helmet to the watching civilians. Ned looked back sourly at him, wondering how the fellow could have the mental or physical energy left to clown.

A civilian shouted to the man next to her and pointed. She was looking at something in the distance.

The trike exploded in a jet of cyan brighter than the sun. The thunderclap of a 20-cm bolt from a tank's main gun shook even the heavy firetruck.

Ned raised his eyes. A tank, streaming stripped branches and pushing a mound of loam ahead of its bow skirts, shuddered its way through a belt of flowering dogwoods a kilometer away.

Ned reached to key his helmet, remembered that the radio didn't work, and checked the load of the 2-cm powergun that he'd ignored since Raff handed it to him. Ned was alive again, fully functional.

"Behind the building, fast!" Yazov shouted through the integral mike. *"Tank coming!"*

The firetruck fishtailed wildly. Westerbeke had failed to react quickly enough, and one of the others in the cab forced the steering wheel over against the driver's grip.

The second 20-cm bolt clipped the nearest of the four free-standing columns across the temple facade. If Westerbeke had made the hard left turn as ordered, at least half the bolt's energy would have centerpunched the vehicle instead of blasting a cavity in a wall of brick and climbing vines nearly a kilometer beyond the intended target.

The column, concrete beneath a marble finish, exploded violently. Head-sized fragments broke the shaft of the next pillar over and hammered the building's front wall. Concussion and flying stone knocked down all those standing on the porch. Calcium in the concrete blazed with a fierce white light.

The pediment lifted with the initial shock. It settled back, cracked, and fell on the twitching bodies beneath. Seeing Telarians killing their own people didn't make Ned feel better about the things he'd done; but it reminded him that this was war, and war had its own logic.

The firetruck pulled down the back of the knoll on which the temple stood—at least a temple in appearance, whatever the Doormanns were using the structure for in present reality. Westerbeke had slowed to sixty kilometers per hour to maneuver: the full tank of water made the vehicle top-heavy as well as sluggish.

Ned bailed off the tailboard, reflexively executing a landing fall, and rolled upright again. Heartbeats after Ned left the firetruck, Raff, Paetz, and Yazov jumped away from it also.

The vehicle continued on, accelerating slowly out of its S-curve.

Westerbeke kept the temple and the knoll itself between him and the hunting tank. The truck climbed a triple terrace of flowering shrubs and disappeared for the moment through an arched gateway.

An air-cushion tank was capable of twice the firetruck's best speed empty, and the half-track's path cross-country was unmistakable. The tank would destroy the truck and everyone aboard it—Lissea included—if somebody didn't stop the tank first.

That was what Ned Slade was here for. Somewhat to his surprise he found he was heading a team. He'd jumped at the side of the building, out of the tankers' line of sight only if he stayed low. The other three mercs scrambled toward him from the rear of the temple.

Ned waved them down. He stood, presenting his powergun and screened only by the mass of the temple beside him.

The tank had covered half the intervening distance. The driver didn't have enough field experience to handle the huge vehicle properly off-road, where the surface was less resistant than paving to highly pressurized air. He should have tilted his fan nacelles closer to vertical to keep a finger's breadth between the ground and the lower edge of his skirts. As it was, the tank plowed a shallow trench across the carefully tended soil.

The tank wasn't alone. Four air-cushion jeeps, similar to those the *Swift* carried, flanked the bigger vehicle. Each jeep mounted a tribarrel on a central pintle.

One of the gunners saw Ned and opened fire. His 2-cm bolts formed a quivering rope that smashed the side of the building like a wrecker's ball, several meters above their intended target.

Ned shot the gunner, shot his driver, and shot the driver of the other near-side jeep. Then he ducked and ran as though he'd just lighted the fuse of a demolition charge.

Which, in a manner of speaking, he had. The tank turret rotated as the two jeeps described complementary arcs and collided in a spray of plastic and bodies. The gunner of the second vehicle, the only crewman Ned hadn't killed, landed like a sack of flour thirty meters from the wreck.

The tank fired. Tribarrel bolts had punched holes in the temple wall, even though the weapon was firing at a slant. The charge of the 20-cm main gun blew the whole side of the building in. Because the concrete had no resilience, the enormous heat-shock shattered it. Refractory materials sublimed instantly to gas. The concussion threw Ned flat and sprayed him with gravel-sized bits of wall.

Either the tank gunner was uncertain about what lurked in the eruption of dust and blazing lime, or he was rapt in a sudden orgy of destruction. The tank fired twice more into the temple, blasting inner partition walls and the furnishings into self-immolating fireballs. Trusses slipped because their support pillars were broken. The main roof tumbled in as the porch had done moments before. A jet of flame-shot smoke spurted from the wreckage.

Ned crawled blindly on his hands and knees, wheezing and trying to blink away the grit covering his eyeballs. His damaged helmet was gone, and the nose filters probably wouldn't have worked anyway.

Hands grabbed and held him as other hands expertly tied a moistened kerchief across his nose and mouth. "I had to get us better cover," Ned gasped when he could speak.

Raff held him; Yazov had provided the field-expedient filter. The dust cloud spread as it settled onto the rubble, covering an increasing area with its white pall. "Paetz," Ned ordered, "take out the jeeps. The rest of you aim low, punch holes in the skirts. It can't move if the plenum chamber can't hold air."

He clambered onto a slab of concrete, looking for a firing position in the shifting wreckage. "Come on, out of sight! And don't shoot at the tank till I give the signal—they'll pull off if they figure what we're doing. Come on!"

Josie Paetz ran out at an angle from the collapsed building. A tribarrel chased the motion. Suspended dust flashed and scattered the concentrated packets of plasma well above the mercenary.

Paetz chose his point, ducked, and then rose again, firing when the two maneuvering jeeps crossed in line with him, three hundred meters away. Both vehicles spun out of control.

The jeep crews were in body armor. The burst of submachine-gun fire—it was only eight or nine rounds all told—wasn't enough to guarantee lethality with hits on armored torsos, so Josie aimed at faceshields. Although the haze of dust combed the bolts and reduced their effect, all four of the targets were dead before the careening vehicles flung them out.

Paetz ran back, hurling himself toward cover. The tank began to swing wide of the crumpled building, keeping two hundred meters clear. The main gun fired again, shocking the ruins like a boot kicking an ash pile.

Larger fragments sprayed outward; finely divided dust *whoomped* up into another mushroom. Ned fell sideways. Broken concrete slid, pinning his right boot. He couldn't breathe, couldn't see.

He flipped the sling over his head so his weapon hung crosswise on his chest, clearing both hands to tug at the weight holding his foot. The individual chunks were small enough, head-sized or thereabouts; but the jagged corners caught at one another like puzzle pieces. Some of them were still joined by twists of finger-thick reinforcing rod.

The main gun fired. The impact lifted Ned free and flung him in a stunning somersault down again on the bed of rubble.

By accident or design, the tank gunner was doing precisely the correct thing. So long as he continued to fire into the wrecked building, there was no chance that the mercenaries lairing there would be able to disable the tank. Disruption from the 20-cm bolts kept the team from aiming accurately, and there was a high likelihood that the huge impacts would kill them all despite the excellent cover the concrete provided.

The tank cruised parallel with what had been the long side of the temple. The turret was rotated ninety degrees from its midline carriage position, so the fat, stubby muzzle overhung the swell of the plenum chamber.

A line of cyan flashes licked across the tank's bow slope. Someone was shooting at the vehicle from straight ahead.

Ned unslung his weapon and leaned against a tilted slab to steady his aim. His vision danced cyan and its orange reciprocal, and his lungs felt as though he was trying to breathe the contents of a heated sandbag.

Herne Lordling stood in the track of the firetruck across the topmost of the three terraces. He turned his submachine gun sideways, loaded a fresh magazine, and emptied the weapon again in a single dazzling burst toward the Telarian tank.

There was absolutely nothing useful the light charges could do to the massively armored tank—

But they could draw the attention of the tank's crew, and they did so. The turret gimballed around to bear on the new target. Ned fired, Raff and Yazov fired, Josie Paetz fired—his submachine gun wasn't going to help any more than Herne's but it didn't matter; this was no time to save ammo.

The skirts surrounding the tank's plenum chamber were steel—thick but not as resistant to powergun bolts as the iridium armor of the hull. Ned and Yazov planted five bolts each along the swelling curve, blowing divots of white blazing steel and leaving holes you could stick your fist through.

The main gun fired. Everything within a meter of where Herne Lordling stood dissolved in a flash of blue so saturated it could have cut diamond.

Raff's first magazine of rockets had HE warheads. They left sooty black scars across the skirts, denting but not piercing the steel. The Racontid reloaded faster than Ned or Yazov. The next four rockets were tungsten penetrators that sparkled through the skirts, with at least a chance of clipping fan nacelles within the plenum chamber, besides.

The cushion of air which should have floated the tank's height roared out through the holes in the skirts. The tank dug its port side still deeper in the soil and sodded to a halt. Its turret rotated toward the ruins again with the deliberation its great mass demanded.

Ned got up and ran, bandolier flapping and his heavy shoulder weapon held out at arm's length like an acrobat's balance bar. The team had disabled the tank, but they couldn't destroy it. There was nothing to stay around for except certain death from the battering the tank gun would give the ruined temple.

The building had been eight or nine meters across, though in collapse the fragments slumped over a wider area. Paetz and Yazov dodged around the rear of the pile and threw themselves down.

Raff had chosen a firing position on the far side of the ruin to begin with. The Racontid vanished to safety in a clumsy jump. His arms and legs flailed like those of a cat flung from a high window.

Ned stepped to a heap on the fractured roof from which to push off in a similar leap. He might break something when he landed six or eight meters away, might even knock himself silly, but the turret was turning and—

The mound was powder over a grid of reinforcing rods. Ned's right leg shot through a rectangular gap. The rods clamped him just above the knee. If they'd caught him just a little lower, inertia would have torn all the ligaments away from the joint. As it was, the pain was agonizing—and the thumb-thick rods held him as firmly as a bear trap.

Ned looked over his shoulder. The tank's 20-cm gun steadied in perfect line with his torso. In the far distance, motion in the corner of Ned's eye marked a second Telarian tank following the furrow dragged by the first. Cyan light so bright it was palpable engulfed the disabled tank.

The massively armored bow slope burst inward from the jet of plasma. Everything within the fighting compartment ionized instantly; ready charges for the main gun and the cupola tribarrel added their portion to the ravening destruction. The fusion bottle ruptured and the turret, a 60-tonne iridium casting, spun into the air like a flipped coin.

For a moment, Ned could neither see nor hear because of the blast. He had closed his eyes instinctively when the muzzle yawned to spew his own death, but eyelids could only filter, not bar, the cyan intensity. The shockwave of metal subliming in the energy flux made the air ring like a god's struck anvil. It lifted the turf in a series of ripples spreading from the point of impact on the tank's bow.

The anti-starship weapon from the gun tower on the eastern horizon fired again. The second Telarian tank exploded. This time the hull shattered. The vehicle's dense iridium flanks flew outward, crumpling like foil in a flame.

Deke and Toll Warson had removed the lockouts from the

fire-control computers, thus turning the captured gun tower into a support base for the teams within the Doormann estate. They'd taken their bloody time about it, but close only counts in horse-shoes—

And hand grenades.

Ned began to laugh, humor or hysteria, he really didn't care. "Hey!" he croaked, "somebody get me out of here! Hey, can anybody hear—"

Yazov's boots thumped on the rubble. Raff had flung the big man halfway up the pile as if he were a sandbag. Yazov scrambled closer, detaching the cutting bar from his belt. His nephew followed him in a similar high-angle trajectory.

Yazov thumbed the bar's trigger to test the tool. The blade hummed eagerly. "Some of them laughed when they saw all the gear I was carrying," he remarked smugly. " 'He'll need a jeep, he can't walk with all that cop,' they said."

"*I'm* glad you've got it," Ned remarked. The veteran sounded perfectly normal: too normal. He wondered just how well Yazov was doing inside.

He wondered how well *he* was doing inside. He'd be all right so long as he kept everything on the surface, though.

"You bet you're glad," Yazov said. He chose a point, set the bar against it, and cut through the mild steel rods with a shriek and a shower of red sparks. "You can't have too much gear when it drops in the pot. You know that, don't you, Slade?"

"You bet," Ned agreed. When the powered blade howled through a second joint, he felt some of the pressure release. He still wasn't free.

Josie Paetz stood beside his uncle, changing the barrel of his submachine gun. He was smiling, all the way through. His face was more terrifying than the bore of a 20-cm powergun.

Yazov made a third careful cut. "There," he said, offering Ned his shoulder for a brace.

"I'll lift him," said Raff, who had climbed the ruin normally. The left side of the Racontid's body was blackened where a nearby bolt had singed the normally golden pelt.

The stench of burned hair clung to Raff, but he seemed to be in good shape regardless. His gentle strength raised Ned like a chain hoist, vertically, with none of the torquing that could shear and tear.

Ned checked his powergun. It had a full magazine. He must have reloaded after firing the second clip into the tank's skirts, but he couldn't imagine when or how he'd done it. "Let's get going," he said aloud.

His right leg hurt like hell, but it supported him. Raff nonetheless kept an unobtrusive grip on Ned's equipment belt as they descended the pile of debris.

"Cutting bars are great when you have to get in close, too," Yazov said conversationally. "You ever do that, Slade?"

"Yeah," Ned said. "Once. Lissea shot him off me."

They headed along the path the firetruck had torn across the grounds. The swale at the base of the terraces would have been boggy, but the landscape architects had run perforated tiles under the turf to a catch basin disguised in the base of a sundial.

"Well, keep it in mind," Yazov said. "Beats hell out of a gun butt. Though a sharp entrenching tool, that can work pretty well too."

Yazov sounded nonchalant, but he looked to the other side as the team skirted the crater of vitrified soil the main gun bolt had punched where Herne Lordling briefly stood. "You know," he added, "I never liked that bastard. I still don't. It's a hell of a thing. I still don't like him."

"I don't think it had much to do with liking," Ned said, wishing that his eyes didn't blur like this. "It was a matter of doing his job. Like we all did."

A smoothly resilient path led through the brick archway. The truck must have followed it, though they couldn't see the tread marks. For the moment, the gun tower that was their destination was out of sight also.

A klaxon moaned. The precise location was lost in the bordering shrubs, but it was close and getting closer.

The team melted into ambush position: Paetz and Yazov beneath flowering branches to the left, Raff in a similar position on the right, and Ned behind the end support of a stone bench set along the path for strollers. It wasn't good concealment, but it would protect his torso against even a 2-cm bolt . . .

Yazov jumped up and ran into the center of the pathway. "Wait!" he cried, waving back to Ned who didn't have a commo helmet. "Wait! She's coming through!"

A three-wheeler skidded around the hedge-hidden corner twenty meters beyond the team. The metal tires chirped as Lissea braked hard to keep from hitting Yazov. She brought the little vehicle to a chattering halt just short of the veteran and raised her faceshield.

Ned stumbled as he ran to the three-wheeler because he couldn't see for tears. "You're all right?" he said.

"You're all right?" Lissea echoed. "You're all right?"

"Ma'am, you're out on this alone?" Yazov said doubtfully, checking the vehicle's tribarrel, still locked in its traveling position.

"It's what I could find after the truck bogged," Lissea said. "The fighting's over. Lucas is in charge. He's called a ceasefire with a general amnesty, and I've accepted."

"That's good," Ned said. "He's smart, Lucas is, but that's *good* too." Then he added, "I'm glad I didn't kill him."

"Come on," Lissea said. "Everybody climb on. This will hold us if we're careful."

"It's an overload," Raff said doubtfully.

"Worse things have happened today," Ned said as he settled himself on the pillion. He put his left arm around Lissea's waist; the arm that didn't hold his well-used powergun.

Ned stood with his hands on his hip bones, staring north from the roof-level banquet hall of the Acme. At the large table placed in the center of the room for the discussions, Lissea and Lucas Doormann worked out the final wording of their agreement with a civilian lawyer each in support. Both lawyers were female.

If you knew where to look and you used moderate magnification, you could see that one of the anti-starship weapons on the Doormann estate's perimeter wall was trained on the hotel. The precaution was probably unnecessary, but nobody thought it was a bluff.

Nobody in his right mind thought it was a bluff.

There had been street traffic all night. Now that dawn had washed away the patterns of head- and tail-lights, the number of vehicles visible through the clear walls of the room increased exponentially. It seemed to be business as usual in Landfall City.

There had been virtually no damage in the city and rural areas outside the estate boundary. Within that perimeter, well—the Doormann Estate had been an enclave on the world it ruled. It would be some time before Telaria as a whole appreciated just what had happened on the previous day.

Ned made a sound in his throat.

"Sir?" said Deye, the Telarian in his late fifties standing at the window a few meters away. Deye was a military man by his carriage, though at the moment he wore ruffed civilian clothes. Lucas had made the Acme his temporary headquarters, but in this room, by agreement, the principals were supported by only two aides apiece.

"I was thinking," Ned said. "About what they're going to say. About us."

Deye nodded seriously. "I lost some friends today, Ensign Slade," he said.

The voices of the lawyers chirped at a high rate like gears meshing. They spoke and gestured simultaneously at the holographic display in the center of the table. The words fell into unison, as if the pair were giving a choral reading.

"But I want to say," Deye continued, "I'm proud to have faced you. I wouldn't have believed anybody could fight at the odds you faced. Fight and win, I'll give you that; you *won!*"

Ned looked at him. *Are you insane? We killed hundreds of people and most of them were civilians. We killed thousands of people, and we were ready to raze Landfall City to the ground if you hadn't capitulated!*

Aloud he said, "That isn't quite what I had in mind. And I . . . haven't quite processed everything that's gone on."

Deye's arm twitched. With a convulsive gesture, the Telarian extended his hand for Ned to shake or reject. He had the air of a man reaching into a furnace.

More embarrassed than he could have imagined ever being, Ned shook Deye's hand. Ned had bathed as soon as they reached the hotel, but he still felt as though his skin was sticky with blood.

"Agreed?" Lucas said on a rising inflexion.

Ned and Deye faced around.

"Agreed!" Lissea said, standing to extend her hand across the table to her cousin. The lawyers bent their heads together for a further whispered conversation as their principals shook on the deal.

Lissea stepped back from the table. "We can have the other parties in now," she said. "I think it will be best for me to present the terms so that they can be quite clear that I *am* in agreement."

"Yes, a good idea," Lucas said. He raised the multifunction stylus he'd been using as a light pen and spoke into the opposite end.

The door to the hall opened. "Yes sir?" said the attendant, a solid-looking woman named Joyner. She had been chief of Lucas Doormann's personal staff before yesterday's disaster wiped out Telaria's governmental bureaucracy.

"Send in the . . ." Lucas said. He paused, groping for a word other than "survivors." His attorney whispered to him.

"Send in the successors in interest, Joyner," Lucas said.

No one in the Acme wore a uniform, much less battledress, today. Ned wore ultramarine trousers and a teal jacket. The fabric was processed from the tendrils of a colonial invertebrate which floated in hectare-wide mats across the seas of Tethys. Ned looked more like somebody's date than a—whatever he was.

But when Joyner's eyes fell across him, her face congealed in a mixture of awe and terror.

Thirty-odd chairs had been arranged in a single row set forward from the room's flat partition wall. Ushers guided a file of men, women, and children from the doorway to their places. The principals sat; guardians, a mixture of attorneys and spouses out of the Doormann bloodline, stood behind the chairs of their underage principals. Some of the children were infants in the arms of mothers or nurses, but the range extended through adults in their fifties.

Grey and Duenna Doormann, Lissea's parents, sat in the two

end-seats. They watched their daughter with as much suppressed nervousness as the others in their company did.

Lissea eyed the gathering. "Mesdames and sirs," she said. "Master Lucas, acting in his own behalf and for yourselves as agent, has come to an agreement with me regarding my claims against the Doormann Trading Company."

One of the infants began to cry. Its mother offered a bottle.

"The shares of my branch of the family, previously voted by the late Karel Doormann, have been transferred to my control." Lissea continued. "I have voted those shares in favor of Lucas Doormann to fill the position of President of Doormann Trading left vacant at his father's death."

There was a collective sigh of wonder and relief from the assembly. Two of the guardians began to whisper, then broke off when they noticed Ned watching them.

The infant cried louder. Its bottle bounced down onto the hand-loomed carpet brought in for the occasion. The mother lifted the child close to her face and began to croon under her breath.

"I myself," Lissea said, "will proceed to Alliance to set up an office there for Doormann Trading. I'll be traveling with my consort, Carron Del Vore, who has interests and expertise in the Twin Worlds. The recent opening of the Sole Solution to free trade will cause massive structural adjustments on the Twin Worlds. There are huge profits to be made by the companies which are first on the ground. We—"

The infant began to wail. Its mother rocked and stroked her child. Tears were running down the woman's cheeks. The man standing behind a neighboring chair bent over with a disapproving look to say something.

"The baby is all right," Ned said.

Everyone stared at him. The leaning man looked like a beast caught in the headlights.

"Babies cry," Ned said. His face muscles were as stiff as a gunstock. "It's all *right*."

Lissea glanced over her shoulder. She nodded, turned again, and said, "Master Slade is correct."

Clearing her throat she went on. "Doormann Trading Company will be in the forefront of the new expansion beyond the Sole Solution. I expect we'll be able to double our gross trade figures within the decade. Even with the higher margins due to long Transit distances, net increases should be in the order of twenty percent."

The mother took a soft block from her bag. The infant chewed it and gurgled.

"I would expect to be absent from Telaria for the foreseeable future," Lissea said in a cool, dry voice. "My father, Grey, will act as my agent when required, though all decisions regarding the normal running of Doormann Trading will be made by the president 'as before."

She looked across the row of her relatives and their representatives. Only a few of them would meet her eyes.

"Are there any questions?"

A seated woman of thirty or so, overweight and overjeweled, looked at Lissea, opened her mouth—caught Ned's expression from the corner of her eye—*I wasn't even thinking about her!*

—and closed her mouth without speaking.

"Lissea and I," Lucas Doormann said, "have discussed yesterday's events and the situation that gave rise to them. Lest there be any question, let me say that everything that happened before today is a closed book. Doormann Trading Company is starting fresh, with a solid structure and bright prospects."

He looked at Lissea and added, "I appreciate the confidence Lissea has shown by supporting me for the position of president. I intend to show myself worthy of that confidence by focusing on the company's future. *No* one will be permitted to undermine that future by word or action."

The sitting and standing lines of representatives faced Lucas Doormann, but many of them watched Ned out of the corners of their eyes.

No one in his right mind thought it was a bluff.

"Very good," Lissea said, verbally gaveling the meeting closed. "I'm informed that the president will call an organizational meeting for the new board within the next few days. I may still be on Telaria at that time, but I won't be at the meeting. Therefore I'll take leave of all of you now."

She bowed stiffly to the representatives, then glanced over her shoulder. "Ned," she said, "I need to see you for a few minutes in my suite."

Lissea started for the door. Her lawyer got up and reached toward Lissea's shoulder for attention. Lissea batted the hand away. "Not now!" she said. Joyner opened the door as Lissea swept toward it with Ned silent at her heels.

The hallway was packed with aides, attendants, and Doormann guards identifiable by the blue collar flashings on their civilian clothes. The security personnel broadened the corridor they already held open between the banquet hall and the bank of elevators.

Lissea got in with Ned and touched 12. The whole twelfth story had been converted into a suite for her and her burgeoning household. Ned waited till the elevator had dropped to midfloor and touched EMERGENCY STOP. A chime sounded three times before he got the access plate open with a tool from his wallet and switched off the alarm.

"We can talk in my suite," Lissea said. She licked her lips and added, "Carron isn't there."

"That's all right," Ned said. He had to force himself to meet her eyes. "I wanted you to know that I'm going back to the *Swift* to pick up my pay from Tadziki. I'll ship out then. I'm not sure where to."

Lissea backed against the side of the cage with a thump. "Ned, I want you to come to Alliance with me. I'll *need* you on Alliance. S-s-somebody I can trust."

"No, I'm going to travel for a while," Ned said. "I . . . have some things to think about."

He was staring at his own haunted eyes in the polished brass wall of the elevator cage. He'd looked away without realizing it.

Lissea took his hands. "Listen to me," she said. "Carron understands. But I made a promise to him, Ned. I can't . . . I shouldn't . . . break a promise like that. He put his life on the line."

Ned grinned wryly. "Yeah, he did," he said. "Carron's a decent guy, and he's got a lot of guts. I wish you both well."

"Ned!"

He looked at her again. Embarrassment forced his grin into a rictus.

"Don't you *care?*" she demanded. "I'm offering you everything I can. You know I am!"

"Lissea," he said, "I fought for you, I did things for you that I'd never have done for myself. I'd partner you anywhere in the universe. But I'm not anybody's consort. And I'm not *anybody's* puppy!"

He reached past her and touched EMERGENCY STOP again, releasing the cage.

Lissea's face was white. "Things can change, you know," she said harshly. "It might take time, a few years even, but I waited longer than that to get justice here on Telaria. You've got to take the long view sometimes, Ned!"

The cage stopped. The door opened onto a foyer full of servants and recently hired bodyguards nervously awaiting the arrival of the stalled elevator.

"I do take the long view," Ned said. "I want to be able to live with myself. Good-bye, Lissea."

She stepped out of the cage with her back straight and her face composed. Ned touched LOBBY.

As the door closed, he thought of calling, "Lissea, I love you!" But that would just have complicated matters.

Ned walked up the ramp of the *Swift*. Part of the engine-room hull plating was off. A mobile crane prepared to lift out one of the drive motors.

A rehab crew from the dockyard had made a pass over the main bay already. The bunks and lockers had been removed, the spray insulation stripped and replaced, and a fresh coat of robin's-egg-blue paint applied.

All that was fast work, but the *Swift* had become the private yacht of Mistress Lissea Doormann, the controlling stockholder of Doormann Trading Company. The vessel would carry her and her immediate entourage to Alliance as soon as its reconditioning was complete.

Tadziki sat at the portable data unit placed before the aft bulkhead. Carron Del Vore was with him. Carron gave Ned a plaster smile.

"Hey, trooper!" the adjutant called. "The Warsons were just in, asking about you. How did the business go?"

Ned grinned back, slipping unconsciously from one persona to another because of Carron's presence. "Slicker 'n snot," he said, watching the prince blink in disgust. "Full amnesty, full pay and bonuses. The only thing Lucas would have called a deal-breaker was if Lissea had insisted on staying on Telaria. She already knew that was impossible after all the people we'd killed."

Carron nodded twice as though priming a pump to bring up his words. "Our new duties on Alliance should be very interesting, shouldn't they, Slade?" he said in a voice resembling that of a hanging man's.

"*Your* duties," Ned said nonchalantly. "I'm going to—I don't know, knock around a while. I've got no apologies for anything we did to get through the Sole Solution, but—"

His mouth quirked. "There's more widows and orphans on the Twin Worlds just now than I want to look at."

Tadziki watched Ned with a raised eyebrow, but he didn't enter the conversation.

"Ah . . ." said Carron. "Ah. I'd understood you'd be accompanying Lissea as her personal aide?"

"I regretted turning the offer down," Ned said evenly. "But I thought it was better that I do so."

Carron swallowed. "I see," he said with obvious relief. "Ah. Do you chance to know where Lissea is now?"

"Back in her suite in the Acme," Ned said. "At any rate, that's where she was going when I left her after the negotiations were complete."

"Master Slade, Master Tadziki," Carron said, nodding to either man, "I'll leave you then. Good day."

Tadziki waited for the Pancahtan to stride down the ramp before saying, "A better day for *him* than he expected to be having a few minutes ago, anyway." Then he added, "You all right, Ned?"

"Via, I don't know," Ned said honestly. "I *will* be all right."

He looked around for someplace to sit. Apart from Tadziki's chair and the navigational consoles forward, there was nothing.

Tadziki slid a software file sideways and offered a corner of the portable data unit.

"No, that's all right," Ned said. "Look, I just came to draw my pay. I—"

His vision blurred for a moment. "I'd kind of like to get off Telaria without seeing the rest of the crew, do you know? I—"

He was choking. He swallowed. "Tadziki," he said, "they're the best there ever was. If I have grandchildren, I'll tell them I served with the Pancahte Expedition, with all of you. But when I see your faces, I think about things that I'm not ready to handle just now. Do you understand? Do *you* understand?"

"As it happens . . ." the adjutant said. His fingers called up a file. He loaded a credit-transfer chip. "I do."

He hit EXECUTE; the data unit chuckled to itself. He looked up at Ned. "You'll get over it," he added. "I don't say that as consolation— it isn't consolation. But everybody gets over it in time, you and me . . . and your uncle did, I'm sure."

The unit spat the loaded chip halfway out of the top slot. Tadziki pulled the chip the rest of the way and handed it to Ned.

Ned looked at the value imprinted on the face of the chip. He shook his head. "It's a lot of money, isn't it? For a soldier."

"It's never the money," Tadziki said. "Nobody does it for the money."

He smiled sadly at Ned. "Do you think you've proved you're a man, then?" he asked.

Ned blinked. "Is that how you see it?" he said.

"How do *you* see it, Ned?"

Ned looked toward the bulkhead and through as much time as he could remember. "I think . . ." he said, "that there's a guy named Ned Slade, a person. And I learned that there's a big universe out there, and that he hasn't seen much of it yet."

His face broke into an honest grin. He reached across the data unit. "It's been good to know you, Tadziki," he said. "With luck, we may meet again in a while."

"I'd like that," Tadziki said as they shook hands. To Ned's back, as the younger man walked out of the *Swift*'s hatch for the last time, Tadziki added, "When you're ready."

Ned watched through the fence surrounding Berth 41 as the integral cargo-handling machinery of the *Ajax* finished stowing within the vessel's hold the contents of a lowboy. The emptied lowboy whined away on its multitude of full-width rollers. The waiting line of eight similar vehicles jerked forward by fits and starts.

The *Ajax* was a mixed passenger/freight vessel displacing some four kilotonnes. She was configured for operations on less-developed worlds, where the port facilities might be limited to human stevedores and animal transport. On full-function ports like that serving Landfall City, the *Ajax* docked at outlying quays and still loaded as quickly as the port's own systems could manage at the more expensive berths.

The load that had just gone aboard the *Ajax* was small arms and ammunition.

Whistling "You Wonder Why I'm a Trooper" under his breath, Ned walked to the berth office, an extruded-plastic building set into the fence. Three sides were bleached white, but there were still traces of the original pink dye around the north-facing window- and doorjambs. A balding man in his mid-thirties stretched at the desk within. He covered his yawn when he saw Ned.

"Can I help you, sir?" he asked, politely but with a slight wariness. "I'm Wilson, the purser."

"I was wondering where the *Ajax* was loading for," Ned said.

The walls of the small office were covered with holovision pinups of both men and women. The images ranged in tone from cheesecake to pornography that would be extreme on nine worlds out of ten. Apparently it was a tradition that the purser or supercargo of every ship using Berth 41 tacked up his or her taste.

"Looking for a job?" Wilson asked, eyeing Ned carefully.

Ned wore a casual tunic and slacks, brought from Tethys and stored on Telaria. The garments were pastel green and yellow respectively, with no military connotations.

Wilson gestured to the rickety chair before his desk. "Go on, have a seat."

"I'm not certificated," Ned said, sitting down. "I was just noticing your cargo."

Wilson frowned. "Look," he said defensively, "I know what you're thinking, but you're wrong. This isn't anything to do with that business yesterday. And we're not gunrunning; we've got all our licenses."

Ned laughed. "In broad daylight, out of Landfall City?" he said. "I know you're straight. I just want to know straight *what?*"

Wilson relaxed again. It was a hot day. His jacket and saucer hat hung on a peg behind the open door. "Well, it's like this," he explained. "A pharmaceuticals firm from Magellan, they tried to set up a base on an unidentified planet they'd found. It doesn't have a name and I don't have the coordinates—that's a trade secret. All I know is it's a jungle."

Ned nodded. When his head moved, the image of one of the pinups—a woman with Oriental features—performed an act that Ned would have thought was impossible for a human to achieve.

"Well," Wilson continued, "the folks from Magellan went in, and they got handed their heads. Literally. There weren't enough of them left alive to lift ship, and half the rescue force got killed besides. After that, they knew the size of the operation it was going to take."

The pinups were tacked one over another in multiple layers. The image that had caught Ned's attention was stuck directly against the wall, but later-comers had carefully avoided covering the woman's amazing abilities.

"Magellan couldn't fund anything like that alone," Wilson said, "so they did a deal with Doormann Trading. Doormann supplies hardware and the capital to hire a support force. Magellan provides the science staff. And the coordinates, that's the big one."

He tapped his electronic desk. "We're carrying the Doormann Trading share to Magellan. I don't know if they'll hire us to take part of the expedition from Magellan to the new site or not."

"They'll be hiring on Magellan, then?" Ned said. "Guards, I mean."

Wilson shrugged. "I can't imagine they wouldn't be," he said. "Curst good rates, too, I shouldn't be surprised. But if you're thinking we might give you passage on tick against your hiring bonus . . ."

The purser's voice trailed off. Ned noticed that Wilson didn't flatly bar the possibility.

"No, nothing like that," Ned said as he fished from his pocket the credit chip Tadziki had paid him a few hours earlier. He put the chip on the desk before Wilson. "If you've got a cabin open, you've got a passenger."

Wilson's eyebrows rose when he saw the amount printed on the chip's exterior. "We've got cabins," he said, poising the chip at the edge of his desk's processing slot. "Only thing is—"

He looked up. "We're going to lift as soon as we've got the cargo loaded. Midnight, I'd guess, maybe an hour or two later. Is that a problem?"

Ned shook his head. "Suits me fine," he said. "I'll have my baggage sent over immediately."

Wilson pushed the chip in far enough for the transport mechanism to take over. He entered the class and destination codes onto his keyboard. "We're getting a bonus for fast delivery," he explained as he typed. "That's why we're in a hurry to lift. With all that brouhaha yesterday, I thought it was going to hold us up. But the new bosses, they say the deal's still on."

The desk chuckled to itself as it processed the data. Wilson smiled and stretched again. "Hey, wasn't that something yesterday? I've been talking to a couple of the port police. Via, what a hell of a business!"

Ned nodded. "That's the word, all right," he said. "Hell."

A new chip, imprinted with the lower amount of the first chip less cost of passage, sprang from the output slot.

Wilson slid it over. "Here you go," he said. "Just show up an hour before liftoff or take your chances. We've got your identification from the credit transfer."

The personal data from Ned's credit chip appeared on a small screen inset at an angle into the desktop. The purser glanced down as he referred to it, then blinked in astonishment. "Slade?" he said. "*Edward Slade of* Tethys?"

Ned dropped the credit chip into his pocket again and stood up. "That's me," he said.

"But blood and martyrs, Master Slade!" Wilson cried. "You're the guy? You're the one who took out two tanks with a submachine gun yesterday?"

"Me?" said Ned as he walked out the door. "No, but that sounds like something my uncle Don might have done."

The Berth 41 office was closed when Ned returned. Wilson lounged at the wicket of the fence with an armed crewman. Beyond, the *Ajax* gleamed in the beams of the positioning lights set in pits in the concrete.

The purser waved cheerfully at Ned's approach and called, "You're in plenty of time, Master Slade. We've stowed your baggage—four pieces, that was?"

"Four," Ned agreed, stepping through the wicket. Much of Ned's own gear was dress clothing, which he couldn't imagine needing on Magellan or thereafter. He was keeping the clothes, though. They were a link to . . . to home, to civilization; to life.

The lowboys had discharged their cargo, but the vessel's three holds were still open. A pair of service vehicles in Doormann Trading blue were parked before the hatches, and several figures there gestured conversationally.

The sailor with Wilson stared at Ned. Ned wondered what the purser had been telling the man.

"Also," Wilson said with a smirk, "your friend just came aboard. She'll be waiting in your cabin."

"Partner?" Ned said.

Wilson and the sailor exchanged quick glances. "Ah, yessir," Wilson said carefully. "A Mistress Schmidt from Dell. She said she was going to give you a sendoff to Magellan. Ah—is there a problem, sir?"

Ned grinned. He felt light enough to float into the starry sky. "No problem at all," he said as he walked down the light-taped path to the *Ajax,* to the future—

And to Lissea Doormann.

AUTHOR'S NOTE

The earliest form of the legend of Jason and the Argonauts can be reconstructed only from literary fragments and vase paintings. In this version, Jason appears to have sailed west, into the Adriatic, rather than east to the ends of the Black Sea. Readers with an interest in Greek myth will notice that I've adapted portions of this *Urmythus* in the plot of *The Voyage*. Most significantly, the original Jason doesn't sow the dragon's teeth. Rather, he yokes the bronze bulls to battle the water monster which guards the Golden Fleece.

I don't mean to imply that I ignored the *Argonautica* of the third century B.C. poet Apollonius Rhodius. On the contrary, Apollonius was my inspiration and main source.

The problem facing Apollonius is similar to that of a modern writer who intends to rework ancient myths. Apollonius was a cultured man working in a period of high civilization. His material, however, was that of the Heroic Age and would inevitably be compared to the use made of the Heroic Age by Dark Age writers like Homer (the two Homers, in my opinion).

The result is oddly disquieting. Apollonius was a very skillful writer. His characters are well drawn and their motivations are perfectly understandable to a modern reader. The problem is that the events and activities Apollonius describes are generally those of a much harsher period; a period that *wasn't* civilized, by his standards or by ours. The result reads like a saga about sensitive Vikings or the autobiography of a self-effacing quattrocentro duke.

The partial failure of an excellent craftsman like Apollonius was a warning to me. To achieve what I believe is a more suitable tone for my adaptation, I reread the *Iliad*. Frankly, Homer's stark vision of reality is closer to that of my own mind anyway.

Apollonius wasn't merely a negative model for me, either. Many of the classical authors had a remarkable talent for sketching minor characters with a line or two. Apollonius was near the forefront of that group.

The members of the *Swift*'s crew are generally the characters whom capsule descriptions in the *Argonautica* evoked in my mind. Thus Apollonius' Idas became my Herne Lordling; Teiamon and Peleus became the Warson brothers; Calais and Zetes became the Boxalls (though here I mined Propertius as well); the young Meleager became Josie Paetz, while his two uncles were combined into the character of Yazov; Periclymenus became Raff—and so on.

Most (though not all) of the *Swift*'s layovers are from points Apollonius describes in the course of the *Argo*, though I've significantly reduced the number as well as changing their sequence. I've tried to maintain Apollonius' rough balance of events on the outward voyage, in Colchis, and on the return.

Because some readers will want to know the originals from which I built my fictions, and because (based on my past experience) most reviewers commenting on the sources will get them wrong, the equivalents are as follows:

Telaria/Iolcos;
Ajax Four/Mt Dindymon;
Mirandola/Lemnos;
Paixhans' Node/Salmydessos in Thrace;
Burr-Detlingen/the Isle of Thynni;
the Sole Solution/the Planctae (the Clashing Rocks);
Buin/the Island of Ares;
Pancahte/Colchis;
Wasatch 1029/Trinacria (which isn't really Sicily;
   but then, I don't suppose Colchis was much the way
   Apollonius describes the place either);

Kazan/a combination of Crete (which Talos guards)
    and the Po Valley;
Celandine/a combination of the Brygaean Islands
    and Drepane (Homer's Phaeacia);
Dell/Mt Pelion

Apollonius ends his poem just as the *Argo* comes back home to harbor. There's reason for his decision—the same reason that Eisenstein halts the action of the *The Battleship Potemkin* where he does: what comes next is pretty horrifying. I went on and described the return as well; partly because it is a major part of the myth, but primarily because I find it morally necessary—for me—to show precisely where certain courses of conduct and tricks of thought lead.

The use of force is *always* an answer to problems. Whether or not it's a satisfactory answer depends on a number of things, not least the personality of the person making the determination.

Force isn't an attractive answer, though. I would not be true to myself or to the people I served with in 1970 if I did not make that realization clear.

Dave Drake
Chatham County, NC